T0013453

JEN WILLIAMS lives in London wit[...]
She started writing about pirates and [...]
has never stopped. Her short stories [...]
anthologies and she was nominated Best Newcomer in the 2015
British Fantasy Awards. *The Silver Tide* is the final novel in Jen's
spectacular Copper Cat trilogy, and follows *The Copper Promise*
and *The Iron Ghost*.

Praise for *The Silver Tide*:

'Expect dead gods, mad magic, piracy on the high seas, peculiar
turns and pure fantasy fun'   *Starburst* magazine

'*The Silver Tide* does not fail to take us on a non-stop ride'
                                                  SciFiNow

'*The Silver Tide* is massive, wide screen, surround sound story-
telling at its very best'   www.ebookwyrm.blogspot.co.uk

'The perfect ending to the series'   *SF Crowsnest*

'An enthralling adventure of pirates, dragons, gods – and the Black
Feather Three'   *Sci-Fi Bulletin*

'A cracking book'   *Falcata Times*

'Swords and sorcery at its most ingenious and entertaining'
                                        www.lynns-books.com

'An utterly outstanding and thrilling ride'
                              www.brizzlelassbooks.wordpress.com

'I've loved every minute of this story, and it's one I'm going to
fiercely miss'   www.overtheeffingrainbow.co.uk

'If only all fantasy was as addictive as this. . . Highly recommended'   www.theeloquentpage.co.uk

Praise for *The Iron Ghost*:

'Williams has thrown out the rulebook and injected a fun tone into epic fantasy without lightening or watering down the excitement and adventure. . . Highly recommended'   *Independent*

'The second outing is as entertaining as the first, being absolutely stuffed with ghoulish action. There is never a dull page' *SciFiNow*

'A highly inventive, vibrant high fantasy with a cast you can care about; fast-moving enough to ensure there is never a dull moment'   *The British Fantasy Society*

'Just as magical, just as action packed, just as clever and just as much fun as its predecessor. . . You'll find a great deal to enjoy here'   www.fantasy-faction.com

'Atmospheric and vivid. . .with a rich history and mythology and colourful, well-written and complex characters, that all combine to suck you in to the world and keep you enchanted up until the very last page'   www.realitysabore.blogspot.co.uk

Praise for *The Copper Promise*:

'Fresh and exciting, full of wit and wonder and magic and action, *The Copper Promise* is *the* fantasy novel we've been waiting for'   Adam Christopher

'*The Copper Promise* is dark, often bloody, frequently frightening, but there's also bucket loads of camaraderie, sarcasm, and an unashamed love of fantasy and the fantastic'
    Den Patrick, author of *The Boy with the Porcelain Blade*

'*The Copper Promise* is an excellent book, stuffed with all the ingredients of sword and sorcery mixed to a fresh new recipe. It's a shamelessly good old-fashioned blood-and-thunder tale, heroic fantasy the way it's meant to be'
    Joanne Hall, www.hierath.wordpress.com

'The characterisation is second to none, and there are some great new innovations and interesting reworkings of old tropes. . . This book may have been based on the promise of copper but it delivers gold'   Quicksilver on Goodreads

'A wonderful sword and sorcery novel with some very memorable characters and a dragon to boot. If you enjoy full-throttle action, awesome monsters, and fun, snarky dialogues then *The Copper Promise* is definitely a story you won't want to miss'
                          www.afantasticallibrarian.com

By Jen Williams and available from Headline

The Copper Promise
The Iron Ghost
The Silver Tide

THE SILVER TIDE

JEN WILLIAMS

headline

Copyright © 2016 Jennifer Williams

The right of Jennifer Williams to be identified as the Author of
the Work has been asserted by her in accordance with the
Copyright, Designs and Patents Act 1988.

First published in Great Britain in 2016 by
HEADLINE PUBLISHING GROUP

First published in paperback in 2016 by
HEADLINE PUBLISHING GROUP

3

Apart from any use permitted under UK copyright law,
this publication may only be reproduced, stored, or transmitted, in
any form, or by any means, with prior permission in writing of
the publishers or, in the case of reprographic production, in accordance
with the terms of licences issued by the Copyright Licensing Agency.

All characters in this publication are fictitious and any resemblance to real persons,
living or dead, is purely coincidental.

Cataloguing in Publication Data is available from the British Library

ISBN 978 1 4722 1116 3

Typeset in Sabon LT Std by Palimpsest Book Production Limited,
Falkirk, Stirlingshire

Printed and bound in Great Britain by CPI Group (UK) Ltd, Croydon CR0 4YY

Headline's policy is to use papers that are natural, renewable and recyclable
products and made from wood grown in well-managed forests and other
controlled sources. The logging and manufacturing processes are expected
to conform to the environmental regulations of the country of origin.

HEADLINE PUBLISHING GROUP
An Hachette UK Company
Carmelite House
50 Victoria Embankment
London EC4Y 0DZ

www.headline.co.uk
www.hachette.co.uk

For Mum,
(who is thankfully nothing like Devinia)
With love.

PART ONE
The Poison Chalice

1

Chen stood on the back doorstep, feeling the sweat cool on his skin. The moon had painted the clouds with light, and they hung in the sky like ghostly courtiers paying homage to their queen. Behind him, the roar of the tavern was constant, even at this time of night; the Banshee's small company of ships had made port at Two-Birds that morning, and there were a lot of thirsty men and women with coin to spend. For Chen, cook and occasional scrubber of pots at The Blinkered Inn, this meant a long night in a stuffy kitchen. The Blinkered was on the outskirts of the crowded town, where the buildings ended and the rest of the island began, but it was worth the uphill walk for ale that had only been watered down a touch, and, in Chen's opinion, the best double-meat stew Two-Birds had to offer.

It was a hot night, as most nights on Euriale were. Sometimes the heat would make Chen's scars itch, and each scored line would become a map of his mistakes, his conflicts, his triumphs. Sighing, he slipped a finger under his eyepatch and scratched at the sweat gathering in the puckered hole that had once been his eye, lost when a line snapped in a storm; it had snaked out of the night like a lightning bolt and turned his eye to jelly in an instant. Chen had seen men have their heads sliced from their necks in such accidents, so he had considered himself lucky at the time. Chen, or Screaming Mad Chen, as he'd been known in those days, believed in looking on the bright side. The Graces had been with him that day.

A figure leaned out of the door behind him. It was Molly, her hair gathered into a kerchief and a look of extreme irritation on her face. Chen could see sweat glistening on her forehead in the moonlight. 'I've got another six orders here, Chen. When you've quite finished taking the air, do you think you could give me a bloody hand?'

Chen drew himself up to his full height.

'I'm collecting ingredients, woman. Don't you fuss me now. Some of these ingredients, they need to be collected at night. Or do you want just any old stew?'

Molly rolled her eyes at him.

'Don't you pull that cook shit with me, old man. Just get what you need and get back in here, or I'll find some other one-eyed fraud to boil up this slop.'

Chen waved a hand at her and she disappeared back inside the tavern.

'Slop indeed.'

He left the step and headed to his garden. He had planted it himself over the last few years, buying seeds from the ships that sold such things, watching over the seedlings, even going as far as to cover the more fragile plants with an oilcloth when the worst storms hit. This small garden, his job at The Blinkered Inn – this was his retirement, of a sort. He had sailed with several crews over his long life, and hadn't regretted a single moment of it, but his bones were too old for sea voyages now. So, it wasn't exciting and Molly gave him no respect, but it was better than dying at sea. Better than watching a cutlass open your guts, or drowning in the deep, the weight of the sea pushing you down into the dark.

Chen bent and plucked a sprig of colder's fern, smiling faintly as the crushed leaves gave off a peppery scent. He stuck them in his apron pocket and began a quick circuit of the garden, picking herbs for that night's stew, as well as for tomorrow's breakfast. What he'd said to Molly wasn't complete bullshit; some plants were better picked at night, their flavours sealed in by darkness, and not sweated out by the sun. He chuckled quietly. He was getting to be a poet in his old age. Screaming Mad Chen,

4

dithering under the moon and fussing over herbs. Well, bollocks to it, he thought. The men he'd sailed with would have laughed at him, but most of them were dead.

He paused at the furthest reach of his garden. It backed on to the wild woods, and the trees loomed over him like a bank of storm cloud. That was the end of Two-Birds, pirate port and town, and the beginning of Euriale itself. As he looked at that dark mass, some of his good cheer leaked away. He supposed it suited a pirate to grow old on an island such as Euriale – always close to danger, always close to death – but at night-time, in the dark, the usual bravado and jokes didn't quite erase the sense of foreboding. You only ever left Two-Birds by sea, you didn't venture beyond the town, and you certainly didn't go walking in those trees after dark. Those who did, didn't come back, and that wasn't a story made up to tell around a tavern fire. That was the cold truth.

'Cursed place,' he murmured, and he scratched beneath his eyepatch again. His skin felt livid with scars, just as though the newest one wasn't over a decade old. 'Poison. That's what it is.'

As he moved to go, his thoughts already turning to the next batch of stew, something pale at the base of the nearest tree caught his eye. It was a clutch of moonroot mushrooms – he'd tried to cultivate them in his own garden several times, and they had never taken. Now here they were, growing just a few steps from his small, neat fence. Growing not in Two-Birds, but in Euriale. The distinction was important.

Chen cleared his throat and glanced back at the tavern. Lamps shone at every window, and beyond it, the gathered lights of Two-Birds curled along the bay like a constellation of impossibly bright stars. Just looking at it made him feel a little braver.

'I'm Screaming Mad Chen,' he muttered to himself, before stepping over the fence. He scampered to the treeline, trying not to notice how quickly he was moving, or how his heart had started to beat faster. Immediately it felt colder, and the pleasant scents of his garden were lost. Instead, he could smell the thick, wild scent of the island; it smelled of animal dung and rotten things and madness.

'Bloody nonsense.'

He knelt and quickly picked several handfuls of the moonroot. Once he'd had a chance to wash these and steep them, tomorrow's stew would be the best he'd ever made. He allowed himself a smile, pleased with his own luck and no small bravery, and stood up to go back to his garden. Beyond the trees he was startled to see a man standing in the dark, lit from within by some sort of strange, bluish light. The man was tall and broad, his hair curling close to his head. From what Chen could make out, he was handsome, his strong jaw smooth, his posture straight and true. The man seemed to be looking at him, and then he turned away.

Chen would never know why he followed him into the trees. He simply dropped the last of the moonroot and went after him, stepping from the light into the dark. The man was already some distance away, moving silently between the tree trunks. Chen caught sight of a section of his broad back, still lit from within with that strange light, and then a glimpse of the back of his head, and then he was no more than a distant glow. Chen stumbled, holding out one hand and catching on a nearby trunk for support.

'What am I . . .?'

Chen blinked rapidly. It was like waking up after dozing off by the fire; sounds seemed louder, lights brighter. There was a rustling in the trees that seemed to come from all around, although there was no breeze to speak of.

'Stupid old man.' He took a few rapid steps backwards. The trees pressed in on all sides, their darkness suffocating, but despite the closeness he felt terribly exposed. 'I must be getting feeble.'

He turned back, searching for Two-Birds' lights through the trees. Thick vines hung everywhere, obscuring his view.

'Graces be damned.'

The glowing figure had been an odd shadow, or a bit of moon magic. Perhaps he'd mistaken the mushrooms, and just the touch of their skins had given him a strange dream. He'd made a mistake, a big one, but it wouldn't matter. He'd go back inside, and it wasn't as if he'd *tell* anyone about it, oh no . . .

There was a low thud, and Chen was pushed violently forward. Only a lifetime spent keeping his balance on storm-lashed decks stopped him falling to his knees. He looked down to see something long and glistening sprouting from his chest. It took him a second to realise that it was the head of an arrow.

'You shouldn't have left your world, godless one.'

To his right the darkness between the trees shimmered, as though the air was as thick as water, and a woman appeared. Chen would have sworn that seconds ago that space was empty, but she was utterly solid, no ghost made of blue light. In the gloom he could make out that she was short, with skin as white as paper and untidy black hair that came down to her jaw and curled under there. She was beautiful, with almond-shaped eyes and a full mouth painted red, but a shadow lay against her neck. Chen narrowed his eyes at that, sure it was familiar, but the pain in his chest was starting to push all other thoughts aside.

'I . . . why would you? I was just . . .'

She came closer. The woman moved with grace through the undergrowth, barely making a sound, and she wore a strange combination of fur and leathers, beads and bones and other trinkets at her ears and wrists. In her hands was a pair of long curved swords. She was not carrying a bow.

'You have entered the world of the Twins now.' She smiled at him, and Chen felt his bladder release in a sudden hot torrent. It was the smile of a wolf. 'Such as you must stand in sacrifice.'

She looked over his shoulder and nodded, and a man came out of the shadows, a bow held loosely in one hand. He did not simply appear out of the air as the woman had done, but he moved just as silently, and he wore dark clothes.

'He will do,' she told the new man, her tone kind now. 'A bit scrawny for your first, maybe, but we will find the meat on him.'

Laughter came from beyond the trees. Chen looked around, trying to see who was there, but the woman reached out and pushed him to the ground. He cried out; the stench of the island had increased when she had touched him, and it felt like an invasion. He didn't want to die here, with that stink in his nose.

'Please,' he said, aware from the taste of blood in his mouth that he was as good as dead already. 'Please, I can give you coin. I spent most of it, but I hid some too. I can tell you where, I can—'

The woman laughed. Now that she was closer Chen could see that the shadow on her neck was a tattoo – it covered her neck, reaching up to the line of her jaw, and apparently continued below the leather vest she wore. It was too dark to see what it depicted.

'Old pirates,' she said, almost fondly. 'Always the same offers, the same threats. This is the disadvantage of meat that can talk.' She looked up to the man with the bow and held out one of her swords. 'Make the cuts the way I taught you, and the gods will bless our feast this evening.'

2

Wydrin passed the folded cloth across the table. 'Go on. Have a look.'

Frith glanced up at her, frowning slightly. The chik-choks house was busy, full of the gentle clatter of men and women moving their pieces across their game boards, the murmur of quiet conversation and the occasional disagreement. Their own board had been colonised by several empty glasses, the game pieces – crystal monkeys, as was Wydrin's preference – scattered to either side. Frith had picked up the game after only a few demonstrations and was dangerously close to winning his first match. He suspected this was why Wydrin had developed a habit of disrupting the game with elaborate orders of drinks.

'What is it?'

She nodded at the cloth. 'Nothing awful, I promise. Well, a bit awful.'

Frith picked up the material and unfolded it. Inside was a small piece of gold, rounded and dented into a familiar shape. 'Wydrin,' he said, 'is this a tooth?'

She nodded. 'Not bad work, either. Bit flashy for my tastes.'

'And why am I holding a tooth?'

Wydrin picked up her glass and took a gulp. 'That was left for me outside our room this morning. Wrapped in parchment, my name scribbled on it. Nothing else. No note, no instructions.'

'You left the room this morning?'

'I went out to get some fresh air. You were still asleep. It was as if you were worn out or something.' She gave him a look over the top of her glass, and Frith smiled. It was strange, even now, to smile like that, but her green eyes demanded it. He put the gold tooth down on the chik-choks board.

'Do you know why someone would send you a gold tooth? Is someone paying a debt they owe perhaps?'

Wydrin laughed, although he noted the bitter tone of it. 'You could say that. You remember when you went swanning off to Whittenfarne to learn your mages' words?'

'Of course.' Without thinking about it, Frith's hand moved to the staff leaning against the chair next to him, fingers briefly brushing against the words carved there. These days Selsye's staff never left his sight.

'Seb had buggered off too, so I went back to Crosshaven, and—' She paused, swirling the last of the mead around the bottom of her glass. 'Well, I got involved in some stuff I probably shouldn't have. Pirate business.' He could see real regret in her eyes, not an expression he often associated with Wydrin. 'I helped a man called Reilly rob a man called Morgul, but the stupid little bastard pushed it too far, and a lot of people died. It was a bloody mess.'

Frith raised his eyebrows. 'You made some enemies then, I assume.'

She shrugged. 'It's not the first time it's happened. I had to leave Crosshaven for a while, which was fine because we ended up, you know, having to deal with the god of destruction in the form of a dragon.' She waved a hand airily.

'I do seem to remember something like that.'

'But when I came back I was careful. I asked around. Checked all the usual sources, and everything suggested that the Morgul situation had blown over. Those seeking revenge were apparently sated, and no one was muttering my name in dark alleys any more. Or no more than usual. And then this.' She tapped the tooth with the end of her finger. 'Reilly had a gold tooth. He thought it made him look dashing.'

'So it's a warning.' Frith leaned back in his chair. 'A threat.'

'It seems so.' Wydrin put her glass down, knocking over one

of the crystal monkeys. 'Nothing I can't handle, but it might be worth—'

There was a crash from the front of the chik-choks room. A woman had just walked in and thrown the door back with more violence than was strictly necessary, catching the edge of a nearby chair and scattering game pieces. The man at the table stood up angrily – his drink appeared to have landed in his lap. He began shouting at the woman, who stood looking at him with a faint expression of curiosity on her face.

'Oh *shit*,' said Wydrin.

The woman looked as though she was in her fifties, with deep red hair tumbling in an untidy cloud to the middle of her back. It was braided here and there, Frith noticed, and tied with black ribbons. Her skin was tanned, and she wore salt-blasted leather trousers and vest, with a black silk shirt underneath. There was a pair of well-used cutlasses at her belt, along with a range of smaller daggers.

'Who is it?' There was a look of sheer alarm on Wydrin's face now. Frith rested his hand on the staff. The solidity of it was comforting. 'Is this one of the pirates you've angered?'

'You could say that.'

The man was still shouting, his face growing redder and redder. The woman with the cutlasses seemed to grow abruptly tired of it, and in the middle of his rant she reached out with both hands, grabbed hold of his shirt, and brought her forehead up smartly to meet his nose. Even across the other side of the room, Frith quite clearly heard the crunch as small bones shattered. The man howled, pressing his fingers to his face as blood flowed from his broken nose.

The woman turned away from him, her eyes scanning the room for her next victim.

'By all the Graces . . .' Wydrin stood up and waved frantically. 'Hello, Mum!'

Wydrin called for another round of drinks and fetched an extra chair from a nearby table. Out of the corner of her eye she could see the proprietor watching her with sudden attentiveness – even in Crosshaven, they didn't get too many brawls in gaming houses, and she could tell that she had rapidly become his least favourite patron. She ignored him.

'Frith,' she said, as her mother took the offered seat. 'This is Devinia the Red, notorious captain of the *Crimson Sea Witch*, scourge of the Bararian flotilla, first pirate to sail the Shadow-Bone Pass without smashing her ship to pieces, popularly referred to as the "Succubus of the Silent Sea"—'

'No one has ever called me that,' put in her mother, evenly.

'. . . The Eighth Wonder of Crosshaven, or the Terror of the Torrent,' continued Wydrin. 'She is wanted in several countries with rewards healthy enough to set you up for life, if you live to claim it. She is also my mother.'

'Thank you, Wydrin, that's enough.' Devinia looked her over, her dark blue eyes narrowing. 'You do not look to have changed much since I saw you last.'

'And when was that?' asked Wydrin. She felt the brittleness in her tone and was powerless to change it. 'Three years ago? Four?'

'Possibly.' A waiter arrived with their drinks, and Devinia peered with interest at the flagon of ale set before her, but did not move to drink it. 'It's the *Poison Chalice* now, not the *Crimson Sea Witch*. I have a new ship.' She transferred her icy gaze to Frith. 'Who is this, then? Where's the other one? The big one?'

Wydrin grimaced. Frith was looking at the pair of them with a faintly stunned expression, but he recovered well.

'Madam, I am Lord Aaron Frith of the Blackwood. It is an honour to meet such a distinguished lady, especially one with such a remarkable reputation.'

Devinia raised her eyebrows. There were a few beats of silence.

'An honour, is it?' Devinia turned back to Wydrin. 'Where did you find this one?'

'Frith and I have been travelling together for a while now. Saving the world from dragons, mad mages. That sort of thing.'

'So I have heard,' said Devinia, leaning back in her chair. Her face remained cool, disinterested, and Wydrin felt a flicker of irritation. It was as if fighting dragons and foiling evil magic was a regular occurrence, something Devinia did on a slow day perhaps, when she was bored. 'Stories of the Black Feather Three abound in every port. I thought it was your usual ploy of spreading elaborate rumours, but the same tales were being told everywhere and, of course, your brother can attest to the reality of your dragon.'

Quickly, the irritation turned to anger. She didn't say it outright, of course she didn't *say* anything, but the accusation was there in the slight downward turn of her mouth.

'Jarath is *fine*,' said Wydrin, with more heat than she intended. 'I saved him. We saved him.' She glanced up at Frith, who said nothing. 'He's a pirate, Mum, like you. He's hardly a bloody stranger to risk.'

'A stranger to dragon fire though,' replied Devinia, before shaking her head as if knowing Wydrin wanted to argue the point further. 'That's not why I'm here, anyway.'

'Then why are you here? Not that it isn't a pleasure to see you of course, out of the blue and with no prior warning.' And in truth, it was good to see her. Devinia had a few more lines at the corners of her eyes, and the first few grey hairs were beginning to show at her temples, but otherwise Devinia looked as she ever had; strong, immovable and defiant. And like a spectacular pain in the arse. 'Why exactly have we been blessed with your presence?'

Devinia cocked her head slightly.

'This is your new young man, isn't it? That's why you're showing off?' Before Wydrin could answer, she carried on. 'I'm here, Wydrin, because you have shown yourself to be an extremely capable sell-sword with a remarkable reputation won in a short space of time. You also have some interesting friends, with some interesting abilities.' She glanced at the staff leaning against Frith's chair. 'And so I have come to ask you if you would like to join me on a small adventure.' For the first time, Devinia smiled, just a little. 'I think it might be your sort of thing.'

Wydrin sat back in her chair, suddenly wary. She could count the occasions that Devinia had asked for her assistance on the fingers of one hand, and still leave enough to hold a tankard of mead. She looked at Frith, who shrugged his shoulders minutely.

'Oh? Exactly what sort of adventure are we talking about, Mum?'

Devinia leaned forward over the table, lowering her voice. 'You remember the island of Euriale?'

Wydrin frowned. 'Of course. It's where the port town of Two-Birds is. You took me there often enough as a kid.' Catching Frith's questioning look, she turned to him slightly. 'Two-Birds is a pirate town, full of – well, people like my mum here. Beyond Two-Birds, though, there's nothing but wild jungle. It's generally believed to be cursed.' She smiled. 'I was a terror for stories about Euriale when I was a kid.'

'Some of those stories involved gold,' cut in Devinia. She took a sip of the ale. 'Gold and treasure, and wonders unlike any other place on Ede, all hidden at the very centre of the island.'

Frith shifted in his chair. 'And you expect me to believe no one has yet claimed this treasure? When the closest town is full of pirates?'

Devinia gave him a cool look. 'Whether the island is cursed or not, it certainly is dangerous. No one has been known to survive more than a handful of days when venturing into the island.'

Wydrin shook her head. 'It hardly matters anyway, Mum. Unless you have some magical way to get to the centre of the island without getting killed?'

'Actually, you're the ones that have that.' Devinia leaned back and crossed her arms over her chest. 'I just have the map.'

Wydrin snorted. 'A map of the interior of the island? No such thing exists. Nothing reputable, anyway.'

'I have one and I assure you, it certainly is real.' And then to Wydrin's surprise, her mother turned away from her and addressed Frith directly. 'The problem, Lord Frith, is one of transportation. The island of Euriale is split by a great spiral of waterways that lead to the very centre, banked all along the way by high cliffs of black rock. With the right vessel it would be possible to sail almost all the way—'

She paused as Wydrin scoffed into her drink.

'But Euriale *is* dangerous. Small boats and ships are surely doomed, overwhelmed within days.'

'Overwhelmed?' asked Frith. 'Overwhelmed by what?'

'The local wildlife,' replied Devinia dryly. 'The only reliable way through would be with a big, tough ship, one where the crew are kept as far away from the water as possible. A ship like the *Poison Chalice*.'

'But Mum—'

Devinia silenced her with a look. 'The difficulty is that the *Poison Chalice* is a ship with sails. And once we're deep in those waterways with the cliffs rising on either side of us, we will lose most of the wind we need to move. The waterways are deep, but they are also cramped, and the *Poison Chalice* has no oars to keep her moving when we are becalmed. This is where you come in, with your staff and your magic.'

Frith toyed with one of the crystal monkeys on the table. 'I'm not sure I follow.'

'I've heard the stories of the Black Feather Three.' Devinia tipped her head to one side. 'You can hardly avoid them, around here. I've heard all sorts about what you can do with your magic.'

'Are you asking him to move your entire bloody ship for you?' Wydrin shook her head slightly.

'I am asking him to provide our means of propulsion.' Devinia looked directly at Frith. 'What do you think? Is it possible?'

For a long time Frith said nothing. He looked at the staff, leaning next to him. Wydrin knew that he was limited to the words that Selsye, long-dead mage and crafter of the Edeian, had carved into the wood itself, but she also knew that, thanks to the ministrations of the mad mage Joah Demonsworn, he now knew more about the elusive magic than anyone else on Ede. Thinking of what that had cost him caused a bitter taste to flood Wydrin's mouth. She fidgeted in her chair.

'I think it is possible,' he said eventually. And then he nodded, more certain of himself. 'Yes, I believe so. I have the word for Force, and the ability to send it in several directions at once. And my mastery of the spell itself has vastly improved. I could sail your ship for you.'

Devinia's mouth quirked up at the corner. 'You can leave the sailing to us, I just need you to provide a fair wind. What do you say?'

Frith caught Wydrin's eye, and she saw that he was open to the idea. There would be treasure, yes, and adventure, but more importantly there would be a way to use his knowledge of the Edenier, something she knew he had been craving. And there was Sebastian to think about. She had been avoiding that problem for too long.

'It seems you have gained yourself the services of the Black Feather Three, Mum.' Wydrin took a sip of her mead. 'Now we just need to discuss the fee. There will be no family discounts, of course.'

3

Sebastian slipped into the crowd, pushing to the front easily enough. From the corner of his eye he saw a few men and women turn to him angrily, but once they caught a glimpse of his broad shoulders and muscled arms, they quickly turned back to the action in the pit. They were here to watch a fight, not to pick one.

It was a busy day at the Marrow Market, and the air was full of the smell of roasted meat and spilt beer as the people of Crosshaven sought out their afternoon's entertainment. Sebastian leaned on the wall at the edge of the scale pit, peering down like everyone else. At the bottom was around a foot of water, still stained pink from the last fight. Sebastian remembered that one well. He had won so much coin that the gaffer had started to give him a curious look, but that hadn't stopped him from going back to bet on this fight too. Let him look. Let them all look. He took a skin from his belt and had a gulp of toka, relishing the burn as it worked its way down his throat to his empty stomach.

'Introducing our next combatants, ladies and gentlemen.' The gaffer stood at the far side of the pit, with his twin daughters to either side. They were both lean and strong, blond hair pushed back from faces that looked like they'd been born already bored by life in general. In their arms they held a pair of sun-lizards, held securely at the neck. Each lizard was two feet long, with a narrow snout lined with sharp teeth. 'On the right, we have Icefang, who has won his last two games.' One daughter brandished the lizard she was holding easily enough, although Sebastian knew them to be heavy creatures. Icefang was pale blue and dotted with yellow markings from the end of his snout to the tip of his tail. Sebastian reached out instinctively and felt the cold thread of the lizard's mind there waiting for him – the animal was relaxed, inert almost. It was a veteran of the pits. 'And on my left we have Sourcrest, in his first ever bout.' The second daughter stepped forward, and this lizard was a pale salmon-pink, with a deep brown belly and rolling yellow eyes. When Sebastian reached out to this one he took an involuntary step back; its mind was jumping all over the place. The lizard could smell the blood in the water, and the hands at his throat were too hot, too alien. He wriggled in the woman's grasp, opening and closing his long snout. 'I trust you have all placed your bets, ladies and gentlemen? Then let us begin.'

In unison, the two women stepped forward and dropped the sun-lizards into the pit where they landed with a splash. The blue lizard, Icefang, immediately scurried to the far side, pressing itself to the wall. The other, Sourcrest, thrashed for a while, snapping its jaws at the air in confusion. There was a cheer from the spectators, shouts of encouragement and derision.

'I'm not doing it,' murmured Sebastian to himself. His hand went to his beard, tugging on the bristles there. 'I will just watch. No more than that.'

The blue lizard scampered along the bottom of the wall, sending waves across the water. The pink lizard was still confused, shaking its head back and forth, when the other one came for it, shooting across the pool and sinking its teeth into the animal's scaly flank. There was a roar of disgust from the crowd – so easy! – and the pink lizard scrambled away, its blood tainting the water.

'What's the point of this?' yelled a woman standing to Sebastian's right. She had pale blond hair falling in a braid over one shoulder, and she was shaking a fist at the gaffer on the other side of the pit. 'We've come to watch a fight, not feeding time!'

Sebastian looked back down. The pink lizard was limping badly now, while the other was openly stalking it. They moved in tight circles, the water filling with blood.

'I won't,' said Sebastian again, and this time it was loud enough that the blonde woman heard him. She looked up, her face creasing with confusion. 'I won't do it again.'

But it was no use. Already he was reaching out to the pink lizard, his mind touching its own, a sliver of silver, so cold and yet frantic. He felt the shape of it clearly in his mind and very carefully he surrounded it. *Listen to me*, he said, uncertain that the lizard would understand but trusting his tone to convey the meaning. *Listen to me, do as I say.*

With the barest push, the lizard's mind was encompassed. In the pool it went rigid, and for a few seconds the blue lizard was confused. The prey wasn't retreating as it expected.

'Go on, then!' screamed the woman next to Sebastian. 'Finish the bastard!'

Sebastian peeled apart the lizard's mind, splitting the silvery threads until he found the part he wanted. As ever, it was easy, as easy as it had been with the wyverns – this part of them was always close to the surface. The need to fight, the urge to taste blood. He felt his own pulse quicken in response.

Kill.

The pink lizard leapt at its rival, jaws suddenly wide and lethal. It landed on the other and rolled with it through the water, sending up a splash high enough to soak some of the spectators. There was a cheer at this, but as the lizards fought and the water churned, it became difficult to see exactly what was going on.

Sebastian tugged at his beard. He didn't need to see. He could *feel* it.

In a few moments it was all over. The pink lizard stalked away, leaving the shredded carcass of its enemy in the water. The blue lizard lay on its back, its guts open and ragged, and all around coin changed hands as they prepared for the next fight. One of the blonde sisters produced a long stick with a hook on the end, and attempted to retrieve the body.

Sebastian turned away, breaking the link with the victorious lizard. He could feel its disorientation now the fight was over, and that somehow was the worst part. He took another gulp of toka from his pouch, trying to wash the taste of blood from his mouth, when a hand landed heavily on his shoulder.

'Hey, Seb. Still betting on the scale pits?'

He looked down into Wydrin's open face. She sounded cheery enough, but he could tell from the creases on her brow that this was not where she had hoped to find him. It was still the first place she'd looked though; he could tell that from her frown too.

'I am,' he said shortly. Frith was standing just behind her, scanning the crowd with his usual expression of caution. 'What is it? A job? Just tell me where.'

Wydrin sighed. 'It's a little more complicated than that. Come on, let's go get some food. You look like you need something hot inside you.'

'Your mother is back in Crosshaven?'

Wydrin nodded as she took a bite from her steaming slab of lamb. It was wrapped in thin brown bread, already soaked through with grease, and the butter was burning her fingers. 'She asked after you,' she said. They stood off to one side of the meat vendor, letting the crowd part around them. Sebastian had refused her offer of food at first, but she had insisted. He was too pale these days, his cheeks too hollow. Frith had accepted a small portion of the meat, holding the bread carefully with gloved hands. 'I didn't tell her you look like shit, but she'll see that for herself.'

Sebastian took a slow breath, looking around at the press of people as though he wanted to be elsewhere. 'And?'

Wydrin shrugged. 'My dearest mother wants us to travel with her to Euriale. She has a map of the interior of the island, something long thought not to have existed at all, and there are some tall tales about what might be hidden there.'

Sebastian frowned. 'Euriale? I know the name.'

'The notorious pirate port of Two-Birds is situated there,' said Frith.

'Yeah, Two-Birds,' Wydrin continued. 'Devinia would take me there when I was small sometimes. Full of pirates, taverns, pissing

20

contests. The island itself is largely unknown and unexplored though—'

'– because it is considered to be incredibly dangerous,' finished Frith.

Sebastian looked down at his food, considering.

'All right,' he said eventually. 'But why would Devinia want us along on this little venture? From what I remember, Wydrin, she is more than formidable, and travels with a crew who would swim across the nine seas and back for her.'

'Apparently, we have special skills.' Wydrin winked at Frith, who wore his staff slung across his back. 'Experience in the field, extreme quick-wittedness, good looks. And she needs Frith's magic to get there.'

'I have no special skills,' said Sebastian flatly. He still hadn't eaten any of the food.

Wydrin rubbed the back of her hand across her mouth, her levity vanished; this was something they'd been dancing around for months. 'Seb, whatever happened with Ephemeral and the brood sisters –' she paused, uncertain of what her next words might provoke. 'Whatever happened with Dallen, you are still one of us. One of the Black Feather Three.'

Sebastian looked away from her. There were a few beats of silence between the three of them, filled by the general din of the Marrow Market. Out of the corner of her eye she could see Frith looking solemn. After a moment, Sebastian threw the wrapped meat parcel down onto the ground – not in an angry movement, but in a gesture of defeat.

'As far as I can see, Wydrin, the only skills I have are to alienate those I love, and to fail in my responsibilities.' When she opened her mouth to protest, Sebastian held his hands up. 'I will still come with you, if that is what you wish. I can still wield a sword well enough, after all.'

'We leave two days from now,' said Frith softly. 'From the Fair Winds dock. Sunrise.'

Sebastian nodded once, before turning and heading away into the crowd. Wydrin sighed and rubbed her greasy fingers across her leather vest.

'It will do him good to be away from here,' said Frith.

'I don't like it.' Wydrin shook her head. 'Sebastian has never shown any interest in these things before.' She gestured vaguely in the direction of the fighting pits. 'But now it's all he does, in between drinking toka and brooding. The Sebastian I knew would have found the scale fights barbaric, but now he watches them like he's hungry for something. Our good prince broke his heart, and now it's like he's not really here. As though he left part of himself in Skaldshollow.'

Frith looked away, his expression darkening. 'Skaldshollow was a cursed place. There is much I wish I could have left there.'

Wydrin threw away the last of her lamb. She no longer had much of an appetite. 'And now we head off to another cursed place. Let's hope this one has rather more treasure and fewer disasters.'

4

The *Poison Chalice* was, Frith reflected, rather like Wydrin in one sense: it took an awful lot to get it moving in the morning.

Eventually, they sailed from Crosshaven at midday, with the sun a bright coin in the sky, and a busy sea channel to negotiate. Frith leaned against the guardrail as they moved, watching the bustling city port grow smaller as the ship sailed away from the island and into the larger archipelago. He could see other islands dotted around, brown blurs distorted with heat haze and smoke.

The *Poison Chalice* was easily the largest ship he'd ever been aboard. She was, Wydrin had told him, a galleon, and he had to admit the grandness of the name seemed appropriate. She was a tall, sturdy ship built of shining dark wood, with raised, boxy-looking hindquarters and three great masts hung with enormous cream-coloured sails. Above the crow's nest flew a red flag with a black border and a silver cup at its centre. The figurehead that clung on the prow of the ship depicted a fierce-faced woman with pale-blue skin; her long white hair was strewn with delicately carved shells and crabs and she wore a silvery shift that appeared to be made of scales. Wydrin had told him the figure was supposed to represent one of the Graces. One arm reached out, fingers clutching a long silver chain that glittered in the bright sunshine. She looked, in his opinion, formidable. All in all, he thought the ship suited Wydrin's mother down to her salt-stained boots.

Having grown up in the middle of the Blackwood, Frith's only experience of boats had been the occasional summer's day at the lake, punting around in an elaborate rowboat his father had had made for his wife. Thinking of it, he smiled slightly. Those memories were now so distant they almost seemed to have happened to another person. Had he truly once lived in a castle, with a mother and father and two brothers? His hair had been brown then, and he'd had only the one scar; a small oval depression on his upper arm, a souvenir from the afternoon he and Leon had pretended to be the leaders of the Steadfast Seven with daggers stolen from the armoury. Leon had laughed hysterically, until he had seen the blood soaking into his brother's shirt.

Everything was so different now. Absently, he pressed a hand to his chest, where the Edenier no longer boiled inside him. The mage magic he had taken from beneath the Citadel had once leapt at his command, but now it was gone; all erased by the Edenier trap, a device that stripped magic from men and women like a practised hand skinning a rabbit. It had been worth it to stop Joah Demonsworn, who had been a mad man and a mass murderer, but all he had left now was the *knowledge*, a maelstrom of images inherited from the lunatic when they had shared their memories.

There was nothing left but the knowledge of magic, and the fear that to use it would take him down the path Joah had followed.

Frith took a deep, slow breath, tasting the salt in the air. 'I barely recognise myself these days,' he murmured.

A shadow fell over him. He looked up to see Sebastian, a faint smile on the knight's gaunt face.

'You and me both, my lord.'

'I am glad you chose to join us, Sir Sebastian.'

Sebastian grunted. 'It's not like I had anything pressing to deal with.'

Frith looked back out to sea. There were seagulls high above them, a promise of white against the blue. It was a fine day.

'Wydrin worries about you,' he said eventually. 'She shows it by trying to annoy you more than usual, of course. But she is worried.'

'Lord Frith, you forget that I have known Wydrin for many years.' Sebastian turned towards him slightly. 'I have no doubt you have a greater knowledge of her underclothes than I could ever need or want, but don't presume to think you know her better than I do.'

The anger was a sudden thing, clogging Frith's throat. 'You dare to speak to me so?' He was thinking of his staff, wrapped within a length of oilcloth, locked in a long wooden box in their cabin. If he had it now . . . 'I am sure I do not need to remind you what we have all been through together.'

The tense expression on Sebastian's face faltered, and he shook his head. 'I am sorry, Frith. Truly.' He tugged at his thick beard, glaring at the horizon as if the answers to his troubles lay somewhere along that bright edge. 'What you said about not recognising yourself. That cuts closer to the quick than I would like to admit.'

Frith cleared his throat. He was reminded of his childhood again, of a quiet castle with very few people of his own age. It had been difficult to make friends. 'You can talk to me. If it would help.'

Sebastian smiled faintly, and for a brief moment he looked very much like the smooth-faced knight Frith had met for the first time in the Hands of Fate tavern. 'Thank you. I shall bear that in mind.'

Before Frith could reply, they both turned at the sound of footsteps behind them. The ship's first mate, Kellan, a tall bearded man with hair greased back into a tail and vanbraces wrapped in multicoloured scraps of cloth, was approaching with an elderly woman at his arm. She was short and wiry, with grey hair and deeply tanned skin, and there was a wine-coloured birthmark on her right cheek, faded and creased with age. She wore a long-sleeved green shirt, and at her waist there was a thick leather belt, glittering with a variety of knives.

'Gentlemen,' said Kellan, 'I thought I should bring Augusta Grint to meet you. She is the ship's medic, although of course, I very much hope you won't be in need of her services on this voyage.'

The old woman glared up at the two of them, her eyes as

bright and beady as a jackdaw's. 'Well,' she said, addressing Sebastian, 'you're a biggun.'

Sebastian paused for a moment, before nodding shortly. 'You are not the first to have said so, Mistress Grint. It is my pleasure—'

'You, though – I don't like the look of you.' The old woman reached out and grabbed hold of Frith's forearm. It took all of his self-possession not to gasp – her grip was incredibly strong. 'Been ill, have you? I won't have anyone bringing illness onto the *Poison Chalice*. I've got enough to bloody deal with.'

Frith wrenched his arm away. 'I was injured, but it was some time ago and I am quite recovered, thank you. You are the ship's medic?' He glanced at Kellan, who was grinning with every sign of enjoyment.

'Ship's medic? Nursemaid to a bunch of ninnies, mostly. General dogsbody, more like.' Augusta grimaced, deepening her considerable wrinkles. 'You're thinking, the baggage is too old. Too weak. How can she treat the sick? I'd be surprised if she could lift a spoon, let alone a bone saw.' She stepped up and poked Frith firmly in the midriff with one bony finger. 'Let me tell you, you long streak of piss, I could have your leg off in seconds.'

'Augusta has been with Devinia all of the captain's life,' added Kellan with an expression of innocent helpfulness.

'Oh, she was a bleedin' nightmare!' cried Augusta, apparently glad to have a crack at her favourite subject. 'All knees and freckles and that ridiculous hair of hers.'

'You knew Devinia when she was a child?' asked Sebastian.

'Of course I did. I was on the ship that picked her up. Merchant vessel, taken badly, blood in the water. Nowt left alive on board but rats and one scruffy little kid hiding under the bunk.' She paused. Frith sensed that she'd said too much. 'Anyhow, we took her on, and here we are. I've never questioned that girl's orders, not once, and she gets some bloody foolish ideas in her head, let me tell you. But this, messing about with Euriale . . .' She trailed off, then glared up at Kellan. 'You know better, laughing boy. Why haven't you said anything to her?'

Kellan shrugged. 'I merely do as my lady instructs.'

Augusta snorted. 'I would suspect you'd lost your balls, boy, except we've all heard the evidence of those, night after bleedin' night.'

'You do not approve of the journey to Euriale, I take it?' put in Frith, desperately trying to steer the conversation into less horrifying territory.

The old woman seemed to shrink somehow then, and some of her bluster ebbed away. 'Course I don't. It's a bad place. Unnatural. Cursed. No one with any bloody sense would sail into those waters. If I had my way we'd never set foot on the island, and that goes for bloody Two-Birds too.' She patted absently at the knives on the belt. 'What's there is best left alone.'

'And what is there?' asked Sebastian. Frith was surprised to see that he looked angry again, as though the old woman were lying to them.

'Ghosts,' said Augusta. 'Ghosts and wolves.'

It wasn't the cabin Wydrin remembered from her childhood, of course, but she recognised many of her mother's possessions: the big black iron teapot, stained with tea and age, the blue crystal sugar pot with its silver spoon. The giant sword with the curving blade, much too large for Devinia to actually wield, but kept in her cabin because it was beautiful, emeralds shining in the hilt like frozen pieces of summer. And the great map of Ede pinned to one wall of the cabin, painted onto parchment and filled in at the edges with various outlandish monsters. It had been her favourite when she'd been small, she remembered now. Her father would point to the places with the strangest names, and tell her wild stories about his adventures there; it had been one of his favourite games. Pete Threefellows had always been the most outrageous liar.

Devinia, who was sitting at the desk covered in more recent, legible maps, saw her looking. 'What do you think of the new ship?'

'Well, it's not the *Crimson Sea Witch*.'

Devinia grunted. 'You always were too sentimental to be a pirate.'

'You really took it from old Tom Dogget?'

'That particular storm had been brewing for years.' Devinia leaned back in her chair, looking out of the small port window. 'We'd been crossing each other's paths more and more often, and there were rumours that he saw the *Sea Witch* as encroaching on his territory. More interesting were the rumours that his crew were sick to the back teeth with his ravings. I decided, in the end, to give him the fight he kept dreaming of.' Devinia looked up, her mouth briefly curving into a smile. 'I don't think he enjoyed it half as much as he thought he would.'

'And now you have the biggest, baddest ship on the Torrent.' Wydrin watched her mother raise her eyebrows at her use of that term – the Torrent was what pirates called the stretch of five seas that formed an irregular belt around the belly of Ede: the Sea of Bones, the Yellow Sea, the Stony Sea, the Demon's Strait, and the wide hot expanse of Y'Gria's Loss. 'And you want to use it to explore Euriale, of all places?'

Without answering directly, Devinia shuffled through the maps on her desk before sliding one on top of the others. On a map, Euriale resembled a pie that had been dropped from a great height and shattered into a rough spiral pattern. It was mostly round, with the port town of Two-Birds clinging to its outer rim, and then you could follow the wide waterways directly into the heart of the island, circling ever inwards with jagged cliffs of stone and jungle towering to either side. Except no one in their right minds did that, because Euriale was cursed. Not even the people of Two-Birds would map it – in fact, the people of Two-Birds would be the last to attempt such a thing; they lived with the ghosts and monsters of the island every day.

Wydrin picked the map up, peering at it critically. It certainly seemed more complete than any map she'd seen of the island before.

'Where did you get this, then?'

'I have my sources,' said Devinia. 'You'll see that it *is* possible to get a ship almost all the way to the centre of the island, despite what we've thought for all these years.'

Wydrin put the map back on the table. 'When I was little, Augusta used to tell me stories about Euriale. That if you wandered into the trees, you never came back, that the spirits that lived in there would eat your soul and walk around in your empty skin.' She waved her hands about for emphasis. 'That the island hated people, that it would eat anyone foolish enough to wander away from Two-Birds.'

'Do you believe in those old folk tales now, Wydrin?'

'Mum,' Wydrin sat down in the chair on the opposite side of the desk, 'these days I have very good reason to believe in all sorts of shit. Or haven't you heard *my* stories? A dragon under the Citadel, the resurgence of mage magic, an army of terrible dragon-women, a living mountain, demons and blood and gods only know what.'

'*Your* stories now, are they?' This time Devinia's smile was cold. 'You truly are weaving the legend of Wydrin Threefellows, the Copper Cat and slayer of dragons.'

'Mum.' Wydrin took a slow breath, closing her eyes briefly. Here it was, then – that quick flash of anger, always close to the surface. 'You're missing the point. Those things all sound like stories told by vindictive old women who like to keep their charges awake all night with bad dreams, but I know them to be real. I have the scars.' She held up her hand where the skin in the centre of her palm was dented and pink – a remnant of her time joined to the mountain spirit, when a piece of Heart-Stone had nestled there.

Her mother didn't look at it. Instead, she stood up and walked over to the great ornamental sword hanging on the wall. 'There are other stories about Euriale. Do you remember those?'

Wydrin sighed heavily and fiddled with the maps on the desk. 'There were lots of stories, but Augusta preferred the bloodthirsty ones.'

'Treasure at the heart of Euriale. So much of it, you would need the biggest, baddest ship on the Torrent to carry it all back.' Devinia touched her fingers to the emeralds glittering in the sword's hilt. 'And more than that. Magical items, secrets that have been kept for centuries. The island was once known as the island of the gods, did you know that? Every god, every demon, every limping spirit creature had a temple there, or a shrine, or a pile

29

of blessed rocks. It was the very heart of Ede.' Devinia turned back, and her eyes were shining. 'Imagine what we'll learn there, Wyd.'

And that was the truth of it. Wydrin leaned back in the chair, looking at the expression on her mother's face with a weary sense of defeat. It was knowledge that Devinia craved, it always had been; to know more than everyone else, to hold the secrets, to get to the impossible places before everyone else. It was the great secret of her legend – Devinia the Red, Terror of the Torrent and ruthless pirate, feared and adored in equal measure, would step around a pile of gold coins if it meant she could discover something completely new. The giant sea chest that took up a good portion of her cabin was full of books rather than booty – notes collected by Devinia over the years, even sketches and maps she'd drawn herself. It was locked at all times, and as far as Wydrin was aware, only she and Augusta knew its true contents.

'Is it worth the risk though, Mum?' asked Wydrin, although she knew she'd already lost this argument. 'How do you even know this map is accurate? New ship, all done up and shiny. Don't you want to keep it that way? You've no real idea what we'll find in that place.'

'Ah, but now I have you, don't I?' Devinia came back over to the desk and briefly rested her fingers in Wydrin's hair. 'You and your new, dangerous friends. Magic, and the Black Feather Three. I have certainly heard *those* stories.'

'Oh yes,' said Wydrin, folding her arms over her chest. 'And we have such a great track record with this sort of thing.'

5

The island was alive around her; the soaring hunger of the hunters, the murmuring heartbeats of the hunted. The slow, green tide of the trees, reaching up and up. Estenn crouched on a thick branch some twenty feet above the ground, hidden in a crowd of fleshy green leaves. In the distance she could see the dancing white light of the bay, curls of smoke smeared by the wind. She sensed a flurry of activity in the port; a new ship had recently docked, which meant the chance for everyone to make some coin. The weight of her curved swords at her waist was comforting, and she knew her place on the island as clearly as she had ever done. The Eye called to her, even now.

She looked down to see a pale-blue figure moving slowly through the trees, just as on the night they had taken the wizened old pirate. They were coming more frequently now; the same figure, lost and wandering about the trees, glowing with its own inner light. You did not live in the wilds of Euriale without coming to expect the unusual – Estenn smiled slightly at the very idea – but she knew that this was something different. It was a sign. A sign that her time would be soon. The Eye of Euriale was opening.

In one smooth movement, Estenn stepped over to the trunk of the tree and slid back down to the ground, barely making any noise. When her feet were back in the mulch of the island, black soil and rotten leaves pushing up through her toes, she allowed herself to *become less*. She barely had to think about it now, after all these decades. One moment she was there, a solid presence under the trees, and the next she was a shadow, a cold space in the air. The ghostly blue figure to her right paid her no attention, although so far the ghosts seemed uninterested in anyone at all, even if you went right up to them and waved in their faces. Just one more mystery of Euriale.

Moving silently through the trees, she approached the figure and circled it slowly. Its own inner light blurred the details of its face, but she could see that it was a man, tall and broad across the shoulders, hair curling close to the scalp. He wore strange clothes, a mixture of robes, tunic and chainmail, and on his feet were leather sandals that laced up to the tops of his calves. Estenn thought back to the distant days before the island, when she had been so impossibly young. Had the men of her home dressed like that? She thought not. Certainly the slavers who owned the ship that had snatched her did not. There was something regal about the figure, in his bearing as well as his clothes.

'What are you?' she murmured, watching as the figure walked on. He appeared to be looking for something, or else he was lost. 'Are you a sign for me, strange one? A message from the Twins?'

Her men and women had reported the same ghostly figure all over the island, even small groups of them stumbling through the forest together. A few had made it down to the town itself, floating through the streets of Two-Birds. Estenn had to wonder what the townsfolk thought of the ghosts. It would be one more thing for them to be afraid of.

Not so Estenn. Turning her back on the figure, she ran deeper into the forest, letting her feet carry her back to their small settlement. As she ran, she could feel the island growing around her, edging towards something unknown. She always felt it in this way – the heartbeat of the island moved her own blood – but just lately there was something new. The world had changed in some significant way, and the island was reacting, coming to life, or *bringing life* . . . Estenn smiled as she ran, feeling a tightness in her chest as she contemplated what that could mean. It wouldn't be long now, and Res'ni and Res'na would call her to their service. She was sure of it.

She saw the first of their perimeter scouts at the top of a steep slope. He was deep in the foliage, well hidden and certainly invisible to any fool that might wander along, but not invisible to Estenn – the art of not being seen was her own, after all. Coming closer, she watched him looking all around, his face grown suddenly tense. He wore black paint on one side of his face, white on the other, a mark of respect to the Twins – and yes, he couldn't see her, but he knew something was near. That was good.

Stepping forward, Estenn let herself become visible again, standing in clear view so as not to startle him too badly. Immediately he stood up.

'Emissary.' He nodded, almost bowing. He was young, this one, only stolen from the town in the last few years, and he was still half terrified of her. She could see him glancing nervously at the twin wolf tattoos that encircled her neck and shoulders. 'You have been far?'

'Down to look at the bay, Cully, to watch their comings and goings.' She placed a hand on his arm and rewarded him with a smile. He was frightened now, but eventually he would come to love her, as they all did. Estenn the Undying, Estenn the Unseen, Emissary of the gods, Chosen of the Twins. 'Anything to report?'

He swallowed hard. His eyes were still drawn to the snarling wolves at her throat – Res'ni and Res'na, gods of chaos and order.

'Only the ghosts, Emissary. They are everywhere now. We've seen seven just today, all within walking distance of the base.'

'Signs from the gods, Cully,' said Estenn, looking beyond him. 'They are an echo of something, I am sure of it. I will speak to the Spinner today. You never know when he might have something useful to say.'

'Yes, Emissary.'

She left him to his watch and headed up the slope. There were signs now that she was nearing home – skulls propped on sticks and wedged into tree hollows, their smooth foreheads painted black and white, banners of bird feathers and bear skins hanging from the trees. There were more scouts hidden here. It was possible to feel them all around, warm human presences against the alien fog of Euriale.

Further up and she was through the thick circle of trees that sheltered the settlement, walking amongst the lean-tos and the huts, the smell of cooking fires and sweet, burning flesh. Her people nodded to her, lifting their painted faces and smiling. She smiled back, tasting their love on the back of her tongue. It was good.

At the far side she came to a hut that was bigger than the rest, and with four guards at the entrance. They stood aside as she approached, revealing the dark entrance to a sloping underground tunnel.

'How is he today?'

The tall woman with auburn hair in plaits answered. She was holding a long spear in one hand.

'Same as he ever is, Emissary. He moans, he stinks the place up, he doesn't like the food.'

'Thank you, Gen. But remember, he is a creature of the island. We owe him our respect, whatever his mood.'

The woman called Gen blanched slightly, and nodded. 'Of course, Emissary. Forgive me.'

Estenn ducked past the guards and walked down the low earth tunnel. There were oil lamps wedged into the soft dirt every ten feet or so, and she could smell their thick scent, along with the wild odour of Euriale's dirt. And another, stranger smell. That was the Spinner.

At the bottom of the tunnel was a wide chamber, the ceiling festooned with tree roots pushing through from above. There was another guard down here, a girl of around fourteen, one of the children to be born within the group – a true child of Euriale. Estenn smiled to see her.

'Not on patrol, Ivy?'

The girl stood up from where she was crouching, the huge shape of the Spinner rising behind her. 'It is my honour to keep the Spinner company today, Emissary.'

'I'll take over from you for a short while. Get some air.'

Ivy nodded once and left without looking back. Estenn stood

for a moment, looking at the shape crouched in the corner. It was big, the rounded top almost brushing the ceiling, and it was covered with blankets and bearskins. Only near the ground was there a gap, and through this stuck a long, spindly limb, ending in a curved hook. There were bristles lining the inner curve of the claw, and the skin that covered the limb was a glistening black. She could just make out the lower shard of a piece of the Spinner's pearlescent armour, shimmering where it covered what she chose to call his leg, for want of a better word. As she watched the claw flexed in and out, almost beckoning, and the covering of blankets and furs shivered.

'To what do I owe the pleasure, Estenn of Euriale?'

The voice was old, deep, and shivered inside her head like a tuning fork. Most of her people could not stand to hear it, and many of them hadn't even seen the face it issued from. It didn't make it any easier to take.

'Can I not just pass the time with you, Spinner? You are happy enough to talk to Ivy.'

'Time? How much time though? You have slipped free of time, Estenn, as you have slipped the bonds of sight.' And then before she could respond, 'Ivy is still young. If she left now, she might not become as warped by the island as you have.'

'So you were telling her to leave? Dripping your poison into her ears?'

'With what is coming, she will be safer if she left now. You all would.' The Spinner made a brief, high-pitched humming noise. Estenn resisted the urge to cover her ears. 'Euriale was not meant for human souls. The cradle of Ede is no place for mortals.'

'So you keep saying.' She took a few steps forward, watching as the limb drew closer to the main body of the Spinner. 'I've come to talk to you about that, actually. There are ghosts walking the island, images of the same man, painted in blue light. They are everywhere, even walking the streets of Two-Birds. Do you know what they are?'

The great bulk of the Spinner shivered all over.

'Signs and portents, ripples from the opening of the Eye.' And then, more urgently, 'You *must* let me go, do you not see? The cycle is starting again, and I must be there to birth it. I am the Spinner, it is my job, my purpose. New life will be beginning, in the heart of all-gods isle, and I must spin for it, I must ease its passage, it is dangerous for all, it is . . .'

Estenn sighed. The Spinner would do this often; become over excited, lose focus. She went over to the side of the chamber and picked up one of the lamps. Holding it out towards the blankets, she watched the claw flex convulsively.

'You are burbling again. You know I do not appreciate that.' She crouched, holding out the lamp so that the bright circle of heat and light fell directly on the exposed limb. 'It has been a while since I burned you.'

The Spinner still made the high-pitched humming noise, but when he spoke again his voice was slower.

'You play with things you cannot possibly understand, Emissary.' He used her title without anger or irony. 'The Eye of Euriale is opening, and those forces cannot be bent to a human will.'

Estenn grinned. 'Are you so sure I am human?'

The Spinner was quiet for a moment. 'The island has changed you,' he said eventually, his voice oddly sad. 'Given you life beyond your years, a strength that you should not have. You walk in its shadows and its secrets, but it comes with a price. You cannot see that any more, because it has broken your mind.'

She ignored that. The thing was always telling her she was mad. 'The Twins have chosen me to be their weapon.' She pressed her free hand to the tattoo at her neck. 'And they have given me the gifts I need. I will do what is necessary.'

'The last secrets are still hidden from you,' said the Spinner, sounding defiant again. 'There is that at least. I will not tell you, no matter what you do to me.'

'Don't be so sure about that.' She rested the hot rim of the lamp against the bare skin of the Spinner's leg, and the creature shrieked. There was a hiss and an alien stink. 'There is a lot of you to hurt, and many more limbs we can cut off.'

The Spinner shivered and moaned, but said no more. After a moment, Estenn made her way back out of the tunnel.

6

Nestled in the blue heart of Y'Gria's Loss, Euriale grew on the horizon like an ink spot in water; dark, chaotic, wild. As the *Poison Chalice* drew closer, Sebastian could see tall black cliffs fringed with explosions of green foliage, trees festooned with vines and bursts of exotic blooms of all colours. Almost hidden underneath this broad stroke of riotous nature was a smaller example of the human sort: the pirate town of Two-Birds was a crowded collection of ships and buildings, cosily squeezed into the island's natural bay. There were multitudes of flags, most of them black, and as they neared the port he could hear them snapping in the wind; a natural counterpoint to the cries of the gulls that wheeled overhead.

He was so absorbed in this spectacle of colour and activity that he didn't notice Kellan standing next to him until the other man spoke.

'Quite a sight, isn't it?'

Sebastian turned to him. He didn't like to be taken unawares, but his mind always seemed to be elsewhere lately. The captain's first mate was standing with his arms crossed over his chest, an expression of benign amusement on his face. Despite the growing heat of the day, he still wore the elaborate vanbraces and gloves that Wydrin said were his particular affectation. Sebastian forced down the initial surge of irritation.

'There are so many ships already at port,' he said, gesturing to the confusion of wood and masts and flags that threatened to blot out the town entirely. 'I'm not sure they have the room for us.'

Kellan nodded, still smiling. 'Not to worry, they always find room for us somehow. The captain is not the sort of person you turn away from Two-Birds, not if you want to keep your lungs breathing easily in your chest.'

'This isn't the first time you've been here?'

'Oh, not at all.' Kellan grinned, a brief flash of white splitting his black beard. 'We're old hands here. And I don't expect you'll be a stranger here for long – your companion Wydrin is already planning on giving you a guided tour of *all* the taverns, one after the other, I believe. The captain wants to take on more supplies before we head on into the island, so you've plenty of time to nurse your head tomorrow.'

Sebastian winced despite himself. 'Oh, good. Will you be joining us for the tour?'

Kellan smiled, and slapped Sebastian on the shoulder as if they were old friends. 'Alas, I have other business on Two-Birds this evening. You will have to face that fate alone.'

Long after sunset, Sebastian found himself following Wydrin through the door of what she promised would be the last tavern of the evening, a place right up at the edge of the town, pressed against the looming curtain of the jungle. He had to hope she was telling the truth. His stomach felt as though it were building up for its own tropical storm.

Frith was leaning on the door frame with an expression that suggested he was concentrating very hard on something; possibly staying upright or not throwing up. He clasped his staff to his chest, fingers white at the knuckles. 'How many taverns is this now?' he said to Sebastian, his voice low and urgent. 'What number are we on?'

'Something in the upper-tens.' Sebastian grimaced. It was hot in the tavern, and noisy, as they had all been so far. He could smell ale and cooking meat. His stomach cramped. 'I lost count somewhere after The Blistered Coin.'

Frith nodded seriously, as if this were what he expected. 'I hate pirates,' he said, with feeling.

Ahead of them, Wydrin was already ordering at the bar, her voice cutting over the general hubbub. A harassed-looking woman with a kerchief holding her hair back was taking her order, already slamming tankards down onto the bar top. When they caught up, Sebastian held up one weary hand.

'Do you have any food left? Anything at all would do, at this point.'

The woman raised an eyebrow at him. 'We've still got some stew. Not as good as it used to be, not since I lost my last cook, but it'll settle your stomach some.' She disappeared through a door behind her, where Sebastian could just make out a stove and a cloud of steam.

'Good call, Seb.' Wydrin took a swig from her ale, before dragging over a couple of stools. 'And for the Graces' sake, Frith, sit down before you fall down.'

The young lord gave her a cool look before sliding onto the stool and propping his staff against the bar. 'I don't suppose this place serves wine?'

Wydrin ignored him. The serving woman came back, three bowls of hot stew balanced carefully on her arms. Sebastian took them gratefully, before passing her a handful of coins.

'I've heard you do the best stew,' said Wydrin, poking the surface with her spoon. 'Best stew on Two-Birds up at The Blinkered Inn, is what I've heard.'

The woman frowned and fiddled with her kerchief. 'Used to be. Chen was a pain in the arse, but he knew how to throw a bowl of grub together.'

'What happened to him?' asked Sebastian. Asking questions kept his mind off how the room was gently tilting back and forth like they were still at sea.

'He went out back one night,' the woman jerked a thumb over her shoulder, 'and I think he went into the trees.' She looked for a moment like she might say something more, but then she shrugged, having apparently reached the end of the story.

'Into the trees?' Sebastian took a slurp of the stew. It was hot and a touch too salty, but it wasn't ale, and for that his stomach was grateful. 'What happened to him then?'

To his surprise, the woman glared at him. 'He went into the *trees*. Around here, that's enough.'

With that she turned and bustled off up the other end of the bar. A man who was drinking next to them leaned over. A deep scar twisted its way down his face, turning his left eye white. He grinned at Sebastian, revealing a mouthful of brown teeth.

'Not been to Two-Birds before, squire?' The man looked them over, nodding to himself. 'Nope, fresh meat, the lot of you.' He peered at Wydrin a little closer, screwing up his good eye until it was nearly lost in a net of wrinkles. ''cept this one, maybe. Well, if you'd been here before, you'd know not to go into the trees. Euriale eats those that venture too far from the lights. Screaming Mad Chen, he went out for a walk, didn't come back. Happens all the time.'

'You mean people get lost?'

'Oh no, squire. People gets taken. It's a hungry island, this one. We live under the sufferance of a ravenous beast.' He shifted in his seat, frowning at Wydrin now. 'Don't I know you, girl? You look awful familiar.'

'You've probably met my mother,' said Wydrin, looking tired for the first time that evening. 'Devinia the Red, Terror of the Torrent, blah blah blah, pain in my arse.'

'No, it's you I've heard tell of.' He jabbed at her exposed arm, where the inked sharks curled around her elbow. 'Wydrin of Crosshaven, the Copper Cat.' He looked up at all three of them. 'The Black Feather Three. My brother sails up north – can't be doing with it myself, too bloody cold – but at the end of this last crab season he came back with all sorts of tales. A mountain that got up and walked, an entire city of the dead.' The man sniffed, his tobacco-coloured whiskers bristling. 'And I've heard other stories too. That you were part of that mess at Sandshield. Dressed up like one of those Graceful Ladies, and sneaked a band of rival pirates right into Morgul the Biter's treasure room. A bloody business. A lot of men and women died that night. Good and bad.'

Sebastian looked at Wydrin, watching carefully for her reaction.

Her disastrous caper at Sandshield had happened while they were apart, and she very rarely spoke of it. Sebastian suspected she carried a significant weight of guilt over the lives needlessly lost there, and guilt was unusual for Wydrin. Eventually she sighed and leaned an elbow on the bar, one hand drifting closer to her dagger Frostling at her hip. 'And do you have something you want to say to me about that, old man?'

With a prickle of unease, Sebastian realised that the rest of the tavern had gone eerily quiet. There was still a murmur of conversation, the occasional knock of glass against wood as people moved their drinks, but he could sense an alarming amount of focus on their small group. Wydrin had warned him about the tooth she had received, and had mentioned that possible danger was coming their way. At the time, he had barely taken notice. When *wasn't* danger coming their way?

Before the old pirate could answer, Frith lurched forward, brandishing his staff. Tendrils of white light flickered up and down it like a miniature lightning storm.

'If you do have something to say, you'd best say it to all of us,' he said, scowling in a manner Sebastian found very familiar. 'But beware of the consequences.'

He struck the staff on the ground and a small fireball, roughly the size of an orange, popped into existence in front of them. Frith gestured with the staff, and it floated towards the scarred man, bathing his face in light so intense that the old man cried out and turned away.

'I didn't mean anything by it!' He stumbled back, half falling off his stool. 'You're all mad, the lot of you!'

'Hoy!' It was the woman behind the bar, her kerchief askew. 'You can't bring bloody fireworks in here, what are you playing at?'

Sebastian stood up, and touched Frith's elbow. For a moment the young lord swayed on his feet, and then the fireball winked out of existence. 'Wydrin, perhaps we should take our friend outside for a spell?'

They left via a side door, Wydrin's arm around Frith's waist. Outside there was barely any breeze at all, but it was still cooler than the tavern had been, and Sebastian took a long, slow breath. The jungle loomed off to their right, a curtain of darkness that felt too solid. Sebastian looked at it out of the corner of his eye, suddenly feeling an odd sense of superstitious dread. He was reminded of when he walked the Demon's Throat as a young novice. There had been that same feeling of a greater presence, something bigger than you could imagine, watching you in the dark.

He looked away, and tugged at his beard. How much ale had he had? With what they'd all seen, it wasn't that surprising that he was jumping at shadows.

'Here, sit down for a bit.' Wydrin led Frith over to the low stone wall that marked the perimeter of the tavern. 'Really, I thought you lordly types would be able to handle more ale. I mean, don't you spend half your time drinking wine out of silver goblets? Watered wine with breakfast, mead with dinner, iced wine with supper—'

'Wydrin, if you say wine one more time,' Frith held up one hand, his fingers trembling slightly, 'I am going to make a mess on your boots.'

'Perhaps I should go back in and bring out the stew.'

'Why are we here, Wydrin?' Sebastian turned back to them. He could still feel the trees at his back. 'What has brought us here, of all places?'

Wydrin looked up at him, pausing in the act of rubbing Frith's back. Despite how much she'd had to drink, how much they'd all had to drink, Sebastian could see caution in her eyes. It was one of the tricks of the Copper Cat – she was never quite as drunk as you thought she was.

'You know why we're here, Seb. We're the Black Feather Three, seeking out adventure, coin, stories to tell around the tavern table.' She waved a hand, half smiling. 'This is exactly the sort of place we'd end up.'

Sebastian shook his head. 'And it doesn't have anything to do with proving something to your mother?'

Wydrin's eyebrows shot up at that, and even Frith shifted in his seat on the wall. 'Look, we've all had a few pints, so maybe we should just—'

'We keep throwing ourselves at ludicrous situations, again and again. Haven't we done enough damage? Haven't we caused enough trouble?' The world was spinning again – Sebastian squeezed his eyes shut, urging everything to keep still. 'The people we've hurt, the lives lost because of us. And here we are again, on a cursed island. We should go home, or at least start trying to find one. You two should be enjoying the time you have together, not looking for more inventive ways to get yourselves killed.'

Wydrin stood up, her fists clenched at her sides. 'So we should go back to Crosshaven, where you can spend your days fiddling the scale fights and drinking yourself into a stupor? That's a much better plan.'

Sebastian frowned. 'How do you know I'm scamming the scale fights?'

'Oh please, your name is mud all over the Marrow Market!' Wydrin threw her hands up into the air. 'We had to get you away from there, if nothing else. I'm not blind, Seb, I know something is wrong. This is like the demon all over again – too proud to admit your mistakes!'

'This coming from you!' Sebastian could feel his voice rising, but could do nothing to stop it. 'The queen of reckless decisions, the mistress of questionable behaviour!'

Frith laughed, and they both looked at him in surprise. He covered his mouth, shaking his head, before something behind them both caught his eye. The young lord sat up, his features suddenly much more sober. 'What is that?'

Sebastian turned to see a shimmering figure of blue light emerging from the trees at the edge of the woods. It was tall and broad shouldered, dressed in robes and chainmail, although the light was too bright to make out the features of its face. The figure passed them slowly, making not a sound at all.

'Augusta said this place was riddled with ghosts,' whispered Wydrin. 'I can't believe the old baggage was right for once.'

Sebastian opened his mouth to answer, and found he could not. The sight of the pale-blue figure had stilled him, thrown a hook in his heart and captured it. There was something about it that was deeply familiar and deeply alien at the same time. He remembered seeing the wyverns for the first time, feeling that silver thread thrumming in time with his own soul – but this was no dragon, and as far as he could tell, no dragon-kin. So what was it?

The figure continued on down the cobbled path towards the centre of Two-Birds, and then, before it reached the lamps on the next street, it faded, then vanished. When he closed his eyes, he could still see the faint imprint of it, haunting the inside of his eyelids.

Wydrin put a hand on his shoulder, the tension in her voice now replaced with concern. 'Seb? Are you all right?'

For a moment it was difficult to think. He swallowed hard, and nodded. 'I believe so. Although I've completely forgotten what we were talking about.'

7

Wydrin rose early the next morning, a fat slice of sunshine cutting through the slats, laying a warm hand across her forehead. She expected to find Frith asleep next to her, in the deep death-like sleep of the horribly drunk and soon to be hungover, but the narrow space next to her was empty, and after a moment she heard a splash from the small room next to the main chamber. Slipping out of bed, she padded across the floor, moving silently out of habit.

Frith was standing next to the big washbasin, pressing a wet piece of cloth to his forehead, rivulets of water running down his face. His white hair was damp, and sticking up in all directions. She paused by the door frame, taking a moment to admire the taut muscles of his stomach, the sharp angle of his shoulders. The light coming through the slats lay across his brown skin like bands of gold, and Wydrin experienced the odd tightening of the chest she often felt when she and Frith were alone together these days. There had been other men, of course, men with whom she had spent pleasant evenings and memorable afternoons, but being with Frith made her fingers itch for her daggers, filled her with an indefinable need to fight, to protect. She remembered how Xinian had mocked her – a fool willing to die for love, but not to live for it. She supposed this was living for love, and in truth it made her uneasy. It was dangerous and exposed, like walking a taut rope over a great drop.

'If I were an assassin, I could have killed you eight times over by now.'

Frith turned at the sound of her voice. There were dark circles under his eyes but he smiled at her wanly. 'I seriously doubt that. I have the Copper Cat in the other room, watching my back.'

'I'm certainly watching *something*.'

She came into the room and saw his staff propped against the wall. It was never far from him. Seeing the direction of her glance, Frith's face grew serious again. He was never far from that, either. 'I get the impression your mother is more interested in the staff than me.'

She gave him her best filthy look. 'Like mother, like daughter.'

He shook his head at her, almost laughing but not quite. He threw the piece of cloth back in the basin. 'It's dangerous, Wydrin. I feel that now more than ever.' He crossed the room to the staff and briefly rested his fingers against it. 'Storing what Edenier I could in the staff seemed like a good idea at the time – the idea of a desperate man – but it haunts me now.'

Wydrin crossed her arms. 'Selsye made the staff, and I've no doubt she was a decent sort. She wasn't Joah. She wasn't anything like Joah, and never could be.'

Frith's lips thinned at the mention of the rogue mage's name. 'No, she wasn't like him, but I was.'

'Frith—'

'The Edenier trap. I finished it when Joah Demonsworn couldn't.' He turned towards her, but his eyes were glassy now, staring off at something she couldn't see. 'I spilled blood for it. I killed a man, for no other reason than the pursuit of power. One in a long line of terrible things I have done.'

'It's not the staff that haunts you, it's that demon-tainted mage bastard.' Wydrin stepped lightly from one foot to another, feeling herself getting angry and knowing it was foolish. The man was dead. She had cut his head from his shoulders with her own blade. 'We've all done things we regret.' Unbidden, Sandshield appeared before her, fire pouring out of the doors, men and women with their heads burning like torches. She hadn't meant it to end like that, but when had good intentions ever stopped terrible things happening? 'What happened at Skaldshollow, we have to put it behind us – you, me, *and* Sebastian.'

He came back to her then, his grey eyes finding hers. Instead of the fire at Sandshield she remembered standing in his castle on the day before they went chasing the dragon, the pad of his thumb brushing the underside of her wrist.

'We don't have to forget everything that happened in that cold place,' she said. 'I have a couple of good memories, at least.' Wydrin stepped up and kissed him, sliding the flat of her hand over the smooth skin of his back. No scars now, thanks to the deal she'd made with the demon Bezcavar. No visible scars, anyway. 'You stink,' she said, when they broke apart. 'Do you want some breakfast?'

Outside the air had been washed clean and the cobbles under her boots were damp. The rain had moved on, but Wydrin could smell it still in the air, mixed with sea salt and the wild, thorny scent of the jungle that crouched behind Two-Birds. She had left Frith up in their room, still trying to wash away the scent of stale wine, and she had it in mind to wander down to the western part of the pirate town, where she dimly remembered the best eateries to be.

When she had been small, Devinia had brought her to Two-Birds a number of times. It had been one of Wydrin's favourite places to visit, so full of noise and colour and very much like her home of Crosshaven, and yet not quite. Whereas Crosshaven was as old and as ingrained as the stones it perched upon, there was a fragility to Two-Birds, a dangerous sense that the town could be gone again at any moment, either wiped away by a storm, or raided by a bigger gang of criminals. She remembered how the rain would come in like a grey curtain, solid and loud, roaring across the ocean and dousing the small town in minutes. She remembered storms that howled and crashed waves up the small cobbled streets – people had been washed away and lost – and long days of blistering heat that had left her too hot to move, sprawled on the deck of her mother's ship with a huge palm leaf over her head for shade, or drinking iced wine with her feet dangling over the side of the pier. Always, Augusta had had her beady eye on her, warning young Wydrin not to venture beyond the borders of the town, and for once she had listened. You had to be a fool not to recognise the danger of Euriale. It was not a place for children to go wandering.

And now we're sailing right into the bloody middle of it.

She followed the winding street downwards, passing ramshackle houses, warehouses, taverns and butchers. It was like any busy town, with men and women heading here and there on their daily business, except there were more scars on display, more missing eyes and absent limbs. Life on the sea was hard; hard enough for retirement on an island like Euriale to seem like a good deal.

Walking on she came to a small market square. Across the wet stones there was a tall wooden building painted white, complete with a bell tower and a giant rusted bell. There was a pair of red doors at ground level, with a great grinning skull painted across them. This was the home of the current mayor of Two-Birds; once a year the pirate captains would goad themselves into a rough sort of democracy, voting for one of their number to be the official head of the pirate town. Devinia had told her more than once that it meant very little – who could really be said to be in charge of such a bunch? And who could possibly enforce their wishes? But it was a figurehead position, someone to look to when an official word was wanted, when someone was needed to blame. Wydrin privately suspected that the reason Devinia dismissed the title was because she herself had yet to win it.

Pausing in the centre of the square, her quest for food quite forgotten, Wydrin tried to remember who held the position currently. Lamefoot Jameson? Edgar 'The Fury' Sims? Around her men and women were setting up their stalls for the day, heaving stolen goods out of sacks and giving them a spit polish. Then, as if she had summoned the figure by thinking about it, the red doors of the Mayoral Tower opened, and a tall, broad-shouldered woman stepped out into the morning light. She wore a long leather great coat, stained and scuffed with use, and leather boots that looked equally battered. Her hair was short, so blond it was almost white, and she had a high forehead, so that her hair seemed to be straining backwards from her face. There was a wide slash of red greasepaint across her mouth, an affectation that reportedly caused the crews of the ships she attacked to run in fear; when she bellowed her war cry, it almost looked as though her head were splitting in two. Wydrin was familiar with the effect, as she was familiar with the woman who employed it. Inwardly, she sighed. Ristanov the Banshee was a well-known rival of her mother's, and likely the last person she wanted to see as mayor, but there was the thick golden chain around her neck with the fat golden skull pendant dangling from it. No one ever said pirates were subtle.

There was movement behind the tall woman and another figure stepped out into the daylight. This one Wydrin recognised straight away; Kellan still wore his tattered vanbraces, and he looked like he'd had a late night. Wydrin had been ready to walk away, eager to put some space between herself and the Banshee, but this was too curious not to question.

'Hoy!' She waved at them and jogged over before either of them had a chance to depart. 'I was looking to get some breakfast, Kellan. Any suggestions?'

Kellan looked faintly pained, while Ristanov placed her hands on her hips. 'Ah, Wydrin, you're up and about early,' he said. He fiddled with one of the rags tied around his left arm, and then shrugged. 'Should be easy enough to find food around here.' Wydrin said nothing, simply beaming up at the pair of them with a carefully innocent expression. After a moment, Kellan cleared his throat. 'I take it you know Carlita Ristanov, also known as the Banshee, current mayor of Two-Birds?'

Wydrin grinned a little wider. 'I do believe we've never actually met.'

'Devinia's whelp,' rumbled the Banshee. She had a low, throaty voice, still thickly accented from her native Bararia. 'Not the one that calls himself the Crimson Scar. The other one.' Ristanov peered down at Wydrin. Her eyes were so pale a blue they were almost colourless.

'Congratulations on making it as mayor.' Wydrin nodded seriously, trying to convey how deeply impressed she was that the

Banshee had managed it. She watched with pleasure as the taller woman's mouth turned down at the corners. 'That is quite the achievement.'

'It is a vote, as well you know,' said Ristanov. 'The captain that is considered most capable, yes.'

'You must be very proud.'

Kellan took a slight step forward, almost coming between the two of them, but not quite. 'Did you want something at the Mayoral Tower, Wydrin?'

'Not especially. Did you?'

Kellan grinned. 'Just updating our records, making sure your mother's acquisition of the *Poison Chalice* has been recognised. We don't want anyone turning up later to argue about it.'

Wydrin tipped her head to one side. It was true that there were ledgers in the Mayoral Tower, a rough history of the pirates affiliated with the island. It was up to each captain how often they updated their own records.

'Your mother caused some ripples when she took Tom Dogget's ship as her own,' Ristanov sneered, distorting the slash of red greasepaint. 'Even pirates have a code, yes.'

Kellan laid a hand heavily on Wydrin's shoulder. 'True enough. Well now, shall we find ourselves some breakfast, Copper Cat of Crosshaven?'

For a moment Wydrin wanted to argue the point further – it would, in many ways, be a fine start to the morning to draw her sword against this woman – but she had long since been out of pirate politics, and had no real desire to get involved again. She shook Kellan's hand off and sketched the Banshee a brief bow. 'Absolutely. If I stand here too long I shall get a sour stomach.'

When Wydrin and Kellan were across the square and down a side street, Kellan gave her a sidelong look. He was smiling a little ruefully.

'I take it from that little exchange that you know about the history between the Banshee and your mother, then?'

Wydrin nodded. Ahead of them she could see an open hut where a man was roasting chickens on a spit. They were glistening and fat, and the smell of cooked meat and butter wafted up the alley. Her stomach growled.

'I know that four years ago Devinia was in the midst of taking a fat little trading schooner out on the edge of Emmet's Bay when Ristanov the Screecher came out of nowhere to put a hole in the side of my mum's ship, and in the resulting chaos made off with the goods. And then, six months later, my mum caught up with her north of Onwai and returned the favour.'

'And so it has been going on ever since,' said Kellan. He did not sound concerned. 'Banshee isn't liked by many, but she is respected. Which is why she's the mayor now, as much as your mum doesn't like it.'

'Hey, you want one of those chickens?'

For the first time Kellan looked pained. 'I don't eat meat.'

Wydrin raised her eyebrows at that. 'A pirate who doesn't eat meat? No salted pork rations for you?'

'It's the smell,' he said shortly, and then turned away as she bought one of the hot roasted chickens, wrapped in brown paper.

'It doesn't bother you then,' she asked as they made their way back up the alley, 'that Devinia's worst enemy is the mayor of Two-Birds now? It doesn't strike you as a problem?'

'Not a problem as such. An opportunity, maybe. You know what pirates are like, kid. When do they ever like each other? Two-Birds is like throwing a bunch of angry tomcats in a crate and doing a little dance on top. It's all one-upmanship, a big group of show-offs competing to be the biggest show-off. And now your mother has the biggest ship of them all.'

'One big pissing contest,' agreed Wydrin absently, passing the parcel of food from one hand to the other. The butter was burning her fingers. 'Is this what this is all about? The Banshee is lording it up over Two-Birds so Mum turns up and prepares to explore the inner heart of Euriale, supposedly an impossibly dangerous task. Do you know where she got this latest map, by the way?'

Kellan turned to her, and for a moment the look he gave her was too avid. She frowned slightly.

'Sad to say, I don't know all of your mother's secrets, Wydrin of Crosshaven.'

Kellan seemed distinctly unworried by Devinia's plans, and by the potential for trouble posed by Ristanov's presence, so much so that Wydrin had to wonder if he truly understood the dangers of either. However, Kellan was Devinia's first mate, and Wydrin had never known her mother not to choose the shrewdest of her crew for that role. He might look like a grease-covered idiot, but she knew there would be more to him than that.

'I've got a hungry mage to feed. I'll see you on deck, Kellan.'

8

The moon was rising over an ocean of deepest indigo when Frith finally emerged from the leather worker's shop, his coin purse significantly lighter but his boots, his belt, and the special sword-strap he'd had made to carry the staff across his back, all oiled and in fine order. It had been a lot of work and on short notice, but the woman who'd served him had been unperturbed, apparently well used to unusual jobs late in the evening. Now Frith stood on the doorstep, looking down across crowded roofs to the sea below. The rains of earlier had cleared swiftly, just as Wydrin had said they would, and now the night sky was a hectic explosion of stars.

He turned to head further up the hill, the staff held comfortably in his right hand. Frith liked to carry it when he could, using it like a walking stick of sorts – the gods knew he'd had experience of using such – as it meant the Edenier was always at hand, with only a thought needed to summon it. This was the closest he could get to the power he had once wielded, when the magic had churned in his chest. Now there was a silence inside him, the raw magic replaced by a tumult of knowledge and images – knowledge gifted to him by the mad mage Joah Demonsworn. The only Edenier he had access to now was stored in the staff, ready to do his bidding but forever one step removed. He took a slow breath, reminding himself that without the genius of the Edeian-crafting mage Selsye, a thousand years dead, he wouldn't even have that.

Two-Birds was particularly busy at this time of night, the scent of alcohol and cooking food everywhere. He was eager to get back to their rooms, to spend one more night of relative peace with Wydrin before their adventures moved them on elsewhere, but as he crossed the small market square his eye fell on a stall full of cunning little daggers, their shining surfaces like liquid silver under the lamps. On an impulse he moved closer, catching the attention of the vendor, a short dark-skinned man with a string of pearls around his neck.

'Can I help you, sir?' he asked. His voice was soft and his expression grave. 'I was just about to pack up for the night, but always glad to have one more customer.'

'Yes, I . . . I'm not sure.' Frith looked over the man's wares, frowning slightly. 'Give me a moment.'

The man nodded to him, and began to fold up the cloth hung over the back of his stall. When Frith remained quiet, the man began to pack away the knives and daggers, but at that moment a flash of light like the moon on water caught Frith's eye. He held up his hand. 'Let me look at this.' He picked up the knife. It was short and wide, and its fat handle was made of smooth dark wood. Embedded into it was a piece of mother-of-pearl, carved into the shape of a shark. The blade itself was sharp enough, and curved on one side. 'How much for this knife?'

The seller looked up at him, a considering expression on his face. 'It's not for you, I'm guessing?'

Frith scowled slightly. 'How could you know that?'

The man shrugged, and pointed. 'Guessing by the brooch at your neck and the arms sewn on your cloak, sir, you prefer a griffin or a tree motif.'

Frith blinked, surprised despite himself. 'You are quite correct.'

'For a dear friend then, I'm thinking. A lover, even.'

All at once Frith remembered buying silver trinkets outside the Storm Gates. The vendor had asked him if they were for his sweetheart, when at the time he had thought Wydrin dead. A familiar sick feeling washed through his guts.

'I don't have time to haggle. Just tell me your price.'

The man relented, holding his hands out in a gesture of

peace. 'For you, sir, two silver bits. It's a fine knife, I think you'll agree.'

Without saying any more, Frith passed the man the coins and took the knife, wrapping it carefully in a scrap of offered fabric before slipping it into the bag at his belt. He was glad he'd found it, but the whole conversation had dredged up memories of the Desert of Bones and his time there – his desperate grief for Wydrin, and the man he had killed to power the Edenier trap – and now his evening felt soured. He was still brooding over it as he left the market square to head further uphill, cutting through side streets to avoid the main crowds, and perhaps that was why he failed to notice the three figures that followed him down one particular dark alley. His first clue that anything was amiss was a throaty chuckle from directly behind him.

'In a hurry are you, lordling?'

Frith spun around, belatedly taking in his surroundings. There were three men behind him, their faces partially hidden in the poor light, although one of them, a man with a ragged scar dividing his face, looked familiar. 'What do you want?'

'What does anyone want?' said the fattest one. He was bald, the light of the moon casting a ghostly silver coin on his shining head. 'Job security, a warm hearth, a sense of peace in one's life—'

'Shut up,' snapped the one with the scar. 'We know you, you posh bastard. Lording it up in The Blinkered Inn. And we also happen to know that that thing you're carrying is worth a few bob.'

'This?' Frith gestured with the staff. He could feel a familiar quickening in his chest – not the Edenier any more, only his own growing rage.

'The stories have reached us, even out here in the arse-end of Y'Gria's Loss.' This was the third man. He had lank hair hanging in his face, and had produced a dagger. He was weaving it back and forth in front of him, as if already carving flesh. 'The Black Feather Three, the Copper Cat and her pet mage. A mage's staff has got to be worth something, that's what we reckon.'

Frith nodded. He gripped the staff with both hands now,

and the magic was licking at his palms, eager to be free. 'By all means,' he said, 'you are quite welcome to try and take it from me.'

The fat one and the one with the knife charged him, apparently hoping to simply knock him to the ground. Frith pictured the mages' word for Force, imagining it flying from his mind to the Edenier trapped inside the staff, and almost instantly his fingers tingled. A wave of faint purple light burst from the staff lengthwise, catching both men across the stomach and throwing them back up the alley. Frith heard the twin *oofs* as the breath was knocked from them, and he savoured the fierce burst of satisfaction. Without giving them a second to recover he pictured the word for Ice and sent a cone of glittering white brilliance up the alley that welded their boots to the cobbles. The other man, the one with the scar, had hung back against the wall. Of course, reflected Frith, this one had seen him use the staff in the tavern, and knew it was no mummer's trick.

The thief looked frightened now, and he was scrambling backwards, his comrades both moaning on the ground. Frith turned quickly, meaning to swing the staff in a one-handed arc to give the thief a good crack on the skull, when something connected solidly with the back of his own head.

Black stars burst in front of his eyes and he staggered, dropping the staff and falling almost to his knees. Inwardly, he cursed himself – he'd been concentrating on the men in front of him, not listening for footsteps in the alley behind him – Wydrin was always telling him he was no street brawler. A big man with a club in his hand stepped past him and snatched up the staff before Frith could react. He was covered in bristly black hair, his beard swamping the lower half of his head like a thistle. Frith touched a hand to the back of his head: no blood, but it was difficult to focus.

'Oh no, I think I get to play with it first.' The staff looked like a toothpick in the bearded man's meaty hands. He shook it at Frith, then looked aggrieved when nothing happened. Wincing, Frith climbed to his feet.

'Don't mess about with that!' snapped the one with the scar.

'You might scratch it, and those things fetch more when they're perfect.'

'I just want to try it out.' The bearded one swung it again, poking at the air. The parts of his face that Frith could see were turning red. 'How come it's not working? I want to make ice like he did.'

'You are a fool,' said Frith in a low voice. 'You think such knowledge is for everyone? The Edenier is art, poetry. Power.' Frith blinked. His head was throbbing. 'You are like a bear holding a lute.'

'What're you talking about?' The bearded man screwed up his face in confusion. 'He's bloody mad, this one.'

'Here, let me show you.' Frith reached out and placed his hand flat on the staff. The magic inside sang, and he fed it the word for fire. Bright coppery flames erupted from the other end, blasting the bearded man directly in the face. For a moment the alley was filled with orange light, and the man fell back screaming, his head ablaze. Deftly, Frith snatched the staff from his arms as he collapsed, before spinning back and sending a wave of ice towards the scarred man, welding him to the wall up to his neck.

'Perhaps I am not a street brawler,' he said to no one in particular, 'but I do have my tricks.'

He paused, checking that the knife with the mother-of-pearl handle was still safely in his bag, before leaving the alley. He took care to tread on the prone figure as he passed.

For Sebastian it was an unsettled night. His room at the Blind Pig was large and well furnished, with wide windows loosely covered in gauze – a nod towards Devinia's standing and the Black Feather Three's own infamy – but it felt stuffy and close, the wild jungle scent of the island thick in the air. Finally, after an hour of kicking blankets off and turning from one side to another, he gave up on sleep and went to the table instead. The *Poison Chalice* was due to leave at dawn, turning away from the safety of Two-Birds and heading past the Cliffs of a Thousand Sorrows, and from there deep into Euriale. It was going to be a long time before he slept anywhere other than a cramped ship's bunk, and he should get what rest he could, but every time he started to drift towards sleep, the same images would swim in front of his eyes: a tiny green plant miraculously untouched by dragon fire, the look of horror on Prince Dallen's face as the brood sisters swarmed the Narhl camp, the Second sneering at him, daring him to accept his true nature. Dawn was a long way off, but there would be no sleep for him tonight.

He poured some wine from the jug on the table and took several large gulps. It was sour, and too warm, but it eased some of the tension in his shoulders. He sighed and armed a layer of sweat from his forehead. It was enough to make him long for the winters of Ynnsmouth. Except that he couldn't go back there, either.

'Dallen would not like this place,' he murmured to himself. 'Too bloody hot by half.'

A movement by the windowsill caught his eye. Putting the goblet down he saw that there was a tiny lizard, no longer than his smallest finger, perched on the wooden ledge. At the same moment he recognised it for what it was – *dragon-kin*, part of his mind whispered – and he felt the thin sliver of silver in his mind. It seemed to thrum softly, a tiny slip of consciousness nestled within his own. He could feel its alertness, poised always on the brink of fleeing, and how it could hold itself utterly still until that moment. Sebastian swayed on his feet, unable to separate himself from the mind of that tiny creature, and then his awareness snapped back. He cried out, stumbling awkwardly into the table and the lizard fled, vanishing out the window with a flick of its tail. Wine ran across the wood where it had sloshed out of the goblet. It had almost been like being back with the brood sisters, the blood they shared with him making him constantly aware of their dragon nature.

'Isu be damned.'

Sebastian ran a hand over his sweaty face, ignoring how his fingers were trembling. He tried to think of Isu, the great mountain of his home, the god-peak to which he had once sworn his sword – there had been so much solace in the snowy silence of Ynnsmouth. Instead, he went to the window, pushing the gauze aside. Outside the street was lit by a single oil lamp high on a post, painting the cobbles and the ramshackle buildings opposite in orange and black. There was no breeze, but at least the air beyond the window had a clear sky above it and . . . his breath caught in his throat.

At the top of the street a soft blue light was growing, building like some sinister sunrise. He'd seen that light before, outside The Blinkered Inn. He leaned out of the window, his heart beating thickly in his chest.

Why this? Of everything I've seen, why does this move me?

The pale ghostly figure came into sight. Just as it had the night before, it moved slowly, almost as though it was lost. The robes flung across the figure's back flapped and twitched as though caught in a wind blowing in another world. Despite the heat of the night Sebastian felt goosebumps break out across his arms. He watched the ghost walk down the street, hardly daring to breathe, until the figure was below his window. It stopped and looked directly up at him.

Sebastian jumped back so suddenly that he whacked his head on the window frame. Wincing, he leaned back out to look down on the face of the ghost. The figure was still looking back up at him, and although it was difficult to see his features through the bright glow, he thought he could make out the smooth planes of his face, the darker furrow of his brow. Sebastian thought the figure looked worried, or confused. And then, as he watched, the ghost began to fade away, evaporating like marsh mist. In a handful of seconds, the street was dark once more.

9

The *Poison Chalice* moved out of Two-Birds' bay under a canopy of relentless blue sky, turning as she did to sail along the coast. Wydrin stood on the deck with Augusta, watching as the cliffs of Euriale surged up on their port side. Here the black rock was spotted with strange, brightly coloured trees that clung to deposits of dark brown earth, while thicker vegetation crowded the tops of the cliffs like a shock of unruly hair. Even from here it was possible to see life in that jungle; birds of azure and russet, the darker flicker of monkeys moving through the branches. The crash of the sea against the cliffs was a constant rush and roar. Wydrin took a deep breath of salty air, feeling a surge of excitement. This was a wild place.

'What a shit hole,' commented Augusta.

Wydrin looked down at the older woman. Never tall, she had shrunk with her advancing years, and the hands she looped through the belt at her waist were knuckley and swollen. 'Where's your spirit of adventure?'

Augusta raised her eyebrows, black eyes glinting. 'Spirit of adventure? I'll bloody give you spirit of adventure.' She sniffed. 'When we all get torn to bits by sea beasts, or someone eats something poisonous and I'm scraping up the leavings of their guts, then you can talk to me about bleedin' spirit of bloody adventure.'

Wydrin smiled. 'You always did hate this place.' Next to them the island was curving gradually in on itself, and the *Poison Chalice* was following. She was fast and trim, moving through the sea with barely any effort at all. Around them the rhythms of rope and sail were smooth, almost comforting to Wydrin's ear. When Augusta did not reply, she looked down to see the old woman frowning, a distracted look on her face.

'It's got a dark history this place, girl. A bloody one.' She looked up at Wydrin then, squinting into the sun. 'Your mother won't have told you, I suppose. As she shouldn't, it's none of her bloody business.'

'What are you talking about?'

The older woman took hold of her arm, squeezing none too gently above the elbow. 'Come on, let's sit down for a moment. I don't have the stamina I used to have, although I'd thank you not to pass that around.'

They sat together on a couple of crates, Wydrin noting how the older woman winced as she sat. She'd never known Augusta to get weary; the old woman had always been an alarming powder keg of energy.

'What is it, Nan?' she asked quietly. 'What is it about this place really?'

Augusta smacked her smartly on the thigh. 'Don't be calling me that, I'm no one's gramma.' Her face had softened a touch though. 'I came here once when I was younger than you. Much younger. I bet you didn't know that.'

Wydrin shrugged. Augusta had always been a pirate's medic. It did not seem that surprising that she'd visited Two-Birds as a youth. 'That must have been a *really* long time ago.'

Augusta smacked her leg again, a little harder this time. 'Cheek. When I was a girl, the biggest trade in these parts was slavery. Big ships with people stuffed down in the hold, packed in like cattle. Mostly they were from Bararia, these ships, and they would raid to the east, on the southern coast of Onwai, and down through the Farsky Islands.' Augusta pursed her lips. 'I say they raided, but of course this was mostly legitimate business then. Sail up, as bold as you please, and just take people. Rip them from homes and families, take them to the other side of the world.'

Wydrin looked up at the cliffs passing slowly by. Slavery was a dirty word in Crosshaven. Ships thought to be trading in human lives were either chased out of the archipelago or forcibly boarded. 'Even in Crosshaven?'

'Oh yes, even in your precious Crosshaven. And it still goes on, girl, so don't you be getting any high ideas about how much better things are now. It's just that those that do it stay out of civilised waters.' Augusta scowled, creasing a new pattern of wrinkles across the wine-coloured birthmark on her cheek. 'There are still plenty of us what remember the Storm Days very clearly, very clearly indeed, but back when I was a girl, that was just simmering under the surface. Back when I was a girl, you could sail into Two-Birds with four hundred men, women and children in the belly of your ship and no one would turn a hair.'

The Storm Days. Long before Wydrin's time, but she'd heard the stories often enough; a great uprising against slavery that had spread from the outer islands of Crosshaven right across the Torrent. Ships burning, blood in the water.

'It gives me no pleasure to tell you this, girl, but I served aboard one of those ships myself. A lone woman in Two-Birds – you took what work you could.'

Wydrin glanced down in surprise, but Augusta wasn't facing her. She was looking down at her boots. 'You served on board a slaver?' She couldn't quite keep the disapproval from her voice. Augusta's head snapped up, a familiar glint of fury in her eye.

'Like I said, I took what work I could get. I served as a bone saw, mainly for the crew, but there were times when I was sent below too. When a woman was pregnant, or there was an illness below the decks.' She touched a hand to her forehead, and her fingers were trembling slightly. Wydrin felt a stab of unease. In all the years she'd known Augusta, she'd never seen her so unnerved. 'The things I saw, girl.' She shook her head abruptly. 'We were in dock at Two-Birds, and another ship came in. It was called the *Starworm*, and it quickly got around that it carried a terrible illness with it, something that was burning through the cargo like a wildfire. The people. It was killing them.'

Augusta sniffed again, shifting on the crate. Her tough brown boots were peeling at the toes.

'I had a bit of a reputation by then, you see, and the captain of the *Starworm* sent for me. Asked me what I thought he should do. By then, more than half of them were sick. The smell of that place, down there in the dark. I knew, girl, I knew I couldn't do it any more when I smelled that, when I saw their faces. I'd seen a lot of illness by then, but I didn't know what it was. Something they'd brought with them from Onwai, no doubt, growing thick and nasty in the dark and heat. I told him that he needed to clean the lower decks thoroughly, wash everything down with vinegar and scorpion oil, scrub it till the place squeaked—' The old woman paused. Wydrin kept her silence. 'That same day he sent off for the oil and the vinegar. I saw them roll the barrels up from the dock. And then I watched them throw the sick overboard, still all chained up together, hands and feet bound with iron cuffs.' Augusta's voice shook, just a touch. 'All of them into the water, anyone who was ill, or who looked ill. More than a hundred, a good portion of them children, drowned in Two-Birds dock.'

Wydrin swallowed hard, feeling cold despite the hot sun overhead.

'It was one of the things that led to the Storm Days, of course. Stories passed from slave to slave, leading to the bloodiest uprising the Torrent has ever seen. But I shall never forget that. Watching the barrels roll up the deck, and watching the men and women fall, most of them too sick to scream. There are sharks in these waters, of course.'

'What did you do?'

'What could I bloody do?' Augusta gestured angrily at the cliffs as though it were their fault. 'I told them to stuff their job, and never worked on a slaver again. Too bloody late, of course. I have blood on my hands, as much as I tried to wash it off with good honest piracy. Some things you can never really leave behind.'

Wydrin felt a stab of real alarm. The colour seemed to have drained from the old woman's face, and she thought she'd never seen her looking so frail. And on the back of that fear, she felt a surge of anger. Did Devinia know about this? If she did, what business did she have bringing Augusta back here?

'Are you all right, Nan?'

Augusta snorted. 'Am I all right? I'm an old woman, that's what I am. An old woman who got to live out the days of her life and didn't die vomiting in the hold of a ship, iron cuffs round my ankles, or drowning with my family chained up next to me. Of course I'm bloody all right.' She shook her head abruptly. 'My point is, this place is cursed. It's not a place where people should be.'

At that moment, a shadow fell over them both. Wydrin looked up to see towering black cliffs on either side of the ship as the *Poison Chalice* turned inwards, following the wide waterway into the interior of the island. Suddenly out of the wind it was possible to hear the cries of birds and monkeys all around.

Wydrin stood up. A cold feeling had come over her as they sailed out of the open sea and into the shadow of Euriale. She tried to put it down to Augusta's horrifying history lesson, but there was a sick twisting in her gut, a feeling she'd long since come to trust as a warning. Every instinct was telling her to leave this place, to put her back to it and get away as fast as she could. There would be an ending here, she could feel it. A severing of bonds.

By the Graces, she thought, *there is something terrible here, and it's looking for us.*

She looked around and saw Sebastian and Frith sitting together on another cluster of crates. They were playing cards; Frith's head was bent to his hand, an expression of fierce concentration on his face, while Sebastian was looking past him, watching the ebb and flow of activity on the deck. On the back of her sense of unease came a wave of affection for them both, and her hand drifted down to Frostling. The worn leather of the grip was a comfort to her.

Whatever it is in this place that means us harm, let it come, she thought. *I'll tear its throat out.*

'Sebastian, pass us the bottle behind you.'

It was late, and they were gathered in Devinia's cabin. Wydrin was fetching goblets from a chest filled with sawdust, while Frith and Devinia herself stood over the map table. Sebastian passed Wydrin the bottle of wine from the table behind him, and she swiftly removed the cork and poured them each a glass. The *Poison Chalice* had made anchor, and in the morning Frith would begin his duties with the Edenier, providing the wind that was now hidden from them. They had already practised twice, on the way from Crosshaven, and Sebastian thought the young lord was eager to get started.

'I'm still not sure why this is considered such a dangerous journey,' said Frith again. He was glaring at the map as though it were refusing to give up its secrets. 'I've seen nothing especially threatening so far, save for the occasional angry monkey. Judging from your map, the *Poison Chalice* should have little difficulty navigating to the centre of the island. And you're telling me this has never been achieved previously?'

'Lots of people have taken their ships this way, certainly,' said Devinia evenly. 'It's just that none of them have ever come back.'

'There are monsters,' said Wydrin. She shrugged at the look Frith gave her. 'Really Frith, who are we to scoff at rumours of monsters? We passed two wrecks already today. We were lucky that the *Chalice* can wriggle around them.'

Sebastian took a sip of his wine. He had seen the wrecks too – black skeletal fingers covered in green seaweed, poking out of the sapphire water. There had been no obvious explanation for them, no rocks in the shallows or signs of fire.

'She also has eight cannon, the Black Feather Three, and a crew made of flint and knives,' said Devinia. She poked at the map. 'We're going to do it. I *will* be the first to reach the centre of the island.'

'It will still be dangerous,' said Sebastian, his voice low. They all turned to look at him. 'There will be monsters, or other pirates, or dark magic. Things hidden in the hills, history we shouldn't be disturbing.' He met their eyes, one by one. 'And men and women will die. Your crew will die, Devinia. Screaming, frightened and in pain. If it is one thing I have learned, it's that death is everywhere. Is gaining the centre of Euriale worth the price, Devinia? Are you willing to let your own people die for it?'

Devinia's dark blue eyes narrowed. The edge of her mouth curled in what was almost a smile. 'These men and women your heart bleeds for, Sebastian. Who do you suppose they are? Priests and nursemaids, perhaps? A pack of frightened children?' She threw back the rest of her wine in a single gulp before she continued. 'They are the crew of the *Poison Chalice*, the crew of Devinia the Red, Terror of the Torrent. Men and women who live for battle and plunder.' She cocked her head slightly. 'Not so different from yourself, from what Wydrin has told me.'

Sebastian glanced at Wydrin, who looked stricken. 'That's hardly what I said, Mum.'

'The battle of Baneswatch, commanding the brood sisters and the wyverns, fighting alongside mountain savages.' Devinia raised an eyebrow. 'He sounds like a warrior to me. The sort that legends are written about.'

Very carefully, Sebastian put his goblet back down on the table. 'Forgive me, I need to get some fresh air.' He saw from Wydrin's expression that she intended to follow him out, so he gave her the tiniest shake of his head. 'The heat of this place disagrees with me. I shall be back shortly.'

Up on deck it was relatively quiet. He saw men and women tending to the tasks that kept a ship in good health, whilst a handful of others stood watch. The deck was filled with orange light from the lamps that hung everywhere. Beyond the guardrail the cliffs were a dark, solid presence, the sea a whisper against their hull. The air was full of the thick, wild scent of the jungle, and the high lonely calls of the creatures living in the trees passing above them.

He walked away from the main source of activity, heading towards the rear of the ship. It was darker here, the shapes of barrels and ropes looming out of the shadows. Heading for the portside, he looked down to catch the glimmer of lamps and starlight on the water. There was a section of lower ground; a long length of rocky beach sat at the bottom of the cliff, half concealed by thick foliage.

And there was the blue light again.

Sebastian felt his heart stutter in his chest. The ghostly light painted the leaves of the bushes with a glow like diamonds, and, as he watched, the figure stepped into view: the tall man with broad shoulders, hair curling close to his head. Sebastian couldn't tell if he was imagining it, but it seemed to him that the ghost was clearer, and he was able to make out small details that had been lost in the light before. His clothes had a slightly military bearing, and he wore an ornate belt at his hip. The figure looked up at Sebastian, and their eyes met.

Sebastian looked back across the deck. There was no one close to him. His broadsword and other smaller weapons were wrapped carefully in his own bunk, along with his heavier mail and armour; he wore only his metal-plated greaves and bracers, more out of habit than anything else, and a small knife at his belt. Quickly, he began to pull on the straps of the last of his armour, loosening and then carefully placing them on the deck. Next he took off the light cotton cloak, unfastening the badge of Isu as he did so. He looked at it for a moment before placing it on top of his cloak. Eventually, he stood in his trousers and shirt, his wide leather belt and his boots.

The figure was still there, watching him. Without thinking too closely about what he was doing, Sebastian pulled himself up onto the guardrail. He looked over his shoulder once, half expecting Wydrin to have appeared out of nowhere to tell him he was being an idiot, but he was alone.

Standing up straight, he felt the world turning around him. There was a sense of something new beginning, or ending. It didn't seem to matter which.

Sebastian dived off the ship into the black water, barely making a splash.

PART TWO
The Wolf with Two Faces

10

'The passengers are here, Captain.'

Captain Allgood looked away from where his crew were readying the harpoon for travel and met the eyes of Reese, one of the youngest boys to serve on board *The Huntress*. The lad's face was ashen.

'Well? What are you telling me for? Show them to their bunk.' Allgood waved at the boy irritably. He didn't like dealing with passengers; they were a useful source of extra coin, but they didn't stay quiet and still like the rest of his cargo. He turned back to the harpoon, peering critically at the ropes and chains. Next time they made port in Onwai he was going to have the whole thing looked over, refitted, if necessary. It had been a hard season up in the northern seas, and the ice and salt took their toll.

'I think, Captain, that you might want to come and . . . have a look.'

Allgood turned back. Reese looked unsettled, and this was a boy who had jumped into the sea armed only with a spear, often finishing the job where the harpoon had failed. He was strong and wiry, and not easily scared.

'If you're wasting my time, lad, I'm having your rum ration.'

He followed the boy back down to the gangway where the crew were rolling on barrels of provisions. Behind them the port of Kortstone was quiet, shrouded in mist. Two figures with hoods stood to one side, letting the men and women with the barrels and sacks past.

71

'If the Narhl has changed his bloody mind, I'm keeping the fee,' Allgood muttered to Reese. 'I told him. I said, "such as you has no business going so far south", but there's no telling those savages anything.'

'I don't think that'll be the problem, Captain,' said Reese faintly.

As they approached, one of the figures stepped forward. She wore decent travelling leathers, a thick woollen cloak with a deep hood covering her face, and a pack slung over one shoulder. The pack appeared to be tied with strips of a wide variety of strange materials: rough hessian, blue ribbons, a strip of red silk. The figure wore gloves.

'Hello, yes, I'm Captain Allgood,' the Captain said. 'This is *The Huntress*. She's a working boat, as you can tell, so I don't really have the time for chit-chat and social niceties. My boy Reese here will show you to the space we've cleared. Meals are twice a day, you get the same as the rest of the crew, so don't moan or Graces save us I *will* feed you to the first sea monster we find.'

The figure nodded once, and pulled back her hood. 'Thank you, Captain. That all sounds quite sufficient.'

Allgood took an involuntary step backwards. 'I . . . what . . . who?'

'I *told* you,' muttered Reese next to him.

The woman had skin as green as a ripe apple, and eyes that were yellow from lid to lid, with a black slit in the middle: the eyes of a snake. Her hair was silvery white and tied back into a long braid. When she smiled, he saw that her teeth were pointed and sharp. She was beautiful, and frightening; like the sheer drop from the side of a cliff, or the rolling bank of cloud that announced a storm.

'What are you?' Allgood finally formed a sentence. His fingers were scrabbling for the knife at his belt, with little success. He was not a man who had a lot of experience with fighting; his targets were taken down by harpoon and spear from a distance. 'I will not – I will not have monsters on board this boat.'

The green woman frowned slightly. 'I believe my husband has spoken to you and brokered our passage aboard your ship. Is there a problem?'

'A problem?' Allgood swallowed hard. 'Your husband is Narhl, and I got no problem with the Narhl, but you—' He shook his head. His fingers had found the knife, but he hadn't drawn it. 'By Ede's soil and seas, what *are* you? I've never seen owt like you before.'

The woman drew herself up to her full height and raised a single eyebrow. 'Have you journeyed the entire span of the globe, Captain Allgood? Have you scoured every inch of Ede's soil and sea? No? Then you do not know all of her mysteries.'

Allgood shook his head. He felt lost. He wished that Reese wasn't standing there watching him.

'I can't – I can't just—'

'Captain Allgood, I am a peaceful person. I do not have to be, but I am.' The green woman smiled a little wider, revealing more of her pointed teeth. 'I simply wish to travel to the destination as discussed with my husband. I will be no trouble to you or your crew. Unless you or your crew invite trouble. We are paying you handsomely, are we not?'

Allgood puffed his breath out through his lips. The green woman's husband had given them more coin than they would likely make from hunting this season, and Allgood's threat about keeping the money whatever happened now felt distinctly rash. Behind the woman, the other figure had come closer, and he could see a sliver of distinctive Narhl skin beneath the hood. The man had been skinny for one of the men from the frozen north, not obviously a warrior, but his eyes had a wild cast to them. Allgood found abruptly that he didn't feel much like denying this pair what they wanted after all.

'All right. Fine.' He took a deep breath. 'What should I call you, then?'

'My name is Ephemeral,' said the woman seriously. 'It is my own name. I chose it.'

'Are you certain about this, Terin?'

They were finally in their bunk, a tiny room down some steps, just opposite the hold. It was good to be away from the curious eyes of the crew. Ephemeral sat with Terin on the narrow bed.

73

'Absolutely.' He nodded once. He smiled. 'We've spoken about it a lot.'

Ephemeral shifted on the bed. Her husband was not a typical Narhl. He was wiry and thin, a thinker rather than a fighter. His hair, brown streaked with grey, was wild and untidy, his small beard dotted with pale blue lichen. His eyes were dark blue. She still found his features fascinating, and could not grow tired of looking at them. And there was the way he looked at her. Without flinching.

'It could be painful for you. Dangerous. It could kill you eventually. The warmth.'

He tipped his head to one side. It was a thing he did when he was thinking. 'I have walked that line all my adult life, my love. The flames grant me visions sometimes. Imagine what I might see in a place where the sun beats down all day?' He smiled. 'Besides, we are already here. We both know we must go. Isn't this true?'

Ephemeral nodded, and took his hand in hers, the marbled pebble patterns of his skin against the flat green of her own. 'Your people do not leave the Frozen Steps often.'

It was a momentous thing he was doing. She could feel that in her blood, in the way his kin had looked at him before they left.

Terin nodded. 'We are trapped there, really. Bound by the cold, bound by the mountain. Our connection to the frozen lands makes travel anywhere uncomfortable. But, Ephemeral, there is so much I must see.' He squeezed her hand. 'There will be *libraries*.'

Ephemeral smiled, but it felt too tight on her face. She led him into danger, this peaceful, kind-hearted man.

'I do not know where he is exactly,' she said. She pressed her free hand to her chest. 'But I feel it, in here. There is something wrong. And it grows worse, all the time. The link between us is faint, because we are so far apart, but I feel it, keenly. I feel my father in our shared blood. I have to find him, husband. I must help him, if I can. Tell me,' she shifted on the bed again, 'tell me again what you saw when the flames took you.'

Terin nodded, his long face growing serious. There were faint burn marks up both of his arms and, she knew, across his narrow chest. His people did not approve of his fire-trances, but they would listen when he told them what he saw, because they knew the truth of it.

'I saw a man with a black beard and black hair, a man with blue eyes and an unknown mountain in his soul.' Terin's voice was entirely normal, but his gaze shifted over her right shoulder, staring off into nothing. 'There is a sword in his hands and a great weight on his heart. He moves into darkness now, and there are wolves in between the trees.' Terin's brow creased slightly. 'There is an evil in the forest, something god-fed, and I can't see it clearly. It moves, and it hunts, and it wishes . . .' Terin shook his head, as though the words wouldn't quite form. 'It wishes great harm for the world. I can't see it clearer than that. And the man moves closer to this darkness, and a great maelstrom of change. It is a chaos that will take him beyond the reach of the fire-trances, beyond my sight.' He blinked rapidly, coming back to her. 'That is all I remember, my love. I am sorry it cannot be clearer.'

She reached up and placed her hand briefly against his cheek. His skin was still cold, which was a blessing. 'You see much,' she said with feeling. 'But you must promise me, Terin. If it becomes overwhelming – the heat, the strangeness of the places we go to – then tell me. I will take you back, if you need me to. I will not risk you.'

'I will be fine.' He smiled again. 'I am not like my kin. I want to see the world.'

'Even so, I will watch you,' she said firmly. 'And if I decide we must leave, then we will leave.'

Terin nodded once. There were a few moments of silence between them. All around, they could hear the crew preparing to leave Kortstone. The cabin they had been assigned was cramped and smelled of fish. For the first time, Ephemeral allowed herself to feel a shiver of excitement. She was truly journeying out into the world now, with no one to advise her or hold her back. The decisions she made from now on were her own, for better or for worse.

'You miss your sisters,' said Terin suddenly.

Ephemeral looked down at her own hands. It would be some time before she saw another like her, she knew that much.

'They will be fine,' she said, with more assurance than she felt. 'Crocus and Havoc are busy. Indigo is keeping King Aristees on his feet. Toast is so taken with the wyverns, I doubt she noticed that I left.'

'They will all miss you,' said Terin. 'They look up to you.'

'My sisters walk their own paths now.' And with that, she felt a small throb of pride. 'They know their own names, their own minds.' She tipped her head to one side, mimicking the motion he made when he was thinking. 'We will see so many places, Terin.'

Terin grinned. 'Ephemeral, you are my strength. Without you I would still be cowering in the snow somewhere, waiting for visions to transport me. Now I sail across oceans, towards adventure and the unknown. And libraries!'

'And libraries,' agreed Ephemeral. 'We will find my father, and we will save him if we can. After that, the libraries of Ede are ours.'

11

They appeared just as Estenn was taking her midday meal. It was a fine hot stew, spiced with herbs grown in the jungle of Euriale, steeped in the juices of fruits they had picked themselves. The meat – that tasted akin to pork, but wasn't – was tender and fell to pieces as her spoon touched it. Ivy and Gen appeared at the entrance to the Emissary's home. The younger girl looked distressed, while Gen simply looked angry. Estenn put down her bowl and gestured to them.

'What is it?'

Ivy sidled over the flagstones that were set into the earth at the entrance, clearly unnerved at entering such a holy space. Estenn made her home in an old temple to the Twins, one of the very few stone structures in their sprawling camp. It sat at the heart of their dwellings, a low building of pale-brown rock crouching close to the black earth like a wolf ready to spring. There was no door, just a dark entranceway of square rock, and on the floor beyond the flagstones were the remains of an old mosaic made of black and white tiles. If they filled the place with strong lamps it was still possible to see how one side had depicted Res'na, a white wolf against black, and Res'ni, black and snarling against a snowy background. There were two altars at the back of the squalid room, and Estenn fancied she could still smell the old blood that had been spilled there, particularly at night when the moon was full. She kept only the barest furniture in there, and slept on the stones. It was her place as the Emissary.

'It's the Spinner. He's sick,' said Ivy. She glanced up at the altars, lit now with long, thin beeswax candles. She pressed the palms of her hands flat to either side of her face, a brief entreaty of blessings from the Twins. 'He's shaking all over and won't calm down.'

'He's pitching a fit or something,' added Gen. She wouldn't quite come over the threshold, preferring instead to lean on her spear just outside the entrance. 'I think you should come and see, Emissary.'

Estenn put the bowl down on the flagstones and got to her feet.

Outside, the settlement was busy. Following Gen and Ivy she weaved around men and women performing their daily tasks in the sweltering heat, receiving nods and grateful smiles as she passed. One or two called out to her: 'Bless you, Emissary', 'The Twins give you strength, Emissary'. She passed the cooking pits, where red-hot embers cooked the meat they had carefully skinned and speared on spits. These were tended with special care, as cooking the meat was considered an act of worship to the wolf gods themselves.

Another guard stood at the entrance to the Spinner's enclosure now, a thin man with grey hair and a pirate's scars across his back and chest. He met Estenn's eyes with a frown but didn't say anything. He didn't have to; Estenn could hear the Spinner's howls from where she stood.

'Stay here,' she told the three of them firmly.

She ventured down into the dark, snatching up a lamp from the ground as she passed it. When she reached the Spinner's enclosure, she paused. He had thrown off the blankets and the sacking they covered him in, but she could not see him clearly because he'd also knocked over the lamps they kept in his chamber. She silently thanked the Twins for this small mercy.

'What has happened?' she asked, not troubling to keep her voice soft. 'Why are you causing such a ruckus?'

The Spinner howled again, a wild, discordant keening. It

sounded as though it came from several throats at once, and Estenn could feel her hair trying to stand on end. The creature was shivering all over, and in the dark she could see his complicated limbs scraping at the walls.

'You must be calm,' she told him. 'If you do not calm yourself, I will have them all down here to restrain you. Dirty human fingers, corrupting your skin. Is that what you want?'

The Spinner wailed once more, and then gave a great convulsive shudder. Orange lamplight ran sickly over rounded scales of pearlescent armour; they seemed to run like wax as she watched. She squeezed her eyes shut to try and keep the sight out. She had seen a great deal that was strange during her years on Euriale, but the Spinner's true form was still difficult to process.

'It is coming!' cried the Spinner, his voice still full of strange harmonies. 'It pierces us, tears back the centuries.'

'What is?' asked Estenn. Despite her misgivings she held out the lamp, bathing the Spinner in uncertain light. 'What is coming?'

The Spinner scraped his claws against the wall, peeling away clods of clay. 'I felt it, of course I felt it, how could I not? It draws near, and it brings with it everything I fear. The ending, and the beginning. The time of birthing.' The Spinner drew his various limbs inwards, like a dying spider. 'You,' he said, and now the voice was a whisper. 'You will destroy the cycle even as you seek to extend it. The birthing comes, and the key approaches.'

Estenn shook her head. The Spinner was raving, worse than she'd ever seen him. Had something come to the island that she wasn't aware of? She crouched, setting the lamp down by her feet, and pressed her hands and feet to the dark soil, curling her toes so that they dug into the dirt. She knew the island like no other: it was a part of her, and she was a part of it. The scent of Euriale was wild in her nostrils, and that alien power was just below her fingertips. Without thinking about it, she began to *become less*, fading from view as she gave herself over to the will of the island. As ever she sensed the slow building of power. Soon, yes, it would be soon, but was there something else?

Her eyes snapped open in the near dark, and she became visible again. There was some new magic that had not been here before, at least not while she had lived on the island. It was akin to the magic here, but it was a different shape. She thought of how the Spinner had described it as a key. Slowly she stood, and became aware of the Spinner watching her.

'No,' he said, his voice a whisper now. 'You mustn't. You mustn't.'

Ignoring him, she turned and walked back up the passage. Out in the bright daylight she met Gen, Ivy and the old man. They were watching her anxiously, although she could already see how relieved they were that the howling had stopped.

'Gen, who has the westward patrol this afternoon?'

The woman with auburn hair stood a little straighter. 'Anine, Emissary.'

Estenn nodded once. 'Go and tell her to keep an extra eye on the waterways today, and for the next few days. Tell her that if she sees anything to send a runner to me immediately.'

Ivy's eyebrows shot up. 'Emissary, you think someone is bringing a ship in?'

Estenn tipped her head to one side, sucking at a tooth. There was a shred of meat caught in it. 'Someone is coming, yes,' she said. 'Or something.'

12

Frith stood on the deck of the *Poison Chalice*, the staff held in both hands. It was very early, and still quite dark in the canyon of the waterways, while above them the strip of dawn sky was pale pink and threaded with stained clouds.

'We're ready for you, Lord Frith,' came Devinia's voice behind him. 'We've lost our fair wind now, and the currents aren't to be trusted. It's down to you.'

Frith nodded once, picturing the word for Force in his mind. They had practised, of course, out in the open sea, but here there were walls of sheer rock to either side, towering over the ship. A mistake here – too much force, in the wrong direction – could be disastrous. He could feel the eyes of the crew watching him, and he could feel Wydrin watching them, too, no doubt ready with a sharp word if any of them should pester him. He smiled slightly at that, and closed his eyes.

The word for Force was clear in his mind. With it, he pictured the three big masts of the *Poison Chalice*, festooned with sails. They surrounded him; he could hear the creaking of the wood. He had been concerned at first that he could only push the magic one way, that the force would have to be pushed directly ahead of him, as though he were physically moving it himself, but after some thought, he realised it was entirely possible to split the force into separate, flexible strands, and these he could direct wherever he liked. It was Joah's knowledge, of course; the collective wisdom of a man who had spent his life studying the Edenier and the Edeian. He had also spent his life torturing and murdering innocent people to please his demon benefactor, but that hadn't stopped him sharing the knowledge with Frith when he thought he could be his brother in arms. Frith frowned, trying to put that from his mind, but, as ever, he found he couldn't leave it behind completely. Over the last few months, new knowledge had been rising to the surface; new words, new ways to combine magics, things he'd never contemplated suddenly making a strange kind of sense. It was clear that he'd picked up more than he'd originally thought during Joah's 'crossing session'. He did not like to think about that too closely.

'Any time you're ready, Lord Frith,' said Devinia.

Sighing, Frith lifted the staff and reached out with the word. Nearly invisible tendrils of force flowed from either end, colourless but showing as a disruption in the air, like heat rising from baking stones. He directed them effortlessly, up and out and away from each other until they curled against the canvas of the sails. He was rewarded with the flat *crack crack crack* sound as the sails filled with his magic and a sudden shifting of the deck underfoot as the ship surged forward. He opened his eyes, and after a moment there was a ragged cheer from the crew. The *Poison Chalice* was moving sedately down the waterway, black cliffs passing them on either side. Devinia approached and slapped him heartily on the shoulder.

'Good work,' she said. 'Keep that up, and we'll let you know when you need to stop.'

She stepped away, already barking orders at her crew, and Wydrin appeared at his side instead. 'How does it feel?' she asked.

'It is fine,' he replied shortly, holding the word in his mind. 'It is as I expected.'

'Does it tire you out? How long do you think you could keep it up for?'

Frith shot her a look. 'You doubt me?'

Wydrin grinned. The day was brightening all the time, painting her untidy hair in golden colours.

'Devinia would wear you into the ground if she thought it

would aid her. And I would prefer you to have some energy at the end of the day.' Her smile faltered and she looked around. 'Where is Sebastian, anyway? I thought he would come up to see this at least. I haven't seen him since he went off to sulk last night.'

It was difficult to shrug whilst holding the heavy staff in both hands, so Frith tipped his head. 'I do not think Sebastian is as interested in this voyage as you might hope.'

Wydrin sighed. 'You may be right.'

Frith kept the magic up for a good couple of hours, enjoying the movement of the ship under his feet and the sense of controlling something so enormous. When eventually he insisted on a break, he staggered back a few steps as he let the word go and was surprised to find that the staff was hot to the touch. He felt light-headed too, and gratefully took the beaker of water passed to him by Kellan. Having negotiated an hour's lunch with Devinia, he had just turned away to head below decks when he realised there were raised voices behind him. Wydrin and a short woman with dark skin were standing close together, looking with confusion at something in the shorter woman's arms. He went over, still reeling slightly as the staff tingled in his fingers.

'He wouldn't just leave them there, Bernice,' Wydrin was saying. She picked something out of the bundle the shorter woman was holding, and the sun winked off Sebastian's enamelled badge. Frith remembered it well; it had been the only thing that had saved the big knight from the rogue Gallo's blade.

'I found them on the deck, half hidden by the crates,' said Bernice. She had Sebastian's thin summer cloak in her arms. Her brow was furrowed, and Frith could guess what she was thinking from the downward turn of her mouth. 'We need the decks clear, and I thought it was passing strange because no crew would just leave their belongings out in the air like that, where someone might come a mischief.' She paused, eyeing Wydrin with obvious concern. 'They were near the guardrail, Wydrin.'

'And you did not see Sebastian?' asked Frith.

'No one has seen him this morning at all,' said Wydrin. She didn't look worried, not yet, but she did look annoyed, which

Frith knew was only half a step away from worried for Wydrin. 'We should go to his cabin, and—'

There was a rapid flurry of shouts from all around the ship, and to Frith's surprise the deck under his feet lurched abruptly to one side, nearly pitching him straight into Bernice, who was much better at keeping her feet. The short woman dumped Sebastian's belongings on the deck and ran, responding to some call Frith had missed.

'What's going on?'

The deck lurched back the other way, the cliffs to the right looming very close. Frith could hear splashing, too, the normally calm water crashing against the hull. The crew were all moving now, dashing across the deck. Wydrin took hold of his arm.

'Let's go look.'

They raced to the far side, but before they reached the guardrail something enormous crashed into it, splintering wood and throwing them back. It looked to Frith like some sort of giant orange slug, glistening with transparent slime and pocked with fleshy suckers. It stretched, the very end of it becoming long and tapered, and it slid rapidly across the deck, nosing back and forth as though blindly searching for something. Next to him, Wydrin swore loudly and drew the short sword she called Glassheart. As if sensing the danger the thing swung back towards them both, and Frith realised that it was a tentacle rather than a slug; the great bulk of it was still below the ship somewhere. He looked back the way they'd come and saw that the fleshy tentacles were all over the ship. The men and women of the crew were already attacking with swords and daggers, trying to drive it back.

'Don't just stand there gawping,' Devinia had appeared behind them, both cutlasses drawn. She looked distinctly unruffled. 'Chop the bastard thing back into the sea.'

Wydrin was ahead of her, jumping forward and bringing Glassheart down with both hands. The sword struck the tentacle with an unpleasantly meaty chop – Frith was reminded of afternoons wasted in the kitchen at Blackwood Keep, watching the cook prepare a carcass for dinner – and the rubbery flesh peeled back, weeping yellow fluid. At the same time, the ship canted sharply to one side again, this time so violently that Frith was sure they would be smashed to pieces on the rocks at the base of the cliffs. He fell into the guardrail, struggling to keep hold of the staff. Another tentacle, bigger and longer than the rest, reared up on the other side and made a spirited swipe for their central mast. There was a shrill scream from behind him and Frith turned just in time to see an unfortunate man swept over the side.

Pushing himself away from the rail, Frith tightened his grip on the staff and summoned the words for Fire and Ever. A ruby stream of flames leapt from the end of the staff, snaking up like a whip to curl around the biggest tentacle. It drew back instantly, flopping heavily against the sails before sliding back over the side. Frith turned the staff, meaning to use the flames against the next tentacle he could see, when a sharp elbow caught him in the ribs.

'Are you trying to set fire to my bloody ship?' Devinia gave him an outraged look. There was yellow slime on both her cutlasses.

Frith opened his mouth to retort, but the *Poison Chalice* rocked again and now they appeared to be sinking: the monster was trying to drag them under. He summoned the word for Cold instead, and sent a blizzard roaring across the deck to freeze two of the tentacles solid, where they promptly stuck to the deck.

'Here.' Devinia grabbed his arm and half dragged him to the one bit of the deck that wasn't taken up with tentacles or frantic crew members. 'Quickly,' she said, 'Fill our sails and get us moving. We must pull away from it.'

Frith looked back. Wydrin had drawn Frostling too now, and had joined three other crew members in repelling a particularly thick tentacle. He lifted the staff in both hands and summoned the Force spell, filling their sails in an instant. The *Poison Chalice* groaned like a ship in a storm, and the creature behind them gave a long rumbling roar, so low it set Frith's teeth on edge.

'That's it,' cried Devinia. She stood next to him, ready to defend him should any tentacles get too close. 'Keep going!'

Frith took a deep breath, trying to ignore the chaos around him. The force surged out of him, filling every sail to breaking point. He could hear the creaking of the masts, could feel the resistance in his own arms. Around him the deck was now slippery with slime and yellow blood. There was a crash, and his face was abruptly wet with spray, but he kept his eyes ahead, focussed on the sails.

'Ye gods and little fishes!' Wydrin's voice was clear over the cacophony. 'How many arms does this thing *have*?'

The *Poison Chalice* shifted, surging forward in the water, and there came another low roar, now curiously closer than it had been. Frith heard the cries of the crew and felt the hairs on the back of his neck stand up. Next to him Devinia had turned to face the threat, and was letting fly a stream of curse words to rival her daughter's vocabulary, but he didn't look. He couldn't – if he let the force pushing their sails dwindle for the smallest moment, they would have no chance of escaping the monster's clutches.

'Keep going!' called Devinia again. 'For the love of the Graces, keep going!'

There was another ear-splitting roar, followed by the corresponding screams of a few unlucky crew members, and then with a surge that to Frith seemed to almost lift them out of the water, the *Poison Chalice* was away. There was a huge splash to either side as their sudden speed sent waves crashing against the cliffs, and at that moment Frith did dare to glance over his shoulder. He saw something enormous boiling in the water, a burnt orange slab of glistening muscle, studded with a single wet eye and riddled with reaching arms, and then it was gone, slipping back under the turbulent water.

Estenn leaned back against the tree, lowering the eyeglass for a moment. Next to her, Anine and Gen were watching her carefully. The three of them were hidden within the treeline, and in the heavy shade their black and white faces looked stark.

'Well, that is interesting,' she said, striving to keep her voice level.

'What is it?' demanded Gen. 'The stick produced fire, and then ice. I have never seen such, not even on Euriale.'

'It is certainly a relic of the old days,' said Estenn. She licked her lips, which were suddenly very dry. 'A relic of the true days, when the gods were with us, and the Twins walked among these trees. It is, in short, exactly what I have been waiting for.'

She lifted the eyeglass again and the big ship below leapt into focus again. She could see the men and women moving rapidly across the deck. There was an older woman with wild red hair bellowing orders. She had lost sight of the white-haired man with brown skin who had wielded the strange wooden staff. She guessed he had gone below.

'What do we do?' asked Anine. She was quieter than her cousin, and had a tendency to wait until it was time to ask pertinent questions. 'Do we take it?'

Estenn bit her lip, counting the men and women on the deck, and the cannon in the ship's broadside. They looked to be well armed, and disciplined too, especially for a pirate vessel.

'They may be too large for us,' she said. She turned, looking up from the waterway that housed the ship to the curving path it cut through the island behind them. From their high vantage point it was possible to see parts of the trench, and there was movement there too. It seemed that the ship with the interesting passengers had company it was unaware of: a parasite travelling in their wake. Estenn smiled, feeling her heart quicken.

'We will wait, and see,' she told Gen and Anine. 'I think the gods are looking to bless us again, very soon.'

13

Moments later, the crew were back to work. Devinia had them on the deck, buckets and mops in hand, swiftly washing away the yellow blood – if that's what it was. Wydrin turned away from them with a sick feeling in her gut. As distant as Sebastian had been lately, he would not have sat idly by while the ship was under attack. With a nod to Frith, who lowered his staff and followed her, she headed below deck.

Sebastian had been assigned a narrow cabin that was just about long enough for him to stretch out in, adjacent to the one she was sharing with Frith. Wydrin pushed aside the heavy red fabric that hung over the door to see an empty bunk. She hadn't really expected anything else, but still she stood there for a moment, glaring at the empty hammock as though she could will Sebastian into appearing there.

'He's not here, is he?' asked Frith at her shoulder. It wasn't really a question.

'What has he done?' Her voice sounded too small to her own ears, so she cleared her throat. 'He's made some dodgy decisions in his time – and I can hardly criticise him for that – but to abandon the ship in the belly of Euriale.' She stepped fully into the narrow cabin, looking around for any clues. 'That's stupid, even for Sebastian. Even for me.'

Frith stepped around her, and opened the long sea chest at the foot of the bunk. Inside was Sebastian's broadsword and other small weapons, wrapped in their oilcloth.

'He did not take these,' said Frith. 'Why would he leave the ship unarmed, unless he—'

'He would not do that,' said Wydrin, although a terrible, cold feeling was sweeping up from her feet, so suddenly that she felt almost faint with it. Could he have decided to take his own life? Could she have been so blind as to have missed such torment? When Prince Dallen had walked away from him, it had broken his heart, but she had trusted that he would come out the other side of that sadness eventually. Sebastian, always the level-headed one, always the speaker of sense. This was the sort of battle she could not win with daggers, and it frightened her badly.

'We'll have to go back,' she said, meeting Frith's eyes. 'We'll take one of the skiffs back the way we came. I need to know what happened.'

Devinia was not convinced. Back up on deck she stood with her arms crossed over her chest, scowling openly at Wydrin. Her hair had been bound back into a loose tail, although pieces of it had come away, framing her stern face. Her mother rarely wore a captain's hat, preferring to wear black ribbons in her hair.

'You must be jesting with me,' she said. Next to her, Kellan was still organising the clean-up; the monstrous creature hadn't done any serious damage, but had torn one of their smaller sails, while Augusta was doing her own rounds, tending to the injured crew. 'You expect to take a boat and row it back up the waterway? Here, in Euriale? Across the path of the thing we just barely escaped?'

'We've been all over this ship, and Sebastian isn't here,' said Wydrin. 'He must have left the ship late last night, when no one was watching.'

'Late last night, we were some distance away,' said Devinia. 'Your lordling here has pushed us along at a fine rate. You know how dangerous this place is, Wydrin. A skiff will not survive. You will not survive.'

'I don't have time to argue about this, Mum. I need to go back and look, and Frith is coming with me.'

Somehow Devinia managed to look even more outraged. 'It's not enough that you must get yourself killed, but you have to take our only means of propulsion with you? What will happen if we should face another beast like the one that nearly sank us? Should we sit here quietly while it peels us to pieces, waiting for you to come back?'

'So now we're your sole protection too? The Devinia the Red I grew up with needed no mage for protection!' Wydrin could feel her voice rising, and struggled to control it. She could see Kellan watching her with interest, and knew that much of the rest of the crew would be doing the same.

Devinia was now shaking her head with disgust. 'Always too reckless, never thinking things through. This is why your brother is the captain of a ship, and you are a grubbing sell-sword—'

'Madam,' Frith's voice was low and stern. He stood with the staff held at his side. 'This is Black Feather Three business. The three of us have bonds that are not so easily severed, as I'm sure you have bonds with your own crew. This is not something we will compromise on.'

For a moment Devinia appeared to be speechless. She looked from Wydrin to Frith, and back again.

'Fine. Go, then, but know, Wydrin Threefellows, fabled Copper Cat of Crosshaven and unending bane of my existence, that you carry my life, and the lives of my crew, in your pockets. And if you sink that skiff, I'll follow you into the afterlife and tan your bloody hide myself.'

They set out on the ship's skiff at midday, the sun filling the narrow waterway with simmering heat. Everywhere Wydrin glanced, the water was too bright to look at, dancing and painting vivid after-images under her eyelids. Frith sat opposite her while she rowed, the staff held across his lap. He looked uneasy as they made their way out of the shadow of the *Poison Chalice*. Wydrin deliberately did not look up at it; it was easy to imagine Devinia glowering over the rail at them as her precious ship sat becalmed in the water. Instead she kept her eyes ahead, looking for anything unexpected in their path.

'Should I not help you with the oars?' he asked.

Wydrin shook her head, leaning back into the pull and feeling her muscles bunch with the effort. 'I want both your hands free should we come across any trouble.' She tossed her head to move her hair out of her eyes. 'Keep watching the water. We're hoping we're too small for that slug thing to take much notice of. The *Poison Chalice* probably gave it a good bump on the head on the way past.'

Frith nodded, although he looked less than pleased with her words. 'And how far back will we go? We cannot be sure when Sebastian left the ship.'

Wydrin pushed, and pulled, pushed, and pulled, feeling the drag of the oars through the water. She wondered briefly what might be beneath them right now, watching their slim shadow pass overhead.

'We know that he must have left between the time we were all in the cabin together, and when we set off this morning. I know roughly where we started when you took over propulsion of the ship – the cliffs grow suddenly higher there, and the way is narrower.' She paused. Sweat was breaking out over her back. 'Also there was a large rock standing out of the water that looked a bit like a cheerful monkey.'

Frith raised an eyebrow. 'If you say so.'

They moved steadily on, and soon the *Poison Chalice* had dropped out of sight, lost around the sharp bends of the waterways. It grew quieter to Wydrin's ears; the raucous birdsong and the cries of the monkeys seemed further away, and the sounds of her oars cutting through the sapphire waters felt muffled. She realised that the general noise and energy of her mother's ship had to some extent been shielding them from the eeriness of the island.

'Look at that.'

She looked up to where Frith pointed, her heart in her mouth, but it was a flock of birds flying overhead, like black shards of glass against the sky. She blinked once. Not birds.

'Bats,' she said, and put her head down to the next stroke. The water was calm and they were moving quickly, but her heart told her it wasn't quick enough.

'We get a lot of bats in the Blackwood,' said Frith. 'They did not look like bats. Their heads were too long.'

Wydrin shrugged awkwardly. 'This whole place is weird.'

Frith did not reply, but he held the staff a little tighter.

It took them some time and Wydrin's back was full of a dull, warm ache, but they reached the cliffs she had in mind. Wydrin manoeuvred the little boat around so that they did a rough circuit, moving from one side of the cliffs to the other. On one side was a pile of rocks and black sand poking out of the water. She took them over until the wooden hull scraped against the miniature shore. Frith hopped out and pulled it in further, and Wydrin got out and helped him. When they were happy the boat wasn't about to abandon them, they looked around at their surroundings.

'Well,' said Frith, 'it does indeed look like an overly happy monkey. Ede truly is a world of wonders.'

Wydrin elbowed him, and they set about exploring the small space of sand and rock. It didn't take long.

'Here, look.' She crouched on the ground and pointed. There in the wet, grey sand were clear boot prints – the prints of someone with very large feet. 'He made it this far,' she said, trying not to let the relief show in her voice. 'He did not just perish in the water.'

Frith went to the very edge of the sand and looked up. The cliff face loomed over them, black and forbidding. Here and there short wizened trees with deep purple blossoms clung on for their lives, and they themselves held birds' nests of grey and green. Tiny birds, no bigger than the end of Wydrin's thumb, buzzed in and out like busy gemstones. 'And where did he go from here, then?' he asked. 'There is nowhere to go save back into the water.'

Wydrin ran a hand through her hair. It was stiff with salt already and growing curlier by the day. 'There is a way up,' she said, after a few moments of staring at the cliff face. She pointed to a place where a section of stone had fallen away, a long time ago. It had left a series of narrow ledges; all of them quite far from each other, but not impossible to reach, if you happened to be quite tall. 'It wouldn't be an easy climb, that's for bloody sure, and I wouldn't like to do it, but if you were desperate . . .' She pursed her lips, wondering just how desperate Sebastian had been. 'If you were desperate, I reckon you could make it. And he wasn't wearing his sword, or any of his heavy armour. Remember when we were trapped in Temerayne and we had to climb that wall of ice in a hurry? He made it then.'

'I remember some of that day, yes,' replied Frith wryly.

A glint of something blue caught Wydrin's eye. She stepped around a pair of jagged rocks and found a blue-glass globe nestled in the black sand there. She picked it up and showed it to Frith. He looked at her and she saw both worry and sympathy in his eyes, and somehow that made it worse.

'He must have dropped it,' she told him. 'He wouldn't leave this behind deliberately. It was one of his most treasured possessions.' *Along with that stupid badge of Isu*, she added silently, which he most certainly had left behind – discarded on the deck like an old boot. Frith said nothing. Abruptly, Wydrin felt her chest fill with anger, and she closed her fingers firmly enough to make her oar-bruised hand ache. Why would he do this to them? They were the Black Feather Three. He was her sworn brother.

'So,' she said. 'When I see him next I'm going to shove this globe so far up his—'

'He went up the cliff,' said Frith. 'He left the ship in the dead of night, swam to this sorry pile of rocks, and then hauled himself, soaking wet, up this cliff face. So now what?'

Wydrin looked up at the towering stone wall. 'SEBASTIAN!'

The tiny birds in their wizened nests all fled as one, filling the air with emerald buzzing, while overhead larger birds and animals gave panicked calls.

'SEBASTIAN! If you can hear me, I've got a bloody bone to pick with you!'

There was no reply. Wydrin dropped her hands to her sides. She grimaced.

'We could climb the wall too,' she said, not quite looking at Frith. 'It wouldn't be very easy, not now that you don't have the magic to lift us into the air, but we could do it. And then what? At the top of the cliff is a bloody great smelly jungle.'

'And meanwhile, your mother's ship languishes, stranded,' Frith added. 'If we made it to the top, I do not expect Sebastian to be standing there waiting for us.'

'We would have to track him through the trees, and he was the only one of us that was any good at tracking.' She looked back at Frith. 'Unless you have a knowledge of forest lore that you've been holding back, growing up in the Blackwood and all.'

He drew himself up slightly. 'I was a lord. Or the son of a lord, at least.'

Wydrin turned back. She felt helpless and angry. They knew he had gone this way. There was nothing they could do about it. After a moment she felt Frith's hand rest on her shoulder. She leaned into it, and he spoke softly into her ear.

'I am sorry, Wydrin. Truly.'

She let out a long sigh. When they had passed into the main body of Euriale she had felt that cold sense of severing, and she had dismissed it. Already, one of their number was lost.

'Perhaps he is heading back to Two-Birds.' She forced herself to say the words, hoping they would bring some comfort. 'He was never particularly keen on this adventure. Perhaps we have asked him to move on too soon after Ephemeral, and Dallen, and that whole bastard mess at Skaldshollow. He could have decided to go back, and he would have known that Devinia would not have lent him a boat.' She swallowed. 'It is not so far to Two-Birds from here.'

Frith nodded, although she noticed that he didn't voice an opinion one way or another. 'What do we do then?' he asked. 'Where do we go from here?'

'We go back to the *Poison Chalice*,' said Wydrin, still looking up at the cliff. She slipped the blue-glass globe into her own pocket. 'And we hope that Sebastian can bloody well look after himself.'

14

Sebastian stood under the tree and listened to the storm passing overhead, the near-solid rain turning the black earth to an oily slick around his boots. He could hear nothing but the percussion of rain against leaves and the deep-throated rumble of thunder, just starting to move away now. The mineral scents of water and jungle were thick in his nose.

Euriale was a place of wonders. In his short walk from the cliff edge he had seen many things that were new to him – a large grey cat with tufted black ears and enormous protruding incisors, slipping away between the trees, flightless birds with long legs and banded beaks, and a small crowd of reptiles about the size of chickens, all walking on their back legs, tiny forelegs held delicately before them. These last Sebastian had paused to watch. They had been bright green, their long narrow heads with eyes like chips of onyx, and when he'd taken a step towards them they had all scattered as one, only to move back into their group, watching him with beady eyes. He had felt their keen lizard minds, fragments of silver wire in his head.

The rain stopped almost as abruptly as it had started. Sebastian stepped out from the shelter of the tree into a freshly dripping world. Now the thunder had departed he could hear bird calls all around him, and the whoops and hollers of monkeys in the canopy. He moved off, stumbling through bushes and the tangle of undergrowth, dimly aware of small creatures fleeing from his blundering.

He walked all day, with no clear idea where he was heading or why. The sun set, turning the fragments of sky overhead molten orange, and then, when night did come, it was with a darkness so thick that it was almost suffocating. Sebastian kept moving until he could no longer be sure of his footing – it would not do to wander straight off the edge of a cliff in the dark – and finding a relatively clear patch beneath a clutch of trees he built the best fire he could with green twigs and dry leaves. The smoke was black and smelled terrible, but he felt safer with its yellow light on his hands and face. There was that big cat to think of, which even now could be approaching his makeshift camp, eyes like moons easily piercing the darkness. He shifted, missing the weight of the broadsword at his back. With sudden clarity, the foolishness of his actions loomed up to seize his heart.

'What have I done?' he said aloud. In the distance, a monkey appeared to hoot with amusement. He shook his head. 'You're right. That's not the question I should be asking. I know what I've done. I just don't know why.'

Except that wasn't entirely true. There was a mystery here, something that had seeped in around the edges of his mind, obscuring everything else. The *Poison Chalice*, with its crew ready to risk anything for the sake of adventure . . . it had all seemed to smell of death to him: deaths he wouldn't be able to prevent, or deaths he would actively cause. He remembered the smoking slaughter of the battlefield in Relios after Y'Ruen had blessed it with dragon flame; he remembered following the brood sisters into King Aristees' camp, watching with satisfaction as they tore to pieces the Narhl soldiers holding his lover captive. He remembered the resurrected dead of Skaldshollow, mindlessly rushing at him with sharpened bones protruding from their bodies; he remembered cutting them down, and feeling the glory of the slaughter. And then Dallen watching them leave, raising a hand in farewell – his grief for his own people driving the final wedge between them.

Sebastian held his hands over the meagre flames. He did not need the warmth, but that small feeling reminded him he was alive. His traitorous mind called up a picture of Wydrin, who would have long since discovered he had left the ship. He imagined her scowl, and then her growing alarm as she realised he had gone. She would probably insist on looking for him, had probably already had that argument with her mother. On that count, at least, Sebastian was fairly certain: they would never find him, not in this labyrinth of a jungle. Absently, he slipped his hand into his pocket, seeking the blue-glass globe Crowleo had made for him, and his stomach dropped a little when his fingers found nothing. It must have fallen out, probably on his climb up the cliff face. His memory of Isu, and of Crowleo's act of kindness – gone. Likely, he would never see the Secret Keeper's apprentice again, and now he had lost the only thing that connected them. He swallowed down the wave of guilt. It was better this way. No one would have to die because of him.

A shivering cry rent the air over his head, and Sebastian found his hand reaching automatically for the short sword that was no longer on his belt. Just a bird, he told himself, but it hadn't sounded like a bird. It had sounded much larger. He thought of the small running lizards, of how different they had felt. It was something about this island. Perhaps it was cursed, just as Wydrin claimed.

It was some time before he relaxed enough to lie down by his small fire, but eventually he did, curling his body around it as best he could. In the dark hours of the night he slept, and dreamed of a ship full of the scent of flowers, and an unrelenting heat.

The next day, Sebastian had a sighting of the blue ghost, the first since he had climbed his way up the cliff face. One moment the trees were full of deep indigo shadows, the last light of the day painting bark orange and grey, and the next, everything was lined in pale blue fire. Sebastian turned, startled, to see the eerie figure standing just a few feet away from him, almost too bright to look at.

'Who are you?' he said. His voice was thick from a day of near silence. He cleared his throat. 'What are you doing here?'

The ghost seemed to consider him for a moment, and then it walked on past him, disappearing into the trees ahead. Sebastian followed, stumbling to keep up, and although that ghostly figure faded into nothing, another took its place, some distance ahead. Sebastian picked his feet up and ran, determined to catch up with the ghost this time. Again, when he'd caught up with it, the figure faded into nothing, only to be replaced with another further ahead. Sebastian ran on, stomping through small bushes and weaving around trees. The light was fading swiftly and he felt sure he was being led into some sort of trap – and there could be no question that the figure was leading him – yet he could not stop. Here were the answers he was seeking. He didn't know why yet, but he was sure of it.

It was so dark by the time he reached his destination that he very nearly fell over it. His boots met solid stone, and a tall building loomed up ahead, lit only in moonlight. He could make out very little save for an odd steeple poking above the treeline, and just ahead of him a small courtyard paved with dark red stones. The final ghostly figure that had led him here had vanished.

Cautiously, Sebastian stepped over the low wall that surrounded the courtyard, taking a moment to note that the red stones shone as though they were wet, and headed towards the entrance. The empty doorway was arched at the top, and in the gloom he could just about make out a carving above the lintel; it looked to be a many-legged creature of some sort. Beyond the door, there was nothing but pitch-blackness. Sebastian paused there, willing the blue ghost to appear again. The darkness beyond the door did not feel threatening – on the contrary, the urge to walk over the threshold was strong – but for all he knew there could be nothing but a great hole in the floor, or something equally hazardous. He forced himself to step away, and instead resolved to make his camp on the stony courtyard. The sticks he'd collected the night before were now dry in his belt, and the fire came much easier this time. Around him, the calls of monkeys and birds welcomed the night.

'This is where it meant me to come,' he murmured to the flames. 'I am sure of it. This place must mean something.'

Sitting cross-legged by his fire he saw now that the red stones were actually made of glass – great red-ruby cobbles that absorbed the firelight and cast it back in a crimson glow. Sebastian ran his fingers over them, marvelling at their smoothness – there wasn't a scratch that he could see. He thought of the magical glass in the Secret Keeper's house. Was this more of that? Did these glass stones also hold secrets? Or a warning?

'Why do you trespass here, stranger?'

Sebastian looked up with a start, his hand once more reaching for the weapons that weren't there. A tall man stood over him; he wore a robe, a shirt of mail, and leather sandals that laced up his calves. He was completely solid and real – even in the firelight Sebastian could see that his skin was a deep warm brown, and that the epaulettes at his shoulders were bright gold – but he was also the ghost. The ghost made real, finally.

15

'I – trespassing?'

'This isn't the sort of place you wander idly about.' The man came around the fire, and belatedly Sebastian realised that he had not heard him approach at all. He scrambled to his feet. 'You are not supposed to be here.'

The man was scowling slightly. He was tall, almost as tall as Sebastian, and his hair, which appeared to be dark, was a mess of short curls. His chin was clean shaven, and from what Sebastian could see he carried no obvious weapons.

'Who are you?' Sebastian managed to get out. 'What are you doing here?'

The man looked away, out into the dark. He seemed annoyed. 'My name is Oster. That seems right. I know that much, I think. I am here because . . . this is where I must be.' He turned back, scowling, and for the first time he seemed to take in Sebastian's tense stance. '*I* belong here. The question really should be what are you doing in this place?'

'You led me here,' said Sebastian. He could feel the darkness inside the building behind him, the thick darkness of the jungle all over, and this one small point of light. 'We all saw you in Two-Birds, but you were like a ghost. A ghost made of blue light.'

The man who had named himself Oster frowned and shook his head. 'I did no such thing. You've imagined it. You trespass here, on the isle of the gods.'

Sebastian ran a hand over his face, and then tugged at his beard. 'Sebastian,' he said finally. 'My name is Sebastian Carverson.'

'You are the first person I have exchanged words with, Sebastian Carverson.' He did not seem pleased about it. 'This is all wrong. This is not as it should be.'

And with that he sat down by the small fire, staring into the flames. After a moment, and with no other choices immediately available, Sebastian joined him.

'What else can you tell me?' he asked.

'This wasn't how it was supposed to be. I do not understand what has happened. I almost know things, they hang on the edge of my knowing, but I shouldn't . . . the Spinner should be here.' He scowled, as though just talking about it annoyed him. 'There is no sense in telling you any of this. You won't understand.'

'I came here to find you,' said Sebastian, feeling foolish as the words passed his lips. 'Can you tell me why?'

Oster glared at him. 'Why should I be able to tell you that? There are other people in this place. Did you know that?'

Sebastian blinked at the change of subject. 'Do you mean at Two-Birds? The pirate town to the north-west of the island – surely you came from there?'

'No, not there, in the jungle itself. In the cradle of Ede.' Oster leaned forward, and the firelight painted his face in broad shapes. There was something unsettling yet familiar about his face, Sebastian decided, as though he'd seen it carved into a crumbling wall somewhere. It was the face of an ancient king; it did not belong to this age. 'There shouldn't be people here. They walk on sacred ground.'

'The cradle of Ede,' said Sebastian. He was over his alarm, and now he was fascinated. Oster's eyes glittered with fierce intelligence, yet very little of what he was saying made sense to Sebastian. 'What do you mean by that?'

'You see that building behind you?' Sebastian turned and looked. 'It is a temple to a god that existed on Ede long ago. They called her Effrafi, and she was a god of the sun. We sit on her fire-stones, and this was her place, when the world was young. If you were to walk beyond the temple and down the dip that parts the earth behind it, you would find a small pile of glassy black rocks. Underneath that, if you dug down deep enough, you would find the bones of both a man and a horse, buried alive for the honour of Qio, a god who was ancient before Effrafi's name had ever been spoken. Walk north-east far enough, and there is a series of depressions in the earth, eight clear lines, one each for the Eight Mercies. Blood was spilled in those ditches once. People have come here for centuries, building their temples and their shrines, and then they left again. It was important that they left. This was never a place for humans.'

Sebastian stared at him. 'How can you know all this?'

Oster didn't answer immediately. For a time he looked off into the dark. When he turned back he almost looked sad. 'This is only the surface of what I should know. Something has gone wrong.'

He leaned forward, wrapping his arms around his knees in a gesture that made him look much younger. As his cloak fell away, Sebastian saw something he hadn't noticed before; along his bare right arm was an incredibly elaborate tattoo, seemingly traced in silver ink. It was of a dragon. Sebastian caught his breath.

'That is extraordinary work,' he said in a low voice. Oster followed his gaze and then held his arm up as though he hadn't seen it before himself. The dragon curled around his entire arm, from his wrist up to the top of his shoulder. Every minute scale, every curved tooth and horn, glittered with impossible detail.

'You shouldn't be here,' said Oster again. 'People build their temples and shrines, and then they leave, and we have time—'

Abruptly Oster reached across the fire and shoved Sebastian hard in the chest with surprising strength. At almost the exact same moment there was a clatter against the glass stones, and Sebastian registered an arrow bouncing off into the dark, inches from his leg.

'Enemies,' murmured Oster. He was on his feet now, his face tense. 'The wolves are coming.'

Sebastian stood up and looked around. There was a great deal of movement in the trees, and he thought for a moment that he saw men and women there – five or six of them at least. Their

102

faces were oddly divided; one side black, one side white. Then there was a crackle and a smear of light to his right where Oster had been standing. A great force flung him to one side and he landed hard on the fire-stones. He rolled instinctively, bringing himself to his feet in time to see a brightly shimmering shape moving between the trees. There were screams now, shouts from the men and women he'd seen there. Sebastian rubbed his fingers across his eyes and blinked rapidly – it was difficult to make out what was going on, and that thin silvery line that linked him to the brood sisters and other dragon-kin was *thrumming* inside him, making his heart pound.

'Oster? Where are you? What's going on?'

The only answer was a shout of pain from the dark trees. Sebastian ran across the crumbling courtyard and vaulted the low wall easily, but when he reached the trees he could see no one.

'Oster?'

There was a groan off to his left. Pushing aside the undergrowth he spotted movement on the ground. A young man, his face painted black and white, lay on his back, clutching his stomach. Sebastian could see little else in the dark, but he recognised from the way the man was moving that he had been badly hurt.

'Who are you?' asked Sebastian. 'Where are the rest of you?'

The man groaned, rolling his head towards him. The white paint stood stark against the dark bristles of his beard. 'The Emissary . . .' He gritted his teeth before continuing. 'She must be told. The Spinner . . .'

'Who is the Emissary? Why did you attack us?' When the man didn't reply, Sebastian nudged him with his foot. 'The man I was with. Did you see where he went?'

The injured man gave a sort of strangled laugh. 'That was no man. The Eye of Euriale, it opens.' He shivered all over. 'It opens!' The man reached out with one hand, as though to grab at Sebastian, and then he lay still.

'Damn it. Isu give you peace.' Sebastian stood up. Now that he listened, he could hear footsteps approaching him through the trees. He moved into a fighting stance, but it was Oster who appeared, still carrying no weapons.

'You are alive, then.'

Sebastian shook his head slightly before replying. 'What happened? One moment you were with me, the next—'

'Enemies in the forest. I could smell their ill intent.'

'I didn't realise there were any people on the mainland of Euriale. Everyone seems to think this place is populated solely by monsters.'

For the strangest moment, Oster looked offended. When he didn't reply, Sebastian continued, wondering what he could have said. 'This man mentioned an emissary, and a spinner. What happened to the others?'

'I dealt with them,' said Oster shortly. 'You say he mentioned the Spinner?'

'I said he mentioned *a* spinner. Who is *the* Spinner?'

Oster ran a hand through his tightly curled hair. 'If they have him, they must have him against his will. That would explain a lot.'

'It doesn't explain anything to *me*,' said Sebastian, wincing faintly at the echo of Wydrin in his words. 'Oster, who are you? Who were those people?'

Oster turned to look at him. The moonlight was like a halo, lining him in silver, and his face still held an expression of barely contained anger. Sebastian wondered what colour his eyes truly were. 'It shames me, but I must demand that you help me, Sebastian Carverson. I must find the Spinner, and you must help me do it.'

The night was still, the heat oppressive. Sebastian looked at the strange man in front of him, sensing that he was walking into more danger; heading towards death again, death that he had left the *Poison Chalice* to avoid. But this was the mystery he'd been searching for; he knew it by the ghosts that had led him to the sun god's temple, and by the powerful waking of the dragon blood inside him.

'I will come with you,' he said. 'Where else do I have to go?'

16

The name of this new ship was *The Piebald Knight*, and Ephemeral tried to take that as a good omen, but every day her unease grew. Every day her stomach was a nest of snakes.

They travelled ever southwards and, as expected, the days grew warmer and longer. The ship sailed under an impossibly wide sky, blue from corner to corner, and hanging in it was the fiery sun. Ephemeral had come to think of it as an enemy. Only at night were they safe from its unwavering heat, and then there was the agonising wait for sunrise, dreading the strip of silvery pink light that appeared on the eastern horizon. When she had travelled across Creos and Relios with her sisters, she had barely thought about the heat – they thrived in it, born as they were in dragon fire – and in those desert lands the very clay underfoot had been uncomfortably warm, the sun touching everything like a brand. But things were different now. Terin suffered, and the sun was an enemy.

She stood on the deck, looking out across the glittering blue expanse of the sea. It was, the captain had told her, the sea known as Y'Gria's Loss. The ship was the type known as a 'junk'. Somewhere beyond her anxiety Ephemeral turned these new words over in her mind, marvelling at them and feeling the now familiar thrill of knowledge gained. She loved the shape of this small ship, the segmented curve of the sails. *The Piebald Knight* carried twenty crates full of the dried petals of a certain orchid, the captain had told her, greatly prized in the southern lands as a means to make both perfume and poison. *That is what this place is*, thought Ephemeral. *It is perfume, and it is poison.* The scent of the orchids seeped up from the hold until everything was permeated with it.

The captain approached her. She was a short woman with olive skin and black hair, her braids bundled up under a wide-brimmed brown hat, which was tied with a length of pale-green silk. She eyed Ephemeral warily, and Ephemeral pretended not to notice.

'Madam.' She bowed slightly, as was her custom. 'The winds are brisk, and we make good time today.' Around them the small crew bustled about, or took their leisure with smoking pipes. Ephemeral and Terin were the only passengers; she had learned quickly that that was the best way for them to travel. 'Is there anything I can get for you?'

Ephemeral looked at the shorter woman. Of all the captains they had sailed with so far, Captain Lichun had been the kindest. She forced herself to smile.

'Perhaps just a bowl of cool water, Captain Lichun, if it isn't too much trouble. And that drink you brought us yesterday. Terin seemed to find it some comfort.'

Lichun smiled and half bowed again. 'Of course. I had a bottle hung from the ship overnight, so that the sea might cool it for you. I will have it brought to your cabin.'

When the captain left her, Ephemeral ventured below decks. In such a small ship their quarters were very cramped indeed, but thanks to the unusual cargo they did not smell half as bad as other places they had stayed. She had covered the small porthole window over with a piece of sacking, so it was dark in the room, and she could just make out Terin's slim figure on their narrow bunk. He lay stripped down to his underclothes, and his body was covered in sweat. At the sound of her entering the cabin, he lifted his head wearily. 'Is that you, my love?'

She placed a hand on his shoulder, squeezed it, and took it away. 'How are you feeling?'

He smiled. 'Good. Bad. I edge closer to true visions all the time, even as I feel it pushing my body beyond what it can take.'

There was a rickety stool next to the bunk. Ephemeral sat

on it. The Narhl came from a cold land of endless snow and brief days – the sun that they saw was milky and pale, a shadow of this enemy that now pursued them. So closely tied were they with the Frozen Steps that to experience heat was actively harmful to them. Terin was a fire-seer, a Narhl who used warmth to induce visions, so he had slowly developed a higher tolerance for heat than was generally seen in his people. However, the endless warmth of these southern seas were taking their toll on him, as she had feared.

'You must rest,' she told him. 'Do not seek out the visions now, Terin. You do not have the strength.'

He shook his head, barely flattening the thin pillow he lay on. 'I must suffer it, Ephemeral. It is the place of a fire-seer. To seek further than anyone else. I . . .' His voice trailed off, and she heard him take a long breath. 'I believe I will see truths that have long been hidden.'

There was a soft knock at the door and the ship's boy stepped in. He was a pale lad with a shock of yellow hair on his head like dandelion fluff. His eyes were very wide as he brought over the bowl of water and a tall bottle of blue glass. He looked from Ephemeral to Terin and back again, as if unsure who he was more curious about.

'Thank you,' said Ephemeral, taking both items from him. He looked down at the claws on the ends of her fingers, and she saw him swallow hard. All at once she felt a desperate longing for the Frozen Steps, where the brood sisters were no longer a novelty. 'You can go.'

The boy left reluctantly, as though he wanted to watch them for a while longer. When he'd gone, Ephemeral dipped a cloth in the bowl of water, and was pleased to find that it was reasonably cold. She held it to Terin's forehead, who sighed with pleasure.

'I have to admit,' he said, 'I would give much for that bowl to be full of ice. Or to be able to put my feet into a freshly fallen mound of snow. To feel a cold wind.'

Ephemeral put the bowl down, and opened the bottle. A strong scent of alcohol rose from it. 'Would you like some of this?'

Terin nodded, and took the bottle from her. It was a drink the captain called turtle gin. It was very strong.

'Does it ease the pain?'

'It helps a little,' said Terin, before taking a few more gulps. He passed the bottle back. 'My body aches continually, but the liquor relaxes my muscles.'

'We will turn back,' said Ephemeral abruptly. 'We will head north quickly, until the temperature drops again, and you can rest properly. I will pay the captain all the coin we have left, and if she won't take us, I will force her.' Ephemeral glanced to where her sword stood, propped up in the corner of their tiny cabin. 'She is a wise woman, and will not oppose me. Not if the lives of her crew are at stake.'

'Ephemeral, no.' Terin took hold of her hand, and pushed himself up in the small bed. 'We both knew the dangers of this journey when we started. I will not turn back just because it has become uncomfortable.'

'But you could die,' said Ephemeral. She knew she shouldn't speak so bluntly, that a human wouldn't have said such harsh words to one they loved, but it was not in her just then to be subtle. 'This heat could kill you.'

'No one knows that better than me.' To her surprise, he grinned. 'I am a heat-seer, remember? I have danced that line every day of my adult life, ever since I saw the ghost-lights in the northern sky and they spoke to me. Listen to me, Ephemeral. This morning, a shard of the dawn sun fell on my skin—'

'But I covered the window!' cried Ephemeral, horrified. 'You should have been safe.'

'Listen,' said Terin again. 'A beam of sunlight fell on my arm and I focussed all of my being on that piece of warmth. It granted me a vision. It comes easier than ever now.'

'What did you see?' she asked, her voice hushed.

Terin's face became serious. 'Much that convinces me that we were right to leave to find your father when we did. I saw a wild place, full of boiling heat and life, full of so much that is alien to me. There is a place, in the centre, like a web.' Terin pursed his lips. 'I cannot quite find the right words. But I felt . . . creation,

Ephemeral. New life, boiling into existence. It was beautiful, and dangerous. I saw your father, and he was alone. He was without his sword. He was heading towards this place, heading towards the heart of both destruction and creation. A shadow came with him, a blue shadow.' Terin shook his head. 'Again, I am not sure of the right words, but I knew in the vision that he would be lost to us, if he kept going in that direction.'

Ephemeral took a slow, deep breath. 'Did you see anything else?'

'Wolves,' said Terin immediately. 'Wolves in the forest, wolves shaped like people, with blood on their lips. There is a she-wolf, the leader of their pack, and she is the hungriest. I could taste salt, in the vision, and there was a strange noise, like a keening child.' He shrugged. 'That is where it ended.'

They sat together in silence for a while. Ephemeral could hear the sea, and the call of birds. The smell of the dried orchids was overwhelming, and she was too aware of how warm it was, down here in the dark. What would her sisters be doing now? she wondered. Did they sense the trouble their father was in as keenly as she did? She thought of Crocus, the sister she felt the most kinship with; when she had left the Frozen Steps, Crocus had been learning to fly the wyverns, eager to take them to the furthest reaches of the Narhl territory for hunting expeditions. Ephemeral had suggested they visit Skaldshollow, where the people of that city were still struggling to rebuild their lives – it was important, she felt, to maintain the small bonds they had built after the defeat of Joah Demonsworn. King Aristees had been sceptical, and she did not know if her advice had been acted on. Perhaps she would never know.

'You are sure, then?' she asked him, knowing that she'd already asked this question a hundred times, and still needing to ask it. Humans changed their minds all the time, after all. 'You are sure we must keep going?'

'We must, Ephemeral.' Terin looked solemn now, his long hair framing his bony face. 'And not just for Sebastian, either. I fear that all who walk the surface of Ede may be in danger.'

17

'One of the patrols didn't make it back last night.'

Estenn lowered the eyeglass. They had been inching along the top of the cliffs, following the progress of the big ship far below. Some hours ago one of Euriale's unpredictable fogs had blown up, and she had been lost to view for some minutes. It had been impossible for Estenn to see what had happened to the ship during that time, but she was willing to bet it wasn't pleasant. The fogs of Euriale never were. Touching her fingers to the wolves at her throat, she turned to face the messenger.

'Who led them?'

'Barrett.' The young man licked his lips. It happened, every now and then, that her people would vanish. One or two, taken by the island. She considered it the price they paid to survive in such a place, but to have an entire patrol go missing was rare. 'Five people. Didn't come back.'

'Perhaps they are lost.' This also happened occasionally. The island was disorientating; it got under your skin and twisted your internal compass. One of her men had once complained that if you were out under the trees for long enough by yourself, it was like being very drunk. She stood up, stretching the muscles in her back. She'd been sitting in one place for too long, just like the big ship. 'Or perhaps they did not let Euriale into their hearts and minds. You know that I have told you that the only way to survive this place is to embrace it.' Estenn looked to

Gen. 'Any word from Two-Birds on what this ship is and who she carries?'

Gen nodded eagerly. 'The place is rife with gossip of it, Emissary. The ship is the *Poison Chalice*, captained by Devinia the Red.' Estenn would often send one or two of her men and women to wander the town, especially when it was busy. Information was always useful. 'They say that she has her daughter Wydrin with her, and the rest of the Black Feather Three.'

It was like suddenly being doused in cold water. Estenn caught her breath, and forced herself to keep her expression neutral, while her heart thundered in her chest. The magic they had seen suddenly made sense.

'That is interesting indeed. Tell me, Gen, what is it we know of the Black Feather Three?'

The young woman with auburn hair stood up a little straighter, proud to be called upon in this way by the Emissary. 'They are the mercenaries who banished the mighty Y'Ruen, taking her glory from this world. One of them is capable of the long-lost art of mage magic.'

Estenn nodded, her face breaking into a grin. She looked round at her followers, who looked back at her uncertainly. 'It explains what we have seen. The staff that produces flames and ice. It's an artefact from long ago, surely stolen from under the Citadel.' She straightened up and looked back down to where the ship sat, sails currently empty. 'It is the key the Spinner spoke of, and I will take it. And I will want to talk to this Wydrin of Crosshaven too, she who took our last god from us. I would like to talk to her very much.' She raised the eyeglass again and traced the waterway back. Some distance behind the great fat ship, and hidden from her by the twisting black cliffs, were three smaller ships – sleek raiders with sails and oars. They had been hunting the bigger ship for days, but now they were closing in. 'Their pursuers are so cautious, hiding in the wake of the larger ship, letting her attract the attentions of the island, but they won't dawdle for ever. Soon.' She smiled to herself. 'Soon we will have a distraction sent from the very gods themselves.'

*　　*　　*

111

'They definitely came this way.'

Sebastian paused to touch the thick fleshy leaves of the bush that hung over them like a bower. At head height a few of them were smeared with greasy white paint – like that worn by their attackers. Ahead of him, Oster nodded.

'I can smell them all over this part of the forest.'

They moved on, Sebastian jogging to catch up. They had been walking since dawn, and Oster showed no signs of tiredness. In daylight, Sebastian had been able to see that the cloak he wore was a deep, dark red, and the oddly military leather skirt that came down to his knees was studded with brightly shining steel. The coat of mail he wore over his brown woollen tunic was made of bright silver and looked brand new. His eyes were a pale tawny colour, striking against the deeper brown of his face. Sebastian found it difficult to look at the tattoo. The coils of the dragon shimmered against the man's muscled arm as though they might move at any moment.

'Have you seen men and women with painted faces in this place before?' he asked.

Oster turned to him, opened his mouth, and then shook his head. 'I have not, no. Although that isn't to say that they haven't been here for a very long time.'

'I thought you said you were born in this place?'

'Born . . .' Oster seemed dissatisfied by the word. 'I am from here, yes. And I know a great deal about it. I know the names of every god, demon, sprite and spirit honoured here. I know to whom every brick or stone was consecrated. I know that this is oldest place on Ede, and I know that the Spinner is not where he should be. But there are gaps. My own history . . . These newcomers are too recent.'

Sebastian tugged at his beard. He was rapidly coming to realise that asking Oster questions only seemed to result in more questions. He tried again with one he'd asked earlier.

'Why are you here alone? Surely you must know other people here? Or are you a recluse of some kind?'

Just ahead of him Oster reached up and pushed back a low-hanging tree branch and waited for Sebastian to pass under. 'I know I should not be here alone. There should have been others.

112

And the Spinner is not here. This is all wrong.' He scowled. 'I must find out what has happened.'

They passed out of the trees into a small glade. Powerful sunshine lit the small space with emerald light. There was grass here, coming up to the top of Sebastian's boot, and in the centre it was possible to see where it had been stamped down.

'Here, look.' He pushed past Oster and walked up the small incline. In the middle of the grass were the remains of a large fire – dark ash, pieces of charred wood. He poked at it with his boot. 'They made camp here.'

Oster appeared at his side. 'We grow closer, then. They must have come from somewhere.'

Sebastian bent down and plucked something from the ashes. It was a long bone, half as long as his own forearm. It had been severed at both ends, and there were gnaw marks along its length. Something about it felt wrong. He poked around in the rest of the ashes and drew forth a section of ribcage. He looked at it for a moment, before dropping it abruptly.

'These are human bones,' he said. He was remembering the battlefield at Relios, and the smoking remains of the Ynnsmouth knights. Ip, the seed of a demon waiting inside the child, had skipped from body to body, looking for any flesh that might still be edible. 'The people we hunt are cannibals?'

Oster picked the bones up himself, turning them over in long-fingered hands. After a moment, he sniffed at them.

'Yes, human flesh.' There was something in the way he said it that made Sebastian pause, but then Oster turned, looking back the way they'd come. 'Can you feel that?'

Sebastian opened his mouth to ask him what he was talking about, but then he did feel it. A powerful thrumming in his blood; the silver thread that connected him and the brood army and the other dragon-kin was suddenly singing. There was something in the trees. Something big.

'Who are you? What *is* this place?' He pressed a hand to his forehead, dizzy. He wondered, distantly, if Ephemeral could also feel this, up in the Frozen Steps. It felt that powerful. 'Please, Oster, you must tell me—'

The trees below them shook, and an enormous monster emerged. It was twice as big as a horse, its horned back brushing the lower branches. It was covered in thick leathery skin that was a deep olive-green, and sections of it – the broad curve of its back, the tops of its stubby legs – were covered in tough-looking yellow plates. The monster's head was like some sort of marriage between a lizard and a bird, its long snout ending in a lethal-looking hooked beak. When it opened its mouth to make a short, huffing snort, Sebastian could see rows of peg-like teeth.

'What is that?' he breathed. He could feel it in his blood, the cold intelligence of it. The monster had turned towards them, and snorted again, louder this time. There was no mistaking the challenge in the noise. It stomped its forelegs, and Sebastian felt the ground tremble under his feet.

'A child of Euriale,' breathed Oster. 'The cycle has begun again, and new life is being created.' He shook his head. 'This is all wrong. I should know this.'

The animal lifted its head and gave a short, trumpeting roar.

'We should move,' said Sebastian, not taking his eyes from the monster's giant form. 'Whatever it is, we've annoyed it.'

'Wait,' said Oster, and he stepped away. The tattoo on his right arm seemed to catch the sun, and then it was shining with its own internal light.

'Oster?'

The light bloomed, a golden flash that seared itself on the inside of Sebastian's eyelids. The shape inside the light that was Oster began to twist and change. Sebastian stumbled backwards, trying to make sense of what he was seeing. Where Oster had been was a long serpentine shape of gold and white. At first, he took it to be a wyvern – like the mounts of the Narhl, it was long and sinuous, but it had no wings and the legs were longer. The creature's head was more akin to that of Y'Ruen, festooned with twisting horns, long jaws lined with sharp teeth. Its eyes were amber, its scales cream, lined with gold. As he watched, it opened its long jaws and hissed at the monster at the bottom of the clearing. Its tongue was black.

114

'Oster? Is that you?'

To his alarm the dragon creature responded to his voice, whipping its long head around to glare at him with narrow eyes, before it crept across the clearing. Its ridged tail swept from one side to the other, and Sebastian could hear it brushing through the grass.

'That's why I can feel it in him,' he murmured. The pounding in his dragon blood was now impossible to ignore. 'The dragon blood is in him, too.'

On some level he knew that it would be wisest to melt back into the trees, but instead he stood and watched, transfixed, as the golden dragon reached its reptilian cousin and appeared to greet it, pressing its narrow snout to the neck of the other creature. The monster lifted its own head and snorted.

We mean no harm here, brother.

Men were here. They darken the trees.

We are not men such as them.

Sebastian gave a low cry. He could not hear them, but he knew what they were saying, all the same. It was similar to when he had fought with the brood sisters and had known their feelings, shared their pain. Their thoughts had been so close to him then, and now it was as though a barrier had been stripped away.

The big monster with its leathery skin huffed once more – Sebastian felt its awareness passing over him briefly – and then it turned back and disappeared into the trees. The bright dragon with cream and gold scales curled round on itself, the coil of its tail shifting like a snake, and then it was consumed with light again. When it died, Oster was standing there once more. He ran a hand distractedly through his hair, and caught Sebastian's eyes.

'What are you looking at?' he demanded.

18

It was late, and a light rain was falling. Frith, released from his duties for the night by Devinia, made his way below deck to the med bay. For the last two days Wydrin had stayed by the woman Grint's side, helping where she could and tending to the sick. They had passed through an unnaturally thick fog, and some of the crew had come out of it covered in huge, pus-filled boils. That in itself was unpleasant enough, but a number of those had subsequently come down with a fever, and so far, five had died from it. The old medic Augusta Grint had been wild with frustration, barking orders and demanding clean water. None of it had helped – Frith had watched as the bodies were sewn into spare pieces of canvas and tipped over the side, while Devinia spoke quiet words to a stunned crew. Now there was only a single patient left, and as he entered the narrow room he found Wydrin crouched by the bed. The air was thick, full of the mingled scents of dried blood and sharp vinegar.

'How is he?'

Wydrin looked up at his voice. Her eyes were bloodshot, and her hair lay lank across her forehead.

'He sickens, like they all did.' The still figure on the bunk was a boy of no more than sixteen, his skin looking yellow under the lamps. 'Augusta has no idea why this one has lingered so long while all the others were carried off so quickly. This little shrimp should have been the first to go.' She leaned over and placed a wet cloth against the boy's forehead, squeezing a little so rivulets of water ran down his forehead and cheeks. The boy didn't react. 'Ship's boy, only been with them for a year. His name is Antrew.'

Frith came closer, the staff still gripped in his hand. He wanted to go and get some hot food; the rain, though light, had soaked him to his skin. More than that he wanted to spend a few hours alone with Wydrin in their cabin; so much time alone on deck with his own thoughts was unsettling. His thoughts would turn to the Edenier trap and how it had opened like a black flower when it had received its blood sacrifice; to the many rooms inside Joah Demonsworn's Rivener – the great machine had contained a new nightmare in every cell. Time with Wydrin was all that seemed to ease his mind these days.

'Where is Augusta?'

'I sent her off for a nap,' said Wydrin. She put the cloth back into a basin by the bed. 'She was nodding off in her chair.' She paused to stifle a yawn.

'You look as though you could use a rest yourself.'

She looked down at the boy and rubbed her fingers across her eyes. 'I don't want to leave him, in case he wakes up. Or in case he . . .' Her words trailed off, and she scowled. 'Trust Devinia to bring him to this place. Antrew and all the others who've died today. None of them should be here. Pirates are used to dangers – rival ships, bad weather, lack of decent food and water – those are the risks of a life at sea. Not this. This place is unnatural. We shouldn't be here, but my mother won't see that. To her it's just another place for her to stomp into with her big boots on.'

'I believe Sebastian felt the same,' said Frith. He saw Wydrin wince. 'But it was always his choice to come.'

'Sebastian –' she looked up at him then, and he saw the stark worry in her eyes. 'What is he bloody playing at, Frith? He could be anywhere by now, he could be dead, and there's nothing we can do about it.'

Frith opened his mouth to reply when from above came the thunder of boots on deck, and a chorus of shouts.

Frith turned to the stair. 'What now?'

'Oh something else going horribly wrong, I expect,' said Wydrin, and she stood up, pulling Glassheart from its scabbard.

Devinia the Red had been standing at the helm, resting her hands on the wheel. They weren't moving, but it gave her comfort to feel the smooth wood under her fingers. To either side the black cliffs of Euriale towered over them, and the night sky was thick with cloud, obscuring the moon and stars and giving them a night as dark as any she'd seen. Lamps had been lit all over – more, even, than Devinia thought was necessary, but the crew were uncomfortable here and she supposed she could understand that. Even so, it made her uneasy. The island slept around them like a giant, restless beast, and here they sat in the centre of it, lit up like a whore's bedroom. To be so visible went against every instinct she had.

'Evening, Captain.'

Kellan came up the stairwell, looking behind Devinia at the dark that followed them, before joining her at the wheel. The fine rain had stopped, but his hair and beard were dusted with shining droplets.

'Kellan. How goes it?'

He looked away from her again, as though he expected some great monster to loom up out of the dark. For all she knew, it could.

'Only Antrew left, Captain. He lingers, and Augusta can't say for sure which way it will go.'

Devinia nodded slowly. She could smell smoke on the air now, very faint. 'And the rest?'

Kellan shrugged. He was always reluctant to deliver bad news. 'The crew are with you, as ever. But they're nervous. They're playing cards and dice, and drinking their rum, and they're swapping stories. You know the sort. A friend of a friend who wandered away from Two-Birds, and they found him the next day missing all his skin. That sort of thing.'

'All pirates tell those stories. And how much more delicious they must be, with this view?' She gestured to the cliffs surrounding them. 'Keep an eye on it, Kellan. We've only just started to make our way into the interior of the island, and I don't need them losing their nerve before—'

It was the tiniest noise that gave it away, but Devinia had been at sea for many years, and she knew the sounds of a ship better than her own daughter's voice. It was the soft *clonk* of a wooden oar against the edge of a boat, so soft and careful she almost didn't hear it. And it didn't come from her ship. It came from behind them.

Instantly Devinia extinguished the lamp next to her and turned around to peer into the dark. Kellan opened his mouth and she silenced him with a gesture.

The waterway behind them was a shifting mass of black; ink below them, velvet above. She could see nothing, but there was that scent again; the smoke of a torch recently extinguished. That and the sound of an oar. The *Poison Chalice* had no oars.

Without taking her eyes from that view, Devinia knelt and retrieved a specially made flare from a wooden alcove in the helm. She had bought them on their last trip to Onwai; a cunning mixture of powders and explosives that produced a powerful light. With her forefinger she tugged the loop of fabric that acted as a trigger and threw the whole thing, overarm, across the rear-most guardrail. Halfway through that slow arc the flare surged into life, lighting the space beyond the *Poison Chalice* with brilliant blue light like a falling star.

Crawling along behind them in utter darkness were three sleek raiding ships, each of them filled with men and women bristling with weapons. They had been sneaking up on them, so slowly, so carefully, following the beacon that was the *Poison Chalice*. Before the flare hit the water and fizzed out Devinia saw a woman stand up in the prow of the nearest ship; she wore a dusty greatcoat, and her face was slashed with a streak of red greasepaint.

Devinia turned, already bellowing, already drawing her weapons. The bastards had been sneaking up from behind them, hiding from danger in the wake of the larger ship.

'Attack!' she cried. 'We are under attack!'

Kellan was down on the quarter deck already, barking instructions to the crew. Devinia spun back to look at her enemy and immediately had to duck as an arrow zipped past her right shoulder. She snarled – arrows were a coward's weapon.

'Come up here, Ristanov, and show me your steel! You will have to board me to take this prize!'

There came an answering crow of laughter. 'Perhaps I will stay down here and poke you full of holes. Even the fattest sow will bleed to death eventually!' The woman's crew roared at her response and clashed sword against sword.

Devinia backed away. It was all very well exchanging pleasantries, but she had several immediate problems. First, the ship was stuck with her rear in the face of the enemy ships, and her cannon were all facing to either side rather than directly behind. Second, they could not race away; even with Lord Frith powering their sails with his magic, they were like a rat caught in a maze.

'Get ready to fight,' she called to her crew. 'I want to cut that smile from the Banshee's face myself!'

Wydrin and Frith appeared on the deck, their faces twin moons of surprise.

'You! Mage boy! Use that fire of yours to keep them back! Wydrin, oil down the sides of the ship – I want those bastards slipping right off.'

The *Poison Chalice* was a well-ordered ship, but the crew were already rattled, thanks to the tentacled monster and the burning fog, and for a few moments everything was chaos. Devinia caught sight of Lord Frith dashing towards the rear of the ship as she made her way down, sending bright fire balls behind them, but the lookouts in the rigging were already shouting that the ships were coming alongside, two to port, one to starboard. There were shouts, voices raised in anger that she didn't recognise, and despite their best efforts, there were men and women climbing over their sides. In seconds, fights were breaking out all across the ship.

A man with scars across his bald head lurched out in front of her. Devinia met his sword with her own cutlass, pushing him back easily before dealing a blow to his shining scalp that would leave more than a scar. She stepped over his body, bellowing more orders. There were so many strangers here now, so many of the Banshee's men, and where was the bitch herself?

'Kellan? Where is Kellan?' She couldn't see the first mate anywhere. A young sailor known as Freckled Freya stumbled past her, so she grabbed her shoulder. 'Turn the mainsail to starboard, now. Stop gawping at me and obey your captain!' The girl ran as though her trousers were on fire, while Devinia turned to bellow at Frith. The young Lord had taken to sending cones of ice over the guardrail.

'Lord Frith! Get over here and earn your place in my daughter's knickers!' She saw him turn, a mingled look of confusion and outrage on his face. He paused to crack the end of his staff into the face of an invading pirate, before running over to her.

'Madam, I really must—'

'Can you fill the sail from this side? With as much force as you can muster?'

'I can, but that would—'

'Just do it.'

For a moment she saw a dark look in his eye, but he held his staff aloft and the sail filled as she willed it. There was a groaning all over the ship and the *Poison Chalice* suddenly lurched to one side, so abruptly that the black cliffs to the right of them loomed alarmingly close. In seconds, they could be dashed to pieces, but instead she heard a chorus of screams as the longboats that were alongside them were crushed between them and the cliffs.

Devinia had been in battles before – many, in fact – and was familiar with the way that the fear and anger could stretch and distort the perception of time. She also knew that panic could turn the tide of a battle, that a single act could change everything. But never before had she witnessed so many things going wrong so quickly.

Lord Frith released his grip on the spell and the *Poison Chalice* righted herself violently, pushing a wave against the opposite cliff that came back and showered them with spray. Out of nowhere Kellan finally appeared, straining against the rocking deck with a look of black thunder on his face. Devinia opened her mouth to shout a command to him, then found her words snatched away as her first mate walked up to Lord Frith and punched him solidly on the temple. Her daughter's lover crashed to the deck as though his bones were made of jelly, and the mage's staff fell from his fingers, rolling with the motion of the ship.

In an instant Wydrin was there, standing over his body, the staff snatched up and held securely. Devinia could see her daughter shouting at Kellan, could see him shouting back, but could not make out the words. She ran, meaning to come between them before her daughter could do real damage – perhaps Kellan had thought Frith meant to destroy the ship, not realising the order had come from her.

'Stop it, the pair of you!' Around them, the fighting was fierce. 'We haven't got time—'

Kellan spun and pushed his knife smartly into her stomach. She took a sharp breath, her fingers automatically trying to grip the handle, but Kellan had already pulled it out. Blood filled her silk shirt, obscenely hot.

'Nothing's ever straightforward, is it?' said Kellan in a pained tone of voice. Devinia stumbled backwards just in time to see Wydrin screaming, bringing the staff around in a wide arc to connect with Kellan's stomach – *too slow, silly child*, thought Devinia faintly, *a dagger would be faster* – but he stepped away so that the blow only caught at his hip.

'What are you doing?' Devinia pressed a hand to the hole in her gut. It felt deep. 'What have you done?'

'What have *we* done, you mean?'

Devinia turned. The Banshee stood behind her, grinning widely. The slash of greasepaint across her mouth was like a wound. Dimly Devinia was aware of Wydrin fighting, Wydrin calling her name, and Kellan holding her back. She gritted her teeth, forcing herself to concentrate.

'Get off my ship, you grinning lunatic.' With one hand she brandished her cutlass. 'Or I'll use your guts for rigging.'

The Banshee grinned all the wider.

'Full of bullshit to the end, yes. I will kill most of your crew I think. For the foolish mistake of sailing with you. And then I will kill you slowly, for the foolish mistake of thinking you could best me. That, and sleeping with your first mate.'

Devinia looked to Kellan, but he was fully occupied keeping

Wydrin away from him – her daughter still held the staff in one hand, using it defensively, while her short sword stabbed and whirled like a stinging insect. For the briefest, shining moment Devinia felt a queasy mixture of pride and fear. *I should not have brought her here.*

'Shut your hole.' Devinia turned back and leapt forward, meeting the woman sword for sword. There was no time for fear or pain here, there was only the fight: only survival, and who wanted it more.

She was quick, leaving no time for the Banshee to think. It was her only chance, to put a burst of strength behind her sword arm and drive the woman back, hoping for a lucky strike. The Banshee opened her mouth and screamed, her pathetic gimmick meant to scare pirates witless. In response, Devinia spat in her face.

'Couldn't face me on the Torrent, could you?' she called, hoping her voice sounded stronger than she felt. 'Had to sneak up behind me on your belly like a snake.'

'Old woman, you talk too much.'

The Banshee struck forwards and then up sharply, pushing Devinia's cutlass to one side. It was the sort of move Devinia could normally deflect through sheer strength, but the wound in her stomach was rapidly pumping out her last reserves of that into her sodden clothes. She gritted her teeth, bringing the sword up again as quickly as she could, but it was too late. The Banshee snapped forward, striking Devinia on the temple with the pommel of her sword. Abruptly the deck seemed to suck at Davinia's knees and, before she was truly aware what had happened, she had sprawled on the boards, and the Banshee had one booted foot pressing down on her wrist. She felt her cutlass drop from her numb fingers.

'There you are, old woman. Yes. On the deck where you belong. Perhaps I will make you scrub it before I flay you, yes.'

Devinia screwed her eyes shut and then opened them, trying to see properly. The Banshee's face was a dark shadow hanging above her, but beyond her head she could see the clouded sky. And something was moving in it.

'What's that?'

There must have been genuine curiosity in her voice because the Banshee turned away from taunting her and looked. Devinia could tell from the way that she straightened up that she'd seen it, too. Three shapes floated down towards them, looking like great birds with rigid wings, except that as they got closer, Devinia could see that the wings had intricate wooden frames, with a material not unlike canvas stretched across them. Underneath these strange contraptions were three people – two women and a man – and they floated down in a tight spiral, obviously looking to land on the deck.

'What bastard nonsense is this now?' murmured Devinia.

The Banshee had left her and was stalking back towards her own crew.

'Eyes to the skies!' she called. 'I want them caught and held too!'

But the newcomers were fast. Devinia watched them land, almost at exactly the same time. Immediately they threw off their makeshift wings and brandished long curved swords that looked wickedly sharp. Two of their number made short work of the men and women who were close by, while the other – a short woman with pale skin, black hair and a tattoo that covered all the skin below her chin – seemed to look around casually, as if searching for something. There was a shifting of the light – Devinia blinked rapidly, convinced her vision was fading – and the black-haired woman faded from view.

Grunting with the effort, Devinia forced herself to sit up. There was a cold feeling in her guts that had nothing to do with the stab wound.

'Wydrin!' she cried, 'get out of here! Now!'

She caught sight of her daughter, still fighting, blood thick on her sword, and then she pitched forward, as though an invisible force struck her from behind. Wydrin stumbled, leaning on the staff for support, and then the other two strangers descended on her. Devinia saw the ropes then, saw the sack go over her daughter's head. She surged to her feet, ignoring the way the world tipped around her like it was rolling off its axis.

'WYDRIN!'

It was too late. The woman with the black hair had reappeared, and in the midst of the chaos and the blood, they dragged Wydrin to the guardrail with the sack now pulled smartly down to her torso. Together they lifted her up, and dropped below out of sight.

19

Wydrin had been aware of sudden movement behind her, a shadow that shouldn't have been there, and then the world went dark. Her nostrils filled with the smell of old sacking, and she could feel rough hessian weave against her face. Instinctively, she brought her arms up, slashing wildly with her sword and trying to keep her attackers at arm's reach, but someone delivered a hard blow to the top of the arm holding the staff and she felt it go numb. The staff was snatched away from her and she crumpled over as someone punched her solidly in the stomach.

'Get her over the side,' said a low voice just near her ear. 'Fast and quiet, give them no time to think. And handle that thing carefully.'

Another blow, this one to the side of her head, and Glassheart was ripped from her fingers. Wydrin growled and tried to throw herself out of range, but her head was ringing and strong arms were forcing her back towards the guardrail. There was a moment of alarming disorientation as she was shoved against the rail and then over it, before being lowered somehow into empty space. She kicked wildly, cursing and even biting at the sack but before she could get a clear idea of where she was she hit solid wood again. The sound of water was much closer here.

'Frith!' The last time she'd seen him, he'd been unconscious on the deck, and her mother had been bleeding from a wound in her stomach. Nevertheless, she called for them: 'Frith! Devinia!'

Someone struck her again, and for a time she was lost to the dark. When she came back to herself her head was between her knees, and it took a few moments to remember what had happened. There was the rippling sound of oars through water, and she could no longer hear the chaos of the ship. Taking a slow breath, she held herself very still.

'I know you are awake now.' The voice was low and female. 'Do not try to pretend otherwise. It would also be a mistake to try and escape. While you were unconscious we tied you more securely, and a dip in the waterways now would be a quick way to drown.'

'Who –' Wydrin paused and cleared her throat. Her head was pounding. 'Who are you? You're not the Banshee, and I don't think you're her crew.'

'I am Estenn the Emissary.'

Wydrin shifted slightly. Her arms had been bound; firmly, but not tight enough to be painful. 'I have to tell you, Estenn, that's an impressive title, but I have no bloody idea who you are. Why have you taken me? Where are we going?'

'I have taken you for the glory of the gods.'

Wydrin barked laughter at that. 'You took me to please your gods? They are going to be very disappointed. From what I remember, godly sacrifices tend to be virgins who wear a lot of white. Well, I don't want to dash your dreams, but—'

'You will not talk idly of the gods,' said the woman mildly. 'Not in front of me.'

'Oh, we are going to get on like a house on fire.' Wydrin tensed her shoulders, trying to ease the ache in her head. 'Can you take this bag off? It's not helping my headache any.'

There was a pause, and the sack was pulled up. It was still night, and the small boat they travelled in had a single oil lamp at its prow. There were two people at the oars and two others at the prow, all with hoods up, while facing her on the bench opposite was a woman with a heart-shaped face, ghostly in the lamplight. She wore a mixture of furs and leathers, and bracelets bristling with small charms circled her arms. There was a tattoo at her throat, a sprawling, intricate thing that covered her skin like a blanket of shadows, and she sat slightly forward, her hands held loosely together. Wydrin sensed a great potential for movement from the woman; this was someone constantly alert and ready to act. It was a skill she valued in herself, and once again she cursed her own stupidity at being taken so easily. *I will never hear the last of this from Mum.* If Devinia was still alive, of course. She took a breath, forcing herself to remain calm.

'Why did you attack Devinia the Red? She is not an enemy you make casually. I wouldn't kidnap her daughter either, to be honest.' Wydrin shifted on the bench. To either side were the cliffs, dark and silent. There was no sign of anyone else. 'I don't often say this, because she already has the ego of a pirate, but she is a bit of a nightmare when crossed.'

The woman who had named herself Estenn smiled slightly, a slow curling of one corner of her mouth. 'I have heard the talk of Devinia the Red in Two-Birds, and I have also heard of her daughter, Wydrin the Copper Cat of Crosshaven. Not a pirate, but a sell-sword.' She tipped her head slightly to one side. 'Well, I did not attack your mother, Wydrin of Crosshaven. Though when we left her, she looked fairly beaten to me.'

Wydrin sat back, keeping her face carefully neutral. These people were not with the Banshee, but Ristanov had certainly been there. And Kellan, the worthless backstabbing scum. What was happening back on the *Poison Chalice*? It seemed likely that the crew had been overwhelmed, and would now be at the mercy of the mayor of Two-Birds.

'I will ask you again,' she said. 'Why have you taken me? And where are we going?'

'I am taking you to a godly place,' said the woman. 'And I feel we have spoken enough for now.'

They rowed on for another hour, until the inky night sky had turned a bruised indigo, still heavy with cloud. At some signal Wydrin didn't spot, the boat coasted over to the right-hand side, coming up close to a long length of black sand at the edge of the cliff. She was shoved from the boat with little ceremony, and as they stood together in the dark a long rope ladder rolled down from the very top of the cliff.

'I am cutting your bonds now,' said Estenn. 'You will notice that you are unarmed, while we are carrying a variety of sharp objects. You will climb the rope ladder and meet my soldiers at the top, and you will not try to escape. I'd rather not spill your blood after all this effort, but I am not averse to the idea.'

Wydrin glowered at her, rubbing some feeling back into her numb arms. Everything was aching – her head, her arm, her stomach – and the last thing she wanted to do was climb a rope ladder up a towering cliff in the dark, but as she stood there one of the hooded figures pulled a dagger from within her jacket, letting the scant light run along the blade. She sighed.

'Whatever you say. But I've heard that this island is very unlucky. Cursed, even.'

'Not for the children of Euriale, it isn't.' Estenn gestured with her sword. 'Go. There will be people waiting for you at the top.'

Wydrin turned and pulled herself up onto the ladder. Immediately, her bruised arm shouted with pain and her head swam, but she gritted her teeth and forced herself to move. Hand over hand, as quick as anyone raised on ships, she made her way up the ladder. As she did, she looked back the way they'd come, half hoping to see the *Poison Chalice* come lurching round the corner, but there was nothing. At the top she reached up and strong hands took hold of her forearm and tugged her up and over. There were more hooded figures; two with bows, and three with swords. The one who had lifted her up was a woman with braided auburn hair; she had painted one side of her face black, the other white. They all had.

Wydrin opened her mouth to comment on this, when Estenn climbed up behind her. The eyes of the hooded people all moved to her, and Wydrin caught their joint expressions of affection and awe. There was no doubt that she was their leader, and a beloved one at that. The other three followed up, the last one with Frith's staff tied carefully to his back. Once they were all safely up, Estenn gestured to him and he took the staff from his back and handed it to her. She took it greedily, and turned it over in her hands, running her fingers over the carvings there.

'Light,' she snapped. 'Bring me more light.'

Two more oil lamps were summoned, and they stood by the side of the cliff in a soft pool of warm yellow light. Wydrin looked beyond them, into the blackness of the trees. Here she was, then, in the wilds of Euriale, and she wasn't dead yet, although she found she wasn't sure how long that state of affairs would last. It smelled wild here, it smelled dangerous. This was not a place that wanted human company.

When she turned back, the woman who had named herself Estenn the Emissary was holding the staff in both hands, judging its weight.

'It is beautiful,' she murmured. 'A true relic of the golden age. When this artefact was crafted, all the gods were alive and Ede was as it should be. This item has seen the glory of the world. I swear I can feel it.'

Wydrin snorted. 'It is a particularly lovely stick, I'll give you that.'

'And I will use it to restore the glory of the gods,' continued Estenn, ignoring her. 'This will be my key, the path to the old magic.'

'That is what this was all about?' Wydrin felt her mouth split into a grin. She shook her head, and then laughed with delight. 'You wanted the staff all along?' She paused as another delicious thought struck her. 'And you took me to what? Give you information on it?' Wydrin threw back her head and laughed some more. 'I don't know anything about magic. You gods-addled idiots!'

Estenn moved so quickly that for a moment Wydrin could have sworn that she vanished from view. There was a deafening crack and Wydrin fell to her knees, a slow white star exploding in front of her eyes. She forced herself to look up, to get her bearings. Estenn the Emissary stood over her, with the staff in her hands. There was a smudge of blood on the end of it.

'When I have restored them I will feed you to the Twins,' she said. Her face was eerily calm again. 'Slowly. But first, we will talk.'

20

The pirates were still arguing.

Frith watched them from his place on the deck. His hands were bound behind his back with rope, and the clouds above were keeping the night dark even as they crawled towards dawn. The surviving crew had been locked up below decks save for Devinia, Augusta and himself – as they were their most important prisoners, the Banshee and Kellan apparently wanted them kept close.

He lifted his eyes to the pirates. Kellan was pacing by the mainsail, his hands curled into fists at his sides, while the Banshee stood with her arms crossed over her chest, an expression of bemusement on her face.

'The ship is intact, yes?' she said. In the fighting, the red paint across her mouth had been smudged into a pink smear. 'I do not know what your problem is.'

'Intact! She's intact, all right, and stranded. We were using the staff to propel the ship. What do you propose we do now?'

The Banshee shrugged a shoulder. 'We leave the *Chalice* here, under guard. We travel the rest of the way in our own ships. We are faster than this bloated hulk.'

Kellan was shaking his head again. He had done a lot of that over the last hour. 'Travel into the centre of Euriale on ships that sit that close to the water? You are insane.'

'You are a coward,' the Banshee snorted. 'I have come this far in them. It is quite simple. We take our ships into the centre of this island, take what is hidden there, and come back. Once we have stripped this hulk and removed the ballast we can bring other ships, and tow her back. We have the map now, yes.' She patted the leather of her long coat. 'The dangers of this place are mostly stories told by easily scared pirates. Like you.'

To Frith's left he felt Devinia shift. She was weak, and had lost a lot of blood, but it seemed she still had the energy to be angry.

'You won't last until midday!' she called. 'It's one thing to hide in the wake of a larger ship, letting us catch the eye of anything that might be waiting. Quite another to take your bilge-heaps into the island alone. I ask only that you take me with you, so I can watch as you get torn to pieces by the monsters that wait for you.'

The Banshee looked over, a grin splitting her red mouth. 'Oh yes, you must come with us, Devinia the old. I will need something to feed the monsters.'

Kellan glanced over at them. 'You forget,' he said to the Banshee, 'that gold was only part of my payment.'

The Banshee frowned again. 'There is little I can do about that. What is no longer here, I cannot give you.'

Frith felt a bony elbow poke him in the ribs. He turned to see Augusta peering up at him, her lips folded into a thin line.

'That pair of idiots will argue until the island opens up and eats them both,' she said. 'Here, can you reach my belt?'

He looked down. The old woman's medical kit with its collection of knives had been removed from her, but she still wore the sturdy leather belt. It was, he noticed, branded with images of leaping hares, of all things.

'Yes? What of it?'

'On your side, there is an item wrapped in black felt, tucked into the band. They missed it, the useless bastards. Can you see it?'

He could. Frith glanced back over to Kellan and the Mayor of Two-Birds to make sure that they still had their attention elsewhere, and then shifted around so his back was pressed to

Augusta's side. With his fingers he felt along the belt until he found the item and pulled it free.

'Good lad,' said Augusta, her voice still low. 'Unwrap it, but carefully. You don't want to cut your bloody fingers off.'

Slowly, Frith peeled away the wrapping. He felt what must have been a bone handle and a short length of sharpened steel. Holding it gingerly, wary of injuring himself, Frith turned it over in his fingers, until the sharp edge of the blade was pressing against the rope that bound his hands. He pushed back and forth, and felt fibres give away under the pressure.

'That's it, you've got it,' murmured Augusta. 'Cut yourself free lad, and we can get us all out. Devinia will rush that bastard, and we'll take the ship back.'

Frith said nothing, concentrating on cutting the rope. Wydrin had been taken by persons unknown, snatched and carried off over the side in the middle of the chaos, along with his staff. No one knew who these kidnappers were, and, thinking about it, he felt a rising tide of cold panic in his gut. Wydrin, taken from him, when he was more powerless than he had been in years – no Edenier, no staff, no griffin to take them to safety. All at once it was too easy to remember the desperation that had led him beneath the Citadel. It was unacceptable, to be powerless like this, when the life of the woman he loved was in danger.

The ropes were loose. He flexed his wrists, pulling his arms gradually free. They were stiff from being in one position for so long, but that didn't matter. They'd get plenty of exercise soon enough.

'Are you done?' asked Augusta. She sniffed. 'We'll take the ship back, lad. Pass the blade to Devinia, and we'll take the *Chalice* back – alone, if we have to.'

'A pirate with half her blood missing and an old woman, against all these pirates? While Wydrin is in danger?' Frith sat up, giving his legs a few brief seconds to get their blood flow back. 'I have one chance, and I must take it. My apologies, but I care nothing for your ship.'

He stood up and turned towards the guardrail. There was a squawk of outrage from Augusta and a shout from Kellan, but he was already running. One of Banshee's men appeared from the left, arms outstretched to grab him. Frith ripped the knife across his stomach, feeling it catch and tear there before his momentum carried him past. The blade caught in the other man's flesh and he left it, and then he was vaulting over the rail. His stomach turned over as he fell down into the dark, and then he hit the water. It was like a solid wall of ice, knocking the air from his lungs and crushing his limbs. He forced himself to open his eyes into a world of shifting darkness. He could see nothing, and then a trail of bubbles zipped past him: an arrow. They were firing arrows at him.

Gritting his teeth against the urge to drag air into his already burning lungs, Frith kicked out frantically and began to swim. It was difficult, in the dark and freezing wet, to tell if he was even going in the right direction, but he kept under the water for as long as he could, until the burning in his lungs became too much. He surfaced briefly, snorting water out of his nose, to find that he was some feet away from the *Poison Chalice* – he had managed to jump further than he'd realised, but not quite far enough. He could see figures on the ship, outlined against the light from the lamps, and they were notching arrows. Quickly he turned away, kicking frantically with limbs that already felt too heavy to move.

'Stop firing!' That was Kellan's voice, clear and echoing against the cliff face. 'He's the one that knows how to use the staff.'

The Banshee shouted in response, apparently unconcerned about the potential importance of the missing staff and after a few seconds a fresh barrage of arrows pattered the water around him. Frith took a deep breath and forced himself to submerge again, trying not to think about what it would feel like to take an arrow in the back.

When he came back up for air, the ship was further away, and ahead of him the waterway took one of its sudden turns. Beyond that he would be out of sight of the *Poison Chalice*, which was a bit of luck, but he could also see a skiff, probably the same one he and Wydrin had used earlier, peeling away from the side of larger ship. They were coming for him after all, then. It was time for him to get out of the water, if he could.

Putting the last of his strength into it, Frith swam for the turn, hoping that he would make it before the ship caught up with him. Eventually, the cliffs cut off his view, and once out of sight he could see that to one side there was a ragged section of rocks at the bottom of the cliff. With no other option, he swam for it, dragging himself out of the water with some difficulty. There were small stunted trees on the rocky outcrop, and so he made for these, hiding himself behind them as best he could.

After a few moments the skiff came into view. Frith pressed himself to the ground, ignoring the rocks digging into his ribs and barely daring to breathe. The boat slowed, obviously looking for him, but beyond the lamps of the *Poison Chalice* it was still dark, and the light they carried would only make it more difficult to see him. After a few moments a terrible screeching call echoed between the cliffs, coming from further down the waterway – one of the strange creatures that called Euriale home was making itself known in the night. Frith watched as the men in the boat exchanged hurried words – he could almost see the exact moment they decided to give up – and then they turned around, heading back around the bluff of the cliff. They were lost to sight quickly.

Frith remained where he was for a time, just in case they changed their minds. His clothes were soaking and heavy, and his head was still thumping where Kellan had cold-cocked him. He had escaped the ship, but he had no map of the island, no weapons, and no idea where Wydrin was or who had taken her. At least now he could move, he told himself. At least now he could take action, instead of waiting on the deck of a ship with strangers. He felt a brief pang of guilt at leaving Devinia and Augusta behind, but they had known the risks. If he died on this island, at least he could die knowing that he had been looking for Wydrin. She would have come for him, if he were lost. He knew that with an unshakeable certainty.

Standing up, he squeezed some of the water from his shirt. The clouds of earlier were starting to draw away, letting through some of the watery dawn light, and as his eyes adjusted, he saw that the cliff face was pitted here and there with the stubby trees; they clung on to the rock in clusters. He thought that with a bit of luck he would be able to make his way up.

'Wherever you are, I am coming for you, Wydrin. I swear it.'

Devinia watched as the men came back on board, conspicuously lacking Lord Frith or his body. Kellan was on them immediately, his brow furrowed in an expression she'd never seen on him before.

'Where is he?' snapped Kellan. 'Don't tell me he out-swam you?'

One of the men shrugged sullenly. 'Something got him, didn't it? This place, it's full of monsters. Bloody thing came up out of the water, took a big bite, and carried him down. We'll not be seeing him again.'

Devinia frowned. All that power and knowledge, lost with one man.

'That's right,' said another sailor, nodding rapidly. 'It was a big thing, whatever it was. We didn't stick around to be eaten too.'

The Banshee chuckled. 'I think he has learned his lesson not to go swimming in Euriale.'

Kellan rounded on her, still scowling. 'This is no joke. That man was our only chance of ever using the staff.'

Ristanov shrugged. 'The staff is also gone, so what does it matter? We follow the rest of the plan as agreed.' She cleared her throat and spoke louder, so that her crew could hear her. 'Red Watch, you will be staying on the *Poison Chalice* for now. Black and Yellow, you are with me. Store what you need here, and make ready to leave at dawn. Kellan, get Devinia the elderly and her crone there ready to move.' The Banshee grinned suddenly, splitting her red face. 'I really do wish to feed them to monsters.'

'Stupid wee bastard,' muttered Augusta next to her. 'If he'd bloody listened instead of running off, we'd be fine. Now he's fish food, we're stuck with that Bararian bitch, and you can imagine how much Wydrin will sulk when she finds out about this.'

'Be quiet,' snapped Devinia. 'I'm listening.'

'Oh that's right, you don't take any bleedin' notice either,' carried on Augusta in the same tone. 'Don't know why I bother speaking at all, the Graces know you're all so wise, that must be why we're sitting prisoners on our own bastard ship.'

Kellan came over to them. His face was a series of harsh lines, with not a trace of the easy humour she had come to expect from him. It was the face of a completely different man, and she wondered how she could have failed to spot it.

'You're coming with us,' he said shortly. 'Be ready to move.'

'Did she pay you well, you little whore?' asked Devinia sweetly. 'You know what happens to pirates like you? Seagulls won't eat what will be left of you, in the end.'

'Generally, pirates like me get rich,' said Kellan, with a touch of his old humour, but then he knelt in front of her and his face was stiff with fury again. 'I have yet to receive my payment, actually, but I will claim it in full eventually. Your daughter, Wydrin Threefellows of Crosshaven, the so-called Copper Cat, was to have been my payment, to do with as I would.'

Devinia stiffened, and she heard Augusta tut at her.

'Don't move so much,' muttered the old woman. 'You're already bleeding like a festival pig.'

'Oh yes,' Kellan grinned to see the anger on Devinia's face, 'I was going to cut her up nice and slow. Make you watch, maybe. And when I find her again, *and I will*, I will do it.'

'Why?' asked Devinia, her voice hollow.

In reply, Kellan pulled at a strap on the vanbrace on his left arm, yanking it loose and then peeling them back. It occurred to Devinia – too late, her mind whispered, it comes to you too late – that she had never seen him without them, even when they had bunked together. Under the vanbrace the skin on his arm was a deep angry red and the flesh was twisted and melted. It had been a considerable burn.

'I was there,' he said, his voice low and deadly. 'On Sandshield, with my brother, when your daughter and her friends fired the hall of Morgul the Biter. I got this', he brandished the arm at her again, 'trying to pull my brother out of that nightmare. Very painful, but not fatal. I got my brother to a boat and took him away from that place. He was a blackened ruin. He moaned at

137

me to kill him, to put him out of his misery, but I wouldn't, because I believed I could get him to a healer in time. He died just as we were pulling into port at Crosshaven.' He sat back on his haunches; all expression had left his face. 'The smell still haunts me. Sickly and sweet, like a roasting pig.'

Devinia shifted, pressing her hand to the wound in her gut. 'Why not just seek her out and kill her?' she asked. 'Why work your way aboard my ship?'

'Oh, she's been away, and well protected, since. I wanted to hurt her and all who love her, in as many ways as possible.' He smiled warmly, and it was so like his old face that Devinia felt disorientated. 'I thought that ruining her mother's life would be a good start, before cutting her to pieces.'

'She's gone.' Devinia forced herself to grin back at him. 'Only the Graces know where to. You won't find her.'

Kellan stood up. His face was blank again, as though they were discussing the weather. 'Don't you worry, Devinia. I will have my prize.'

21

Wydrin's captors were relentless. They marched her on through the jungle for that entire day, pausing only to let her take small sips from a water skin they carried with them. When the sun began to set, filling the spaces between the trees with a bloody, ruby light, they came to a low building half lost in the trees. Here, Estenn gave orders to make camp. A few of her soldiers – as Wydrin was coming to think of them – moved off into the trees to keep watch, while the others built a small fire in the centre of the ruins. The building itself was made up of interlocking circular rooms, although there was little left now save for low walls of crumbling yellow brick. The floors looked like they had once been covered with fine mosaics; now they were broken and lost in creeping weeds. Wydrin was made to sit by the fire and, after a time, Estenn came and sat opposite her.

'You could have picked a place with a roof,' said Wydrin. She stretched her legs out, groaning slightly. Walking all day with no rest over rough terrain had not been kind to her feet. 'It'll piss down later, and then we'll be in for an uncomfortable night.'

Estenn gazed back at her across the fire. The woman's eyes were black, her lips a startling red against the pallid tone of her skin.

'No, it won't rain tonight,' she said eventually. Wydrin had the strangest feeling she'd been listening to some internal voice. 'The early morning, perhaps.'

'Who are you?' asked Wydrin. 'I mean, really, who are you? Who would live on a cursed island? And what sort of people follow you? Aside from the fact that you've kidnapped me from my mother's ship and hit me with that bloody staff, I am actually curious to know.' She smiled slightly. 'Curiosity was always my greatest weakness.'

Estenn touched her hand to her throat, stroking the inked skin gently. Wydrin could see dark dirt under her fingernails.

'I am a woman with many names, and many pasts,' she said eventually. 'Maybe you, the Copper Cat of Crosshaven, can understand that more than most.'

Wydrin raised her eyebrows slightly. 'So you know who I am?'

'We keep one ear to Two-Birds at all times,' said Estenn, 'and you have been the source of considerable gossip over the years.' She sat back slightly, her legs crossed underneath her. 'You were meant to come here, I think, with the staff. Perhaps it would be good for you to know why I do what I must do. It is a story all the world must know, eventually. Ede must learn from its mistakes.'

'How long is this going to take?' asked Wydrin. 'I like to have a drink when I'm listening to longwinded stories, if you've got anything to hand.'

Estenn ignored her. 'I was born in Onwai, some . . . time ago. I was the youngest of seven sisters, so I was given over to the Golden House of Worshipfulness to eventually become an acolyte there. I went at the age of seven, and started my studies of Benoit, the Walker of the Path. I was a good student, I studied hard, and truly I loved Benoit. I learned his Eighteen Laws of Peace by heart, and I excelled at the Three Golden Paths of painting, poetry and music. When I turned seventeen I was blessed by the Mother to become a novice, and I was sent to Pathania to spread the word of Benoit. Myself and four of my fellow initiates were to sail there on a ship called the *Indigo Ribbon*. The journey would take three weeks.' Estenn paused and took a small flask from her belt. She unscrewed the cap and took a sip from it. 'I've not told this story for some time, and it makes my throat dry.' She offered the flask, and when Wydrin nodded she gently threw it to her. Inside it was a very sweet, very thick wine. Wydrin took three quick gulps and passed the flask back. 'A week out from Onwai, our ship was taken by slavers. Those who resisted were killed. I was very young, and very frightened. I had only ever known the green mountains of Onwai, and the peace of the Golden House. I was terrified. Myself and the other novices were chained down in the hold of the slaver, where we stayed for another three weeks. One of my friends died of a fever, chained next to me, much closer to me than you are now. Another tore up rags and forced them down her own throat until she choked to death.' The woman's dark eyes sparkled in the firelight. 'I was sold twice over the course of five years. My first owner was a Pathanian merchant who bought me to teach his children to read and write. That place wasn't as bad as some. I had a small, bare room of my own, and I was given kitchen scraps to eat. Every night in that tiny room I would recite the lessons of Benoit and look for the good in my life. I trusted to the greater good that eventually I would be delivered from this misery, and that I would find my way back to Onwai and the Golden House. But Pathania, as I'm sure you know, is a land of plagues. Red coughing fever swept through the city and my owner's children both died. I sat at night in my small room, listening to them cough and cough, tearing their lungs to pieces inside their own chests. When it was all done, he sold me. What good is a slave to teach children when there are no more children?'

She paused again to take a sip of the strong wine. Wydrin leaned forward. 'A city in Pathania? Slavery has been outlawed in Pathania for decades. Are you telling me he openly owned slaves and nothing was done about it?'

Estenn looked at her for a moment, as if judging how much to tell her. 'This was long before the Storm Days swept the beginnings of civilisation across Ede. That particular uprising was still two decades away.'

'Hold on,' said Wydrin. 'The Storm war was over fifty years ago. That would make you . . .' Wydrin shook her head. The woman's skin was clear and unlined, and her body was lithe and obviously strong. There were no grey hairs in that black mane, and no crow's feet at her eyes. She looked no older than thirty, if that. 'You would be more than seventy years old.'

Estenn moved her head. It was not quite a nod. 'Do you want to hear the rest?'

Wydrin frowned, and then shrugged.

'I was sold to a mining operation on the western coast of Relios. There are chunks of precious minerals hidden in seams deep in the rocks of that country, and I was one of the people who worked to find them. That was considerably worse than being a scribe for a wealthy merchant. The earth in Relios is red, and riddled with soft clay. It doesn't make for safe mining shafts. I saw lots of slaves die, and narrowly escaped death myself many times, while I worked until I became a shadow of a person. I did not know who I was any more. I had no life of my own. I still recited Benoit's lessons, but they had become just words to me, which, of course, is all they ever were. Salvation and wonder do not lie in human hands.

'Eventually, the mine ran dry and I was sold again. Back onto a slaving ship I went, all hope of recovering myself long since lost. The ship took on supplies at Two-Birds, and that was when, finally, my destiny came for me.'

Estenn shifted on the ground. The firelight made her features a mask.

'The captain of the slaver took a handful of us into Two-Birds with him. He fancied that perhaps he could pass us off quickly to some willing ship's captain, or perhaps to one of the brothels. While I was in the town, a young woman helped me to escape. I will never know why.' Estenn looked up and met Wydrin's eyes. 'That was when I found Euriale.'

'You went into the island?'

'Where else could I go? I was so obviously a slave, without a single coin to my name, and I was terrified by my sudden freedom. I had been a slave for years, and knew nothing else. More than anything, I wanted to be away from other people. Men and women had only ever brought me pain and false promises. Benoit, with his human teaching, had promised me a kinder world, and then left me to suffer.'

'And you've lived here ever since?'

Estenn sat back slightly. There was a shrill cry from somewhere

142

deeper in the jungle, and the sound of something heavy moving through the trees, not far from where they were. Wydrin looked in that direction, but no one else seemed to be concerned.

Estenn smiled, and it was almost a warm smile; that of someone remembering a distant but pleasant memory. 'That first night, as I slept on the black soil of Euriale, the shadow of a wolf came for me. I was frightened at first, and it hurt, but their need was very great, and they had been waiting for me for a very long time.'

Despite the warmth of the evening Wydrin felt goosebumps break out across the tops of her arms.

'The Twins?' Despite herself, she whispered the words. 'You mean Res'ni and Res'na?'

'An echo of them.' Estenn met her eyes again, and seemed to come back from wherever her mind had been wandering. 'Long since perished, of course, but in this place, the ghosts of gods still walk. Tell me, Wydrin of Crosshaven, how much do you know about the mages, and their citadel?'

Wydrin cleared her throat. 'Well, I've been inside the place, if that's what you mean.'

'Do you know how they trapped the gods inside it?' insisted Estenn.

Wydrin shrugged. 'I know what everyone knows. That they hid some very interesting, very powerful objects inside the Citadel, and when the gods came to take them, they cast a spell. Or something.'

'Doesn't that seem rather simplistic to you?'

'Gods are greedy, and single-minded.' Wydrin shifted on the hard ground. 'From what I saw of Y'Ruen, she thought mainly of what she'd like to destroy and little else.'

Estenn nodded, as if this were the response she had expected. 'What very few people now know is that there was a very specific artefact placed inside the Citadel to lure the gods. A very specific, very dangerous artefact. It was known as the Red Echo, and it was so dangerous that it was stored in two separate parts, so that no one should be able to use it. The Red Echo, it was said, killed mages. It could rip past a mage's magical defences, and kill a great number of them in one, agonising second.' Estenn tipped her head slightly to one side. 'Can you see why the gods might have raced to claim it? The chance to finally wipe out the mages. Imagine if someone had used it? How different the world would be now.'

'Why are you telling me this?'

Estenn pressed her fingers to her throat again. 'You are interesting to me. And sometimes I like to give people a choice. Most of the men and women who are with me now are people I once gave a choice to. I saw you fighting on the deck of your ship. You're a strong woman, and a skilled fighter. You have the shape of a god on your skin, just as I do.'

Reflexively Wydrin put a hand to the tattoo of the Graces on her arm.

'And more than that,' continued Estenn. 'If the rumours and stories are true, you saw Y'Ruen in all her glory. You helped to end her.' Estenn was looking at her very closely now. 'Do you even realise what you did? What you took from the world? Ede has wilted without the presence of her true gods. With Y'Ruen back the world was fresher, more vital, more full of magic. I felt it here, on Euriale, in the cradle of the gods. And then you took her away.' Estenn took a long, slow breath, and when she spoke again her voice shook. 'You *took her away*. I want to understand why.'

'*She* was a dragon,' said Wydrin, unable to keep the disbelief from her voice. 'A bloody great fire-breathing bitch of a dragon, very intent on killing everyone and everything in her path. I saw what she did first hand.' She thought of the *Briny Wolf* burning bright with dragon fire, and the men and women in the water. She thought of Y'Ruen coming back to pick them off, like a dog rooting for scraps. 'I saw her murder and eat people, and she would not have stopped, not until every human was a dusty black mark on a rock somewhere. I *saw* that, while you were sitting out here in your commune for weirdos.'

There was a murmur at this from the men and women standing guard. Estenn held up a hand and they fell silent. 'You cannot understand, Wydrin of Crosshaven. You have not seen across the

144

years as I have. The last of the gods is dead now, and this world needs its gods.'

'Gods?' Wydrin could feel her voice getting louder, and despite the fact that she was unarmed and these people would lose nothing by slitting her throat, she could not stop it. 'Gods, demons, spirits. Do you know what I have seen of gods and what they bring to Ede? Suffering, misery and horror. I have seen men and women burned alive, I have seen an entire city sunk under the sea because a god was *offended*. I have seen gods toy with the lives of men and women, because they have nothing better to do. I have seen apparently wise people exile one of their own because of rules made to honour a god that may or may not be there.' Wydrin turned her head to one side and spat on the ground. 'That is what I think of your gods.'

Estenn stood. Again she seemed to fade from view and abruptly she was there in front of Wydrin. She barely had time to react before the blow caught her, folding her over onto the broken tiles.

'I do not give everyone a chance,' said Estenn evenly. 'Most are wise enough to take it.'

22

Frith stumbled on through the trees.

His sodden clothes had long since dried out in the heat of the day, but now they were clinging to his back with sweat instead. The jungle around him was a riot of colour, noise and movement. He had never been in a place that felt so virulently alive; the forests of the Blackwood were practically a graveyard in comparison. Everywhere there were birds, insects, tiny monkeys and other mammals – all of them buzzing or singing or calling to each other. Even the flowers and plants seemed more alive than was seemly; he saw fleshy green plants with rows of thorny teeth snapping shut around insects that flew too close, and long trumpet-shaped blossoms that released sporadic clouds of glittering golden pollen.

Frith sneezed. It was all giving him a headache.

And, of course, he was lost. Lost in an alien jungle, with no magic, no supplies and no map. When the Edenier had burned inside him it would have been so simple to summon the word for Seeing. That at least would have given him some idea of where Wydrin had been taken, and then he would have used the words for Ever and Fire to burn this stinking forest out of his path until he found her and then he would crush the idiots until their bones—

His footing gave way and he slipped to his knees, half falling into a thorn bush that clawed at his clothes and skin.

For a few seconds the jungle of Euriale rang with a long list of curse words, most of which Frith had picked up from Wydrin quite recently.

When he had exhausted that particular lexicon, Frith pulled himself to his feet. He spent a few moments picking thorns from his clothes, and pushed his hair back from his face.

'I must take time to think,' he said. Around him the cacophony of the jungle continued. 'Wydrin's life could depend on it.'

Beyond the trees to his left was a green pond, overhung with some huge twisted variety of willow tree. He pushed his way through and sat on a mossy rock at the water's edge. On the far side of the water he could see a colony of tiny, silvery frogs wallowing in the mud there. Some of them hopped lazily into the water, raising small plops rather than splashes. Something about that movement, about the look of their grey bodies, tickled at the back of his mind.

'I have no magic, no staff. No supplies, no weapons.' He touched his belt, thinking of the short sword the pirates had taken from him, and even the vicious little scalpel Augusta Grint had given him. The pretty little knife he'd bought for Wydrin was now with her, wherever she was. 'I should have waited,' he murmured, his chest suddenly tight with self-loathing. 'Waited until I was armed again, until I had a force behind me.' But he also knew that he couldn't have done that. When he'd woken up to find that Wydrin had been taken forcibly, cold panic had seized him. It was like Skaldshollow all over again, watching her body spin away through the Rivener, knowing that every chance had been lost, and the dark days after that, when it had been so easy to turn to Joah Demonsworn's blood-soaked magic.

His eyes caught the movements of the frogs again. Perfectly formed and tiny, they hopped in and out of the sludgy water, hopping like little stones—

Frith sat up, holding his breath.

It was one of Joah's memories, one of the ones he'd been left with when Joah had performed a 'crossing', briefly meshing their experiences together; for a time he had looked out through Joah's eyes, and had seen many wondrous and terrible things. Much of it hadn't made sense at the time, but eventually the knowledge had settled like sediment in a pond, and now he knew much of what Joah had – Joah, the greatest mage to have ever lived. The greatest – and the most terrible.

Frith closed his eyes, willing himself to remember the details. There had been a forest – not a headache of colours like this one, but a deep, green forest like that of home – and a young boy with brown skin and barely any flesh on his bones. He had worn nothing but leather belts, and had sat on a great boulder. The boy had small grey stones in front of him, and he had made them jump to his will.

'That was not Edenier,' said Frith, looking back to the frogs. 'It was the Edeian. Magic inherent in the flesh of Ede itself. The same magic that moved the werkens, and riddled the mountains of Skaldshollow and the Frozen Steps.'

He looked around at the trees and the foliage, encasing him in their green cave. The most ancient places were the ones where the Edeian was strongest, and here, he realised, he could practically feel it. Euriale was alive with wild magic. Perhaps that was something he could use.

Frith settled back on the rock, trying to ignore the discomfort and the heat. He forced himself to close his eyes and relax. He summoned the memories, letting himself be lost in them as he hadn't for some time. He saw again the woman in the turquoise silk robe, and the man with the beard and hands covered in gore. He saw Bezcavar again in the human form that Joah had known a thousand years ago, and he saw the Edenier trap, unfinished and still somehow deadly – this his mind skipped away from rapidly before he could dwell on it – and he saw the boy in the forest. Concentrating fiercely, Frith peeled back the layers of the memory. The boy's eyes had been dark green, he remembered, and in truth he wasn't a boy at all, but a spirit of that place. Not a ghost, but a being of trees and water and earth that had taken human form for a brief time. Joah had summoned the spirit and it had shared knowledge with him. Suddenly, Frith understood that as the boy had been the spirit of that place, so Mendrick, a wolf built of stone, had been the spirit of the mountain at

Skaldshollow. The spirits were everywhere, but they took different forms.

More frogs plopped into the pond. Frith stood up. What would a spirit of this place look like? Would it help him? Would it ignore him? Or just kill him outright?

Without giving himself time to think about it, he walked around the edge of the pond, splashing through the algae-thick water, until he got to the muddy bank. He knelt there, giving the frogs a few seconds to get out of the way, and then he plunged his hands into the muck. Immediately, a thick, green stink assaulted his nostrils and he turned his head to one side to take a breath of fresher air. The mud was thick and almost black, gritted here and there with pebbles and ancient frog bones. He dragged his fingers through it, ignoring the way the water was soaking into his trousers, and began to sculpt the shapes that were burning in his mind. Small walls of mud, curving shapes, deeper trenches; it was difficult to get the mud to stay how he wanted it. Distantly he was aware that it was a deceptively complex spell, similar to O'rin's plan a thousand years ago to carve the words of the mages' directly into the Edeian-rich earth, but this was several mage words on top of each other. It was like trying to build a palace with porridge.

Around him, the jungle noises grew quieter. Stillness spread out from the pond like a flood. Frith ignored it.

He pushed deeper, feeling the hard nubs of roots under his questing fingers, dredging up the deepest, blackest mud; it would have the strongest magic in it. He pulled it up in great, wet handfuls, no longer noticing the stink, and he kept building, holding the shapes in his mind as best he could. After a few moments he looked around and snatched up a handful of sticks and foliage from the littered ground next to him and began to construct a rough framework within the muddy pile.

It was a little like making the Edenier trap – the same sense of cold satisfaction at creating something from nothing – but without the creeping horror and sensation of violation that came with using demon-tainted magic. A fly touched his face, and he batted it away impatiently, smearing black mud there. He barely noticed.

149

When finally he sat back from his creation, the sun was creeping towards the horizon and his legs were numb from kneeling for so long. He staggered to his feet, wincing as the feeling came back through bright points of pain.

It didn't look like much, at least not to the untrained eye. His pile of mud and sticks was roughly cone-shaped, and came to just above his knees. Sticks and mud and tiny bones poked out of it, and there were gaps and shapes in there too; Frith could see them in his mind's eye. More than that, he could feel them. Quite different to the sensation of Edenier burning in his chest, the latent Edeian in front of him felt like a warm tickling on his skin. When he held his hands out to it, the feeling brushed at his palms, as though he were facing a fire instead of a pile of mud.

'There was something else,' he murmured. Around him, the birds and the monkeys had fallen silent.

He consulted his memories again, seeing Joah's skilled fingers creating his own shrine of mud. When it was complete, the mage reached into a pocket and produced a small bird made of golden wire, and he'd placed it within the structure. The bird had tiny sapphires for eyes.

'An offering,' said Frith. 'Of course.' He took a step back, and looked down at himself. He had nothing of worth, no weapons, no jewellery. In the dark green cave of the trees, Frith shook his head. All he had were the clothes he was wearing.

After a moment, Frith put a hand to his shirt. There were silver buttons at the throat – each one engraved with either a tiny tree or a tiny griffin, made after their return from Baneswatch. Looking at them made him think of Gwiddion – another friend, lost. He took hold of two and yanked them away from the shirt, breaking the stitching, before bending and pushing them into the thick mud at the heart of the shrine. He stood back to admire his work.

'Please, if you're there, I need your help. If you're there. If anyone is there.' He paused, wondering if there was a certain thing that needed to be said. He consulted his memories again. 'I call on you here, at the heart of Ede.'

'You are more correct than you could possibly know.'

Frith started, feeling the hairs on the back of his neck grow stiff. The voice was low and somehow insubstantial, like the echo of a voice, and it seemed to come from inside his head. At the same time, the pond in front of him grew dark, as though something behind him were casting a large shadow. He could feel a presence, a terrible unseen shape, standing so close behind him that he was sure he should feel its breath on his neck. Frith stood very still. He knew, somehow, that it would be a bad idea to turn around.

'Spirit,' he said. He took a deep breath, willing his words to be the right ones, 'I am honoured by your presence.'

'On an island of shrines and temples, yours is the most paltry,' came the voice again. Frith could read no emotion in it, and no gender. 'But you interest me because you are god-touched. The Destroyer and the Liar. You were present at the end of both.'

Frith blinked rapidly. He knew that, logically, if something were standing right behind him, he would be able to see their reflection in the pond, but there was nothing. Only the deepening shadows.

'I was,' he said after a moment. 'I helped to end Y'Ruen, and I saw O'rin perish, to my sorrow.'

'And so the cycle begins again,' said the voice. 'Or at least it should. What is it you want from me, god-touched one?'

'I need your help,' said Frith. He tried not to rush his words, but it was difficult. Some terrible part of him, perhaps the same part that had seen the construction of the Edenier trap to the end, dearly wanted to turn around and look upon the face of what he was speaking to. 'I have lost someone. She was taken to this island, and is lost somewhere upon it. I need help to find her.'

'I am not a dog you can use to follow a scent,' said the voice. It did not sound angry, but, even so, Frith felt his heart quicken in his chest. 'This is the cradle of Ede. It is my eye that opens. And you dared to summon me for this?'

Frith gritted his teeth. 'I have the power to do so, so I did. I use what I have at my disposal. I must save her, as she would save me.' He took a deep breath. 'I love her.'

The voice was silent for a time. Frith kept his eyes on the dark water in front of him. All of the frogs had vanished.

'The woman you seek. She is one of the Grace's children. Salt in her blood, and fire in her hair.'

'Yes!' Frith almost turned around in his excitement, stopping himself just in time. 'That's Wydrin. You have seen her?'

'She walks my soil,' said the voice, as though this were obvious. 'It's possible to show you where she is.'

'Please,' said Frith, 'that's all I need – some idea of where to start, and I—'

'There will be a price,' said the voice. Frith nodded, not daring to speak. 'The Destroyer and the Liar are gone, so the cycle must begin again, on Euriale, as it always does. The Eye is open. But I feel discord. Something is awry. He who guards is missing from his post, and new life surges unabated. I cannot act, but perhaps you can. Find the one who spins the webs, and set him back where he should be. That is what I ask of you.'

Frith nodded. He barely understood, but there seemed to be little choice.

'If it is within my power, I will do it,' he said, wondering what he had just agreed to. Deals and promises made to demons, gods and spirits: none of it ever ended well.

'Then it is agreed. There is magic you can barely imagine, traveller. I will open your heart to it. Look up.'

Frith looked up to the canopy. As he watched, the long, languid branches of the willows began to lift and peel back, revealing the sky above. It was overcast, and the last orange light of the day clung to the bottom of the clouds with a glow-like fire.

'What am I looking for?'

'Look at the clouds, and see your path.'

Frith frowned, narrowing his eyes. He could see nothing, just clouds and light. There weren't even any birds flying, just clouds that promised rain later and— abruptly he saw it, and he took a step backwards in amazement. There was a break in the cloud, a line, only obvious if you were looking for it. The clouds were moving slowly to the east, but the thin dark line that split them was moving west, and slightly faster than the rest. He could follow it across the island.

'If I follow that, it will take me to her – is that what you're saying?' He turned, too focussed on getting this vital instruction correct, but as he did, noise and colour screamed back into the world. The shadow on the pond was gone, and the birds and monkeys were calling again. After a moment he heard the gentle plop of frogs finding their way back to the water.

He was alone.

23

Estenn's camp was industrious, well-maintained and filled with the smell of cooking meat. Smelling it, Wydrin felt her stomach rumble. She couldn't remember her last decent meal. Estenn had marched them through the forest relentlessly, pausing only for a few hours in the night, and no food had been forthcoming. Now it was mid-afternoon, and the air was tepid, the heat suffocating. Wydrin's fringe was plastered to her forehead with sweat. Judging by her previous visits to Two-Birds, they would have a storm soon.

'I don't suppose there's any food going?' They were walking through the centre of the camp, and everywhere there were men and women with tasks; tending fires, tanning leather, hauling pails of water from a central well. Everyone looked busy, but they all took a moment to glance over at her. She suspected that prisoners weren't often brought into their camp. Or allowed to live very long. 'Even the godless have to eat.'

Estenn, who had been walking at her side while the guards brought up the rear, paused. She pointed over to a nearby cooking fire, tended by two young men. A great side of something was spitted over it, ribs white against red flesh.

'I would offer you food gladly, Wydrin the Godless, but I'm not sure it will be to your tastes.'

Wydrin looked closer at the cooking meat. She felt the worm of fear in her gut grow larger. She could well be in serious trouble here.

'Why would you do that?' she asked, not quite able to keep the anger from her voice. 'There must be plenty of animals to hunt in this stinking jungle.'

Estenn looked at her, amused. In the daylight her skin was smooth and unlined; Wydrin could still see no sign of the many years she claimed to have lived. 'The animals here are children of Euriale, just as we are. Why should we harm them? The men and women of Two-Birds, though,' she nodded towards the fire again, 'they are not worthy to walk the soil of the cradle of Ede. And what better way to keep them away, than by filling the woods with wolves? Besides which, people are much easier to hunt.'

They moved on. Wydrin tried to ignore the smell of roasting meat.

'Where did you all come from?' she asked. 'I know where *you* came from, but it doesn't explain all these others.'

'Not everyone who wanders into the trees is killed for meat,' said Estenn. 'Those who come seeking the gods, or those who have a simple need to escape from Two-Birds – some of those we take in. I teach them how to live here, how to understand the island. A few we have taken ourselves, snatched from Two-Birds as children, and then raised here.'

'You have stolen children? How very godly of you.'

'It is necessary to have new blood sometimes.' Estenn shrugged. 'And now, of course, we have been here so long that children have been born and raised in our camps. The truest children of Euriale. Like Nettle, here.'

They had reached a structure of mud and wood that appeared to shelter a tunnel that led directly beneath the earth. A girl of about sixteen stood on guard at the entrance. She wore a crown of bright blue beads at her temple, and held a spear casually to one side.

'Emissary.' She gave a slight bow.

'Nettle was born and raised on the island,' continued Estenn. 'She knows its heart almost as well as I do.'

'There's a whole world out there, kid,' said Wydrin, addressing the girl. 'All sorts of places where you don't have to live in a sweltering mud pile and hide in the woods – and the dinner choices are a lot more palatable, believe me.'

The girl looked at her with wide eyes, before turning back to Estenn. 'Emissary . . .'

'It's all right, Nettle. Tell her what you know to be true.'

The girl passed the spear from one hand to the other. 'Euriale is the home of the gods, and we are its children. The world outside has forgotten the true gods, and driven them unto death.' She drew herself up to her full height. 'The Emissary has been chosen to bring them back, and we, the children of Euriale, will help her. Ede will see the glory of the gods again. Y'Ruen will cleanse all in her fire, Y'Gria will rebirth the lands and seas, and Res'ni and Res'na will shepherd the dual nature of humanity back into being, while O'rin, father of lies, sets the stories turning once more.'

For a few moments, Wydrin was too stunned to speak. And then she surprised herself by laughing. Nettle and Estenn both looked at her angrily.

'Y'Ruen's cleansing fire? Oh yes, very cleansing. She would kill you all as soon as look at you, and you would welcome it with open arms.' She grinned, unable to help herself. 'Y'Ruen brings nothing but death and misery. You can trust me on that.'

The girl looked confused, but Estenn's mouth was pressed into a thin line.

'This is how the ignorant understand the world, Nettle. Nothing falls from this sell-sword's mouth but lies and self-delusion.'

'Shall I run her through?' asked Nettle, hefting the spear in her hand. 'In the name of the Twins?'

Estenn put a hand on the girl's shoulder. 'Don't worry, Nettle. This one will get what she deserves, in time. We will keep her for a while. Run and fetch Cully and Jake and tell them to take over your guard duty. I will want extra muscle on this entrance for now. Our guest is going to be joining the Spinner.'

The girl ran off, casting one more poisonous look over her shoulder at Wydrin. Estenn took hold of her arm and began to walk her down the tunnel.

'Easy to get them to think what you want when you have a captive audience, isn't it?' said Wydrin. She was wondering what the Spinner was, and didn't want the uncertainty to show in her face. The way was lit with small oil lamps, wedged into the soil. 'That girl knows nothing of the real world, just the poison you have dripped into her ear.'

Close to her, her voice low, Estenn murmured into her ear. 'You are one of the very few people on Ede to have seen the gods in the flesh. Why do you deny them?'

'Oh, I don't deny they exist,' said Wydrin. She thought of flying on the back of a griffin, the sea a twinkling carpet of blue below, while Y'Ruen roared behind them. 'I just happen to believe that you shouldn't have to bow and scrape to someone just because they're bigger than you and have sharper teeth. The gods don't care about you, *Emissary*. They've never cared about any of us.'

Estenn nodded, as though she expected nothing better. 'Let me show you then, Wydrin the Godless, something else very few people have ever seen.'

They had stepped through into a wide chamber. On the far side, almost reaching the ceiling, was a big pile of furs and blankets. It was quivering slightly. Wydrin tried to draw back, but Estenn's grip was strong. She missed the weight of her weapons at her belt more than ever.

'This is the Spinner of Euriale. I brought him here to answer my questions too. He can give you some idea of how it goes.' She shoved Wydrin forward, and she stumbled fully into the chamber. A soft keening noise came from under the blankets. Estenn raised her voice. 'I have someone new for you to speak to, Spinner.'

Wydrin approached the pile of furs and rags cautiously. The keening noise was strange and multifaceted, as though it came from many throats at once, but it was still clearly the sound of someone in distress.

'Hey, it's all right.' She held out her hands to show they were empty. 'I'll help you, if I can. There's no need to be afraid of me.'

Behind her, Estenn laughed softly. She bent down and picked up one of the small oil lamps from the ground.

'You are disappointing, Wydrin of Crosshaven. You turn away from the glory of the true gods, and grub around on the ground with their servants instead. Let me show you what you side with.'

With that, she threw the oil lamp into the centre of the blankets. Instantly the blankets and furs were thrown aside and Wydrin saw a great monster uncurl itself; nine great legs like that of an enormous spider burst out, almost filling the room. She cried out, trying to scramble back, but one of the arms flexed and suddenly she was being dragged through the dirt towards the body of the creature. She got a brief impression of a segmented body covered in interlocking plates of a shining white substance like mother-of-pearl, and more vulnerable-looking sections of black leathery skin, and then she was crushed next to it. Three legs covered in thick bristles curled around to hold her in place.

'Wait! I am not your enemy!'

There was an odd flexing beneath her and she felt the bonds around her legs grow tighter. Peering down past the alien legs that encircled her chest she saw silver strands winding their way up her shins; two of the other legs were pulling them from something she couldn't see, and using them to bind her legs and feet together. Quicker than she ever could have imagined, the web was up to her thighs, and getting higher all the time.

'Estenn!'

The woman was bending to retrieve the oil lamp from where it had rolled on to the floor. She looked amused. Wydrin strained against the limbs holding her in place, only now smelling the alien stink of the creature that held her in its grip.

'You can't leave me here,' she said, hating the desperation in her voice. 'I know about the staff. You need to know what I know.'

By now the strands of web were covering her hands where they were pressed to her chest. The touch of the web was cool and slightly numbing. She tried to ignore the rising panic that was filling her throat.

'Oh, you'll be alive for a while yet,' said Estenn, her tone terrifyingly casual. 'This sort of thing takes ever such a long time.'

With that, the Emissary turned and left the chamber, heading up the rough dirt slope.

'Wait!'

The limbs holding her in place shifted as the web grew higher and higher, but as much as Wydrin struggled to be free the thing was extremely strong, and the web covering her legs and now her arms might as well have been spun from steel. Soon, it would be up to her neck, and when it covered her face, whatever Estenn might think about her chances of survival, she doubted she would be able to breathe through it.

'Please,' she said, 'please stop. I am not here to hurt you. I'm another prisoner, like you.'

The busy legs continued, holding her close and spinning the web. The low keening sound was back, she realised, and it thrummed through the creature behind her so that she could feel it in her own chest.

And then abruptly it was done. The legs curled back out of her vision, save for one which still held her securely to the creature's body. The web had ended just below her neck; when she looked down she could see the contours of her own body outlined in pale silver, as though she were already a ghost.

'There,' said a voice from directly behind her. It was low and deep, with strange harmonies. Wydrin felt all the hairs on the back of her neck stand up. 'Now there will be no distractions.'

24

The beach was black and littered with bones.

Ephemeral picked her way over them carefully, fascinated by the pale yellow of the bone against the charcoal grey of the sand. Some of these bones had been here a very long time, and most of them had long jaws filled with sharp teeth. She did not know what they were, but she found it difficult to look away from them. Next to her, Terin's face was grave. There was a cold wind blowing in from the east, and this had revived him somewhat. It was good to see his grey face clear of sweat again.

These last days had been the hardest part of their journey. When they knew beyond doubt which island Sebastian had gone to, it had taken them some time to find someone willing to sail to Euriale. Everyone had turned them away – most with suspicious looks and several with outright threats. It was, they quickly gathered, a notorious pirate haunt, and to journey there was akin to admitting that you wished to partake in some sort of criminal activity. Eventually, they had gone to the darkest, seediest part of town and located the tavern that smelled most overpoweringly of vomit, and only there had they found a man willing to take them. And when they had stipulated that they wanted to travel to the western coast of the island and not Two-Birds, they had needed to pay twice as much. Still, here they were.

Ephemeral turned to look back to the sea. The man was a tiny dot now, hastily shoving his small boat back out into the wider deep. He had not even wished to put his foot on the sand itself, declaring the place 'cursed'. Ephemeral found this most curious.

'Do you think he will be cursed now?' she asked Terin. 'Do you think we are cursed?'

Her husband looked at her and shrugged his narrow shoulders.

'There are places in the Frozen Steps that are considered cursed.' They made their way up the beach. Clouds gathered above, heavy with a promised storm. 'Beyond the Wailing Hills, for example, is the site of an old Narhl township. A group of travellers came with trading goods – silks, exotic woods, wool, dried fruits – and they also brought with them a terrible disease. In a matter of weeks, everyone in that township was dead. A few bodies were found a mile or so from the town, as the sickening men and women fled to get help. None of them made it.' Terin reached down to pluck an interesting shell from the sand, and placed it in a bag at his waist. 'That place has been considered cursed for a hundred years or so. I have never been there, so I cannot know if to go there is to invite misery.' He tipped his head to one side. 'Perhaps cursed really means it's a place where the memories are so terrible it is best to leave it alone for ever.'

Ephemeral nodded seriously. She wondered if the places that had been destroyed by her and her sisters were now considered cursed, or if the people would try to rebuild the homes they had lost.

They continued on in silence until they reached a rocky bluff of land. There they climbed and pulled themselves up until they stood under the cover of trees. Here, it was warm again, the air wet and close. Terin leaned against a trunk for a moment, pushing his hair out of his eyes. He had already stripped down to his trousers, the long leather belts across his shoulders and chest holding his supplies and his weapons. There were small scars all over his body – remnants of his communing with fire.

'Are you sure?' she said again. 'It might be easier to go to the town first, to see what information we can gather.'

Terin shook his head. 'Your father is not there. He moves towards the heart of this place now. I feel that very clearly.' He smiled at her. 'And I don't believe the people of Two-Birds would much like to answer our questions. We are not pirates, after all.'

'And my green skin and sharp teeth would invite pointed interest.' She sighed. 'The question is, what do we—' She felt a sudden silver shiver in her blood. Ephemeral opened her eyes wide, turning in a slow circle. It was not her father she could feel, but some other sort of kin. Something that was like her sisters, but not quite.

'What is it?' asked Terin in a low voice. 'Are we in danger?'

She didn't answer. Instead she looked up. Above them was a break in the canopy, and as they watched three great flying animals passed overhead. They had leathery wings like bats, but their heads were long and lizard-like, tapering to a point at either end, and they had long narrow tails. They were only visible for moments, as they were flying so fast, but it was time enough for Ephemeral to feel their blood sing with hers. And once she had felt it, she could feel it all around. The island was alive with it: new life, new dragon-kin life. It was everywhere.

Terin's cold hand settled on her shoulder. Abruptly she realised she was swaying slightly where she stood.

'I am all right,' she told him, as firmly as she could manage. 'And I think I now have some idea of why my father came to this place.'

'Here. We are here.'

Sebastian stood with Oster on the edge of a green stone wall, looking down into a deep pit. The other side was a good hundred feet away, and it was impossible to see how deep into the earth it went; the bottom was filled with shadows. The walls below them were carved with interlocking geometric shapes, interspersed here and there with other forms that looked roughly humanoid. Vines and creepers crawled all over the stone, and from where he stood Sebastian could see a few birds' nests clinging to the cracks.

'Where is here?' asked Sebastian.

They had been walking for two days; Sebastian making his way as best he could over the rough terrain, Oster periodically shifting out of his human form and into his dragon form, a golden beast made of light and teeth. He would hunt in this shape, bringing back rabbits and other small mammals for Sebastian to cook over a fire.

It was taking some getting used to.

'This is where he lived,' said Oster. 'The Spinner made his home here, when he did not need to watch over the Eye. And it has been many centuries since the Eye opened last.'

Sebastian peered over the edge. 'He lives at the bottom of that?'

'Yes,' said Oster, apparently seeing no problem with this. 'In the darker spaces, no doubt.'

'Your friend, this Spinner – is he like you? I mean, does he have a human shape?'

As yet, Sebastian had no clear answers for what Oster actually was. The man had appeared to him as a ghost, as many ghosts, and then in the flesh. And when in the flesh, he could change at will into a dragon; a glorious creature of gold and cream scales and bright amber eyes. In this form he was apparently still Oster – still a being capable of thought and reason, yet he was curiously reluctant to answer any of Sebastian's questions. His brow would furrow and an expression of barely checked anger would come over his face, and he would brush it off, or simply walk away. Some of the mystery seemed to be tied up in this Spinner, who, Oster insisted, should have been there to meet him. The fact that the Spinner was missing clearly made Oster deeply uneasy, but again he seemed unable or unwilling to say why.

Sebastian felt as though he were caught on a hook, being dragged along by mystery after mystery. More than once he had wondered if he were hallucinating; if the strange humours of the jungle had simply driven him mad. In a lot of ways that was the most comforting explanation. It was more comforting, at least, than the silver thread of connection that he felt between himself and this strange, angry man.

Oster had been silent for some time, so Sebastian looked over to him. Standing by the great shaft in the ground, they were out of the shelter of the trees, and in the brilliant light his skin was a deep, tawny brown. Despite the days they had spent together his chin was still clean-shaven, the curly mop of dark hair on his head unchanged. He looked up at Sebastian, his face unsmiling.

'Not a human shape, no. I don't believe so.'

'Ah, good.' Sebastian looked back down into the shadowy pit. 'And you want to go down there, of course. I can't see a path.'

'There is one, you just have to be looking for it.' Oster came to his side and pointed to the far side of the pit. 'You see the carving there that looks somewhat like a face? If you follow the long nose down, you can just about see another shadow, cutting across it. That is a visible part of the path.'

Sebastian narrowed his eyes against the bright sun, following Oster's finger. There it was – a suggestion of a horizontal shadow, and then below it and to the left, another. It was possible to follow a sequence of them, gradually sloping down and out of sight, spiralling around the pit.

They walked around the circumference together, picking their way over rubble and long grass the colour of dust. When they got to the place where the path met the top of the wall, Sebastian stopped.

'That looks awfully shallow.'

The path down was little more than a rough series of narrow steps carved directly from the green stone. To the right there was the solid wall, to the left was a yawning drop. To walk down safely it was clear that he would have to lean heavily to the right, pressing his side against the stone at all times. For a moment he was glad he wasn't wearing his heavy armour or his long sword, both of which could have unbalanced him.

Oster was nodding slowly. 'The Spinner does not have much need for conventional paths. You are clearly afraid.' There was a lack of surprise in his voice that was more insulting than a sneer would have been. 'I shall go first.'

Sebastian pursed his lips, attempting to ignore the flare of anger in his chest. He reminded himself that as a child he had walked through the Demon's Throat, alone and in the dark. In the frozen North he had floated down through the empty air into the cursed city of Temerayne. In the Blackwood, he had walked across an invisible bridge. At least he could *see* this path.

'I am not afraid,' he said. 'But there is no need to throw ourselves down there. We will go slowly.'

Sebastian put his foot on the narrow green step. When the entire thing didn't collapse in an explosion of rocks and mud, he stepped fully onto it, and then onto the next one. He kept his right hand pressed to the wall. Behind him he heard Oster step down. To his left, the great yawning nothingness stretched away; he fancied he could feel it pulling at him. Motes of dust danced there, golden in the sunshine. Slowly, one step after another, they made their way down. The walls rose above them like a jade sky, and the cacophony of the birds and monkeys and other animals became muffled, as though they were coming from a great distance away. Sebastian supposed they were.

'Tell me,' said Oster from behind him. 'Why did you come here? Once Euriale was a place of great pilgrimage for men and women, but you do not have the heart of a priest.'

Unseen by Oster, Sebastian smiled bitterly. 'Why am I here? That is a really good question.'

'Where did you come here from?'

'I came here from a place called Crosshaven. It's a little like Two-Birds, only they like to pretend that some of their business is legitimate.' He took a breath against the sourness in his chest. 'My friend is from there, and we were working together. We came here as part of a job but I'm not sure I have the will for it these days. So much has gone wrong in the past.' They were passing a part of the wall that had been carved with great looping shapes – he slid his hand along the curves they made, grateful for the extra hand hold. 'Before that I was a knight, in a place very far from here, a place of mountains and lakes. I wasn't very good at that either.'

'Lakes and mountains, islands of ill repute,' answered Oster gruffly. 'The world is as it ever was.'

'You know something of the world away from this place, then?' Sebastian half turned, almost looking over his shoulder. 'I have told you something of myself. Some people might see that as an invitation to—'

The solid stones under his feet fell away. He heard the dry

rattle of pebbles, the pressure of half a shout forming in his own throat, and then he was ripped away from the wall, a terrible lurch in his stomach as everything solid vanished. He turned as he fell to see Oster still on the path, his eyes wide, and then he was lost in a confusion of green stone and shadow.

Spinning into the dark, Sebastian took a breath – whether to shout or to pray he couldn't have said – when it was abruptly knocked from him. Something huge hit him from the side, grabbing hold of him with crystal claws and curling around him none too gently. He had a brief impression of golden scales, smooth under his fingers like glass, and a bright amber eye.

They fell together, turning and turning, before hitting the floor with a tremendous thump. Oster in his dragon form rolled and rolled, holding Sebastian away from the stony floor until they came to a stop. Then abruptly the dragon pushed him away, sending him sprawling on the stones. For a few moments Sebastian lay still, breathing heavily. When he was sure the ground wasn't about to give away under him, he propped himself up on one elbow, and gingerly patted himself for injuries. There would be bruises, no doubt, but no more than that.

The dragon that was Oster was cautiously lifting its head, black tongue sliding over its teeth. The long tail swished back and forth, scattering dust and rubble.

'Are you all right?' asked Sebastian, and then belatedly, 'And, uh, thank you.'

There was a swirl of golden light, and where the dragon had been there was Oster again, brushing himself down, although he needn't have bothered. Not a single hair was out of place, and his armour wasn't even scuffed. Not for the first time, Sebastian tugged at his beard, feeling very conscious of how unkempt he must look.

'It was foolish of you to fall. A human such as yourself would not survive it.' Oster gave Sebastian a caustic look before turning away.

'Your wisdom is truly astounding,' muttered Sebastian, wincing as he pulled himself to his feet. The bottom of the pit was full of shadows and not much else. Leading off from the great circular stone floor were eight arched doorways. One was bigger than the others, and filled with darkness, while the others looked like they had been blocked up somehow. Trying to ignore how his heart was still pounding from the fall, Sebastian walked over to the nearest one.

It was filled with spider's webs. Not just a few haunting the corners, but a thick barrier of the stuff, great swathes of web as wide and as thick as bed sheets. It filled the doorway with grey shadows, and here and there he could see small shapes caught up in it; lots of birds, the occasional small monkey. Some of the shapes were also covered in the web, small mummified bodies hanging in the dark, but plenty appeared to have just got stuck there – presumably, unable to escape, they had starved to death. It was impossible to see beyond the web.

He walked to the next one, and then the next.

'They are all like this,' he glanced over to Oster, 'all save the largest entrance, here. Why is this one clear?'

Oster shrugged extravagantly. It was dark in the bottom of the pit, but small beads of light peeled along his epaulettes.

Sebastian sighed. 'He is your friend. Do you have any theories?'

Oster scowled at him in the half-light. 'You have many questions. It was never meant to be my place to answer them.' He took a breath, and shook his head. 'The Spinner was not my friend. He was supposed to be here, to serve me,' he said eventually. 'But I have not met him.'

The largest doorway led into a large circular chamber lit with small green glowing stones set directly into the wall – Sebastian had never seen anything quite like them, but they made him think of both the Heart-Stone and Prince Dallen's cold light. There were holes in the walls leading to other, smaller chambers, all empty. Sebastian couldn't help noticing that some of these chambers were in the ceiling, so high up that no human could have reached them easily. The floor was littered with strange items: Sebastian saw the bones and skulls of small animals; leather-bound books, their pages curled and yellow; clay bowls crusted with old food; brightly coloured beads and glass marbles; knives and forks and spoons, the silver tarnished and turning green; a belt made of gold links with a fat golden beetle as a buckle; and, strangest of all, were several masks – these were all piled together in the same corner. A few of them were simple things – white faces with holes for eyes and mouth – while others were more elaborate, depicting women's faces with gold and silver lips and eyebrows.

'What is all this stuff?' Sebastian bent down and picked up one of the masks. Its blank-eyed stare was unsettling.

'The Spinner collects things,' said Oster, as though this were a stamp collection or a rich man's study full of expensive paintings. 'Look at this.' On the biggest wall was another great web, this one apparently made of a thick, silver substance and there were items caught in this web too, small statuettes made from a translucent red stone. Sebastian reached up and touched one, and the whole web vibrated softly.

'It's a dragon,' he said, feeling his throat close up with a fear he didn't understand. 'And these two are wolves.' He walked to the other side of the web to look at the other two, although he already knew what they would be. One was a woman with ribbons of green hair trailing down her back, and the other was a bird with wings spread wide. Next to each statuette was a smear of a thick red substance. To Sebastian it looked like it had bubbled up through the stone itself. 'What does this mean?'

'What do you think it means?'

Sebastian looked at Oster, but could read nothing in the man's face. 'I think it means that all the old gods are dead.' Sebastian swallowed hard. 'Y'Gria, Res'na and Res'ni were eaten by their sister Y'Ruen beneath the Citadel. Y'Ruen herself we pushed from this world. She might still survive there,' he thought of the terrible hole that had opened in Skaldshollow, and the diseased hulk that had tried to pull itself through, 'but she is gone from Ede for ever. And I saw O'rin die. I saw Joah Demonsworn cut his throat open with the god-blade. They're gone, all of them, and your friend the Spinner knew it.'

'All gone,' agreed Oster. 'And the cycle begins again. The Eye of Euriale opens, and new life crawls forth.' He shook himself abruptly. In the gloom, the dragon shape on his arm was glowing faintly. 'This is all wrong. I should not have to explain this, it is not my *place*. I should not even have to speak to you. The Spinner should have been here when I arrived, and then I would have understood it all, but instead I am alone, and the pictures do not make sense.'

They stood in silence for a few moments.

'If you want help finding this Spinner, you'll have to put up with talking to me for a while yet,' said Sebastian, hearing the acid in his voice and not caring. 'Let's look around. Perhaps we can get an idea of what happened.'

Oster nodded, his lips pressed tightly closed, and together they combed through the junk on the floor. Sebastian looked closely at each of the statuettes caught in the web, and then at each of the masks. Oster shifted into his dragon form and scuttled up the walls, filling the chamber with golden light, so that he could slip up into a chamber in the ceiling. After a few moments, his human face peered over the lip of the entrance.

'Have you found something?' asked Sebastian.

In answer, Oster held up his hand. There was a smear there of black and white paint. 'The Spinner was taken from here, by the same people who attacked me,' he said.

'Who attacked both of us,' Sebastian pointed, out, but Oster wasn't listening. There was a look of black fury on his face.

'They have taken my past, and I shall tear them apart for it.'

25

Frith opened his eyes to find himself under a close watch.

The previous night, when it had become too dark to follow the path in the sky, he had found a great hollow tree. The hole where the roots met the earth was big enough for him to crawl inside, and the space within was covered with soft, old leaves. He had curled himself into as comfortable a position as he could manage, and then exhaustion took him. With all the noise and dangers of the island Frith would never have believed that sleep could come so easily, but he slept deeply that night, and had no dreams.

Now bright sunshine painted the world outside his hideaway tree, reflecting off the emerald scales of the three creatures that stared at him. They were small, roughly the size of large chickens, but they were lizard in shape, standing on powerful back legs, with their front legs curled in front of their chests. Their long snouts were lined with tiny, needle-like teeth, and their eyes were bright with curiosity.

Frith kicked out at them awkwardly. 'Shoo! Go away!'

They took a few hurried steps backwards, and then stopped, still watching him. Frith climbed out of the tree hollow, wincing at the stiffness in his back. When they still didn't move, he picked up a rock from the ground and threw it at them. Finally, the creatures scattered, long flexible tails whipping away into the thick bushes.

Frith watched them go, wondering belatedly if they were edible.

Above him, the sky was a mixture of blue and white as a thick bank of cloud moved in from the south. It was possible to see the path there still; a bruise-like line across the pillowy clouds. Today it curved, heading north and then west, cutting across the island. It was time to move.

Wydrin awoke to shadows. It was difficult to believe that she had slept at all, bound up in a spider's cocoon and cradled by a giant monster, but the creature had not spoken again; it had simply held her tightly in place, in the dark. It wasn't, Wydrin had to admit, completely uncomfortable, although the urge to scratch her nose would come and go. She had tried speaking to it, asking it questions, but got nothing in return save for that low keening sound.

She blinked rapidly, trying to wake up fully. There was still an oil lamp in the corner, casting a warm light over the mud walls. The bonds holding her were as firm as ever.

'You know,' she said out loud, 'eventually I will need to pee, and neither of us is going to be very happy about that.'

To her surprise, the creature behind her shifted. First one, then two legs swept down in front of her – covered in black bristles, and here and there a piece of pearly white armour – and picked her up carefully, turning her over and around. Wydrin briefly squeezed her eyes shut, wondering if this was the part where the spider injected her with poison and drank her jellified insides, but when she opened them again she found herself looking at a serene and beautiful face.

'Forgive me,' said a quavering voice. 'I did not have a face to greet you with, so I had to make one. They took all my faces away.'

Wydrin took a slow breath. The face was a finely shaped mask with holes for eyes and a sleek point of a nose, made of the same pearly white substance as the creature's armour. There was a thin white stick protruding from the chin, and this was held in one bristly claw – a surprisingly dexterous appendage, she noted. She could see some of the bulk of the creature now – a fat purple abdomen, patterned with bright orange spots like eyes – and behind the mask was . . . Wydrin felt herself go very still. The mask was beautiful, but not big enough. Behind it she could see many sets of bulbous eyes, red and black, and several sets of mandibles, busily working away. The claw tightened its grip on the mask, and the creature's body shivered all over.

'Now I have the correct face, we can speak in a civilised manner,' said the creature. Wydrin couldn't quite see where the voice was coming from; the mask covered up that part of its head. 'Don't you think?'

'Yes,' said Wydrin, keeping her voice as neutral as possible. She wished fervently for the weight of Frostling at her side. 'It is good to, uh, meet you.'

'I am the Spinner.' The mask dipped slightly in a parody of a bow. Wydrin wished it hadn't. 'What are you?'

'I am a sell-sword. My name is Wydrin Threefellows, the Copper Cat of Crosshaven.'

The Spinner shivered all over, apparently impressed with this. 'A fine name!' The legs shifted, and the Spinner held her out further as if for better inspection. 'A name crafted for adventures, no doubt.' The voice became lower. 'I tend to know about these sorts of things.'

'Well, you've got that right.' Wydrin smiled despite herself. 'In the last few years I have seen more adventures than any one woman should see. Demons, dragons, giant walking mountains—'

Abruptly the Spinner pulled her closer, so that her face was only a few inches away from the mask, and what the mask concealed. The legs circled her again, squeezing her arms and her chest.

'*Yes, yes*, you *know*, don't you? You can tell me! You must tell me, now, please. I know the histories and yet I do not, do you see? I hear the songs and I sing them, but I never *feel* them.'

Wydrin coughed, trying not to panic. If the Spinner squeezed her much harder, she wouldn't be able to breathe.

'I can tell you. But I won't be able to if you crush me to bits.'

The mask quivered, and the pressure eased off a little. 'That is good, yes? Now you can speak. You must tell me of it all, little adventurer.' One of the legs descended from above and touched the top of her head, pushing her hair back from her face. 'You will tell me *now.*'

'Of course, no problem.' Wydrin cleared her throat. 'Where to begin?'

At midday, the weather had begun to change. A hot wind had blown in from the east, scattering the clouds from the sky and leaving it a pure, blameless blue. Frith had watched it happen half incredulously, as his only clue to Wydrin's whereabouts was blown to tatters. Without the clouds, the path was invisible.

He had been trudging his way up a seemingly endless hill when the sky cleared, and now he found himself at the foot of a small structure built of black stone. He'd seen many similar ruins on his way; often in the distance there would be a broken spire, or the trees would part to briefly reveal a pile of rocks. For an apparently uninhabited island, it certainly had a great many signs that humans had passed through here. What had Devinia said? That is was an island of gods, and people had built shrines here for them.

'Crowded with gods and demons and spirits,' he muttered to himself. 'The Blackwood truly must be the quietest place on Ede.'

He climbed over the low wall, now mostly fallen into rubble, and walked under the low roof of the temple. It was good to get into the shade for a little while, and besides which, he wasn't going anywhere until the cloud cover was back.

Inside was a small broken altar, stained and crusted with thick yellow moss, and the floor was broken by crowds of thick thorny bushes. There were fat purple berries on the bushes, some so ripe they had burst onto the floor, and the stones were littered with pips where small animals had feasted.

Frith picked a handful of the berries. They looked very similar to those that grew on a bush in the Blackwood – spinster berries, they were called – and the old cook at Blackwood Keep had been especially fond of making pies from them. Of course, he was half a world away from Litvania now, and there was something off-putting about berries that had grown in the dark.

He popped one in his mouth and chewed cautiously. The fruit burst open, so sweet it was almost sickly. Cook, he remembered, had tempered the sweetness with salt and lemons. He smiled slightly at the memory, and picked a handful, placing the fruits into a corner of his shirt. When he had a decent amount he went back out to the crumbling wall and sat on it, intending to sit there and eat berries until the clouds came back. It was possible the berries were poisonous, of course. It was equally possible he would find nothing else to eat and starve to death out here, hopelessly searching for Wydrin. He ate another berry, and spat out the pip. They certainly tasted like spinster berries.

Thinking of the cook's pies made him think of his mother. She had died when he was very young, and the thought summoned an image of her bedroom door, open just a crack. Through it he could see the thick gauze curtains that covered her bed, and the suffocating fog of incense. The healer, a tall thin man dressed in black, stood at the back of the room like a shadow. Frith remembered how he had hated the man, with his long pale hands and the silk kerchief he wore over his mouth. Even when his mother had seemed to be getting better, the healer's eyes were always sad.

He turned from that memory to a happier one. His mother had been inordinately fond of spinster-berry pies, and whenever the cook was making one she would come and find him. They would sneak together into the kitchen, and steal samples of things as the cook prepared them. Now, of course, Frith realised that Cook must have been aware of their game, but his mother had always let it feel like they were being cheeky, just for the sheer delight of it. It had made the pies taste all the sweeter.

Half lost in his thoughts, Frith glanced down to the wall next to him and was alarmed to see one of the green lizard creatures from earlier perched on the rocks next to him. He was just wondering if it truly was one of them, if it had tracked him all the way from the hollow tree, when its long narrow snout shot out and it sank its teeth into his hand.

Frith leapt up, yelping with pain and simultaneously throwing the lizard off. It shot away into the shadows of the broken temple.

'You little bastard!' Frith took a deep breath, glaring first at the dark space where the lizard had vanished, and then at his wounded hand. There was a neat V-shape of puncture wounds, both on the fleshy pad of his palm and across the bony ridges on the back of his hand. They were oozing blood freely, and already the skin around the marks was red and inflamed.

'I need to wash this,' he said out loud. He looked around. A hole in the ground nearby had caught water from one of the recent storms. He stumbled over to it and plunged his hand in, wincing as the bite marks burned. When he lifted it back out, he had to pick away a dead leaf from between his fingers. The bite marks were still livid, and, if anything, his hand was turning redder. He looked back up to the sky: finally, there were clouds, but they were far to the north. They would be slow in coming.

'Well, there was no poison in the berries,' he said, scowling at the clouds. 'No poison in the berries at all.'

26

'The entire city, sunk under the sea?'

Wydrin nodded, looking up at the ceiling. She was lying on her back now, still bound up in spider silk. The Spinner had placed her carefully there while she was talking, and now he moved back and forth out of the corner of her eye, rearranging the blankets and furs. It was difficult to see much of the creature, in the gloom and bound as she was, but she caught glimpses of long black legs and a shining white carapace. It was not reassuring.

'Under the sea, but Res'ni had sealed it over, so I assume that the people of Temerayne slowly starved to death. By the time we were there, no one was in much of a state to answer questions.'

'Res'ni, always so wilful,' said the Spinner. Just out of sight, his arms were working busily. 'Such a temper. The opposite of her brother in every way. Yes.'

Talking about the gods and the Black Feather Three's recent adventures seemed to have calmed the Spinner down; the fraught tone had eased from his strange, discordant voice. Wydrin was glad, although she was starting to wonder what would happen when she ran out of things to tell him.

'You knew Res'ni well, did you?' It seemed ludicrous to her, but then the last few years had taught her that life was always waiting to drop some new nonsense on her head.

'I know them all, at the beginning.' The Spinner scuttled over, suspending his great fat body above her. He still held up the small mask, a serene moon hanging in the dark. 'I deliver them from the Eye, while it is in flux.' The giant spider shivered all over. 'As it must be now, the Eye is open and I am not there, I am trapped here by the ignorant—'

'Well, Frith had a good idea where the sword was, you see,' Wydrin said loudly. The Spinner stopped shivering, and the mask dipped once, as if in gratitude. 'He had seen the fate of the sword in Joah Demonsworn's memories. We headed across the city, skeletons and dust everywhere you looked. By that time there were things watching us, sea monsters gathering in that mockery of a sky. Frith led us to the tomb where Joah Demonsworn had his final confrontation with Xinian the Battleborn – she was brilliant, by the way, I'll tell you more about her later – and her lover Selsye. We also found Selsye's staff in the tomb, dropped when Joah killed her. She was one of the greatest Edeian crafters of the golden age of the mages.' Wydrin shrugged. 'Or that's what Frith tells me. Her staff turned out to be bloody useful – over a thousand years old and Frith managed to get it working. Anyway, I snatched up the god-blade, eager to be out of there, but of course it was a trap, and—'

'I knew it!'

There was a flicker of light from the far corner, and suddenly Estenn was there. Wydrin could have sworn that the corner was empty seconds before. The woman's eyes were wide, a look of triumph on her face.

'How long have you been there?' asked Wydrin, straining to look over her own chest. Estenn ignored her, instead stalking over to stand in front of the Spinner, who was cowering in the corner again.

'The key you wished to keep from me? I have it.' Estenn was utterly unafraid of the Spinner, facing him down like he was a frightened child. 'That staff is an object of Edeian and Edenier, an artefact of the ancient times. It is my key, sent by the gods themselves. Do you dare to deny it, even now?'

The Spinner shivered all over. The pale mask wavered and dipped. Wydrin wriggled back and forth, trying to put some distance between her and the two of them.

'You mustn't, you mustn't.' The Spinner's voice was a low rumble. 'The cycle has ended, and a new one has started. If you go back, if you travel through the Eye, it will, it will—'

'It will *work*,' spat Estenn. She had drawn one of her long curved swords, and as she spoke she jabbed at the Spinner, puncturing her words with stabbing motions. 'The gods have delivered me the staff and this woman, because it is my destiny to save them. I will correct the mistakes of the past, and our delicate human world will tremble.' She turned back, as though remembering that Wydrin was there. 'You, Wydrin the Godless, I will save for Res'ni,' she said, gesturing with the sword. 'Yours will be the first flesh she feasts upon.'

Wydrin laid her head back on the ground. 'Oh good. Thanks for that.'

Estenn gave a brilliant smile, and stalked out of the chamber. Wydrin could hear her shouting to her guards, issuing orders in a tone that allowed no argument.

'If I could just go a few weeks without meeting some gods-obsessed lunatic that would be—' Wydrin stopped. The Spinner had dropped the mask, and was busily covering himself in the blankets and furs again. The giant creature was shivering all over.

'What's wrong? What did she mean, anyway, about passing through the Eye? I'm assuming she's been on this cursed island too long and it's pickled her head. Right?'

There was no answer from the Spinner. Instead he covered himself with the last of the blankets, and grew utterly still. Wydrin lay in darkness, listening to the gentle trickle of earth from the ceiling.

but Sebastian could hear the disappointment in it keenly. Or perhaps he felt it. 'We will not find his camp today. Why must humans keep stopping? You are so easily distracted.'

'No,' said Sebastian. He couldn't have said what it was that made him feel that they should hurry. Perhaps it was the undercurrent of Oster's confusion, mixing with his own blood, or perhaps it was that growing surge of awareness of everything around him. Something was happening on this island, and it concerned the missing Spinner; of that Sebastian was certain. Waiting until morning to continue to track this man did not seem like the most prudent course of action. 'We will have to force it out of him.'

Without pausing to think about it further, Sebastian broke cover and ran directly at the man, who currently had his back to them both as he prepared his fire. Hearing the crackle of undergrowth, he started to turn, but Sebastian was already there. He twinned his hands together and brought them down as a single fist on the back of the man's head. Due to the angle of the man's shoulders it was an awkward blow, but Sebastian was a good head taller than he was, and significantly heavier, and the man collapsed to the ground with a startled 'Oof'. Before he could do anything more than start to turn over, Sebastian gave him a sharp kick in the ribs and then settled his boot on his neck.

'Hello,' he said, 'I need to ask you some questions.'

The man reached for a sword on his belt, so Sebastian settled his full weight on his neck. The man made some strangled noises.

'Make him tell us about the Spinner, and then kill him in the dirt.' Oster appeared next to him. In the low evening light, he almost resembled his ghost-self again. 'Humans should return to the dirt.'

'Only if he turns out to be less than useful.' Leaning down, Sebastian removed the sword from the man's belt and slipped it through his own. It felt good to be armed again. There was also a bow and a set of arrows in a quiver on the ground, but Sebastian had never mastered archery. 'Are you going to be useful?' He eased off the pressure slightly so that the man could answer.

'What do you want?' spat the man.

'My associate here is looking for a friend of his, and we have reason to believe that you people know where he is.' Sebastian shifted his weight again. 'He is known as the Spinner.'

The man's eyes widened and he tried to roll away again, so Sebastian kicked him firmly in the small of his back. He howled with pain.

'That's not the answer I'm looking for.'

The scout took a deep breath. 'I am a true child of Euriale, and you can't force me to do anything! The Emissary will bring the old gods back, and then you will all cower before us.'

Sebastian glanced over to Oster. He showed no reaction to the man's words. Sebastian reached down and dragged the scout to his feet, giving him a brisk shake as he did so. 'What are you talking about, bringing the old gods back?'

The man's eyes brightened until it looked like he was running a fever. 'She can do it! The Spinner told her everything she needed to know, and she will bring their glory back. The world will be built again in their image, and the children of Euriale will be at the heart of it.'

'You do have the Spinner, then.' Sebastian pushed the man against a nearby tree, briskly rapping his head against the bark. Dimly, he was aware that he didn't want to be doing this. Wasn't a life of violence what he was trying to walk away from? Yet the surge of Oster's emotions was impossible to resist. His anger was satisfying, powerful. 'A simple yes would have done. Where is he being kept?'

The scout laughed and attempted to spit at Sebastian, succeeding only in dribbling down himself. 'I'm not telling you anything. The Emissary was right, we are the chosen, and the rest of you will burn in the fires of—'

Next to him, Sebastian sensed the pulse of shimmering light that meant Oster was changing his shape. The scout's eyes grew so wide he thought they might fall out of his head.

'As you can see, my associate isn't in the mood for lectures.'

Oster's long snout shot forward, opening slightly to reveal rows and rows of gleamingly white teeth. The scout screamed: a high, wavering sound of pure terror. Sebastian shook him again, forcing the man to meet his gaze.

'What are you?' the scout burbled.

Sebastian kept his voice as steady as possible. 'You could help us to find out. Or I could feed you to him. It's up to you.'

Through the silver link between them, Sebastian could feel how much Oster wanted to kill this man. *We need him*, he tried to say back. *We need him for now.*

'The creature is in our camp, in a chamber under the ground. The Emissary has been keeping it there while she questions it.'

'Great.' Sebastian grabbed a fistful of the man's tunic and yanked him away from the tree. 'You can show us where it is.'

28

Devinia lay on her back, listening to the liquid sound of oars slicing through the water. She and Augusta were prisoners on the Banshee's largest raider, *The Dragon's Maw*, a sleek little vessel that sat high in the water. The sails were tied away and the Banshee's strongest oarsmen were at their posts, pushing the ship on as smooth as silk. They moved with efficiency and strength, and leapt quickly to their captain's orders. It was all very annoying.

''Ere, sit up.' Augusta poked her in the shoulder with a blistered boot. 'I need to change the dressing on that wound of yours.'

Devinia shifted her eyes. The old medic was framed in sunshine, so that her grey curls looked like a silver halo. 'It's a waste of linen, old woman.'

Augusta nudged her again, none too gently this time. 'Less of the old, Red, or I'll show you what a proper gut wound is like.'

Reluctantly, Devinia sat up. Around her, the black cliffs moved smoothly past on either side. The rain they'd seen earlier had passed as quickly as it had arrived, and now the sky was blue and it was difficult to believe that there had been any rain at all. Augusta wasted no time in yanking up Devinia's shirt. She poked around with her short, blunt fingers, muttering under her breath. Kellan had at least had their arms untied, as though to suggest that an injured woman and an elderly medic were of no real threat. It was insulting, but there were heavily armed pirates to all sides and their chances of escape were very slim indeed.

'It's knitting together better than I'd have expected,' Augusta said eventually. 'You always were a tough little bugger. It'd take more than one stab in the guts to put you down, I've always said that.'

'What you've always said is that if you weren't around, I'd have been chopped up into bits and sold off for leather years ago.'

'*Hrm.* That as well.' Augusta pulled out her own shirt and began to carefully tear a long strip from the bottom edge. When that was done she tore off another piece and wadded it up into a soft square. Devinia closed her eyes tight, and opened them again. The pain in her stomach had lessened, but the loss of blood was still making her head swim.

'What are you doing?'

'You see any medical supplies around, do you? You imagine Big Gob over there is going to give us any?' Devinia glanced over at the Banshee. The woman stood in the prow of her ship, watching the waters ahead of them. The long coat she wore was surely too hot for the stifling weather, but she kept it on anyway. It was all part of her image, like the red greasepaint.

'I suppose not.'

'Stop your bloody whining then.' Pushing her arms out the way, Augusta pressed the pad to Devinia's wound, before securing it as best she could with the long strip of linen. 'It's better than nothing.'

Devinia lowered her voice. 'Wydrin is out there, somewhere. Out in the wilds of that jungle.' It wasn't quite a question.

Augusta sniffed. 'You're asking me what I think happened to her? And how am I supposed to bloody know? Flying mad people, come down here, snatch her away in the middle of a boarding. And then that lordly piece with the white hair takes *my bloody knife* and leaves us to it.' Augusta settled back, glaring around at the pirates that surrounded them. To either side of *The Dragon's Maw* were two more narrow ships, both showing some minor damage but nothing significant. They were moving faster now, as some of Ristanov's crew had been left on board the *Poison Chalice*. Not Kellan though. He was still here. Devinia had seen him earlier, poring over her own map. 'What I can tell you, Red, is that Wydrin has an even thicker bloody hide than you, and she inherited the infernal luck of Pete Threefellows, too. I don't know who took her or why, but I reckon they'll be regretting it shortly.'

Devinia felt a smile crack her dried lips. 'That's true enough.'

The old woman shifted on the deck, sweat beading the sallow skin on her cheeks and forehead. Augusta refused to complain about it, but sitting out unprotected in the heat was punishing for her. The Banshee's men only seemed to bring them food and water as an afterthought, and the heat was relentless, even when the cliffs afforded a little shade. ''Ere, what's this racket now?'

There was a volley of shouts from the ship ahead of them, and Devinia looked up to see the air filled with golden light. She blinked rapidly, trying to make sense of what she was seeing.

The black cliffs to either side were covered in what initially looked like a natural formation of gold crystals. Long and angular, they shone so brightly in the sun that they were difficult to look at, and clustered on the rock like barnacles. To the right, the formation was so thick near the top of the cliff that it loomed over them, looking impossibly heavy, while to the left the crystals were thicker nearer the water. Devinia sat up, trying to get a better look. The crystals on that side almost seemed to form steps, and they led up to a dark hole in the rock.

'Have you ever seen anything like that?' she breathed to Augusta.

'Course I bloody ain't. I've never seen gold that looked like that either. What do you reckon it is?'

'Riches.' A shadow passed over them, and the Banshee was there, a grin splitting her ruddy mouth. 'Exactly what we came here for, yes? Get up, Devinia the Grey. I'm putting a landing party together, and you get to be the first over the threshold, just in case there are any exciting traps or creatures waiting. A great honour I do you, yes?'

Devinia curled her lip, ready to tell the Banshee to go fuck herself, but the captain slid a throwing knife from her belt and casually turned the blade towards Augusta.

'I wouldn't refuse the honour, Devinia the Grey,' she said mildly. 'Or I will have to amuse myself some other way.'

Devinia pulled herself to her feet, ignoring the way her poorly healed wound tugged at her skin. 'Let's get this over with.'

They bound her hands behind her back again, tighter than was necessary, and then Kellan led her to a small skiff, where two other men waited, all riddled with scars and twitchy with gold-lust; Ristanov did not apparently feel the need to accompany them on this first exploration. They made the short trip across to the golden ledges and stepped awkwardly out onto the slick gold crystals. With Kellan coming up behind her, Devinia climbed up each step with some difficulty, her tied hands making it difficult to balance, until she stood at the entrance to a short dark corridor carved directly into the rock. At her back, Kellan ordered the two pirates to bring their torches. Buttery light filled the passageway and a door at the end became clear. The wood looked a deep dark red to Devinia's eyes, and it had been carved with multiple skulls, bulging out of the wood in alarmingly life-like fashion. The light did not seem to reach into their eye sockets. At about waist height, several skeletal hands reached out to form three shallow bowls.

'On you go,' said Kellan. 'The captain was very insistent that you should go first.'

Devinia bit down her reply, promising herself bloody vengeance at a later date, and slowly walked up the short tunnel, taking care to walk as lightly as possible in case there was anything underfoot that might trigger a trap. She thought of Wydrin, and how the girl had made this sort of nonsense her stock in trade. Piracy was much simpler.

Up close, Devinia could see that the carvings of the screaming skulls were unspeakably old. Rot was evident in several places, turning the red wood flaky and weak, and she could see hundreds of tiny holes where numerous insects had left their mark. The cupped hands were dusted with what looked like the remains of ancient offerings; dark threads of what might once have been silk, and several old coins, rusted into flat black discs. Hesitantly, she leaned her shoulder against the wood and pushed. Nothing moved, but she could feel a faint breeze through the cracks in the wood.

'There's a space behind here,' she said.

The two pirate meatheads elbowed her to one side, inspecting the door themselves.

'There's no handle,' said one of them. His nose had been broken so many times it was now more of an afterthought than a feature.

'Perhaps we put something in these bowls,' said the other one. The parts of his face that weren't criss-crossed with scars gave home to a carroty beard. 'We put something in the bowls and it's an offering to the gods, see, and then the door swings open with a loud creak, right, and beyond it is a glittering room full of gems and gold and winsome priestesses, wearing silk and that.'

Devinia raised an eyebrow. This one had imagination at least. 'Or you could kick it down,' she suggested. 'The thing is nearly rotten through.'

'Do it,' snapped Kellan.

The carroty one stood to one side, looking sheepish, while the other lifted a meaty leg and proceeded to kick the door in. It took only two blows to break the door, and a further three to clear the wood out of the way so that they could pass through. Devinia felt a faint pang at the loss of that piece of history, but what lay beyond the door chased that quickly from her mind. Next to her, the scarred pirate blew air noisily through his lips.

'Bloody hell,' he said. 'I was only bloody right.'

The only thing the chamber was missing was a gaggle of winsome priestesses. It was carved from the black rock of the cliffs, and filled from corner to corner with gold; heaps of gold coins crested against the walls, ornate bowls studded with gems were overflowing with jewellery, while chests stood open to display more riches. The torchlight shone off the gold and filled the chamber with an opulent glow.

'Torrent's tits,' muttered Kellan, his eyes wide, before turning to the two pirates, who were grinning inanely. 'Fill the sacks you have, and then go back to the ships for more men. I don't want to linger anywhere too long in this place, but we won't be leaving any of this behind, either.'

Devinia stood to one side as they pushed past her, eager to get their hands on the gold. She scraped her boot through the coins on the floor, noticing as she did so that they seemed to be covered in some sort of red dust. Peering closer, she could see that there were fibrous pieces of something plant-like amongst it too. A weed, perhaps, that had grown around the treasure and then rotted away to nothing.

'It must kill you, to see all this and know none of it will be yours,' said Kellan.

'You think you will getting a fair share from that lunatic?' she asked, but her eyes were on the two pirate thugs. They were cramming fistfuls of coins into the sack, their fingers rapidly covered in the red dust. Very soon it would be too heavy to carry between them, and they would have to go back for assistance. 'You've done what she needed you to do. You're living on borrowed time, and I think you know it.'

Kellan ignored her, stepping away to explore the rest of the chamber. 'What's this?'

At the back of the room beyond the heaps of coins was a statue of a man. It looked as though it was carved from the same red wood as the door, and it was completely unadorned save for a crown of gold that sat on its head. There were no features to the statue, and the crown itself was simple and plain, particularly in comparison to the elaborate pieces on display. There was more of the fibrous red material on the statue and covering the crown, and as Kellan reached for it, Devinia was briefly filled with the urge to shout at him to leave it alone. It was an instinctive reaction, like watching someone reaching for the handle of a pot left to grow red with heat over a fire. The urge passed, and she watched with a trepidation she didn't understand as he plucked the crown from the statue and turned it over in his hands. Nothing happened.

'This is a fine piece. There's some sort of engraving here.' Kellan absently wiped his hand down the front of his shirt. He no longer bothered with the vanbraces that hid the burns on his arms. 'I may keep this for myself.'

Reaching up, he slid the gold band over the top of his head to rest against his ears. Immediately, the ground under their feet lurched and trembled, sending a cascade of coins across the floor. Kellan opened his mouth to speak, and instead they heard a chorus of panicked voices from outside.

'Quickly, move,' he snapped. 'Get back outside, now.'

Devinia jogged back down the short passageway to daylight, and faltered on the golden crystals there. The Banshee's ships waited in the blue water below, and she could see the crew standing, all looking in the same direction. A giant golden man was stepping out of the cliff opposite.

'What by all the gods?'

It was a figure made from the gold crystals, a rough human shape with giant craggy shoulders and thick, jagged arms. The head, such as it was, gave the impression of a fierce, bearded face, with two deep recesses glowing with red fire serving as eyes. The thing stood over fifty feet tall, looming over the ships, and Devinia thought she could make out a pattern across the gold crystals – odd geometric shapes repeated in lines of red fire. The figure pulled away from the cliff entirely, sending a shower of dust and dead leaves down onto the ships below, and then stepped heavily into the water. There it stopped, staring straight ahead at where they stood on the opposite cliff. When it stood, it was utterly still, as if it were completely inert again.

'It's a monster!' The pirate with the ginger beard had dragged the sack of coins out into the daylight, but now it slipped through his fingers as he gawped at the giant. 'Or a god, or a demon, or some other bloody thing that's going to eat us and—'

Kellan pushed past the man, almost throwing him down the steps. He had both hands to his head and was pressing his fingers to the band of gold there. Devinia watched him, feeling a coil of fear move through her gut.

'No,' said Kellan. 'It's none of those things.' His eyes were wild, and the colour had drained from his face save for two bright spots on the tops of his cheeks. 'It's something else, and I can feel it in my head.'

29

They got Kellan back to the *Dragon's Maw*, the ginger pirate gripping the top of Devinia's arm tight enough to bruise it. Ahead of them, the giant golden figure stood unmoving, looming over the narrow ships.

The Banshee met them as they came aboard. Her pale-blue eyes were bright, caught between fear and anger.

'What is this?' she barked at Devinia. She pointed savagely at the golden figure. 'Do you know what it is?'

Despite her own curiosity and alarm, Devinia took the time to arrange her face into a sneer. 'You truly are an idiot. How would I know what this bloody great monstrosity is?' She tipped her head slightly to one side. 'You might do well to ask your partner in idiocy here, though.'

The Banshee turned her icy gaze to Kellan and seemed to look at him properly for the first time. Devinia saw her eyes widen slightly. 'What is this thing on your head?'

'I can feel it,' said Kellan. His fingers ran over the crown again, touching it lightly with his fingertips. 'It's in my head. It's been still for so long, but now the sun warms it again.' Devinia noticed that he had some flecks of the red material on the tops of his cheeks and across the bridge of his nose. They must have fallen from the crown.

'What are you talking about?' snapped the Banshee.

'That thing seems to have stepped out of the cliff at the exact

190

moment this fool put the crown on his head,' said Devinia. 'I'd say the two are connected, wouldn't you?'

Kellan shook his head and lifted his eyes to the golden figure. 'It's like . . . the word for Growing, Becoming –' he frowned slightly – 'but also the Sun. Daylight is a part of it.' He stopped, and then smiled with genuine pleasure. 'The Dawning Man, that's what they used to call it.'

'Who called it that?' asked Devinia, but at that moment Kellan reached out a hand, and the Dawning Man did the same – one great golden fist lifted into the sunshine. Golden reflections peeled across the water, and there were shouts from the Banshee's crew, a mixture of fear and wonder.

'It obeys me!' Kellan grinned. He lifted his other arm and touched his hands to his head, and the Dawning Man copied him. For one absurd moment Devinia was reminded of a game Pete had played with Wydrin when she was very small. He would clap his hands in a certain sequence, and she would copy, with the sequence becoming more complicated each time. She blinked that memory away.

'You are controlling that thing?' asked the Banshee.

'I just think, and it does what I ask. I don't even have to move. Look.' The Dawning Man took two sudden steps forward, sloshing through the water and sending a wave towards the nearest ship so that it rocked violently.

'Be careful,' said the Banshee, but she was smiling now. 'Such a thing, under our control. I think that might be quite useful, yes.'

'It's old magic,' said Devinia. 'You don't know what you've awakened here. You'd do best to leave it be. Take the crown off and leave it behind. There was enough gold in that chamber to make your trip up here worth it on its own. Take the gold and go, but don't dabble in this.' She was remembering the moment of alarm she'd felt when Kellan had picked up the crown, but the Banshee laughed at her.

'Gold, and the power to move it, that is what I have now, Devinia the Grey.' She turned back to the two pirates standing next to Kellan. 'Take a team of men and start moving everything out of that chamber and onto the steps. And then our Dawning Man here is going to help us load up the ships.'

Kellan nodded absently. There was a red band of inflamed skin on his forehead where the crown rested, and lines of sweat streaked his cheeks. Devinia was shoved back to where Augusta waited. For a few moments they watched in silence as the Dawning Man strode slowly across the waterway to the cave, where the Banshee's men and women were hurriedly emptying the chamber of its treasure. The giant golden figure bent, and scooped up the sacks as if they were filled with feathers rather than gold, before depositing them on the ships. The figure, despite its size and apparent weight, moved with grace and accuracy. It was, Devinia had to admit, a wonder to behold.

'If she fills her hold up with all that, she'll be hanging low in the water,' pointed out Augusta. 'Won't be so bloody fast then, and it strikes me that this is the sort of place where speed might be useful.'

Devinia looked at her, an eyebrow raised. 'That's all you have to say about this?'

Augusta shrugged. 'Bloody great golden monster. What is there to say?' She lowered her voice. 'Wydrin told us about stuff like this. Creatures made of stone that could walk around, powered by some sort of spirit magic. That didn't end well, and I don't imagine this will either.'

'I suspect you're right.' Devinia looked up as a huge shadow passed over them, the Dawning Man's arms full of sacks. In the bright sunshine, a golden halo shone around its head, and the red light within its eye sockets was a dull embers glow. 'The question is, will we still be here when it goes wrong?'

'I know this woman's blood.'

Ephemeral shifted on the tree branch as Terin leaned over her to get a better look. They had climbed up here to watch the ships after having followed them for around a day, and now the ships had been still for some time, anchored next to a portion of the cliff covered in a glittering, gold substance. Some time ago, a giant figure had broken away from one side of the cliff, and was now obediently moving backwards and forwards across the waterway, although it was difficult to see quite what it was doing. It was extraordinary, but it was the figure with long red hair that interested Ephemeral.

'Your eyes are better than mine,' said Terin, a touch dryly. In the shade of the tree he had perked up. 'They all look much the same to me from up here.'

'It is more than sight,' said Ephemeral. 'It is the way she moves, and the smell of her.'

'You can scent her too?'

Ephemeral nodded, not looking at him. 'It's faint, but it's there, and it's all the stronger because I recognise it.' She narrowed her eyes at the distant figure. 'She is not Wydrin Threefellows of Crosshaven, but she is blood to her.'

'A relative?' Terin pushed his hair back from his face, damp with sweat. 'But the woman Wydrin is not here, and neither is Sebastian.'

Ephemeral shook her head. 'It is difficult to sense Sebastian now, because of all the –' she waved a hand, encompassing the whole island – 'all the dragon-kin here, but I know he's not on those ships. I do not think that it is a coincidence that blood of Wydrin is here. This woman may know where they are.'

'You are right, my love, but the red-haired woman is obviously a prisoner. I doubt we could just walk down into their midst and question her.' He lowered his voice. 'And then there is the golden werken.'

Ephemeral looked back at him, noting the disgust in his voice. In the northern lands, a people called the Skald had made beings out of rock, and perverted the spirit of the mountain to make them move around, forcing them into slavery. The Narhl had gone to war over it. 'You believe this is the same magic?'

Terin touched the stone pendant that hung at his chest – a piece of home. 'I sense no mountain spirit here, but this island is far from empty. My love, this place is crowded with spirits. It presses in on me at all sides. I don't know what the golden werken is, exactly, but I do not think it is good.'

'Then we must help blood-of-Wydrin,' said Ephemeral firmly. 'We will watch them for a time, and when the opportunity comes, we will strike.'

30

Frith leaned heavily on the tree trunk, looking down into the clearing.

His hand was a hot, itching mess. He was trying not to look at it. The flesh was red and swollen, pulling the skin tight like a full wineskin. It was throbbing, too, a regular thump-thump that seemed to coincide with the bursts of black stars that were growing at the edge of his vision.

Still. The clearing. That was what he had to focus on. Because this was where Wydrin was.

The path in the clouds had led him here, after another day's walk through the steaming jungle. Below him was what appeared to be a busy settlement, dotted with mud huts and cooking fires. He could see men and women swarming around it like ants around an ant hill. He took a ragged breath – these had to be the people who had taken Wydrin. There was a tree stump in the centre of the clearing that had been painted white on one side, black on the other, and as he watched, men and women came and left offerings at the foot of it. It was too much to hope that Wydrin would be in plain sight somewhere.

'Now what?' he said aloud. His situation was, if anything, worse than when he'd dived from the *Poison Chalice*. He still had no weapons, no magic, and now he had a poisoned hand and, if he wasn't mistaken, a fever too. He supposed he might be able to navigate his way successfully down this steep hill and into the clearing, but he doubted he had the strength to do anything other than pass out when he got there, or perhaps, if he were lucky, aggressively vomit over their boots.

Frith swallowed, clinging a little tighter to the tree.

At least that would be doing something. If he could just get close to her, things would be clearer. It was that, or stand here watching the camp until something else occurred to him, or the fever took him completely. If nothing else, he needed to see her. He would not stand to have Wydrin taken away from him again.

He stood up as straight as he could, and took a few more deep breaths. With the last of his strength he would move stealthily down this hill, keeping watch at all times, and he would study the edges of the settlement. From there, he would figure out where Wydrin was being held, and under the cover of night—

A heavy hand landed on his shoulder. He looked around to see a stocky man with his face painted black on one side and white on the other.

'Out for a stroll, are we?'

Wydrin lay in the dark and listened. Since Estenn's outburst, there had been a great deal of noise from beyond the tunnel leading to the chamber. It was difficult to make out details – the mud walls muffled everything – but she recognised the rhythms and the tones. They were making ready for something, presumably whatever it was Estenn intended to do with the staff, or the 'key', as she called it. The Spinner had continued to be silent, despite all her coaxing attempts to get him to talk. The keening noise would come and go, but that was all.

'Spinner, something is going on up there. It would be a good time for us to rush the guards, wouldn't you say? Spinner?'

There was no response, but there was a murmured conversation from the tunnel entrance, and then the soft thud of boots on mud.

'Someone is coming,' said Wydrin in a low voice. She tensed, straining against the bonds that held her. A trio of dark figures appeared at the entrance to the chamber.

'We're to just leave him?'

'The Emissary is all fired up, you saw her. She doesn't have time for this.' The figure in the middle was thrown roughly onto the ground. 'And we have what we need, anyway. Come on.'

The two guards left, while the figure on the ground moaned and rolled over. Wydrin caught her breath and tried to sit up.

'Frith? Frith, what are you doing here? What happened on the ship?'

He looked up at her and smiled faintly. In the dull light from the single oil lamp she could see that he was pale, his face smeared here and there with mud. She could also see sweat on his forehead.

'This is my daring rescue. Can't you tell?' He climbed to his feet, lurching to one side as he did so.

'Are you all right?'

He shook his head. 'I was bitten by some lizard creature on the way here. Haven't been feeling at my best since.' He staggered over to where she lay, and fell to his knees again. 'Wydrin. Your mother's ship, it was overwhelmed. I'm sorry. I got away when I could. When I left, your mother and Augusta Grint were still alive.'

Wydrin winced. Pushing aside the anger and the fear, she tried to think of what Devinia would do. Concentrate on what they could change, of course. 'There's no time to worry about it now. My mum can look after herself.'

Frith nodded, although he looked less than convinced. He looked at the silvery bonds that wrapped her body. 'What is this? How do I get you out of it?'

She tipped her head towards the corner where the Spinner still sheltered under his blankets. 'Those are his doing. I don't think he means any harm, but he's confused.'

As she spoke, three of the Spinner's long legs rose out of the pile of blankets and fussily pulled them closer to the bulk of his body. Frith cleared his throat.

'And what is that, exactly?'

It took some time for Wydrin to fill him in. All the while the creature she named as the Spinner did not speak, but instead quivered slightly beneath his blankets. Periodically, Frith tried to tear the bonds that surrounded her, but it was like trying to tear through wire. It cut at his hands, and his left hand was already so swollen as to be of no use.

'So this creature, the Spinner, has been a prisoner of the woman you speak of for some time?'

'She has been torturing information out of him, I think. I have seen burn marks on his flesh, and he is afraid of her.' She lowered her voice. 'Look at the size of him. Do you think they could keep him in this chamber if he weren't afraid?'

Frith looked over at the pile of furs and blankets. Sweat was soaking his shirt, and his head was throbbing, but Wydrin was here. He blinked sweat out of his eyes. 'Torture becomes its own prison. It can bind you, and ruin you.' He forced himself to his feet, and took a few steps towards the towering mass of blankets. 'Spinner, I am Lord Aaron Frith of the Blackwood. A friend of yours sent me to help you.'

The quivering under the blankets seemed to pause.

'Who? Who sent you?' The voice was unlike anything Frith had heard before. He pressed his lips into a thin line and forced himself to concentrate.

'I do not know the being's name,' he said. 'But I believe it to be the spirit of this place. I asked it for help, and it gave me a path to this camp. It asked me to look for you. It was concerned . . . it was concerned that you were not where you should be.'

The blankets shivered again, and a high-pitched keening noise filled the room.

'They took me!' cried the Spinner. One bristled claw edged out from under the furs, scratching at the mud floor. 'The Eye is open and I am not there to shepherd what comes through. And now she intends to travel through it, to take her knife and twist it in the past so that all comes unravelled. Oh, oh the cycle, it will all be ruined, and I cannot—'

'It's all right.' Frith could feel his body recoiling – there was an instinct to put distance between himself and this many-legged creature – but there was something else too. There were layers of magic to the Spinner, new and alien magic he had never felt

197

before. He wasn't even sure he *could* have felt it before. He thought of the spirit he had spoken to at the pond, how it had told him it would make him 'open to magic'. Frith reached out and placed his hand on the black flesh of the Spinner's leg. He could see scars there, as Wydrin had said. Burn marks. Frith felt a twisting in his gut, and his head pounded all the harder. 'They have hurt you, but they won't do it again. We are here to help you.'

'That's right,' said Wydrin. Her face was a pale shape in the shadows. 'We're the Black Feather Three. Remember what I told you? Stopping people like Estenn is all part of our job.'

'We just need you to talk to us,' continued Frith. 'Tell us, as calmly as you can, everything that is happening here. We need to understand. And then we can help.'

For a time, no one spoke. Frith sat, his hand on the Spinner's leg. The pain in his hand was like a banked fire, hot and constant. Eventually Wydrin spoke up, her voice low.

'The main force has left the camp. I've been listening. Whatever it is Estenn intends to do, she is on her way to do it.'

Frith nodded, but when he spoke it was to the Spinner. 'They have hurt you, cut you off from all hope. In the end, all your days and nights became the same – a litany of pain, and a desperate struggle to hold on to what you are. The prison closed in all around you until the safest thing was not to move, not to speak. Perhaps, you think, if you keep very, very still, they will forget you are here. You make yourself a small thing, in the desperate hope that you can cling to the last pieces of what you are.' Frith looked at the ground, remembering. 'In the end, all that was left of me was my anger. It was enough for my survival, but to live, I had to accept the help of others. We are here to help you now, Spinner. There is some trust left in you, I think.'

After a moment, the blankets shifted.

'There is poison in your hand,' said the Spinner. His voice was calm now, if still uncertain. 'I can feel it through your skin. I can help.'

Frith nodded. 'I would be very glad of that.'

The blankets and furs shifted and fell away, revealing the vast bulk of the Spinner. Frith kept his face still and his head down as multiple legs flexed and twisted around him. Two claws gently took hold of his injured hand and turned it over between them. Oddly, Frith was reminded of the nanny who had cared for him as a child; when he had a splinter in his finger or had grazed his knee, her careful touch had been the same.

'Yes, poison,' said the Spinner. 'And from something new, too. Without me there to sculpt the webs and tend the Eye, new life is spawning with no restrictions. Hmm.' Two more legs appeared, turning a strange substance between their claws – it looked to Frith like liquid moonlight, a white shining fluid that shone with multiple colours, much as Gwiddion's wings had. As he watched, the Spinner pulled this substance into long tremulous shapes, twisting and re-forming all the time.

'What are you doing?' asked Wydrin from the floor. 'I can't see.'

The Spinner ignored her. Almost faster than his eye could follow, the deft claws spun the pearly substance around Frith's injured hand, quickly forming a glove that clung to the swollen flesh. It was blessedly cool, and almost immediately Frith felt better.

'What is this?' he asked, his voice hushed. The Spinner curled the last of the substance around his fingers, and then drew his claws away.

'The shell will harden, drawing out the poison,' he said in a matter-of-fact tone. 'When it is done, it will simply crack and fall away.'

'Thank you,' said Frith. He held up his hand. It now looked as though he were wearing an exquisitely crafted glove made of mother-of-pearl. Already he could feel the sweat drying on his forehead. 'You can make extraordinary things, Spinner.'

'It is my purpose', said the Spinner softly, 'to care for life, to see it to fruition.'

'Hey, this is all brilliant and everything,' called Wydrin, 'but do you think you could let me out of this cocoon now?'

Frith looked up at the Spinner. He was holding a white mask, of all things, that appeared to be made from the same stuff as the healing glove. The Spinner shrugged – no easy feat with nine legs.

'I put you inside that to keep you safe,' said the Spinner, in a slightly reproachful tone. 'They cannot harm you if I keep you close.'

Even so, he stepped over Frith – such grace for such an enormous creature – and scooped Wydrin up into his many arms. Frith felt a surge of alarm at seeing her picked up so easily, but then the claws snipped away at the web holding her in place, and the Spinner placed her carefully back onto the floor. She stumbled, walking awkwardly on legs that had been stuck in the same place for hours.

'I will tell you now,' said the Spinner. 'Tell you all I know. Yes? And then you can stop her?'

'That's right,' said Wydrin. Frith went to her and she kissed him firmly on the mouth, pressing one hand to his cheek as she did so. There would be time for words later. 'The so-called Emissary is going to regret crossing the Black Feather Three.'

31

'The Eye of Euriale is where new gods are born.'

They were sitting in a rough circle, the small oil lamp wedged in the dirt between them. The Spinner had thrown off the blankets and furs, although he still clasped the mask, so small against the bulk of his body. Frith held his injured arm out awkwardly in front of him, the white glove on his hand shining oddly in the lamplight. Wydrin regarded him quietly. He looked like he'd been dragged backwards through an angry bush, but it was him. He was safe.

'New gods?'

'The island has ever been the cradle of Ede,' continued the Spinner. 'When the old gods die or simply fade away, the Eye of Euriale opens again, and new life is born. It is my job to be there for those new lives, to spin the webs as they come through. I sing them their history, I help to shape the forms they must have, and I *control* the process. Without someone to funnel the energies and spin the webs, it – anything could happen.' A quivering had returned to the Spinner's voice – he controlled it with obvious effort. 'Estenn and her soldiers came to me when I was preparing for the Eye to open. In the past, humans have come here and built their shrines, and then they have left again. This is not a place where humans can live unchanged. The magic is too strong.'

'Estenn claims to have lived here for decades,' said Wydrin. 'She also claims to be around seventy or eighty years old, though she looks no older than me. I've also seen her fade away, become invisible. It seems that living on the island for so long has certainly changed her.'

The Spinner dipped the mask in apparent agreement. 'The island's magic has given her long life, and strange abilities. She is a zealot, and Euriale's magic has only strengthened that.' Wydrin stretched out her legs and winced; she still had pins and needles. 'When they came to me, I was surprised. Frightened. I fear I did not put up much of a fight. They pierced me all over with darts, and my consciousness dimmed. When I awoke, I was here. Then there were questions. So many questions.'

Frith leaned forward. 'What does Estenn intend to do?'

'She does not want new gods. She wants the old ones, the ones she has given her heart to. She intends to bring them back.'

'How can she do that?' Wydrin glanced back towards the chamber entrance, but it was still empty. 'Y'Ruen is gone, and O'rin died in Skaldshollow.'

'While the Eye is open, everything is in flux,' said the Spinner. He sounded nervous now. 'All of Ede's history lies beyond it. If she possesses an item forged in Ede's distant past, an item forged in both Edeian and Edenier, she can travel back through the Eye. It is possible.'

'Travel back?' Wydrin cleared her throat. Despite the warmth of the chamber her arms were covered in goosebumps. 'Travel where, exactly?'

'Into the distant past. Back to the time before the Citadel was constructed. Back before the mages laid their trap.'

Wydrin met Frith's eyes. 'She has your staff,' she said. 'If she can go back to that time and sabotage the Citadel, then the gods will never be trapped there. Y'Ruen, the Twins, Y'Gria, the whole bleedin' lot of them will be free.'

'And if the gods are not trapped there, they will continue to exist, waging their wars down through history,' added the Spinner. 'Everything you thought to be true – all of Ede's history – will be changed for ever.'

'This is madness!' cried Frith. 'The mages created the Citadel because the gods were out of control. Their war was destroying

Ede – everyone knows this, it is the oldest lesson in our history books, to change it would be insanity.'

'Of the gifts that Euriale gave Estenn, a crippling madness was one,' said the Spinner sadly. 'She cares not for the consequences, only for the glory of her forgotten gods.'

Wydrin shook her head slowly. 'Can she do this? Is it really possible to travel back to the past through this Eye of yours?'

The white mask nodded frantically. 'Oh yes, certainly. And once there she can unpick the tapestry of history. She is strong, fanatical, and, as you have pointed out, she has abilities a human should not possess. I fear it would not be difficult for her to destroy the mages' plans.'

Wydrin met Frith's eyes. 'We have to stop her before she gets to the Eye. I didn't fly halfway around Ede to put that dragon through the sky only for some madwoman with a tattoo fixation to just bloody pop it back into existence again.'

'There is more to it than that,' said Frith, his voice grave. 'Do you not see? If the gods were not interred in the Citadel, the war with the mages would have carried on, with untold death and destruction. The world as we know it now would not exist. There is no predicting what we might be left with.'

Next to them, the white mask of the Spinner nodded frantically. 'All the threads, undone,' he said. 'The tapestry of history destroyed.'

'What do you want to do?' asked Frith.

Wydrin smiled lopsidedly at him, although a cold hand clutched at her heart. 'Go and save my mum from a bunch of bloodthirsty pirates, or save the world from the tyrannical reign of half-mad gods?' She lifted her hands and then put them back on her knees. 'From past experience, I'd have to say that my mother has always been able to look after herself, whereas the world seems to be getting into this sort of trouble every few months just lately.' She turned back to the Spinner. 'We have to get out of here, my friend, and you're going to take us to this Eye. We'll try to get there first, and stop Estenn the bloody Emissary before she even tries anything.'

'I can take you there,' said the Spinner, his voice quavering, 'but there are men and women outside, and they have knives and darts, fire and lamps that burn, and they poke at me.' The Spinner took a shuddering breath. 'How will we get out?'

'I don't know if you've noticed,' said Wydrin, 'but you're a giant armoured spider. If you want to leave this shit hole, I'm pretty sure you can.'

The keening noise came back, and the white mask trembled in the grip of the Spinner's claw. 'Oh no, no, I make things, I care for things, I weave and I preserve. I cannot threaten, I cannot hurt.'

'You must be strong,' said Frith. 'Get us outside, and we can take care of the rest. There will be weapons out there, and once we're armed again, we can fight our way out.'

Wydrin looked at Frith, noting how he kept his gaze steady. He knew their chances of fighting their way out of the camp were slim, but he was working to build up the Spinner's courage. Without it, they would be doomed.

'Fighting,' repeated the Spinner. 'There will be fighting.'

'Don't you worry about that,' said Wydrin. 'We're professionals. We just need you to give them a bit of a surprise.'

For a few moments the Spinner was silent. Wydrin thought she could hear hammering going on above them, but much less movement now.

'The discordance of the Eye grows worse by the moment,' said the Spinner eventually. 'I can feel it, as though every strand of my web is trembling, and the one who calls herself the Emissary will only make it worse. She will destroy the whole web, if she is allowed to continue.' Slowly, the Spinner rose up on its great legs, filling the chamber with its bulk. 'I cannot allow that. Yes, I will come with you – if you help me, please.'

Wydrin stood up, smiling in the dark. 'Slowly now,' she said, pitching her voice low. 'Let's see what they've got waiting for us.'

Ahead of them the entrance to the tunnel was a bright semi-circle of light. After a few moments, a slim figure came into view, a spear slung casually over one shoulder. As they watched, the figure bent to pick something off her boots, and then stood up with one hand on her hip. From the posture of her body, Wydrin guessed that she wasn't enjoying her guard duty, and wanted to be elsewhere. Of course, thought Wydrin, she wants to be with

Lady Fanatical, busily messing about with history. They waited a few more moments, and were rewarded with another figure coming into view. This was a young man, and he wore his spear across his back. There was a bottle in his hand.

'I think this may be our best chance,' whispered Wydrin. She turned to look at the Spinner lurking in the tunnel behind them. His great bulk filled it, the tiny white mask held in one trembling claw. 'Are you ready, Spinner?'

The Spinner said nothing, although the mask shook so much she wondered if he might drop it.

'Do not worry,' said Frith. He reached up and placed his fingers on the leathery black flesh of the Spinner's leg. 'We will be right behind you.'

The Spinner trembled all over. *If he starts that keening noise again,* thought Wydrin, *we'll have lost this,* but instead he gently placed the mask on the floor, and stepped over them, moving nimbly on his nine legs.

Wydrin had one last view of the two guards outlined against the daylight, and then the Spinner rushed up the tunnel towards them. He could move shockingly fast, and in moments they heard screams as the Spinner barrelled out of the tunnel entrance into daylight. Wydrin was already running, Frith close behind her.

Outside the two guards were on the ground. The girl still lay where the Spinner had knocked her over, a stunned expression on her face, while the young man was struggling to his feet, already reaching for the spear on his back. Frith ran up to him and without hesitation struck him firmly on the back of his head with the solid glove that the Spinner had made him. It cracked down the middle and the pieces fell to the floor, while the young guard pitched forward onto his face, unconscious.

Wydrin kicked the girl's spear away from her grasping fingers and then punched her in the face, breaking her nose. The girl gave an outraged squawk before Wydrin grabbed her by the collar and dragged her to her feet.

'Give me the dagger off that lad's belt,' she said to Frith, who was already reaching for it. He handed her the blade and she held it to the girl's throat.

'Shout for help and I'll open your throat to the sky.'

The girl spat blood from her lips. Her eyes kept moving back to the Spinner, who was crouching next to them with his legs held tightly around his enormous body. Wydrin wanted to look too – she could feel the strangeness radiating off him like a fever – but she kept her eyes focussed on the girl.

'You're too late.' The girl wriggled in Wydrin's grip, so she pressed the blade more firmly to her neck. 'The Emissary is already on her way to do the work of the gods. You're all going to die.'

'I don't know, kid. If I were you, I'd avoid the whole "you are doomed" speech and try complimenting me instead. I'm not in the best of moods as it is.'

She looked around. The area by the tunnel entrance appeared to be deserted, but she could still hear the sounds of hammering coming from nearby.

'Where is everyone?' she asked the girl. Next to her, Frith was flexing the fingers on his left hand. It no longer looked infected at all.

'We must now prepare for the changing of the world,' said the girl. She pushed her lower lip out like a child told to go to bed early. 'The godless will die screaming soon enough.'

'The girl is an idiot,' said Frith evenly. 'Perhaps we should go and look for ourselves?'

Wydrin nodded. They walked down the dirt track together, Wydrin dragging the girl with the dagger at her throat, while the Spinner came along behind them, looming like a tame storm cloud. Trees pressed in at either side, filled as ever with the cacophony of bird song and the calls of other animals making their homes in the trees. In the clearing at the bottom of the track they found the rest of Estenn's cultists.

'We prepare ourselves,' said the girl again, a note of pride in her voice. 'When the old gods are restored to us, they will know that we alone have remained loyal and not forgotten them.'

'Did I tell you to speak?' said Wydrin, but with little bite. Her attention was taken by the scene in the clearing. The remaining members of Estenn's fanatics – mostly, from the looks of them, the old and the young and the sick – were busily building a shrine in the middle of the square. The tanning racks and cooking fires had all been cleared away, and the small wooden shacks they lived in had been torn down; the wood was being repurposed to build this new message to the gods, alongside what looked like an awful lot of human bones, picked clean and carefully bleached until they shone white. Wydrin saw a great wooden dragon curling around in a circle, its wings made of human thigh bones, splayed against the ground and bound together with sheets of what looked like thin pinkish leather – she didn't want to dwell too long on what it might actually be. Inside the circle created by the dragon was a tall wooden woman, her roughly carved face still oddly beautiful, with braided jungle vines falling from the back of her head making up Y'Gria's famous green hair; her gown was a clattering weave of human rib bones. Off to one side Wydrin saw what must have been their depiction of O'rin; a squat figure covered in a cloak of glossy leaves, its head that of a great owl, with two plates of shining metal as his eyes. *He didn't look like that*, she thought, distractedly. *They've got his beak all wrong.*

And rising above the rest of them, two enormous wolves, their mouths open to bare snarling teeth, surely collected from every type of animal that inhabited this stinking island, along with many donated by those men and women foolish enough to venture beyond Two-Birds. One was painted white, the other black. Res'na and Res'ni, twin gods of order and chaos.

As they stood there, one or two of the cultists noticed them, and turned to watch, although no one seemed especially alarmed.

'You have escaped the chamber,' said one old man. He had plaited his beard into two points, one side of which he had covered with thick black paint. More of the cultists turned towards them, and Wydrin pressed the dagger a little closer to the girl's throat.

'Very observant,' said Wydrin. 'I can see why Estenn keeps you people around. Where's everyone else? Is everyone in this clearing? Answer my questions or see your little friend here bleed into the dirt.'

The old man shrugged. 'It hardly matters now,' he said in a patient tone of voice, as though explaining something to a well-meaning idiot. 'Kill the girl, or don't – she has been a true servant of the gods, and they will not abandon her. The new age of the Twins starts soon.' He took a breath, and then continued. 'The Emissary took our best fighters with her to the Eye of Euriale. As the new age approaches, the island itself convulses with joy, and it can be a dangerous time, even for one as gifted as her. Those of us who cannot fight or travel swiftly, it is our job to prepare the first message to the gods, so that they might recognise their true servants.' He gestured to the elaborate shrine taking shape behind him. Next to him, several other men and women nodded in agreement. 'This is our last task.'

Wydrin looked around at the dismantled shelters, the filled-in fire pits.

'What do you expect to happen?' asked Frith next to her. 'Truly?'

The man with the pointed beard drew himself up to his full height. 'We will be risen up, as the chosen ones, and live with the gods themselves.'

Wydrin barked laughter, and gestured at the shrine with her dagger. 'If Y'Ruen suddenly appears back in the world, she will burn you all up in the blink of an eye. She won't even see any of this. She cares nothing for you. She cares nothing for human lives at all. None of them do.' *Save for O'rin, maybe*, she added silently.

The old man peeled back his lip in a sneer. 'No, it is you who will burn.'

Wydrin shook her head in disgust. 'Fine, whatever makes you happy, I suppose. How long ago did Estenn and her favourite idiots leave?'

'At dawn yesterday,' replied the old man. 'It will be very soon now. Very soon.'

Wydrin took the dagger away from the girl's throat and shoved her forward, as hard as she could. She sprawled into the dirt with a cry.

'We are already more than a day behind,' said Frith in a low voice. 'We have little hope of catching up with her, let alone getting to the Eye before Estenn.'

'Actually,' the Spinner cleared his throat behind them, 'I had an idea about that.'

32

'Are you sure that this is wise?'

Frith stood watching Wydrin oil her sword, carefully cleaning it and its scabbard before reattaching it to her belt, alongside the small knife with the mother-of-pearl shark on the handle. They had found her weapons in a storage hut off to one side of the square; none of the cultists left behind by Estenn made any move to stop them, so absorbed were they in the completion of their strange shrine. As they feared, there had been no sign of Frith's staff; Estenn would have ensured that she took her key to travelling to the past with her.

'I don't see that we have much choice, not if we want to catch up.' Wydrin held up Frostling, balancing it on the palm of her hand as she peered down the blade. 'And the Spinner wants to help.'

Frith looked up. They were outside the settlement now, in a thick copse of trees. The Spinner seemed to prefer being up in the canopy to walking along the ground, and he hung above them, a dark nightmarish shape half hidden in the branches. There was, Frith couldn't help noticing, a twisted mass of scars where his cluster of legs joined his body – it must have been quite the job to remove the Spinner's leg, but it seemed Estenn had been determined. Frith felt a slow spark of anger in his chest, and he prepared to nurture it.

'You will be perfectly safe,' came the Spinner's querulous voice. 'It is the swiftest way to traverse the isle of the gods.'

Frith sighed. Wydrin, having adjusted her sword belt, came over and took his arm. Her red hair fell over her forehead in a messy clump, and she smiled at him lopsidedly. 'Let's face it, at this point, we've done things a lot more ridiculous than this.'

He nodded once. 'I follow where you lead.'

She turned to the Spinner. 'We're ready,' she said. 'As ready as we're likely to get, anyway.'

The Spinner trembled, before lowering himself towards them on a thin wire of spider web. Seeing that many-legged shape descending on them so swiftly made all the hairs on the back of Frith's neck stand up, but he forced himself not to flinch. Not while Wydrin stood next to him.

'Which of you would like to go first?' The Spinner sounded almost shy.

'I will.' Wydrin stepped forward and lifted her arms up. 'I've done it before, more or less.'

The process was very quick. The Spinner swept Wydrin up with his many legs, handling her as delicately as a nurse holding a newly born child. He turned her round and round, spinning his silvery web at the same time, gradually covering her lower body, and then her upper half, in the web. This time, Wydrin kept her arms up out of the way so that they were free of the silver threads. She settled Frostling, secure in its scabbard, by her side so that she could reach it if it were needed. Once she was covered, the Spinner tucked her up next to the great bulk of his body, attaching her there with more thread and ribbons of web. When it was done, she waved down at Frith cheerily enough.

'Are you now ready, Lord Aaron Frith of the Blackwood?' the Spinner asked in a solemn tone.

Frith took a slow breath. They had wasted enough time already. 'Do it,' he said.

The Spinner snatched him up, bristled legs handling him as if he weighed nothing at all. When the first loops of web closed around his legs, it took all his strength of will not to kick out against them. Instead, he pursed his lips and let it happen, trying not to think about the alien intelligence now rendering him immobile, or the drop to the forest floor below. The web strands were firm but not overly tight, and soon they covered him up to his chest. Like Wydrin, he kept his arms out of the way.

When the Spinner was satisfied with his work, Frith was positioned next to Wydrin, tucked next to her as gently and as firmly as a child being put to bed. He looked at her, and saw his own bemusement mirrored on her face. She grinned at him, and Frith found himself laughing uneasily. For a moment, everything in his life seemed too strange. What had happened to the straightforward life his father had planned for him at Blackwood Keep? There would have been no magical giant spiders in that life, no word-magic, no dragons or gods. But then, he suspected there wouldn't have been as much laughter in that life, and certainly no red-headed sell-swords.

'You are ready,' said the Spinner. There was an unmistakable note of pride in his voice. The white mask dipped into their field of view, held at the end of one hairy leg. 'Shall we go?'

'Let's do it, Spinner,' said Wydrin. 'We've got some catching up to do.'

The mask nodded once, and then swept out of sight. Abruptly the world spun around them and Frith gasped as his stomach turned over; the Spinner was climbing up, up into the very tops of the trees, moving with a fleetness that Frith could barely have guessed at. The ground vanished from view, and instead they saw the dark interior roof of the forest, lit with a glow filtered green through a thousand leaves, and fractured with the dense nests of monkeys and birds. He heard Wydrin exclaim next to him, her voice filled with wonder, and then they were off, shooting through this hidden world at remarkable speed. They moved up and down as the Spinner picked their route across Euriale, sometimes swinging so low that they saw the forest floor again, sometimes so high that they broke through the canopy entirely to catch brief glimpses of the emerald ocean that surrounded them.

Frith reached over and took Wydrin's hand, squeezing it firmly. 'If I should vomit, please do not tell your mother.'

* * *

'There it is, look.'

Sebastian pointed down the hill where it was just about possible to make out wisps of smoke from cooking fires. The scout they had captured slouched between him and Oster, looking moodily at his feet. Once they had found the well-worn trail, they had hardly needed the scout to guide them, but Sebastian did not want to kill him just yet.

'It is close,' agreed Oster. He nodded, and then looked back over his shoulder to the dense foliage behind them. All was quiet, for now. 'We will not make it before they catch up, I think.'

Sebastian shook his head. The morning before, they had been swarmed by a pack of lizards that ran on their back legs. Each of them came up to Sebastian's waist, their mottled leathery skins giving them the colours of the trees. Their teeth had been sharp, their eyes hungry, and Sebastian and the scout had only survived by scrambling up the nearest tree. Oster had turned into his dragon form and curled his body around the trunk of the tree, opening his jaws and challenging the creatures. Hisses and roars had been exchanged, until the smaller lizards retreated, swarming back into the trees where they were lost to shadows again, but Sebastian had felt their reluctance keenly: a silver shiver in his blood. When he'd asked Oster if he'd been able to communicate with the animals, he had just shrugged. 'I could exchange little more than impressions. I tried to tell them that we weren't food or a threat, but in their minds we are slow moving, and full of warm blood. I warned them off by my size alone, I think, but they will be back.'

And so they were. For the last day both he and Oster had sensed the strange lizards at their backs, following just out of sight. Sebastian could feel their hunger as an echo of his own, clouding his mind and making it difficult to concentrate. They were being hunted.

'There's little we can do either way,' said Sebastian. 'Let's get down the hill, and hope they wait for us to be behind some wooden walls before they attack.'

With Oster keeping one heavy hand on the scout's shoulder, the three of them moved rapidly down the slope. Sebastian saw a number of what he took to be markers – wooden stakes painted black and white, some topped with skulls – and then they were into the settlement itself.

'Where is everyone?' He gave the scout a small shake, but the man just looked down at his feet.

They headed to the centre of the settlement, passing extinguished cooking fires and partially dismantled huts, until they came to what Sebastian supposed passed for a village square. All the people were here, surrounding a great wooden shrine; they knelt in the dirt with their heads bowed, utterly silent. Sebastian looked at the shrine itself, and felt a worm of worry twist sickly in his gut.

'You there!' He called to the group of people, but no one answered. No one even looked around at him. They stayed silent, their attention focussed on the hastily built wooden idols that towered over them. 'Answer me!'

When nothing happened, he turned to the scout. The man's eyes were wide, and transfixed by the shrine.

'What is going on?'

'It is time,' he said in a hushed voice. 'The Emissary has gone to the Eye of Euriale to restore the gods.'

Abruptly he pulled away from Oster's grip, displaying a strength they hadn't guessed at. He stumbled over to the crowd of prostrate worshippers and fell to his knees with them.

'I haven't finished with you,' said Sebastian. The hunger of the lizards was making him irritable. Without thinking about it too closely, he concentrated instead on the silver thread that was Oster's presence. 'You will tell us where the Spinner is being kept or I will kill you.'

'It hardly matters now,' called the scout, not looking at them. 'It's north of here, at the edge of the settlement. There's a tunnel that leads to a chamber.' He paused, then added, 'kill me if you want, my place is here now. We lend our strength to the Emissary.'

Sebastian sighed, and started walking north. 'Come on, we'll get no sense out of this sorry lot.'

In any case they found the chamber quickly enough. There were deep scuff marks in the dirt outside, and other strange prints that Sebastian couldn't identify. On the ground by the entrance he found shattered pieces of what looked like a white glove. He turned them over in his hands.

'This is made from the same material as the masks we found in the Spinner's home,' he said. 'I'm sure of it.'

Oster nodded, and picked up a discarded oil lamp at the entrance and rekindled it, casting orange light into the dark mouth of the tunnel. Sebastian put the white shards into his pocket.

'Is there anything more you can tell me about the Spinner?' he asked Oster. 'Anything that might be useful to know before we go exploring in the dark?'

Oster looked at him, his expression closed. 'Nothing that you need to know, human.'

Sebastian looked away, suddenly missing Wydrin and her instinct for lies. She would know if he were leading them into a trap. Oster was arrogant and haughty, and yet at the same time Sebastian could feel how lost he was through the strange connection he felt to the man – the thread that connected them spoke of no lies. It was very disorientating.

They walked together down the dirt tunnel, and although there were more of the strange scuff marks, the chamber below was empty. Sebastian was unsure whether he was relieved or disappointed.

'He was here,' said Oster. He had wedged the oil lamp into the dirt and was standing next to the packed dirt wall. He rested his fingers there lightly. 'I can smell him. The shape of him filled this place for some time.'

There were lots of furs and blankets heaped into one corner, all permeated with a weird, alien funk, and wiry strands of silvery material were strewn across the floor. Sebastian took the broken pieces of the glove out of his pocket and turned them over in his hands. He thought of the Second – how he and the brood sister had hunted in the woods together, her yellow eyes fixed on their prey.

'Oster, how is your sense of smell?'

The other man looked up in surprise.

214

'I mean, not now, as such, but when you're . . . in your other guise. Are you aware of scents?'

'Of course,' said Oster. 'The island is alive with smells like colours, a riot of them. My perceptions are much greater than a mere human's.'

Sebastian held out the shards, and Oster took them, a faintly bemused expression on his face. 'Good. We know he was here recently, and now we know that he's left. I think you could follow that scent, when you're in your other form. There can't be many other things that smell like the Spinner.'

Oster narrowed his eyes. 'The Spinner's scent would be unique, as he is.' He tipped the shards to his face, his nostrils flaring. 'It is very clear, and will become clearer. I think—' He stopped, and shook his head. 'Can you feel that?'

A second later, Sebastian did. A great silver rumble, building in volume, roared through his blood. For a moment, the room spun around him and he thought he might fall to his knees, but Oster's arm was there, steadying him.

'What is it?' he asked, although he already knew. The lizards were coming.

They ran out of the tunnel and back to the square. The men and women of the camp were still there, motionless in the dirt.

'Get up, you idiots!' Sebastian yelled, waving his arms even though none of them were looking at him. 'There is danger coming here, and fast. You need to get to shelter.' He looked around. 'If you're out of sight you're probably safe.'

The men and women did not move. Next to him, Oster shrugged.

'Here, you.' Sebastian went over to the scout who was still kneeling in the mud, his forehead pressed to the dirt. 'Those beasts we ran into before are nearly here. You know what'll happen when they arrive.' He poked the man in the ribs with his boot, but he didn't move. 'They're nearly here, and they're hungry.'

'The gods will protect us,' muttered the scout directly to the mud. 'We are the children of Euriale, the chosen few. We must send our strength to the Emissary – that is our only task now.'

Sebastian swore and stepped away. The proximity of the lizards was making it difficult to think clearly.

'We should go.' Oster glanced to the south. 'They're in the settlement now. They are coming.'

As the words left his mouth, Sebastian saw them; beasts moving at an alarming speed, their reptilian necks stretched out before them, teeth flashing in the sun. The hunger they brought with them was a crashing wave.

'You cannot speak to them?' asked Sebastian, knowing it was useless. He and Oster were already turning, already running. 'As you did the other . . . monster?'

'They are too new,' said Oster. 'The Eye brings them forth with no thought, no reason, and we share less and less blood. And I feel no urge to protect those who took the Spinner from me.'

Sebastian glanced back just before they reached the treeline. He saw the great lizards piling into the square and stopping, apparently surprised by the bounty that met them. They called to each other, strange fluting noises like birds. Sebastian saw a couple of the worshippers look up at that, finally distracted from their strange vigil, and he saw the look of horror that passed over their faces.

'There's nothing we can do,' he muttered, wondering whom he spoke to.

They slipped into the trees as the first screams split the air.

33

'It is the only way. We are simply not covering the ground fast enough.'

Sebastian looked up from the simple supper he'd prepared himself. They were now some distance from the cultists' base – far enough to feel reasonably safe from the swarm of lizards that had overrun the camp. Oster had had no trouble picking up the Spinner's scent, and had moved with increasing purpose, so swiftly that Sebastian had struggled to keep up.

'It's weird.' Sebastian took a bite from the fruit he'd found. It tasted like an apple, but the flesh was softer. 'I have only the faintest understanding of what you are, and I – well, I wouldn't be comfortable with it.'

Oster turned to him too sharply, his amber eyes ablaze. 'We must hurry! It's not just the absence of the Spinner. It's the island itself. The life that spawns here is growing out of control. I can feel it all around, restless and chaotic. You saw the creatures that swarmed the camp.' He looked more closely at Sebastian. 'And I know that you felt them, too.'

Above them the sky was violet, the edges pink with the setting sun.

'I don't know what you mean.'

For a moment, Oster said nothing at all. Then he shook his head. 'Is this what humans are like? Desperate to avoid the truth? Or so dense that they cannot see what is right in front of them?'

He bared his teeth in what was almost a grin. 'Except human is not what you are. Not completely. You seek to ignore that which lifts you above warm-blooded idiot kin, because you are a fool.'

Sebastian bit his lip to keep himself from surging to his feet. To fight with this man – or whatever he was – would only end badly for him. He forced the anger down, determined not to dwell on Oster's words. 'You know nothing of me.'

The silence drew out between them, filled with the hoots and calls of the animals and birds that surrounded them. Was it Sebastian's imagination, or did the very calls sound more agitated? Were there more of them? If Oster were right, and Euriale was in the grip of some sort of mass population surge, then the little town of Two-Birds could be in a lot of trouble. The pirates there were good at turning their backs on the mysteries of the island, but what if it came looking for them with tooth and claw?

'I can make it easier for you,' said Oster. Sebastian looked up in surprise. Oster's voice was softer, and he was looking away into the night. 'I will go slowly at first, until you are used to it.'

Sebastian found himself thinking of the night he had spent outside the cave with Prince Dallen. *We could take it slowly*, he had said. He turned away and threw the remains of the fruit into the bushes, hoping that Oster didn't see the colouring of his cheeks.

'All right,' he said, standing up and wiping juice on the backs of his trousers. 'I will try it at least.'

Oster met his eyes briefly, before nodding and looking away. He stepped back from Sebastian to give himself room, and then light began to peel off him in waves, white and cream and gold. Sebastian watched with his eyes half shut against the glare; it was extraordinary, every time he saw it. When the lights died away, there was Oster the dragon; twenty feet long and glittering with shining scales. The great reptilian head turned towards Sebastian and fixed deep amber eyes on him. It was strange, but that haughty look was becoming familiar, in both of Oster's forms.

Cautiously, Sebastian moved to the dragon's side. His back was ridged with spines and small, tough horns, and underneath the white and gold scales muscles clenched and unclenched. There certainly didn't appear to be anywhere comfortable to sit.

'Wait a moment,' he told Oster, before walking back to the treeline. There were plants with huge fleshy green leaves, each as big as the piece of stone slate his mother had used to knead her dough on. He picked several of them, before stripping length after length of wiry vine from a tree twisted with the stuff. Finally, he took off his outer shirt and folded it up into a rough ball; it had seen better days, anyway. 'Hold still.'

With some difficulty he put together a makeshift saddle, or at least a padded area on Oster's back held in place with tough vines. Once seated there he could reach forward and take hold of the longer horns growing out of the dragon's neck. He shifted in place, trying to distribute his weight evenly. It wasn't as ungainly as he'd expected.

'This is as good as it's going to get, I think,' he said aloud. After a moment, Oster lurched forward, and despite himself Sebastian yelped. The sense of strength just below him was unnerving; he was reminded of the sea wyverns of the northern lands, and how they had surged through the water like knives.

There was something else though, too. He placed his right hand flat to the scales on Oster's side, and felt that silvery bond between them open like a flower in his mind. Oster seemed to sense it, and moved a little faster, weaving between the trees easily, his long tail curling on behind them.

'You *were* born here,' said Sebastian, his voice hoarse with wonder. Through Oster he could feel the living island, the tenuous heartbeat of all that lived here. It was obvious now that Oster was deeply connected to it all, as was everything that spawned under its trees. 'We can go faster,' he said, then added, 'if you wish.'

He knew then that Oster could not stumble, could not take the wrong path or get them lost. It was unthinkable. Oster was a child of Euriale and dragon blood roared in his veins. They could not fail.

There was an answering rumble from Oster, as though he agreed, and they sprinted off through the jungle together.

34

'I think that's going to be tricky to travel across, even for you, Spinner.'

Frith turned – awkward in his spider-web harness – to look at Wydrin as she spoke. They hung in the branches of a tree taller than any he'd seen in the Blackwood, and her unruly hair half covered her face. The tree was perched on the edge of a cliff, and below them was a lagoon, the water a deep, rich blue. On the far side was a wide stretch of beach, the sand bone white, and lying like a great beached whale was the wreckage of a ship, the furthest tip resting on the sand and the bulk of it in the water. It was bigger even than the *Poison Chalice*, and though it was in pieces and had clearly been there for decades, he could tell it was of a shape and a design he had never seen. The wood was a deep, ruby red, the planks so tightly fitted that the thing almost looked like it had been carved from one single piece of wood. There were great holes in it, spoiling its beautiful shape, and here and there tall trees had grown up through it. Not just decades lost, he told himself, but centuries.

'We could go around,' he suggested. 'Follow this cliff edge and find the far side.'

'It would take too long,' said the Spinner. 'I can feel everything changing, even now. She grows closer to the Eye, and everything spins further and further out of balance.' The Spinner shivered all over, shaking their cocoons so that they swung slightly back and forth. It wasn't a pleasant sensation. Wydrin reached over and squeezed Frith's arm, although whether she meant to give support or take it he couldn't tell. 'If we don't stop her, if we don't stop Estenn and she passes through the Eye, oh . . .'

'It's all right, Spinner, we won't let that happen. Will we, Frith?' She squeezed his arm again.

'No,' he agreed. 'You can count on the Black Feather Three, Spinner. How do you propose we get across there?'

The Spinner climbed down the tree a short way and scrambled to the edge of the cliff. Wydrin and Frith hung suspended beneath his belly, the drop yawning below them. Frith squeezed his eyes shut briefly, and forced himself to look away from the blue water they were hanging above.

'The big stick that points out of the broken boat,' said the Spinner, pointing with one bristled claw. 'You see that?'

'The mast,' said Wydrin. The enormous wreck had split into three pieces; the central part was still partially upright, the tall central mast intact and pointing almost true. Beyond it was another section of the broken ship, with another, smaller mast; this one was nearly lost in a forest of green and brown vines, and the holes in the decking and the hull looked as deep and dark as caves. 'It looks reasonably sturdy.'

Frith looked at her again, and she gave him the tiniest shrug.

'I can shoot web towards it,' said the Spinner. 'Make a line for us to cross on. Assuming the mast, as you call it, is sturdy. Then we can move over to the next mast, and from there, the far cliff.'

Frith opened his mouth to speak, and then shut it again. The giant mast was not so far away from them, and the dark red wood it was carved from looked solid enough, but for the Spinner to attach his web to it and climb across would mean being flung across mid-air for a reasonable distance.

'If we go around,' said Wydrin quietly, 'we may not catch up with Estenn in time. And the first we'll know of it will be the thunder of Y'Ruen's wings – not trapped in the Citadel after all, but free these past thousand years to do whatever she likes. I don't know what goes on in the minds of gods, but I doubt she has any kindly feelings towards us.'

'And that's if Ede hasn't already been destroyed by the gods warring with the mages and each other. If Estenn gets through before we can stop her, we will be living in the results of whatever she chooses to do to the past.' Frith sighed, and shifted in the makeshift cocoon. 'If you believe it is our best chance, Spinner, we will take it.'

The Spinner didn't reply, but crawled up to the very edge of the cliff and teetered there for a moment. Just below them the wreck split the lagoon like some great carcass, and Frith forced himself to focus on the mast. It would be easy, he told himself. The Spinner would not misjudge the distance.

The fleshy abdomen behind them convulsed once, and they saw a shining bolt of web go arcing out across the water. It hit the mast head on, and then the Spinner lurched forward, swinging downwards abruptly so that his heavy body hung below the line he had cast. Next to Frith, Wydrin gave a small cry of surprise, and then laughed.

The Spinner scrambled down, legs pumping busily. Their view wobbled and changed; one moment it was the sky, dotted here and there with tiny white clouds, and then they would see the cliffs, or the still, blue water below. Sooner than he thought possible they were there, and the Spinner was scrambling up to the top of the mast. Now they were on the broken ship, it was possible to see exactly how rotten it was; ragged holes in the decking were fringed with virulent jungle weeds, thick with thorns and fleshy purple leaves. The wood itself was black in places, rotting away to a thin fibrous shell. Frith craned his neck, trying to look at what was directly below them, and was alarmed to see the same creeping black rot all around the bottom of the mast.

'Quickly now!' he said, raising his voice. 'To the next part of the ship before it—'

With a deafening crack the mast snapped in two, and Frith felt his stomach trying to crawl out of his throat as they abruptly dropped towards the deck. The Spinner's stomach muscles flexed again and suddenly they were flying along a new line, not towards the next, equally rotten mast, but speeding towards the broken prow. The angle was slightly off and they crashed awkwardly onto the deck, the Spinner rolling with his legs curled protectively around both of them, until they came to a stop at the bottom of the rotten forecastle.

'Shit,' said Wydrin, 'that was a bit too close for my liking.'

Frith opened his mouth to agree with her, only to see a pair of baleful yellow eyes staring at them from the huge hole in the deck. They were joined by another pair, and another. 'This ship is not uninhabited,' he said, striving to keep his voice steady. 'Spinner, if you would be so kind, I believe we should leave.'

Wydrin twisted around in her cocoon, trying to see the Spinner's face. 'I think he's stunned, Frith. He took quite a smack when we landed.'

As she spoke, a monster rose up from the hole in the deck. It had leathery skin like a lizard, and finely boned wings like a bat. An elongated head filled with flat peg-like teeth turned to regard them with eyes the colour of curdled cream, and then it opened its long mouth and screeched at them. Three more identical creatures rose up behind it, all screeching and beating their wings.

'Spinner? Spinner!' Wydrin elbowed him in the guts, but there was no response. The winged monsters came closer, cawing and snapping their jaws like agitated crows. Some took to the air, pounding them with the wind from their wings, while others skittered towards them on awkward-looking back legs, using the stunted claws at the tips of their wings as appendages to drag their bodies forwards; these were clearly animals that spent most of their time in the air, when they weren't nesting inside the wreckage of ancient ships.

'We may have to make a run for it,' said Frith. As he spoke, one of the beasts stretched out its long leathery neck and nipped at the end of one of the Spinner's legs.

Wydrin cried out. 'Get away, you big ugly bastard!' She pulled Frostling from the scabbard wedged to her side, and awkwardly began to chop away at the silvery threads holding her in place. The flying beasts edged closer, their heads cocked in an expression that was both curious and predatory. Frith waved his arms at them, and shouted.

'Come and get me, you brutes!'

The closest one, a creature with skin rippled yellow and green, turned its long head towards him and snapped its jaws together. It hopped forward on its stunted rear legs, and gave a short bark of annoyance.

'Swiftly, Wydrin,' Frith pulled against the bindings holding him in place, knowing it was useless.

'I'm going as fast as I can. This stuff is bastard hard to cut.'

The last of the threads popped free and Wydrin half jumped, half fell from her cocoon, landing heavily on the deck and drawing her short-sword Glassheart in one smooth movement. She swung a wide arc at the gathered monsters, startling them so that they drew back momentarily.

'Wydrin!'

She turned and threw Frostling towards Frith, who surprised himself by catching it easily. He turned its sharp edge on the silver threads.

'Shit, there's even more in the hull.' Wydrin planted her feet, trying to look everywhere at once. 'We're going to be surrounded in seconds.'

'We'll have to make a run for it.' The Spinner's web was unreasonably tough, even against Frostling's wickedly sharp edge. There were at least ten of the flying beasts now, with four of them in the air, their huge wings beating them with blasts of wind. As he watched, they began to circle round, pinning them in. He had only cut down to the middle of his stomach, and his legs were still trapped. 'Wydrin, go! Quickly, while there's still a way out!'

She glanced back at him over her shoulder, an outraged look on her face. 'And leave you here? Not bloody likely.'

'Go! I mean it!' His hands were sweating, his grip on the blade slipping. One of the flying beasts, obviously growing bolder now, scampered forward and snapped at Wydrin, catching her on the arm. She cried out in pain, stumbling backwards, and Frith saw spots of blood spatter the deck. 'NO!'

There was no boiling surge of Edenier in his chest, but for the barest second Frith felt as though he were outside himself – as though he were linked to the water and the air of this place.

He could feel the rotten wood below them, holding up the remains of the ship. It was already so old, all it would need would be a little push . . . there was a thunderous crack from far below and the entire ship shifted slightly to the right. Wydrin stumbled and had to scramble to stop herself from falling down the hole, while several of the flying beasts took to the air, screeching with outrage.

'What was that?' cried Wydrin. Frith shook his head, too surprised to answer – his heart thundered in his chest as though he had just run up a hill – and then behind him came the Spinner's voice, groggy and confused.

'The island, she calls,' he said.

'Spinner! Quickly, you must let me down!'

Without questioning him, the Spinner brought his claw deftly across the remaining web holding Frith in place, and he dropped down to join Wydrin on the deck. He didn't land as neatly as she did, and winced as his feet took the impact.

'Spinner!' called Wydrin without looking at him. 'Can you move? Can you get out of here?'

'I don't know. I am hurt. Everything is strange.'

Around them, the winged creatures were drawing in again, snapping their beak-like jaws together. Frith edged closer to Wydrin, and they pressed their backs together.

'We have to keep them from him,' she said, shifting into a fighting stance. 'Don't lose my dagger. I'm very fond of it.'

'Fine. Don't get killed. I'm very fond of you.'

She glanced over her shoulder at him, grinning widely, and as if they'd been waiting for her to look away, the animals surged forward.

'Look out!'

It was like being thrown into a nest of spitting snakes. The flying lizards were in an instant frenzy, snapping and lunging at them, and it was all Frith could do to swing the dagger back and forth. Keenly he longed for the Edenier; how easy it would be to throw these creatures back, to burn them or blast them with ice until all were dead.

One creature leapt forward and slammed its bony head into

Wydrin's midriff. She flew backwards, crashing to the deck. She sagged there briefly, the short sword loose in her hand. Frith turned and sank the dagger into the monster's leathery hide and felt a searing moment of satisfaction as it screeched with pain, and then it flicked its enormous wing at him and he was flung to the deck himself. There was an ominous creaking from below him, and he had a moment to wonder exactly how awful it would be to fall through into the dark, no doubt to be torn apart by an entire host of winged monsters.

A strong hand on his shoulder pulled him to his feet.

'Keep moving, princeling.' Wydrin's face was ashen, her right arm wearing a sleeve of blood. 'I say we get to the side and jump over, swim for it. If we get to the beach, we can—'

There was a resounding crash and the entire ship trembled. Wydrin and Frith clung to each other as the flying creatures all took to the air at once, like starlings startled from a tree.

'What now?'

Another monster was crawling its way over the shattered edge of the wreck: a giant, glorious lizard of cream and gold scales, its eyes like beautiful amber lamps. Frith immediately thought of Y'Ruen – only that old god matched this creature's glorious lethality. It was a dragon, and on its back was a wild man with black hair and beard, a sword held in one hand, and a look of triumph in his eyes.

Before either of them had time to react, the dragon surged across the guardrail and landed amidst the flying creatures, its jaws closing around the neck of the nearest one with a sickening crunch. The monster, instantly dead, was dropped back through the hole in the deck and then the dragon leapt, bringing down those that were trying to flee. The man riding it swung his sword and cleaved a chunk of flesh from the flank of the nearest monster, and it, too, crashed to the deck. In seconds, the flying monsters that had so menaced them were lying in pieces on the remains of the deck, their thick scarlet blood soaking into the red planks. Those that had escaped were already small shapes against the sky, fleeing for some other part of the island.

For a few moments, there was silence. The great golden dragon stood with its snout in the air, snorting like a dog tracing a scent. The man on his back was cleaning his sword with a rag, before sliding it reverentially back into its scabbard. Something about that movement, the sheer practised care of it, tickled at the back of Frith's mind, but he caught a small gasp of pain from Wydrin and the thought was lost.

'Are you all right?'

She nodded at him ruefully. 'Bastard thing bit right through my leathers. I'll have a scar, I expect, but without my armour I wouldn't have had a bloody arm.'

He pushed her hair back from her face and kissed her firmly. His heart was still beating too fast. Briefly she pulled her fingers through his hair and pressed herself to him. It was all right. She was alive. They were both alive.

'Wydrin?'

They both turned at the sound of that voice. The man with the wild hair and beard had dismounted from the dragon, and was approaching them warily. He held out one hand, as though to stave off a blow. Belatedly, Frith recognised the clear brow, the kind blue eyes. He felt a rush of something in his chest, quite unlike the Edenier, and to his surprise he found himself grinning. Next to him he felt Wydrin take a startled breath, and then let it out. He squeezed her arm, wanting her to know he was there for her.

'Sebastian!' she cried. 'You absolute fucking shithead!'

35

Wydrin had hit him, and then hugged him, and then hit him again.

Sebastian's sudden reappearance had seemed more extraordinary to her than the dragon who had turned back into a man, but now that they were all safely off the wreck and camped on the narrow beach, he could see her eyes returning to Oster again and again. There would be a time of questions now, although Sebastian couldn't imagine how they could possibly answer them all. Euriale was truly an island of mysteries.

'So that is the Spinner?'

The enormous spider-like creature was crouching off to one side, its legs held protectively around it. They had managed to coax it away from the ship and onto the sand, but it hadn't spoken a word since, and now it was quivering slightly and humming under its breath.

'He is healing himself,' said Oster in way of an answer. They had built a small fire as the daylight bled from the sky, and they sat around it now, bedraggled and blood-stained.

'And who are you again?' asked Wydrin pointedly. Sebastian had scavenged some berries and root vegetables, and they had shared them out around the fire. Between her words, Wydrin chewed on the end of something that was almost a turnip. She didn't look too happy about it. Frith had torn off a piece of his shirt and they had used it as a makeshift bandage for her arm. 'Because I don't think I have that clear in my head yet.'

Oster glared at her. 'I am Oster. That is all you need to know.'

Wydrin gestured wildly with the root vegetable. 'That's all you have to say? You don't think the turning into a dragon bit requires more explanation?'

Oster shifted where he sat. 'It is the Spinner's job to give explanations. He was to explain everything to me. It is not my place to answer questions, and certainly not yours to ask them of me.'

'I was to sing him his history,' murmured the Spinner. His voice was high and faraway, as though he spoke to someone in a dream. 'His history, his new, shining life. Each of them were to have been new and perfect, but the Eye is in flux, in flux.'

'Spinner?' asked Wydrin. 'Are you with us again?' But there was no answer.

'Obviously, something went wrong on the *Poison Chalice*,' said Sebastian. 'Why are you even on the island?'

'I could ask you the same thing!' said Wydrin, raising an eyebrow, but then she shook her head. 'It was a bloody mess. We were boarded, and I was kidnapped by this insane god-freak called Estenn, the same one who took the Spinner here prisoner. She has some ludicrous plan to go back to the time of the Citadel and stop the mages before they imprisoned the gods. She wants to bring them all back.'

'What?' Sebastian paused with a handful of berries halfway to his mouth. 'Why, by the love of Isu, would anyone want to do that?'

'She is a fanatic,' put in Frith. The young lord looked bedraggled and dirty, but his eyes blazed beneath the mop of white hair. 'Her followers call her the Emissary, and she believes it is her purpose to restore the elder gods to Ede.'

'After we went to all the trouble of getting rid of the last two, accidental and otherwise,' put in Wydrin.

'And what's more, apparently it is possible. This Eye of Euriale that the Spinner tends can act as a portal back to the past. My staff was created when the Citadel was built – it is her key to travelling back there, and now she has it.' Frith leaned back, the fire casting his face into angular shadows. 'She wants to create a world where the gods were never banished, where they lived to

229

bring the war between them and the mages to a bloody conclusion. Ede as we know it could be destroyed.'

Sebastian shook his head slowly. There was an anxious twisting in his gut, and he could feel it reflected in Oster. The silver thread that connected them vibrated with it. He could feel anger there too.

'So, we have to get to this Eye thing,' said Wydrin. She paused to chew a particularly tough piece of tuber, her face screwed up with mild distaste. 'Before Estenn does. Legs here knows where it is,' she gestured over her shoulder at the Spinner. 'He was carrying us there before that wreck turned out to be full of monsters.'

'Is there anything we can do to heal him faster?' Frith addressed Oster. 'For all we know, Estenn is already there.'

Oster shook his head, looking affronted. 'How should I know that? It was the Spinner's duty to counsel me, and thanks to the actions of these zealots he is now incapable of this. It is I who have been misused and betrayed here. I may not know my histories, but I know that I was not birthed in the Eye to provide you with answers to your inane questions. I have no interest in being useful to you.'

'Don't be ridiculous.' Wydrin stood up, chucking the last nubbin of tuber onto the fire. 'You're a dragon, and you're on our side for once. I would call that pretty useful, whether you like it or not. Sebastian, would you take a brief walk with me?'

Wydrin watched her friend out of the corner of her eye as they walked a short distance down the beach, leaving the orange glow of the fire behind. His long black hair was tangled and wild, matted in places with dirt, and his beard was the bushiest she'd ever seen it. His clothes were ragged and filthy, and he'd lost some weight, but his eyes were bright, his face animated. He simultaneously looked better and worse than when she'd last seen him.

'So what did you think you were bloody playing at?'

Sebastian sighed, and turned to look at her. 'I'm not sure I can really give you the answer to that, Wyd. I just had to get away. From the death, the fighting, the wilful courting of disaster. I

230

wanted peace, and it felt like we were sailing back into danger again.'

Wydrin cleared her throat. 'Well, you've done a great job of avoiding all that.'

Reluctantly, Sebastian smiled, and then shook his head. 'Perhaps I am cursed. After all I have done, I wouldn't be surprised.'

Wydrin made a disgusted noise. 'You left us, in the middle of the night. No goodbye, no note. At least when you abandoned me last time you had the good grace to scribble on a piece of parchment for me. I thought . . . I thought you were probably dead, Seb.'

'I could not talk to you about it. I didn't know *how* to talk about it, so I thought it best if I—'

'You are my sworn brother!' She stopped, and took hold of his arm. They stood together in the dark, the bloated moon hanging above. She didn't know if she wanted to strike him or embrace him again. 'We are partners. You abandoned me!'

'Wydrin, you do not need me any more. You have Frith now, and I know that you are happy. I would not lessen that, for anything in the world.'

Wydrin threw her hands up. 'I love you, Sebastian, but you don't half talk some horse shit sometimes. Who says that I *need* you? Who says that I need Frith? We are better together, all three of us – that's the truth. If the last few years have taught me anything, it's that. And are you trying to tell me that because I have taken a lover there is no room for anyone else in my life?'

To her surprise, Sebastian laughed. It was genuine, and it eased her heart a little.

'I know better than to tell you anything.' He shrugged. 'I see the bond there is between the two of you, and I know that Frith would tear the world apart to protect you. Probably quite literally. And that you would skin anyone alive who dared give him so much as a funny look.'

A low wind blew up, chasing the sand between their boots. Wydrin sighed, and punched Sebastian lightly on the arm. 'Just stop running off on us. It's the Black Feather Three, and don't you forget it.'

They stood in silence for a time, listening to the calls and shrieks of the animals hidden in the trees. The wild scent of the jungle was mixed with salt here, and the acrid scent of the sand. Wydrin thought of their walk up the Sea-Glass Road – it had been so hot, the air full of spice and the filth of the city. It felt like a hundred years ago.

'You realise your new friend is some sort of god?' she said idly, watching the expression of surprise that moved across Sebastian's face. 'A very handsome one, too. Much preferable to old O'rin beak-face.'

'What are you talking about?'

Wydrin turned to face him. 'Both Estenn and the Spinner described this place as the cradle of Ede, Sebastian. The old gods are dead, and there are new ones being born. It is the Spinner's job to bring them forth. What is Oster, if he is not a god?'

Sebastian looked back to their fire, his eyes wide. Oster and Frith were sitting in silence there, the dark bulk of the Spinner squatting behind them like a lost shadow.

'That can't be, can it? I mean, he . . .'

'Seems so normal? Apart from when he turns into a shimmering golden dragon, you mean?' Taking pity on him, Wydrin threaded her arm through Sebastian's and turned him to walk back to their small camp. 'Trust you to have a crush on a god, Sebastian.'

36

The treasure had been tainted. Devinia was almost sure of it.

She had watched the Banshee's men and women handling the sacks, piling gold into the waiting casks they had brought with them, and had noticed how their hands had been tinged with the red dust afterwards. She had thought little of it at the time, and then, days later as they sailed up the waterway with the Dawning Man following on behind, it had seemed like every crew member she saw was covering his or her mouth to cough, or was rubbing at his or her chest, an expression of faint discomfort on their faces. The hatchet-faced woman who had brought them their last two meals had what looked like a bright red sore at the corner of her mouth – Devinia saw Augusta glaring at it with professional interest – and she had staggered as she'd walked away, even though the waters were calm.

And then there was Kellan.

On the fourth day, Augusta and Devinia had been summoned to the captain's cabin on board the *Dragon's Maw*. The place was a mess; dirty clothes were slung in the corners, plates covered in the crusted remnants of food littered the table, sticky goblets were everywhere. Ristanov stood by the single window, her arms crossed over her chest, while Kellan was slumped in the chair. It was gloomy in the cabin, and his face was cast into shadow.

'You were a medic, yes?'

Augusta frowned at the question. 'I'm the *Poison Chalice*'s sawbones, if that's what you're asking.'

'You are our medic now, crone,' snapped the Banshee.

'What happened to yours?' asked Devinia. 'Even you can't have been stupid enough to sail up here without someone to patch up your wounds.'

'He died,' said the Banshee. 'One of the very few of my crew to die when we took your ship.' She sniffed. 'Old one, you will look at Kellan. He is ailing for something. You will cure him.'

Augusta barked laughter. 'Paw at that scumbag's carcase? Why, you can go fuck yourself, girl.'

Banshee nodded to the guard behind them, and Devinia felt the cold press of steel to her throat.

'Refuse, and I will bless my cabin with the blood of Devinia the Red,' said Ristanov shortly. 'My patience is a small thing today. Do you understand this, crone?'

Augusta sighed dramatically. 'Fine. Cut my arms free then, unless you want me to examine the wretch with my eyes alone.'

Her bonds cut, Augusta took a moment to rub vigorously at her wrists, before approaching the man slumped in the chair.

'What seems to be the trouble?'

Kellan lifted his head, and Devinia caught the dull gold sheen of the crown. She had yet to see him take it off. 'I have a fever, is all,' he said, his voice thick. 'It's the air on this island, bound to make anyone ill.'

Augusta bent over him, tutting under her breath. Devinia watched as she pressed her hands to Kellan's face.

'Any chance of a bit more light? It's darker than a devil's arsehole in here.'

With every sign of reluctance, the Banshee lit a pair of oil lamps, filling the room with a dirty yellow light. Augusta stepped back, her shoulders stiff. 'That ain't no fever, lad, or have you not looked in the mirror lately?'

Stepping away from her guard, Devinia peered over the old medic's shoulder. Kellan was pale, with dark circles under his eyes, and where the gold touched his skin there was a creeping red growth. It was fibrous, furry almost, and Devinia was reminded of the strange red dust in the chamber.

'What is it?' asked the Banshee.

'How should I bloody know?' Catching the angry look the Banshee threw her, Augusta softened her voice. 'Looks like a skin disease to me, but I haven't seen anything like it before. He's burning up, but his sweat is cold. His heart is beating like he's been doing circuits of the deck.' She bent over slightly, looking Kellan straight in the eye. 'You need to take that crown off, son. Even if it isn't causing what you've got, you need to get some air to the infected area.'

'I cannot take it off,' mumbled Kellan. 'The Dawning Man listens to my every thought now. It obeys me. I live *through* it.'

'You should stop,' said Devinia. 'Put down anchor for a while, wait for this to pass.'

'And wait here for the island to destroy us?' The Banshee shook her head. 'There is still much to see here, yes. And the Dawning Man is now our bodyguard.'

'It's old magic, you fool, and you don't know what you're playing with.' Devinia looked back at the red growths on Kellan's forehead. She felt ill just looking at them. 'My daughter encountered magic like this, and it led to the deaths of hundreds—'

'No one is interested in your bitch daughter!'

Devinia looked up in surprise – the Banshee sounded truly unhinged. Next to them, Augusta reached out to pluck the crown from Kellan's head, and he surged to his feet.

'You will not take it from me!' he bellowed. 'I hold the power here!'

There was an answering flurry of shouts from outside, followed by a piercing scream. The Banshee ran from the room, pounding up the stairs, followed by her guard. Devinia and Augusta shared a look, before following them out onto the deck.

The Dawning Man stood in front of the *Dragon's Maw*, shining like a beacon in the sun. In its great golden fist was a man, apparently plucked straight off the deck. He was screaming, his legs kicking helplessly against the solid crystal fingers holding him in place. From one of the ships someone fired a volley of arrows that clattered harmlessly against the creature.

'What are you doing?' Ristanov yelled the question at the Dawning Man, before turning on Kellan, who had emerged from below decks. In daylight, it was painfully obvious that the man was sick; the red moss-like growth on his forehead stood out in stark contrast to his papery white skin. 'Stop this!'

Kellan seemed to stare straight through her, and the Dawning Man turned and slammed the unfortunate man into the cliff face. There was a crunch of multiple bones being broken, and then it smeared the remains across the black rocks, before dropping what was left into the water. The glistening red trail was dry in moments under the punishing sun.

The Banshee rounded on Kellan, her arms held out as if to shake him. 'Why would you – what do you —'

'I am not taking the crown off,' said Kellan mildly. He looked almost bored, and completely unaware of the eyes of every crew member now watching him closely. 'The power of the Dawning Man is too valuable to just cast away.'

Ristanov looked wild for a moment, as if she might strike him, and then she thought better of it. Instead, she stalked back down the steps to her cabin, ignoring the stares of her crew, and after a moment, Kellan followed her.

Devinia met Augusta's eyes, and realised that the old woman had spotted exactly what she had too; when the Banshee had raised her arms, there had been flecks of the red growth on the underside of her wrists. Whatever it was that Kellan had, it was catching.

37

The Eye of Euriale was almost in sight.

Estenn paused to wipe burning sweat from her forehead before it could sting at her eyes. The site itself had not been easy to find – she supposed that there were whole sections of Euriale that were simply much easier to traverse when you were a giant sentient spider – and now they were met with more obstacles. The Eye of Euriale resembled a small, artificial hill, one built of concentric blocks of pale green rock, each half as tall as her. This in itself would have been difficult enough to climb, but it was covered in thick swathes of spider web. The stuff was thick and silvery, so tough that they could not simply push it aside, but had to cut through it with their sharpest blades. They all had pieces of it stuck to them now, patches of gossamer silver that clung to skin and to leather like glue; she could feel plenty of it in her hair, but was resisting the temptation to yank it out.

So close now. She took a slow breath before hauling herself up onto the next level of stone. Gen scrambled up next to her, a hatchet clutched in her fist.

'Emissary, it is nearly time.' The girl's face was flushed, her eyes watering as if she might cry. 'You will bring the old gods back for us, and Ede will be made anew.'

Estenn smiled and briefly squeezed her arm. 'And you will take your place in history, dear Gen. You have all worked so hard to get us here. The Twins will raise my followers up above all others.'

It was the right thing to say. Gen beamed at her before attacking the webs with renewed enthusiasm.

There was a cry from above them – one of her people, a lithe young man who had once been a ship's boy, had reached the very top, and he stood silhouetted against the sky, his arms raised in triumph. Estenn felt a stab of annoyance. She should have reached the top first: she was the Emissary. It was her destiny to look into the Eye of Euriale and skewer its secrets. Plastering a serene smile on her face, she hauled herself up the next block, and then the next, slashing wildly with her sword. When at last she stood below the final ring of stones, two of her soldiers reached down to pull her up. This too annoyed her, but she relaxed into it, letting it become an act of ascendance. She would reach the Eye of Euriale by the sweat of her followers – it only made her more worthy.

'My people.' She turned with her arms spread wide, towards those who still climbed. They were all nearly at the summit now. 'The age of the Twins is about to begin.'

One or two of them cheered, and she smiled indulgently. Turning away, she walked to the very edge and looked over. She took an involuntary step backwards, and hoped that no one saw. She bit the inside of her cheek to keep from crying out.

The Eye of Euriale surged beneath her like a whirlpool of eldritch light. It seemed to reach for her, as if it had been waiting all this time just to see her, to claim her as its own. There were flickers of lightning down there, silent and yet full of violence, and she could almost feel the new life waiting to burst forth. No matter. There would be no need for that, not when she had set history back on its rightful course.

Reverentially, she slid the wooden staff from the straps holding it to her back, and held it securely in both hands. This would be her key.

'Children of Euriale!' They were all there now, the select group she had chosen to accompany her to the Eye. Each of them wore the markings of the Twins, and they all looked appropriately awe-stricken. She grinned, unable to hide her joy. 'We are here on the cusp of history! I go now, as your Emissary, to change the

238

world for the better.' She thrust the staff into the air. 'Join your brothers and sisters at the shrine, and wait for the world to be renewed!'

She stepped up to the very edge and closed her eyes. This was it. Whatever happened now, she would be free of this world.

'Heads up, wolf lady!'

Estenn's eyes snapped open in time to see an enormous shape barrelling across the void towards her, multiple legs outstretched. She had a moment to recognise the ridiculous little mask that was clutched to the creature's head, and then the Spinner landed on her, knocking her off the step and onto the block below.

Estenn screamed with rage and scrambled for her sword.

'What is the Spinner doing?' cried Oster.

'I think that's called taking the initiative, kid,' said Wydrin. Estenn herself was out of sight, but her soldiers were all around the steps, and every one of them was armed. Wydrin unsheathed both her weapons and passed Frostling to Frith, who took it with a nod. 'Speaking of which, your little trick with the dragon thing would be really useful right now.'

Oster looked confused for a moment, and then his human form dissolved into a cascade of lights. Not waiting to see what he would do next, Wydrin nodded to Sebastian. 'Let's get to the other side and make sure she's down.'

If Sebastian had been troubled lately, it made no difference to his skills as a warrior. With his borrowed sword he charged at the oncoming cultists, using his size and strength to take the bite from their attacks, before striking with solid, well-placed blows. Wydrin saw them fall from the corner of her eye as she whirled and stabbed, her stance slightly wider as she fought with her short sword. Frith came on behind them, finishing off anyone who still looked lively enough to attempt a second attack.

At the far side they were met with a fresh wave of soldiers, and for a moment Wydrin lost sight of Sebastian as they surrounded him, moving to take down the most obvious threat. She ran to the step and looked down, only to see the Spinner with his legs curled protectively over his body. Estenn was perched on top of his fat body, the staff shoved back in its belt and a long curving sword held high in one hand. It was already thick with black blood, and the Spinner's mask was spattered with it.

'No!'

Estenn brought the sword down, burying it in the taut fleshy mound that was the Spinner's unprotected belly. He shrieked, a high inhuman sound that seemed to press against Wydrin's eardrums, and all his limbs trembled.

'You'll pay for that, you bitch!'

Wydrin braced herself to jump down, planning to land directly on Estenn and knock her clear, but the light around the woman twisted and bent oddly. Wydrin had a brief impression of her pulling the sword free, and then she was gone.

'Shit.' She turned to Frith, who had just caught up with her. 'Did you see where she went?'

The air to her right seemed to grow thicker somehow, and all at once a curved blade was sailing out of thin air towards her face. Instinctively, Wydrin brought up Glassheart to intercept it, wincing at the impact.

'You will not take this from me!' Estenn's face was twisted with rage, her black eyes shining. Frith brought Frostling down in a silvery flash, paring open the flesh on the woman's arm, and she leapt back with a cry. Immediately, Wydrin pushed forward, hoping to strike with Glassheart before she could get her guard up again, but the woman was unnaturally fast and caught the blow on her blade.

'You have to stop!' They traded more blows, faster and faster, the ringing of their blades like discordant music. Wydrin let her instincts take over, willing Frith to stay back. 'You haven't seen what these gods can do! You would destroy us all!'

'I would remake the world!' snarled Estenn. She lunged forward, getting under Wydrin's defence briefly and searing through the leathers on her left arm. Wydrin punched out with the pommel of her sword, catching the woman on the chin hard enough for her to stagger backwards, but it wasn't enough to take her down. 'And all the unbelievers will burn!'

'You are an idiot!'

There was a chorus of screams from the other side of the Eye. Wydrin glanced up to see Oster in his dragon form, his jaws wide and gleaming. Sebastian was next to him, broadsword flashing in the afternoon light.

'No,' said Estenn. 'I am the Emissary.'

In one fluid movement she sheathed her sword and drew the staff from its belt, while her other hand slipped a throwing knife from her jerkin and flicked it towards Wydrin, almost casually. Wydrin twisted to one side so that it did little more than nick her shoulder, and then Estenn was leaping over the edge of the pit, Frith's staff held triumphantly in one hand.

Wydrin ran to the edge, feeling Frith close behind her. There was Estenn, already a tiny figure plummeting into the heart of the Eye, and then she was consumed in green light. A great white hole opened up there, a shifting caul of diamond light, and beyond it Wydrin could see red sand, and the daylight of another age.

'Quickly!' she said to Frith. 'We have to follow her through before that hole closes!'

He met her eyes steadily. 'How will we get back?'

'If we don't go now, there won't be anything to come back to.'

She expected him to disagree, or at least to question her. Instead he took her hand.

Wydrin looked up to the other side of the pit. Sebastian was there, one hand raised. Most of Estenn's soldiers were dead or dying. He moved to the edge, Oster close behind him. They had had the same idea.

'Well, then,' said Wydrin faintly, 'I suppose we're all idiots together.'

She squeezed Frith's hand in her own, and they jumped into the churning Eye of Euriale.

PART THREE
A Parting of the Ways

38

As she passed through the Eye, Estenn dreamed.

She knelt, gathering her heavy robes in one hand, and set the taper to the candle. The light blossomed in the cramped bunk room, illuminating the carved wooden figure on their makeshift altar. It was her turn to make the acquiescence, so she settled herself as comfortably as she could on the wooden boards and prepared to contemplate the face of Benoit, the Walker of the Path, Blessed in Name and Spirit. The carved figure was a good one, given to them by the Sacred Mother herself, and judging from the paintings and sculptures that adorned every corner of the Golden House of Worshipfulness, it really did look like him. There was Benoit's clear brow, the faint, forgiving smile, the twist of beard that curled from the bottom of his chin. Sacred Mother claimed she had seen him once, amongst a crowd of his followers, when she was just a girl. Estenn took the clay ampoule from within her sleeve and poured a small measure of the oil into the bowl in front of the figure. The scent of heartsblossom and Mother's Lament filled the bunk, growing stronger as the heat from the candle warmed the oil.

Quiet moments. Estenn would think of them often, over the long, long years of her life.

She had been murmuring the first canticle, preparing her mind to walk the First Path, when the door of the bunk had crashed open. The candle and the oil had been scattered, and Estenn had looked up to see a man she didn't recognise, a man with skin as white as a fish's belly, a lattice of purplish scars on his midriff.

'We've got another one here,' he'd said over his shoulder to someone she couldn't see. 'Is this ship full of little girls?'

Estenn had stood up then, holding herself straight, as all students of the Golden House were taught to do.

'We are making our first pilgrimage.' Some part of her knew that her words were pointless. What had happened had already happened; her life as she knew it was essentially over. She knew that by the man's scars, and by the dirty knife at his belt. Even so, these were words that needed to be said. 'We are people of peace, envoys from the Golden House and advocates of Benoit, the Walker of the Path.'

The man barked laughter at her, his pinkish eyes creased with mirth.

'Don't much matter what you *was*, girl. If you don't want your guts around your ankles, you'll do as you're bloody well told.'

Years passed in a green haze inside the Eye. Estenn saw that time wasn't a line to be followed, but a tumult to be lost in. Everything she thought of as herself was spooling away into the torrent – so easy to be obliterated, in this swirling of years – so she focussed all of her will, drawing the pieces back together again. She would not come so far only to be destroyed by a mindless force.

It was another time, on an island she would come to call home. Two owners later and she stood in the docks of Two-Birds, the last in a line of dirty, diseased slaves. Someone new would be buying them, but Estenn had long since lost interest in the bartering of her own flesh. She stared down at her feet instead, glad only that they were no longer in the hell that was the hold of the ship. The floor here did not shift beneath her bare feet, and there was sunlight on her head. She focussed on these things, drawing her will into a tight, narrow thing. Benoit had taught openness, an awareness of all things; life had taught her to hold herself close and deep inside, where no one else could reach. Benoit could go hang.

'Let me have a look at you, kid.'

A firm hand pressed her shoulder briefly, and the touch was so unlike that of her captors that she looked up. A young woman stood in front of her, short with a curvy waist, her hair a mess of dark curls. She had a port-wine birthmark on her cheek.

'Have you been sick lately?'

Estenn shook her head. This was a medic then, someone employed by the new or the old owners to check the merchandise over. The woman was frowning, her eyes travelling over Estenn's emaciated form, the bruises on her arms and neck. As Estenn watched, the woman glanced back up the line to where business was being done. She saw the woman come to some sort of decision.

'Here, I need to look in your eyes.' The woman led her a few steps away, supposedly to find better light, and made her tip her head up to the sky. 'Look up for me, kid.'

Estenn did as she was bid, and felt the woman's thumbs brush the bony mounds of her cheeks. As she did so the woman spoke in a low voice that only Estenn could hear.

'You've no shackles on. This idiot has had so much horn-root this morning he barely knows how many limbs he has, let alone how many slaves. There's an alleyway directly behind you. Follow it to the end and you'll come to a side street. Head north and you'll find a tavern called The Iron Bullock. If you go to the kitchens and tell them Grint sent you, they'll give you a bowl of soup. You get all that?'

Estenn rolled her eyes back down to look at the medic, and gave the tiniest nod.

'I'll be back there later tonight. I can help you get off this bastard island.'

'Why?' murmured Estenn. It was the only word she spoke to the woman.

'Does it matter to you?' The woman looked uncomfortable now, and she took her hands away from her face, glancing back up the row of slaves again. 'Go now. Don't run. Walk like you have every right in the world.'

I do, Estenn would have told her, but instead she did as she was bid, walking calmly out of the daylight and into the shadow of the alley. As swiftly as that, her days as a slave were over.

It was growing closer, she could feel it. A world that brimmed with magic, the Ede of a thousand years ago – still god-touched and sacred. In the confusion of the Eye, Estenn tried to move towards it, knowing that her tiny movements meant nothing at all but unable to resist doing so. The Twins were calling her home, finally.

She ate the soup, but did not wait for the medic. Instead, Estenn wandered back out onto the streets of Two-Birds just as the sun was setting, painting the cobbles and the windows with lurid orange light. She knew that she must look a sight – the tunic and leggings she wore were of decent quality, but she had spent weeks in the fetid hold of a slave ship, and the stink was like a second skin. Luckily, Two-Birds was hardly the most respectable of towns, and no one challenged her.

She moved up and down the streets, letting her feet take her where they would. The soup and the ale had filled her belly and she felt oddly at peace, despite the uncertainty. It was more than the food – it was the simple ability to walk where she wanted to, knowing that the decision was her own. Perhaps they would catch up with her and that would be the end of this brief freedom, but somehow she didn't believe so. There was the start of something new here; just as the scarred man bursting into her bunk had changed her life, so would the actions of the woman with the port-wine birthmark. She wouldn't be going back to the slave ship.

Something else was calling.

Eventually she came to the edge of the small town, and stood before the towering trees that marked the start of the wild part of the island. She stared at them as the shadows grew long. There had been a great deal of talk about this place in the holds of the slaver. The port of Two-Birds was a pirate town, but the island of Euriale itself was dangerous. Everyone knew it.

Estenn cast a look over her shoulder. Below her Two-Birds was coming alive for the night, lamps easing into life like errant fireflies. Down there was another path, another life. If she stepped between the trees now there would be yet another path, and it would be as different to the other as sandpaper was to silk; she could feel that keenly. She thought of the teachings of Benoit, with all his talk of paths and openness. He had spoken of study, of quiet contemplation, of restraint and the betterment of man. Next to the wild forest, thrumming with its own alien power, Benoit and his ideas seemed small and foolish: a child's idea of truth.

'I am done with the ways of men,' she murmured.

Estenn stepped into the cursed forest just as the last light was draining from the sky, the wild, alien scent of Euriale closing around her, as green as the Eye she fell through. Somewhere in the distance, a wolf raised its head and howled.

39

The yawning sensation in her stomach stopped, and Wydrin found herself kneeling in rich, black soil. For a moment she thought they hadn't gone anywhere at all – that perhaps the Eye of Euriale had spat them back out and they had landed in the jungle somewhere – but when she looked up she saw strange twisted trees, unlike anything she'd seen on the island, and the light was different. She staggered to her feet.

'Where are we?'

The others were picking themselves up, and Wydrin turned in time to see Estenn glaring back at her, black hair framing a face that had gone paper white.

'Wait!'

Before Wydrin could move, light twisted around the Emissary and she vanished, slipping off amongst the trees. Next to her, Frith was struggling to get up. At the sight of his face, she brushed thoughts of pursuing Estenn aside.

'You look half dead!'

Frith took a slow breath. Like Estenn, his face was ashen.

'I've had more pleasant journeys. Did you – did you also see your past?'

Wydrin took his arm and pulled him to his feet. The tall, pale trees were thick on all sides. 'I saw bits and pieces, yeah. As we went back through history, I suppose we went through our own, too.'

'There was a great deal I would rather have forgotten,' said Frith. He squeezed her arm, and then stepped away, letting her know he could stand by himself.

Sebastian and Oster came to them, Sebastian's sword already in his fist. 'She went through the trees behind you,' he said. 'We shouldn't give her too much of a head start.'

They started off, moving as quickly as they could, although the close proximity of the trees made that difficult. They had slim, spindly trunks, and the bark was flaky, the crumbling edges faintly purple. Far above their heads, branches reached up to a cloudless blue sky. It was, Wydrin realised, aridly hot, with none of the humidity of Euriale. She forced herself to look around as much as possible, watching for the odd fracturing of light that Estenn used to conceal herself. She couldn't have gone far.

'I do not think we are in a forest,' said Frith.

'What?'

He nodded at their surroundings as they ran. 'The trees, they are too regularly spaced, and there are no other plants growing in this soil. Just the trees. I believe we are in a garden of some sort.'

'A garden? Are you telling me we came a thousand years into the past to land in someone's herbaceous border?'

'Well, hardly herbaceous—'

'Hoy, you there!'

A figure in loose-fitting white clothes lurched out from behind a tree trunk. He was a deeply tanned man in his fifties, with a shock of grey hair that stuck up as though he frequently ran sweaty fingers through it. He wore a silver torq around his neck, with a yellow crystal hanging from it; there was a mage word carved there, although Wydrin could not have said what it was. His hairy feet were confined in brown leather sandals.

'Greetings,' began Sebastian. 'I wonder if—'

'How'd you even sodding well get in here, that's what I'd like to know.' The man marched up to them, brushing soil from his hands. He wore a belt with several clear bottles attached, sloshing with liquid. 'This is supposed to be the bloody sacred groves, and instead it's like bloody market day, trespassing idiots on sale. I'm just sitting there, tending the trees, when something comes charging out of nowhere and treads on my bloody feet. Couldn't even see what it was! Now I've got you lot, a bunch of Unbound, if I'm not mistaken, stomping around—'

'I will not be spoken to like this,' protested Oster.

'Where were you trodden on? Back the way you came?' Wydrin made to push past the man with grey hair, but he threw back his sleeves to reveal forearms bound with strips of silk. Next to her Frith give a low cry.

'Oh no you bloody don't!' The man raised his hands and twin ribbons of white light curled from his palms. Wydrin went to draw her dagger, only to feel both hands grow painfully cold. Before she could do anything else, her hands snapped together and a ring of glittering blue ice crackled into life, encircling her wrists in cuffs as hard as steel.

'You're a mage,' said Frith. He too had his wrists bound, as did Sebastian and Oster. The latter was looking at the ice cuffs with growing anger.

'Oh, I see we have been infiltrated by geniuses,' said the man, rolling his eyes. 'Come on, you're coming with me.'

He held his hand up, as if he would do them further mischief. Wydrin caught Sebastian's eye, and saw him give a tiny shake of his head. They needed to know what the situation was here, and if they had even appeared where they expected to be. Getting into a fight now would likely end badly.

'Oster, trust me,' said Sebastian in a low voice. 'It is safer to be pliant for now.'

The mage led them through the trees until, abruptly, the neat forest ended, and they were stepping over a low red brick wall. To Wydrin's surprise, they were in the middle of a courtyard; tall arched passageways met them on every side, while windows high in the walls caught the midday sun and reflected it back in brilliant white squares. There were more men and women out here, all wearing loose white clothing of various cuts and materials. Some of them had their sleeves rolled up, or wore robes with no sleeves, and all of them had silk tied up to their elbows, all inscribed with mage words. The men and women glanced over at them curiously; some carried books, while others looked as though they had recently travelled a great distance, their leather boots dusty, the cuffs of their trousers stained. Of Estenn, there was no sign.

'I'll take you to the common room,' said the man, who was studiously ignoring the curious looks of his peers. 'You can wait in there, and the Commander can deal with you. I don't have bloody time for this. Do they think those trees will grow themselves? I can hardly be expected to perform my duties if I also have to be escorting trespassers all over the bloody place.'

Sebastian tried again. 'Forgive us, we did not know we were trespassing. It's very important that we—'

'Didn't know?' hooted the man. 'What? Did you just trip over the walls of the Arkanium and land right in the middle of the sacred grove?'

He led them under an arch, where the shade briefly gave them welcome relief from the relentless sun, before urging them up a set of steps. A pair of men wearing crimson vests and the dour expressions of guards fell in behind them; they were unarmed, but their biceps were thick with strips of painted silk. At the top of the steps they emerged out into the open air again, to find themselves walking along battlements looking out over a city of red clay and smoke. Sebastian caught his breath.

'It's Krete! We're actually here. The Eye brought us here.'

Wydrin looked out over the city, a tight feeling in her chest. There was no Sea-Glass Road of course, and where the Citadel should crouch above the city there was instead a confusion of red stone and wooden scaffolding; it loomed off to their right like an ant's nest, riddled with workers building a monument that would stand for a thousand years. *Until we brought the whole thing down*, thought Wydrin, feeling faint. *Until we left it in ruins.*

The rest of the city was eerily familiar. Buildings of yellow and red brick crammed in close together, with more constructed of wood and grey stone than Wydrin remembered. There was also slightly more space, with wide thoroughfares lined with carts and market stalls. Someone had actually put some thought into the layout of the city, at one time. It was something that had never occurred to her in the seething mess that was the Krete she knew.

'Fuck me sideways,' she murmured.

The mage and the guards led them down a short flight of steps and through a set of tall wooden doors. The room inside was large and spacious, and full of bright daylight from the wide glass windows that looked out across the city. Otherwise it was sparsely decorated, with three long tables that had obviously seen a lot of use, while mismatched chairs were scattered around the room. There were threadbare tapestries on the walls.

'Don't steal anything,' snapped the mage. He made a sharp gesture with his hands and the ice cuffs melted and fell to pieces. With that he disappeared through an interior door, while the guards took up position on either side of the room.

'It's not like there's anything worth stealing anyway,' said Wydrin. There were a few moments of silence, and then everyone started talking at once.

'This is an outrage! I will change my form and smash these windows, and then we can be gone—'

'Did you see the way he wielded the Edenier? Such casual precision! If I could just—'

'These people mean us no harm. If we can find a way to leave quietly, without doing any damage—'

'Hold on, hold on!' Wydrin held up her hands, and then lowered her voice, conscious of the men on the doors. 'We have to think about where we are. And *when*. The man who brought us here was a mage – as well as a gardener, apparently – and the men and women in that courtyard also looked to be mages. We appear to have landed right in whatever passes as the seat of power for the mages of this time.' She looked at Frith. 'I'm assuming, prince-ling, that you've done a fair amount of reading about the mages since we were, uh, last here. Where do you suppose this is?'

Frith frowned at her. 'Much of the history of the mages has been lost.' He crossed his arms over his chest. 'But the memories shared with me by Joah Demonsworn have given me access to details that no one else could possibly know. I would guess that this Arkanium is a place I glimpsed in his recollections where he

254

once came to learn. There were a great many powerful mages in residence, and he was pleased to have the opportunity to study here.'

'There is no building like this in modern Krete,' said Sebastian, a note of caution to his voice. 'Nor even a hint of one.'

'And no mages either,' said Wydrin. She looked at the tapestries; they were too faded to make out much. 'These people are fighting a war against the gods, and we can see their plans taking shape.' She nodded towards the windows, where it was still possible to see the beginnings of the Citadel. 'We're here to stop a woman who wants to destroy their plans. I'm telling you, these people are our natural allies. What's our alternative? Run around Krete and hope we just bump into the woman who can make herself invisible at will? Fight our way out of a building filled with men and women who can use magic as well as I use a blade?' She tugged a hand through her tangled hair, still full of the alien stink of Euriale. Her arm was sore from their tussle with the flying monsters, and the makeshift bandage had stuck to her skin. 'We need to try at least. Let's just hope this Commander person is reasonable.'

Xinian the Battleborn put the pieces of parchment back down on the desk, and rubbed her neck, trying to loosen the stiff muscles there. What she wanted, more than anything, was a long, hot bath and a full night's sleep. Just to wash away the desert grit would be a start, but Archmage Reis wanted her report on the night's action, as well as her thoughts on the Citadel's progress. She sighed, glaring down at the carefully sketched plans. It all meant very little to her – layering Edeian spells with Edenier was Selsye's speciality, not hers – but Reis cared little about that. He would want to know if they could protect the Citadel while it was constructed, if Xinian's troops could keep the enemy busy until it was finished. Xinian frowned, thinking of the men and women they had already lost. How many more would they lose, to keep the gods from Krete while they worked? And all for a plan that had such a whiff of desperation about it that half the men and women who served under her would not meet her eye.

She turned away from the desk, suddenly tired of looking at the plans. She would do what she could to make it work, and the rest . . .

'The rest is up to the gods,' she murmured, smiling bitterly. She reached for the bottle on her desk. Xinian's rooms had seen better days – she spent very little time at the Arkanium now, and their resources were as low as they'd ever been – but the Mistress of House knew to keep a bottle of Pathanian wine chilled, should she arrive home unexpectedly from the skirmishes. Xinian poured herself a glass and gulped it down in three quick swallows. There was no time for the leisurely bath, but the wine cooled her throat and cleared away some of the Kretian dust.

'Commander?' A voice came from outside, followed by a hesitant knock.

'What is it?'

A mage she vaguely recognised peered around the door. His face was red from exertion or too much sun. He looked her up and down, his eyes growing wide. Belatedly she remembered how she must look: her leather gear was still thick with mud from the last battle, her cloak torn and burned at the edges. She had taken a small injury when a shard from a boulder had hurtled in her direction and slashed across her forearm; the arm that ended in a smooth stump was crusted with old blood. She felt a flicker of irritation, and waved at him brusquely.

'Well? Spit it out, man.'

The man's face turned blotchy, and he swallowed hard before continuing.

'Commander Battleborn, we had some trespassers. *Unbound* trespassers. I mean, we still have them. We've taken them prisoner. I have, I mean. They're in the common room, the one we use to meet traders and merchants and their ilk.'

Xinian poured herself another measure of the wine and drank it down. Her skin was prickling under her clothes.

'Common folk trying to sneak in the gates again?' She shook her head. 'They believe it will be safer in here, if the gods come. It is idiotic, but it is hardly a matter for the martial commander of the mages. Inform the head of the guards, or, if you're feeling especially malicious, the Mistress of House.'

The man squirmed. 'Begging your pardon, Commander, but these aren't any common folk. They look like sell-swords to me, and they just turned up in the middle of the sacred grove. No one but a mage should be able to get in there, and yet there they bloody were, standing there clear as daylight.'

Xinian paused with her hand on her glass. The sacred grove was one of Selsye's projects. She wouldn't want strangers blundering about amongst her trees.

'Sell-swords, you say?'

'Dirty tavern brawlers,' said the man. 'Although', he drew himself up to his full height, 'perhaps that's just what they want you to think. Maybe they're spies. Spies for the gods themselves.'

'Very well.' Xinian rubbed a hand over her smooth head, consciously recalling the Word that was tattooed there: Forbearance. 'Take me to the prisoners.'

40

At night, when the ships were still and darkness filled the waterway, the decks rang with the sound of coughing and misery. The Banshee's crew were sluggish, going about their duties with slow hands and thick heads, as though they'd all been at the rum the night before, while Kellan himself was rarely seen, preferring to stay below decks. Devinia and Augusta huddled together on the deck, next to an oil lamp. Carefully, they peeled back their sleeves to expose their skin to the light, and examined each other's faces for signs of the red growth. It had become something of a routine. The man who stood guard over them had it on his shoulder – a creeping tendril of it peeked out from under his shirt – and he scratched at it continually, a faint expression of distress on his face that Devinia was quite sure he was unaware of.

'Nothing,' said Augusta, relief evident from every crease on her lined face. 'Unless you've got it growing in crevices that aren't so easy to check, I'd say we're free of it.'

'Let's not think about that, shall we?' Devinia murmured. 'We must be among the lucky few. Every man and woman I look at is scratching at themselves, and even accounting for the lack of hygiene on a pirate ship, that's unusual. How have we missed it?'

'We didn't touch the gold directly,' said Augusta. 'It comes from that, no doubt. Could be a disease, could be a curse.' She rubbed her own arms briskly, although the night was balmy. 'When I think about how close I came to snatching that crown off his stupid head . . .'

Devinia nodded, consumed with similar thoughts. She had been in the chamber with the tainted gold, had breathed in that stale air. Could the red moss be growing in her lungs even now, poisoning her from the inside out?

In the stillness and the dark, a pale blue light flared to the west of the ship. Instinctively, Devinia clambered to her feet. The guard grunted at her to get back down, but she ignored him, peering out across the water. At the base of the cliff was a small patch of rocky ground, and on it stood a slim man with an unruly beard and hair that came down past his bare shoulders. He held a ball of blue light in his hands, and in the harsh glow she could see that his skin was a motley collection of strange colours. Something about that tickled at the back of her mind, but then the man stepped forward, smiling.

'Ahoy, ship!' he called. 'I bring you a cure for your ills! May I come aboard?'

A crewman stepped forward with an oil lamp. 'Who are you?' he barked. 'How did you get there?'

'I am a wandering hermit, come from the island,' said the man with the blue light. He had a strong accent but his words were well spoken and clear. 'I go where there is suffering, and alleviate it if I can. I am a holy man, if you will accept such an arrogant assumption.'

The babble of talk from the crew increased, and then Ristanov appeared on deck, striding across to the guardrail, her back stiff. The red moss had grown along her hairline and in a thick clump under her ear. She didn't grin as often as she once had.

'What cure do you bring us?'

'My name is Terin. To my own people I am a seer, and I bring you knowledge that will cure your affliction.' He slipped the blue light into a pocket. 'May I come aboard?'

'You know this is a diseased boat, and yet you would come aboard?'

It was difficult to read the man's face in the shadows, but he seemed to grow solemn. 'It is my destiny to do so.'

'Fine. Bring the fool. I will gut him myself when he proves to be useless, yes. It will give us some entertainment.'

The man, who called himself Terin, was brought on board. Devinia watched as he was marched up to the forecastle where the Banshee received him; now that Kellan stayed largely below decks, Ristanov seemed to prefer being under the open sky. Devinia edged as close as she dared, her guard too distracted by his own woes to call her back into line, but the conversation between the pirate and the strange man was too low to make out. Some long moments passed, during which Devinia half expected to hear a blood-curdling scream as the man was gutted, or a splash as he was simply thrown overboard, but eventually he was led back to where she and Augusta sat. His arms had been bound behind his back, and the burly pirate pushed him towards them with a grunt.

'Well, I don't reckon that went how you hoped,' said Augusta. 'What are you, some sort of lunatic? Did you bargain for gold? Believe me, you don't want any of the gold they're carrying.'

'Not at all,' the man called Terin nodded formally at them both. Up close his body glistened with a film of sweat. 'Ladies, I had a vision that I would lead these good people to their salvation – the completion of my destiny is all the gratitude I require.'

'Oh, I bet Ristanov loved that,' said Augusta.

'But the captain requires that I be firmly restrained in the meantime. She is very cautious.'

'What have you promised her, exactly?' Devinia lowered her voice. 'These people are dying. It's possible you could catch whatever it is they have.'

'But it appears you have been untouched, which I am glad to see.' There was an edge to his smile – a sense he was hiding something – but then he cleared his throat and the moment passed. 'There is a lagoon, not far from here, with extraordinary healing properties. I have promised Captain Ristanov that I will lead you all there.'

'A magical lagoon?' hooted Augusta. 'She really must be desperate.'

'I would say she is, wouldn't you?' said Terin, that shine to his eyes appearing again. 'Desperate enough to go ever deeper into this cursed island, in the hope of undoing what has been done.'

'You're one of those northern people, aren't you?' said Devinia. The pieces had suddenly dropped into place. 'My daughter spoke of your tribe. From what she said, it would be very dangerous for you to come this far south.'

'It is true, I am less than comfortable in this sweltering place. And when the sun comes out again, I may have to hope that Captain Ristanov is kind enough to provide shade.' He settled back against the barrels and smiled at them both. 'But for now I believe I am exactly where I need to be.'

Ephemeral had never been in a place so saturated with life. It filled the trees, thrummed in the air around her, shifted under foot.

She was cutting across the way they'd come to head towards the great basin of still water they'd passed some days back. It was perfect for their plan, or at least she hoped so. It was difficult to keep her thoughts in line, with so much life pushing at her every sense.

Her foot splashed into shallow water, half hidden by the dark canopy of leaves overhead, and she paused. All at once she felt as though she had stumbled into someone's home; the bushes here had been clipped short by blunt teeth, and stumps of trees, the raw inner flesh pale and exposed, sprouted every-where from the cool green water. Someone had methodically pushed the trees down, carefully clearing them away until there was room to cultivate this muddy space of water and green plants. She thought of the homes she had invaded as part of Y'Ruen's army, beating down doors and slaughtering the fright-ened people inside. It felt like part of someone else's life, a story told to her by a friend, perhaps, or more likely, an enemy. If she let her mind settle on it, the details would come back: the boy who had said it was his birthday, whose throat she had torn out with her claws . . . It was different, she told herself; where once she had invaded, now she explored. The difference was important.

'I have made a choice,' she said aloud. 'The choices are mine.'

She took a few more splashing steps through the water and came up short as her boot knocked into something solid beneath the surface. At the exact same moment, a delicate silver echo shivered through her blood.

'Who is here?'

She peered down at her foot. Next to it was a large bulbous shape, dark blue in colour, and covered in raised ridges. There was another one next to it, and beyond it, three more. With a start she realised that the entire pool was filled with the round blue shapes. Without thinking too closely about why she was doing it, Ephemeral knelt in the water and gently pressed her hand to the object, taking care not to rake her claws across it. It was leathery to the touch, and as warm as her hand. And when she touched it, she sensed a new life within – new dragon-kin life – a faint silvery presence that seemed to reach out to her own blood. Unseen by anyone, a wide smile split her face.

'It is an egg,' she said to the hum of the insects. 'They are all eggs.'

She straightened up and looked around. There had to be around twenty eggs in this shallow pool. She was very aware that it was vital she get to the lagoon before Terin did. He would be leading them there now, using his charm and mysticism to bring the pirates into their chosen place of ambush. It was important that she was there first, so that she could lie in wait. Only then would they have a chance to save blood-of-Wydrin, and perhaps learn more of where her father had gone.

Still, the pirates were ill and moving slowly. They would have to follow the twisting waterway to the lagoon, putting days on their journey, while she could cut directly across the island.

Sinking to her knees in the water and mud, Ephemeral placed her hands on the two nearest eggs and opened her mind to the silvery presences within. They stirred, instinctively reaching out to her, and she felt the curling of their minds around her own. It was, she realised with delight, like being back in the birthing pits below the Citadel, her sisters all pressed in around her, closer than skin. For these creatures, this was the birthing pit, these were their sisters. And they accepted her as if she were one of them.

Ephemeral closed her eyes, glorying in the contact of their burgeoning minds, and reached out to the others in the pool. The lagoon could wait for a little longer.

41

Frith stood by the wide windows, looking out across Krete. It seemed the city had once been a near-civilised place; the streets neater, the air free of smoke. It was possible, if he half closed his eyes, to see what it would become, in a thousand years or so. The sense of displacement was huge and unnerving, doubled by the men and women they'd seen in the courtyard. They had all worn the mages' words around their arms, just as he had done, when the Edenier burned inside him. For a moment, the feeling of loss was so enormous that he had to lean on the window frame as the ground seemed to drop away from his feet. To be here, in the golden age of the mages, when he had so recently lost that power himself . . . What could he have done with the power here? What could he have achieved? With a shiver he recalled Joah Demonsworn's ravaged face, twisted beyond all recognition. Sometimes no power is the wisest choice, he reminded himself. Power led to a knife in your hand, a series of empty rooms, and blood. Always blood.

'Are you all right?'

He turned at Wydrin's hand on his shoulder. Her face was dirty, the leather armour she habitually wore even muddier and more scuffed than usual. He felt his heart lighten at the sight of her.

'I never thought to find myself here,' he said. 'If I'd known, when I first met you in this city . . .'

She smiled lopsidedly. 'If I'd known, when I first saw your grumpy face—'

The door behind them banged open, and a tall figure stepped through. Frith opened his mouth to say something, and then shut it rapidly. He looked to Wydrin, who was grinning.

'I am Commander Battleborn.' Xinian stepped into the room and dismissed the guards with a terse nod. 'You have been caught trespassing at a time of war. Do you want to give me a good reason why I shouldn't have you all executed immediately?'

'By all the gods.' Wydrin came forward eagerly, as if greeting an old friend. 'you're taller in real life, Xinian.'

Xinian frowned. In the bright daylight of the well-lit room, Frith could see traces of mud and dust on her brown skin, and her eyes were bright and full of life. When he had first seen Xinian the Battleborn, she had been a confused collection of grey shadows, an echo of a person in a place drenched with magic.

'You've heard of me, then,' she said, looking uncomfortable. 'That will not save you.'

'Of course.' Frith watched Wydrin put away her smile with some difficulty. 'Commander, we need to tell you something very important, and we don't have much time—'

'You have no time at all,' snapped Xinian. She looked over them all, her eyes narrowing. 'None of you are mages. What were you doing in the sacred grove, and, more to the point, how did you get there? Who are you working for?'

'Commander,' Sebastian stepped forward. He looked like a wild man – his beard was tangled and his clothes were little more than rags – but Frith saw Xinian take in his military bearing and the even tone of his voice. She seemed to relax slightly. 'Our story is, I am afraid, an unbelievable one, and we have very little time to tell it. What you must know, first of all, is that you are all in great danger.'

'A greater danger than the gods that threaten to destroy us at any moment?' snorted Xinian.

'It's your defeat of the gods that's in danger,' said Wydrin. 'Please, Commander, we're here to help you.'

At that moment, the room filled with a deep blue light that pulsed on and off, while a high-pitched wavering shriek sounded from outside.

'The southern wall is breached.' Xinian turned to the door immediately. 'Guards, put these four in the dungeons and report to the wall. We're under attack.'

She marched out the door, and the guards came back in, hands raised.

'We don't have time to be stuck in dungeons right now.' Wydrin sighed. 'Sebastian?'

The big knight stepped forward, but before he could reach them, Oster had slipped into his dragon form, nearly filling the wide room. The guards staggered back, their faces slack with shock. With one flick of his tail Oster threw them both to the floor, their cries of alarm lost under the strange wailing noise from outside. Before they could get up, Sebastian neatly knocked them both unconscious with the pommel of his sword. Oster shook his great dragon head from side to side, before the lights consumed him and in the dragon's place was a tall man in gleaming armour once more.

'No human is putting me in a dungeon,' he said. 'Bad enough that they think to confine me in this room.' Sebastian, Frith noted, had seemed unsurprised by this move; they acted as though they were warriors with a battle-forged bond, and yet surely they had only known each other a few days.

'We should follow Xinian,' he said. 'We need more of an idea of what's going on.'

They emerged into a stone corridor filled with men and women running in all directions. Frith saw more mages, hastily tying silk strips around their wrists, and men and women in more conventional armour too, swords at the ready. They followed the corridor east and down a wide spiral staircase, until they emerged in a wide hall that had seen better days. There were enormous oil paintings, covered in a thick layer of dust as if no one had had a chance to clean them for some time, and other arcane items were left in corners, half covered in dirty sheets. They followed the crowds out into another spacious courtyard, small white stones crunching underfoot. A pair of wide black iron gates had been thrown open, and they filed out into the city itself.

The wailing noise was even louder out here, and seemed to be emanating from a row of squat stones along the top of the city's southern wall. They pulsed with the same blue light that had filled the common room. Out here they caught sight of Xinian again – she was already on top of the wall, standing with about twenty men and women wearing deep crimson vests and leggings, their arms bright with bindings. She was barking orders at them and pointing up at the sky.

'What is it?' asked Wydrin. 'I can't see a threat.'

'There is someone nearby,' said Oster in a toneless voice. The man looked faintly puzzled, as if there were a sound just on the edge of his hearing. 'It is . . . so old.'

The wail of the alarms was suddenly drowned out by thunder from directly above. Frith looked up in confusion to see dark clouds billowing out of a blameless blue sky. Sheets of lightning shimmered threateningly, and around them the bright day turned as dark as late evening. Xinian was still shouting orders, and the mages on the wall shuffled into a formation of some sort.

Wydrin's face was turned up to the sky, her skin lit with flashes of white light.

'What the fuck is that?'

The dark storm clouds twisted apart and a huge, snarling wolf head pushed its way through, eyes rolling and jaws agape. It was an ephemeral thing made of light and darkness, of swirling vapour and crackling lightning, but as it loomed above them Frith found himself half crouching as if it might reach out and snap them up with its teeth. He thought of the towering Judgement of Res'ni in the sea beyond Turningspear, a monument to a lost city and a warning to fear the god of chaos.

'Don't let it manifest!' called Xinian from the walls. As she spoke, the rows of mages, with one practised movement, sent a barrage of blue light arching up into the dark clouds. The bolts of light fizzled there, seeming to land like errant falling stars before winking out, but for a few seconds the vision of the wolf faded. Then it howled.

'Hold your lines!' called Xinian over the noise. Next to Frith, Wydrin was holding her hands over her ears. 'It's Res'ni, she will try to confuse you!'

The pitch of the howl increased in volume and discordance; this wasn't a single wolf, these were hundreds, and they all ran for the sake of blood lust. Around them, a rough wind began to blow, as though they stood in a very localised tornado. Debris and litter from the city began to shoot around the cobbles in circles, and then larger objects were thrown into the fray. Frith saw a leather-bound book go flying past, the pages fluttering madly, and a sack of straw, spilling its contents in all directions. The items were spiralling up and out, crashing into walls and the mages under Xinian's command. Frith staggered, and he realised it wasn't wind at all; it was a storm of pure magic.

'We need to get out of here!' he said to Wydrin, shouting over the deafening howls. 'Find something to hold on to!'

The giant manifestation of Res'ni threw its great lupine head back and forth, eyes rolling in their sockets. The mages threw up another volley of the blue energy, but this time it seemed to have little effect. Frith felt Wydrin grab hold of his arm, and then a cart, fully loaded with sacks of grain, spun into the air in front of them. They both stumbled backwards, feeling the pressure of the force-storm battering them back and forth. Men and women were screaming, some attempting to flee, but then forced back as the confusion of debris grew thicker. With the dust in the air it was becoming difficult to see. Xinian was a smudged figure on top of the wall, occasionally lit by her own magical energy.

A wooden bucket flew towards them out of nowhere and struck Frith high on his shoulder, spinning him away from Wydrin. He looked up to see Sebastian crouching over a pair of terrified-looking children, using his body to shield them from the worst of the storm.

'Form up! Now!' It was Xinian's voice, carried to them briefly on the wind and then snatched away again. 'All of you, I want all of the Edenier focussed here, on the back of its throat! On my mark!'

He saw her raise her arm, the one that ended in a stump, and watched as a thick fork of purple light snapped out of the end and up towards the image of Res'ni. It flickered deep inside the beast's mouth, and then was followed by many more forks of bright energy, from the hands of the men and women gathered on the walls and in the courtyard. The dark clouds that made up the wolf's head suddenly paled, as though they were ink washed away by water, and for a few moments the pitch of the howling increased.

'She's bloody done it!' cried Wydrin. 'Look, I can see pieces of the sky again—'

As she spoke, a spike of lightning from the dying clouds stabbed down and struck the wall just to the right of where Xinian stood. There was a deafening crack and the sky was full of flying red rocks, raining down on them all with lethal force. Frith saw a jagged chunk flying towards them, a smear of red across his field of vision, and then everything became momentarily darker, as though he stood under a great shadow. He thought of the spirit in Euriale, who had promised to open him up to magic again. The flying rocks, the panicking people; all was still. He looked at Sebastian, who had grabbed the two children to his chest and continued to shelter them with the bulk of his body. Oster stood just beyond him; he was staring at the place where the wolf had been with an expression of confused horror. And Wydrin. A shard of the wall, no bigger than a penny, had already hit her, catching the skin above her temple and cutting her. Her blood was redder than the rock, a bright shout in the shadow. He remembered the fight in the great hall and how Leon had gone down senseless from a single blow to his head.

This would not stand. Not again.

It was not like the Edenier. Rather than a boiling in his chest, it was as though every fibre of his being – every hair, every piece of skin, every drop of his blood and tissue – lit up with purpose and sang with energy. He reached out with his will and cast the stones away, and even as the world slipped back into motion around him, he noted with satisfaction how they crumbled into ancient dust.

Good, thought Frith, and then on the heels of that, *what is happening to me?*

Darkness flew in at the edges of his vision. There was power, so much of it, and it left like the coursing tide.

42

'Frith? Can you hear me?'

Wydrin was bent over the young lord's prone figure where they had laid him out on a deeply cushioned chaise longue. His face was pale, and there was a lot of red dust in his hair, but he was murmuring in his sleep, which Sebastian took to be a good sign. He looked around the room, and willed Frith to waken soon. They dearly needed someone to explain what had just happened, and, Isu knew, he had no clue.

They had been taken not to the dungeons or even to the bare room where they had waited before, but to a set of untidy rooms he took to be Commander Xinian's own. He had the distinct impression that she had wanted them out of the way as soon as possible, and that she wanted to be the first to question them. Xinian herself had left them some time ago, saying that she needed to check in with the guards on the northern gates, but that she would be back. Her expression as she left suggested that there had better be answers awaiting her when she returned.

Sebastian turned to Oster, who stood near the tall windows that opened on to a narrow balcony. The glass was lined with gold, and glittered in the sunshine, although it clearly hadn't been cleaned for some time. Oster's face was tense, and he watched the sky constantly.

'What is it?'

'I knew that creature,' said Oster without looking at him. 'I

269

knew her. Or I almost did.' He squeezed his eyes shut and shook his head. 'It *almost* makes sense. But I can't quite . . .' He turned to face Sebastian then, and his eyes were desolate. 'The Spinner is dead. He was supposed to sing me my histories, tell me all our stories, and then I would have known. But now he is gone, and I am here.' He gestured angrily at the city beyond the window. 'This is not my time, I know that much, and all the knowledge I should have is lost.'

Sebastian pressed his lips together into a firm line. He had no words of comfort for Oster. This was exactly what he had wanted to avoid. They had headed straight into danger, and once again they had dragged innocent bystanders along with them. Standing in the bright light of the window, Oster seemed to shine with his own inner glow, and his mail gleamed as brightly as it had when he'd first met him. There was no sign of stubble on his smooth jaw, and his dark hair remained artfully tousled. Sebastian remembered Wydrin's words, and felt a curl of unease move through his stomach. Oster was not human, and not a bystander to what had happened in Euriale. He would do well to remember that.

'You did not need to come with us,' said Sebastian. 'You didn't have to jump into the Eye.'

Oster turned to him, scowling. 'It was obvious that you needed my assistance,' he said, drawing himself up to his full height. 'And you still do.'

'I thought that it wasn't your place to serve humans? Besides which, Wydrin and I have been looking after ourselves for some time,' said Sebastian. The silvery link that ran between the two of them was thrumming with this new tension. It was making his head ache. 'If anything, we've had more than enough of dragons and dragon-kin. If that's what you are.'

Oster took a step towards Sebastian, as though they were preparing to fight. 'Of all people, you say that to me? I may not know who I am, but at least I am trying to find out. At least I am not hiding from it.'

'Lads, if we could leave the tiffs for later?' Wydrin was giving them a caustic look over her shoulder. 'I think Frith is coming round.'

270

With more relief than he wanted to admit, Sebastian stalked away from the window and came back to where Wydrin crouched. Frith's eyes flickered open, and he winced before attempting to sit up.

'Take it easy, princeling. You hit the deck fairly hard back there.'

'It feels like it.' The young lord's voice was hoarse. 'Where am I?'

'In Xinian's own apartments, would you believe?' Wydrin grinned. 'She is every bit the hard arse in life as she was in death, isn't she?'

'What happened out there, Frith?' Sebastian put his hand on Wydrin's shoulder, and she pressed her own hand to it briefly. 'You started glowing, and the broken stones—'

'I really do not know.' Frith ran his fingers through his white hair, making it stick up at odd angles. 'It was magic of some sort, but not Edenier.'

The interior door opened, and Xinian stepped back through, a wary expression on her face. At some point she had unstrapped the heavy shoulder armour she had been wearing and now carried it tucked under one arm.

'I do not need to tell you that this is not the best time to be causing trouble at the Arkanium, and in truth I am deeply weary and sorely tempted to just have the lot of you consigned to the dungeons and locked away for the foreseeable future. It seems it's not just a case of turning up in the sacred groves unannounced – there is also the matter of two unconscious guards you left in the common room.' She set the armour down on a low table with a crash. 'However, your white-haired friend here saved a number of lives earlier by disintegrating a shower of dangerous debris, apparently in an instant.' She peered closely at Frith, who had dragged himself into a sitting position. 'He wears no silks and no cuffs, has no mage words that I can see on him, and I cannot feel the Edenier in him. And yet we all saw him light up like a torch as the rocks were destroyed. In short, it looks like no mage magic I've ever seen, and I have seen a lot of it.'

She went over to a tall cabinet of dark wood and removed a bottle of wine and a tray of goblets.

'You wanted to talk to me,' she said, as she brought the tray and the wine back to the low table. 'So talk. Start with your friend here and what he can do.'

'I can speak for myself,' said Frith, some of the old anger back in his voice. 'And I know little more than you do. The wall exploded, and everything seemed to stop.' He paused and looked down, his gaunt face thrown into shadow. 'I wanted the rocks out of the way so I . . . moved them.'

Xinian poured herself a glass of pale-yellow wine. Sebastian noticed that she didn't offer them any.

'You *are* a mage, then?'

Frith caught Sebastian's eyes briefly. How much to say, that was the question?

'I *was* a mage,' he said, 'but I no longer possess those abilities. The story behind that is a long one.'

'And we don't have time to tell it,' put in Wydrin. She had perched on the edge of the chaise longue next to Frith, and now she leaned forward, her hands clasped before her. 'Commander, we have tidings regarding the Citadel plan. You really do need to hear them, and sooner rather than later.'

Xinian frowned at them all. Outside of her armour she was a tall, wiry woman with powerfully muscled shoulders. Sebastian had not seen her ghost in Skaldshollow for more than an instant, but she cut an impressive figure in flesh and blood.

'I suppose the lives saved by the wall have bought you that much,' she said eventually. 'Tell me what you think you know.'

It took some time to explain, and Sebastian was happy to let Wydrin do it. Well versed in the telling of tales, she carefully talked around their origins a thousand years in the future, and focussed on the immediate threat: the woman who could make herself vanish, the woman who hated the mages, the woman who was working on the side of the gods. During the telling, Xinian finally offered them the wine, and they all drank of it gladly. When Wydrin's tale was done, Xinian retrieved a second bottle from the cabinet and refilled their goblets without asking. The expression she wore was grave.

'And you are sell-swords hunting this Estenn down?'

Wydrin nodded. 'Aside from all this, she has stolen something very valuable from us, and murdered a good friend. She will feel the kiss of my blade before all this is done.'

'This is not good news.' Xinian sat on the low table, goblet held pensively in her hand. 'And it could not come at a worse time.' She sighed heavily and glared around at them all. 'The exact details of the Citadel plan are known only to the higher echelons of our leaders. That this woman knows all about them suggests that we have a traitor in our midst.'

'Forgive me, Commander, but that damage is done,' said Sebastian. There was no way to explain to her that the details of the plan were simply historical fact where they were from. 'Now we must move to stop her, and as quickly as possible.'

'When she captured me, she spoke of this artefact, the Red Echo. She said it was the main piece of bait you used – you are going to use.' Wydrin cleared her throat. 'I think she plans to use it to destroy the mages before you have a chance to capture the gods.'

Xinian's mouth turned down at the edges. 'It certainly has the capability to do that. The Red Echo is an artefact forged at the very dawn of the time of the mages, and in truth we barely understand it. The power contained in it is immense.'

'That has to be her first move,' said Wydrin. 'She will locate the artefact, and steal it. Where is it being kept?'

Xinian's eyes grew cold. 'It is kept in two separate pieces, at two separate, *secret* locations. It is quite safe.'

'Oh, great.' Wydrin shook her head. 'I'm sure that's fine, then. Look, I've just told you that this woman can turn invisible, a power even you people don't possess, and that she knows your plans when supposedly only your big high-and-mighties know them. Don't just trust this problem to go away. The risks are too great.' Wydrin took a breath. 'Believe me.'

Xinian looked away, shaking her head. 'This is the last thing Reis needs. If word gets around that an agent of the gods knows of the plan and intends to sabotage it, then his opponents will finally have the excuse they've been looking for to rise up against him. It will shake the Mage Concordance to its very core. Worse, it could be all-out civil war.'

'Who is this Reis?' asked Oster. Sebastian glanced up at him in surprise; he had kept his silence throughout Wydrin's tale.

Xinian raised her eyebrows, pressing her bald head into wrinkles. 'You do not know of the Archmage?'

'I am not from these parts,' said Oster, his voice utterly flat.

Xinian snorted. 'And I thought Reis's dreaded boot had walked every part of Ede. The Archmage commands the mages in this time of war. It was he who pushed for the Citadel plan, and his will that now drives it through.' She paused, and took another gulp of wine. 'We've been fighting this war for over ten years, and we are run ragged. If the Citadel plan should fail before it has even started . . .' She grimaced. 'He will lose the precarious grip he has on power, and it will be easy for the gods to destroy us, for we will all be busy fighting ourselves.' She put the goblet down and Sebastian saw her cast it a rueful look, as though she blamed it for her loose tongue. 'The number of people who know about this must be kept to an absolute minimum.'

'Let us go, then,' said Frith, his voice low. 'We know this woman, and we can track her down and stop her. We can retrieve our property, have our revenge.' He looked up, and his eyes were storm dark. 'It's the sort of thing we are quite good at, if I do say so myself.'

'The Black Feather Three,' said Xinian. 'That's quite a name for a group of mercenaries.' She paused. 'There are four of you.'

'Again, it's a long story,' said Sebastian.

Xinian stood up. She looked very tired, and Sebastian felt a twinge of sympathy. A soldier's duties were never at an end.

'Fine,' she said shortly. 'I have no energy to argue with you, and no people I can spare to watch over you anyway. You shall travel to the two locations I mentioned, and search for this agent of the gods. I will have you assigned to rooms here for the night, where you can rest and have a wash. From the smell of you all, you need it even more than I do.'

'Commander, perhaps it would be best if we left immediately?' Sebastian said, keeping his tone carefully polite. 'The danger to you and your people is so great—'

'I mean, can't you just magic us all there and back really fast?'

274

put in Wydrin. She glanced at Frith, and then shrugged. 'That's a spell you can do, isn't it?'

Xinian half smiled. 'You really aren't from around here, are you? That particular form of magic has been lost to us almost since the war began, along with several others that were especially useful. Travelling from one place to another in an instant, or even just using magic to look at a remote location – we have to use the Edenier itself to ride the Edeian energy that exists in a cocoon around all of Ede –' She held up her hands and cupped them together, before dropping them again, shaking her head. 'In short, it is dangerous magic, all the more dangerous now. When we move through the Edenier and Edeian like that, the gods can find us almost instantly, and in that instant we are vulnerable.' She frowned. 'We found that out at the cost of many mage lives, at the beginning of this war.'

'These secret locations – I take it they're some distance from Krete?' asked Wydrin. 'I'm assuming you wouldn't keep something so dangerous close to a major city.'

'They are far, yes, but we have developed new methods of travel. Take the time to rest now, while you have it. I will send a steward shortly to show you to your rooms.' She walked over to the door and paused there, a small, bitter smile on her lips. 'Do not fret, the methods we have are still fast, and certainly faster than anything this Estenn will have at her disposal.'

43

Ephemeral had meant to leave when the sun set, but then the first of the eggs had hatched.

She was walking carefully among them, feeling their minds brush against hers and murmuring soothing words. She wondered where the mother was, or if these were the sorts of creatures where the eggs were hidden away, then left to fend for themselves. She had read of such things.

One of the eggs began to tremble, and as she watched, the thick leathery hide was pierced from the inside. A dark hole opened in the side of the egg, and then something poked through: a narrow reptilian head, its scales pale blue and shining, dotted here and there with a darker colour, like splotches of ink. It opened and closed its mouth, baring rows of minuscule teeth, while tiny forearms waved about under the water. Ephemeral stared at it for a moment, perplexed, before her stomach turned over. She had assumed that these creatures were at home in water, but clearly this one could not breathe. Perhaps the eggs had been placed here and the area flooded some time later; it certainly rained often enough on the island.

Without pausing to think, she reached down and plucked the infant animal from the wreckage of its shell and held it up out of the water. It was surprisingly heavy; a long tail curled underneath it, lined with scaly bumps, and at its shoulders were two clumps of fibrous tissue. Ephemeral was holding it up to peer closer at these growths when several of the eggs began to twitch near her feet. The time had come, and they were all hatching at once.

With a cry of dismay, Ephemeral tucked the infant into the top of her pack, ignoring its outraged squawk, and bent to rescue another from the tepid water, followed by another. Splashing backwards rapidly she found a muddy hillock rising out of the pool and deposited the newly hatched lizards there, before rushing back for the others.

Some time later she stood at the foot of the hillock, soaked from head to toe and streaked with mud. She had saved all of them, and now found herself looking at a writhing nursery of stumbling, squawking dragon-kin creatures. They were all shades of blue.

'Your mother will be along presently, I expect,' she told them. Reaching out for their minds, she tried to show them an idea of what mother was. The chorus of squawks increased tenfold, and several fell over. She cleared her throat, trying to think of an image for 'Mother' that wasn't an immense dragon-god. Instead, she tried to summon the feeling of safety and closeness she had experienced in the birthing pit, encouraging them to take comfort in each other. In response, she felt their minds questing back at her. They were bright and curious.

'She is probably hunting,' she said aloud, although she could sense no larger creatures nearby, and the last light of the evening was rapidly leaking from the sky. 'Hunting to provide food for you, her young.' She thought of Y'Ruen again, filling the battlefield with boiling flame. 'Mothers can do that.'

There was a trilling squawk from her side, and she looked down in surprise at the baby dragon-kin she had put in her pack. She had completely forgotten about her, and now the creature was staring up at her with bright orange eyes.

'I must go,' she told the creature with the ink splotches across her knobbly forehead. 'Terin will be leading them to the lagoon even now, and I must be there first.'

A warbling cry echoed through the trees, and as one the infant dragon-kin drew together, some of them waving their long heads back and forth, searching for the source of their fright. Ephemeral tried to imagine leaving them alone in the dark, in the hope that their mother would return, and found that she could not do it. Not all mothers were reliable, after all.

'I will stay with you until dawn,' she told them firmly. 'Just until the sun comes up. You will be much braver then.'

Devinia watched with distaste as Augusta settled her blunt fingers against the crewman's chest, pushing him back onto the floor. They were below decks, in the shallow stinking place that was serving as a sick room. Five of the crew were down here now, too ill to work, and Augusta had been roped in full time to care for them, although it was blindingly obvious to everyone that there was nothing she could do. Devinia was supposedly assisting her, which largely added up to fetching buckets of cool water and holding down the patients when they raved, which was frequently.

'Settle down, lad, settle down,' Augusta said firmly. The man twisted under her touch, his eyes rolling. The red moss covered the left side of his face, completely obscuring one eye and colonising the inside of his nose, and for the last hour or so he had been shouting random phrases, gibbering as though in the grip of a terrible fever. He quietened for a moment, and Augusta pushed a damp cloth against what was left of his forehead. 'It's in his eyes, up his nose, in his ear. I'm telling you, it's getting in their brains. They're stable for a while – unwell, uncomfortable, in pain maybe – but once it gets inside their heads, this is what you get. Poor bastard.'

'Oh yes,' said Devinia dryly. 'My heart bleeds. Perhaps next time they'll think twice before stealing my ship.'

Augusta tutted at her. 'You're a pirate, you fool, and so are these poor bastards. You fight and you steal and you kill each other, fine, but no one should have to go like this.'

Abruptly, one of the patients next to them sat up, a look of wild panic on her face. The red moss-like growth covered both her forearms, and she scratched at it violently, heedless of the damage it was doing to her skin.

'Get it off me!' she howled. 'It's inside me. *Get it off!*'

Augusta and Devinia wrestled with the woman, Augusta muttering soothing things into her ear until she rested back against the floorboards, shivering violently.

'Old woman? I need you in my cabin.'

Devinia looked up to see Ristanov standing in the doorway. She had taken to wearing a hooded cloak rather than her long coat, and her face was cast into shadow, only one side of her mouth showing.

'I've got enough to be getting on with down here, thanks,' snapped Augusta.

'I will not tell you again.'

Devinia laid a hand on Augusta's elbow. 'Come on. Save your energy for more useful fights. That's what you're always telling me, isn't it?'

Grumbling, Augusta got to her feet and with Ristanov following along behind them they made their way to the woman's cabin. Even with the stench of illness clouding her ship and the encroaching itch of the moss covering her own face, the Banshee was ever watchful.

Inside the cabin one oil lamp and a smeared window cast a dirty light. The place had only got more untidy since Devinia had seen it last; discarded clothes littered the floor and the air was thick with the smell of old food and sour sweat. There was a figure slumped awkwardly in a chair by the nailed-down table. After a moment, Devinia realised it was the man called Terin.

'This one sickens too now,' said Ristanov, the disgust in her voice barely disguising the fear underneath it. 'I doubt he will live to reach this lagoon he claims will cure us.'

Terin shifted in the seat, lifting his narrow face to the light. His mottled skin was glistening with sweat, and he shivered as though in the grip of a fever, but there was no sign of the red moss as far as Devinia could see.

'See to him,' said the Banshee. It was clear that she did not want to stay a moment longer in the cabin than she needed to. 'If he is going to die, have him thrown over the side. I do not have the space for more sickening men.' She left without looking back.

'It is the heat.' Terin smiled at them weakly. 'It builds in these small spaces, and it leaches my strength from me.'

'Devinia, fetch me that bucket with the water in, and a cloth. Hurry up now.'

Terin smiled gratefully as Augusta pressed the wet cloth to his forehead. 'We need to move you out of here,' said the old medic. 'It's doing you no bloody good at all.'

'Being up in the direct sunlight is not much better, I'm afraid,' said Terin. 'And the captain likes to keep me away from the others, I think.'

'What are you doing here, northern man?' asked Devinia, watching him closely. 'You are very far from home, and you are suffering for it. What possible business could you have on Euriale?'

Terin didn't answer immediately, instead glancing into the dark corner of the cabin where the shadows were gathered like a shroud. 'I am a visionary,' he said eventually. 'A seer. It is my destiny to walk the paths of strange places, and be granted visions for it. This is how I saw the lagoon that will heal your people.'

'They are not my people,' said Devinia sharply.

'Nevertheless, it's where we all must go,' he said, unperturbed by her tone. 'When the fires took me, I saw it as clear as new ice. There, in those waters, the sickness shall be washed away.'

'Fools.' The voice came from the shadowed corner.

'What the bloody hell is this now?' Augusta dropped the cloth back into the bucket.

With her eyes adjusting to the dark, Devinia could just make out a ragged figure lying on a narrow bunk, propped up on one elbow. It was emaciated, a man made of sticks and bones and pieces of torn shirt. There was a golden band circling his forehead, and his eyes were wet and bright.

'I am their future,' said Kellan. 'I am the Red King come again.'

Devinia took a few cautious steps forward, willing her eyes to see more even as the bile rose up in the back of her throat. Nearly every inch of Kellan's skin was covered in the red mossy substance, and those pieces that were still clear had turned a deep red, inflamed colour. Most of his hair had fallen out, and his beard now only remained in sorry tufts. His eyes, burning like stars beneath his golden crown, were utterly sane.

'I can almost see it, in my head,' he continued. 'What it was like, when the Red King ruled. It . . . it itches on the very edges, the very edges of what I can see.' He reached up and pressed red fingers to his eyebrow, as though he could push the knowledge in. 'I will see it all in the end, Devinia.'

'This is what you get,' she said, feeling a small knot of pleasure in her throat and nursing it, nurturing it. 'This is what you get for fucking with me and mine. As slow and painful deaths go, I could hardly have imagined a better one for you.'

'I am not dying, you idiot,' said Kellan. He raised himself further from the bunk, and Devinia saw with some alarm that there was still a wiry strength to his body, even as all the fat was burned away; muscles stood out with strange clarity under skin as red as a ripe apple. 'I am becoming. You'll all see eventually.'

'He talks like this often,' said Terin quietly. 'The captain spends less and less time here.'

'Because she is afraid of what I will be,' hissed Kellan. 'She hates to see me with such power. She wants the crown, but she's too scared to take it.' He laughed, a sound like dry stones being thrown together.

'Or maybe she doesn't much like the look of what it does to your complexion,' said Augusta. The old woman had retrieved the wet rag and was compulsively wiping her fingers on it. 'Because I'm telling you, son, you look like something that fell out of a sick dog.'

'I have power you can't understand!' He sat up abruptly, and a moment later the ship rocked hard from one side to the other, and there was a chorus of cries from above. 'I could crush this ship between my hands if I wanted to.'

Devinia imagined the giant golden figure standing over the *Dragon's Maw*, golden crystal arms ready to turn it into a pile of splinters.

'That's what I'll do,' said Kellan, although his voice was growing weaker now. He leaned back against the bunk, breathing hard. 'I'll show you all, when it's finished.'

'When you're finished, you mean,' said Devinia softly, but Kellan had already closed his eyes, drifting back into a feverish sleep. There were a few moments' silence between them all as the cries of alarm from above dissipated. Augusta blew air out through her lips, and dunked the rag back in the bucket.

'So, lad. How far away is this bloody lagoon of yours?'

44

Estenn staggered into the shadow of a pile of huge red rocks and dropped to her knees. She let herself become visible again, the first time since arriving in the city. She had moved through the strange trees and then through the courtyards of the palace until she'd located an open gate. The city itself had been overwhelming, with its noise and its smells, and the sheer number of people. For a few moments it had frightened her badly; the noise and clatter of Two-Birds was nothing to such a place, and she had longed for the peace of Euriale with a sudden painful keenness. It was easier to hide, to become a ghost, and she had slipped out of the city and into the surrounding desert. She had been walking for hours, keen to put some space between her and the raucous reality of Krete.

The overhanging rocks had created their own small cave, so she crawled a little further in, glad to be out of the blistering sun. Trees. That was something else she missed: trees and shade.

'I am here,' she said aloud. Beyond the cave she could see the blue of the sky, untainted by cloud, and the golden sands of the desert. In her time, this place had long since been destroyed by the passage of the gods, turning sand and rock into a strip of gleaming green glass. She had never seen the Sea-Glass Road herself, but had heard the tales, like everyone had.

She sat up and unfastened her sword belt, laying the blades carefully on the sand next to her. She took a small bag from within her pocket, and shook into her palm five tiny figures carved from bone. There was a woman, a dragon, a bird and a pair of wolves. She pressed them carefully into the sand in a loose circle. Next, from the same bag she took two small glass jars, one containing black paint, the other white. With her finger, she smeared a quantity of each around her eyes: black for the left, white for the right. When that was done she settled back into a relaxed posture, and prepared herself for prayer. Distantly she wondered about the camp at Two-Birds, and whether her people had prepared the shrine as she had instructed them to do. Of course they had. They followed her without question.

Estenn closed her eyes.

'Y'Gria, Y'Ruen, O'rin, Res'ni and Res'na, a true one names you. A true one entreats you.'

She repeated this for some time, focussing on the small bone figures in front of her. Each of them had been carved from the bones of men and women who had been foolish enough to wander away from Two-Birds and into the heart of the island. Their flesh had been consumed in an act of worship to the Twins, their hair and skin dedicated to Y'Gria, the Mother. These were the tokens she kept with her at all times.

Nothing was happening.

Estenn pushed her sweaty hair back from her face and shifted her legs, trying to get comfortable. She was here, in the Ede of the past, where the gods were real physical beings of great power. Of course they would hear her prayers here. She simply had to be patient.

'Y'Gria, Y'Ruen, O'rin, Res'ni and Res'na, a true one names you. A true one entreats you. Y'Gria, Y'Ruen, O'rin, Res'ni and Res'na, a true one names you. A true one entreats you.'

Silence. Estenn snorted with frustration and stood up, stretching out the muscles in her back. There was a steady ache there, and it was distracting her. The journey through the Eye, and the effort of maintaining her own invisibility had drained her. She simply needed to rest.

As she came to the mouth of the shallow cave, she saw two dark figures walking towards her. They came slowly, but as they

283

grew closer she was able to make out some details. One was a man, his skin so dark a brown it was almost black, and he wore loose white trousers made of linen that billowed in the wind. Across his narrow chest were long strips of white silk embroidered with a silver pattern of interlocking squares, and he wore a simple white cap with a long sweep of fabric that protected his neck from the sun. The figure next to him was a woman, and she stalked across the sand with a wide grin on her face. She was as pale as milk, and her hair was a shaggy grey mane, although to Estenn's eyes she looked very young; certainly no more than twenty. The woman wore black rags and torn black trousers, and long tatters of black fabric dragged behind her in the sand like a trail. Her lips looked colourless and dry, but she grinned all the same.

'Hello there!' called the woman. She lifted a hand in greeting.

Estenn took a step back towards where her swords lay on the sand, and the urge to become invisible again was strong. She resisted. There was something about the two figures that was oddly familiar . . .

'What's the matter? Don't you talk?' called the woman. They came up until they were a few feet away. The man glanced at Estenn, his eyes dark, and then looked away again, apparently disinterested. The woman stared avidly, and her eyes were a hazel colour so pale that it was almost yellow.

'I talk,' said Estenn. 'Who are you?'

'Oh!' The woman in black laughed, rocking back on her heels with the merriment of it. 'That's quite a question, coming from you. Do you really have to ask that, weeping one?'

Estenn opened her mouth and closed it again. Her heart was beating too fast. It was possible to see a strange shadow hanging over the two figures now: a shape like two great feral creatures with long snouts and sharp ears. The woman grinned all the wider.

'The Twins,' murmured Estenn, her lips numb. 'I – Why do you call me that?' Her knees felt weak, threatening to throw her to the ground, but she sensed very strongly that to fall in front of these two would be to invite death. It would be like baring your neck to a wild animal.

'The weeping one?' The woman tipped her head to one side. 'Because you are a little weeping creature, a thing of prey and desperation. All of you humans are, and you are so afraid.' The woman's teeth were very white. 'What is it you want, weeping one?'

'The mages have a plan to kill you.' Estenn wanted to phrase it better, but the words fell from her mouth like stones.

'Of course they do.' The man spoke for the first time. His voice was quiet, scholarly. 'It is what they have fixed their minds upon for the last decade.'

'It's the Citadel, the one they are building now,' said Estenn. 'They plan to trap you inside it.'

The woman who was Res'ni tipped her head back and laughed. It was a pure, joyous sound.

'Trap us? Trap *us*? That is very fine.' She reached up as if to wipe away a tear of mirth from the corner of her eye. 'Those little spell-spitters couldn't catch a mouse.'

'They can do it, I have seen it,' said Estenn. Looking at the two figures was hard now. They seemed to phase in and out of her vision, sometimes appearing as a man and a woman, sometimes appearing as something else altogether. 'I mean, I know that it happens. Please, they plan to place the Red Echo in the deepest chamber and lure you there. I can get it, I can use it to kill them, but you must not go to the Citadel, not even—'

The force of the blow threw her backwards so that she collided awkwardly with the red rock. Estenn cried out and slid down onto the sand. The man, Res'na, shook his head slowly.

'You try to command us? You call us weak? You call us foolish?'

Estenn gasped air into her winded lungs. 'No, please, you must listen—'

'Your little human weepings are of no concern to us,' said Res'ni. She was still smiling. Estenn wondered if the woman ever did anything else. 'But you are interesting.'

Res'ni stepped forward and, standing over Estenn, gestured to the tattoo that curled around her chest and neck. 'I like this,' she said. 'Why do you wear this?'

'I am your servant,' said Estenn. There was a heat coming off the woman, like a fever. 'Your loyal servant, always. I am your emissary.'

Res'ni knelt down next to her. Up close, she smelled rank, like wet fur and old blood. Behind her, Res'na still stood impassively, his face a mask.

'So you will kill the mages for us, will you, little weeping one? Achieve what we have so far failed to do?'

'I will do it,' said Estenn. 'The Red Echo can kill them. I will steal it, and use it on the mages.' She took a deep breath. 'I will not let them take you from the world.'

Res'ni chuckled and glanced up at her brother. 'Interesting. Yes, I like you. Here, I will give you a gift.' The woman reached out and took hold of Estenn's unresisting hand. Immediately, there was a tearing sensation in her palm, as though the flesh there had burst apart. Estenn screamed, and Res'ni pressed her hand all the harder.

'It's just a little bit more of what you already have,' crooned Res'ni. 'A little bit more, and I have fashioned it into a tool for you. Am I not a generous god?'

The pain intensified and, desperately, Estenn tried to shuffle away from the woman, but her grip was unbreakable. Lights flashed before her eyes, and she wondered briefly if she were about to pass out. *If I faint here, I could die.* And then the pressure on her hand was gone and Res'ni, wolf god of chaos, was standing over her, grinning.

'How does it feel?'

Estenn looked down at her hand. There was a gouge across the centre of her palm, the edges of her wounded flesh standing up proud, but rather than blood spilling from her hand it was as if the cut had already healed over, leaving a wide band of diseased-looking purple flesh. As she turned it back and forth, it seemed to glimmer oddly, as if that deep bruise colour hid distant stars. She blinked rapidly. Fresh sweat was prickling her forehead, and she felt as though she stood on the edge of a deep, bottomless pit. Everything turned around her slowly.

'What have you done to me?' She pushed the words through numb lips.

'I have given you a great tool, small weeping one,' said Res'ni. 'Fashioned from your own madness, with a little sliver of something that is mine to give. Use it wisely, if you wish to aid us.'

'Please,' Estenn looked up at them, but the pair of figures were a blur now: one smudge of white, one smudge of black. 'Do not go to the Citadel. I can kill them for you, and I will. But do not be lured. Do not . . .'

The sand rushed up to meet her, and she heard the faint laughter of her gods as the darkness closed in.

45

Wydrin padded around the apartment, assessing the objects and paintings and tapestries for their potential worth, and their potential suitability for being secreted away in her pack and permanently lost. Not, she admitted ruefully to herself, that she would actually do it. The Copper Cat was practically a respectable adventurer these days, and besides, Xinian had given them these rooms, and she owed Xinian a great deal – in more ways than one. The Xinian that she would one day be, at least. After her death. Wydrin picked up a small golden trinket from a dusty shelf and turned it over in her fingers. It looked like a tiny globe, with land masses picked out in smooth jade. She put it back on the shelf with a sigh and turned to Frith.

'We've stayed in worse places.'

'That's for certain.'

They had taken a long, hot bath – hot water was of no consequence to the mages, as they could heat it with a single word – and dressed their various wounds. Xinian had had new clothes brought to them; Frith now wore black and grey wool, with a half-cloak lined with rabbit fur and fastened with a silver pin thrown over one shoulder. They had even given him new boots of tough black leather. Wydrin had been glad to accept a new leather bodice and vanbraces, both of fine quality – deep red-brown leather pierced with silver studs that shone – and a new shirt and trousers. It wasn't until they had taken their old clothes off that Wydrin realised quite what a state they had been in. Washed and dressed, with food in his belly, Frith looked almost his usual self, save for a haunted look in his eyes. She caught him, once too often, staring thoughtfully at his hands or looking off at nothing, and she feared a resurgence of the melancholy that had seized him in the aftermath of Skaldshollow.

'Are you all right?'

He looked up from where he was fiddling with the pin on his cloak. 'I am fine. The journey has left me somewhat fatigued, that's all.' He gestured at the room, taking in the thickly woven carpets and cabinets of dark wood. 'The glory of the mages in their prime. It is something, is it not?'

'It is.' She came over to him and fixed the pin in place, before smoothing her hand across his chest. 'How did we lose all this? The power and the wealth? Those beacons on the tops of the walls that warn of danger – I'm sure there must be more examples of magic used as commonly as buckets and brooms, and we've nothing like this.'

'We lost a lot when the age of the mages ended,' said Frith. 'But if that vision we saw in the sky is the price to pay for such progress, then I'm not sure we're not better off.'

Wydrin snorted. 'Good point, as ever, princeling.' There was a plate of food on the table. Wydrin picked up a pastry and popped the whole thing in her mouth. It was full of cream. 'Bloody hell, thish is good.'

'I just wish I still had the Edenier,' said Frith. He was looking away from her now, his expression distant. 'To be here, in this time, having so recently lost –' He stopped and shook his head. 'Without the Edenier trap I would have lost you. We all would have died in that miserable, frozen place, and Joah Demonsworn would still be harvesting souls with his Rivener. But even so.'

'You miss it,' she said, rubbing flakes of pastry down the front of her bodice. 'You miss having that power.'

He looked up. His eyes were full of anger now, but she knew it was not for her. 'Don't you see, Wydrin? If I miss the power, I am a monster. I saw what it did to Joah, how it twisted him and made him less than human. I did things I can never forgive myself for, and yet part of me wants it all back. Part of me is still the person who killed a defenceless man at the Storm Gates. I'm still the person who left Sebastian to die by the shore of the mages' lake.'

Wydrin blinked in surprise and put the plate of pastries back on the table. 'You still think about that?'

'Of course I do!' He picked up a goblet of wine and drank it down in one gulp. 'How the two of you have forgiven me for it, I do not know.'

'Well, if I recall correctly, I punched you in the face for it at the time, so I think we can move past it. As for Sebastian, the two of you have saved each other's skins so often I think that particular slight is long since buried. You are not a monster, Frith. Don't you see?' She touched his face lightly, tracing the line of his jaw. 'The fact that you even ask yourself these questions proves that you're not.'

He smiled and, snatching up her hand, kissed the palm of it gently. Wydrin felt her heart beat a little faster. Ridiculous, but this was what he was able to do to her.

'I would take it back, if it were offered,' he said softly. 'That is what frightens me, Wydrin. And now there is what happened outside the wall.'

'What do you think it is?'

'I do not know. It felt different to the Edenier, as though my entire being were suffused with a great energy. And for a few moments it felt like I stood outside time.' He shook his head. 'It doesn't make sense. The Edenier trap should have wiped all of that from me, and I thought it had. Yet when I was lost in Euriale looking for you, I was able to use the Edeian to summon a spirit. Perhaps there is something left behind, after all.'

'You know, of all the places to find out what's going on,' Wydrin gestured around at the room, 'a big palace full of mages is a good start.'

'Except that I suspect that to tell them too much of what we know could be disastrous. What if something we do here changes our lives in the future? Meeting Xinian, what could that have

290

changed already?' He pressed his fingers to his forehead, as though he had suddenly come down with a headache. 'It is too much to think about. We must stop Estenn, and if we find answers along the way, I will have to be satisfied with that. We cannot take too many risks.'

'You know what else this place is good for?' She unfastened the pin on his cloak with one easy movement. 'The bed in the next room is enormous.'

Sebastian stood with the straight razor in his hand, staring at his reflection in the mirror they had given him. He had taken not one, but two baths, and spent some time combing out the knots in his hair, which was as long and as unruly as it had ever been. Now it was clean and secured back in its braid, something he had not done properly for some time, but his beard still looked like something that might grow under a bush somewhere.

'I could cut it all off,' he said aloud to the empty room. 'A clean shave might make me feel more human.'

He reached up and tugged at his beard, turning his face first one way, then the other. What would there be under the beard? He looked older than he remembered, the fine lines at the corners of his eyes deeper than they had been, his cheeks gaunter, and the scar given to him by the demon Bezcavar remained a livid purple slash across his cheekbone. If he shaved off his beard, would he see the face of the young Ynnsmouth knight he had once been, fresh-faced and naïve, as yet unbroken? He doubted it.

Sighing, Sebastian put the straight razor back down by the bowl and picked up a small pair of ornamental scissors instead. A trim would be enough. He worked slowly, snipping away pieces of black hair until the beard took on less monstrous proportions. As he worked, he noticed new scars across his bare chest and arms, some lying across old scars like a patchwork. To his surprise, he realised he couldn't recall where they were all from any more. Save for the one on his cheek, of course.

Beard tamed, he put the scissors down and splashed water over his face, and as he did so he felt a silvery tremor inside. His first thought was of Ephemeral – in the snowy wastes of the Frozen Steps, a thousand years in the future – but it was Oster who stepped through the door. Grimacing slightly, Sebastian snapped up a robe from a nearby chair and wrapped it around his bare waist, but Oster barely seemed to notice his nudity. Instead, he stalked into the room and sat down heavily in a chair. A second later, he stood up again. He was still wearing the fine armour he'd had on when Sebastian had met him.

'Oster, what is it you want?' Sebastian patted his face with a piece of dry linen, trying not to feel self-conscious. 'I am busy here.'

Oster blinked at him as though surprised to find someone else in the room. He shook his head. 'They took me to a room and left me there. I wasn't sure what I was supposed to do, so I came and found you.' He sat down, and stood up again. 'I feel strange about what I said to you earlier. I cannot rest until I understand it.'

Sebastian held in a sigh. 'Did you not take a bath? They left you new clothes. It would be a good idea to change into them before we are on the move again.'

Oster paced over to the bed, where Sebastian's clothes had been laid out. He picked up a shirt by its sleeve and peered at it critically. 'I believe what I am wearing is more appropriate for who I am,' he said eventually.

'And who is that?'

Oster put the shirt back down again. 'I am Oster, born of Euriale. My history is long and glorious, my lineage is full of pride and fury.' He turned back to Sebastian with a look of genuine confusion on his face. 'That is not why I am here.' To Sebastian's alarm, Oster strode over to him and took his arm firmly. He did not seem to notice that his skin was still faintly damp. 'The tension between us. It unnerves me. I demand that you help me understand it.'

To his own horror, Sebastian felt a faint heat rushing to his cheeks. Oster's amber eyes were full of unhappiness. Sebastian suddenly felt the vulnerability of the other man and it moved him, even as part of him was appreciating the fine planes of Oster's face, the golden tint of his eyes.

'I'm not sure that I can.' The silver thread that connected them seemed to thrum, and Sebastian stepped away, feeling faintly dizzy. 'We have all been through a lot over the last few days, and our tempers are bound to be frayed.' He walked over to the bed and picked up the shirt they had left him. It was blue silk. He held it up, indicating to Oster that he would like to get dressed now. 'You should go back to your own room, use the hot water they have given you, get some rest.'

Oster nodded, but rather than leaving, he went back to the chair and sat down. 'Tempers,' he said, in a musing tone of voice. 'Being angry, or furious. My family have been known for their tempers, and what they can do when roused. I sense that much, it's just the details that are lost to me.'

Sebastian sighed, and while Oster was looking the other way, he attempted to climb into his clothing as quickly as possible. The other man kept talking.

'I was never meant to be alone in that place. The Spinner should have been there to birth me, to bring me forth and spin my stories so that I might know my own history. Instead, he was kidnapped, and then murdered. I must work everything out alone now. It is unacceptable. This Estenn woman must pay for the damage she has done me.'

'You are not the only one she has wounded, Oster,' said Sebastian. Then he added quickly, 'Will you say what it is you are, then?'

For a long time Oster said nothing. Sebastian concentrated on buttoning his shirt, letting the other man have time to think.

'The vision in the clouds we saw outside.' When Oster eventually spoke, his voice was softer than Sebastian had ever heard it. 'I knew her because we are the same. That creature that so terrified the people of this city – that is what I am.'

Sebastian fastened the last of his belts, giving himself time to think. Wydrin had told him this, of course – a professional liar herself, she was always one to see through to the truth of others.

'What you are saying, Oster, is that you are a god,' he said quietly. 'Do you understand that?'

Oster turned around and looked at him. 'Of course I do. Do

you take me for some sort of human idiot?' Then he added, 'That shirt suits you well.'

Sebastian blinked, and shook his head. 'How can that be, Oster? Gods don't just turn up wandering about in the woods.'

The young man shrugged. 'They do if they come through the Eye and find no one to greet them. I thought that when I found the Spinner everything would make sense again, but now he's gone, and I am in a place already populated with my kind.' He stood up. 'Much of what has happened makes little sense, but I do know that I should not be here. Each time has its own gods, and when they perish, new gods are formed.'

'A cycle,' agreed Sebastian. 'The Spinner spoke of a cycle. And you were the start of it, but he was killed before it could be completed.'

'The gods who are here already, if they find me, if they find out what I am, Sebastian –' Oster shook his head. 'Tempers, as I said. My ancestors are known for them.'

It felt strange to hear his name spoken with Oster's newly softened voice. 'You are a dragon, don't forget that.' Sebastian took a slow breath and forced a smile on his lips. Perhaps Oster wasn't the only one who needed to confront who he was. 'And those of us with dragon blood are hardly defenceless.'

46

The *Dragon's Maw* inched away from the main waterway and down the side channel, its sister ships following on after, and, behind them, the looming presence of the Dawning Man.

Devinia watched from the deck as Terin leaned heavily on her shoulder, the sun beating down mercilessly on them both. She had over the last few days unwittingly become his carer, while Augusta rushed around trying to help those crew members brought low by the red moss. Devinia kept the cool water coming, helped him to walk when he was too weak to do so, and brought him up to the deck when the Banshee summoned him. The guards still followed them around, but they were less watchful, more concerned with their own problems. An opportunity would present itself soon, Devinia was sure of it, even if it meant that the entire crew of the *Dragon's Maw* would have to drop dead, and that was looking more and more likely.

'Follow it east,' said Terin, his voice wavering. 'It will bear east, and lead us to the lagoon.'

The Banshee shot him a single look, saying nothing, and then barked a series of orders to her crew. Oars flicked and dragged through the water, severing the sunlight into golden shards.

'How much further?' asked Devinia in a low voice.

'Another day, perhaps.' Terin paused, before adding, 'They move more slowly because of the creature they bring with them. They would be wisest to leave it behind.'

Devinia chuckled, a bitter taste in her mouth. 'It can smash ships, and it's made of gold. Good luck convincing any pirate to leave that thing alone.' She paused. The waterway had grown significantly narrower, and the ships were sliding into single formation. 'What do you think it is, truly?'

Terin turned to look at her. His face was gaunt, his hair hanging in matted strings. 'The man called Kellan spoke a lot, in the cabin. Not to me, but to spirits, I believe – spirits of a history that is long gone. The Dawning Man is a remnant of that forgotten time, and Kellan is feeding it his soul to give it life again.' Catching Devinia's incredulous look, he shrugged the tiniest amount. 'I come from a land of ghosts and magic, my friend. This place is no different. A people called the Skalds built things similar to the Dawning Man, beings of rock powered by a force they didn't understand.'

'My daughter spoke of such things. She's always been liable to tell tall stories, so I took much of it with a pinch of salt. Now, however . . .' Devinia glanced back over her shoulder. Behind them, the Dawning Man followed on, an impossible thing painted in gold and burning red. She turned back to Terin. 'Will the lagoon really save them?'

'Oh yes,' said Terin. 'I am certain that your salvation waits for you there.'

'No, you must go back!'

Ephemeral turned around, glaring at the trees that pressed in behind her. She couldn't see them, but then she didn't need to. They were keeping just out of sight, but their minds were shimmering presences all around – a song sung in silver. She waited for a moment, hoping that she would hear their retreat, but there was nothing.

'You can't come where I am going. You should wait where you were hatched. I'm sure your mother will be back soon.' Ephemeral turned and walked on, stomping through the thick undergrowth, and almost immediately she could hear the patter of their clawed feet following on behind her – they were quiet, but by no means silent. They hadn't learned that skill just yet, and it seemed there was no one to teach them.

Straightening her shoulders, Ephemeral put them firmly from her mind, closing down her link to the silvery web that was everywhere in this place, and marched forward. She pictured Terin – dear, sweet Terin – who would be almost at the lagoon by now. His life was in the hands of people she neither knew nor trusted, and worse than that, she had asked him to do it.

Quickening her step, she forced herself to remember their binding ceremony. Narhl marriages always took place on a full moon, and it had been a particularly beautiful night. They had journeyed to a distant cliff, the frozen lands stretching away beneath them in silver and black and white, and then the Narhl King himself had built a swirling cone of ice around them, hiding them away from the world. They stayed within the cone together all night, alone, until the first watery rays of the dawn had melted the ice away, revealing them as man and wife. Ephemeral remembered how the ice had filled with a deepening glow as the sun rose, how Terin's smiling face had been painted with its light, and she had felt more at home than she had ever felt, even as the cold pinched and seared her skin. That was what she must remember now. Terin was her home and her responsibility – not these new, directionless lives.

Something nudged at her leg, and she looked down to see the dragon-kin she had briefly carried in her pack staring up at her. They were growing fast, already so much bigger than they had been. The stunted nubbins on their shoulders were taking shape, uncurling. *Wings*, thought Ephemeral, a tightness in her throat. *Just like Mother*. It was also a reminder that she could, if she wished, fly away from them.

'Inky, you must all go back.' Now that one of them had emerged, there were multiple snouts edging out from behind tree trunks and from within bushes. Their minds pushed at her own. 'You're the eldest. You should convince them.'

The small dragon-kin at her feet took no notice of this, leaning heavily on her leg instead, almost like a cat after its tea. Ephemeral pursed her lips. They were too young to understand the danger they were in.

'I am already late,' she told them severely. Multiple orange eyes watched her, unblinking. 'I must be swift now, or Terin will be at the lagoon without me, lost . . .' Her voice trailed off. Next to her, Inky opened her mouth wide, showing off her teeth.

'Follow me, then,' she said, reaching out for all their minds at once, whilst marvelling at how easy that was. 'Come with me, little ones, and we shall hunt as we go.'

Ephemeral ran into the trees, and the tide of dragon-kin came on after her.

47

Xinian the Battleborn led them through a broken courtyard teeming with men and women, and they came to a part of the Arkanium that looked much older than the surrounding buildings. Three grey stone walls were still standing, and the mages had built a new roof over the top, the wood still pale and raw. As they approached, a pair of mages guarding the entrance bowed deeply to Xinian and moved swiftly out of their way, while a short woman in crimson vest and leggings hurried over. She wore thick fabric strips around both burly arms.

'Commander!' The woman had frizzy auburn hair held back in a stained kerchief, and at the sight of Xinian her eyes were bright with excitement. 'We weren't expecting you. What's happened? Are we going out on a raid? Do you need my assistance?'

'Silvain, I require the use of two of the carapacers. Get them ready.'

The woman raised her eyebrows. 'Of course, Commander.' She ran back into the building ahead of them.

'What I propose,' said Xinian as they walked into the echoing space, 'is that you split up. Two of you check on one piece of the artefact, two of you check the other. They are kept some distance apart, as you can imagine.'

'That's fair enough,' said Wydrin. 'If we split up, we can cause trouble faster.'

299

Xinian narrowed her eyes at this. 'To use this method of transportation, you will need mage assistance.'

Inside the hall was a tall wooden screen. As they approached, a pair of men folded it back, revealing two large blocky shapes. Silvain was there, pressing her hands against their shiny flanks with a look of intense concentration on her face.

'The carapacers,' said Xinian. 'This is what we use now that our transportation spells are too dangerous. There are only five in existence.'

They looked like a pair of giant beetles made of shining green metal. As they got closer, Frith saw that what he had taken for shell casings were engraved with the looping forms of mage words, and these were what Silvain was pressing her hands to. As she did, each one glowed briefly with a pearly light. There were two lamps mounted to the front of the green domes, which only enhanced the insectoid impression, and underneath he could see what looked like stunted gold legs mounted with springs.

'How do you get around on these things exactly?' asked Wydrin.

'You're unbound?' asked Silvain, looking up from her task. Frith caught the curious look she shot Xinian, but the Commander apparently decided not to notice it. 'Ah, well, they essentially run on a sort of magical clockwork. We wind them up,' she pressed her hand to one of the mage words, and waited for it to wink with light, 'and let them go.'

'Fascinating.' Not quite able to help himself, Frith joined Silvain by the carapacer device, peering closely at the symbols etched into the green metal. 'You fill it with Edenier somehow?'

'Sort of,' said Silvain, looking mildly impressed. 'We store the magical energy within it, and then whilst on board we use the Edenier to steer it. And then, when it runs out, we top it up again.'

'They are not here to learn the intricacies of the Edenier, Silvain,' said Xinian, a cold note in her voice.

'Can I ask why they are here, then?' asked Silvain quickly. 'The unbound are not normally allowed to just wander around the Arkanium.'

'Do you see them wandering?' Xinian glared at the woman, and then gestured at the carapacer with the arm that ended in a stump. 'Two of you will travel with me, and Silvain will accompany the others to our other destination, since she is so curious. Who is going where?'

Frith saw Wydrin exchange a glance with Sebastian. 'Frith and I will travel together, and Sebastian and Oster will take your other contraption.' She grinned. 'That's at least one decent sword arm on each team. One of us is bound to run into Estenn, but I hope it's me.' She touched the dagger at her hip, and Sebastian nodded.

'This woman will not get anywhere near our strongholds,' said Xinian. She walked around to the side of the nearest carapacer, where a short rope ladder hung from its broad top. 'But I promise that she will regret attempting to disrupt our plans. Silvain, show your guests to their transport. You'll be making a trip to Relios today. Threefellows and Lord Frith, you are with me.'

Xinian gestured to Silvain, who hurried over to receive quiet instructions. Frith saw the woman's eyes widen, and then she was dismissed. Xinian turned away from her and climbed the rope ladder that hung down the side of the carapacer, and then dropped down into an alcove that Frith couldn't see.

'Looks like we're splitting up again,' said Wydrin. 'I can't say that I'm pleased about that.'

Sebastian nodded gravely. 'If all else fails, come back to Krete,' he said. 'We can regroup there, if we need to. Do you remember where the Hands of Fate tavern was?'

Wydrin grinned. 'Of course I do. It was the beginning of this whole mess.'

'It is unlikely to be there now,' said Frith.

'Whatever is there currently, that will be our meeting place, even if it's a half-built street.' Sebastian shook his head slowly. Behind him Oster stood, silently watching them. 'It's still too much to take in. That we have travelled this far—'

'I suggest you get a move on,' called Xinian from above them. 'Or we'll have to charge the 'pacers anew.'

Abruptly, Wydrin hugged Sebastian, squeezing him fiercely. The big knight smiled and kissed the top of her head – how long, Frith wondered, had it been since they'd seen a genuine smile from him? When Wydrin released him, Frith took his hand and clasped it firmly.

'I will see you both again,' Sebastian said, but his smile faded as he said it. 'I swear it by Isu.'

They climbed into their 'pacers. The tops of the contraptions were hollowed out and upholstered with cushioned silk. Frith noticed that there were more ropes attached here, made of dark green braided silk. Xinian positioned herself at the front of the seating area, her legs crossed. She gestured and the big lamps on the front of the carapacer flickered into life. Next to them, Silvain settled herself at the front of the other carapacer with an undisguised expression of cheerful anticipation on her face as Sebastian and Oster climbed awkwardly in behind her.

'Shall I lead us out, Commander?' she called across.

'If you must,' said Xinian. 'Be careful of us as you leave.'

Silvain nodded, and held her arms up in front of her. As they watched, two oval-shaped sections of the shining green metal lifted up, and a pair of shimmering wings emerged, composed of emerald light. For a moment they seemed to flicker in and out of existence, and then they began to move, so quickly that they became a brilliant green blur. The carapacer shuddered and then lifted jerkily off the ground. It hovered there for a few seconds, and then it glided swiftly forward, out of the hall and into the bright sunshine of the courtyard. They could see Silvain shifting in her seat, murmuring words under her breath and then the carapacer shot forward, curving up into the sky until it was lost from sight.

'Extraordinary,' breathed Frith to himself. He turned back to Wydrin and was surprised to see her face solemn. He lowered his voice. 'What is it?'

'Saying goodbye again,' she said. 'It feels like a mistake.' She looked up at Frith, her green eyes like smoky jade. 'When we sailed down the waterway into Euriale for the first time, I had this feeling – like this would be the end of something. When we found Sebastian again, I decided I was just being ridiculous, but here we are again, and that feeling hasn't left me.'

Frith found that he did not know what to say to this. The

carapacer jerked, and abruptly they were lifted up into the air. There was a faint hum, just on the edge of hearing; the sound of many spells working in conjunction at once. It reminded him of the Rivener.

'Hold on now,' called Xinian from the front. The carapacer shuddered once more, and they coasted gently out into the courtyard. Around them, mages were watching, no doubt wondering where their greatest military commander was taking a pair of unbound civilians. The Edenier wings buzzed frantically, and before Frith could quite prepare himself for it, they swept up into the air, leaving the Arkanium far beneath them. Frith peered over the side, and felt his stomach turn over. Riding Gwiddion had been one thing – the griffin was a solid beast of muscles and fur and intelligence – but the contraption beneath them felt all too frail.

'Just once, I would like to walk somewhere,' murmured Wydrin. Then she shouted over to Xinian, 'didn't you say these things eventually wind down? What happens then?'

Xinian glanced over her shoulder at them, the bright sun winking off her bald head. 'I would tie yourselves in, if I were you.'

48

Estenn settled the final rock into place, pushing it into the sand firmly, and her mind came back to her with a snap.

She straightened up and looked around. She was dimly aware that for the last hour or so she had been moving rocks around under the punishing desert sun. Her head was throbbing and the skin on her face was tingling. The line of rocks marched off across the red sand, turning and bending here and there to a design she couldn't even guess at.

'Why have I done this?' she murmured to herself. Since the visit from Res'ni and Res'na, her mind felt clouded, all her usual iron purpose thrown to the winds. 'I should not even be here, I should be travelling, I must stop them. I must.' The world spun around her and she squeezed her eyes shut. 'I have a task to perform. For them.'

She opened her eyes and looked at her hand. The ridge of purple flesh no longer hurt, but it felt very warm, as though it were infected. For all she knew, it was.

'Why would she do that?' she asked the empty desert. 'I am here to save them.'

A whirring noise from above caused her to look up. Hanging in the blue sky was what looked a giant green beetle, its wings beating in a brilliantly glowing blur. As it descended, it kicked up puffs of red sand all around, and Estenn held her hands over her face to keep it getting in her eyes. The strange object landed just beyond where she had been placing her rocks, and a tall man with a bald head jumped out. He was in his fifties at least, and stocky, and he had some sort of ornate sigil tattooed onto his scalp. He wore an olive-green cloak over travelling clothes that looked both unsuitable for the desert and as though they had recently seen a lot of hard use. He looked furious.

'What do you mean by this?' He gestured towards the rocks. Behind him, a man and a woman were watching her from the back of the strange flying contraption.

Estenn cleared her throat and willed her mind to recover. 'What are you talking about?'

'The wolf, woman! I assume this was you, since you are standing there with sand all over your hands and a gormless look on your face. What do you mean by it?' Now he was closer Estenn could see that his arms were criss-crossed with long lengths of white silk, all of them painted with words. A mage, then. This was one of the people she was here to kill. She thought of her swords, lying in the sand.

'Who are you?' she asked, and was pleased to see a spasm of anger cross his face. This was good. She was feeling better already.

'I am Archmage Reis, you unbound whelp. Do you mean to call the gods here? Is that what you're doing?'

Estenn looked at the rocks. She supposed that, from above, the pattern of them might make some sense.

'It's a wolf? That's what it looks like?' she wondered aloud.

'Pretending ignorance now, is it?' Archmage Reis scowled. 'As unbound, you hardly need to pretend to that. Of course it's a wolf. What are you? An agent of the Twins? Or just one of these raving fanatics who believes we should let them crush us into dust?' He shook his head in disgust. 'Either way, we'll take you with us to the Arkanium. Xinian can deal with you.' He turned and gestured to the man and the woman still waiting for him. They climbed out of the contraption. Estenn felt her heart grow lighter. It all seemed obvious now. They had given her a gift.

'You are the Archmage?' Her face split into a genuine smile. The man frowned in response, looking confused. 'Your fame reaches further than you realise.'

She stepped forward, and before he could react she took hold of his hand with both of hers and squeezed it. The wound on her palm burned with sudden ferocity, and she watched with pleasure as the Archmage's eyes widened with surprise.

'What are you doing?' he cried.

'I'm just giving you a gift,' she said softly. 'The gift of faith.'

He yelped with pain and yanked his hand away. His two attendants sprinted over, but it was too late. Reis lifted his head, and his eyes were wild. He held his hand out in front of him, and there was a bright purple mark on his palm, throbbing with strange colours.

'It's just a little more of what you already had,' said Estenn. 'The paranoia, the rage, the need for control. I've just given your true nature rein. How do you like it?'

'Sir, are you all right?' The man was young, his brown skin as yet unmarked by lines. Before he could react, Estenn lunged and pressed her hand to his cheek, and felt the madness bite. The woman, who was quicker off the mark than either of her male companions, lifted her hands to summon some mages' spell, but Archmage Reis gestured and she was suddenly a flaming, screaming torch. The scent of burning flesh filled Estenn's nostrils, and she smiled. It was one of the familiar smells of home.

'You will take me where I need to go,' she said, pointing to the strange flying machine. 'You will take me to Whittenfarne now, lord of the mages, and then I will kill you all.'

49

As soon as they were in the air, Silvain was full of questions. She kept glancing over her shoulder at them and shouting her queries against the wind, which Sebastian couldn't help feeling wasn't the most reassuring behaviour for the person apparently keeping this strange craft in the air.

'So who are you people? You can trust me. The Commander does, she pretty much tells me everything anyway. So there's no harm if you do tell me.'

Sebastian looked over at Oster. The young god turned away.

'I am Sir Sebastian Carverson,' he said, leaning forward so that he might be heard more clearly. 'This is my friend, Oster.'

'And you're what? Swords for hire?'

'It's complicated,' said Sebastian smoothly. 'Can you tell us where we're going?'

'I suppose you'll see for yourself soon enough.' Silvain shifted in her seat and the carapacer tipped slightly, turning them to the north-west. Below them orange sands undulated like waves. 'We're heading for Relios. Do you know the region?'

'I'm reasonably familiar with it.'

'You've probably heard of Ashbless Mountain, then. It's a volcano, but it blew itself all to hell a good hundred years ago now. The small towns and villages that surrounded it were wiped off the map, and no one has been able to settle it since. It's an empty shit hole of a place.'

'So the mages have a base there?'

'We have a base hidden *inside* the volcano. It's called Poledouris, and very few mages have been there, let alone unbound. So I guess you should be honoured,' said Silvain. 'Oh hold on, looks like we might have trouble.'

Sebastian sat up, trying to look over Silvain's head. At the same moment, Oster spoke.

'There's more of them here,' he said, his voice pitched low. 'I can feel them.'

At first Sebastian could see nothing out of the ordinary. They were flying roughly fifty feet above the sand, and ahead he could see more desert, some stunted trees, and the occasional pile of rocks. They passed over a steep dune and were faced with the remains of a burning town. Sebastian realised that the smell of smoke had been in his nostrils for some time.

'What was this?'

Silvain shook her head. 'Oh some bloody place. Might have been Zakrnthos, or Maylabria – they were both small towns around here, I can never keep them straight. It's nowhere at all now.'

The fires were starting to burn down, and as they passed over Sebastian could see the broken black shapes that had once been houses. He couldn't make out any people, although he wasn't sure if that was a good or a bad sign. The flesh on the back of his neck tingled, and he looked up into the blue sky, half expecting to see the might of Y'Ruen hanging above them, holding their fiery deaths in her throat, but there was nothing.

'Was this the work of the dragon?' he asked, dreading the answer.

'No, it was *her*. Shit.'

Out of the wreckage ahead of them, a strange billowing shape was emerging. At first Sebastian had the confused impression that it was some sort of enormous jellyfish, something ensconced within delicate plates of soft tissue, and then he saw that there was a woman at the heart of it – a giant woman around twenty feet tall, her skin bone white and her hair the deep green of a forest. Great curling ram's horns pushed through her mane of emerald hair, and below the waist her body split into multiple questing tendrils, like the roots of a tree. She was floating up from the burnt town like a sea current carried her, and she held a fiery trident in one hand.

'It's Y'Gria,' said Silvain, who was already frantically changing the course of the carapacer. There was no mistaking the fear in her voice. 'Oh shit, oh shit.'

'But Y'Gria was the goddess of growth, of new life. They called her the Mother,' said Sebastian. Even as he spoke, the giant woman turned her eyes on them, and there was no mistaking the promised threat in that gaze. Her bloodless lips curved into a smile. 'Surely she wouldn't be responsible for this?'

'Are you kidding me?' cried Silvain. 'They all hate us, and she's the bloody worst. At least the others are half mad, or easily distracted. This one is just a – a giant bitch.'

'For new things to grow, the world must be made anew,' murmured Oster. 'She has given up on you all. She is eager to start again.'

The carapacer was lurching to one side, turning rapidly to get out of Y'Gria's line of sight. Sebastian could feel it shaking with the effort. He curled his hands more tightly around the ropes, and hoped the whole thing didn't just rattle itself apart.

'Hold on, boys,' called Silvain, 'I'm going to try some evasive manoeuvres.'

Sebastian gave a startled yelp as the carapacer dropped suddenly, taking them briefly behind a tall tower that was still burning in places. Y'Gria vanished from sight, but as the carapacer righted itself and skimmed around a corner, she appeared right in front of them. This close, Sebastian could see the smooth skin of her belly – she had no navel. Y'Gria smiled at them warmly. The tendrils that hung below her looked like they were covered in pale bark, but they twisted and moved as easily as flesh.

'Where do you think you are going, my little insects?'

Her voice was warm honey, a hot summer's day when everything smelled of growth and fecundity. Sebastian shook his head, disorientated, and then Silvain turned the carapacer on a pin and they were arcing up into the sky at a rate that pushed Sebastian and Oster to the very back of the cushioned seat.

In less than an eye blink, Y'Gria was there ahead of them again, looming out of nowhere, her thick green hair swirling as though she were underwater. To Sebastian's surprise, Silvain stood up and held out her arms. A bolt of bright orange fire flew from her fingertips and crackled across the god's beautiful face, and for a few seconds Y'Gria drew back, apparently startled. Silvain threw another bolt of fire for good measure before wresting control of the carapacer back and sending them zooming low across the rooftops. Sebastian found himself reaching for his sword, but the speed of the carapacer was pushing him back into the seat – he couldn't even stand, let alone fight. He reached across and grabbed Oster's arm.

'You have to help her!' he shouted. 'You have to change!'

Oster looked incredulous. 'If I do that, they will know what I am!'

Sebastian shook his head, barely able to believe what he was hearing. 'That will hardly bloody matter if we're smeared all over the ground!'

Oster pulled away from him, and the entire carapacer shook alarmingly. Sebastian looked up to see Y'Gria cutting them off again, and this time she was reaching for them. Her fingers brushed the buzzing wing on the right of the craft and for a few seconds it winked out of existence. Silvain was screaming obscenities at the god, punctuated with bolts of fire and lightning, but Y'Gria no longer seemed perturbed by this. She smiled indulgently, like a mother watching her offspring attempt something especially taxing, and then she struck the carapacer with her trident. Bright flames crawled across the green metal, burning with extra brilliance as they passed over the mages' words engraved there, and both wings stuttered and died.

'No!' Silvain threw herself forward, casting a sheet of ice across the fire, but it was too late. With a lurch the carapacer dropped like a stone, going into an awkward spin.

Sebastian had time to see Y'Gria reach down, as fast as a snake, and grab Silvain before she dropped out of sight. He heard the young mage woman scream, saw more fire, and then he was out of the carapacer and spinning towards the ground.

Not here, he thought, *not so far from the mountains –*

The rocks and sand rushed up to meet him.

50

Wydrin leaned over and ran her fingers over the smooth metal of the carapacer's outer shell. The mages' words engraved in the side shone with a faint pearlescent glow, and as her hand passed over them she felt a tingle in her fingertips. Below them was the bright rippled surface of the Creosis Sea. Xinian kept the carapacer moving smoothly, heading steadily east; so far she had refused to name their destination. Wydrin looked at the back of the woman's bald head, noting her rigid posture and well-used armour. It wasn't right, she mused, to know so much of someone else's future. No one should have such knowledge. The whirring of the carapacer's wings caught her eye and something else occurred to her.

'Hey, Xinian. These things aren't alive, are they?'

The mage cocked her head, but did not turn around. 'Of course not. They are simply imbued with magical energy. Eventually that runs out and the wings will stop beating.'

Wydrin caught Frith's eye, and he shrugged the tiniest amount.

'Yeah, I've heard that sort of thing before,' said Wydrin. She looked down at the scar in the middle of her hand, and thought of Mendrick's calm, cold voice. There had been a few dreams since Skaldshollow, ones where she saw Nuava and the Destroyer – the enormous werken she and her aunt had made to battle the Rivener – disappear into the terrible hole Joah Demonsworn had summoned. In the dreams she saw young Nuava die, crushed by unknowable forces on the other side of existence, and she heard

Mendrick silenced, the voice of the mountain gone for ever. She would wake up from these dreams with her heart racing, and in the dark Frith would slip his arms around her and say nothing. He had enough of his own bad dreams to know not to ask.

'I can feel the magic of these contraptions,' said Frith quietly, so that Xinian could not overhear. 'Edenier laced over Edeian. It is similar, but not the same, as the werkens.'

'Should you still be able to sense that?'

Frith shook his head. 'I would have thought not. But the spirit I met in Euriale appears to have changed more than I realised.'

'If you have something useful to say, I would like to hear it,' called Xinian in a sour tone. 'Technically speaking, you two are still my prisoners.'

'We were just admiring these weird machines of yours,' said Wydrin, plastering a smile on her face. 'Being able to build things like this must be enormously useful. I imagine it helps a lot of people.'

For a few moments, Xinian didn't answer, and Wydrin wondered if perhaps she hadn't heard her. When she did answer she sounded reluctant to speak at all.

'Machines such as these are very rare. The skill to wield both Edenier and Edeian at the same time is known to only a handful of people. You will be meeting two of them when we reach our destination.'

'Still, there must be a lot of good you can do for ordinary people. For the unbound, I mean.' Wydrin slapped the metal. 'Just one of these, moving trade goods around, for example. Faster and cleaner. Building materials too.'

'Such things . . . we have been at war for a very long time. Of course, Edenier must be used for the betterment of humankind, but for now . . .' Xinian's voice trailed off.

'All of your resources are taken up with this spat with the gods?'

'This *spat* has been going on for over a decade. Thousands dead, more injured and forced out of their homes.' The carapacer juddered slightly, and Xinian corrected their course with a gesture. 'We do what we can to protect the unbound but we are stretched thin. Every year, we edge closer to total defeat.' Her voice became firm. 'That is why the Citadel *must* work.'

'They must pay,' mused Frith in a low voice. 'Whatever the cost. Even if it costs a thousand more lives, even if they must drive the gods under the ground and watch as their own magic leaks away.'

Wydrin gave him a look, but he just shook his head wearily.

The carapacer flew on as the light faded from the sky. When full night fell, they landed on a tiny island where a ring of bright beacons sat burning with alchemical light. Xinian lit a fire and they made camp as well as they could, eating from a small supply of bread, meat and ale Xinian had brought. The mage had them up again at dawn, pausing to press her hands to the mages' words engraved in the hide of the carapacer before piloting the beetle-shaped craft up into a sky newly clouded with mist. The air grew chillier, and the sea below was lost from view. Wydrin shuddered, and drew the hood of her cloak up over her head.

'We are close now,' said Xinian.

'How can you even tell where we are?' Wydrin gestured at the thick banks of pale mist that pressed at every side. 'This is like swimming through soup.'

'I have made this journey a great number of times,' said Xinian. 'The skies around the Nowhere Isles are usually thick with fog.'

As if to contradict her, the air around them suddenly exploded with light and flame. Wydrin cried out, feeling the skin on the right side of her body sting with sudden heat, and the carapacer pitched to one side. The fireball that had missed them by inches sailed off into the fog, which hissed into nothing at its passage. Frith was shouting and pointing, and an old nightmare descended on them from above: Y'Ruen, huge and vital and real, every single blue scale shining like the lost sea below them. The great dragon opened her mouth and roared and she was impossibly close – Wydrin could not understand how the tiny carapacer could share the sky with such a creature and survive – the smell of her breath was carrion and smoke and war.

'Hold on!' called Xinian from the front. Wydrin grabbed the rope and twisted it around both fists before the carapacer shot forward, diving into the mist like a startled rabbit. Next to her, Frith was bracing himself at the back of the compartment. Wydrin sat up and looked behind them to see the dragon curling lazily around, huge wings beating the mist away. Her huge reptilian head followed them slowly, as though she had already lost interest, the yellow eyes shining in the gloom like lamps.

'She's not coming after us!' cried Wydrin, scarcely able to believe their luck.

'She's easily distracted,' said Xinian. She cast a brief glance over her shoulder. 'Y'Ruen prefers the glory of the battlefield, the pleasure of incinerating hundreds at once. To her we are barely worth the effort, especially as only one of us is a mage.'

'Well she's changed her tune,' murmured Wydrin.

'The problem is her daughters,' said Xinian. 'Where Y'Ruen is, her daughters won't be far behind.'

'Daughters?'

An instant later the first one hit the side of the carapacer, with enough force to nearly tip them all out. The figure that scrambled over the metal side was humanoid, with a loose shirt of golden scales hanging over a body covered in thorny ridges and thick, scaly skin the colour of a frog's underbelly. The woman's face was oddly bat-like, twisted around a huge gaping mouth lined with yellow fangs easily an inch long. Her head was bald, with wide pointed ears, and a pair of leathery, bat-like wings poked from her back. She had a blue crystal sword clutched in one hand, and when she opened her mouth she hissed like a cat.

'She has daughters here too?' Wydrin gestured at the woman with Glassheart, casting an outraged look at Frith. 'We have to deal with the bloody brood army again?'

Frith had scrambled to his feet. He held his own short sword, and the wind whipped his hair back and forth. He shook his head at her, half in bewilderment. 'It's the dragon's brood, but not woken by Sebastian's blood. Look at it! There's nothing human in there at all.'

As if to prove his point, the monstrous brood sister opened her mouth and hissed again, before leaping down into the compartment, sword whirling. Wydrin threw herself forward, getting her sword in and catching the crystal blade on it, before thrusting up with Frostling to bury the dagger deep under the brood creature's ribs. The dragon woman squealed as black blood bubbled up from her greenish skin, and Wydrin forcibly pushed her back over the side. Wings flapped feebly for a moment, and then she was lost in the mist, but out of the fog more winged shapes were approaching.

'Xinian? Can you move this thing faster?'

'What do you think I am doing?' snapped Xinian in response. 'You'll have to keep them off us.'

'Watch out!'

Wydrin turned to Frith's warning in time to see three more brood sisters landing on the carapacer – their feet had long curved toes, almost like talons, and as they scrambled for purchase, their claws scratched through a section of the mage words, and the illuminated portion flickered and died. The carapacer juddered and dropped a few feet through the air.

'Shit!' Xinian turned and shot a bolt of energy over one shoulder, striking a brood sister who had just gained her feet squarely in the chest. She was knocked backwards and lost in the fog, but another landed in her place. 'You have to get them off before they tear this thing to pieces.'

'Not a problem, Commander!' Wydrin surged forward, Frith at her back, and they met blue crystal swords with their steel. The blades clashed, sending discordant music into the air, and Wydrin felt a surge of disorientation; all at once she was back in the Citadel that would exist in the future, surrounded by the brood sisters while Sebastian bled to death on the floor next to her.

'Get back!' Frith smashed the pommel of his sword into the face of the nearest brood soldier, and brought the sword round in a wide sweep to take out the legs of another that perched on the shell of the carapacer. Wydrin stabbed out wildly, letting her instincts take over even as the part of her that stood back from battle and watched for opportunities to strike took note of the shadowed shapes pursuing them through the mist. They were like a carcass attracting flies.

315

'There are too many of them, Xinian!' She jerked her sword free of one body, before crashing it against the blue crystal of another sword. One of the brood sisters leapt down and landed squarely on Frith, knocking him to the floor of the compartment. Wydrin saw the creature's hands close around his throat, but she was already moving, bellowing something unintelligible. She threw herself at the sister and they both fell violently against the side. The carapacer dipped wildly and they went over the side together – Wydrin heard Frith's anguished cry – and then she was clinging to the grip of Frostling, the blade embedded between two metal plates as she dangled from the side of the carapacer. The brood sister clutched at her, and she felt a bright sliver of pain as the claws pulled two bloody tracks across her legs, and the creature beat her wings once, twice. Wydrin yelped as she was dragged up into the air, the yawning nothingness of the mist hanging below her, and then Frith had her arm.

The brood sister was alarmingly strong, but Frith threw all his weight backwards, and the claws lost their grip on her leg. Wydrin and Frith fell back together into the compartment, but not before a large section of green metal flipped up from the side of the carapacer and spun away into the gloom. The carapacer shuddered, and the green glow of the wings stuttered, and then died completely.

For a few dizzying moments the carapacer fell, and they scrambled desperately for the ropes. Several of the brood sisters who had alighted jumped back off, apparently startled by the sudden drop.

'Xinian!'

'I can't hold it, I can't—' The carapacer shuddered and the dive slowed, minutely. Xinian held out both arms, the silk ties flickering in the wind like sand snakes. The Commander was trembling all over with the effort.

'She is keeping us up here with the Edenier alone,' said Frith. 'I doubt she will be able to do that for long.'

Wydrin opened her mouth to reply, only to see four more brood sisters looming out of the fog.

'We have to keep them off her until we can land somewhere.'

She jumped forward, blades at the ready, Frith at her side,

316

when a brood sister fell on them directly from above. Wydrin crashed to the cushioned floor, the air crushed out of her lungs by a pair of knees on her chest. A twisted, bat-like face loomed down at her, and there was nothing human in the eyes at all – nothing but hunger and a need to tear things apart. As if it were a sign for all of them, several more brood sisters landed on the craft, and the whole thing rocked wildly from side to side. Wydrin tried to bring her dagger around to sink it into the creature's side, but a horned foot stood on her wrist and pressed until she thought the bones would break. She couldn't see Frith.

'Get off me, you ugly . . . bat's arse.'

The creature leaned back, opening its mouth so wide that Wydrin thought the top of its head might fall off. It was undoubtedly the action of an animal about to rip a throat out, and Wydrin bucked her hips desperately, trying to throw it off.

And then Frith fell back into view. He had a wound at his neck and his eyes were wild, but as she watched he began to glow, just as he had at the wall in Krete – first with a faint, wavering light, and then a shining white blast. He reached out a hand towards the brood sister that had her pinned, and its skin began to twist and turn grey. The creature screeched, holding out its hands in horror – a gruesomely human gesture – and then the skin crusted and began to fall away. Underneath, the brood sister's flesh had turned to brittle dust, and within seconds there was nothing but a yellowed skeleton sitting astride Wydrin – and then that crumbled away too, lost in the wind.

'What did you—?'

Frith was still burning with the light. He turned away from her, and with a gesture all of the brood sisters were collapsing into dust, their skins wrinkling and splitting, their eyeballs withering and falling back into their skulls, before collapsing into nothing. Within seconds, they were all gone, and the floor of the compartment was filled with a greyish powder, already being whipped away by the wind.

Frith turned to her, and through the glow she could just make out his expression of complete confusion. He opened his mouth to say something, and then the light winked out. Frith dropped

317

to the floor in a dead faint, his body completely boneless, and for a frightening moment the carapacer dipped and Wydrin thought he would be thrown clear. Instead, he rolled to the side and came to rest there. Wydrin scrambled over to him, ignoring the blood weeping from her own leg. She pulled his head into her lap and felt for a pulse; it was there, rapid but faint.

'By all the gods,' she pressed her lips to his forehead, and tasted sweat, 'what was that all about, my love?'

'What happened?' shouted Xinian. She turned to look at Wydrin, and it was obvious that the mage was close to exhaustion. The fingers she held out to either side were trembling. 'Where did the dragon's creatures go?'

'Technically, I think they're in the creases of your upholstery, and there's a reasonable amount in my hair.'

Xinian looked less than pleased by that answer, but she shook her head and turned back to her task.

'Well, we're about to land, whether we like it or not. Brace yourself.'

51

'So, how broken is it?'

They had landed, for want of a better word, on a tiny island of black rocks that barely deserved the description. Wydrin recognised the black sand and stunted trees of the Nowhere Isles from her journey to Whittenfarne – Frith might even have had some idea of where they were, but he had yet to regain consciousness. He lay by the small fire they had made, wrapped in Wydrin's cloak, a bandage at his throat. The scratches across her legs had been painful but shallow, at least. The carapacer sat off to one side, leaning drunkenly, the golden legs that supported it having taken a lot of damage when they had crashed into the rocks. Xinian stood next to it, running her hands over the battered metal plates.

'It is fairly broken,' admitted Xinian. She scowled as she pressed her fingers to the mages' word in front of her. It did not light up. 'Our descent has rattled the pieces apart, and we would need an Edeian crafter to move them back into place to cover the missing panel. I can recharge it with Edenier, but it is beyond my skill to repair the rest of it.'

'And how far are we from our destination?'

'Not so far, but too far to walk it, even if we could scurry across water,' said Xinian sourly.

'Did Y'Ruen know we were coming?' Wydrin asked in a low voice. 'Might she appear again?'

Xinian turned her frown onto her. 'It was a random attack. Y'Ruen delights in bringing death, but she does not have a strategic mind. She simply kills anything that moves. I am more interested in your friend there. What happened to him? How did he destroy the dragon's daughters?'

Wydrin looked back over to Frith. His breathing had slowed, and he now appeared to be sleeping normally. 'If I knew, Xinian, I would tell you, believe me. And I'm sure you will batter him with questions as soon as he wakes up, but for now I suspect we'd all be a lot happier if we could get off this stinking bloody island. How exactly are we going to do that?'

Xinian stepped back from the carapacer and to Wydrin's surprise gave it a single vicious kick.

'The people at our destination knew we were coming,' she said. 'Eventually they will wonder where we are, and eventually they will come looking for us.'

Wydrin grimaced, thinking of the scattered islands of the Nowhere Isles; numerous and continually lost in thick mist, they made the archipelago of Crosshaven look positively organised. 'We'd best get comfortable, then, because I reckon that might take them a while.'

'There's no time.'

They both turned to look at Frith, who was stumbling to his feet. Wydrin held her hands out.

'Oh no, princeling, you stay where you are. Rest is what you need, and you've lost a lot of blood.'

'Not as much as you,' he said, gesturing at her leg. 'And yet you are up and about, ordering me around as ever.' He shuffled over to them, moving as though every step exhausted him. 'I can help you. With the device.'

Xinian shook her head at him, unable to contain her consternation. 'You! And what are you, exactly? No mage, no Edenier burning in you, no silks and no tattoos and yet you turned the dragon's daughters to dust. You are not coming anywhere near any mage artefact until you tell me what you are.'

Frith regarded her steadily. 'For the greatest military commander the mages ever knew, you are foolish. I have told you already

320

that I do not know what that power is when it moves through me.' His shoulders were bunched together and he was holding himself carefully – he was angry, and it was exhausting him. 'But you waste our time asking me again, when you know full well I have no answers. Every moment we spend stranded here gives Estenn more time to unite the pieces of the Red Echo, and then all of your people will be dead.'

In a swift movement born of long practice, Xinian drew her short sword and levelled it at Frith's throat.

'You would do well to speak to Xinian the Battleborn with more respect.'

'Hold on.' Wydrin took a slow breath, watching the edge of the blade. Any threat to Frith was unacceptable, and her instinct was to draw Glassheart and put a quick end to this, but that way lay madness. Frith, for his part, did not move but remained staring at Xinian – Wydrin wasn't sure if he were too bold or too exhausted to move. 'You both need to step back for a moment here.'

'Your people arrived in the middle of the sacred grove, and you have no answers but plenty of threats.' Xinian jabbed the sword at Frith. 'And now you expect me to let him take apart one of Selsye's creations?' Xinian bared her teeth. 'I have no reason to trust either of you.'

Wydrin shook her head, feeling her own anger fill her throat. It would not help, she told herself sternly. Not now. 'No reason to trust us, except that we just kept a bunch of bat-faced bitches off your back? Xinian, we are not your enemy. What harm can it do if Frith looks at the machine? We are stuck here for a while anyway.'

Xinian hissed softly through her teeth and lowered the blade. 'Do it, then,' she snapped. 'Be mindful it does not blow up in your face.'

Frith knelt in the black sand, slowly moving his hands over the green plates of metal. Beneath his fingers he could feel the faint lines of energy that marked the Edeian that had formerly held this contraption in place – they stood out in his mind's eye like

321

glowing lines of emerald green. Through the filter of Joah's memories it was possible to see how the pieces fitted together, how they had been slotted into a latticework to increase the efficiency of the Edenier. It would be relatively easy to move everything back into place, if they had the correct tools. He retrieved a memory of Joah sitting on a wooden scaffold, huge plates of blistered iron hanging in front of him. It had been the monstrous Rivener he was building, the tattoos on his arms prickling with steadily increasing heat as he'd warmed the plates and turned them to his design. In the memory he could feel Joah's warm satisfaction as the net of Edeian closed into place, and it was a good memory. It was almost possible to forget that he had murdered hundreds inside the Rivener for the sake of his demon patron, that men, women and children had died inside the iron walls in pain and terror. There was power here, yes, and the satisfaction of making something entirely new. There was also madness and death. He had to remember that. He had to.

'Can you make it work?'

He rubbed a hand over his eyes and looked up to see Xinian glaring down at him. Too well it reminded him of her standing over his bunk in the Rivener, calling him shadow-mage and entreating him to defeat Joah.

'We lost several plates of metal during the fight,' he replied. 'Without them, the net of Edeian is broken and there is nothing holding the spells in place.' He looked around, thinking out loud. 'If we can use something to bridge the gaps and mend the net, it's possible we could recharge enough of the mages' words to fly us a short distance.'

'What do you imagine you could use to bridge these gaps?'

Frith stood up and brushed some of the black sand from his knees. 'These islands are thick with Edeian.' He thought of O'rin, building his own trap for the gods underneath the rocks of Whittenfarne. Edenier, written in the fabric of Edeian. 'Mud, stones, grass. It all contains Edeian. I am fairly sure I can use them to bridge the gaps in the net.'

'You want to repair the carapacer with mud?' Xinian raised a single eyebrow. 'Then you can fly in it alone.'

'As Wydrin said, we lose nothing by trying. Will you help me? I will need you to use the Edenier.' He paused, feeling shame colour his cheeks. 'I will also need you to help me collect the materials. I still do not have my strength back.'

Xinian narrowed her eyes at him. 'You truly do not know how you killed the dragon's daughters, do you?'

He bit down a sigh. 'I do not. It was like everything was still for a moment, and I grabbed hold of them and *pushed* . . .' He pressed his lips into a thin line. 'I cannot explain it.'

Xinian unfolded her arms. 'Come, show me what you need. At least moving about will keep us warm.'

They collected armfuls of stones and the long blue grass that grew in untidy patches on the island, and Xinian scooped a quantity of gritty black mud onto a torn piece of cloak. While Wydrin sat by the fire and rested her leg, they stripped the grass down and bound it into long thin ropes. With these they secured the flattest stones to the areas of the carapacer missing its metal shell – underneath was a sturdy wooden framework – with Frith carefully turning each stone in place until the strongest veins of Edeian were lined up with each other. It was longwinded and tedious work, but Xinian did not complain; she simply asked questions, and helped where she could. When the stones were as secure as they could make them, they slopped handfuls of the gritty black mud on the bare patches.

'Is this really necessary?'

Frith nodded hesitantly. 'It all contains Edeian. It's strongest in the stones, but the mud has a sort of background glow. This makes it sturdier.'

Xinian snorted. 'The last thing I would describe this mess as would be sturdy,' she said, but she carried on spreading the mud all the same. When that was complete, he watched as she reactivated the mage words one by one.

'We are still missing words. It will not fly without them.'

'Yes,' said Frith, trying to picture it all in his mind. He was aware that he was no longer referring to Joah's memories, but working on his own instincts. 'I thought that we could—'

'We've got company!'

They both turned to Wydrin's voice. She stood by the fire now, and beyond the beach in front of her a boat loomed out of the fog. It was a traditional ship of the Nowhere Isles, built of pale wood with a monstrous figurehead looming at its prow to ward off evil spirits. The vessel came close to the beach and a figure jumped from the side, splashing into the shallows. Next to him, Frith sensed Xinian's posture grow relaxed as his own grew tense – he had seen this woman before.

'I thought I might find you here,' called the figure, splashing up the beach. She wore a long brown coat with many pockets – Frith could see rolls of parchment poking out of them here and there – and she had blond hair, long enough to reach her chin and then cut in a straight, no nonsense line. When he had seen her last, in the memories Xinian had gifted him with, her hair had been long and coiled on top of her head. That day would be many years from now, he hoped.

'Selsye.' For the first time, Frith heard genuine warmth in the Commander's voice. 'I should have known you could find us. How did you do it?'

Wydrin was standing. Frith suspected he was the only one who noticed how close her hand had been to her dagger, but it dropped away now. Selsye advanced up the beach, smiling. Behind her there were a few men on the sleek boat, slipping their oars and taking little notice of them.

'Reports of Y'Ruen in the skies, my love,' said the blonde woman. She nodded cheerily to Wydrin as she passed her. Wydrin nodded back. 'I thought there was a good chance you would experience, uh, bad weather.' Her smile faltered at the sight of the carapacer. 'I calculated your likely direction of approach, and then figured out which of these dreadful little islands you might pitch up on. I waited a bit, you know I'm no pessimist.' She glanced at Frith and nodded to him merrily enough. 'But when you were late, well, I thought I would take the *Dire Heart* out for a little punt.' She turned back and waved enthusiastically to the men on the ship. One of them half raised his hand back. 'It's quite exciting, weaving our way around these little islands. Very nearly ran aground a few times. So, who are these people? It looks like the 'pacer took some serious knocks.' She frowned briefly. 'This was my favourite one, too. I called it Ted.'

Xinian took the opportunity to get a word in edgewise. Frith suspected she'd had a lot of practice. 'You got my message?'

'I did, yes, although I can't say I understood much of it. Fanatics, betrayal, sell-swords, it was quite the read. Oh!' she turned back to Frith. 'Are these the sell-swords? They look the type.' She grinned encouragingly.

'I am Lord Frith of the Blackwood,' said Frith. 'This is Wydrin Threefellows, the Copper Cat of Crosshaven.'

'Goodness!' said Selsye, clearly delighted. 'And you've come all the way out here for what, exactly?'

Frith exchanged a brief glance with Wydrin. This woman was relentlessly cheerful and extremely polite, but he also sensed a hint of steel underneath the courteousness. He could tell from Wydrin's carefully neutral face that she felt it too. This was, he reminded himself, the mage who had faced down Joah Demonsworn side by side with Xinian Battleborn.

'It is a long story, Selsye,' put in Xinian, 'and there's a lot you need to know, but it's very possible the plan has been compromised.' She glanced over to the ship. 'And the collection may be in danger.'

'I see.' The merriment faded from Selsye's face. 'Then we should get back to Whittenfarne swiftly. We can send a team back here to retrieve the 'pacer –' She paused, her head tipping slightly to one side. 'Have you been tying bits of grass around Ted? And . . . rubbing mud all over him?'

Xinian cleared her throat. 'I thought we might be stuck here for some time, so I somewhat unwisely took advice from our guests.'

'I sought to repair it as best I could,' said Frith hotly. 'It was, if you recall, the only plan we had.'

'No, that's interesting,' said Selsye. She walked past them to lay her hands on the carapacer's hide, now half hidden in black mud. 'I can see what you were doing. Patching up the Edeian with the natural background glow of it. You have even lined up the strongest lines of force, so that it will hold together naturally,

325

like when you fill an oil-lined bag with water and it inflates.' She looked to Frith, all her previous foreboding gone. 'You are a crafter?'

'I . . . have some talent in that direction,' admitted Frith. He could almost hear Wydrin repressing a chuckle.

'But that's wonderful!' cried Selsye. She took hold of his hand and shook it briskly. 'There are so very, very few of us, you know. We're much rarer than mages, did you know that?'

'It must be rarer to be both a mage and a crafter,' said Wydrin quietly.

'You are quite right,' said Selsye. 'The Edenier sometimes runs in families, and sometimes it does not, but if a mage procreates with another mage, there is a reasonable chance you will birth a child with the Edenier burning inside them.' Just behind Selsye, Xinian wore a faintly pained expression. He suspected that they had stumbled over one of her partner's favourite subjects. 'But there is no predicting the birth of an Edeian crafter. To be able to see the magic in the earth, sea and stone, to recognise the patterns of it and then know how to use them –' Selsye shook her head slowly. 'It is a rare gift.'

'Indeed.' Frith thought of Joah, peeling apart his mind to get at his secrets, whilst the rogue mage's knowledge had seeped through to him. He had paid quite the price for this gift.

'And what you've done here, with no tools and no decent materials. It's really quite extraordinary!'

'Selsye, we must go now,' said Xinian. 'If we're right, we don't have a lot of time.'

'Of course, of course. Come on, into the ship. Ted will have to fend for himself for a while.' As one they moved down the beach, while Wydrin paused to kick sand over their small fire. 'Lord Frith, we will take you to Whittenfarne and you will see the history of Edeian crafting in all its glory. And I have a friend you really must meet.'

52

Pain dragged Sebastian towards the light, against his will. It would be easier, more comfortable to stay down in the dark, but awareness seeped back as every part of his body started to ring with a new ache. He grimaced, and his face felt strangely stiff. He pressed his fingers to his cheek lightly, and recognised the sticky, powdery feel of dried blood.

'Ow.'

Sebastian opened his eyes. He lay on a cold marble floor, a distant vaulted ceiling built of the same material hanging over his head. There was an odd scent in the air, a mixture of wild flowers and sea salt. Cautiously, he sat up, wincing as a whole new set of aches and pains let themselves be known. It felt as though he'd fallen down a set of stone steps and taken great care to hit a different part of his body on each one.

'You are awake then, my little oddity.'

Sebastian looked around. He appeared to be on the floor of the biggest throne room he'd ever seen. Huge marble pillars disappeared into the shadows of the ceiling, while one side of the room was given over to a great silver chair, entwined with carvings of twisting vines and orchids. A woman approached from this throne, moving with unhurried grace.

She is not human, he told himself. *Whatever she might look like.*

'Y'Gria,' he murmured. She no longer looked like the tentacled giant that had menaced them from the burning town. Now she was a tall woman, with skin the colour of burnished gold and tresses of wild green hair that fell unbound down her back. Ram's horns still curled at her temples, and now she wore a long dress made of yellow silk that brushed the marble floor. It was obvious she had legs rather than roots, and for that Sebastian was absurdly grateful. Abruptly, he remembered their last moments on board the carapacer and how the young mage accompanying them had screamed. 'What of Silvain?' he asked aloud, staggering to his feet with some difficulty. 'Where is she?'

'I killed the mage,' she said. 'As I will kill all of them, eventually. I would have killed you too, but you fell from the mage contraption you travelled in, so I thought I didn't have to.' She smiled faintly. 'But then your companion changed his shape into some other creature and caught you as you fell. You tumbled and rolled around on the ground, and I thought perhaps the impact had killed you anyway.'

'Where is Oster?'

'He's being looked after. Do you know what he is, human?'

Sebastian shifted his weight, trying to think. The sword and the knives were gone from his belt; as little good as they would do him here anyway. Oster had said that the gods did not like each other, that they naturally fought amongst themselves as beings who believed themselves to be above everything else. He had been afraid that they would know him for what he was, but if Y'Gria had him in her power, it was likely she knew what he was now anyway. The question was, what would she decide to do about it?

'He is my friend,' he said. Amusement glinted in her eyes.

'That is all you have to say?' She came closer, until she stood in front of him. They were of a height, and she peered keenly at his face as though looking for something in particular. Sebastian felt the hairs on the back of his neck and arms stand on end. The sense of danger and threat came off her in waves, and inevitably he was reminded of crouching on the field at Relios, Y'Ruen hanging over the Ynnsmouth knights, their fiery doom boiling at the back of her throat. 'When I came for you both, this being

328

you call Oster stood over your unconscious body and growled at me.' She grinned, apparently delighted. 'I was fascinated. Such as he has no need to feel loyalty to such as you.'

'Oster is an unusual man.'

'Man? That is not the form he took as he defended your body. Although, that's not the whole story either, is it?' She placed a hand on his arm and leaned closer, as though she would be able to scent the answer to her question.

'Why are you killing all the mages?' asked Sebastian, buying time. 'What is this war really about?'

'You ask such questions of a god?' Her tone was imperious now, and she snatched her hand away. Almost immediately, her expression softened. 'Truly? It is about our mistake. The ancestors of the mages struck down and killed the very first god, and ate her flesh. They carried the Edenier within them. They were young, and we hoped to see them as allies. Can you imagine? You would think the fact that their ancestors were murderers would be sufficient warning, but even gods can be fools. We lifted them up, gave them the Words to better control the power they had. For a time there was peace and growth.' She paused, gazing across her great throne room. She almost looked wistful. 'It was my time then. But they grew dissatisfied with what we'd already given them, so they clamoured for more. Demanded more. They sought to be gods themselves.' She gave Sebastian a rueful look, and for a moment he was shocked by how human it looked. 'Believe me, I have enough brothers and sisters as it is. They had to be discouraged. When they refused to step away from this destructive path, we resolved to destroy them. Things got out of hand. We are always a step away from fighting, my siblings and I. It is simply our nature. Why just the mages? Why not everyone? Why not each other? Why not the world? Burn it all down and start again.'

Silence rang in the great hall.

'But they called you the Mother of All Things. Y'Gria the Green, god of growth and new life. How can you do this?'

'You people have never really understood us.' Y'Gria laughed. 'Mother of All Things. Relationships with mothers can be tricky, I think. You see this flower?' She held out her hands to him to

329

reveal a tiny clump of delicate blue blossoms nestling in her palm. As Sebastian watched, the blooms multiplied until they dripped from her fingers. 'It's called Ashwort. Not the prettiest name, but it is a pretty flower, and it's my favourite. Ashwort grows most abundantly where there have been forest fires. Something about the broken down vegetation really perks them up. New life, in the midst of destruction. It is the oldest cycle.'

Sebastian took a slow breath. 'This is how you justify the deaths of thousands? Because you want to wipe it all clean and start again? That's not how life works. You don't get to just wipe away your mistakes and not deal with the consequences of them. If you know what Oster is, then you know he is part of a cycle. Your cycle.'

Y'Gria looked up sharply. The blossoms vanished from her hands.

'And that part I do not understand. And you – what are you, little human? You smell like my sister, and you are dragon-kin. Neither of you makes any sense.'

'What are you going to do with us?'

'I could kill you, or I could hurt you until you told me what I wanted to know,' she said firmly, but Sebastian sensed some uncertainty all the same. 'But this is a confusing time for young Oster, and I do not want to upset him unnecessarily. He is family, after all.' She smiled. 'So for now, you are my guests.'

With that she walked back towards the throne and vanished – she simply faded from view and was gone, as though she'd thought of somewhere better to be on the way there. Shortly after that a tall door appeared in the smooth marble wall, and with nowhere else to go, Sebastian stepped through it into a summer's garden.

He stood for a few moments, blinking in surprise. The place was full of brilliant sunshine, the sky above perfectly blue. There were lush lawns lined with flower beds that had burst their borders, shedding pink and yellow and white blossoms, and petite trees with glossy green leaves, heavy with orange and yellow fruit. When he turned in a circle, he saw that the gardens appeared to be attached to ancient ruins of some sort – graceful arches of pale stone burst from greenery on all sides, and the door through which he'd entered the garden was set into a great crumbling wall. The place was warm, and lazy with the hum of bees. It was impossible not to feel slightly more at ease, with the heat warming the top of his head and the sweet scent of flowers in his nose. He pursed his lips and tried to concentrate.

'Sebastian?'

Oster was standing underneath one of the taller trees, turning something over and over in his hands. As Sebastian drew closer, he saw that it was a peach.

'From all the stories I've heard, I'm fairly sure it's a bad idea to eat the fruit of the gods.'

'You spoke to her, then?' asked Oster. Then he added, 'She didn't kill you.'

'Y'Gria seems to find me more interesting alive, which I think is at least partly down to you. What, she wonders, does a young god like yourself want with a mere mortal?' Oster glared at him, and Sebastian looked away, faintly embarrassed for reasons he couldn't pinpoint. 'You saved my life,' he said, in a more solemn voice. 'Again. Thank you.'

'If you would just stop falling off things . . .' Sebastian looked up sharply, but Oster's face was as closed as ever. 'The mage died. I – they are so fragile.'

'Yes, we are,' said Sebastian. 'Y'Gria is dangerous. You were worried that the gods here would find out what you are. She knows, but she hasn't killed you either.' He paused. 'Can she actually kill you?'

Oster ignored the question. 'She spoke to me. It was not what I expected.' He took a bite from the peach, and chewed thoughtfully for a moment. 'She told me she knew my glory for what it was from the moment that she looked at me. That I could never hide what I was.'

'Flatterer,' remarked Sebastian.

'Y'Gria told me I could stay here if I wanted. That I was welcome.' He shifted from foot to foot. '*She* is not what I expected.'

'She still killed Silvain,' pointed out Sebastian. 'She has killed thousands in this war, and I think she has an agenda of her own.'

331

He looked around again, wondering if the god was listening to them somehow. 'We have to get away from here.'

'Have you seen the edge?' asked Oster.

Sebastian followed Oster out from under the trees, taking a narrow path of pale blue stones. He expected them to come to a wall, to see more gardens on a level below this one, or perhaps the roofs of more ruins – they were clearly in a roof garden of some sort – but they reached the edge of the lawn and it dropped away into nothing. Thousands of feet below them was the red-clay land of Relios, made neat and tidy by sheer distance. Sebastian could see the remains of a town, a collection of rubble that looked like little more than a broken goblet from here. He could see a shining ribbon of gold that was a river, and long rows of fruit trees in an orchard, as regular and as small as the stitching on a shirt. As he watched, a white wisp of cloud flew by under them. Whatever they stood on, it was moving, he realised, and a wave of dizziness washed up from his toes. He staggered back a few steps, and Oster snorted with amusement.

'Again. You are always falling.'

'What is this place?'

'It is her palace, although more rightly it appears to be a very large and disorganised garden growing on and around the central throne room. I have explored it, climbed up over the walls and the rooms – they are all gardens, every one. Some are indoors, and some have partly fallen away to nothing. Some contain herbs and plants for medicines, some have poisons and mushrooms, or climbing plants that cover the walls so that you can't see the bricks any more. There was a room that just had thorn bushes inside.' He turned to Sebastian. 'I would not go exploring on two legs,' he said quite seriously. 'There is much here that is unstable.'

'And we're just hanging up here, in the middle of the sky?'

'That appears to be the case.'

Sebastian dared himself to look over the side again, ignoring how his stomach was trying to crawl up through his throat. He was thinking of O'rin's Rookery, hidden away at the top of a mountain. He supposed this was another way to avoid visitors.

'Quite the prison.'

332

'There is food, on platters in random places,' said Oster. He looked as though he were trying to figure something out. 'And places to sleep. They look quite comfortable. For humans. It is like she's trying to make it comfortable for us. To make us welcome.'

'You are wondering why she hasn't just killed me, when she has killed so many others.'

'No,' said Oster. 'She feels the dragon blood within you, and that perplexes her. She asked me about it, but I didn't have any answers to give. I am wondering if I was wrong. I know so little of my family, and she knows a great deal of my history. When she was birthed from the Eye of Euriale, the Spinner was there to sing her the songs of the gods.' He resolutely did not meet Sebastian's eye. 'Perhaps she will share that knowledge with me.'

'In exchange for what? Oster, at this time in history, the gods are killing thousands. Not just mages – they're tearing entire cities from the map in the midst of their war. Y'Gria herself told me she wishes the world to burn so that they can build it again.' He lowered his voice. 'If they are not stopped, humankind will be destroyed.'

'And why should I care about that?' Oster turned to him. The bright sunshine gleamed off his tawny skin, and filled his eyes with banked embers. He was impossibly beautiful, and all at once difficult to look at. It was obvious what he was; Sebastian could hardly believe he hadn't seen it straight away. The silver tattoo that wasn't a tattoo at all glittered. 'I am a god. It is not my place to care about how many people Y'Gria has killed.'

'Your place? Your place isn't here at all, it's a thousand years in the future!' Sebastian took a slow breath. Silvain's final scream was haunting him. 'We have to get out of here and away from her, Oster. We have to stop Estenn before she gets to the artefacts.' When Oster didn't react, he added, 'She killed the Spinner, remember. She took your histories from you.'

Oster met his eyes. 'And this place might be my only chance to regain them. You can always resume your journey without me. You merely need to find a way down.'

*   *   *

Sebastian spent the rest of that day exploring Y'Gria's garden palace. As Oster had warned him, there was no sensible layout to the place: lawns would end abruptly over empty sky, and sets of stairs led up to nothing. He saw trees that clung to the very edge of their soil, roots hanging out to grasp at empty air, and more than once he came to a halt as the steepness of a hill threatened to encourage him to take a very sudden tumble. It was as if several palatial gardens had collided in mid-air to create this strange confusion of ruins and foliage. The only part of it that seemed to adhere to any sort of plan was the gigantic cold throne room, but he could not find the entrance to that again – he suspected that the great chamber was only accessible when Y'Gria wished it to be.

Gradually, the sun began to set, filling the endless blue sky with pink and orange light. Sebastian explored some of the interior rooms, and as Oster had promised, these were as filled with plants and trees as the rest of the place, and here and there he found platters of food resting on mossy hillocks, as if waiting for him. He picked food off them as he went – sweet, sliced ham and peaches, fat yellow cheeses and ripe red apples.

As night fell, he found himself back in the outer gardens. There was no sign of Oster. He wondered if he had transformed into his dragon form, and was at this moment climbing over the broken roofs, or if Y'Gria had taken him into the throne room again.

To the west, the sky was a purple bruise, shot through with the last streaks of orange light yet to fade from the clouds. He could see a mountain range there, and a distant pall of smoke. Once, when he had been small, he had been required to learn the names of all the mountains in Relios. They weren't sacred, like Isu and its brethren, but it had been important to know them, all the same. If he wasn't mistaken, that was Ashbless, the ancient volcano where the mages were keeping half of the Red Echo. They weren't that far away at all, not really.

'I will have to find a way off this thing soon,' he murmured to himself. 'Or else bring the whole bastard thing down.'

53

Whittenfarne was a place transformed.

When he'd last been there, Frith had spent weeks on the island and had developed a healthy hatred of the place, with its splintered black rocks, stunted trees and shallow pools of foul-smelling water. It had been a desolate landscape of stone and mists, the only brightness the patches of tough blue grass that sprouted here and there. There had been nothing else of note, save for the giant mage statues and O'rin's little conical huts woven from grass.

The statues were still there – as they approached from the western side of the island, one loomed out of the mists towards them, a woman with her hands held out – and the Nowhere Isles were as foggy as ever, but now there was a small wooden harbour clinging to the edge of the island, and it was busy with boats and people. The wood was shining and well-maintained, and there were several small buildings clustered there and at the foot of the statue. He could see men and women in thickly furred robes, moving crates and sacks back and forth. Selsye's men brought the little ship into dock neatly enough, and they climbed out onto the sturdy pier. Frith looked around, trying to get his bearings. Had he been to this part of the island? It was impossible to recognise much.

Xinian was already barking orders to the mages present on the dock, who appeared to be officials of some kind. Judging from the expressions on their faces, their hopes for a quiet day had fled at the sight of Xinian's sour countenance.

'I want the wards doubled,' she snapped at the nearest woman, who nodded hurriedly. 'Keep a closer eye on everyone who comes into the dock, and no unbound is to be let within sight of Lan-Hellis, is that clear?'

'Lan-Hellis is our stronghold here,' said Selsye, who was ushering them past the confused mages towards the small buildings. 'Well, I say stronghold, but it's actually a place of study and learning. Everywhere is a stronghold these days. Everywhere needs to have walls and wards.'

'This is where the artefacts are kept?' asked Wydrin in a low voice.

Selsye nodded once, biting her lip slightly as she did so. 'It is my, uh, honour, to curate the collection of artefacts. As a crafter of Edeian as well as a mage, I have a particular interest in magical objects.'

'Selsye is our foremost expert in the field,' said Xinian. 'As much as she doesn't like to boast about it.'

The blonde woman waved a hand at her dismissively. 'No one else enjoys sitting around and looking at old things quite as much as me, that's all.'

'Apart from your little shadow, of course,' added Xinian, an amused twitch at the corner of her mouth. Frith watched the two mages exchange a look, but could not guess at its meaning, and then they moved beyond the buildings to meet a horse and cart.

'No magical transportation?' asked Wydrin innocently.

'You would like to try falling from the 'pacer again, perhaps?' asked Xinian. Wydrin rolled her eyes.

The horse and cart was driven by a mage in thickly furred robes, a scarf piled so high around his neck that they could hardly see his face. They followed a path of white gravel that had been cut into the black rock itself, curving and weaving around the bubbling pools of acrid water that Frith remembered so well. The mists came and went, rushing in to festoon their hair and clothes in icy droplets, then slinking away to reveal sections of the desolate island in abrupt tableaux. More than once, Frith spotted mage words carved into the sides of the rocks themselves, or directly into the uneven ground and filled with the same white gravel.

These, he suspected, were some of the wards that Xinian had spoken of.

'How long has this Lan-Hellis been here?' asked Frith. Selsye tipped her head to one side, giving him a considering look.

'Centuries, of course. Lan-Hellis is legendary. The mages built it on the foundations of a much older building. It has likely always been a place of ancient magic, which is one of the reasons we study here. We are all drawn here, eventually.' She sounded wistful, gazing out across the rocks and mist with genuine affection. Frith kept thinking of the time he had stumbled into a pool and been bitten by a lizard. He had hoped never to return to the miserable place. 'And of course, Lan-Hellis already had such an extensive collection of artefacts, it made sense to start gathering together what we would need for the Citadel within its hallowed halls.'

'And there she is,' said Xinian, a wry note in her voice, and then in a lower tone, 'Give me Creos any day. This place is too damn damp.'

Frith looked up and felt his breath catch in his throat. Next to him Wydrin sat up a little straighter. The mists parted and Lan-Hellis loomed out of the fog like a ghost suddenly made solid. His first thought was of the Spinner, and the brief glances of the creature's true face – Lan-Hellis seemed to crouch on the black rock like some great, blind insect. Five huge white domes dominated the building, shining dimly with their own inner glow, while all around it were twisted spires of black rock, reaching up towards the shrouded sky almost as though they had caught it in some moment of terrible cataclysm and frozen it there. There was a huge arched gate, which they were heading towards, lit with brightly glowing white orbs, and there he could see a small group of men and women in black robes. As they approached, the light within one of the giant white globes fluttered strangely – Frith was reminded of a moth at a lamp, sending shadows of its wings all around the room – and most of the mages who had been standing at the gate suddenly went inside. He could tell by their hunched shoulders and rapid footsteps that whatever the dimming of the light meant, it was not good news. Next to them, Selsye pursed her lips.

'More attacks,' she murmured. 'Y'Gria must be talking them round.'

'What are the big white things, then?' asked Wydrin. The cart had stopped, and at Xinian's signal they climbed out. 'Other than a way to make your fancy mage building look like it has eyes.'

Selsye half smiled. 'In a way, they are eyes, of a sort. Think of them as . . . magical lenses. Within the globes are teams of mages, casting spells to monitor the gods and their movements. They are very difficult to track, and can shield themselves easily, but it is possible to pick up traces of Edenier from their actions. Those traces increase significantly when they target us, or a city, or a village. Sometimes it can reverberate back towards us, and then the lights go out.' She pulled her robes closer around her. 'There will be a lot of mages up there tonight with nasty headaches.'

'All right, Selsye,' said Xinian smoothly. 'These unbound don't need to know all our secrets.'

'Just the secrets that might save our arses, if you don't mind,' said Wydrin. They were led towards the gate, where the guards on duty gave them curious looks but said nothing. Inside was a huge shadowy hallway, cold and damp, with various odds and ends piled up against the walls. Frith saw more paintings and tapestries on the walls like the ones in the mage stronghold in Krete, but these all looked darker, older.

'Right, then, let's get this over with,' said Xinian briskly. 'We will go to the chamber now where the Red Echo is kept. You will see we are in no danger of losing it, and then we will lie in wait for this Estenn of yours, and take her prisoner if she arrives. Once that is done I will personally cart you both back to Krete and get on with the work I'm supposed to be doing.'

Selsye cleared her throat. 'If Lord Frith here is an Edeian crafter, then I would really like to spend some time with him. There is much he can learn here, and judging from his instincts repairing the 'pacer, we may even learn something from him.'

Wydrin raised an eyebrow at Frith and spoke in a low voice. 'Like I said before, this could be a good place for you to get some answers. Me and Xinian can check on the Red Echo together.'

Xinian groaned. 'Fine. Selsye, show him your toys, if you must. Wydrin of Crosshaven, you're with me.'

Xinian marched away down the hall and Wydrin had to scurry to keep up with her. She cast a quick look over her shoulder to see Frith disappear through a doorway, and then Xinian took a sharp right down a narrow corridor. They passed men and women in long dark robes, their face preoccupied, nervous even. *These are a people at war*, Wydrin reminded herself. *People who have been at war for years. No wonder they look jumpy.*

'So you keep your most valuable artefacts here?' she asked to fill the silence.

'Some of them,' replied Xinian. 'They will stay here until the Citadel is complete and ready to receive the items. To bring them all together too soon would be dangerous. So many magical artefacts in one place can cause a certain . . . bending of reality.' She shook her head slightly. 'Selsye is better at explaining these things.'

'No, that makes sense,' said Wydrin, half to herself. She remembered the strange atmosphere under the Citadel; the odd sense of foreboding, the feeling that you were being watched. And that was after the artefacts had had centuries to change the world around them.

'And, of course, the gods can sense that much magic together in one place. Which is what we're banking on.'

They came to a door with two mage guards, a pair of skinny young men. Xinian must have caught the sceptical look that passed over Wydrin's face.

'Believe me, Yohan and Rafe here are two of our strongest mages. They could kill you with the merest eye blink.'

The two young men looked faintly perplexed, but they bowed slightly as they passed through the door. Wydrin tipped them a lazy salute.

Beyond the door was a large circular chamber made of smooth white stone and lit with bright lamps. The floor was covered in pale dust. There were high windows in the room and Wydrin could just make out shadowy figures standing beyond them, watching.

'This is the Moon Room,' said Xinian. 'It's the only way in and out of our artefact room. As you can see, anyone walking across here is very visible to the people in the galleries. And there are always people in the galleries.'

Wydrin nodded, impressed despite herself. As they walked across the room, she noticed that her boots left big obvious prints in the dust. On the far side they came to a circular panel in the wall made of black wood. Xinian reached into her shirt and pulled out a silver object on a long golden chain. It looked to Wydrin a little like a snake with a bird's head, and when Xinian pressed it to an impression in the door, the shape of it twisted and changed to fill the shapes there. Wydrin heard a soft hiss, and then a metallic series of clicks before the round door swung open. Xinian stepped to one side.

'I would remind you at this point, Wydrin Threefellows, that as formidable as the guards are on the Moon Room, I am a hundred times more powerful. Touch anything in here without my say so, and I will be handing you back to your Lord Frith in a small wet bag.'

Wydrin held her hands up, unable to keep from smiling. 'Are you suggesting I'm a thief, Commander?'

Xinian's mouth twitched at one corner. 'I've seen your type before, usually sneaking around the edges of battlefields, looking for what they can steal. Get in the room.'

Wydrin stepped through the circular opening. The room beyond was gloomy and crowded. She got an impression of many figures and shapes looming in the dark, and then Xinian stepped through. She gestured and a number of small lamps fluttered into life in the ceiling. Wydrin was reminded of her father's warehouse back in Crosshaven – there were dozens of boxes and crates, some of them sealed up, some of them open and spilling sawdust onto the floor. There were other items, glass boxes on top of pedestals, containing strange objects she could hardly guess at the purpose of, and other, larger things leaning against the walls and shrouded in cloth. The place smelled of dust, and old things, and another, stranger scent that made her think of Euriale. After a moment she realised that the hair on the back of her neck was standing on end – there was magic here. A lot of it.

'Selsye has been cataloguing.' Xinian gestured at the general chaos as if this explained the mess. 'Some of it has been packed away ready for travel, but Selsye cannot help but examine it as she goes. This represents an extraordinary collection, gathered from all over Ede. It is the wealth of the mages.' She paused, frowning slightly. 'All to be sacrificed, to end this war.'

'It's like when you're clearing out your cupboards,' said Wydrin, walking down a strip of floor space that had yet to be taken up with boxes. She ran her fingers over a crate. 'You find all this stuff you haven't thought about in years, letters and keepsakes from another part of your life, and you can't help picking them up and thinking about all the time that has gone by.' She looked up as they passed a huge glass case. Inside it was a very old sword made of a strange, dark red metal. It glittered oddly, as though something inside it flowed like water. 'I imagine it's like that, only much more so. What is this?'

'The singing sword of Breem. They say it absorbed the souls of everyone it killed, and the wailing noise it makes as you swing it is the sound of them crying out.' Xinian raised an eyebrow. 'Selsye has been leaving that one until last, I think. She says it feels dirty, no matter how much they clean it.'

'And this?' Wydrin had stopped by another glass case. This one held a pair of gauntlets, made from steel and a shining white metal Wydrin didn't recognise. They were beautiful, the links and joints crafted with a grace that spoke of jewellery rather than armour. Wydrin patted the glass, her fingers itching. The gauntlets looked priceless.

'Those? We know very little of them. Selsye calls them the Hands of the Tower because they were found in some ancient ruins in Pathania. They confer on the wearer great strength, apparently.'

'Were there any matching pieces? Any armour that went with them?'

'No, nothing else was ever found.'

'They're beautiful—'

'Yes. Shall we move on?' Xinian laid a hand on her shoulder and, none too gently, steered her away from the glass case. Wydrin cleared her throat.

'So where is this Red Echo, then? What does it look like exactly? Is it already crated up?'

Xinian took her to the back of the room, and stopped. She sighed, and then knelt on the floor and knocked sharply on a wooden hatch concealed there.

'Everything all right in there?'

Wydrin stood still, blinking and wondering if perhaps Xinian had lost her mind, when a piping voice floated up from the floor.

'Hello? Is light?'

Xinian straightened up. 'There you go. As you can hear, the Red Echo is fine. And I think you'll agree that our security measures are sufficient. Shall we go?'

'Hold on a minute.' Wydrin peered down at the hatch in the floor. It was made of plain wood, with a simple bolt across it, and it was half hidden by the swatches of cloth covering the boxes and crates. 'Are you telling me the Red Echo is a person?'

'I am not telling you that, no,' said Xinian. The impatience in her voice was clear. 'It is complicated. And that is only half of the Red Echo.'

Wydrin knelt down and placed her hands on the wood. 'Hello? Are you all right? Are you alone down there?'

'Dark, no lights!' The voice sounded very young, and confused. 'Who? Commander?'

Wydrin stood up. 'What is that? Are you keeping a child down there?'

Xinian shook her head, frustrated. 'No. It's complicated, ancient magic. It is difficult to explain. Perhaps Selsye—'

'Show me,' said Wydrin. She lifted her chin slightly. 'I've come all this way. I want to see it.'

They stood for a few seconds in silence, Wydrin with her arms crossed over her chest, Xinian with arms straight by her sides. Eventually, Xinian gave a great theatrical sigh.

'Fine. We will go down there briefly, but don't get it all excited.' She crouched down and pulled the bolt across before lifting up the heavy hatch. From below came a strong waft of a dusty, papery scent. There were plain wooden steps descending into darkness. Xinian gestured to the hatch. 'If you're so curious, you can go first.'

Keeping one hand on her dagger, Wydrin descended into the gloom. Xinian followed, summoning a ball of light above her fingers. The glow revealed a small, bare room with a dusty floor. At first Wydrin could see no one at all in the room, and then she spotted a tiny figure, almost like a doll, sitting in a corner with its knees up to its chin.

'This is your terrible weapon?'

The figure stood up, tiny limbs working. It had a smooth bald head, narrow arms and legs, and even minuscule fingers and toes, but it looked as though it were made of faded, yellowed parchment. There was writing all over it, densely packed words written in black ink covering every inch of its papery skin, and its face was a collection of bumps and shadows hinting at a human shape. Wydrin felt a shiver of recognition; this creature was a cousin to the culoss, the small folk they had met inside the Citadel, left behind by the mages to maintain the magical wards.

'Light? Is there?' The voice was surprisingly loud for such a small figure.

'How long have you been down here?' Wydrin took a step forward. 'What are you?'

The papery figure held out its papery hands, displaying the words written there. 'I am spell. No words, in the dark. No time. I am Echo.'

Belatedly, Wydrin realised that the walls were scratched all over with writing. She turned to Xinian. 'How can you keep it down here like this?'

'It's not alive, Wydrin.'

'But it can talk! It can think, it can miss the light. Why not at least keep it up with the boxes and crates?'

'It was made centuries ago, pieced together by mages much wiser and more skilled than us,' said Xinian. She looked angry now. 'The Red Echo is an incredibly dangerous spell, and it is best kept out of sight. I thought you knew this.'

'If it's so dangerous, why haven't you destroyed it?' Wydrin advanced on Xinian, squaring her shoulders. She was thinking of Mendrick, and the quiet certainty of his voice. 'Better to keep it

343

around in case you need it? Or is it that you suspect it is alive, and you do not want the guilt of ending its life?'

'Enough!' Xinian held up her arm, the one that ended in a stump, and a small ball of fire popped into existence above it. Behind them, Wydrin heard the Echo take a few hurried steps backwards, its paper feet rustling. 'You are a guest here, Wydrin Threefellows, and we have been more than accommodating. I think you will agree that the Red Echo is sufficiently protected. It is time for you to leave.'

Wydrin took a slow, deep breath. She had to remember why they were here. 'I want to come back,' she said shortly. 'I want to talk to it for a bit longer.' She swallowed down her own anger with some difficulty. 'Please, Xinian. You can watch me down here, or get someone else to do it. But I need to know more about this. It might help us catch Estenn.'

Xinian's eyes blazed, but with a gesture the ball of fire vanished. 'You and Selsye will drive me to the grave. Too bloody curious by half. Fine, I will give you some time with the spell. The gods know that Selsye keeps coming down here to talk to it – she thinks I don't know about that, of course, but she isn't the best liar.' She gestured with her head towards the wooden steps. 'Come on. For now, I want to increase our security and make sure everything is locked down. Your thief isn't getting in here.'

Half defiant, Wydrin turned back to the small papery figure, and forced herself to give it a smile. 'I'll come back, Echo. I'll bring some light, if I can.'

54

'I fear we must talk honestly about your magic, Lord Frith.'

Frith looked up to see Selsye smiling at him. She was leading him down a damp and draughty corridor lit by guttering candles. Her hair was dishevelled from the journey, although she didn't seem to have noticed. Looking at her, he couldn't help but remember the memory Xinian had given him; a brave woman throwing balls of green fire over the side of a tomb, the stone lid flying back and striking her in the face. The blood, the sound of her bones breaking. He swallowed and looked away.

'What do you mean?'

'Xinian described to me what happened when the dragon's spawn attacked you, how you shrivelled them into dust. This is not a magic I am aware of, Lord Frith, and I don't mind saying that I know pretty much all there is to know about Edenier and Edeian.' She cleared her throat. 'That's not as grand as it sounds. Basically, I read a lot. I have always read a lot. And I've spent much of my life here at Lan-Hellis, furthering the study of magic.' She grinned suddenly. 'There isn't an awful lot else to do on this island, as you can imagine. No, the magic Xinian described is something entirely new. Do you know how I've longed to find something new, Lord Frith?' He opened his mouth to reply, but she carried on. 'Besides which, you *feel* strange to me.'

They walked up a flight of steps, and Frith shivered. It was growing colder the further up they travelled, and the black walls seemed to radiate damp. He thought of the miserable weeks spent training under O'rin. At least there was a roof over his head now.

'I feel strange to you?'

'I'm sorry, I'm not being terribly clear. It's not easy to explain, even to those who have been trained. I can sense Edeian, you see. I have spent years sharpening my sense to it. I can even sense Edenier, to an extent. Most trained mages can do that.' She turned to look at Frith as they made their way up another long corridor. This one was lined with doors, all shut. 'I can sense a residue of both in you, which is unusual in itself. And something else too, something I've never felt before. Where did you learn to do it? What you did to the dragon's creatures?'

Frith shook his head, unsure what to say for the best. 'I honestly cannot tell you. It seems to be something I have acquired since we arrived here.'

'And what did it feel like?'

'I was angry. Wydrin was in danger. Everything seemed to slow down, to grow faded.' Frith bit down on his words. He did not want to speak of this, but Wydrin was right; if he was going to find out what this was, this was the best place to do it. 'I concentrated on them. I wanted them gone, so I *pushed* them. I pushed them while everything else was still.'

'When you say you pushed them—'

'Through time,' said Frith. The sudden realisation was like being doused in freezing water. 'I pushed them forward through time.'

Selsye stopped, staring at him. For a moment he thought she was going to call him a liar, or call for guards to take him away. Instead, she gave a joyful shout of laughter. 'That is incredible! Come on, there's no knowing when Xinian will attempt to spirit you away from me, so I must find out what I can.'

She led him up a steep flight of stairs at the end of a dark corridor, and opened a hatch in the ceiling. They emerged into a room of brilliant light, and it took a few moments for Frith's eyes to adjust to the glare. By the time he could see clearly again he realised they must be inside one of the giant globes they had seen from the outside. The smooth white walls of the globe rose around them on all sides, appearing to be made of some sort of clouded glass – he wondered briefly what Crowleo would make of it – and the floor was covered in hundreds of silk strips, some painted with mage words, others blank. It was impossible to see what the floor looked like through them, and Selsye cheerfully kicked them to either side as she strode across the chamber to the thin figure standing facing away from them.

There was a moment, so brief, like a cold finger pressed to the back of his neck, and Frith almost guessed before the man turned around. Instead, he felt a sudden surge of foreboding so strong that it was like drowning.

'Joah,' cried Selsye, 'you could at least keep them all in one pile instead of chucking them all over the floor. Xinian would have kittens if she saw this mess.'

The man turned around. It was Joah Demonsworn, alive and breathing, so much younger than when Frith had last seen him, and with no sign of the madness that had so gripped him. He had an open, handsome face, his brown eyes were kind, and he turned to Selsye with the slightly startled look of someone who had been deep in thought. His hair was bound back in a loose tail and his beard was short and carefully maintained – the beard, perhaps, of a young man who isn't very good at growing them yet.

'I am so close to a solution though,' he said. He was holding something between his fingers, a thin sheet of nearly transparent material, a mage word painted on it in black ink. Frith barely noticed. He thought of Joah calling him Aaron, of him saying they were brothers, and how he had sent a bolt of lightning to Wydrin's heart, blowing her clean off her feet and ripping her from his arms. Heat prickled in his fingers, and there was a roaring in his ears. If the Edenier had still been within him, he knew that Joah Demonsworn would have been a smoking corpse.

'Lord Frith?'

Frith took a breath, and realised that Selsye had been speaking. He'd heard none of it. 'I'm sorry?'

'I was just introducing you to my assistant here,' continued Selsye. Joah was peering at him curiously. He wore a simple tunic of olive green, and loose trousers bound into furred boots. His arms were criss-crossed with multiple lines of silk. 'Well, I say assistant, but he knows more than I do these days. He hardly ever sleeps, I can't keep him from study.' She touched Joah's shoulder, briefly, fondly, and Frith thought: *He will kill you. Years from now he will kill you and the woman you love.* 'Lord Frith, this is Joah Cirrus, our most promising student, and a fellow crafter of the Edeian. Joah, our guest here has an unusual instinct for the craft. Xinian brought him to Lan-Hellis for, well, complicated reasons, but I reckon we can make good use of him while he's here.'

Joah stepped forward, a shy smile on his face. 'It is an honour to meet you, Lord Frith,' said Joah. 'Anyone who has impressed Mistress Selsye in so short a time must be a crafter of great skill indeed.'

'Ye gods, Joah, please don't call me that.' Selsye grimaced at him. 'You make me sound ancient, and I'm barely older than you.'

There was a moment's silence, and Frith realised that he still hadn't spoken, and they were beginning to think it strange. He cleared his throat. 'The honour is mine,' he said, fighting to keep his voice level. 'This place is truly extraordinary.'

'We do a lot of magical experimentation here.' As she spoke, Selsye absently began to collect some of the silk strips from the floor, winding them around her arms as she did so. 'Joah, what is it you are working on at the moment?'

The young mage held up the strange diaphanous material again. 'I am trying to develop a way of easily and swiftly bonding a mage word to an object, or indeed, a person.' He nodded at the silk strips Selsye was clearing away. 'Our current system is wasteful and long-winded. It is possible to have the words inked directly into your skin, of course, but that carries a degree of risk – what if the person doing the inking gets his lines slightly wrong? I am crafting a material that can be inked ahead of time, and will bond on contact. Here.' He bent down and cleared away some strips with one hand to reveal a leather-bound book. Carefully, he laid the material over the cover, and there was a sharp hiss. The mage word glowed pale blue for a moment, and small curls of grey smoke began to rise from

348

the book. Joah sighed, and then stamped out the tiny flame. 'It's almost there,' he said. 'It will be enormously useful.'

'And that reminds me,' said Selsye, smoothly cutting into his flow. 'Our guest has demonstrated a very unusual form of magic, something I have never seen before.' She caught Frith's alarmed look, and shook her head ever so slightly. 'Do not be reluctant, Lord Frith, Joah can be trusted with what you told me. If anyone can help unpick this for us, it's my assistant.'

Joah tipped his head slightly to one side. The light in his eyes was easy enough to read: hunger. Did Joah already know about demon magic, or was he still looking for the power that would give him the edge over other mages?

'Thank you, but I fear we will not be here for very long.' Frith forced a smile on his face. It felt too tight. 'Once we are sure the situation is secure, Wydrin and I have other business to attend to.'

'Then we shall be swift, as Mistress Selsye suggests.' Joah nodded, his voice warm. He could be kind, Frith remembered. He could be generous, and his need to expand the knowledge of the mages was genuine. But he had murdered for that knowledge, over and over again. 'Please, tell me everything you remember, and in as much detail as you can.'

'So, what do you think?'

They had been housed in what Frith took to be one of the small rooms normally reserved for students of Lan-Hellis. There was a washbasin, a small wooden chest, and a basic straw bed piled with furs and blankets. There was a narrow window too, although there was very little to see out of it – just the sweeping darkness of Whittenfarne, and distant ghostly lights. He and Wydrin sat on the bed together, sharing a loaf of bread and a bottle of wine. Wydrin had her legs crossed, and he could tell from the set of her shoulders that something had unnerved her. He didn't want to add to that, but could see no way of avoiding it.

'Joah is here,' he said simply.

Wydrin looked up, startled, the hand not holding the bottle of wine dropping towards her sword belt. He shook his head hurriedly.

'Not *here*. In Lan-Hellis. He is Selsye's assistant, of all things. This is obviously some time before he becomes their worst nightmare. She called him Joah Cirrus, which was his name before they crowned him Joah Lightbringer. Long before Joah Demonsworn.'

'If he harms you—'

'I do not think I am in danger from him. No more than anyone else is, anyway. I would be willing to bet that he hasn't met the demon yet, although perhaps his mind turns in that direction.'

'And he is Selsye's assistant?' Wydrin looked horrified. She passed him the bottle and he took a gulp of wine before answering.

'Yes. She is proud of him. They are both eager to help me figure out this new magic of mine. I don't see how I can refuse their help without raising awkward questions.'

'You could kill him,' suggested Wydrin. 'Or I could kill him. I would be fine with that. I've already done it once.'

'Believe me, I did think of that. If I had had the power I once had, he would already be dead.' Frith clenched his fist, breaking the bread he held into crumbs. 'But we do not know what killing Joah would do. Besides which, there would be no explaining it to Xinian or Selsye. Say that we killed him for crimes he hasn't committed yet? We would be imprisoned immediately, or killed outright, and then Estenn would retrieve the Red Echo and all would be lost anyway.'

Wydrin rubbed crumbs from her hands, and then swiped them off the blankets. 'By the bastard Graces, why do things just get more complicated for us?'

'When I saw him, when I heard his voice . . .' Frith looked back to the narrow window. There was nothing but darkness out there. 'I remembered it all at once. The Rivener, O'rin dying on the floor, losing you. The way that he just peeled open my mind, my memories, and took what he wanted. He saw my love for you and was jealous of it. Used it against me, and you suffered for it.'

'But we came through it.' She leaned forward and squeezed his knee, looking at him steadily. 'We all did.'

Frith put his hand over hers. He thought of the blade in his hand, the Edenier trap opening like a dark flower. And the hunger that lived inside him now, the same hunger he'd seen reflected in Joah's eyes that night.

'What of the Red Echo?' he said, stepping away from the memories. 'It is secure?'

Wydrin sat back, grimacing slightly. She took the bottle and took several long gulps before wiping a hand across her mouth. 'It's not a thing at all,' she said. 'It's a culoss, or something very like it. Do you remember those?'

Frith smiled faintly, despite himself. 'Of course I do. I blew a few of them up, if I remember correctly.'

'Walking bags of dust and worm guts,' said Wydrin, returning his smile reluctantly. 'But they fought on our side in the end, against the newly arisen brood army. You know, if we'd just listened to them in the first place, none of this would have happened.'

'And I would have walked away from you and Sebastian and into another life. A bitter, twisted existence, dreaming of revenge, of justice for my family, knowing I could never have it.' Frith looked down at his hands. Once they had been scarred, his fingernails all torn off with pliers. 'And I would never have had you. I have always been selfish, it's true, but in this I cannot bring myself to feel guilty. Wydrin, I would not give you up for anything.'

'And you'll never have to,' she replied, an unusually serious tone to her voice, but when he looked up she was breaking the bread into more pieces. 'They keep it down in the dark, in a cellar under the main room. It can talk, and it calls itself Echo, but it is just a spell, Xinian tells me. Somewhere there is another one just like it, and together they form a piece of magic so powerful it could destroy the mages.'

'Hopefully Sebastian will be there by now,' said Frith, hoping he sounded more certain than he felt.

'There have been no messages from their other stronghold,' said Wydrin. She shifted on the bed. 'I can't help feeling like we've made a mistake somewhere. We shouldn't have split up again. It puts us all in danger, and I can't say why.' She shook her head, and he saw a flicker of anger pass over her face. 'There is too much we don't know, and it makes me nervous. I hate being nervous. I want to get out there and stab something.'

Frith put the last of the bread aside and shifted over until he could put his arm around her. She stiffened at first, refusing to be mollified, but he leaned down and kissed her hair, and then the warm skin of her neck. She looked up at him, and he was glad to see mischief dancing in her eyes again.

'Lord Frith, are you attempting to distract me with sex?'

'I am,' he said, 'it's true. I am occasionally capable of entirely selfless acts.'

She laughed delightedly at that and slid her fingers between the buttons of his shirt. His heart eased a little. If nothing else, there was always this. Always. He tried not to think of the darkness outside the window.

55

For the first time the Narhl man looked uncertain.

They had finally reached the lagoon, the ships at anchor near one of its sandy banks. Tall trees towered to all sides, a wall of green foliage so dense it seemed to suck light from the place, and the water was crystal blue. Even if Terin hadn't claimed that the waters had healing properties, Devinia thought the place looked inviting – after days on board the *Dragon's Maw* under the blistering sun, the idea of a quick swim was very attractive – but still he held them back. Terin's eyes moved constantly, searching the treeline for something she couldn't guess.

'Well?' snapped the Banshee. Her face was a patch of darkness within her hood, her bare arms marbled with the furry red growth. In some of the more advanced cases, the red growths now resembled fibrous thorns, bursting up through the skin. Ristanov's arm bristled with them. 'We have come to your precious lagoon, greyman. You will heal my people here, or I will cut your throat myself and let you bleed out in this water, yes. What are we waiting for?'

Terin turned to her, his face solemn. 'My apologies, Captain, but this is not an instant process. First of all I must meditate so that I am at one with the spirits here, and then I must commune with them. I can ask the water spirits to heal you, but if I just blunder in, making demands . . .' He smiled faintly. 'I am sure you understand the importance of democracy, Captain.'

The Banshee stiffened, her head twitching back so that for a brief moment it was possible to see her face. Devinia caught sight of one wild blue eye in a thicket of red, and then it was gone.

'Perhaps, priest, I will just butcher you here. Fresh meat for dinner, yes. That may do my crew more good than your prayers.'

'Oh, great.' Augusta appeared behind her, wiping her hands on a scrap of cloth. Her broad, wrinkled forehead was pink with sunburn. 'So we came all the way out here for nowt, then? If you're going to just kill the fool we could have done it days ago and still be picking his bones clean now.' Augusta shook her head in disgust. 'Let him do his business. If it doesn't work, you've still got his skinny hide to fillet.'

Ristanov hissed through her teeth at the old woman, but when she turned back, she waved a dismissive hand at Terin.

'Do what you must. The crew need to rest, anyway.'

'I would like to go down into the water,' said Terin immediately. 'I will be able to commune more directly with the water spirits that way.'

For a brief moment Devinia thought Ristanov would strike him, she looked so irritated, but instead she turned away. 'Devinia the Grey, get your charge into the water. You could use a bath.'

With no small difficulty, she and Terin were lowered down into the shallow water, swimming until they could put their feet on the sandy bottom. From the ship, the Banshee had a team of three men with crossbows trained on them, just in case they decided to take their chances within the island.

'I hope you know what you're doing,' said Devinia. 'Ristanov has never been an especially patient woman, and that shit on her face isn't putting her in a good mood.'

'Everything is as it should be,' he replied. The water came up to their waists, clear and cool against their skins. Terin crouched, letting the water lap against his chest, then his neck. He closed his eyes and breathed out slowly. 'Almost everything, anyway.'

'This is you meditating, is it?'

He sighed and swept his hands through the water slowly, causing a thousand shards of light to jump across the surface.

'You could say that. This is a beautiful place, but it is so hot. How can anyone live in such a place?'

'I'm beginning to think no one should.' Devinia glanced back at the ship, eyeing the crossbow bolts still aimed at them, before edging a little closer to Terin. 'Are you going to tell me what this is really about?'

Terin opened his eyes and looked at her, his dark blue eyes suddenly shrewd. A smile touched the corner of his mouth. 'All I can say, my friend, is be ready to move. And a friend of the Copper Cat says hello.'

Devinia caught her breath. 'You know Wydrin? Do you know where she is? I need to—'

'What is this?'

They both turned back towards the ship at the sound of the voice. A withered figure, half wrapped in a long grey cloak, was standing by the guardrail, watching them. Kellan hadn't troubled to cover his head like the Banshee had, and Devinia noticed the men with crossbows edging away slightly. They were all infected, but even so, no one wanted what Kellan had. In the daylight he was an especially alarming sight. The ring of gold on his forehead was too bright to look at.

'What is this?' he repeated, turning to look at the Banshee, who was watching him carefully. 'Our most prized prisoner going for a little dip?'

'The priest claims he must meditate in the water before the lagoon will provide the cure for our sickness.' Ristanov's voice was tight. 'It amuses me to have Devinia the Grey do menial tasks such as this.'

'Nonsense!' boomed Kellan, holding up stick-thin arms to the sky. The grey cloak fell away and they saw the red ruin of his chest. 'There is no cure for this! We are becoming, we are *changing*, we—'

'I am the captain here, Kellan!'

His narrow head whipped towards her like a snake, and behind them the Dawning Man lurched into life. Huge golden shoulders twisted under the bright sunlight and it took several steps forward, sending waves across the previously calm water. For a few seconds

355

Devinia thought it would simply bring its giant feet down on the ships and shatter them into splinters, but instead it stepped around them, sloshing water to all sides, and bore down on the two small figures in the shallow water. Its huge shadow fell over them, glowing red eyes like baleful lamps. Devinia shoved at Terin, pushing him in the chest.

'Get away from me, it's me he wants to kill,' she said quickly. 'He might even forget you're here if you can get out of its line of sight.'

Terin took hold of the hand pushing him away and opened his mouth to say something, but the huge golden figure was raising its right fist into the air, blotting out the sun.

'Terin, get away!'

Abruptly the fist came whistling down, and Devinia raised her hands over her head, knowing it was pointless but unable to disobey the reflex. The fist crashed into the water next to them, sending up a huge spout of water, that then fell and soaked them both. Devinia gasped, blinking water out of her eyes, but the Dawning Man was already turning away. She braced her legs as fierce waves lapped at them, threatening to push her over. Next to her, Terin was wiping water from his face with a bemused expression.

'I could kill you all, at any time,' Kellan was saying on the deck of the *Dragon's Maw*. He seemed to be addressing the whole crew, but his eyes were trained on the Banshee. 'Remember that. Remember it well.'

With that he turned away, heading back below decks, whilst the Dawning Man stood dormant once more.

56

Hunting was going surprisingly well.

The small dragon-kin were noisy and undisciplined, tending to swarm on prey as soon as it came into sight, and they had lost several meals because of it. But often their sheer numbers would win, particularly against flightless animals too surprised to move quickly. Once they had brought their prey down they would fall on it immediately, tearing the flesh to pieces so swiftly that it was often little more than a red stain on the grass by the time Ephemeral saw it. Inky, the dragon-kin with the dark splotches over her forehead and snout, was always in the midst of the action, jaws snapping eagerly. She was already slightly bigger than her siblings, and her wings were unfurled now, although she had yet to use them. They were all so much bigger than they had been. The fresh meat was filling them with strength, Ephemeral was sure of it.

They hunted, and they kept moving, heading always towards the lagoon. Even so, they did not travel as quickly as Ephemeral wanted. For a few hours they would make good progress, and then a beast would wander across their paths and they would all be lost to the hunting fever for a time – Ephemeral included. She would come back to herself with a guilty start, blood on her hands and on her tongue, the pure shining web of her connection to the kin fading as the hunting fever passed, and then she would be awash with guilt.

Terin, Terin, Terin, she reminded herself, his name like a talisman against the desires that might wash her away. It was like being with her sisters again, but with none of the discordance that had eventually split them. There was just a shared purpose, a singing in the blood, and the knowledge that they hunted to feed – not, as it had been, for the sheer pleasure of destroying what was whole and untainted. Despite their shapes, there was nothing of Y'Ruen in these young souls, and for that Ephemeral was grateful.

'We'll rest here, Inky.'

The sun had set, filling the spaces between the trees with red light and then deepening shadows. They were not far now, she told herself. They would sleep tonight, and be refreshed enough to travel quickly, arriving at the lagoon late the next day.

Ephemeral found a space at the foot of a tree where the foliage formed a reasonably soft mat and made herself as comfortable as she could. The dragon-kin gathered in round her, finding their own spaces and pressing their bodies close together; for comfort rather than warmth. Sensing the comfortable silver web that was their joint presence – already some of them edging towards sleep – Ephemeral let herself relax. All around her, the island was alive, bright with magic, and, nearby, Terin shared the same darkness.

Ephemeral dreamed. She stood in front of a great ring of concentric stones covered in dusty spider webs. It was dusk, and the sky was full of lavender light, while the stones seemed to hum with a power she didn't understand. There was something at the heart of them, something dangerous. She wanted to climb the stones and look at it, but at the same time fear clutched at her heart. There was a flash of lightning from the clear sky and suddenly there was a tall figure on the steps, his broad shoulders covered in a ragged cloak, his chin thick with a black beard. Ephemeral's heart leapt at the sight of him, and she made to move towards him when a great dark shadow passed over them both. She knew the shape of the shadow like she knew her own name, but when she looked up there was no dragon in the sky.

'It's all right, Ephemeral, she's not here,' said Sebastian. 'You don't have to worry about her any more.'

His eyes were kind and blue, as they always had been. The shadow passed over them again, and despite his words Ephemeral looked up for a second time, expecting to see their death circling in the sky, but there was nothing. When she looked back, Sebastian was gone, and her heart was wrought with the worst pain she had ever experienced. She knew with a terrible cold certainty that she wouldn't see him again – it didn't matter that this was a dream, the truth of it sang through every vein. Sebastian was gone where she could never follow.

She awoke in the dark, her heart hammering in her chest. The night felt cold and dangerous, and there was an alien wetness on her cheeks. Ephemeral curled in on herself and sought out the minds of the dragon-kin, looking for some small comfort, any comfort at all.

57

'I'm not even certain I could recreate it again at will.'

Selsye had taken Frith to a great, draughty hall in the centre of Lan-Hellis. It was the tidiest place he had seen so far; the floors had been swept and polished, and the walls were hung with tapestries and paintings that were well cared for. There were low wooden tables with glass cases, and inside these were various items displayed on cream silk. On a bench at the far end, Joah was busily arranging a selection of objects in a row.

'Try not to worry about it too much,' said Selsye. Her blond hair was pushed back with a green kerchief. 'These are just the first of our experiments to try and gauge the range of this magic of yours. And its effects. No pressure here, Lord Frith, only curiosity.' She grinned at him sunnily. Frith grimaced.

'It also seemed to have a debilitating effect on me,' he said reluctantly. 'I passed out after I used it in Krete, and in the carapacer. It took me some hours to come around.'

'And we shall be very careful indeed. Xinian gets very annoyed if I knock any guests unconscious. How's it coming, Joah?'

'Nearly there.'

Frith looked around for something to distract himself. Over to the right there were a number of larger items on display – a set of armour that looked as though it had been made for a giant, a great curling snakeskin, as wide as his own body at its thickest part and dotted with shimmering ruby scales. And—

'What, by all the gods, is that?'

Selsye looked up and broke into a grin. 'Monstrous, isn't it? And "by all the gods" is right. Lord Frith, meet Tia'mast, a god who lived long before this current crop were a twinkle in anyone's eye.'

It was a giant reptilian skull, or at least part of one. It filled an entire corner of the hall by itself, raised up on a low plateau of dark wood. It didn't appear to be made of bone, but of a green crystal, just like the Heart-Stone. He could see the smooth crease of its long snout, the gaping section of the eye socket, and the top half of the right side of its jaw. When it was whole, Frith guessed, it would be about twice the size of Y'Ruen's head, and she had been big enough to swallow a man without having to bite off any bits. The teeth were each as long as the length of Frith's arm, from middle finger to elbow. Tia'mast must have been mighty indeed.

'A dragon. How can you have the skull of a god?'

'Oh, it was excavated from a quarry in Onwai, long before my time I'm afraid. It's been at Lan-Hellis for centuries. I have to admit, I barely notice it any more but I suppose it is quite striking. On festival nights the new students tie brightly coloured bows around his teeth.' Selsye cleared her throat. 'I suppose that isn't very respectful, but high spirits and that. Joah?'

'All ready.'

Reluctantly, Frith turned away from the giant skull fragment. On the bench Joah had arranged several pieces of fruit, a loaf of bread, and a few other objects that Frith didn't recognise.

'Lord Frith,' Joah gave him a nod that was almost a bow, 'what I propose is starting with this apple here. See if you can push it, as you did with the rubble and the dragon's spawn.'

Frith frowned. It felt ludicrous to be trying this here, particularly with Joah Demonsworn looking on. Every time he caught sight of the man he felt a surge of anger, and it was getting harder and harder to contain. He fought it down, and concentrated on Selsye instead, who was nodding encouragingly.

'Fine.' He closed his eyes, trying to remember what the magic had felt like. It didn't boil in his chest like the Edenier had, but surged throughout his entire body. He had felt it in every nerve ending. He reached for that feeling, trying to summon it through memory alone, but there was nothing. He opened his eyes.

'This is a waste of my time.'

'Please, Lord Frith, you must have patience.' Selsye's face was solemn now. 'There is plenty of time, no need to rush.'

Frith scowled. He pictured again the instances when the magic had come to life. The first time had been by the wall, when Res'ni had threatened to bring the stonework down on them. A chip of stone had struck Wydrin on the temple and cut her skin there. He had seen her blood, and then everything around him had just stopped. Likewise, on the carapacer, Wydrin had been forced to the floor, a monster about to rip out her throat. The sense of losing her had been so clear, so sharp. The power had lit up inside him at the very thought of it. And now he thought that there had been another occasion too; on the rotting ship when the flying lizards attacked, he had *pushed* there too, and the deck had shifted. Had he performed this magic then without realising it? He supposed it was possible. It was his will that was the key – not the mages' words, and not the magic in the world around him. It was his *will*.

Frith held out his hand to the apple on the bench. He took a slow deep breath and willed the rest of the world away, concentrating only on the apple. Everything else could just *stop*.

He thought he heard Selsye murmur something next to him, but then she seemed to fade, as did Joah. The hall grew dim, with only the apple remaining as a bright, lively thing. He could feel the reality of it, the solid flesh ripe with juices, so perfectly itself in this place and time. He could change that.

Frith *pushed* the apple. His body tingled all over and as he watched, the apple's skin turned brown and blistered, and then as the flesh inside rotted away it collapsed. He pulled back in shock, but not before the fruit sank down onto the bench in an oozing pile.

'Oh my goodness!'

Frith stumbled, his head spinning, and a strong hand grabbed hold of his arm. In a daze he watched as Selsye ran to the bench, and poked at the mess that had once been an apple.

'You did it.' She turned back to him with an expression of amazement. 'You aged the apple in front of our eyes. And it was just as Xinian described – you glowed with an inner light.'

'This is not Edenier.' With a start Frith realised that the hand supporting his arm belonged to Joah. He shook him off abruptly and stepped away, willing his legs to hold him. Joah gave him a distracted look, then continued. 'And it involves no crafting, so it's not Edeian. A combination of the two, perhaps?'

Selsye nodded thoughtfully. 'That could well be the case. But I have never heard of such a combination. Lord Frith, do you think you could manage a few more demonstrations for us?'

Frith swallowed hard. There was already a deep fatigue in his bones and he longed for a hot bath and a few hours' sleep, but the sense of satisfaction when he had pushed the apple through time had been sweet. He was eager to feel it again.

'I will stay close to you,' said Joah. 'I will not let you fall.'

'I will be fine,' said Frith, not quite able to disguise the edge in his voice. 'I do not require your assistance.'

Over the next hour Frith successfully shrivelled two more apples, a peach and a potato, and turned the loaf of bread black with mould. At the end of it he felt exhausted, but exhilarated. It was true, then – magic had not completely forsaken him, despite the Edenier trap.

'Well, we have successfully reduced the kitchen's fruit supply,' said Selsye. She was gently tossing the shrivelled potato from one hand to another. 'Lord Frith, I understand that you are a private person, but is there anything you can tell us that might aid our understanding? You are obviously a naturally talented Edeian crafter, but I understand you told Xinian that you were once a mage, but that you aren't any longer?'

Joah looked at him in surprise, his brown eyes concerned. 'How is that even possible?'

I did it to destroy you, thought Frith. *I did it to stop the monster you eventually became.*

'That is private,' said Frith. 'I would rather not talk about it.'

'But Lord Frith,' started Selsye, 'if we are to figure this out, we must be in possession of all the facts—'

'Try this one now,' said Joah. He had walked over to the bench and picked up a small stone object. 'I want you to try pulling this time. You've pushed these others forwards. Can you do the reverse?'

Frith bunched his shoulders. He was tired, he wanted to be away from these people. He wanted to be with Wydrin. 'What is it?' he asked irritably.

'It's a relic,' said Joah, affably enough. 'As for what it truly is, perhaps with your help we can find out. Pull, remember.'

Selsye shrugged. Frith closed his eyes, and evened out his breathing. Once this was done, he would go back to their room and await her there. He wouldn't have to speak to anyone.

The room grew still. He looked at the object, seeing it properly for the first time. It was a vague lump of reddish rock, obviously deeply carved once but now smoothed and worn away by time. He stilled the room, felt it grow dim, and *pulled* the rock backwards. The sensation was slightly different, but the satisfaction the same: before his eyes the anonymous rock began to bulge and grow, seeping into a shape he had been unable to guess at. In seconds he could see that it was a rough statuette of a woman, her breasts and stomach exaggerated in their fullness. Golden seeds popped into existence on her brow, a tiny delicate crown, and in her arms, a horn spilling with corn. This was what it had been hundreds of years ago, before time had eroded her away, and he had restored that.

He gasped, and the room popped back into reality. Despite the gloom it hurt his eyes. Joah and Selsye were both crowding around the little statuette, and Frith leaned against the nearest table, trying to regain his strength.

'It's such a beautiful little thing!' cried Selsye. 'And it depicts Queen Aliyah of Pathania, if I'm not mistaken. Crops sprouting from a horn were always her motif. Extraordinary!'

Joah turned to look at Frith, a look of frank amazement in his eyes. And something else too. Something more familiar. 'I didn't

364

believe you'd really be able to do it, but you did, brother mage. Imagine, imagine what we can learn from this.'

Frith leaned heavily against the table, too tired to speak. *What we can learn, indeed.*

58

Y'Gria had invited them to dinner.

Sebastian entered the giant throne room cautiously, with Oster following on behind. Where previously there had been empty space there was now a long table of shining red wood, set with glittering silverware. There were spaces for five diners, and there were several elegant bottles of a pale golden wine, but no food as yet. Y'Gria herself stood by the table, a welcoming smile on her face. Her green hair was pulled up on top of her head and secured with a net of golden wire, and she wore a sheer white dress, embroidered at the hem and the throat with a repeating spiral pattern, like the ram's horns that curled at her temples.

'Oster, it is good to see you,' she said evenly. 'Are you enjoying the gardens?'

'They are extraordinary,' he replied. The young god looked as nervous as Sebastian felt, and he walked around the table, putting it between himself and Y'Gria. 'They remind me of—'

'Of Euriale?' Y'Gria nodded, and gestured to the table. 'Please, have a seat, little brother. It's true, I've taken many plants from our island home. There is something comforting about it, don't you think?'

Oster sat down at the far end of the table. When Sebastian remained standing, Oster glanced up, frowning, before turning his attention back to Y'Gria.

'Should Sebastian sit also?'

Y'Gria gave him the barest glance, as if she had only just remembered he was there. 'Of course. He is your friend, little brother, so he is welcome here.'

Sebastian sat to Oster's right, and without waiting to be asked, picked up a bottle of the golden wine and poured himself a glass. The wine of the gods smelled like a late summer night.

'You remember Euriale, then?' he said, taking a small amount of satisfaction from the twitch of irritation that moved across Y'Gria's face. 'The Spinner told us that Euriale was the cradle of the gods. Where you are all born.'

'I have no interest in answering your questions, Sebastian Carverson,' she said sharply.

Sebastian put the glass down and met her eye levelly. 'I do not mean to upset you, my lady.'

'I do wish to know about Euriale though,' said Oster. He leaned forward in his chair. 'I want to know about everything. The Spinner wasn't able to tell me.'

'He wasn't?' Y'Gria raised a single, perfect eyebrow.

'The Spinner was killed,' said Oster shortly. 'Before I could speak to him.'

Y'Gria seemed slightly taken aback by this information, but the confusion only lasted a moment. Sebastian watched her creased brow grow smooth again as she dismissed the Spinner's death as unimportant.

'Well, that knowledge is your birthright, little brother,' said Y'Gria smoothly. 'And it will be yours in good time, I promise. I can tell you everything you need to know. Ah, our other guests have arrived.'

Sebastian had heard nothing, but he looked up to see two figures advancing across the throne room. One was a tall, thin man with dark skin and a pinched expression of weariness about his face. He wore loose white trousers and a cord around his neck which was studded with wolf teeth. The other figure was a woman, short and pale, and her hair was a matted grey mane, tangled here and there with bones and sticks. She grinned at them wolfishly as she came.

'Dinner?' she cried. 'With the family? Are those horns of yours growing on the inside of your head now, Y'Gria?'

The god of growth and life turned graciously to her new guests, and swept a hand towards the table. 'Can we not sit and have a civilised conversation? Once every few hundred years or so?'

'It has never served us to do so before,' said the man. His voice was deep and steady. 'I must then assume that this must serve you in some way, Y'Gria.'

'Res'na, must you be so dramatic? Sit down, both of you. Please. A truce, just for the time it takes us to break bread.'

Sebastian clenched his fists under the table. These were the wolf gods, the twins Res'na and Res'ni. He thought of the silent city of Temerayne, doomed to lie for ever at the bottom of the ocean, thanks to Res'ni's anger. Thanks to her madness.

'Oh you do make me curious, Y'Gria,' said Res'ni. She sat down at the table opposite Sebastian, and gave him a sunny grin. It made his flesh crawl. 'Although it seems you ask us to eat with mortals. A long way to come for you to insult us, you green-haired bitch.'

'Mortals?' asked Y'Gria smoothly. 'Do look again, little wolf sister.'

Res'ni narrowed her eyes. Res'na, who had taken a seat to the right of Y'Gria, turned to her sharply. 'You will explain this.'

'Our little circle has grown, Res'na,' she said. 'Oster is one of our own, lost and adrift in this world. The other one, the mortal, is something else – a mystery for me to solve, I think.' Y'Gria paused, clearly taking pleasure in the impact of her words. 'Shall we eat?'

Sebastian looked down to find his silver plate filled with food; thin slices of rare red beef, fleshy dark mushrooms, and a pile of steamed greens. The smell of it wafted up to his nostrils and all at once he was starving. It curdled his stomach to think of eating what Y'Gria provided, but there was no telling where his next meal would come from, and he would need his strength. He gathered up his knife and fork and ate a slice of the beef. It was bloody on his tongue and the taste of it woke the hunter in him. He took several more mouthfuls before he realised that no one else at the table was eating.

'How can this be?' demanded Res'ni. 'There can be no one

but us. We are the lords of this realm, with no usurpers.' She peered closely at Oster. 'Where did you come from, boy? What are you really?'

'He is a god,' snapped Y'Gria irritably. She waved a hand, and the course on Sebastian's plate vanished to be replaced with a whole cooked fish, its silver scales dotted with capers. Hesitantly he took a bite, and he thought he'd never tasted anything so good – it seemed made of his memories of Ynnsmouth, the fresh lake-caught fish that his mother would cook on the hearth, filling the house with good, wholesome smells.

'One that we just did not know about?' Of them all, Res'na looked the most discomfited. He sat on the very edge of his seat, his fingers resting lightly on the table as though he might up and run away at any moment.

'It hardly matters,' said Y'Gria. 'Do you not see what this means, wolf-brother? Now there is another of us, we can stand together against the mages, now we do not need *her* and the liar—'

'Oh this again!' crowed Res'ni. She turned a delighted look on Sebastian and tipped him a wink. 'Talk of alliances, of standing together against the mage-scum, of an agreement that we are all equal. I will tell you again, then, Y'Gria, that it is not in our nature to band together. You are a fool.'

'Res'ni, if you would just listen—'

'Do I need to remind you of my nature?' Res'ni planted her palms down on the table and the tableware began to rattle and jump. A bottle tipped over and spilled wine like liquid gold across the red tabletop.

Y'Gria pushed her lips into a moue of distaste. 'Really, Res'ni. Must you?'

'You seek an alliance?' The words were out before Sebastian had realised he was going to speak aloud. He watched with some trepidation as Res'ni turned her attention to him. The plates stopped rattling. Next to her, Res'na was watching him as though he were distant weather approaching on the horizon.

'She is always seeking an alliance, little human. Y'Gria, big sister, wants us to work together to kill the mages, to wipe

369

them and your entire laughable race off the face of Ede. Kill them all, start again. But that isn't the whole truth of it.' She crashed her fist into the table, and laughed at how the cutlery jumped. 'She seeks to lead us. To be the head of the family, because that is what she secretly believes she is. It will not happen. Ever.'

'Res'ni, you talk nonsense.' Y'Gria sounded melodramatically weary. 'Don't you see? With Oster on our side now we will be all the more powerful. We need to turn our hands to the same purpose for once.' She gestured carelessly at the table and the food changed again; now it was fruits, still wet with dew. 'No more of this wandering Ede, killing a mage here and there, tearing a country half to pieces and then leaving it to the ravens. No more casting cities to the bottom of the ocean and then using your influence to inspire a generation of artists.' Y'Gria raised a perfect eyebrow. 'Do not think I am unaware of your proclivities in that regard, wolf-sister.'

'What makes you think Oster is on your side?' Sebastian said into the brief silence. Again, all eyes turned to him. 'You've barely let him speak.'

'You are the one who should not be speaking, mortal creature,' hissed Y'Gria. She turned her fingers and the peach he held in his fingers was a fat, wriggling beetle. He cried out and dropped it to his plate. 'I could empty your steaming insides onto the table. So you will hold your tongue!'

'He is right,' said Res'na. His voice was steady. 'Who is to say this stranger would stand with us? He is not our family.'

'I do not know what I am,' said Oster gravely. 'I ask you to tell me. Please, give me the stories I am owed.'

'And would you stand with us, then?' asked Y'Gria eagerly. She was suddenly intent, a hawk on the wind who has spotted her prey far below. 'You would be our ally?'

To Sebastian's surprise, Oster looked over to him, a questioning look in his amber eyes. When Sebastian didn't respond, Oster turned back, a closed look on his face. 'I have no other loyalties.'

'Do you see?' Y'Gria pointed a finger at him triumphantly. 'This one is the edge we need. We just need to stand together. Fate has delivered him into our laps, and it is time to start this world over again. I just need you to listen—'

'Enough of this!' Res'ni stood abruptly. For the briefest second, Sebastian saw not a young woman with wild hair but a great black wolf, its ruff bristling with aggression, yellow eyes like moons, and then it was gone. 'You presume too much, as usual, Y'Gria. I am disaster and disease and chaos, I am not a force to be moulded to your whims. I answer to no one, and I am not impressed by your pretty youth here. Throw him back to the Eye, or let me eat him.' She bared her teeth at Oster, and her madness was almost a scent in the air. 'He would be more use to me that way.'

'Will you not listen?' The sheer frustration in Y'Gria's voice almost made her sound human. 'Do you not see what we can achieve if we work as a single force?'

Res'na rose slowly from his seat. He gave Y'Gria a cold look, somewhere between revulsion and pity. 'It is not in our natures to do so, Y'Gria, Mother of the Fields. As you have known since we all crawled forth from the Eye.'

Later, Res'ni came to him in the gardens, under a bloated moon.

Sebastian had found a bower so heavy with fragrant purple blossoms that he thought it was possible to sit under it without being seen, but Res'ni advanced towards him out of the gloom as though he sat in broad daylight. Foolish, he told himself, to hide from gods.

'I really do not have the slightest idea what you are doing here, mortal creature,' she said. She stood over him in the dark, hands on her hips, and for the strangest moment he was reminded of Wydrin.

'I'm sure I don't know what I'm doing here either,' he answered, amiably enough. It seemed wise to stay amiable with this one.

She snorted amusement, and then prowled around him. He tried to keep one eye on her without obviously following her movements. The back of his neck prickled; it was the same feeling as being in the woods, being tracked by something larger and hungrier than you.

'You and the new one, there is a link between you. That is very strange. Even stranger, this link smells of my sister. The one that Y'Gria would rather not talk about.' She tipped her head to one side. Out of the light she was just a shaggy shape in the dark, and it was easy to see the wolf in her again. 'What are you to him? His body-slave? His companion? He defers to you, watches you when you are not looking.' She sniffed. 'It is not seemly for a god to behave that way with a mortal.'

Sebastian raised an eyebrow. 'Oster? Mostly he sees me as someone who fails to answer his questions, and brings him to places he does not wish to go. I am a nuisance.'

'If you were a nuisance, he would have ended you,' pointed out Res'ni. 'What is the story? Perhaps I can read it in your blood.'

Faster than he would have believed possible she was under the bower with him, her hand at his throat; it was like being held in a gauntlet of steel. He tried to push her away, but he might as well have been flailing against stone. Her other fist was in his hair and she yanked his head back, exposing his throat. As quick as a dog sneaking scraps from the table she bit him, nipping with unnaturally sharp teeth, tearing at his flesh. Sebastian cried out but she was already stepping away from him, wiping her hand over her mouth. She had a thoughtful expression on her face.

'Interesting. Dragon in your blood.' She shrugged. 'Nothing about it makes sense. But that is the sort of thing that pleases me. The question is, what does this Oster get out of it?'

Sebastian stood, pressing his hand to his neck. It was difficult to tell how bad the wound was in the dark, but he could feel his own blood, hot and slick against his palm. He gritted his teeth against a wave of dizziness.

'He gets nothing from me,' he spat.

The light under the bower changed, and Oster in his dragon form was suddenly there, pushing Res'ni aside with a curl of his long, golden-scaled body. She stumbled back, startled, and bared blood-stained teeth. She growled, a low threatening noise in the back of her throat.

'Don't pick a fight you can't win,' she suggested. 'You are practically a babe, newly born and mewling.'

372

The golden light of Oster's scales grew in brilliance and once more it was the man standing there. 'I don't believe you're welcome here any more. If you will not help Y'Gria, then she wants you gone.'

Res'ni laughed. 'Is that what you are going to do, infant? Curl up under Y'Gria's breast and hope that she mothers you? It is against our natures to work together, which she knows very well. She doesn't want family unity, she wants dominance. Why do you think that Y'Ruen isn't here? The dragon would tear her to pieces as soon as look at her. As she would with any of us.'

'Go away,' said Oster, his voice flat. 'You are of no interest to me.'

Res'ni grinned, and then slowly licked her lips, smearing the last of Sebastian's blood. 'And you are even less than that to me. Enjoy your mortal, if he doesn't bleed to death.'

She jumped away into the shadows and was gone. Oster turned to Sebastian, his brow furrowed. 'She has harmed you?'

'She gave me a fair old nip,' said Sebastian, trying to force a smile. 'I don't think it's too deep.'

'Come out here where it is lighter. Let me see.'

Sebastian stepped out of the bower. Y'Gria's floating palace had passed out of the clouds and the gardens were pooled with stark silver light, turning the trees and plants and flowers into creations of cold steel. Reluctantly, he took his hand away from the wound – he could feel the ragged edges of it under his fingers – and Oster peered at it closely.

'What are you going to do?' he asked Oster quietly. 'Y'Gria wishes to destroy the mages. You know we came here to stop that happening.'

'The mages aren't my people,' said Oster. He sounded distracted, distant. 'Humans are no concern of mine. Here, this plant.' He turned away from Sebastian and bent to a nearby bush, plucking several thick leaves from its stubby branches. 'They will help the wound heal. The plants here are plants from Euriale, and I know them.' He pursed his lips. 'There is so much I don't know, but I know that.' Next he took hold of his cloak and carefully tore a long strip from the hem, leaving it ragged. It was, Sebastian realised, the first time he had seen Oster's clothes look less than perfect.

'You don't have to—'

'Let me do this.' Leaning in close, Oster bound the leaves against the wound in Sebastian's neck, tying the fabric firmly. Sebastian held his breath. Immediately, the pain in his neck lessened.

'Do you not see, Oster? What point is there in binding this wound for me, if you help Y'Gria to kill the mages, to raze Ede of all human life? I would be one of the ones she kills, and even if she didn't, I would have to stand against her. I am human too.'

Oster glared at him, amber eyes burning. 'You are different. I feel it. You feel it.'

Sebastian shook his head slowly. 'No, I'm not, not really. I share a bond with dragon-kin, it's true, and I was a fool to try to ignore that. But in the end, I will always be your enemy in this war.'

A cloud scudded across the moon, and for a moment Sebastian couldn't make out the expression on Oster's face.

'But you are . . .' Oster shook his head abruptly, his face creased with anger. 'If you cannot stand with Y'Gria, then you must at least stand with me. You are the only – it is the only way I can keep you safe from the others.'

'Oster, I have made too many poor choices, and caused too much suffering, to betray my people now.' Sebastian caught a breath and held it. He realised that as much as it was the truth, he did not want to tell Oster this. 'If you choose this path, I cannot come with you.'

The anger that flitted over Oster's face then was easy to read. 'Then Y'Gria will kill you, and I will be free of this confusion.'

He stalked away into the night, vanishing as swiftly and as easily as Res'ni had.

59

Augusta's knife pierced the grey skin and sliced downwards in one easy movement. She hooked her blunt fingers under the flap and pulled it back, revealing a dense mat of fibrous red material within the dead man's chest. The guard standing over her, tall with scars across his bald head, made a helpless sound of disgust at the sight of it.

'What is the point of this?' The Banshee stood in the doorway, hanging back from the rest of them. Devinia watched her carefully, wondering if she could get the knife from Augusta and stab it into Ristanov's throat before the guard got between them. It would be a dirty fight, in a small space – she, armed with a scalpel, against two pirates armed with daggers and swords. She pulled her eyes away from Ristanov and watched Augusta.

'I'm trying to learn what this sickness is,' said Augusta. 'This poor bastard is helping me. If I can get an idea of what it's doing to the body, maybe I will be able to figure out a way to stop it. Or lessen it somehow.' Her voice had taken on the distant quality it often did when she was concentrating on her work. Devinia doubted she was even aware of the impatience in the Banshee's voice. Another cut, and the mess below the skin was further revealed; it was like looking down into a red, alien jungle. Ristanov edged closer, her mouth turned down at the corners, half her face hidden under a thick layer of the red moss. 'Will you look at this now? On the surface it's just these fibres, but underneath it's forming actual cords, and they're wrapping themselves around the bones, like a creeper climbing a tree.'

Devinia pursed her lips. There was a strange smell, too, sweet and corrupted like over-ripe fruit. There was too much saliva in her mouth, and all at once she thought she might vomit. Swallowing hurriedly, she looked up to see an identical expression on the Banshee's face. Their eyes met, and she could almost hear the other woman's thoughts: *growing inside me, turning my flesh to mulch*.

'I have had enough of this!' Ristanov was trying to sound angry, but Devinia could hear the fear beneath it. 'That priest will heal us today or I will tear out his guts!'

She turned on her heel and stomped up the steps. After a moment, Devinia, Augusta and the guard followed her.

It was an overcast day, the blanket of cloud turning the lagoon's water a dead-eyed silver. Terin still stood in the shallows, his arms held out to either side, his back to the ships. The men with the crossbows were still there too; they had lowered their weapons, but kept an uneasy watch on the meditating Narhl man.

'You, priest!' The Banshee stepped up onto the guardrail. She had given up on the hood, and now her ravaged face was a red smear in the murky daylight. 'You have had more than enough time to commune. You will heal us now, or you *will* die, yes.'

Slowly, Terin lowered his hands and turned slightly towards them. Devinia could already see the apologetic cast to his face, and she felt a stab of annoyance. Couldn't he see that there was no more stringing the woman along?

'My captain, I fear I am not quite ready. This is a delicate process, and the spirits cannot simply be bludgeoned into lending their help.'

'Enough!' The Banshee gestured to the crossbowmen. 'Take aim. I want him alive when I drag him back on board, so aim for somewhere painful.'

Devinia found her attention caught by something on the coast. It looked like movement in the trees, but as soon as her eyes found it, it was lost again. She blinked and turned back to the man in the water – for the briefest moment he appeared to be looking in the same direction, and then he was turning his face back to the Banshee. Had he seen what she had seen too?

'Wait! My apologies, Captain. The spirits, they are moved by your plight. It is time.'

'Time?' Previously so full of righteous anger, Ristanov now sounded uncertain. There was the tiniest seed of hope in her voice, terrible to hear. 'What do you mean, priest?'

'Please,' he said, and gestured at the shallows where he stood. 'Bring your men and women down here. It is time to bathe in the healing waters. Time to wash away the illness.'

For a few seconds there was silence. Devinia looked over and met Augusta's eyes; she shrugged minutely.

'Yellow watch, you will go first,' said the Banshee. When no one moved, she gestured at the water. 'Get in there, do what the priest says. We will see if he can give us what he promised.'

Men and women began to move, stripping off heavy leathers and sword belts before climbing down the sides and wading out into the shallows. Once the first few went, more and more joined them from all three ships, until Devinia was sure that it had to be more than just yellow watch down there, but the Banshee said nothing. She was waiting, she realised, until she was sure there was something to this. If anyone was going to be made to look a fool, it wouldn't be Ristanov the Banshee.

'Good, this is good.' Terin beamed at them all, waving them in. He waded backwards until he found a boulder poking out of the water and climbed onto the top of it. His narrow chest gleamed wetly, like a mottled stone in a stream. He glanced once behind him, into the black trees, and then he turned back to them, smiling kindly. 'That's it. Cover yourselves in the healing water, soak in it. The spirits are coming.'

'I feel better!' cried one of the men in the water. The red moss covered his throat like a scarf, and lined each of his dreadlocks in red. 'I feel better already. The magic of the water, it's real!'

Ristanov took a step forward, watching the bathers intently. Devinia wondered what Kellan was doing, hidden below in the shadows of the ship.

'That's it, that's good,' called Terin. 'Now I want you all to sink below the water so your arms are under, yes, all the way up to your neck, that's good. That's exactly where I need you.'

Terin's posture suddenly became tense, and he reached out with both hands as if to pluck something invisible from the air. The good-natured, slightly absent-minded smile dropped from his face to be replaced by an expression of absolute concentration.

'Cold, come to me.'

Even on the ship, Devinia felt it. The temperature dropped abruptly, a wave of cold that made her draw a surprised breath, and then let it out in a puff of white vapour. The water around the bathers turned cloudy, and then rigid with a layer of ice. The men and women down there cried out, some of them sensible enough to try and stand up fully so their bodies weren't trapped, but none of them made it: the ice was too sudden and too thick.

On his rock, Terin stumbled slightly, visibly exhausted by the feat he had just performed.

'What is going on?' cried Ristanov. She was echoed by her crew, voices raised in confusion and anger. 'What is this? Kellan!'

Before anyone could react, a dark shadow rose from the tree-line and descended on them. They were, Devinia realised as her stomach turned over, a clutch of flying lizards, with wings like bats, leathery blue skin and bright orange eyes, and they had their jaws open wide, revealing row upon row of shining teeth. She thought of her son, Jarath, and his tales of the great dragon that had destroyed his ship, but she saw no fire; instead the dragon-like animals fell onto the ships, jaws snapping and tails flailing. Men and women ran to arm themselves, and she saw crossbows fired. In moments everything was chaos.

'Augusta?'

She turned in time to see the old woman burying her scalpel into the neck of the man who had been guarding them. She twisted the blade once, finding exactly the right part of the neck, and then stepped away neatly before she could be caught in the torrent of blood. The man fell to his knees.

'What are you bloody gawping at, Red? I reckon it's time we made a move, aye?'

Devinia pulled the dying man's sword from his belt, savouring the fierce stab of triumph at the weight of cold steel in her fingers again, before turning back to the fight. Everywhere she looked there were men and women fighting off the dragon creatures. Up close, Devinia realised that their wings had made them seem bigger and fiercer than they actually were – now they hissed like snakes, snapping and squawking at the crew. A figure climbing over the guardrail onto the ship caught her eye – she had green skin and white hair, and a wicked-looking dagger clutched between her pointed teeth. Catching Devinia's eye, she took the dagger from her mouth and shouted at them.

'Get to Terin!' she called. 'Quickly, blood of Wydrin!'

'What did she call me?'

Augusta was already tugging her to the side of the ship. Behind them, Terin had been performing more of his strange magic and the ice was holding the ship where it was.

'Watch them!' Ristanov was screaming. 'Don't let them escape!'

Two pirates and the Banshee herself came for them, blades flashing – in the overcast light they looked like shambling corpses, their faces and chests streaked with the gore-like moss. Putting her body between them and Augusta, Devinia swept her stolen sword back and forth, keeping them at a distance. 'Come and meet your deaths then, idiots!'

The two pirates ran at her, bellowing, and it was almost too easy. The sword danced in her grip, so long missed, and the first fell screaming, his guts in his hands. The second took a slice to her arm and fell back, looking around for help. Ristanov hissed in disgust at them both, raising her own cutlass high above her head. Moving faster than she had done for days, Devinia ran at the pirate mayor and brought a fist down in the middle of her face before she could react. Her nose made a flat *crump* as the bones disintegrated, and while the Banshee staggered, Devinia tore the sword from her hand and threw it to the deck, before grabbing the woman by the throat and pressing the blade under her chin. Other crew members had converged on them, their eyes wild. Devinia edged back towards the guardrail, dragging the Banshee with her.

'Come near me and I'll cut your captain's sorry throat,' she said. The woman with green skin appeared at her side.

'We must go now,' she said in a matter-of-fact tone. 'We must go before—'

There was a screech of metal, and the Dawning Man lurched into life, red eyes blazing. Devinia took hold of Ristanov and threw her bodily over the side – marvelling briefly at how light the woman was – and then helped Augusta over, before jumping herself.

They landed awkwardly on the ice, Ristanov rolling bonelessly to a stop, obviously unconscious. All around them the trapped crew cried out, caught in the ice, as the Dawning Man started to move.

'To Terin! Quickly!'

Barely knowing what she was doing, Devinia grabbed Ristanov by the hair and hauled her across the ice, while Augusta, suddenly surprisingly spry, sprinted towards the rock where Terin stood. They got there just in time to see the Dawning Man take a series of steps, one straight through the *Forgotten Sun*, crushing it into a mess of splinters and ice. The dragon-like creatures all took flight again, heading back into the trees, and a wretched figure appeared on the deck of the *Dragon's Maw*. It was Kellan, his teeth very white in his crimson face.

'Where do you think you are going, Devinia? Have you forgotten what I am now?'

'Oh great,' muttered Augusta. 'Who woke that bastard up?'

The Dawning Man crashed through the ice between them, heedless of the men and women trapped there. It would be on them in seconds.

'I'm not sure that I can,' Terin was saying, his voice no more than a whisper. Devinia looked at him to see the young man pale as milk, dark circles under his eyes. 'Ephemeral, I don't know if I can.'

'You must,' murmured the green-skinned woman. 'I know how strong you truly are, my love.'

The Dawning Man loomed above them. Terin extended one trembling hand, and again the temperature dropped drastically. Caught in the middle of it, Devinia gasped, feeling the cold pinch at her face and steal the breath from her lungs. The air was filled with a brittle cracking sound and the water immediately surrounding the rock turned white, freezing the Dawning Man's legs where they were. It faltered, and for a moment looked like it might just fall over, and then it simply stopped. From behind it they heard Kellan's howl of frustration.

'We'll have seconds, if that,' said Devinia. She gathered the limp body of the Banshee and flung it over her shoulder. A threat to the captain's life might keep the pirates from their backs for a moment, and at least she would have the pleasure of killing her slowly at a later date. 'Make for the trees, and run as far as you can.'

60

The stew was watery, with more potato than meat to its name. Wydrin chased a scrap of what she thought might be lamb around the edge of the bowl with a chunk of bread.

'You would think they'd have better food here,' she confided to Frith. 'Remember that feast under the Citadel that Gallo gave us? That was proper bloody food. There was a ham as big as your head.'

'I am surprised they have any food at all,' said Frith. 'Whittenfarne isn't the most attractive stop for trading vessels.'

They were sitting at one of several long tables, eating a late dinner with around a hundred black-clad student mages. The dining room was in another large draughty hall – Lan-Hellis appeared to be riddled with them, with no particular thought given to their layout. It made Wydrin think of a rabbit warren – a warren filled with pasty young men and women who didn't get out enough. At a table at the head of the room, Xinian and Selsye sat with several other mages, obviously of a higher rank. Joah was there too – when Wydrin had seen him for the first time, Frostling had found its way into her hand without her even having to think about it. Her head had been full of Nuava, the girl who had ridden a great stone monster to her doom in an effort to stop him from taking more lives, but Frith had slipped a hand around her arm and murmured in her ear, and Frostling went back to its scabbard unbloodied.

'How is it going? With the magic lessons?'

Frith looked up at her, his grey eyes serious. Over the last few days he had grown obviously weary, dark circles appearing under his eyes, and he slept deeply at night, not stirring until morning. 'I am gradually learning how to control it,' he said. He glanced around at the mages sitting closest, and lowered his voice. 'It becomes easier to summon. I would not have thought that I would end up back on Whittenfarne, learning how to control magic again. But we are no closer to understanding where it comes from. Joah asks me endless questions, and I know he senses that I am holding back. Selsye is kinder. I think she believes that I lost the Edenier due to some sort of traumatic event, and will not force me to talk of it.'

She's not that far wrong, thought Wydrin. Out loud, she asked, 'Do you have any ideas in that direction?'

'I think it was the spirit on the island,' he said. He swirled his spoon through his untouched stew. 'I think it magnified something that was already there. And then the Eye brought it into focus. Who knows what sort of magical forces we passed through, to bring us so far into the past? And this magic is time related. It must be linked.'

'Except that you can't really tell them that.'

'No,' he agreed. 'I really can't.'

There were raised voices from the table. Wydrin turned to see that a solidly built bald man in travelling leathers had entered the room, and he appeared to be remonstrating with Xinian. The Commander had stood up, and there was a look of shock on her face. Wydrin felt a shiver of unease move down her spine.

'Who is that, do you think?' The low murmur of conversation in the hall had grown to a hubbub, and Wydrin could see mages at the lower tables staring at the bald man, or leaning their heads together in urgent conversation. The man's face was red, and he was stabbing his finger towards Xinian repeatedly. Next to her, Selsye had half risen out of her chair. Wydrin blinked. Sometimes, when she was sailing with her mother, the air would change in some imperceptible way and they would know that a storm was coming – perhaps it would be hours or days away, but it would

383

always come. In a room crowded with people and no ocean in sight, Wydrin felt that same sense sweep through her; a change of atmosphere that promised some oncoming disaster. It was never wrong.

As casually as possible, Wydrin slid out from the bench, wiping her fingers on her trousers as she did so.

'Stay here,' she told Frith. 'Keep an eye on them. I'm going to check on our little friend.'

She left the hall at a normal pace, not hurrying, not wanting to draw attention to herself – particularly not wanting to draw the attention of the angry bald man currently making Xinian's life a misery. Once out into the labyrinth of corridors, she walked faster. The sense that something had gone wrong was only increasing, and there was a taste in her mouth, brackish and sour, that had nothing to do with the stew. The way back to the artefact room was easy enough to remember and soon enough she approached the door that led to the Moon Gallery.

At first she did not see them. The lamps closest to the door had been extinguished, and the two guards were dark shapes half hidden in the shadows. Wydrin knelt and tried to pull the nearest one upright, but he was limp in her arms, boneless as a doll filled with sand.

'Yohan?'

She pulled her hand away to see it slick with blood, still warm. Rafe hadn't fared any better. Swearing, Wydrin unsheathed her dagger and opened the door to the Moon Gallery. The white powder on the floor had been disturbed; a pair of boots had left their prints – light, but noticeable all the same. The mages who stood in the windows did not seem alarmed. They were talking easily to each other, comparing notes and tying lengths of silk around their arms.

'Of course,' murmured Wydrin. 'If she doesn't want you to see her, then you won't. Hoy!' She cupped her hands around her mouth and yelled up at the windows. A few perplexed faces looked down. 'Raise the alarm, you idiots!'

With that she ran across the Moon Gallery, taking no care with the powder as Estenn obviously had. The door to the artefact room was unlocked and pushed almost shut, resting on its hinges, and that gave her pause. Where had she got the key? Cautiously, Wydrin opened the door.

The room was still and dusty, the lights burning steadily. There was no sign of anyone there, but that didn't mean she was alone. Wydrin advanced into the room slowly, Frostling held at the ready, her other hand hovering over the pommel of her short sword. There was silence, and the smell of old things and raw wood.

Moving as quietly as possible, Wydrin edged her way to the back of the room, keeping close to the left-hand wall. Stark shadows stretched across the floor towards her, and she imagined the tattooed assassin in every one. There was a flare of anger in her chest, and she welcomed it. *Bring her to me*, she thought, *and I'll cut her bloody heart out.*

She reached the far end to see that the hatch in the floor was standing open. If the dead guards on the door hadn't been enough, here was the final proof. She skirted over to the hole and peered down into the dark.

'Echo?' she whispered, unable to help herself. 'Are you down there? Echo?' Inevitably she was reminded of exploring caves with Jarath as children. Echo, they had shouted, and then told each other that it was ghosts who answered them. 'Echo?'

There was the tiniest flicker of shadow to her right and Wydrin was already turning as Estenn appeared out of the dark. She brought Frostling up and across to catch the woman's cutlass against the blade, before forcing it up and to one side with all her strength. Estenn staggered back, perhaps surprised by the force of the blow.

'Where's the Echo?' she spat, but she'd already spotted the sack at Estenn's feet, pitifully small.

'You came all this way to stop me.' Estenn was paler than she had been, the red faded from her lips, and the circles around her eyes looked like bruises. Frith's staff, formerly Selsye's staff, was strapped to her back. 'Wydrin the Godless, you are a fool.'

She brought her curved sword whirling round again, but Wydrin already had Glassheart in hand and they crashed their blades together with a discordant clang. Wydrin tried to push her away again, grunting with the effort.

'You won't get out of here with that thing,' she said through gritted teeth.

'You have no idea what I can do now.' Estenn dropped back suddenly, bringing her hand up with the palm held out flat, the cutlass hanging from her splayed fingers. Wydrin jumped away in time so that Estenn's hand only brushed her cheek, and she felt a sudden heat across her face there, as though she had been slapped. Ignoring the sensation, Wydrin launched herself at the other woman, blades flying. She danced and parried, slapping away each attack with ease. Estenn looked momentarily confused, retreating back against the crates, pushing the hessian sack back with her foot. It was, Wydrin realised, her advantage – Estenn couldn't leave the sack, and it would slow her down no matter what she did.

Frostling slid through the air like liquid silver and sliced a crimson path across the woman's collarbone, spoiling the wolves inked there. Wydrin gave a shout of triumph, and then to her surprise Estenn threw one of her cutlasses at her, the whistling metal barely missing her face. Estenn snatched up the sack with her free hand and threw it over her shoulder, turning to run for the far door.

'Oh no you bloody don't!'

Wydrin sprinted after her, catching up quickly and reaching out to grab a fistful of the woman's thick black hair, twisting it around the pommel of Glassheart. Estenn gave a squawk of outrage and spun round, cutlass flying, and the flat of her curving blade struck Wydrin on her left hand, hard enough for Frostling to go flying from her fingers. Instinctively, she let go of Estenn's hair only for the woman to kick her solidly in the shins. Swearing, Wydrin punched out with her free fist, striking Estenn on her cheekbone. There was a crack, though whether it was from her fingers or Estenn's face, Wydrin couldn't have said.

'Give it up, you lunatic!' she shouted. All at once she felt too hot, as though she were coming down with a fever, and her face was burning where Estenn had touched it. Frostling was missing from her hand, and she wasn't sure now where she'd lost it. 'The gods don't care about you.'

Estenn barrelled into her and they both went over, crashing into the crates and glass boxes. For a few seconds it was a bar brawl; a fight too close for blades, they scrabbled at each other, fingers and fists and knees and teeth. There was a tinkling crash as one of the glass cases smashed to pieces by their heads – Wydrin caught a glimpse of delicate silver links and with a grunt she rolled herself away from Estenn and scrambled towards it. Somehow she had lost Glassheart too, but the Tower Gauntlets were there, lying amongst the broken glass. Stumbling slightly she snatched them up and slid them over her bare hands. There was a sensation, like plunging your hands into hot water, and she made a pair of fists in front of her. The gauntlets were over-sized but beautiful, and she grinned, tasting blood in her mouth.

'All right, then, let's see what you've fucking got.'

Estenn glared up at her as if she were mad. She still had the single cutlass, although she was holding it awkwardly – Wydrin guessed there was a wound on her arm somewhere. All this blood couldn't be hers alone.

'I will kill you, heathen.' Estenn's voice was low and utterly certain.

'You're not doing a very good job of it so far.'

Estenn leapt for her, cutlass flying. Wydrin, always good at anticipating a move, dodged it easily. With the assassin suddenly within reach, Wydrin brought her fist across, missing the woman's chin but catching her full on the shoulder. Estenn flew into the nearby boxes as if she had been thrown from a horse.

'Ye gods!' Wydrin looked down at the gauntlets. 'Where have you been all my life?'

Estenn was already climbing out of the wreckage, although she looked faintly stunned.

'I can kill you with my dagger, which will at least be quick,' said Wydrin. 'Or I can beat you into a pulp with these. Your choice.'

Estenn opened her mouth to reply, when there was a commotion at the far door. Wydrin looked up to see a score of mages piling into the room, their arms covered in fluttering strips of silk.

'You took your time,' cried Wydrin. 'She's here, look, freeze her solid or whatever you do, or just let me finish the job—'

Wydrin looked back, but Estenn had vanished. Desperately she cast around, looking for the tell-tale flicker in the shadows.

'Watch the door!' she called, 'the bitch can make herself invisible, and she's still got a sword—'

Abruptly she was crashing to the floor, a cold encircling her arms, so deep and crushing that she could barely breathe. She gasped, dragging air into her shocked lungs – there was a starburst of ice around her hands, frozen solid.

'What are you doing?' Instinctively, she pulled her hands apart, shattering the ice with the gauntlets. The mages were advancing, their hands held out in front of them as though they approached a wild beast.

'That's the one,' she heard one woman say. 'The Archmage wants her taken down. But carefully. He wants her questioned.'

'Oh for fuck's sake!'

Wydrin rolled over and brought her gauntleted fists down on the stone floor with all her strength. There was a deafening crash and the entire room shook, so violently that she saw several mages thrown to the floor. In the confusion Wydrin scrambled up and ran for the far door, spotting a shadow just beyond the entrance as she did so; Estenn was already leaving. As she streaked past the mages one of them raised his hands to her, a ball of crackling electricity growing between his fingers, and she flung out her right fist, catching him in the chest and sending him flying into the mages gathered behind him.

'Sorry!'

Out the door and across the Moon Gallery, she saw Estenn's footprints appear afresh – she wasn't being so careful this time – and as they emerged into the wider corridor Wydrin realised she could make out the outline of the woman, a darker shape amongst the shadows. Perhaps she had to concentrate to do her little vanishing trick, or perhaps the beating she'd already had had shaken something loose. Ignoring her own aches and pains

Wydrin sprinted after the woman, following her up flight after flight of stairs. The strange heat in her face was now a steady throbbing, making it hard to concentrate. Estenn seemed to know exactly where she was going.

'I can see you, Estenn!' she bellowed. 'And there's no bloody mystical hole for you to jump into this time!'

Estenn crashed through another door and they were out on the roof. The air was cold and damp, with wisps of fog like spirits curling around the jagged architecture. Immediately in front of them was one of the great white globes, lit from within with softly glowing light. Estenn made for this immediately, making a decent job of scrambling up the side, sack swinging back and forth over her shoulder.

'Where do you think you're going?' Wydrin followed, surprised to find that the globes were made of a rough, grainy sort of glass, giving her boots enough traction to climb easily enough. There was a series of shouts from below, and with a sinking feeling Wydrin realised that several of the mages had come out onto the roof after them.

Estenn turned to face her. 'There is nothing you can do.' Her tone was calm, relentless. 'What is happening now was meant to happen. It was always my destiny to save the gods. It was why they saved me, back on Euriale.'

'You saved yourself, you silly cow,' shouted Wydrin. There was a crackle as something exploded, and a fireball arched over her head, followed by another that brushed her arm. Wydrin cried out and stumbled, only for a cone of intense cold to hit her shoulder from the other side. She turned to shout at the mages. 'You should be shooting that shit at her, not me, you idiots!'

She could see their faces in the light from the globe. They looked confused, perhaps uncertain as to the sense of their orders. One of them, a young man with long blond hair, opened his mouth as if to shout at her, but before he got any words out his face seemed to crumple in on itself. He aged rapidly before her eyes, his skin creasing to wrinkles and his cheeks caving in, his blond hair turning grey and then white in the space of a second. His eyes were wide and terrified, and then they, too, fell back into his skull and he was a pile of bones in a black robe, and then less than that – dust. Behind him stood Frith, his hands raised, his body bathed in a strange, shifting light.

For a few moments no one moved – the mages seemed too stunned to act, and even Estenn seemed taken aback by the man's sudden death – and then all was chaos. A handful of mages threw a barrage of spells at Frith but he raised his hands and they, too, died screaming, their bodies rushing to their deaths like mud washed away in a stream.

'Frith?' Wydrin made to move towards him – the light that bathed him coloured him in shades of grey and it made him look incorporeal – but he waved her back.

'Stop her!'

She turned back to see Estenn looking up to the sky, waving the staff over her head as if signalling to someone. There was something up there, something lit up with green lights and swooping down at an alarming speed.

'No one's coming to pick you up, wolf cub.' Wydrin dropped into a crouch and brought the gauntlets crashing down on top of the globe. There was a sound like a thousand bottles breaking and Wydrin fell back down onto the roof, rolling away from the shards of glass while a tower made of white light shot up into the dark sky, briefly illuminating the roiling clouds there before winking out of existence. When she lifted her head the mages were all gone, either destroyed by Frith's new dangerous magic or having fled. Frith ran towards her.

'Wydrin, my staff, she dropped it next to you! Quickly, pass it to me and—'

Estenn appeared out of the darkness behind him, a sudden pale face in the shadows, and the long curving tip of her cutlass burst from the middle of his chest, slick with blood that looked black in the gloom. Frith looked perplexed momentarily, and she saw his questing fingers brush the lethal edge of the blade, as if wondering what it was doing there.

'NO!'

For a long dizzying moment, Wydrin's vision went dark at the edges, and she felt as though it was she who had been stabbed – what else could this pain in her chest be? But then her vision snapped back and she was catching him, catching him as he slid from the end of Estenn's sword. They collapsed together onto the cold black rock of the roof. Dimly, Wydrin was aware that Estenn was getting away, that a carapacer had landed nearby and she was climbing in, but she could only take in the blood, and Frith's dark grey eyes, looking into hers.

'No no no.' Hurriedly she shook off the gauntlet from her right hand and pressed her palm to his face. 'Stay with me, stay, don't you bloody dare go anywhere without me, princeling.'

'Wydrin, I can't . . .'

'You have to listen to me, stay with me, please.' Her voice broke on the words. 'By the fucking Graces, I can't lose you, I can't.'

'I love you.'

She saw his eyes lose focus, and it was the world ending. He grew heavier in her arms as his body grew still, and then a rough hand took hold of her collar and hauled her up and away. She turned to kill this person, to open his throat, and a flash of purple light tore consciousness from her. It was a relief.

PART FOUR
The Black Feather Three

61

Far across Whittenfarne, beyond its lonely hills and desolate wastes, a hunched figure stands in the darkness. He doesn't need light to see by.

The terrain in this eastern part of the island is considered by the mages to be too difficult to bother with. There are too many pools of caustic, foul-smelling water, with too many creeping lizards with needle-sharp teeth waiting at the bottom of them. It was hard enough to carve out a settlement on the western edge – Whittenfarne is always unforgiving. Nothing pleasant or useful grows here and there are few native animals that you would want to look at for longer than a handful of seconds, although the hunched figure is quite partial to the shellfish that cluster in the rock pools. Sometimes he will make a point of spending a day harvesting them, and then an evening cooking them over a fire. There are always more than he needs to eat – and he doesn't really need to eat at all – but it is one of his stubborn little habits, a small pleasure he makes a point of enjoying because he feels keenly that his siblings wouldn't understand it. There is a particular satisfaction to be had in collecting the meat yourself and then cooking it to your specification.

He is not cooking tonight. Instead he shuffles around the pools, pausing every now and then to push a long, grey finger into the black mud. There is little of interest on Whittenfarne, save for the magic. The Edeian here is so strong he can taste it in the air, and it prickles on his skin when the mists swirl around him. That's why the mages keep coming, that's why they built their fortress here.

In truth he is out here checking his traps. They were excavated some years ago, under his careful supervision and to his specific design, and thankfully, so far he hasn't had to use them, although he wonders a little more every day. The war with the mages, and between themselves, spirals further out of control every day. He sees evidence of this wherever he goes on Ede; from far above he sees the burnt towns and cities, he sees the refugees hiding, the devastated crops and blasted land.

They haven't sought him out yet. He clings to that thought, and hopes that he will be left in peace. His siblings have never trusted him. Why would they? It was never his nature to be trustworthy, and the idea of them trying to bring him over to one side or another is ludicrous. Alliances never last, not with them.

There is a series of caws and he straightens up from the pool to see three black birds perched on a nearby rock. They are all watching him.

'You don't much like it here, I know,' he says, amiably waving a finger at them. Inside his cowl his large yellow eyes are creased at the edges. 'The mist gets your feathers all damp, you can't get the smell out for days. I know. But there is so much power here, my sweets. I can't turn my hand against them directly, no, but I can leave something waiting for them. Just in case.'

There were other places like this, across Ede, with similar secrets hidden under the mud and clay and grass. His companions preferred those places, with warm breezes or clear days of crisp sunlight. There were more trees there, for a start. He feels their exasperation against his skin – as light as eggshells. They want to nest, to perch, or to run free. They want to go back to the Rookery and preen.

'Prideful creatures,' he tells them. He unfurls his own wings, shaking their midnight-hued feathers to the darkness. His boldest companion changes his shape and pads over to him on the feet of a great cat. The creature pushes his sleek head into his hand,

and he pats him absently. 'We will go soon,' he murmurs to the griffin. 'Perhaps we will journey to Onwai, no? It's summer there for them now, and it will be so hot that even you will stop complaining.'

All of a sudden, the rocks around him light up as bright as day, and far to the west a column of brilliant white light shoots up into the sky. It comes from the mage stronghold there and it sparks against his nerve-endings as only pure Edenier can. He watches it for a moment, hand lying forgotten on the griffin's head, and then the light winks out. Behind him, the two bird-shaped companions *caw* and *tok* to each other in disapproval.

Perhaps the mages had engineered some sort of terrible accident and wiped themselves out. That, at least, might put an end to the continual fighting and destruction. Ten years of this madness. Sometimes it seemed that the only way it would end would be for one side or the other to cause their own annihilation.

'And maybe I could help with that,' the figure murmurs. He folds his wings away back under his cloak. 'One way or another.'

It has always been his nature to be cautious, to see which way the cards will fall. It was another thing he knew his brothers and sisters could not understand about him, because they were always certain of how they would react: with anger, with generosity, with chaos, with order.

Cards. It had been some time since he'd played cards. He would have to find someone to play with, someone who would not be disturbed by his face but could still play a decent hand of Poison Sally. The griffins certainly weren't any good at it. He supposed he might find himself a disguise of some sort again, something that would let him walk amongst humans without comment, although it would have to be something quite outlandish.

'I keep telling you, if you applied yourselves, you'd be better at it,' he tells the griffin. 'These human games can teach you a lot about how to lie, how to keep your face unreadable.' He glances down at the griffin's long curving beak, black and flawless in the night. 'Yes, well. That's not the point.'

The figure turns back towards the west, looking out to where the bright column of light had been. There is some dark business afoot there tonight, and an ember of curiosity burns in his chest.

'Mages and their squabbles and their quest for knowledge. What could I learn from a mage?' He turns away from the stronghold, putting his back to it with some relief. 'No mage deserves my counsel these days.'

He heads off towards the eastern coast. Perhaps there would be shellfish tonight after all, cooked on the beach under a crescent moon. That would be very fine.

62

The floor of the cell was damp and uneven. Dimly Wydrin was aware that a ridge of stone was digging into her side and gradually making her lower back numb, and there was a fine layer of grit pressing into her cheek. There was nothing in the room at all – no bed, no blanket, no stool, no window. There was a square hole in the door slightly above eye level, criss-crossed with thick black wire, and through that came the weak light from an oil lamp further down the corridor.

She was waiting. There was nothing else for her to do now, but wait. There was no sense wasting her energy shouting and screaming and banging on the door to be let out, because they wouldn't. Eventually, they would have to do something with her, and that would be when she could act. This sort of advice came to her in her mother's voice, in Devinia's dry, serious tones. 'Why are you wasting your voice?' she would say. 'You're achieving nothing here. Wait, and watch. And choose the moment.'

Her mother's voice seemed all too close at the moment, ready to tell her all the ways in which she had failed, to point out all the mistakes she had made. She could hear her speaking as if she were standing in the other corner of the cell, her arms crossed over her chest and a faintly disappointed look in her eyes. *You always were too sentimental to be a pirate*, she would say. *You see what happens, when you love too deeply? When you stay in one place too long? The captain has to stand apart from the crew, has to know her own way. She doesn't need anyone else, because as soon as you do, you are weak. And where has it got you exactly? What are you now?* Worse than the words themselves was the sympathy buried under the disappointment. If Devinia felt sorry for her, then she really had fucked up.

'I am still myself,' she said to the empty room. She lifted her hand and placed it against her cheek. Of all the bruises and cuts she had taken fighting Estenn, the strange burn on her cheek was nagging at her. It felt hot under her fingers, and it was difficult to concentrate. 'I am fast, I am deadly. I am the Copper Cat of Crosshaven.'

You are a shell, replied her mother. *You are hollow.*

'I am broken,' she replied. Her throat was dry. Did she have a fever? Her head was too hot. 'But broken things can still kill. I was stupid, you are right.' Her voice cracked a little – so dry – and her mind cruelly supplied her with a memory of Frith's grey eyes, his seldom-seen smile. 'Really stupid. But even broken things can learn.' She closed her eyes tight, willing herself to put the memories and the pain aside, and focus on what would happen next. What she needed to do.

There were footsteps in the corridor outside. There was a rattle of keys and the clank of a lock being turned, and a heavyset man in long crimson robes opened the door. There were two other men behind him wearing similar garb.

'The Archmage wants to see you,' he said. 'Get up.'

When she didn't move, he took a step into the room and rolled up his sleeves. His arms were thick with mage bindings.

'The Archmage isn't a very patient man,' he continued. 'You will likely only get this one chance to speak, and there's no one else to speak for you. You're alone now, mercenary.'

Wydrin uncurled herself from the floor and dusted herself down. Her weapons had been left in the artefact room, and were no doubt in the custody of the mages now. She felt oddly light without them. Hollow.

'Come on,' the man put a hand on her shoulder and guided her out the door. 'Can't say I'd want to be in your shoes right now. Reis is in a fine old mood.'

They led her out and down several corridors. She tried to remember their layout, in case she needed to know it later, but they seemed to double in front of her eyes. They brought her to a hall where the walls were hung all over with maps of Ede. There was a long table in the middle covered in scrolls and parchment and small bottles of black ink, as well as long lengths of silk. There were men and women standing by the walls, mostly in black robes, but a few with the red robes of the men who had escorted her to the hall, and she saw Selsye standing to one side of the table. Her face was very pale, and she stood with her hands folded inside her sleeves.

At the head of the table was the solidly built bald man who had stormed into their dinner the night before. He had changed his clothes since then and was now dressed in thick olive-coloured robes. His face was florid and blotchy, his eyes too bright. He openly glared at Wydrin as they brought her in.

'This is the one, is it?' he snapped at no one in particular. 'And what about the other?'

'The Edeian crafter Lord Frith is dead, sir,' said Selsye. Her voice was very quiet. As she spoke her gaze flickered over to Wydrin and back to Archmage Reis more than once. 'He appears to have been killed during the fight.'

'As were several of our own,' said Reis. 'One of many things this unbound snake will answer for.'

'Where is Commander Xinian?' asked Wydrin. 'I need to speak to her.'

Reis stood up and took a few steps towards her, his arms behind his back. 'Commander Xinian is currently suspended. The charges against her are many. For making use of two carapacers for frivolous means when we are in the middle of a war. For being taken in by a bunch of agents clearly working for our enemies.' He shook his head. 'Never would I have thought this of her. She was my most trusted . . .' His voice trailed away. 'The other carapacer? We had a report on that?'

Selsye cleared her throat. 'Wreckage from a carapacer was discovered near the remains of Zakrnthos in Relios. There were no bodies found inside or nearby, but it seems likely that Silvain

401

and the two enemy agents have perished.' She looked down at her feet.

Wydrin clenched her fists at her sides. *Sebastian*. 'You brought her here with you somehow,' she said in a low voice. 'The bitch can make herself invisible so it's not that hard to figure out. Estenn came here and took Echo and murdered . . .' She dug her fingernails into her palms. 'I was trying to stop her, *we* were trying to stop her, but you let her get away. She will be going to fetch the other half of the spell now, so how about you stop wasting your fucking time questioning me and get after her?'

To her surprise, the Archmage tipped back his head and gave a harsh bark of laughter.

'Oh yes, this mysterious Estenn. This agent of the gods. Xinian also mentioned her, claimed that's who you said was coming here, but no one saw this woman. There is just you, and your dead friend, and a missing artefact of great value. Oh yes, and several dead mages whose bodies have been turned to dust. This Lord Frith of yours was apparently a very skilled mage, something else that Commander Xinian failed to spot.'

'This is insane!' Wydrin started forward, and felt a hand land heavily on her shoulder. 'Do you seriously think it was us? If that's the case, then why am I still bloody here? Where is the Echo? Who took it, in this big imaginary plan you've concocted for us?'

Reis sneered, gesturing around the room at the mages gathered here. 'Obviously, your plans didn't quite go as you expected, and you got left behind, your fellow agent killed. I am hardly here to explain your little conspiracy.'

'You are out of your mind! If I'm an agent for the gods, then who killed my friend?' She took a breath, willing herself to keep speaking. 'He was stabbed through the chest with a cutlass. If Estenn doesn't exist, then who here killed him? Who here fights with a cutlass?'

Reis turned away from her, gesturing to the guards.

'This is a time of war, Wydrin Threefellows of Crosshaven, and as such we do not have time for hearings and trials, even if I felt you deserved one. Normally agents of the gods would be killed on sight, but we are very close to finishing the Citadel project, and if there are any further moves against us, I want to be able to question you at my leisure. You will be returned to a more permanent cell, and you will stay there for what remains of your life.'

Wydrin was moving before she had consciously made the decision to do so. She sprinted across the room towards Reis, and she had her hands stretched out to wring his neck when a bolt of magical energy hit her side, crashing her into the table. The guards were on her in an instant, wrestling her back to her feet. She kicked and punched at them wildly.

'NO!' she screamed. 'You can't take me back down there! I have to kill her, I have to tear her throat out, don't you see?' Someone grabbed hold of her collar and dragged her partway across the stone floor. The heat from the mark on her cheek was a searing burn. 'You can't take this from me! You have to let me go!'

A fist landed in her gut, forcing the air out of her in one blow. She gasped, still struggling to get away, to shout, but there were five of them on her now, and she was being forcibly dragged from the room. Twisting and writhing, she caught one last sight of Reis, his head already turned back to the papers on the table, and Selsye next to him, watching her go with wide eyes.

63

'You are avoiding her.'

Oster looked up from where he was sitting. There was, improbably, a thick leather-bound book in his lap. They were in the shade of a low stone wall, one of the many ruins that riddled Y'Gria's flying garden. Oster had taken off his bulky shoulder armour, and now wore a simple tunic of soft grey material. The dragon etched on his shoulder looked like the finest silver filigree against his brown skin. He scowled, and turned another page.

'She is angry,' he said. 'She mutters and she spits oaths to herself.'

Sebastian came and crouched down next to him, his hands held loosely between his knees. The sun was hot, the sky they sailed through pitiless and blue. He thought they were over western Relios now, although he couldn't be sure. Somewhere out there, Wydrin and Frith were in danger, and he was stuck here.

'A while ago you told me that your people were known for their tempers,' he said. 'It seems you knew more than you realised.'

Oster snorted, and tapped the book with his finger. 'It is all in here,' he said. 'The legendary rages and quarrels, the fights and the petty revenges. It's a wonder really that she ever thought they would band together as one. Nothing in our endless history suggests it could ever be so.'

Sebastian tipped his head slightly, looking closely at Oster's face. For the first time that he could recall, the man had a fine layer of stubble on his jaw. The dark shadow against his skin conspired to make him look more human somehow, and he felt an uncomfortable spike of desire. Reluctantly, he thought of Oster bursting into his room in the Arkanium, and he turned his face away in case he caught sight of the colour rising in his cheeks.

'Where did you get that?' he said, gesturing at the book. 'I've seen nothing but plants and stone in this place. Y'Gria doesn't strike me as the bookish sort.'

'Res'na gave it to me.' Oster looked guilty now. 'He came to me before he left. He's not like the others, not really. He's not full of hunger and need, like Y'Gria, not full of fever and rage like Res'ni. He is quiet. Measured. He said that it wasn't right that I didn't know my own history, that it was wrong that such an important step had been missed.' Oster frowned slightly. 'I think the idea of it made him uncomfortable. Actually, I think *I* made him uncomfortable. He said something about the natural order, about things being out of balance, but then he shook his head and said, "What's done is done." He told me that he would not help Y'Gria, because it was not how things were meant to be, but he did give me this.' He flipped the cover back. On it were the words: *The Histories of the Gods of Ede* embossed in gold.

'A useful thing to have, certainly,' said Sebastian. 'Is it helping?'

Oster shook his head slowly. 'It would be easier if the Spinner had been there to sing me my stories. The gods have been numerous. There is a lot to read.'

'Give me the highlights, then,' said Sebastian. With a grunt, he sat down next to Oster. The bite on his neck was healing nicely – he had replaced the original dressing with fresh leaves from the plant Oster had showed him, and it was no longer sore. 'What are your favourite bits?'

Oster frowned at him before turning back to the book. There were beads of sweat on his forehead. Sebastian couldn't remember if he'd seen him sweat before.

'In the age of the comet, Danrayus the sun god grew tired of the wars between the humans in the great central continent, and so split the entire thing down the middle, sending each part away to a new place in the sea. The war was ended.'

Despite himself, Sebastian smiled faintly. 'I suppose that is one way of dealing with it.'

'A hundred years after that, Sirena the serpent god brokered a peace between two nations, and they declared her the god of peace and built a great statue in her honour. The remains of it can still be seen today, in the Kitai valley of Onwai.'

'It sounds like the old gods spent a lot of time dealing with conflict.'

Oster turned to another page. 'During the reign of Queen Kenista, Seriil the All-Knowing came to Ede in his human form and took a human lover. From her he learned that he did not know everything after all, and became a much wiser god. It is said that their passion shook the mountains, and Queen Kenista herself blessed the union.'

There were a few moments' silence. Sebastian realised he was holding his breath. 'Oster—'

'I do not understand everything in here,' Oster said, not looking up from the page. 'But some of it, perhaps I can. It is like the knowledge is already with me, and I am breathing it to life with these words.'

Sebastian nodded, thinking of the brood sisters, and how they had treasured books. It was safer to think about than where his mind had been heading.

'What are you two up to?'

Y'Gria appeared from behind a stone grey wall. She wore a shimmering gown of green silk, embroidered at the neck and hem with glittering sapphire insects. Her dark green hair hung loose down her back, and the smile plastered on her face looked false.

'What else can we be doing in this place?' asked Sebastian. He stood up, reluctant to be in a submissive position in front of Y'Gria, and after a moment Oster followed suit. 'We are prisoners here.'

Y'Gria narrowed her eyes. It was clear that she hadn't wanted a reply from him. 'Oster, what do you have there?'

'It was a gift, from Res'na. To help me know my history.'

She was next to them in an instant, her golden fingers snatching the book up from Oster's unresisting hands. 'You accepted a gift from Res'na? Who threw my hospitality back in my face?' Y'Gria's smile grew wider, exposing more of her teeth. 'You of course do not realise, as you are a child, but what you have done is a great insult to me.'

'I am not a child,' started Oster. 'You know that is not how this works.'

'An insult to your sister, who took you in and sheltered you.' Y'Gria shook the book at him, letting the pages flap open. 'Didn't I promise I would tell you everything you needed to know, once our siblings were all in agreement?'

'But they are not,' said Oster in a flat tone. 'They have no interest in banding together, sister, because they do not trust you.'

She cast the book to the ground and slapped Oster so hard across the face that he rocked back on his heels. Before he knew he was doing it Sebastian had moved between the two of them and shoved Y'Gria back. For a few seconds she was too shocked to react.

'You, human. You dare to lay hands on me? I have been far too tolerant of Oster's little whims.'

She gestured, almost lazily, and her slim golden arm grew bloated and pale before splitting into several long twisting appendages with tapered points. Sebastian had a moment to stumble away, before the tentacles shot towards him, wrapping around his neck and lifting him off the ground. Almost immediately the edges of his vision went dark, and he felt his throat being crushed. He tried to hook his fingers around the grasping roots but each one he pulled away was only replaced by another. It squeezed his throat like a strong man squeezing the juice from an orange.

'Leave him!'

There was a cascade of yellow and white lights and Oster was in his dragon form. He opened his long-fanged mouth and hissed at Y'Gria, before launching himself at the god, crystal claws flying. Sebastian was aware of a startled shout from Y'Gria, and then the pressure on his neck was gone. He fell to the grass in a heap, before lifting his head to see Y'Gria and Oster roiling and hissing together, a mess of scales and claws and green-tinged snake-like roots. He scrambled to his feet, wishing that he had his sword.

There was an ear-splitting cry, and the creature that was Y'Gria scampered away, climbing up and out of sight over the stone wall in a confusion of body parts. Oster was shaking his long reptilian head back and forth, green blood on the jagged horns that fanned out around his head.

'Oster? Are you all right?'

The dragon turned its gaze on him, amber eyes wide, and then Oster was back, arriving in a herald of lights. 'Sebastian?'

Oster sagged suddenly as if he might fall, and Sebastian went to him, taking hold of his arm.

'I . . .' Oster looked up at him, his amber eyes full of confusion. And something else. 'I couldn't let her hurt you. Not you.'

'She will be angry with you for this.' There was a tightness in Sebastian's chest. 'You really shouldn't—'

'Everything is confusing,' said Oster, taking his other arm. 'But you, Sebastian. You are the one solid part of my life. Why is that? Why do I need a mortal at all?'

Oster pulled him close and pressed his forehead to Sebastian's, closing his eyes. His skin was warm, like a blessing.

'Please. I need you, Sebastian.'

'Oster . . .'

The young god's lips met his, and all thought of caution was swept away. Sebastian kissed him back firmly, his hand sliding up Oster's arm and touching the shining dragon mark there. The silver link that ran between them seemed to open like a river bursting its banks, and he knew what it was to look through the eyes of a dragon, fast and clever and ancient. He felt the need to live, to run, to hunt, and when Oster's hand tugged at his shirt he lifted his arms up so that he could remove it faster. Oster's tunic went next, and Sebastian had a few seconds to admire the smooth muscles of his chest before the man bent his head to his neck, leaving a trail of kisses across his shoulder. His new stubble was rough against his skin.

'This isn't wise,' he managed, 'not here,' but he was already pulling the man towards him, pressing their bodies together, and all thought of anything else – Y'Gria, the war, the flying palace – was lost in a silvery heat. They fell down into the deep grass together, and Oster pushed Sebastian onto his back.

'There are some very specific things I want you to teach me, mortal.'

64

The voices were with him all the time now.

They were like the itching. So constant it had faded into a faint background buzz, a thing that he accepted even as it was impossible to ignore completely. Kellan looked at his bare feet against the sand; they were as red as raw steak, his toes twisted portions of gristle. He smiled faintly.

'Sir?' A woman with a blue silk scarf tied over her black hair appeared next to him. He had spoken with her often, the sort of career pirate you saw all over the Torrent, but he couldn't recall her name. The voices hushed that information away from him, as if it wasn't important. Perhaps it wasn't. 'Sir, we've made anchor, brought supplies ashore, as you asked.' She paused. They had also fished as much useful stuff as they could out of the water from the ship he had destroyed, but she clearly didn't want to bring that up. She also didn't mention those crew members now stretched out on the sand, too weak to move. 'What would you have us do now?'

'They took Ristanov.' He did his best not to make it sound like a question, but it was so hard to concentrate. On the edge of his hearing, he could hear the murmur of a great many people in a high-ceilinged room. A man was speaking there, and his voice pierced his heart.

'Yes, sir. Devinia the Red and the old medic, they took the captain with them when they fled.' She bit her lower lip, and

410

glanced at the Dawning Man where it stood motionless on the shore. It was late evening, and the thing was a great black monolith traced in the light from their campfires. 'Sir, we should go back. Take what we can salvage and make our way to the *Poison Chalice*. This place has been nothing but poison for all of us.' She was looking at him closely now, and she was unable to hide her expression of horrified disgust. 'Maybe if we get away from Euriale, there's a chance we could heal.'

Kellan cleared his throat and forced himself to focus on her face, to try and see her clearly. There were tendrils of the red infection at her throat.

'And see everything we've fought for, lost?' Kellan smiled, feeling the skin on his face twitch and stretch under the weight of the fibrous red growths. 'We are so close to glory. Can't you see it? Can't you feel it?'

'Kellan, you fool, we're losing people all the time.' She bared her teeth at him, a genuine flash of anger, and then with another glance at the Dawning Man, got herself back under control. 'Not just from the disease. People are running away. They'd rather take their chances in this cursed jungle than . . . It's all falling apart. You have to give this up now.'

'Give it up? Just let them go?' For a moment, an image of Wydrin Threefellows floated in front of his eyes, and it briefly obliterated the whispering voices and even the terrible itch. 'When that little bitch comes back, where will she go? Who will she go to first? Her bitch-mother, of course. And I intend to be there when she turns up, and then I will skin her alive, I will have the Dawning Man pull her arms from her shoulders, slowly, and she will see, you will all see—'

The voices came back in a rush. The pirate woman was watching him with wide eyes.

'You're thinking, I'm not your bloody captain.' He leaned in close to her, taking a perverse satisfaction in how she pulled away. 'You're thinking, fuck the Banshee and her poxy, diseased treasure. Well, I might not be your captain, but I—'

He reached up and touched the tips of his fingers to the golden crown at his head, and his vision flooded with blood. When it cleared away, he was in a stone hall with a roof of clear, glittering glass. Lined up against either wall were ten of the Dawning Men, five on each side; all enormous, golden, and filled with ruby fire. He was sitting on a throne, the weight of the golden crown a burning presence against his forehead. There were people in the hall too, men and women in elaborate furs and robes, all clustered down the far end of the hall. It was their voices he had been hearing, chattering constantly. Now that he was closer, he could tell that they were afraid. This pleased him. He looked down at his hand and saw that it was a twisted, red thing. On the floor below the throne, a young woman knelt on a crimson carpet, her skin impossibly white against the blood-coloured fabric.

'You don't have to do this, Father,' she was saying. Her face was an unblemished moon. 'This can all end with you, here.'

In this strange hall of stone and glass, Kellan raised his withered red hand and watched with satisfaction as his daughter's clear and unblemished cheek suddenly puckered and blistered red, tiny tendrils of the Red Waste spreading rapidly, clawing up her cheek to caress her lower eyelid. His daughter did not cry out or curse him, but her eyes filled with silent tears. Behind her, the cries of the nobles grew hoarser, more angry, and with a rumble, the Dawning Men began to move—

Abruptly, Kellan was back on the beach in the fading light, and the pirate woman was still peering at him in confusion. He took a breath, tearing his fingers away from the golden crown.

'I am not your captain, but I am the Red King reborn!' He spat at her, waving one hand at the Dawning Man in the shadows. 'I will have the revenge that was promised to me, or I will crush every one of you.' He gestured, and the Dawning Man took a ponderous step forward, sloshing water up the beach. 'Gather what supplies you can carry, and follow me. We're going after our escaped prisoners.'

65

Pink.

The light was pink, and it was familiar. It was that, more than anything, that drew him back. He had seen this light before, more than once, but the memory that stayed with him was of a dark night in his own forest, Wydrin watching him with open scepticism as he healed her arm. The magic then had been a force of its own, half leading him, half evading him. It had been the first time he had touched Wydrin's face.

'I think he's coming round.'

'It's too soon. I haven't finished.'

Frith tried to pull away from the voices. They weren't the ones he wanted to hear, and one of them filled him with dread. He wondered where his brothers were. If he had slept in too late, it was normally Tristan who came to rouse him – if he was feeling kind, he would bring a freshly cooked pastry from the kitchen, and if he was feeling mischievous, he would slip a damp towel under the bedclothes. Frith would chase him out of the bed chamber, roaring his disapproval, and Tristan would scamper back down the steps whooping loud enough to wake the whole household.

'Why is he smiling?'

'Please, I'm concentrating. There is so much damage here.'

The light was brighter. Was it the sunset? Frith remembered the Secret Keeper's room of glass, how it had been glowing with pink and orange light.

'He's bleeding freely again. I don't know if I can do this.'

'Be calm, Joah. Anyone else would have lost him by now. Just do what you can.'

There was pain, a dull ache in his chest that swiftly deepened into a burning agony. He was back in the Mages' Lake, and they were torturing him, torturing him as Yellow-Eyed Rin had done. His brothers, his father, they were already dead. Memories came back in a sudden flood, pushed along by the pain, and he struggled to surface, panic tightening his throat. Where was Wydrin? Why wasn't she with him? She had kissed him on the wooden platform of the Destroyer, he had seen her body twist away into the darkness below the Rivener, she had fallen from the griffin, the taste of her skin that first sweet time together in the tavern in the Riverlands – his memories were the shattered pieces of a glass, too confused and too sharp to put back together.

'Oh, no. Hold him still! He will undo it all if he thrashes around like this.'

'Keep working, I'll do what I can.'

She was laughing and placing her chik-choks piece down on the board, she was pushing him back onto a feather bed, her skin like fresh cream against the tawny brown of his own, she was running into a fight, daggers in her hands and a grin on her face, she pushed him from the top of the Queen's Tower, and they fell together.

'Wydrin!'

'Damn it, he's awake. Quickly now, Joah.'

Pink light, and the stench of blood. Frith opened his eyes to see Selsye leaning over him, her hands on both his shoulders, holding him down. Joah Demonsworn was on the other side, the pink light spilling from his hands turning his face into a mask. They appeared to be in a tiny room lit with several oil lamps, and he was lying on a table. His clothes were stiff with dried blood, and his shirt had been cut away from his chest. As he watched, a long wound there sealed up, bathed in pink light. It left a livid purple mark.

'That's all I can do,' said Joah. The pink light faded, and Frith could see how drained the young man looked. His face was damp with sweat. 'It may not hold, even now.'

'You did well, Joah, you really did.' Selsye patted the young man's shoulder and turned back to Frith. 'Lord Frith, I cannot stress how important it is that you lie still for a moment. You will have a lot of questions, but the healing we have done here is very fresh and the wound you had was very serious. Please, just stay where you are for a moment.'

Frith tried to sit up.

'Where is Wydrin? What have you done with her?'

Selsye sighed and pushed him back down gently. 'I don't know why I expect anyone to listen to me, I really don't. Wydrin is fine.'

'But he killed her, he used, he used the Heart-Stone . . .' shakily he lifted a finger to point at Joah, who had sat down heavily on a stool in the corner of the room. Frith squeezed his eyes shut. That wasn't right. 'I don't – is she safe?'

'She is about as safe as anyone can be,' said Selsye dryly. 'She's in one of our most secure cells, and believe me she's doing a lot better than you are at the moment. Here.' Selsye leaned around him and pulled a wide swatch of clean white bandage across his chest. He shifted slightly, and for a moment an agony so complete washed over him that everything in the room grew dim again. When his vision cleared there was a thick bandage over the wound.

'There,' said Selsye. 'Let's hope your body can do the rest, Lord Frith. Joah and I have laboured for hours here, although Joah gave the most – he's our most gifted healer, of course – and I don't even want to talk about the state your back was in, I mean, did that woman even clean her sword?'

'You used the healing spell on me?' Every time he spoke there was a tugging sensation inside his chest. 'Doesn't that—?'

'Have debilitating effects on the mage using the spell? Well, yes it does, but Joah and I decided you were worth the effort.'

'You did?'

Joah was looking over at them, obviously too exhausted to speak. Selsye produced a jug from a table he couldn't see, and handed him a clay cup full of water. 'Here, drink that. Lord Frith, you represent an entirely new area of magical study that could lead to all sorts of breakthroughs in the field. It's possible that what you can do is related to a third type of magic, and I don't need to tell you how important that could be. Besides which, saving your life would be the reasonable thing to do, wouldn't it?'

With some difficulty, Frith sat up and took a sip of water. It tasted sweet.

'I owe you my thanks,' he said eventually. 'Tell me what happened. Why is Wydrin in a cell? Did Estenn escape? Where is Commander Xinian?'

Selsye and Joah exchanged a look. 'This is where it gets complicated, Lord Frith. You may have noticed that this isn't exactly the best place to treat a man who has suffered a sword wound as serious as yours.' She gestured to the small, cramped room. 'This is not our infirmary. The truth is, Lord Frith, no one else saw this Estenn of yours. What they saw was the artefact room broken into, the Red Echo missing, and Wydrin of Crosshaven wearing a pair of stolen gauntlets. Apparently, she then ran to the roof to escape, where you joined her and killed several of the mages who tried to stop her.'

Frith looked down at the water in the cup. He remembered seeing the mages throwing lightning at Wydrin, and he remembered reaching out for them with this new power. They had crumbled before him, turned to dust and bone. When he didn't speak, Selsye continued.

'As far as Archmage Reis is concerned, it is you who are the agents of the gods. Xinian has been suspended from her position, pending further investigation. Wydrin is, as I said, locked in a cell accused of high treason.'

'That is ludicrous.' Frith glared up at them both. 'You know this.'

'There are a lot of questions that need to be asked,' said Selsye. She was wiping her hands on a cloth now, not quite looking at him. 'All of this looks very bad. The Archmage is acting erratically, seeing conspiracies everywhere but refusing to look too closely at any of the facts. He was always such a meticulous man – this is not like him at all. He will not listen to Xinian. He will not listen to me. We—' she shook her head. 'Everyone thinks that you are dead, Lord Frith. We took your body away, saying that we needed to study your remains to see if we could find any clues as to your abilities. They let us do it.'

'Does Wydrin know I survived?'

Selsye met his eyes. 'She thinks you are dead, just like everyone else. She is being watched so closely there is no way to get a message to her.'

Frith pursed his lips, thinking of when he had seen Wydrin fall through the Rivener, her lifeless body twisting away into the darkness. He had thought she was dead then, and it had nearly destroyed him.

'What do we do now?'

'This whole situation is a mess.' Selsye threw up her hands in a little gesture of defeat. 'Xinian is not locked up, but she may as well be, with eyes on her at all times. She is as happy about that as you can imagine. Meanwhile, this Estenn woman could be halfway across Ede now with our artefact.'

'You believe us, then?'

Selsye rolled her eyes at him. 'What did you do? Stab yourself through the back? No one else here save for Xinian or Wydrin would even have a sword on them, let alone know how to use it, and, forgive me, but the red-headed, tough-as-old-boots mercenary is clearly madly in love with you.' Across the room Joah looked up, an unreadable expression on his face. 'No, it was this Estenn woman who tried to kill you, and we already know she can make herself invisible. What worries me the most is that Reis isn't even willing to entertain the idea. Something doesn't add up there, and it's the key to this whole mess. We have to get you both out of here somehow, and we all need to get to Poledouris before this gods-crazy bitch does.' Selsye cleared her throat. 'Please excuse my language, it's been an eventful night.'

'There are other questions we need answers to,' Joah lifted his head to stare at Frith. The young mage sat with his shoulders slumped. 'Do not forget that, Mistress Selsye.'

'Ah. Yes.' Selsye put her hands on her hips for a moment, looking down at the floor. 'How could I forget? Lord Frith, we were wondering if perhaps you could shed some light on this.'

She turned away from him, fetching something from the floor. When she turned back she was cradling his staff in her arms – in the warm light of the lamps he could see every carved piece clearly, the pale wood seeming to glow by itself.

'Ah,' said Frith. 'That.'

'Indeed. This.' Selsye turned it over in her hands, running her fingers over the delicate carvings. 'This was found near your body. A staff of rare, Edeian-enriched wood, carved with mages' words. There are a couple of interesting things about this staff, Lord Frith. The first is that I know this wood. I grow the trees myself in Krete, within the Arkanium. I have been breeding the saplings for years, working to get the wood exactly right so it can be crafted. I would know the grain of it, the smell of it anywhere, and this is my wood. Second, I know that no staff like this exists on Ede, because I haven't made it yet.' She came over to the side of the table, and for the first time he saw something akin to anger in her eyes. 'I have drawn plans to make this staff, Lord Frith. This exact staff. I could show you the drawings I have hidden away in my chambers, but I have a feeling you don't need to see them. Do you have an explanation for this?'

For a long moment, Frith was silent. He could feel Selsye and Joah looking at him, waiting for the answers. It would be dangerous to tell them anything, but he also needed them to trust him. There had to be a way to minimize the danger.

'I will tell you,' he said, meeting Selsye's eyes. 'But I will not tell him.'

Selsye took a step back, still holding the staff to her chest. 'Joah Cirrus just saved your life, Lord Frith. I'm not sure you understand, exactly, the sacrifice he has just made for you.'

'I know, believe me,' said Frith. He deliberately did not look at the young mage in the corner, who was watching him with wide brown eyes. 'I also have my reasons. I will tell you everything I can, but those are my terms. I suggest you take them, if you really want to know what's going on here.'

'It's all right, mistress.' Joah stood up, still a little unsteady on his feet. 'I will leave you now, if it furthers our understanding.'

Joah went to the door and left, not looking back at them. They heard his footsteps echo away up the hall. Selsye glared at Frith, and placed the staff carefully against the wall.

'You had better start talking then, Lord Frith.'

66

Xinian stood with her arms at her sides, staring straight ahead. She wanted to pace the chamber, she wanted to slam her fist down on the desk, she wanted to sweep all the instruments and bottles aside to crash on the floor, she wanted to kick the wardrobe in.

She took a slow, deep breath, and stared at the map that hung over Reis's desk. Control was everything. She must not lose her temper now. She needed to put her case to Reis rationally, in a calm voice. Then he might start paying attention. Reis was on his way, the guards had told her, and that in itself was strange. Whenever he had summoned her before he had always been here waiting – she hadn't thought the man was capable of being late. Stranger still, his chambers smelled of old food and stale wine. As much a soldier as a mage, Reis had always kept his own apartments scrupulously tidy. His chambers here were functional, unlived in, filled only with things necessary for the smooth running of the mage cause. But now there were unfinished plates of food on his desk, cast aside on top of maps and reports, and there were dirty goblets perched on every available surface. The food, the usual basic fare of Whittenfarne, looked largely untouched, and even the goblets were mostly full, as though the man kept ordering meals and forgetting them.

Something is not right.

To her left was a low table of dark wood. It used to house the Archmage's globe, a functional wooden thing with the countries and seas painted in bright colours. Now that was gone, and on a swatch of black material were tiny figures of the gods, carved from yellowed bone. It wasn't actually unheard of for mages to keep idols of the gods – their relationship had ever been a complicated one – but she had never seen such amongst the Archmage's possessions. It was a small thing, but something about it sent a cold needle into her heart.

Behind her, the door opened, and Reis strode into the room. She kept her face forward, staring at the wall like a good soldier.

'Commander Xinian,' he walked round to the other side of the desk. He didn't look at her, instead poking at the maps and papers. 'The dust has settled a little, so perhaps now you can construct some good reasons as to why you thought it a good idea to bring two agents of the gods to Whittenfarne and give them access to our most dangerous artefact?'

Xinian breathed in slowly through her nose. *Control* . . . 'Master Reis, with respect, that is not what happened here. I have already filed a report – it should be on your desk there. Possibly under a soiled plate.'

Reis snorted and sat down heavily in his chair. 'Save me the time and the insolence, Commander. Spit it out.'

Xinian drew herself up to her full height. 'Sir, we were warned of a plot to disrupt the Citadel plan and of an agent of the gods called Estenn, who intended to steal the Red Echo and use it against us. The mercenaries who brought this information to me were in pursuit of this woman for their own reasons, mainly because she had murdered an associate and stolen their property. We proceeded to Whittenfarne to check that the Red Echo was still safely under lock and key, while Silvain accompanied two of the group to Poledouris. When I arrived, everything was as it should be.' She paused. Reis was pushing the remains of what looked like a roast chicken around a dirty plate. His fingers were covered with grease. 'However, we underestimated the Estenn woman. She arrived here and broke into the artefact room, after having murdered two of the guards there. The mercenary known as Wydrin Threefellows went after her, but was unable to stop her. In the struggle, Lord Frith was mortally wounded and the agent we know as Estenn left the island. By means of a carapacer, it appears.'

The silence drew out. Reis pulled a leg off the chicken and began to chew at it noisily, as though he were a dog eating scraps under the table. Xinian pursed her lips, trying to ignore the rising tide of dread in her belly. She couldn't remember ever having seen Reis eat in his own quarters, certainly not in the middle of a meeting with a subordinate. The only sounds in the room were the wet smacks and gristly pops as he made his way through the meat. Her anger, she realised, was swiftly being replaced with desperation.

'Archmage,' she said eventually. 'Do you understand what I am telling you? This Estenn is an agent of the gods and she now possesses one half of the Red Echo. We must contact Poledouris immediately, and send a show of force after her.'

Reis pulled a bone from between his lips, sucking away the last traces of meat. How long had it been sitting there, she wondered? Nothing in the room smelled fresh.

'You hear how it sounds, Xinian. Your story is ridiculous.'

She ignored this. 'I sent you a message, sir, from Krete, warning you of this. Did you not receive it?'

Reis waved a hand dismissively. 'This is a serious lapse in judgement from you. I'd never have thought it, but even the best must fall eventually. I thought you had the backbone to be my second in command. Perhaps *I* have also had a lapse in judgement.'

'Reis!' Xinian took a few steps towards the desk, and then pulled herself back. 'Master Reis, even if you don't believe me, and I do understand that it sounds outlandish, even *if* you don't believe me, we must get reinforcements to Ashbless Mountain *now*. One half of the Red Echo is loose, and she'll be going for the second half next. We have to take steps.'

'It's no longer your concern, Xinian. I am taking you off active duty.'

For a few seconds, Xinian could say nothing at all. Reis was concerned with the debris on his desk again. He picked up an elderly piece of boiled potato and squeezed it between his fingers, covering his hand in mush. She took a step towards the desk, slowly.

'The agent Estenn arrived the same time you did,' she said in a low voice. 'Someone gave her a key for the artefact room. Only myself, Selsye and you have a key to that room. The agent left in a carapacer, flown by a mage.'

Reis looked back up at her. He was smiling, and there was a tiny piece of chicken skin stuck to his lower lip. It was that, even more than the look in his eyes, that chilled her blood. Such a precise man, such a fastidious man. A soldier to his bones. What was this thing sitting at his desk?

'Get out of my sight, Xinian,' he said mildly. 'The concerns of this war are no longer your concerns.'

Xinian nodded. As she left she glanced at the bone figures of the gods. The twin wolves stood at the front of the group, watching her with their hollow eyes. She slammed the door on her way out.

67

Sebastian awoke slowly, holding on to the sense of warmth and well-being for as long as possible. There was sunlight on his face, and the scent of a garden. There was a warm body pressed against his side, and gradually memories from the night before filtered through. He opened his eyes.

'Oster?'

The god lay next to him in the grass, a serene expression on his face. His stubble was thicker than it had been the day before, and there was a grass stain on his shoulder. Sebastian elbowed him, and he grunted.

'What?'

'We have to talk about this. About what we're going to do.'

Oster half opened his eyes. 'I am not so interested in talking at the moment.'

Despite himself, Sebastian half laughed. 'Our problems are still the same as they were yesterday.'

'And yet somehow they seem less important.' Oster looked at him frankly. 'You have so many scars, Sebastian. Do you think that I will, in time, have scars?'

'I think everyone does.' Sebastian sat up, mainly to distract himself from the warmth of Oster's skin. In the morning light the god looked more human than he'd ever done before, more real, and the sight shook him. 'Your sister will know we have done this.'

'If she tries to hurt you, I will destroy her,' said Oster easily. 'Come, lay back here in the grass with me.'

'You're not listening, Oster. As fine an invitation as that is, you have to think now. Y'Gria wants you to help her kill the mages, and the rest of humankind. The longer we stay here, the less time we have to save them. We have to go, and soon.'

Oster sat up. 'Go? Go where?'

'To Ashbless Mountain. We may already be too late, but from there we can join up with Wydrin and Frith again, and track Estenn down.'

'I do not wish to go anywhere.'

Sebastian looked at him. 'But . . . you can't . . .'

'Y'Gria is my family. This is where I belong. She and the others, they may not be perfect, but they understand me. They are helping me to understand myself.'

'May not be perfect?' Sebastian climbed to his feet. 'They are murderers.'

Oster shook his head. 'I knew that you wouldn't understand.' He stood up, moving with his usual liquid grace. There were leaves stuck to his back with sweat. 'Why is this? How can we share what we have shared and you still do not see it? I must learn who I am from them. It's not something I can walk away from.'

Sebastian looked around. His shirt was crumpled and hanging from a bush. He plucked it up and began to shrug it on.

'Family are just a starting point.' He paused, thinking of Ynnsmouth and his mother, a handkerchief tied around the lower half of her face. How she had let him walk past, and not said a word. 'By Isu, you have to let them go. If I've learned anything . . .' He turned back to Oster, suddenly much angrier than he'd realised. 'They're not your family, Oster, they're just cruel ancestors, who should be nothing more than a footnote in history.'

'But they're not,' said Oster, stiffly. 'You brought me to this place, and the Spinner died, and this is what I have. It's all I have, Sebastian, and I will not walk away from it.'

Sebastian retrieved his trousers, and slipped them back on. 'Then I must walk away from you.'

* * *

424

Frith sat on one of the benches in the crowded dining room. He had his head bent low, apparently intent on the bowl of soup in front of him, his hood pulled down as far as it would go so that his white hair was hidden. The pain in his chest, incredibly, had gone from a stabbing agony to a painful throb. Selsye sat next to him, her head up, tense. Joah had promised them a distraction, although Frith did not know the details of it.

'Look, he's coming back.' Selsye sat up. 'Be ready to move.'

Joah wound his way around the benches, a studied look of innocence on his face. He paused next to Selsye.

'Greetings, Mistress Selsye. I have some interesting results from our last experiment. Would you look over them with me?'

'Joah! Of course, of course.' Selsye stood up from the bench, giving Frith a swift poke in the side as she did so. 'It would be instructional for our new student here to see how we work. Come along, Eustace.'

Under his hood, Frith grimaced. They walked swiftly towards the tall doors on the far side of the room. Just before they got there, a terrible shriek rose up from the centre of the dining hall. It was a lonely, maddening sound – the call of a ghost in a moonlit graveyard. Unable to stop himself, Frith turned back to look.

With a deafening crash the central table flipped over and a strange black shape boiled up, a cloud of liquid ink. It was marked here and there with glowing red patches, and as he watched it seemed to twist into a variety of shapes – for a brief moment he saw a great angry cat, a beetle with huge flexing mandibles, an eagle, hooked beak opened wide. It slashed madly at the men and women around it, and all the mages were scrambling to their feet, bound arms outstretched. Spells began to fly.

'By all the gods!'

'Come on,' hissed Selsye, 'we won't have long.'

They left at a pace, leaving the crash and roar of a magical battle behind them.

Xinian marched down the hallway, fist clenched at her side. When she reached the cell, the guard outside it looked horrified to see her. He took an involuntary step backwards.

'Commander Xinian,' he stammered. 'I wasn't told you were coming. I mean, that is to say, you no longer have access. You're not—'

'I'm here to question the prisoner. She has caused me all manner of trouble, and I would like some answers,' she said. 'Do you truly intend to keep me out? Do you think you could?'

The guard shook his head. 'With all due respect, Commander, I have been given my orders.' He stood up a little straighter, and inwardly she admired his nerve. 'I cannot let you in this cell.'

At that moment there was an echoing shriek. Nothing human could have made such a noise and still be heard deep within the bowels of Lan-Hellis. A few seconds later, several magical alarms went off at once. Xinian brought her withering gaze back to the guard, who was staring up the corridor in confusion.

'Well,' she said, 'that sounds serious. I imagine you need to go and see what that is?'

He opened his mouth, then thought better of it and charged up the corridor. She could already hear the sounds of fighting coming from above. Xinian placed her hand over the lock and summoned the word for Fire, focussed down to the size of her palm. After a few moments, molten metal dripped down the door, and she kicked it open.

Wydrin Threefellows waited for her, poised as if to pounce. Xinian held up her hand.

'Not so fast, mercenary. I am here to help, believe it or not.'

For a few seconds Xinian thought the woman was going to charge her anyway – there was a feverish light in her eyes that didn't look entirely rational – and then some of the tension went out of her body. Save for a livid red mark on her cheek the mercenary looked pale, and winnowed away somehow, as though some vital piece of her had been removed. She stared at Xinian without a trace of her normal good humour.

'What's going on?'

The noise of the alarms had increased, and now the unmistakable sounds of a magical battle were floating down to them. Whatever Selsye had cooked up, it was good, but they had a sizeable number of the world's best mages here, and it wouldn't take them long to put things right.

'No time for questions. We're getting you out of here, and we're leaving the island.'

Wydrin nodded once and stepped out of the cell, blinking against the light from the oil lamps. Xinian reached into the bag she was carrying and pulled out Wydrin's sword belt and a long hooded cloak.

'Quickly, put these on. And stay close behind me. Keep your mouth shut until we get outside.'

Wydrin strapped on her sword belt, and something seemed to return to her – some small spark of fire. She shrugged on the cloak and pulled the hood up.

'How are we getting off Whittenfarne? One of your carapacers?'

'We seem to have run out of those,' said Xinian sourly. 'We are arranging other means. Now, follow me.'

68

As she stepped out onto the cold black stones of Whittenfarne the chill wind cut through Wydrin like a knife. She pulled the cloak Xinian had given her closer. In the cell she had lost all sense of night and day, but now she could see that it was late evening, the crescent moon hanging in a largely clear sky like a discarded sickle. Xinian had led her down deserted corridors, a disgruntled look on the commander's face as the sounds of a pitched battle grew fainter the closer they got to the doors. Whatever it was that Selsye had done, it was still going on – the slit windows of Lan-Hellis showed flashes of yellow and purple fire.

'Quickly,' snapped Xinian. 'We can't leave from the western dock in case someone sees us and reports back to Reis, so we have to get to the northern coast, and it's not a pleasant walk at the best of times.' She paused, and looked more closely at Wydrin. 'Will you be able to walk?'

Wydrin glared at her. 'I'm walking now, aren't I?' In truth, she felt better than she had in a while. The poor food and the darkness, the grief and the frustration had conspired to reduce her somehow, but she was still here. And now she was free, with her sword back at her side. Her vengeance wouldn't be denied for long.

They set off across the rocks. Xinian waited until they were a good distance from the looming presence of Lan-Hellis before she produced a small ball of light from between her fingers. Whittenfarne became a ghost world of grey and black, jagged rocks looming like nightmares to every side. Wydrin curled her fingers around the hilt of Frostling, and imagined plunging the blade into the soft flesh of Estenn's neck, the skin parting, the blood surging up and flowing over her fingers. The thought kept her warm. With her other hand she touched the burn mark on her cheek.

It was still full dark when they reached the coast. A slim little ship with a snarling dog figurehead was waiting for them, and they boarded in silence. Xinian exchanged a nod with a heavily scarred woman whom Wydrin took to be the captain, and they moved off into the night, the sea slapping rhythmically against their bow. Wydrin settled on a bench, her head down. She would need to find a whetstone and some oil soon. Her weapons needed tending to.

Eventually, Xinian sat down with her. As they drew away from Whittenfarne the mists flooded in, and the mage's bald head was dotted with beads of moisture. She ran a hand over her scalp and flicked the water away.

Wydrin looked up. 'Are you planning to take this tiny ship all the way to Relios?'

'We're just getting to where we need to be to pick up our next method of transport.' Xinian grimaced and lowered her voice. 'What a gods-cursed mess. Half of me wants to dump you in the sea right here and turn this ship back towards Lan-Hellis.'

'This isn't over,' said Wydrin. 'And I think you know it.'

'Yes, well.' Xinian ran her hand over the smooth stump on her other arm. The strips of silk she had tied up both arms were damp and clinging to her skin. 'We're meeting the others on an island called Umbria. It's on the very outskirts of the Nowhere Isles, barely a part of the archipelago at all, in truth. From there we should make good time to Ashbless Mountain and we'll catch this Estenn of yours before any more damage is done.'

'The others?'

'Selsye, Joah and Frith. They left the island from the western dock – Selsye is still in the Archmage's good books, after all

– so they will get there before us. It seemed prudent to leave Whittenfarne separately. Less chance of us all being caught.'

For a moment the whole world seemed to pitch from one side to the other. Wydrin wrapped her fingers around the bench beneath her, willing everything to be still while a wave of deepest despair swept through her like a sudden black tide. The mark on her cheek burned as though she had been freshly branded. Did she have to hear his name everywhere too? Wasn't the pain she already carried enough?

'Frith,' she said. There didn't seem to be enough air in her lungs to get the word out. 'Frith is dead.'

Xinian's eyes grew suddenly wide. 'They didn't tell you?'

'Didn't tell me what?'

'Selsye had trouble enough getting messages to me, and there hasn't been time – Lord Frith lives, Wydrin.'

It was a knife in her heart. Distantly, she thought she could hear her mother laughing. *What's worse than grief, Wydrin? Hope.*

'Do not play with me, Commander.' Wydrin touched the hilt of her dagger. 'Or I will open your throat in the belly of this ship. I saw him die. They stood me in that room with those mage bastards and they talked about him as if his death were nothing but a footnote.'

Xinian shook her head. 'I think I prefer you with a sense of humour. He didn't die, Wydrin, although it was a close thing. They hid him away and healed him, and then kept his survival a secret. It saved him from the dungeon.'

'They . . . healed him?'

'From what I understand, it wasn't easy, and he certainly should have died, but Joah and Selsye are unrivalled in this sort of magic.'

Wydrin took a slow breath. It *was* possible. She had felt the effects of the healing magic for herself – a pink light that had been like sinking into a warm bath. But what if this was more lies? A joke? She pressed her cold fingers to the mark on her cheek. It was too terrible, this hope. She had thought she could carry on, her heart armoured in vengeance, but here was love again, to make her weak. It was unacceptable.

Strong fingers gripped her forearm, and she looked up to see Xinian, her face creased in discomfort. 'Take heart. You will see for yourself soon enough.'

'How soon?'

Frith stood and watched as Selsye added a small bag of powder to their fire, turning the flames an eldritch green. The grotty little beach they stood on looked all the more sinister in its sickly light. Joah had left some time ago, climbing up over the rocks behind them to go and arrange their 'transport'. From Selsye's expression he had surmised that she wasn't best pleased about this part of the plan, but in general she was quieter than she had been. He suspected this had a lot to do with what he had told her. Reluctantly, he looked over at the long narrow bag resting by the fire where they were keeping his staff. Very deliberately he looked away and out to the mist-shrouded sea. Their ship should be arriving soon.

'I am still not sure I believe any of it,' said Selsye into the silence. She tucked the empty bag away into one of her pockets. 'It is ludicrous. All of it.'

Frith didn't answer immediately. She had, at least, kept her promise of not telling Joah, although he wasn't sure how long that would last. Eventually, he said: 'It would explain a lot though, wouldn't it? The staff, the nature of my own strange magic. It's bending the fabric of time – you said so yourself. I have travelled here from a future Ede, using a similar magic, and somehow it has infected me. Truthfully, did you not think there was anything strange about us? Something slightly out of place?'

Selsye snorted. 'Out of place? You were all bloody out of place, according to Xinian, since you turned up tramping around in my sacred grove.' Her smile faded. 'Perhaps there was something. I don't know. Lots of small things, adding up to an overall strangeness. I don't know what Xinian will say about this. I doubt it will improve her mood, anyway. Oh, speaking of which.'

She nodded to the mists behind them and a ship loomed out of the swirling fog. Frith took an involuntary step forward, his heart beating faster, and then he saw her, jumping down from the side into the shallows. She seemed a little uncertain on her feet, and he found himself splashing down to meet her, ignoring the biting cold water that soaked into his trousers.

'Wydrin?'

She looked up, her face so full of hope and terror it hurt his heart. She was deathly pale, with a single vivid pink mark like a scald on her right cheek.

'By the Graces!' She grabbed him and pressed her hands to the sides of his face, staring at him as if willing him to be real. 'I thought she fucking killed you. I thought you were taken from me.'

'I'm not, I'm fine. Look at me.' She was shivering within his arms. 'Wydrin, are you all right?'

She kissed him then, fiercely, her mouth deliciously warm even as the sea threatened to leach all heat from his body, but when she pulled away there were tears on her cheeks. Frith reached up to push her hair away from her face, and she took hold of his hand and gently pulled it away.

'Wydrin . . .?'

'Hoy, you two, get out of the water already,' Xinian called to them from the beach. 'If you catch a chill, I'm not healing you.'

Frith looked back to the fire. Joah had returned and was deep in conference with Selsye. He opened his mouth to say something else to Wydrin, to draw an explanation out of her somehow, but she was already splashing through the water to the beach. Ignoring the faint throbbing pain in his chest, he followed after her.

69

'You have our means of transport, Joah?'

They were clustered around their small fire, the flames burning orange again. Wydrin found herself staring at Joah Demonsworn. This was the closest she had been to him since they'd arrived at Lan-Hellis, and although it was all too possible to see the man he would become, it was strange to look upon the face of an enemy who had yet to harm you, had yet to steal away the man you loved. At the thought, her traitor eyes slipped back to Frith, who was standing very still, his arms crossed over his chest. Looking at him, she saw the curving blade bursting through his chest. Her cheek burned, and she looked away.

'I have summoned him, yes,' said Joah. 'He likes to be in the earth.' He took a short trowel from his belt and, kneeling down, dug into the black dirt. A few inches below the surface he uncovered what Wydrin initially took to be a shiny black rock, but then a set of segmented legs flexed experimentally at the air, and a large crab sidled out of the hole. It was as black and as slick as obsidian, with a pair of glowing red patches on its smooth back, like embers still warm from the fire. It was about the size of Wydrin's hand, stretched from the tip of her thumb to her little finger.

'Well, I had been having a craving for some fresh seafood lately,' she said. 'You really didn't need to go to all this trouble though.'

'That is no sea creature,' said Xinian, her voice curiously flat. 'It is a demon.'

Wydrin took a step back.

'It is the same being you used as a distraction in the dining hall,' said Frith. 'What is it doing here?'

Joah bent and picked up the crab-shaped thing, holding it up for them to see. It sat in his hands placidly enough. 'First of all, I should say, do not be afraid. This being, who I call Feveroot, has been bound by multiple spells and magics, and is no more capable of harming us than you are able to lift this island above your head. Once, Feveroot inhabited a tree in eastern Pathania, a great thorn tree. It is from that, that I took his name. Inside the tree, he drew animals and birds to him, and compelled them to impale themselves on the long, wicked thorns. The creature fed on the blood as a sort of sacrifice.'

'Demon,' snapped Xinian. 'Call it what it is, Joah.'

Joah nodded. 'Yes, that is what it is, Commander. A demon, a being of terrible appetites that has boiled up from the flesh of Ede itself. It is also a source of great and fascinating knowledge. There are many different types of demons – some prefer to remain invisible, hiding within the bodies of others, while some prefer to haunt certain places and landscapes –' Catching the look both Xinian and Selsye were giving him, Joah cleared his throat. 'I found this specimen when I was travelling through Pathania last year, and with it I discovered how to draw out such a creature, and bind it to my purpose.'

'It will end badly,' said Frith sharply. He opened his mouth as if to say more, and then shook his head. 'You play with something you do not understand.'

'It is all perfectly safe,' said Joah. 'I have bound the creature, and brought it here with me. I commanded it to change its shape in the dining room, to alarm the mages, and then when we had the time we needed, I commanded it to make itself very small and come here. Its powers are limited, but it can carry you where you need to go, and it will obey you. It has no choice.'

'By demon. You want us to travel by demon.' Wydrin reached

up to touch the mark on her cheek but stopped herself. 'I don't know why I'm surprised by anything any more.'

'I – I cannot approve of the use of such magic,' said Selsye quietly. She had her arms folded into her sleeves. 'We barely know anything about it, and Joah is so young.'

'Mistress Selsye, I have learned so much from Feveroot.' The expression on Joah's face was earnest enough, but Wydrin found herself wondering how much Selsye truly knew about his education outside of Lan-Hellis. She looked at Frith to see barely restrained anger on his face, but it only brought back visions of Estenn's sword and she forced herself to look away.

'I am not happy about it either, Selsye,' said Xinian, 'but at this moment, we have very little choice. The transport spells are closed to us, and we have no hope of accessing the last carapacers.'

Selsye nodded once. 'Needs must, I suppose, but Joah, we will be having a long conversation about this in the near future. Assuming that there is a future. In the meantime, I will stay here, and keep close to the Archmage.'

Wydrin raised her eyebrows. 'Is that wise? Reis no longer lives in the land of the sane. You could be in danger.'

'I can look after myself,' she said. The casual ease with which she said it led Wydrin to believe it was true.

'Joah, show us what we need to know,' said Xinian. 'And be quick about it.'

The young mage pushed a loose strand of hair behind his ear. He almost looked nervous. 'We will need a little more space.'

As they followed Xinian and the others back towards the sea, Wydrin felt Frith fall in at her side.

'I need to tell you something.' He cleared his throat. 'I told Selsye where we are from. Where we're really from.'

She looked up at him, unable to help herself. 'You did what?'

'I had little choice. They saw the staff, Wydrin. Selsye has it now. She hasn't made it yet, but she has all the designs.'

'Ye gods and little fishes. What did she say?'

'As you can imagine, she did not believe me at first. But it explains too much. I did not tell her what we know about Joah, or their own fates. Although now I wonder if I should have.'

'Why ruin what they have now? All happiness ends in death anyway. At least Xinian didn't have long to endure before she joined Selsye.'

She felt Frith looking at her then, so she turned her face away, out into the dark.

'Wydrin, are you all right? It's like you can't look at me.'

'I am sorry, but I can't do this any more,' she said. 'It makes me too weak. I thought I could live with it, but I can't. I see it every time I look at you now. I see you die, over and over.'

'What do you mean? Wydrin, what are you talking about?'

'I can't do it,' she said simply. 'I can't go through that pain again. And I would lose you, eventually, and I would be destroyed by it.'

'Better to pretend you don't love me?' The old anger was back in his voice, and even that was a thorn in her heart – memories of journeying across Ede, and the antagonism between them that masked something else. 'To ignore that I love you?'

'You'd get bored of your bit of rough eventually,' she said, almost absently. The mark on her cheek was burning, burning. The crescent moon above doubled, and then tripled. 'How long can I entertain you, really?'

He stopped. 'You cannot think that,' he said. 'You *know* that is not true.'

'Are you two coming? We have little enough time as it is!' Xinian waved them on down the beach.

Wydrin looked away from him and trudged across the sand. After a moment she heard him follow after her. When they reached the others, Selsye handed Frith the long leather bag containing the staff. She shrugged at his startled look.

'Having it around hurts my head,' she said simply, 'and I've no doubt it will come in handy.' With that she turned away.

'This is what you'll need,' said Joah. He took from around his neck a silver chain with what looked like a long glass phial hanging from it. 'Whoever holds this has control of Feveroot, and can command him to change his shape. Now, I will need a sample of your blood. All of you who intend to ride with Feveroot.'

'Why?' demanded Xinian.

'Once a sample of your blood is in the phial, Feveroot is bound to you, and cannot do you harm,' said Joah. Selsye stood off to one side, looking down at her boots, while the demon itself crouched on the sand in its crab shape, unmoving.

'Fine,' said Xinian, unsheathing the dagger at her waist. 'Let's get this over with.'

Joah pulled the stopper from the phial and took a number of thin glass rods from inside. In turn, they each offered up a drop of their own blood, into which Joah dipped a glass rod, before securing it back in the phial. When it was done, he passed the phial to Xinian, who looked at it as if she'd just been handed a soiled undergarment.

'And what do I do with it, exactly?'

'You command him. He speaks, when spoken to.' Joah cleared his throat and addressed the glass-like crab on the ground. 'Feveroot, you have new masters now.'

'I am overjoyed.' The voice was soft, vaguely male. The red patches on the creature's back glowed with each word.

'You will be returned to me, Feveroot. I will want to know that you did as you were told.'

'Oh I expect you will.'

Wydrin frowned. The demon did not sound like Bezcavar. Did demons have different voices? She supposed that would make sense.

'It is ready,' said Joah. 'Now you must tell it what it needs to be, Commander.'

Xinian grimaced down at the glass phial in her hand. 'I just tell it?'

Joah nodded eagerly. He had the air of a man longing to show off a magic trick. Xinian, however, looked as though she'd rather be anywhere else than in charge of a demon. She shook her head, as if she couldn't think of anything at all.

'We have to travel far, and quickly,' said Frith in a low voice. 'Across seas and across the land.'

Xinian glanced at him, and shrugged. Next to her Selsye looked tense, her lips pressed into a bloodless line.

'Be a bird, then. A bird large enough to carry us.'

'As you wish,' murmured Feveroot. The crab seemed to burst apart, a solid explosion of ink-like glass, tendrils reaching up and out. They all took a startled step back, and then it was much, much larger, surging down the beach in a tide of black. Wydrin had a confused impression of shining feathers, stretching up into the dark, and then they were sharing the beach with what looked like a giant eagle. It still looked like it was made of black glass, but now its eyes were glowing a baleful red, and watching them closely. The beak was a curving blade, icy with moonlight.

'Isn't it extraordinary?' exclaimed Joah. 'The things we could learn from this creature, the magic we could master.'

No one had an answer to that.

70

Flying with Feveroot was initially a very unnerving experience.

When it had been time for them to leave, the demon had bent its head low, the tip of its beak scoring a line through the sand, until its back was accessible to them – a smooth stretch of black glass that was warm to the touch, highlighted here and there by glowing red shapes; like a panel in a stained-glass window, but feather shaped. Xinian, Wydrin and Frith had clambered up over its wing and stood awkwardly on that shining surface. Selsye and Joah watched from below.

'Well, this is inconspicuous,' said Wydrin. 'Feveroot, I hope that you don't fly too fast, because I think we'll just be blown off into the ocean.'

'I could hold you in my talons.' The voice came from the glowing red sections rather than the eagle's head. 'I would not drop you.'

'Held in the claws of a demon.' Xinian was frowning. The glass phial now hung around her neck. 'Why does that feel like a bad idea?'

'It cannot harm you,' called up Joah from below. 'Remember, your blood is in the phial. It is bound to you, and must protect you.'

'Wait a moment,' came Feveroot's voice again. Around them, the slick glass-like substance of the demon's body became mobile again – multiple threads of shining obsidian leapt up and over them, interlacing into a lattice. After a moment, some of the empty sections filled in with the glowing red substance. Again, Frith was reminded of a stained-glass window.

'Feveroot, what are you doing?' asked Wydrin. She reached out and touched the lattice work.

'This will keep you from being blown off into the ocean,' the demon replied evenly.

'Fine,' said Xinian. 'Let's get this over with, shall we? Take us across the sea to Relios, and there we shall land. From there I can check for messages from my contacts.' She paused. 'I take it you know where Relios is?'

Feveroot unfurled his wings. 'I am familiar with all places where roots burrow.'

'Good.' Xinian walked to the edge of the cage and looked down to where Selsye stood. Something passed between them then, a shared understanding. Frith looked away. 'Selsye, watch Reis. If anything happens, get a message to me if you can. Stay safe. I love you.'

'I love you too, Xi. And be careful.'

Frith glanced over to Wydrin, but she was standing with her arms crossed over her chest, looking down at her boots. Feveroot spread his great wings, and the others on the beach retreated to a safe distance. The demon crouched slightly, talons scoring great furrows in the black sand, and they were off up into the sky, moving at a tremendous rate. As one, they all fell onto their backsides, and there was a bellow of outrage from Xinian.

'Demon, have a care!'

There was a moment of turbulence, and then the flat surface of Feveroot's back evened out somewhat.

'My apologies,' murmured the demon.

Frith turned to help Wydrin to her feet, but she was already clambering up.

'It makes me miss Gwiddion,' he said, half smiling. 'More so than usual.'

Wydrin smiled wryly, but then looked confused, as if she'd lost her train of thought. She touched the red mark on her cheek, before turning away. 'We shall miss him all the more, if this demon pitches us into the ocean,' she said, without looking at him.

*   *   *

440

They flew on through the night. It was cold, and Wydrin could hear the wind well enough, but the strange barrier Feveroot had erected around them seemed to keep the worst of it out. Beneath them the sea was a stretch of darkness alive with the silver movement of moonlight on waves. Xinian was standing upfront, her hand curled around the glass phial as if she feared that to let go of it was to lose their mastery of the demon, and Frith stood nearby. Every now and then he would glance back to Wydrin, an expression of concern on his face. She had moved to the back of the glass cage and sat crouched against it, her knees drawn up to her chin. She felt feverish and ill, but this was hardly the time to come down with a sickness. Absently, she pressed her hand to one of the glowing red panels set into Feveroot's back. It was faintly warm, and it made her feel oddly dizzy – fever, reflected back at her. She blinked rapidly.

'Feveroot. How did they catch you?'

She only murmured the question, but the response was immediate. A voice answered, matching her own low tones. It came only from the red panel next to her.

'He drew me from my tree as a surgeon draws poison with a poultice. I fought him, but I had never had to fight before and I fought poorly. When I was out he caught me in a cage of spells and bound me to the phial, and to him.'

'In a cage.' Wydrin ran her other hand over the black lattice that kept them safe. 'Why were you in a tree in the first place?'

'Why not?' Feveroot's voice was relaxed and speculative, as though they discussed the weather over a warm pint. 'It was my home, and it was me. I had been living in that tree for centuries.'

'The blood,' said Wydrin. She cleared her throat. 'Joah said that you made birds and animals kill themselves on your thorns. On the tree's thorns.'

'I did,' agreed Feveroot. 'The blood and the pain was sustenance to me.'

'I knew a thing like you once,' said Wydrin. 'Well, I didn't know it, but I spoke with it, more than once. It craved pain. It manipulated humans into providing it. Either by injuring themselves, or by torturing others. It was a nasty piece of work. We destroyed that creature, in the end.'

For some moments, Feveroot didn't reply. To the east, the dawn was turning the horizon a silvery pink.

'The earth craves blood,' he said eventually. 'You have felt it, I think. How the earth nourishes itself with the dead and the lost. It is a natural thing. I am simply the dirt's need for blood manifested into something that can think and talk. There is magic in the soil, the stones and the clay, and where there is a powerful desire, beings like me are called into existence.'

'That's a pretty way of putting it,' said Wydrin. She splayed her fingers over the red light. How could she be so warm and so cold at the same time? 'Sounds to me like you're just another blood-thirsty monster.'

'I don't understand humans,' said Feveroot mildly. 'I took small animals. Birds, rodents, the occasional small cat. I called them to me, and I gave them a kind of ecstasy as they died, becoming one with the tree. Humans cause each other pain every day, in so many ways, sometimes through cruelty, sometimes from neglect. They kill and wound each other over nothing, yet I am the demon?'

'Don't you feast from that too? The pain we do to each other? Bezcavar, the other demon, lived for that.'

When he spoke again the demon sounded repulsed. 'No. The poisons you leak to each other give nothing to me. The purity of physical pain, the slow bleed into nothingness, the sweet taste of blood – that is what I crave.' He paused, then added, 'All of you are in pain now, and I can't use any of it.'

'Oh, I *am* sorry,' said Wydrin, rolling her eyes. 'I shall be sure to open a vein for you.'

'Emotional pain. Who does it benefit? The one who holds the phial is tortured by confusion. Her carefully ordered world has been broken. And the man whose heart you hold is wracked with pain, lost in it, and he has never been far from it. You tell me I am cruel to spear the starling, but why have you done this to him?'

Wydrin shifted. The glass was not comfortable to sit on for long.

'I have my reasons,' she said. Uncalled for, the image of the blade bursting through Frith's chest danced in front of her eyes. She felt him go limp in her arms again. Her head spun, and she leaned heavily on the glass-like surface while her cheek burned like a brand.

'Do you really? Because it is not that you do not love him.' Feveroot's voice took on a speculative note again. 'Hundreds of years old, and I will never understand humans.'

'What do you know about love? You're a demon.'

'Much passes to me in the blood. You are not entirely well. Have you noticed?'

Wydrin pressed the back of her hand to her forehead. The skin there was hot and clammy. She thought abruptly of Augusta, who had nursed her through several illnesses as a small child. All at once she felt terribly homesick. She hoped that Augusta was staying out of trouble, somehow.

'I'm not feeling especially sharp, no. I've picked up a fever at Lan-Hellis. Bunch of sickly mages who don't get out often enough. It was bound to happen.'

'That's not what it is,' said Feveroot. 'You've been touched by something, and it's twisting you all wrong inside. Can't you feel it? It's getting worse, slowly. It is like a tree growing around a rock, twisting its roots all out of shape just to survive.'

Wydrin shook her head and stumbled to her feet. It was a relief to take her hand away from the softly glowing red panel. Without saying another word to Feveroot, she walked to the front of the cage, where Xinian stood looking out over the demon's smooth head. The sea was a blanket of silver, dotted with golden jewels. The cold wind slid over her fevered skin and she shivered violently.

'You can see the coast of Relios now,' said Xinian. 'We will pause there, and then move on.'

'Good,' said Wydrin, 'the sooner the better.' She peered at the distantly rising sun, but the band of light warped and leapt erratically before her eyes, refusing to stay still. She looked down at her boots instead.

A bad time to get sick, she thought.

71

'He's still following us. Persistent little shit, isn't he?'

Augusta passed Devinia the spyglass they had taken from the Banshee, and she put it to her own eye. They were camped on the side of a steep hill, and the thick green blanket of Euriale was spread below them. Looking where Augusta pointed, it was possible to see movement in a clearing at the foot of the hill. Men and women, most of them moving sluggishly, and then a flash of golden light as the Dawning Man passed between the trees. She waited, and there was a distant tearing crunch. One of the trees vanished from view.

'He's tearing the trees out of his way to get to us. I'm almost flattered.' Devinia lowered the glass and slipped it into her belt. 'We need to keep moving.'

'Well, that's going to be a problem, Red.'

Scowling, Devinia turned back to their small makeshift camp. Ristanov the Banshee was lying on her side, her hands tied securely behind her back, although Devinia doubted they needed to restrain the pirate any more. The red disease covered most of her skin, and she moved in and out of a feverish sleep. Sometimes she would wake up, and use her remaining energy to jeer at them, or shout for Kellan to come and get her. The young Narhl man sat some feet away, his head down. The strange magic he had summoned to freeze the Banshee's crew in place, and then to stop the progress of the Dawning Man, had cost him a great deal. The green-skinned woman, who called herself Ephemeral, had explained to them that because Euriale was such a warm place, the magic had been especially difficult. And that was the other problem.

'Where is she?' snapped Devinia. 'She can't just go wandering off. We need to keep moving!'

'She's with the dragon-kin,' said Terin faintly. He shifted his foot slightly so that the sun fell directly on it. 'They are hunting.'

Devinia took a breath and hissed it out through her teeth. 'We don't have time for this.'

'Because we'd be making such good time otherwise?' Augusta gestured at Ristanov and Terin, and then sat down herself, grunting as she lowered her rear-end onto the dirt. 'Face it, Red, we have to rest. My knees are not happy about climbing up this hill as it is, and we're all running on empty. Kellan is slowed by his own sick crew, and all those pesky trees in his way. Unless, of course, you feel like running off into this piss-soaked jungle alone?'

Devinia opened her mouth to give the old woman a suitable reply, when one of Ephemeral's lizards trotted back into camp, followed by four others. Suddenly, all around them the forest was full of the noise of large animals moving through the undergrowth. The dragon-kin, as Ephemeral called them, were growing larger by the day. The one she called Inky snorted at the ground and pressed its wings closer to its back. After a moment, Ephemeral herself slipped between the trees.

'Have a good hunt?'

Ephemeral looked up in surprise. She threw down a clutch of fat rabbits. 'They get better and better all the time.'

'That's not exactly reassuring.' Devinia put her hands on her hips. 'Look, we're going to have to move before we start a fire for those. Kellan is still on our heels, and we have miles to go before we reach the *Poison Chalice*.'

'I do not want to go there,' said Ephemeral. 'That is not where my father is.'

Devinia closed her eyes briefly. 'I told you, I don't know where your Sebastian is. He left the ship shortly after we entered the interior of the island, and Wydrin has been taken, I . . .' She pressed her fingers to her eyes. There had been very little food and water since they had escaped, and her head was pounding. 'We don't have a better plan.'

'He is near the centre of the island,' Ephemeral insisted.

'I am fond of Sebastian, believe me – anyone who can put up with my daughter for that long deserves respect – but it's not enough. If we can retake my ship—'

'I cannot just give up. I must find him.' Ephemeral stopped, and doubt passed over her face like a shadow. 'I don't believe the dreams.'

Before Devinia could ask her what on Ede she meant by that, Terin gave a low cry and fell over onto his side. In an instant Augusta was by him, pulling his head onto her broad lap so that she could peer down into his eyes. The young man was shaking violently, his mottled skin covered in a thin sheen of sweat. Ephemeral came and knelt by him, taking his hand in her own.

'There now, lad, take it easy. Red, do we have any water left?'

Devinia passed her the waterskin from her own belt, although there was little enough left in it. Augusta poured it onto the man's hair, murmuring quietly to him all the while.

'It is the heat,' said Ephemeral. 'He is having a vision.'

'What do you mean?' Devinia came closer, keeping one eye on Ristanov, although the woman appeared to be deeply asleep.

'It is what he does,' replied Ephemeral. 'He is a seer for the Narhl. He experiences the pain of heat, and lets it move him into a trance state.' She took a breath. It was odd, Devinia reflected, to see such an expression of sorrow on a face as alien as Ephemeral's. 'I should never have brought him here. It is too much.'

All around them, the dragon-kin were eerily quiet, watching the scene with their bright orange eyes. Terin twisted weakly and then shuddered once, and opened his eyes.

'Stay where you are, kid,' said Augusta. 'Rest up. We'll find you some more water soon.'

'Ephemeral?'

'I am here, my love. What did you see?'

Terin looked past them, his blue eyes focussing on something they couldn't see. 'A web. Green rocks rising. Blood on stone.' He blinked rapidly. 'Sebastian and Wydrin, they were there, at the centre of the island, but I could see through them, like they were made of ice. I can't . . . There is a great power at the centre of this island. Like nothing else on Ede. It can change everything.'

'Wydrin is still alive?' asked Augusta.

'A great power?' Devinia leaned forward. 'What sort of power?'

'Magic,' said Terin, 'but stronger even than the mountain spirits.'

'Stronger than the Dawning Man? Can we use it?'

Terin shifted his gaze until he was looking at her. 'There is no other force like it.'

Devinia sat back on her haunches and pressed her hand to her mouth. It could all be a trick, a ruse to get them to the centre of the island. She had, after all, no reason to trust these two. They had risked their lives to rescue them from Ristanov's ships, this was true, but why would Wydrin now be with Sebastian? They had not left together. Then, with a lurch, she realised that she had no clear idea how they could retake the *Poison Chalice* – even with the help of Ephemeral's dragon-kin, without Lord Frith's magic the ship was essentially dead in the water. Perhaps she had no real choice at all.

Devinia looked up, meeting Augusta's eyes. The old woman's lips were pursed, as if she knew what Devinia was about to say next and was already preparing not to like it.

'The centre, then. If that's where we need to go, then that's where we'll go,' said Devinia. 'We find Wydrin, we find this great power of yours, and we use it to tear that big golden bastard to pieces.'

72

Sebastian stood at the very edge of the gardens, leaning out over a vast stretch of nothing. The chill wind tugged at his clothes, and below him the red clay of Relios was scarred with black scorch marks and smoking ruins. Y'Ruen had been this way. To the north-west was a mountain range, looming ever closer and half shrouded in dark cloud. Somewhere in that place was Poledouris, the other secret stronghold of the mages, and his original destination.

I could jump, he thought again. It would be so easy, to simply let go of his hold on this section of crumbling wall. A few seconds of noise and wind, and then nothing. It would be better, perhaps, than remaining a prisoner of Y'Gria's while she continued to murder the people of Ede; a prisoner at least until she grew bored of his secrets and killed him herself.

But the urge wasn't there, not truly. Perhaps, when he'd left the *Poison Chalice* and wandered into the jungles of Euriale, he had been despairing enough to want to lose himself in the cursed forests, but things had changed. *He* had changed. Sebastian shook his head slowly to himself. Poledouris was out there, in those shadowed mountains somewhere, even if he couldn't reach it. If Y'Gria took her flying palace closer, there was a still a chance he could get there, still a chance he could make some difference, and while he had that hope he could not give up.

Hope. Sebastian grimaced. *Always more painful than no hope at all.*

'What are you looking for?'

He turned to see Oster approaching through the orchard of apple trees. He no longer wore the heavy armour Sebastian had grown used to, but a simple tunic of fine dark blue wool, the sleeves embroidered with silver dragons, matching the markings on his arm. Sebastian didn't know where he was getting the new clothes from, but he suspected Y'Gria was responsible. He had to admit, they suited him very well.

'Our destination, the mage stronghold of Poledouris. You remember? That was where we were going.'

'I remember,' said Oster mildly.

'The woman Estenn may not have made it there yet. There may still be time.'

'A lot has changed, Sebastian,' Oster came and stood next to him. Since they had slept together he appeared more relaxed, more comfortable in his own skin. The golden light that had seemed to illuminate him from within had dimmed, but it only served to make him more beautiful, as far as Sebastian could see. Now his beauty was a human rather than an ethereal thing – the faint stubble on his jaw, the crease at the edge of his eyes when he smiled, the way his curly hair flattened at the back when he'd been lying down. Sebastian looked away.

'A lot has changed for you, maybe. I still have a duty to fulfil.'

'You don't,' said Oster, as easily as if they were talking about a mild disagreement over what to have for dinner. 'Stay here, with me. Y'Gria would not dare harm you, none of them would. I have read about it in the history that Res'na gave me. So many of my people have taken up mortals as lovers, raised them up above all others and loved them for ever.'

Sebastian closed his eyes briefly. 'Oster . . .'

'And I do love you, Sebastian.' For the first time his voice was ragged, as though it were torn over the words. 'I know that much. When we are together I am at peace. Things make sense, and I understand my place in the world.'

Sebastian stared furiously down at the world passing below

them, not trusting himself to meet Oster's amber eyes. The silvery link between them was a riptide, eager to sweep him away.

'If that is true, Oster, then let us go away, together. Come with me, and leave Y'Gria behind.'

There was a moment's silence. Below them a flock of birds flew past, wings like knives on the wind.

'She is my family, for better or for worse. You cannot ask me to give that up.' Some of the ice was back in Oster's voice. 'Slowly, I am learning about my own history, Sebastian. She tells me some things, every day, and without it I would be lost.'

'And yet you ask me to give up *my* family.' Sebastian turned back to face Oster, allowing himself to feel the anger that flared up in his chest. 'What do you think Wydrin is to me? She has been my sister in arms for years, and if Estenn succeeds, if Y'Gria is allowed to continue her destruction of the mages, then I will lose her. Even Frith, cantankerous bastard that he is –' Sebastian paused, realising as he said it that it was true. 'Even Frith I would count as a brother to me. You ask me to let them die, by staying here with you.'

'But they are just humans.' Sebastian could tell from the way Oster shook his head slightly that he regretted the words as soon as they were out of his mouth. 'I mean, they are not like you. I can feel the connection between us, Sebastian. Please, do you not love me?'

Sebastian took a step backwards, putting himself perilously close to the edge. He thought of Dallen, of Cerjin, even Crowleo. Loving anyone was a curse, as far as he could see.

'You don't . . .'

There was a rustling in the undergrowth around their feet, and the tips of several pale green roots slithered into the open.

'As fascinating as it is to listen to your ridiculous declarations –' Y'Gria's voice preceded her as she stepped out from behind a tree. Her arms were split into multiple twisting tentacles, and her green hair was a wild tangle down her back. 'I think we have some interesting company approaching.'

Following her eager gaze, Sebastian looked back towards the mountains. A green shape was flying down from the foothills, like a giant beetle. It was a carapacer.

'Wait, that could be Wydrin!'

Y'Gria's flying palace was already moving, swooping down towards the carapacer with a violence that made Sebastian dizzy. The world below them was a blur.

'Mage scum, is what it is,' said Y'Gria. She was grinning widely, and as she spoke, she grew larger, her pulsing roots pushing her up into the sky. 'I will tear them and their little toy apart.'

'No!'

It was too late. The carapacer was swerving away, having apparently finally seen what was descending from the clouds above, but Y'Gria was faster. Her tentacles whipped out and embraced the small flying contraption like fronds of seaweed wrapped around a wet rock, and then she was dragging it back towards the palace.

'She's bringing it back here,' said Sebastian. 'Come on.'

Tracking her movements, he and Oster ran around to where she clearly intended to drag the carapacer – a wide stretch of open grass, framed by a series of fallen walls. They got there just as she landed, in time to see the flexing roots drag one figure from the back of the contraption and hold him up to the sky. It was a man wearing scarlet robes, and he pelted her with a few minor spells – Sebastian saw the glitter of ice crystals in the air – before Y'Gria casually pulled him apart like a child pulling the legs off a spider. A hot red rain fell on the grass.

'Wait!'

To a wonder, Y'Gria did stop, but belatedly Sebastian realised it was because of something inside the carapacer rather than anything he'd said. He and Oster staggered to a stop in the clearing as Y'Gria carefully lifted another figure from the carapacer and set it down on the grass.

'This one carries the mark of my sister,' said Y'Gria. 'How unexpected.'

The woman looked half out of her mind with awe, her unruly black hair swept back from her face, the tattoos at her neck a dark shadow. Sebastian felt his skin grow cold. After all this, Y'Gria had brought Estenn straight to him.

Before he knew it, he was running. He saw Estenn turn a

startled glance towards him – did she remember him from the Eye of Euriale? – and she drew her cutlass. He had no weapons, but it was too good an opportunity to miss. Dancing past the blade he moved in close under her guard and barrelled the woman to the ground, using his superior size and strength to hold her to the grass. If she hadn't been dazed by Y'Gria's capture, he doubted he would even have been able to get near her.

She kicked and punched wildly at him and landed a blow directly on his ear that made his eyes water. In the second it took him to recover she had wriggled out, taking a moment to kick him solidly in the neck, and was scrambling for her sword. Sebastian rolled over and took hold of her ankle, yanking her solidly to the ground again.

'Please!' she gasped. 'I am here to help you, Y'Gria of the garden. I am a loyal servant!'

She twisted in his grip and crashed her elbow into his face. His nose didn't break, thankfully, but he felt blood gush in a sudden hot stream. There was a hiss and a shimmer of lights, and Oster was there in his dragon form, horns bristling and amber eyes wild. Sebastian felt Estenn go rigid in his grip.

'Enough!' cried Y'Gria. 'I would like to hear what this servant of mine has to say. It is time for your human pet to still himself, Oster.'

Sebastian pushed himself up on his elbows as a swarm of roots shot through the grass towards him. He had time to see the look of pure hatred that Estenn turned on him – *she is even less sane than when we saw her last* – and then the tentacles were looping round his throat and pulling fast. He tried to stagger to his feet, to get away from them all, but his vision was already growing dark.

Sebastian fell back onto the grass, fingers twisting around roots stronger than any man's arm.

73

The dark mountains floated beneath a pall of smoke and cloud. As they neared the jagged peaks, Frith saw great chasms in the rock, where molten lava winked and boiled as bright as the sun, and the air stank of sulphur. Feveroot brought them in low, under Xinian's instruction, and the air grew hot and acrid.

'Poledouris is not far now,' said Xinian. She was watching the shifting patterns of smoke and stone below them with a careful eye. 'It can be easy to miss, if you are not familiar with the entrance. Which is, of course, the point.'

Feveroot sank lower, walls of smoky grey rock rising to either side of them. Just to their right, the rocks seemed to shift and a cascade of lava surged down the mountainside, sending up a cloud of black smoke.

'Is this safe?' asked Frith. 'The place looks as though it might collapse – or explode – at any moment.'

'Nothing is ever safe,' murmured Wydrin. She was sitting down, leaning against Feveroot's cage with her arms wrapped around her.

'The mages at Poledouris have been holding this mountain together for centuries,' said Xinian. 'It is unstable, and there is a great deal of molten rock at its heart, but they have bound it together with a series of spells. Selsye has even elaborated on them, so that they can use the heat from the lava to warm the rooms and heat their water.' A rare smile touched Xinian's lips.

'She has so many ideas. Sometimes I can barely keep up. Here, demon, around this tall jagged rock. You may have to make yourself smaller, if you can.'

'Of course,' murmured Feveroot. The demon shrank, wide black wings drawing back into themselves – Frith could feel the creature shivering under his boots – and then they were round the corner and alighting at the mouth of a cave. There were two iron brackets screwed into the rock, but both torches were out. Beyond them the passage led into deepest shadow.

'This isn't right,' said Xinian. 'There should be guards out here. We shouldn't be able to just walk right up to the front door.'

The black lattice cage shrank back, and the three of them clambered down onto the rock. Frith pulled the staff from the belt on his back and held it securely in both hands. It felt good to have it back, to have the power at his fingertips again, although he caught Xinian giving him a dubious look and, not for the first time, he wondered if Selsye had told her anything. Wydrin drew Glassheart, and paced from foot to foot.

'Let's get in there and find out what's going on,' she said. Her face was shiny with sweat. 'What about Feveroot?'

'The demon?' Xinian shook her head. 'It can just stay here.'

'Seems to me it could be useful,' said Wydrin. She shrugged one shoulder. 'We don't know what's waiting for us in there.'

'Fine, let's just get this over with.' Xinian told hold of the phial and drew the chain from around her neck. She passed it to Wydrin. 'You can have responsibility for the bloody thing. Keep it out of my way.'

Wydrin put the chain around her own neck. 'Feveroot, change yourself into a salamander, or something.'

'As you wish.'

The great black bird perched awkwardly at the cave entrance became liquid glass again, swirling down to the size of a small black lizard with a fat tail. It was covered in red glowing patches, rather like the pattern on a real salamander's hide. Wydrin bent down and extended her arm, and Feveroot scuttled up it to rest on her shoulder, tiny obsidian claws clutching at her leathers.

'Keep your eyes open,' said Xinian. She lifted her fingers and summoned a small ball of light to hover above her outstretched arm. 'Stay alert. I have a bad feeling about this.'

'Don't we always?' murmured Frith.

'There is blood ahead. I can smell it.'

The demon pitched his words for her ears only. He was a warm presence on her shoulder, heavy and oddly reassuring. As soon as they were out of sight of the cave entrance, she saw that he was right. Two bodies lay on the ground ahead, and someone had apparently taken a sword to them with some enthusiasm. She saw a severed hand lying palm up, fingers curled inwards like a dead spider.

'Estenn has been here,' she said to the others. 'She did have a head start, after all.'

'She could still be here,' said Frith. 'If we're lucky we may catch her on her way out.'

'Luck,' murmured Wydrin. 'Remind me again when we ever had any of the good variety?'

As they walked past the bodies, Feveroot scuttled down from her shoulder and padded silently into the dark pool of blood. Wydrin paused, letting the others get a few paces ahead, before hissing to the demon. 'What are you doing?'

'Just a taste,' replied Feveroot. 'Your mind is swarmed with heat, and is not as rigid as Xinian Battleborn's. It's easier to move under your control.'

Wydrin blinked rapidly. This felt like something she should tell the others, but it was hard to think. 'Well, stop it, or I'll show you how rigid my boot is.'

Reluctantly, Feveroot scuttled away from the bodies, leaving tiny bloody claw marks in the dust. 'Their blood is all wrong,' he said. 'They taste how you feel. It is the same thing that is wrong with you. Can you not feel it?'

'Be quiet.'

They followed the tunnel deep into the mountain. It was warm and smelled of sulphur, the air clawing at the back of Wydrin's throat. Eventually they emerged into a great hall with a cavernous ceiling, stretching off into the dark. The walls were lined with what Wydrin initially took to be a series of long, thin alchemical lights, until she saw that the bright orange light was moving.

'Is that lava?' She looked up. The lines glowed softly, bathing everything in light like a bloody sunset. 'By the Graces, how is this place still standing?'

'It is lava tamed,' said Xinian, a faint note of irritation in her voice. There were statues of men and women in robes towering off to either side of them, carved from red rock, and a big plinth in the centre surrounded by benches carved directly from the rock. On the far side was a huge angular doorway. 'I told you, they have achieved great things at Poledouris. Most of them thanks to Selsye.' They edged into the room, Xinian trying to look in all directions at once. 'The grand mages, they use this place when they want to show off. This hall should be busy, full of people.'

'What is that?' Frith pointed up at the plinth as they navigated their way through the benches. There was a widening pool of blood on top of the stone, and as they watched a series of ripples broke the surface. As one, they looked up, and saw at least twenty bodies hanging motionless near the ceiling. Blood dripped from them in a slow steady rain.

'Oh shit,' said Wydrin.

'I was just trying to tidy up.' The voice came from behind them. A ragged mage in blue and green robes sat up from the bench where she had been lying. Her curly brown hair had been burned off on the right side, leaving her scalp crisped and bloody. 'I thought, get them up out of the way at least, get them out of the *way*, make it easier to clean up.' She shrugged and the effort almost sent her to her knees. 'But it just keeps *raining* . . .'

'What happened here?' demanded Xinian. 'You will answer me!'

'It's the strangest thing,' said the woman, smiling slightly at her own foolishness. 'I can't really remember. There was a woman here who wasn't a mage, and we were all very upset about that, but then she touched me, and have you ever noticed how warm it is here?' Absently she reached up and patted her blackened scalp. 'Too many people, that's what I said. It wouldn't be so warm if there were fewer people here. Some of us decided to thin the numbers.'

'There is madness in her blood,' murmured Feveroot by Wydrin's foot. 'They all have it.'

'You're not fucking kidding.'

'It is the same madness you have, you fool. Can't you feel it?'

Wydrin squeezed her eyes shut for a moment. What had the woman said? Estenn had touched her, and then apparently the mages had all decided to kill each other. Estenn had barely needed to wet her own blade. There was something there, something important, but she couldn't quite grasp it. Xinian was raising her voice to the woman, and her concentration was broken.

'Where is this woman now? Where are the rest of you?'

The mage shrugged. 'I can't think about that. It's taking all my concentration to keep them all tidy.' She nodded towards the ceiling where the bodies hung, motionless. 'The others won't help.'

As if she'd summoned them, there were a series of shouts from across the hall, and a handful of mages sprinted into the room. Wydrin had time to see that their eyes were wild and unfocussed, that most of them were bloody with wounds and burns, and then they were hit with a barrage of magical attacks. She ducked down behind the stone bench as a ball of emerald fire shot over her head.

'Stand down!' cried Xinian. 'I command you!'

Wydrin peeked over the top of the bench and saw Xinian and Frith standing side by side, flinging magical attacks back at the pack of mages. Frith conjured a wall of ice and swept it across the plinth, and he and Xinian used it for cover as they crept forward, but a wild fireball swept past them and caught the woman in the blue robes. She went down screaming, and a second later the bodies that had been hanging near the ceiling were plummeting towards them. Unbidden, an image of the sword bursting through Frith's chest blotted out all other thoughts, and Wydrin's lungs felt crushed with the horror of it.

'Look out!' Without thinking, Wydrin scooped up Feveroot and threw him at the plinth, picturing what she wanted as she

457

did so. In mid-flight, the demon expanded like a roll of black silk to become a great manta ray, the shiny black surface of his back shimmering like water. The dismembered bodies of the mages bounced off him, with only a few hitting the plinth – those that did shattered apart like over-ripe fruit. Wydrin saw Frith glance round at her, his eyes wide, and then his ice barrier was gone, melted under a barrage of fireballs. Xinian stepped out from under Feveroot's shadow and flung a wave of force at the rogue mages, sending half of them skidding back across the room. Their faces were wild, lips peeled back from their teeth in expressions of mindless fury; they conjured their counterattacks even as their bones were shattered against the far wall.

'Stand down!' screamed Xinian again. 'You must stand down!'

'There's nothing you can do,' said Wydrin. It was difficult to breathe still, and the mark on her cheek seared her flesh. She reached up a hand for Feveroot and the demon slunk back to the form of a salamander. 'Estenn has driven them mad somehow. I'm sorry, Xinian.'

Frith met her eyes then, and nodded once. He lowered the hand holding the staff and his body began to glow from within with the strange white light.

'No,' said Xinian, even as she erected another barrier against the mage attacks. 'There must be something else!'

'We can't do anything for what they've got,' said Wydrin. As she said it, she felt a worm of dread twist in her stomach. *And nothing we can do for me.* 'They won't stop until we're dead.'

Frith raised his hand, and several of the rogue mages crumpled inwards, mouths opening wide with terror as their flesh turned to dust. One of those left made a mad dash towards them, and Wydrin stepped forward to meet him, stabbing him quickly through the chest. Even as he died he scrambled at her, fingernails clawing at her leathers, and then he grew still. For an odd moment, Wydrin found she could not look away from his eyes, frozen in a frantic expression in his last seconds of life, and then she pushed him off the end of her sword. The rest of them fell swiftly to Frith's lethal new magic until the light that surrounded him winked out and his shoulders dropped, his face grey. Instinctively, Wydrin went to him and pulled him up by his elbow. Xinian stood watching them, a bereft expression on her face.

'On your feet, princeling, we still have to move.'

'It takes so much out of me,' he murmured. He put his hand over Wydrin's, and the mark on her cheek burned fiercely. She pulled away, wiping the blade of her sword against her leg.

'She will pay for this,' said Xinian. She was looking around at the remains of the mages, her mouth twisted into a bitter line, at the dismembered men and women scattered all over the plinth, at the dusty remains of the others.

'The Red Echo,' said Frith, with some effort. 'Where was it kept?'

She could hear in his voice what they all knew – that they were too late.

Xinian nodded once. 'Follow me.'

The chamber was empty, as they had known it would be. The small space was lit by the softly glowing lava lights, and there were dusty scuff marks on the floor. At least they hadn't kept this half of the spell in darkness.

'What would she do now, Xinian?' asked Frith. Some colour had returned to his cheeks, although he was still holding himself carefully. 'Where would she go with it?'

Wydrin took a slow breath. She was leaning against the wall and trying to make it look casual. 'She will want to kill as many mages in one go as she can. Where is the biggest population of your people?'

Xinian was glaring at the dusty floor as though it might suddenly produce the Red Echo for them.

'Our biggest city by far is Raistinia, in the north of Relios. It doesn't hold the military might of Krete or the knowledge of Lan-Hellis, but it's where most have settled. There are families there, people raising children. Most mages have a home there. If she wanted to deal us the biggest blow, she would get the Red Echo within range of Raistinia. The effects would be devastating.'

Wydrin ran a hand over her forehead and shook the sweat away. Her head was thumping. 'Right. Does this place have a carapacer?'

'Of course.'

'Great. Get yourself on it and as far away from Relios as you can. Go back to Lan-Hellis, or even better, get you and Selsye somewhere in the middle of bloody nowhere.'

'What are you talking about?' Xinian looked incredulous. 'We must pursue the madwoman!'

'That's our job now,' said Frith. 'Do you not see? If the Red Echo goes off while we're in Relios, or while we're on her tail, you will be caught in it, Commander. The weapon kills mages, does it not?'

'What will the rest of your mage idiots do without you?' said Wydrin. 'You need to survive this.' She took her hand away from the wall. 'Does this feel hotter than it did before?'

'Ludicrous.' Xinian glared at them both. 'You truly expect me to put the future of my people in the hands of . . . whatever you two truly are?'

'You have no choice, Commander,' said Frith. '*You* are the future of your people. Reis is mad. Who else will lead them?' He paused. 'Think of Selsye. You have to get away from the Red Echo. We will stop it if we can. We have come a very long way to do so.'

Xinian looked from one to the other, an expression of horror on her face. 'And if you can't?'

'Seriously,' Wydrin stood up away from the wall, 'does it feel like it's getting hotter in here to anyone else?'

There was a terrible pause, during which the entire room shuddered. There was a thundering crack from somewhere far above them.

'The wards.' Xinian was already making for the door. 'With no mages here to maintain the spells, this place will shortly be a working volcano once more.'

In the end Xinian agreed to leave in the carapacer, and Wydrin and Frith watched her go from the back of Feveroot, who had taken the form of the great manta ray again. Xinian flew up into a sky heavy with cloud, a tiny green insect against the grey, and then she was lost to view. She was going, she said, to collect Selsye, and they would figure out what to do from there. She hadn't looked happy about it, but they were coming to the end of their options. Below them, the mage stronghold of Poledouris was collapsing in on itself, sending up plumes of black smoke and showers of red sparks. Frith wondered what priceless mage knowledge was being destroyed under a layer of molten rock.

Wydrin knelt on the demon's back and placed her hand against one of the glowing red spots. Feveroot rippled as though he swam in an invisible ocean.

'To the north then, demon,' she said. 'And you'd better get a wriggle on.'

The mark on her face was livid, her red hair plastered to her face with sweat. There was something in the way she sat that struck at Frith's heart – she was holding herself up when she wanted to lie down. The demon slid through the air, heading up into the clouds until they were coated in a fine film of moisture. Frith saw Wydrin shiver, and then when he caught her eye, she grinned.

'I know, I know, I look like a bag of shit warmed up. If Augusta was here, she'd send me off to my bunk with a flea in my ear.' She shuddered again, and looked away from him. 'No time for that though, princeling.'

74

The red growth on the back of the Banshee's neck was so large now that it was forcing the pirate to walk with her head bowed. Following on behind her, Devinia found she could barely tear her eyes from it. The thing looked vital somehow, as though it were pulsing somewhere inside, preparing for a secret triumph only it knew about. She was, she realised, starting to think of the infection as some sort of separate entity. Ristanov's hands, tied behind her back, were fuzzy red claws.

They were heading towards the top of another hill, edging closer to the centre of Euriale. Ephemeral and her husband had disappeared off into the woods to hunt, while Augusta was somewhere in the treeline to her right, poking around for anything that might resemble a medicinal herb. So far she hadn't found anything useful, and she seemed to be taking it as a personal insult. From behind them they heard the occasional crash as the Dawning Man made its slow pursuit. Devinia wondered how many of the original crew were still alive, or if Kellan followed them alone now. It hardly seemed to matter.

The Banshee tripped and fell to her knees in the dirt, barking a harsh cry of mingled surprise and pain. She struggled for a moment, and then simply knelt with her head down, breath whistling through her nose and mouth.

Devinia watched, and when she didn't get up, nudged her with her boot. 'Keep moving, Ristanov.'

The Banshee tipped her head to one side as though her neck were boneless.

'Why do you not kill me, Devinia the Grey?'

The woman's face was lost under a fibrous mat of red moss, only her eyes recognisable as the woman who had taken the *Poison Chalice*. They were wide and blue, as they had ever been, but now that Devinia looked closely she could see a tiny fleck of red in the white of her right eye. She wondered briefly what that felt like, and then hastily turned her mind in another direction.

'Do you want to die, Ristanov?'

The Banshee made a peculiar gargling noise in the back of her throat. It took Devinia a few seconds to realise she was laughing.

'I am already dead, you know this. It is hardly my choice now.' She coughed and shook her head. 'I did not think you would be the one keeping me alive. I slow you down, I take your water and what scraps of food you have. You wish me to suffer, yes? You want me to feel every inch of this . . . whatever this is.'

'Because of you, my daughter was kidnapped. You stole my ship, and my first mate.' *And the island*, she added silently. *You took the discovery of that from me.* 'I have every right to want you to suffer, Ristanov.'

The Banshee shrugged, the growths on her back quivering with the movement. 'If Kellan had had his way, your brat would already be dead, yes, or worse. We're pirates. We are wolves, not lambs.' She cleared her throat, and then sighed, as if all this talking was wearing her out. 'Maybe it is the old woman who stills your blade. Even now, she looks for ways to save me.' She grinned, and Devinia had to look away. It was like looking at a flayed head.

In truth, she didn't know why she hadn't killed the Banshee or even why she had brought her with them. If they had been at sea, or in a brawl in a tavern, she wouldn't have hesitated. Was her revenge meaningless if she killed a woman who was half dead already? Or did she simply wish to watch her die inch by inch, glorying in her pain and misery?

'Perhaps I think you will be useful, before the end.'

'I can feel it moving inside me,' said Ristanov, as if she hadn't heard. 'I can try not to think about it and it works for a little while, and then I feel it, uncoiling.' She shuddered violently and fell into the dirt, her voice slurring. 'Moving, moving, the Red King is coming, coming.'

Grimacing, Devinia went to the woman's side, but by the time she knelt down, Ristanov had passed out again, her eyes rolling up to the whites. After a moment, Augusta appeared from between the trees, the old cloth she'd tied around her head soaked through with sweat.

'Is she gone, then?'

Devinia shook her head.

'She's right, you know. You should kill the poor bitch. Graces take her, she can't be long for this world anyway.'

'You were listening?'

'Mostly. I always said you were the coldest woman I ever met, Red, ever since you were a girl. Sharp and as cold as steel. But this is cruel, even for you.'

Devinia stood up, scowling. 'Because of this excuse for a captain, Wydrin is lost on this island somewhere. Do I need to remind you of that? Or have you also forgotten all the people who died when she took the *Poison Chalice*?' She thinned her lips, knowing she was lashing out at the wrong person but unable to stop the words. 'I thought you cared about my daughter.'

Augusta rolled her eyes. 'Oh, do shut your gob. You know very well that I love that aggravating little pain in the arse as though she were my own. At least Wydrin is more like her father than you, for which I am thankful. Imagine having to put up with two like you.'

From far behind them came the shuddering crash of another tree being pushed to one side. Devinia took a deep breath, feeling the tug on her poorly healed stomach wound.

'And I'm glad she's more like you than me. I'm sorry, Augusta.'

'Now, don't you go getting soft on me, Red, I can only put up with so much bollocks on one trip.' Augusta reached over and squeezed Devinia's arm with her strong, blunt fingers. 'What's our plan, then?'

'It looks like we're stopping here for now.' Devinia nudged Ristanov with her boot, but the woman was deeply asleep.

'Aye, let's wait for the two lovebirds to get back.' Augusta sat heavily in the dirt and pulled the sweaty handkerchief from her head. 'If they can't find food with a troop of hungry lizards in tow then we really are up shit creek.'

Blood, hot and pounding and panicky. The irresistible movement of prey, the scent of fear in the air, sharp as a blade, and the sweet sense of closing in. Ephemeral took a sharp breath as she ran, savouring the taste of the hunt in the air, and then ahead of her Inky swept down from the canopy and drew her claws along the deer's back. They fell together, Inky's wings keeping her from landing in the dirt. The deer was dead before it hit the ground, the blow across its back severing it from life in some deep, unseen way.

Jogging to a stop, Ephemeral looked around as the other dragon-kin caught up. They were all fast and they all took to the hunt naturally, but Inky was still outpacing them. *She is the leader of their pack*, she thought, and then watched as they shredded the meat of the deer between their teeth, turning it to a red ruined thing in moments. She opened herself to the silvery touches of their minds and felt the satisfaction they took in the hot flesh slipping down their throats, hunger satiated.

'What are you thinking?'

Terin slipped from behind the trees. He had been following them at his own pace. He was still recovering from using the cold summons, and his bare chest glistened with sweat.

'I am thinking that they are not my sisters.'

'Should they be?'

'Of course not.' She gestured to where they were gathered, snipping and snapping over bones. 'Their minds are so bright, so interesting. They are so close to what I am, but also completely different. I do not have the right words to describe it to you. Are you certain that you cannot feel them at all? You are a seer. I thought that if anyone could, it might be you.'

Terin came over to her, smiling faintly. 'I wish that I could, just so that I could share what fascinates you so.'

'I wonder . . . if my father had not woken us with his human blood, perhaps I would be as they are. Pure, not confused. It might have been easier.'

'The crab with the biggest pincers is always the tastiest.' When she looked at him askance, he shrugged slightly. 'A saying from the Frozen Steps. Nothing truly worth having is ever easy. But I am glad to hear you mention your father. I thought perhaps you had forgotten him.'

To her own surprise, Ephemeral felt her face grow hot. Terin was always provoking feelings she did not understand. Normally she enjoyed it. This did not feel so enjoyable.

'Forget Sebastian? How could I do that?' She took a breath, and separated her mind from the feeding dragon-kin behind her. 'I do not know what you are referring to, husband.'

'We came here to find him, but it seems you have found new family instead.' His face was still, his blue eyes calm. For reasons she could not understand, this only made her face hotter.

'I do not know where he is. Devinia the Red does not know, Augusta Grint does not know. I have exhausted the possibilities!' Her hair had come loose from its braid. She began to tidy it up, not quite looking at Terin. When he did not speak again, she softened her voice. 'I can't sense him any more, Terin. Not here, not anywhere. I reach out for him and there is just a blank space. I thought perhaps that it was the dragon-kin, that they took up so much room in my head that I couldn't see him because of it but . . .' Her voice trailed off.

Terin rested his cold hand briefly on her arm. 'Ephemeral. There is something you have not told me.'

Inky raised her head from the carnage and peered over at Ephemeral. She felt the faint questing of her mind, obviously curious as to why she was distressed, and Ephemeral gently pushed it to one side.

'I had a dream. Before I got to the lagoon. It was just a dream. Sebastian spoke of them to me, and Wydrin Threefellows did too. They are not to be taken seriously. They are just pictures your mind paints while you sleep, to keep itself amused.'

Terin frowned. 'This is a place of potent magic. I would be

inclined to look carefully at any dreams I had in this place, especially if they felt important.'

Ephemeral looked away from him. She wanted to be hunting again, to be lost in the purity of the chase. Perhaps the Second had had a point after all. 'In the dream, he was here on the island. He told me that I was safe now. And then when I wasn't looking, he disappeared. I knew that he was gone, that I would never see him again.' She briefly pressed her hand to her chest. 'I knew it here. It was what I did to him, the last time we were together. We said goodbye in an alleyway, and when he was distracted for a moment I left.' There was a tight feeling in her throat. She didn't understand that either. 'I thought it was the best thing to do. He was sad, and wanted to be away from that place. I didn't want to give him a reason to stay.'

They were both quiet for a moment. The dragon-kin had made short work of the deer carcass, and were now nosing around for anything else that looked interesting; all save for Inky, who was watching them both closely.

'What if that was the last time I saw him? I thought I had come to the end of my journey with him, but now I need him again. I did not know that would happen. I do not know *why* I need him.'

'That sounds like family to me,' said Terin. He took her hand, and squeezed it. 'He is your father, Ephemeral. Sometimes we go on needing them, even when they are not there any more. I do not know what has happened to Sebastian, but we will go on looking for him, I know that. There must be answers on this island somewhere.' He paused, looking at the dark red marks on the grass where the deer had been. 'I also know that if we return to the camp with only full dragon-kin bellies to show for our hunt, we may all be on the menu.'

Ephemeral found herself smiling, despite the tightness of her jaw. He could always surprise smiles out of her.

'Another hunt, then. A swift one, for we must keep ahead of our enemies,' she agreed, reaching out for the dragon-kin minds again. 'And we will control our appetites this time.'

75

When Sebastian awoke he was lying face down on cold marble. There was blood on his temple, sticky enough to briefly seal his eyebrow to the floor. He rolled over with a grunt to see Y'Gria and Oster in the midst of a heated argument, with Estenn standing off to one side. The lighting in the throne room was muted, and Y'Gria herself had regained some of her composure in what he was sure was a display of power for the human captives; her green hair was a sleek curtain down her back now, and there was no sign of the teeming tentacles. She stood, her long-fingered hands interlaced in front of her dress, her chin held high. In contrast, Oster was pacing in front of her like a caged animal, his fists bunched at his sides.

'You will not lay hands – or other appendages – on him again. If you want my help, in any sense, you will do as I say.'

'Do stop whining about your mortal, Oster. Can you not see we have a guest? And your creature is conscious again, no harm done.'

Sebastian climbed slowly to his feet, watching Estenn warily. The woman looked even wilder than when he'd last seen her, her black hair a tangled bush, her eyes wide and staring. This was what coming face to face with your gods did to you. She still had the sword at her waist, and there were a pair of hessian sacks by her feet. As he watched, one of them moved. Oster was already holding out a hand to him.

'Sebastian, are you all right?'

He didn't deign to give an answer. Instead he glared at Estenn. 'What have you done? What have you done to the others?'

Estenn's red lips peeled back from her mouth in a sneer. 'I left them for dead, as the godless deserve. They could not stand against me, and now I have the weapon that will destroy the mages.'

There was no obvious way out of the throne room. He could make a grab for the bags at her feet, and perhaps he would get there before she drew her sword or Y'Gria tossed him aside, but then he would have nowhere to go.

'Isn't it wonderful?' said Y'Gria warmly. 'This young woman is a true servant of the gods. She has brought us a weapon, made by their own hands, that will be the mages' undoing.'

Sebastian kept his eyes on Estenn. 'You will destroy Ede,' he told her. 'There will be nothing for you to return to but a smoking ruin.'

'Your Ede, perhaps,' she said. 'That is the Ede that will end.'

Y'Gria raised a single finger. 'I have decided that we must deal them the most devastating blow. The one that will hurt the most. We will take their most beloved city from them – the one where they raise their little mage children.' Y'Gria turned directly to Estenn, a beatific smile lighting her face. 'I will take you to Raistinia, my child, and we will tear their world apart.' Quick as a snake, she turned back to Sebastian. 'You will be kept out of our way.' She shot a look at Oster. 'Little brother, purely out of affection for you I will tolerate your . . . eccentricities, but you would do well to remember who your family are. Stand against me in this, and I will pull your favourite toy to bloody pieces.'

Oster looked as though he might say more, but Y'Gria was already turning away, sliding an arm around Estenn's shoulders.

Feveroot flew low over the parched desert floor, the sleek black curves of his manta-ray form rippling faintly. The sky overhead was clear and the sun was a heavy weight on the top of Wydrin's head, with even the breeze failing to alleviate the thumping behind her eyes. Periodically, she would touch the red mark on her cheek, marvelling at the heat that kissed her fingers. Frith stood near the head of the ray, looking out towards their destination, waiting for the thin blue line of the coast to show itself. Raistinia was a city on the sea, apparently.

'Can you feel it now?' said Feveroot. His voice issued from the red mark nearest her right boot. 'It grows, and it clouds your judgement more and more. You know that it will only grow worse.'

Wydrin squeezed her eyes tightly closed and opened them again, willing her head to be clearer. It didn't work.

'Can you take it from me?' she asked quietly, not really sure what she meant by the question. 'Some demon magic. Make this madness go away. Take it from my blood.'

Feveroot was silent for some time. 'Even if I were free, that isn't within my power. But perhaps I can point you in the direction of help, if your head is too addled to see it.' When he next spoke, the demon's voice issued not just from the red mark by her boot, but from every part of the red pattern that speckled the giant manta ray. 'She knows she is ill.' His voice was louder than she'd heard it before. 'Perhaps you can ease your pain together.'

Frith startled and turned around, his eyes wide. 'Do you address me, demon?'

'He is sharp, this one. I do, Lord Frith.'

Treading carefully, as though he thought the demon might suddenly turf them off, Frith walked over to Wydrin. His grey eyes were narrow with caution. 'You will admit there is something wrong, then?'

'It was Estenn,' she said. 'She did something to me at Lan-Hellis. When we fought in the artefact room, she reached for me and I moved out of the way, but not quite fast enough to avoid being touched. I think she has given me something, the same thing she gave to the mages at Poledouris.' She took a deep breath. It was exhausting just to talk. 'Feveroot could taste it in my blood, as he tasted it on the dead mages. Whatever it was, I don't think she gave me quite enough, but –' She raised her hands and then let them drop back to her knees. 'It was enough to cause me a heap of trouble.'

'And to stop you thinking rationally,' said Frith. He came and sat cross-legged next to her. 'You have not been right since Lan-Hellis, that much is obvious.'

'The stuff about you and me—'

'The stuff about us is nonsense.' He sat up a little straighter. 'Clearly.'

'Frith, whatever she has done to me, it's like she's taken hidden feelings, and then made them stronger. When I thought you were dead –' she paused and wiped a handful of sweat from her forehead – 'I was lost. I am afraid to feel that again. To be weakened again. That is real. I am stronger if I am unattached.'

'I beg to differ,' he said, glaring at her with his storm-grey eyes. 'You went through a great shock, whilst under the influence of some sort of magical curse. But you are stronger than it, and we are even stronger when we're together. I learned that, the hard way.'

Wydrin found herself smiling even as her heart began to beat faster; a wild panic growing in her chest. It wasn't in her to stop loving him. She would always be this weak.

'You seem very sure that I haven't just gone off you, princeling.'

He looked away from her for a moment, staring off at the red and blue horizon. 'There has been a lot of upheaval in my life, to say the least. Much of what I thought to be unending and infallible was temporary, and easily broken. I was wrong about so much.' He turned back to her, the sharp angles of his face etched by the sun. 'But I do know that you love me, Wydrin Threefellows.'

She took a shaky breath – it was like succumbing to the fever, even as she knew the truth of it. She *was* stronger than the madness. She just had to concentrate on that. Easier said than done.

'I would kiss you, you git,' she said, 'but I am incredibly sweaty.'

'You are a fool, sometimes,' he said mildly, as he turned to face her. He touched the line of her jaw, and kissed her firmly. Wydrin felt her head spin, and was glad to hold on to him for a time.

'It is always pleasing when humans see sense,' said Feveroot. 'I have witnessed very little of it since I was taken from the tree. But you are still afflicted, Wydrin Threefellows.'

'There must be a cure,' said Frith. 'There will be healers, ones

471

who are familiar with magic and curses. If that's what this is. We will seek one out.'

'No time,' said Wydrin, shaking her head slightly. 'We race to Raistinia. There's no time to stop to find some wise woman and her herbs.' She pushed her hair back from her forehead. 'I will just have to get through it. When Estenn is dead, when the threat of the Red Echo has been removed, then we can worry about what's wrong with me.'

'The infection grows worse all the time,' said Feveroot. Wydrin thought she could hear actual doubt in the demon's voice – what a different creature this was to Bezcavar, the demon who had tried to kill her in Skaldshollow. 'It could kill you eventually, or cause you to be killed.'

'Why would you care, demon?' asked Frith. His words were short, but he sounded genuinely curious. 'You seem very concerned for a being that thrives on pain and blood.'

'I can only be set free – can only return to my tree – if the blood is willingly washed from the phial with water. If the phial is broken, I will be scattered to the wind, and lost.'

'Don't you worry about me,' said Wydrin, keeping her voice as firm as she could. 'My blades are sharp, and it takes more than a cold sweat to keep the Copper Cat down.'

Privately though, she wondered. In the far distance, the glittering blue band of the sea sparkled into existence, and, sitting on it like a scar, the shadow that was the city of Raistinia. They had very little time, and now more than ever they needed her wits, and her luck. And it seemed she was running out of both.

76

Tove reached up to hang another of the white linen sheets over the line. It was a warm, cloudless day, and the small cobbled courtyard was a pleasant suntrap. Consequently, her charges – her own son of eight years, and her niece and nephew – were starting to get that glassy-eyed look that spoke of a longing for an afternoon nap. That wouldn't do at all. Pulling up her sleeves to display her own finely inked silk strips, she gestured with her fingers and sent a fine spray of ice crystals over the children. Gratifyingly, they shrieked as one.

'Wake up, magelings!' she said cheerily. 'I want to see perfectly formed words from each of you this afternoon, and you won't do that if you're drooling down your tunic.'

'Mum.' Her boy shifted in his chair, wiping droplets of moisture from his face. 'This is *boring*. We could be down at the sea yards. There's a company of mummers come in from Onwai, and Father said they're doing a play with real swords and real blood and—'

'You will call me Mistress Tove during our lesson,' she snapped, more annoyed with him than she wanted to admit. Trist was a good boy, but he didn't yet grasp the gifts he'd been given. The Edenier remained unpredictable to them, as it always had – sometimes it was passed down through the family line, and sometimes it would suddenly appear in families where no one had lifted a single magical finger before. And sometimes, of course, it would skip a child entirely, despite the talents of the rest of her family. She thought of her dear daughter Kaiya, who was with her father today, dutifully learning her sciences. The Edenier was a gift, not to be squandered. Belatedly, she realised that her niece and nephew were watching her with raised eyebrows, apparently waiting for the scolding they expected their cousin to receive. Instead, she turned to the bucket at her side and removed the long brush, already thick with ink. 'Trist, up you get. I want to see the words for Fire, Force and Ever. Quickly now, the lines must be swift and smooth, no faltering.'

Frowning so that his lower lip stuck out, Trist stood and took the brush from her. He approached the white sheet and hesitated there, clearly bringing the correct shapes to mind, but before the ink touched the canvas her niece cried out, pointing above their heads.

'What is that? Oh Aunty Tove, what is it?'

In the blameless blue sky above their heads a giant fist of rock hung in the air, as solid and as real as the cobbles under their feet. It was festooned with vines and flowers, hanging from it like a shifting curtain of greenery. As they watched the shape moved slowly over them, shrouding them in black shadow. It was heading towards the centre of the city. Tove felt her skin grow cold all over, despite the heat of the day.

'Mum, is it the gods? Have they come?'

She looked down at Trist's upturned face. He had already managed to smear ink on his cheek.

'I don't know, my love, I don't . . .'

Except that she did. She had never seen it with her own eyes, but there wasn't a mage alive who did not know the aspect of Y'Gria's floating palace. Indeed, a great number of dead mages had known it very well. The mage guard would be moving into place now, and the special spells that hung over her city would be leaping into life, but even so, terror constricted her throat. It was hard to believe that it was possible to stand against such a thing when you saw it hanging in the sky above you.

'Go inside,' she said abruptly. 'Our lessons are over for today. We will stay inside and –' She swallowed down her fear. *Wait for the nightmare to go away.* 'We'll stay under a roof for now.'

* * *

474

Y'Gria appeared at the bars of Sebastian's makeshift cell, a small smile playing on her golden lips. She had put him down in a dark corner of one of the ruins, and fashioned bars from the roots of an old tree growing above to hold him there. He had tried to break through the twisted roots, throwing himself against them again and again, but although they had bent a little they had never come close to breaking.

'What do you want? Where is Estenn?'

'I thought you would like to see this, good Sir Sebastian,' she said. 'Oster promises that you will behave yourself, and if you don't, I will throw you from my palace walls. How's that? I do hope you will behave, Sebastian, because I would so dearly like to see your face when we destroy the mage city.'

Sebastian stepped back from the bars, not trusting himself to speak. She nodded once, and the crumbling walls grew lively with thick green vines. They slid around his arms and pinned them to his back. He resisted once, feeling alarm as a grip stronger than anything human twisted around his wrists, but then it stopped.

'There. Held securely, I trust.' Y'Gria gestured lazily at the roots, and they shrank back up to the tree above them. 'Come with me.'

Sebastian followed her out of the ruins and into a wide court-yard with neatly cut green grass. There were crumbling grey walls on three sides, and the far side was open to the sky. Oster was nowhere to be seen, but Estenn was there, fussing over her hessian sacks. Y'Gria took him to the very edge, where empty space yawned inches from his feet. It occurred to him that with his arms bound behind his back it would be very easy for her to simply push him out into the void, but then she could have done that any time she wanted.

'Behold, Raistinia.'

It was a jewel of a city, a confection wrought in red-gold and studded with sapphires. Rather than merely spreading next to the sea, Raistinia took the ocean to its bosom; Sebastian saw canals of glittering water dissecting streets of red brick, and large square pools dotted with pleasure boats and barges, fes-tooned with bright flags. The floating palace descended rapidly towards the city, until he could clearly see people moving down the streets and along the canals. Most of the faces were turned up to them, and some were already running. He was reminded of an ant's nest when some bigger creature, a scorpion perhaps, began to tear down the carefully constructed towers of sand.

'We are moving out over the centre of the festering hole, where it is best to deploy the weapon. Isn't that right, Estenn, my child?'

Estenn stood up from the sacks. To Sebastian she looked dazed, as though being in such close proximity to Y'Gria had given her sunstroke. He eyed the bags, measuring the distance between him and Estenn. He could run and use his body to push one or both the sacks over the side. He would likely fall himself. A drastic solution, but there were so few options left.

As if she had read his intention on his face, Y'Gria slipped a cold hand around the top of his arm. 'Now then, Sir Sebastian, I had Oster's word you would behave yourself. Does the word of your lover mean nothing to you?'

'Where is he?' he asked, dragging his eyes away from the sacks. 'Shouldn't he also be here to witness your triumph?'

Y'Gria squeezed his arm, letting her nails dig into his flesh. 'He is in a foul temper for some ridiculous reason, so I have sent him to be alone until he can conduct himself with more grace. Are we ready yet, Estenn?'

'I believe so. There is a small ritual to perform, and then the Red Echo will fall on all of them below.' Her tongue darted out and licked her lower lip. 'Thousands of the godless, dead, by my hand.'

Sebastian saw Y'Gria's eyebrow twitch slightly. 'At our hand, my dear. Do what you must.'

'I will not let you do this,' said Sebastian, trying to meet Estenn's eyes. 'Whatever it takes, I will stop you.'

'Make any move I don't approve of, Sir Sebastian, and I will gut you in seconds,' said Y'Gria almost pleasantly. 'You will be quiet, and watch the will of the gods in action.'

The bags at Estenn's feet trembled, and to Sebastian's surprise a small figure climbed out of one. It looked like a creature made of paper and scrawled with ink; it made him think immediately of the Culoss, the strange little men they had battled and then befriended under the Citadel. They too had been made by mages. After a moment, an almost identical figure climbed out of the second one. They both stood blinking ink-black eyes in the sunlight.

'They are the Red Echo?'

'The mages and their ridiculous confections,' said Y'Gria dismissively. 'Get on with it, Estenn.'

Sebastian tensed, thrown by the apparently living spell. Estenn drew her cutlass and knelt before the two doll-like figures. With tiny movements, she nicked their parchment palms; red grains of what looked like sand leaked from one, black sand from the other. She took their hands, preparing to place them together.

'For the glory of the gods,' she said through gritted teeth. 'For the glory of the Twins!'

Out of the corner of his eye Sebastian saw Y'Gria frown, and then, as he tensed to throw himself forward, hoping to knock Estenn away from the Red Echo, a black shadow descended on them all.

'I've got a bone to pick with you, you gods-crazy bitch!'

He looked up to see an impossible creature of glimmering black glass swooping down on them from the clear blue sky and then abruptly Wydrin was hurtling from its back, dagger already drawn. She landed on the grass and rolled, tucking the blade carefully aside so that it didn't stab her, and then she was back on her feet. The great black creature, which Sebastian realised was shaped like a manta ray, banked round and he saw Frith run and jump from its back too, landing in the grass with somewhat less grace. The strange black manta ray turned and dropped back out of sight.

'What is the meaning of this?' Y'Gria was screeching, her form already splitting into hundreds of twisting roots. 'Who would dare?'

'The Copper Cat dares!' Wydrin waved Frostling in the air, and then caught sight of Sebastian. 'Seb!' She was sweating, and there was a red mark high on her cheek. 'Good to see you alive, we'll catch up in a bit.' With that she ran directly at Estenn. The

77

For a few heart-shattering seconds Wydrin dropped through the sky, Echo clutched to her chest, and then Feveroot was beneath her, tendrils of flexible black glass reaching up and gathering her to his changing form. Despite his efforts she still landed hard, and Echo gave a muffled squeak beneath her.

'Help?'

'Hold on, kid, this is going to get bumpy.' She rolled over onto her back and looked up at the floating palace. She could already see bursts of multicoloured light and errant fireballs as Frith did his best to keep the god creature occupied. Her heart clenched at that, and the fact that Sebastian was up there with him, but they had very little time. If they could get Echo away and hide the spell again, there was still a chance. As she watched, a plume of pale-green tentacles burst from the side of the palace, swirling eerily in the open air. For a moment she thought it was just Y'Gria fighting off Frith's magical attacks, but then the tentacles twisted and shot towards them, moving faster than she would have believed possible.

'Shit! Feveroot, make yourself hawk-shaped. And DIVE!'

The shining black substance of the demon twisted and ran together, becoming lethal speed, and they shot towards the ground at a terrific pace, so quickly that Wydrin felt sure her vital organs had all switched places. Even so, they weren't quite fast enough – a barbed tentacle flashed out from the main cluster and caught at Feveroot's tightly furled wing. Wydrin saw the wickedly sharp thorns tear through the slick substance of the demon's flesh as though it was made of butter, and a bright red burning fluid spattered into the sky, hissing as it hit cool air. Feveroot screamed, a many-throated howl that chilled Wydrin to the bone. The tentacle tore loose and suddenly they were out of reach, but still the glowing red blood of the demon poured from the wound, and they were spiralling towards the ground. Wydrin clutched at the hard feathers at the back of his neck as the city of Raistinia loomed sickeningly close.

'Feveroot? Feveroot, are you with me?'

'I am . . . holding on to this shape.'

Wydrin looked up, thinking that this couldn't possibly get any worse, only to see Estenn sliding down one of Y'Gria's twisting roots towards them. Her teeth were bared, eyes wild. *We're both as bloody mad as each other*, thought Wydrin. The root tip was growing thinner and thinner as Y'Gria attained the extremities of her reach. Estenn had a sack tied at her waist – the other half of the spell, of course. She intended to unite them still.

'I would brace yourself,' said Feveroot. 'For want of a better word, we're about to land.'

Wydrin turned back in time to see what looked like a busy market square filling her field of vision. She saw colourful stalls, and people fleeing from them, and then they were down and rolling, the world a chaos of noise and splintered wood.

When finally they stopped moving, Wydrin uncurled herself and looked around. Echo sat dazed on her lap, while the wreckage of the market lay in disarray around them. Estenn, she was sure, must have come down somewhere nearby. She hoped that the zealot had landed on her head and was currently leaking her brains onto the cobbles somewhere, but the gods did not seem to be on their side lately. Feveroot shuddered beneath her and she slid off his back, passing Echo up to her shoulder as she did so.

'Hold on tight to me, Echo, this isn't over yet. Feveroot? How are you doing?'

The demon turned his sleek hawk head towards her. His eyes

still glowed red, but without their usual fire. 'See for yourself.' He raised the wing that Y'Gria had caught – the glowing substance appeared to have stopped flowing for the time being, but the limb was ragged, pieces of his shiny black flesh peeling back like the petals of some exotic flower. 'Not fatal, but I am greatly weakened.'

'Fuck. I'm sorry.' She pressed the back of her hand to her forehead. Her head was spinning again, and the city smelled strange to her – to one side, a stall that had been selling spices had been smashed to pieces, spilling powders of many colours onto the ground. It was hard to think clearly. 'Can you fly?'

'Not at this size, I'm afraid, and not for long.'

Wydrin looked up. The floating palace still loomed above them, casting a shadow over the city. Distantly she could hear the soft *crump* of magical explosions, and as she watched she saw a ball of bright purple fire arc up from below and hit the palace on its craggy underside. The mages of Raistinia had some understanding of what had come for them and were trying to fight back. She squeezed her eyes shut briefly, ignoring the burning of her cheek. 'Go back up,' she said. 'Make yourself something small, and get back up there without attracting Y'Gria's attention. Help Frith and Sebastian, if you can.'

Feveroot tipped his head to one side. 'Without you commanding me, I cannot . . .'

'Oh right.' Wydrin cast around and saw a stall that had been selling jars of wine. A few of them were miraculously untouched. She uncorked one and used the contents to wash out the inside of the phial, spilling most of the wine over herself in the process. When it was done, she held it out to Feveroot.

The giant hawk collapsed in on itself and became a simple human figure made of black glass. The eyes, as ever, were red. Gingerly, Feveroot took the phial from Wydrin. If anything she thought he looked afraid.

'You understand what you have done?'

'Not really,' she said. 'But I don't have time to worry about it, and I've decided to trust you. Don't make me regret it. Please, get up there and help them.'

Feveroot blinked, and abruptly the human shape dropped away to be replaced by a large bat, the phial clutched in its back paws. The demon shot up into the air, soon lost to sight behind roofs and towers. Wydrin couldn't help noticing that he hadn't agreed to help them at all, now that he had his freedom in his grasp.

'Wydrin the Godless!'

Estenn appeared out of the wreckage of the market, her cutlass already grasped in her fist. Her hair hung over her face, and she was baring her teeth like the ink wolves that circled her neck. 'We have some unfinished business.'

'Oh yes,' said Wydrin. 'That.' She turned and jumped over a pile of broken crates, heading for a side street.

78

It took Frith no more than a second to accept Sebastian's presence, and then he was at his back, cutting his bonds and freeing his arms. He passed Sebastian the short sword from his own belt.

'We must keep her occupied.'

They had time to exchange no more words than that, as Y'Gria was already writhing, splitting into hundreds and hundreds of questing, pale roots. Estenn had vanished over the side, apparently in some suicidal pursuit of Wydrin, but the enraged god was more than enough to deal with. Sebastian fell into an attack stance – the sword was shorter and lighter than his preferred weapon, but the Ynnsmouth knights were trained to proficiency with all blades – while Frith spun the staff between his hands, sending a barrage of orange flame at the bulk of the creature. And creature she was, as Y'Gria's humanity was melting away rapidly – her finely featured face bloated and then ran, becoming something stretched and feral-looking, her mouth splitting into a gaping maw. Several of her fatter tentacles sprouted long twisted barbs, and they began to squirm together like a nest of enraged snakes.

'I have had enough of you!' Her voice was distorted and slurred as her mouth fell open to reveal a long, pointed purple tongue. 'I will not suffer your pestilence a moment longer.'

She swiped at them, a move designed to simply fling them from the edge of the floating palace to fall to their deaths, but Frith moved faster, conjuring a sudden wall of glittering ice to block her tendrils. Almost instantly the ice cracked with the pressure being exerted on it, but Sebastian was already sprinting towards the knotted section where the tentacles joined the main meat of her body. Bringing all his weight to bear on the blow, he struck downwards and severed several of the limbs in one arching movement. Bright blue blood spurted across grass and stone, and Y'Gria bellowed with outrage. Sebastian grinned.

'Quickly,' shouted Frith, 'I will cover you as best I can!'

As more feelers shot across the grass towards him, more shards of ice burst into existence, as well as sheets of orange flame that turned the questing roots black and crispy. Sebastian glanced back to Frith once, to see the young lord holding the staff in both hands, turning it this way and that to direct his magical attacks. The expression on his face was one of utmost concentration and, Sebastian thought, grim satisfaction. Convinced that Frith knew what he was doing, Sebastian let himself fall back into the familiar movements and patterns of his training – the enemy was fast, the enemy was everywhere, but he had a sword in his fist and the fever of battle was roaring through his veins.

Sebastian leapt forward, sword moving in a blur as his blade sliced through tentacle after tentacle. His tunic was soaked through with what passed for Y'Gria's blood, and the old god was shrieking, retreating back against the ruins that cupped the wide lawn. The silvery thread that was his dragon blood was singing, sensing the weakness and fear of its prey, and for once he surrendered to it completely. It was glorious – the simplicity of the fight, the satisfaction of torn flesh. And through that shimmering silver connection he suddenly felt Oster nearby.

Are you there?

There was no answer. Putting it to one side while still drawing strength from it, Sebastian drove on, until he was beneath the bulbous flesh sack that was the main part of Y'Gria's body. He would carve this so-called god up into pieces, and his dragon brethren would feast.

'ENOUGH!'

The rippling flesh of Y'Gria's body expanded, throwing him back over the severed pieces of tentacle that littered the grass. The smooth pale-green node of flesh in front of him split open in a bloodless wound, and a great blind beak lined with yellow teeth burst forth, snapping and questing inches from his boot.

Sebastian had a moment to grasp that this was Y'Gria's truest form – a giant carnivorous plant, all growth and appetite – before it was reaching for him on the end of a long, sinuous neck. Its green throat filled his vision, wet and pulsating, and the beak opened to its fullest extent, ready to snap down over his legs, when something black and shining struck him from one side with enormous violence, rolling him out of the creature's reach. Sebastian scrambled to his feet to find an uncertain black shape pooled at his feet, dotted with glowing red lights.

'It thirsts for blood, as I once did,' said the shape, and before Sebastian could take that in, Frith was at his side. He was still sending multiple fireballs up towards the writhing shape of the god, but his face was wet with sweat now, his white hair slick to his forehead.

'The situation', he panted, 'is not improving.'

Sebastian looked up. Y'Gria had swollen until she dwarfed her own ruins, a pulsating, multi-limbed creature, questing tendrils nosing at the sky, the grass, the stones. The terrible plant-beak that had burst forth from her expanded gut had been joined by two more identical protrusions, their wide mouths creaking open and snapping shut, weaving on the ends of their necks like snakes. Of Y'Gria's human form, there was no sign.

'Isu's balls,' said Sebastian.

Born and raised in Crosshaven, Wydrin had always secretly believed that all cities were a natural home to her – put her down in any confusion of buildings and meandering streets, and she could always take you to the best tavern – but Raistinia was proving itself to be a maze. Alleys she felt must take her to a main street led back on themselves; she burst out onto squares to find that there were no other exits, and the walls and buildings all felt too tall, looming over her like enemies. Stumbling into a small cobbled courtyard she was startled by an ornate fountain, the sound of water splashing over the stones somehow unbearable.

'It's this bloody fever,' she said aloud, leaning against the nearest wall to get her breath back. 'It's pulling everything out of shape. Like trying to run in a nightmare.'

Echo, who was gripping tightly to the back of Wydrin's collar, shifted slightly, papery skin scraping against Wydrin's neck. 'Your blood. Is wrong,' it said in a matter-of-fact tone.

Before Wydrin had a chance to answer, Estenn appeared at the entrance to the courtyard. For a few seconds the expression of steely determination on her face reminded Wydrin of her own mother, and then she was sprinting across the square. Wydrin gathered what wits she had and ran for a set of stone steps leading up to a dark doorway. Inside was a cool wood-panelled room hung with elaborate portraits, and two men in scholar's robes stared at her in shock.

'Get out of the city,' she said as she ran past them. 'Get everyone out, if you can.'

She was sprinting up another set of wooden stairs as she heard Estenn come in the room behind her, and then she was running across a gangway that led over the street to another building. Being back out in the daylight again she blinked rapidly, her head spinning, and she collided lightly with the side. In seconds Estenn was on her, and it was only Echo's tug on the back of her collar that made her sidestep rapidly away, narrowly avoiding Estenn's whirling cutlass. Turning to face the woman, she drew both her sword and her dagger.

'You want to do it here, do you?' She flexed her fingers, twirling Frostling so that it glittered in the dusty sunshine. 'That's fine with me.'

'There is no stopping it,' said Estenn, her eyes wide. 'Can't you see that? I passed through the Eye of Euriale to get here, I have the weapon. It is my destiny to save the gods.'

'Destiny is just a fancy word for people who want their own way all the time. And I came after you, Emissary. Maybe it's my *destiny* to stop you.' She dropped into a fighting stance, ignoring the way the world pitched around her like a ship at sea. 'I will not let you kill all these innocent people.'

'Innocent?' sneered Estenn. 'They took the gods from us, and left us to live in a world without their grace for a thousand years. They made a tiny, grubby world full of men and misery, and they didn't even stay around to suffer it with us.'

Wydrin laughed. It was growing difficult to remember why she was here. Above them, the floating palace loomed like a cancer on the sky. She bit the inside of her mouth, forcing herself to concentrate on the pain. 'The world is always grubby. You don't like it? Make it better. You don't get to wipe it all away and remake it in your image, and you can't rely on gods to sort it out. They don't care about you. They don't care about any of us. We're better off without them.' Tasting blood in her mouth she leapt forward, blades flashing.

Estenn roared and danced forward to meet her, swords meeting in a discordant crash. Keeping Glassheart as a barrier, Wydrin ducked and slashed out with Frostling, but Estenn slipped back out of range. The pressure from Estenn's cutlass removed, Wydrin stumbled, head spinning, and then the other woman began to flicker and fade from view.

'Oh no you don't, that's bloody cheating.' Keeping her eyes on where the woman had been, Wydrin dived forward, Frostling at a point, and was rewarded with a squawk of pain and the pressure of her blade piercing flesh. Estenn flickered back into view, her right arm running with blood, but before Wydrin could react she brought the pommel of her cutlass round in a heavy blow, connecting with the side of Wydrin's head. Her vision dimmed and suddenly her knees were hitting wooden boards. The sounds of the city were muffled, and she felt blood running down her neck to soak into her shirt.

If Estenn had not been so desperate to snatch Echo away at that moment, if she had spent the second it would have taken to cut her throat, then it would have all ended there – it was a thought that would reoccur to Wydrin, over the rest of that long, painful day. Instead, Estenn grabbed at Echo, pulling the small creature sharply towards her. Wydrin surged to her feet, driving the top of her head directly into Estenn's face. There was a crunch of small bones as the older woman's nose broke and a cry of mingled rage and pain, then Wydrin snatched Echo back from her unresisting hand and ran blindly down the walkway. There were men and women in the streets below, shouting and pointing at the sky. If she could just get far away and hide, just for a little while, they could move the Red Echo somewhere else, but Estenn was relentless. Already Wydrin could hear the pounding of her boots, and when she burst into the tower on the far side, she was only a few steps behind.

I should be able to kill her, she thought wildly, running up a spiral staircase with little thought as to where it would take her. *She is good, but she's not as good as the Copper Cat.* Even so, she knew that she had come very close to losing her life. Shame crowded her throat, and she swallowed it down.

Hardly knowing where she was, she burst through a door to find another bridge to another tower. Below stretched a great square pool of glittering blue water boxed in by red-brick walls, and beyond that, the sea itself. There was nowhere else to go. She had run herself into a dead end, again.

'No choice,' she muttered as she ran across the bridge, shoving Echo back onto her shoulder. 'I suppose I will have to bloody kill her now, fever madness or not.' The other tower, she realised as she ran towards it, was actually little more than a lookout post – a wide platform at the top, a beacon ready to be lit against a stormy night.

'Wydrin Threefellows, this ends now.'

She reached the platform and turned, blades ready. The sea was a restless blue roar at her back, and that was a comfort of sorts. She could smell the salt.

'I think you're right about that,' she said, forcing a grin on to her face. *I am the Copper Cat of Crosshaven*, she told herself. *I am the daughter of Devinia the Red. I can take this bitch.* 'If the gods are so powerful and so right, why aren't they down here fighting with you?' She gripped her weapons until her knuckles turned white. 'Think about it, Estenn. If they are gods, why do they struggle against the mages? They're just greedy arseholes with too much power and a tendency to show off.' She took a deep breath. 'You've fought all your life. You're worth more than they are.'

Estenn just shook her head. 'I owe what I am to them. I was made to serve them.'

'If you truly believe that, then you really are the biggest idiot walking.'

There was a moment of silence between them. Wydrin felt the papery scratching of Echo at her back, and behind Estenn the palace hung like a second moon. It was still possible to see bursts of coloured light, and she thought of Frith, still fighting. It made her feel a little stronger.

Then Estenn raised her hand, revealing the livid purple scar on her palm. 'You speak as though the gods have no real power,' she said. 'But they do.'

She squeezed her hand shut, and fear and rage and pain surged through Wydrin like a rip-tide. Wordlessly, she fell to her knees, desperately trying to hold on to a sense of herself as the storm moved through her. The fever that was in her blood boiled over, and she saw everything she feared the most thrust in front of her eyes like garish puppets at a mummers' show – Sebastian lost to her, walking into a cursed jungle never to return; the tip of Estenn's sword bursting through Frith's chest, the awareness in his grey eyes seeping away to nothing.

'No . . .'

She could not escape it. These things would always be waiting for her, there was no outrunning or outfighting the inevitable heartbreak. Dimly she was aware of Estenn standing over her, strong hands tearing Echo away. She heard Echo cry out, and she lifted her head to see the two parts of the spell finally joined. Estenn was saying something, words that had little meaning, and then a storm of red and black sand was swirling up into the sky above the tower, a strange localised tornado that grew larger and larger as she watched. It began to spread out, dispersing through the air like ink in water, and although she was half sure she imagined it, a great cry went up from the city below. Twin shadows, black and red, blotted out the sun.

'They will all die now,' said Estenn, her face split in a beatific smile. 'First this city, then the next, and then all of them will fall.'

Without thinking, Wydrin forced herself to her feet and ran at the Red Echo – two small forms, papery hands joined. She reached down and tore one from the other, clasped what she had to her chest, and leapt from the side of the tower.

79

'To your right!'

Frith hit the ground rolling, the scent of grass and scorched earth strong in his nostrils, as a long tentacle lashed the air where he had been a second ago. He glanced up to nod his thanks to Sebastian, and then he thrust the staff forward again, summoning the words for Fire and Ever. Of all the limited spells he now had at his disposal, this appeared to be the most effective against the creature they fought – slithering roots turned black and crispy under his flames, or drew away before he could reach them. Even so, Y'Gria's ability to expand her body and produce new append-ages was apparently limitless, and the fight was wearing him down.

Not so Sebastian. The big knight was still full of energy, his eyes bright and his face split into a grin as he fought back against the god. He had always been an impressive fighter, skilled and disciplined as well as strong, but Frith had never seen him fight as he did now – there almost seemed to be a silver aura around him as his sword moved in its restless dance. Bezcavar had once named him his 'god of war' and Frith could see why. No sane person would want to face him on the battlefield – he was a man born to be a warrior – but then Y'Gria was neither sane nor, strictly speaking, a person.

To Frith's surprise, Feveroot had returned, and was helping them. He wanted to ask what had happened to Wydrin and Estenn, but there was no time or space to ask – the demon did not fight as such, but used his liquid glass form to shield them and to confound Y'Gria's searching appendages. It was clear that the demon had been injured in some way – spots of smoking blood like lava dotted the grass – but it was here, and it was helping. Frith parcelled away the uneasy questions that arose for later contemplation.

There was a crash, and he narrowly avoided the grasping, teeth-lined beak as it struck the lawn next to him. He sent a ball of fire at its throat, but it twisted away like a child refusing a spoonful of dinner and instead the flames grazed the thick midriff of the god's main body, raising up a welt of deep green blisters. Shrieking, the plant-creature that was Y'Gria scrambled backwards to perch on top of the broken ruins that circled the garden, pale tentacles looping around broken stones and turrets. It would not take long for her to recover, and they were being worn down. Bracing himself for the debilitating exhaustion that would follow, he summoned the new magic, thinking perhaps to turn her to dust as he had Y'Ruen's spawn, but the god slipped through his grasp, refusing to be pinned in one place – it was as if she stood outside time, ageless. He supposed that was entirely possible. But it didn't mean the magic was useless.

'Sebastian, cover me! I have an idea!' In an instant the big knight was with him, his bulk shielding him as Y'Gria's feelers grubbed blindly in the grass.

'What are you doing?' asked Sebastian. He didn't sound concerned, merely curious.

'I'm not sure,' he answered truthfully. 'Perhaps I'll tell you, if it works.'

Frith took a breath, and ignoring Y'Gria, felt everything around him grow still. For a few moments, he stood outside time, and the strange incomprehensible magic filled every inch of him and suffused his skin. He looked down and saw his hand as a glowing shape made of light. He would have one chance only.

He transferred his attention to the ruined wall Y'Gria perched upon. It was possible to feel how it had been when it had been whole – an ornate structure of elaborate towering spires – and he knew instinctively that this was something that Y'Gria had stolen, an ancient ruin that was older even than she. Holding his breath, Frith fixed the ruin within his mind and pushed it back through time as fast as he could, summoning its original structure.

Colour and noise crashed back into the world and Y'Gria's huge writhing body was pierced with towering structures of stone. She screamed, a deafening noise from multiple throats, and Frith staggered backwards and fell onto the grass. Her body was speared, stretched and twisted out of shape, but he barely had the strength left to stand. His vision turned dark at the edges; Sebastian's strong grip on his shoulder stopped him from passing out.

'By all the gods, Frith, how did you do that?'

He opened his mouth, but had no breath left to push the words out. Instead Feveroot spoke. 'It's not over yet. But at least you have made her very angry.'

Trapped by the spires of the reconstructed ruins, Y'Gria was screaming with rage, her body melting into more and more questing roots, coming straight for them. As they watched, the thickest tentacles pushed at the spires holding her in place, trying to crush them into dust. It was clear that she wouldn't be held for long.

'Let her come,' said Sebastian, standing up so that his body covered Frith's prone form. 'I could do this all day!'

There was a thundering roar, the spires fell, and Y'Gria's multiple heads flexed and shot towards them like vipers. With the last of his strength, Frith reached out for the power again, this time capturing the entirety of the floating palace in its aura. In less than a second, the ruins and the gardens expanded like a flower in bloom – broken walls rebuilt themselves, towers shot towards the blue sky, roofs and battlements and courtyards, once shoved together with no thought, suddenly found themselves complete and competing for space where there was none. On the plants in the gardens, Frith worked his magic in the opposite direction – rather than back through time, he pushed them forward. Trees exploded into towering giants, grass grew metres high in seconds, and all around bushes and plants became an impenetrable thicket of briars and thorns. Even as he struggled to stay conscious, Frith felt the floating palace shift beneath him – the sudden change in its weight and shape had broken it somehow, and the smooth magic that had kept it moving so gracefully through the air was now leaking away. There was a jolt, and they all cried out as it dropped some distance before righting itself again.

'What have you done?' screamed Y'Gria through her many throats. 'What have you DONE?'

'This whole thing is going to crash into the ground, and take you with it,' said Frith weakly. 'That's what I've done.'

'In that case, we should leave, I think,' said Feveroot. He was a shifting dark shape around them, orange-red spots bright with anxiety. 'I can probably get you to the ground, or at least halfway there.'

'I'm not going anywhere until I've cut the heart from her,' said Sebastian.

Frith opened his mouth to tell him he was being ridiculous, when one of the newly rebuilt walls to their left collapsed into rubble and the dragon form of Oster burst forth, snarling. There were silver chains on his scaled legs, now twisted into pieces. The dragon opened its mouth wide and hissed, revealing rows and rows of razor-sharp teeth.

'She chained you up?' cried Sebastian.

'Go.' It was Oster's voice, they all heard it, and his great amber eye was fixed on Sebastian. 'There are things I wish to discuss with my sister.'

'Come with us!' Sebastian made to go towards the dragon, but Oster flicked his tail menacingly. 'This place is doomed!'

'Go, while you still have a chance. I won't tell you again.' With that Oster turned and leapt, scrabbling up the newly restored ruins. He struck out at Y'Gria's roots, severing them with quick snaps of his powerful jaws. At once, the old god's attention turned to him, her teeth-lined heads converging on him like a dog scenting fresh meat.

'We have to leave,' said Feveroot again.

With some difficulty, Frith struggled to his feet and touched

Sebastian's arm. The big knight was watching the fight between the two gods with an expression of horror on his face.

'Sebastian, my friend, he has given us a chance. Let us take it.' He paused. 'He is a god, after all. He may survive.'

Feveroot became a great bat, and on his back they left the floating palace, flying awkwardly down towards the city. The demon was still leaking glowing blood, and he moved his wings stiffly.

'What is that?' Sebastian pointed. The city lay below them, a carpet of red and glittering blue, but where the city met the sea proper there was a tall tower, and from that was spreading a great dark shadow. It flowed through the air until it covered half the buildings in a sooty film. And then as they watched, a second shadow spread over it, this one the colour of blood.

'The Red Echo. It can be nothing else,' said Frith. It was hard to speak. If the Red Echo had been activated, what had happened to Wydrin?

'Is there nothing we can do?'

The shadow continued to spread like ink through water, and Frith realised he could hear screaming from below. The people of Raistinia, their doom come upon them.

'Perhaps if we—'

There was a flash of dark light, like being struck on the head, and two things happened almost at the very same moment – the shadow suddenly contracted, vastly reducing the portion of the city underneath its influence, while those parts still touched by the red-and-black shadow were filled with pillars of fire. Flames leapt up from the street, twenty, thirty feet high; a tower of fire for every mage soul caught under the Red Echo's influence. The screaming increased in pitch so abruptly that Frith had to squeeze his eyes shut against it. Such human suffering, and so many lives snuffed out in an instant.

And then the shadow winked out, leaving the city half on fire and covered in a pall of smoke. The damage was done.

80

Devinia had never seen a storm like it.

The sun had been bright in the afternoon sky, and then clouds had swept in like a curtain being pulled, and now the day was as black as the darkest hour of the night. They had been caught out on the side of a steep hill, and now rain was falling in sheets so solid that Devinia could barely see further than her own boots, and the thunder rolled around them constantly, deafening them to all sense of where they were.

'We have to get out of this!' Augusta was clinging to her arm, her grey hair plastered to her head, shouting at the top of her voice to be heard. 'The whole bloody hill is going to be washed away!'

Devinia looked down at her feet and was alarmed to see a rushing current of water washing over her boots, taking debris and mud with it.

'Where?' She ran a hand over her face, trying to clear some of the rainwater from her eyes. 'Can't see anything in this mess!'

There was a flash of lightning and in the brief burst of light she caught sight of Terin, just slightly ahead of them. He was waving, his mouth opening as he shouted something lost in the fury of the storm. Without speaking, Devinia and Augusta hurried to follow him, half blind as they were. After a few moments, Devinia caught sight of what he had been gesturing at: a shallow cave in the side of the hill, little more than a deeper patch of darkness against a confusion of black and grey. They stumbled into it, gasping like beached fish and pressing themselves against the rocky walls. Ephemeral, one strong arm flung around the Banshee's shoulders, followed, her dragon-kin creatures shaking out their wings and squeezing into the tight space.

'By the Graces.' Augusta shook her head, sending droplets of water flying. 'I've seen some storms at sea, some real ship killers, but this.' She folded her wrinkled face into a grimace. Ristanov the Banshee leaned against the wall, and then slowly slid down it, her face slack and her eyes unseeing. 'I wouldn't be surprised if the whole bleedin' island weren't washed away.'

They all paused as a peal of thunder rolled over. Devinia felt the pressure of it on her eardrums. She moved to the very edge of the cave and looked out. The ground beyond the cave was wet and black and shifting; there was no question that they would be stuck in the cave until the storm passed, and even then it was impossible to say what the violence of the weather would do to the landscape outside.

'This place is known for its storms,' she said. 'Sailing Y'Gria's Loss has always been dangerous. At least in a ship, you can try to outrun a storm.' She gritted her teeth. 'We're stuck here.'

'That we are,' agreed Augusta. She squeezed some of the water from her shirt and sat cross-legged on the ground, surrounded by the dragon-kin. Absently, she patted one on the nose. 'Since we aren't going anywhere, I'd like to hear more about this home of yours, young Terin. I got some bits and pieces from Wydrin, of course, but that girl is a born fabricator and I want to hear it from the horse's mouth. You live in houses made of ice, is that right?'

Terin smiled. Soaked from the storm and with the temperature cooler than it had been in days, he looked as bright as Devinia had ever seen him.

'Mistress Grint, we do indeed build our homes from ice, at least in part. We also use stone and coral and other materials available to us.'

'And if heat makes you ill, how do you cook your food?'

'Well, the answer to that is we largely don't. The Narhl diet involves a lot of raw fish.'

497

Augusta made a face. 'Ye gods.'

Devinia sighed and turned back to the mouth of the cave. Behind her, Augusta kept up a steady stream of increasingly incredulous queries while Terin cheerfully answered. After a moment, Ephemeral joined her by the entrance.

'The dragon-kin are alarmed by the storm,' she said, gesturing at where they crouched. All of them were staring out into the night, their eyes like wet stones. There was something very unsettling about the sight. 'It must be the first one they have seen.'

'Do you think Wydrin is at the centre of the island? Truly?'

Ephemeral turned to look at her. In the dark, her eyes were very like those of the dragon-kin. 'I trust Terin's visions. If he saw them there, then that is where they are.'

'Hmm.' Devinia frowned out at the storm. The thunder sounded almost rhythmic now, as though it were a hammer striking an anvil. 'This great magical power he felt. If we can use it, whatever it is, to destroy Kellan, then at least we can make our way back to Two-Birds without being hunted.'

A flash of lightning lit up the trees like the middle of the day, and suddenly it was there – the huge, hulking shape of the Dawning Man, eyes glowing red like faded stars. Devinia felt her stomach drop and she had a brief moment to hope that she was seeing things, that the light and the shadows and her own fears had created the monster, but then it moved, lurching towards them and crashing its huge golden foot into the watery mud. The footsteps of a giant, hidden in thunder.

'We're under attack!' She drew her sword, already noting the shapes running towards them out of the rain, shambling, rain-soaked figures, storm light silver on their blades. 'Be ready!'

It was a bloody, confused fight. Devinia ran from the cave with her sword ready, meeting the first pirate with such violence that the blow near severed his arm at the shoulder, while the storm crashed around them. For the first time, she realised exactly how much she relied on all her senses when fighting; the dark shrouded everything, the roar of the wind and thunder encased them, the stinging rain numbed her skin. She might as well have been fighting underwater.

498

Ephemeral seemed unaffected, moving with the inhuman grace that Devinia was gradually getting used to; men and women fell before the green woman's blade as though they presented themselves to be killed. Devinia felt a brief stab of hope; they had been ambushed, but Kellan's men were down to their last reserves, and there couldn't be that many of them. They could take them here; even with their backs to the hill, it was possible—

The ground beneath their feet shook violently and Devinia was suddenly fighting to stay upright. The Dawning Man was right on them, golden fists swinging. A cadaverous figure, arms held aloft as if to welcome the storm, was bellowing against the cacophony.

'I am the Red King!'

Another flash of lightning seared the sky and Devinia saw him clearly; Kellan was a flayed skeleton, a crimson corpse with eyes rolled up to the whites in his ecstasy, and the thin band of gold still sat on his head.

'You mad bastard.'

The dragon-kin were streaming from the cave, some of them unfurling their wings and leaping into the dark, their jaws open to reveal rows of newly sharp teeth, but the Dawning Man reached out with its enormous fist and plucked one of the lizards from the sky. There was a brittle crunch, which Devinia heard clearly over the storm, and next to her Ephemeral wailed with pain and horror.

'No!'

More of the dragon-kin flew at the Dawning Man, perhaps moved to save their sibling, and the giant batted them down, their broken bodies landing in the increasingly flooded dirt. Ephemeral stumbled, her sword loose in her hand, a stricken expression on her face.

'I can feel them dying!'

'Stay with me!' Devinia took her arm, and then was forced to drop it as a pirate barrelled into her. She killed him easily, grimacing as her fingers slid over his bristling arm, but then the Dawning Man was charging towards them. She spun, trying to shout a warning back to the cave, but it was too late. The Dawning Man stepped over them and crashed directly into the stony ridge, the whole thing exploding in a landslide of rocks and water.

'Augusta!'

More pirates, more blood for her sword. Devinia fought through them, trying to get back to the wreckage of the cave, thinking of nothing else now save for that. The Dawning Man was punching at the rocks, smashing them into powder, while on the hill above them the earth was shifting wetly.

'Augusta! Terin!'

She caught a single glimpse of them in a blistering burst of light. Terin, slim and splattered with mud, supporting a bedraggled-looking Augusta, stumbling away from the pile of rocks. The old woman was clinging to him, her arm held awkwardly to her side, and one side of her face was covered in blood.

'Nan?'

The earth shifted under her feet. From above them, a great wall of mud and water crashed down over the broken rocks and Augusta and Terin were lost to view. Devinia had time only to reach one desperate hand towards where they had been, and the mud and water hit her legs like a solid wave, striking her feet out from under her and carrying her away with it.

81

There was paper and sand between her fingers, and nothing beneath her feet.

Wydrin took a breath, whether scream or curse she wasn't certain, but the violence of her descent stole it from her. She was aware that she'd managed to snatch part of the Red Echo away – a handful of torn parchment and the dusty innards that made up the poor creature – and she'd heard Estenn's sharp cry of outrage before she'd jumped, but she knew it hadn't worked. Even as she fell the air was full of pain and heat, and then she hit the water hard enough to drive all the air from her lungs. The black-and-red sand she still clutched in her hands was washed away and she plummeted into the sea.

I failed.

The water was freezing against her fevered skin, unbearably so, but she made no real effort to swim to the surface. The weight of her weapons was bearing her down, and for the time being she felt happy for it to do so. The water was dark and silent, and above its sheltering roof there were men and women and children dying, because she had failed. The shifting light above her head was filled with the red and orange of fire, so she turned away from it, looking down into the black. Her chest was burning already, and her body ached all over from the impact with the water. Somehow, she knew that her nose was bleeding. *Blood in the water*, she thought, twisting down into the dark. *It's all just blood in the water.*

You called? The voice was three voices in one, the sound of waves breaking against shingles, a distant roar of a forgotten tide, the silence of the undersea chasm. Three sinuous shapes slid towards her through the growing darkness. She felt no terror at the sight of them: only relief that it would be faster than drowning. *Daughter of the salt, daughter of the sea. You join us again.*

Even as her vision grew dark Wydrin felt some confusion at that. *You haven't met me*, she said. *You came to me at Sorrow's Isle, but none of that has happened yet. Not to you.*

There was a swift gurgling noise, like the sound you hear when you are dragged under by a riptide. It was, Wydrin realised, laughter of a sort.

It's all the same to us, said the Graces. They were circling her now, an escort down into the dark. *The sea doesn't change, Wydrin of Crosshaven. The salt is ever the same. And you never listen.*

Listen? Why should I listen? Wydrin watched their arrow-shaped heads, their empty eyes. *You gods are all the same. I've had enough of it. It doesn't matter now anyway. Let me go.*

Gods? We are older than gods, salt-child. Abruptly, one of the sharks swam closer, its tawny striped hide briefly illuminated by the last of the light from above. It bumped into her, none too gently. *You smell wrong. You have some sort of taint on you. We cannot abide tainted water. And you cower, and hide, and wish for it to be over.*

I'm done. I failed, and now there is a city up there suffering for it. Enough is enough, and . . . Wydrin paused. Tainted blood. Feveroot had told her there was an infection in her blood, that it was clouding her judgement. She had turned away from Frith because of it, she had been lost and disorientated on the streets of Raistinia because of it, and now she was drowning because of it – hiding and mewling for peace like a coward, because of the madness Estenn had passed on. Abruptly her heart was hammering in her chest, and her mouth was full of water. It could already be too late.

Help me! She kicked wildly in the water. *Take it from me! Quick, before I bloody die down here.*

That sounds more like Wydrin of Crosshaven. The voices

sounded amused now, but they were still circling, unconcerned. *Salt in your blood, a storm in your belly.*

You're right! She reached out for them. There was almost no light left at all. *I've been tainted, infected by something, but you can take it away. I demand you do this!* She thought of Frith's grey eyes. *I am a child of the salt, remember? But something else has put its mark on me. Can't you taste it?*

The atmosphere in the water abruptly changed. Wydrin felt it as a drop in temperature, and her mouth was so full of the taste of salt she nearly choked.

It is true, came the voice of the Graces. The tone was considering, edging towards angry. *Who would dare to take the sea's own?*

Oh some bloody idiot, I expect. Take me back! Before I bloody die down here!

It was too late. The burning in her chest had spread down her arms, and her legs felt as though they were made of lead. She tried to kick against it, to struggle against the oncoming darkness, but there was no energy left even for that. The light faded, and the Graces were lost in shadows.

There is a mark. The voice of the Graces. *No, child, keep still . . .*

There was a rush of movement through the water, and Wydrin felt her aching body buffeted by unseen shapes. She felt the roughness of their skin under her fingers, and then there was a burst of bright pain across her right cheek as the shark hide abraded away the skin there. She had lost all sense of what was happening to her, but she felt mildly aggrieved. Who was pushing her? Where was that light coming from?

You've a way to go yet, child of the salt.

Suddenly the roar of the sea was the roar of the wind, and Wydrin found herself lying face down on cold wet bricks. She tried to push herself up, only to find a rising torrent of seawater in her throat. When she had finished throwing that up, she stumbled to her feet and touched her fingers to her cheek. It was burning still, but it was the good clean burn of salt in a wound, and when she took her fingers away, they were bloody. And her head was clear. For the first time in what felt like an age, she was free from the spectre of Estenn's madness. Wydrin pushed her hands back through her hair, squeezing out what water she could. She was standing on one of the stone walkways that criss-crossed the sprawling harbour of Raistinia, and ahead of her she could see the watchtower she had leapt from. Beyond that, the city was on fire. There was no sign of Y'Gria's floating palace.

'Right,' Wydrin spat the last of the salt from her mouth and grinned. 'Fuck this for a game of soldiers.'

Y'Gria's palace had left quite the dust cloud.

It had settled somewhat now, but Sebastian found that his eyes were drawn to it again and again. It was at least less painful than looking at the city of Raistinia – Feveroot had managed to bring them to the outer wall, and deposited them by what looked to be a small abandoned trading post, devoid of people but overrun with a creeping purple plant that coiled around the dusty bricks and the remains of market stalls. Beyond the wall, they could hear the chaos of the city as the mages struggled to understand what had happened. The Red Echo hadn't been deployed with complete success – they had seen half of the deadly shadow fall away – but apparently it had been enough to cause a great deal of pain and suffering. The fires were being brought under control quickly at least, with those mages still alive producing blizzards and walls of freezing ice to control the flames. Feveroot had reported this much to them after the brief flight he had made alone over the wall. Now the demon was curled on the sand and rocks in the form of a small fox, although before it had slept it had assured them that Wydrin still lived, and was making her way to the edge of the city – he could sense her blood, apparently. After Y'Gria's monstrous plant form and everything else they'd seen, Sebastian didn't have the energy to question this knowledge.

Frith was sitting on a low wall, his head down, trying to regain his strength. Sebastian was reminded of their night of drinking in Two-Birds, how Frith had stumbled from the last tavern of the evening and sat down heavily, drunk as the lord he was. Reluctantly, a smile touched his face.

'I am glad to see you alive,' he said. 'After we were captured by Y'Gria, I wondered if you had met a similar fate.'

'We almost did,' said Frith. 'Y'Ruen, in all her terrible glory, and what appeared to be a new clutch of brood sisters.' He paused, then shrugged. 'An old clutch, I should say. They did not bear much resemblance to Ephemeral and her kin.'

'Truly?' Sebastian swallowed hard. This news chilled him for reasons he couldn't name. 'The magic you used back there. It didn't look like the magic you've summoned from the staff before.'

'It wasn't. It appears to be something I've been given by our journey through the Eye.' Frith frowned, as though he would have been just as happy not to receive this particular gift. 'A combination of the strange magic that pulled us through to this place and time, the Edeian of Euriale, and the latent knowledge I carry from Joah Demonsworn.' Frith shrugged. 'It is likely I will never understand it.' He stood up, and restlessly pulled at one of the purple fronds sprouting from the wall behind him. 'We saw Joah at Lan-Hellis. He is little more than a student now, but his ambitions are building. He is already experimenting with demons.' He glanced down at the curled form of the being he had named Feveroot.

'Joah? Here?' Sebastian pushed a hand back through his hair. 'This was his time, I suppose, and in his day he was a greatly respected mage. Even so . . .' He looked at Frith, who was glaring at the brambles. 'That must have been strange for you.'

'An understatement,' Frith snorted. 'What of Oster? Do you think he lived?'

Sebastian winced at the baldness of the question. He turned back to look at the distant dust cloud, now little more than a red smudge on the horizon. He could still feel that silver thread between them, and through it he knew that Oster was still alive. For the first time, the connection felt like a blessing rather than a curse. 'He lived.'

Frith cleared his throat. 'Do you wish to go back for him?' Meeting Sebastian's surprised look, he raised an eyebrow. 'You are fond of him, are you not? And he fought for us?'

'Oster has his own decisions to make. Regardless of my feelings on the matter, he needs to make them on his own.' He took a deep breath. 'I think I'm finally starting to realise that I cannot always be responsible for those I love. They must stand or fall on their own.'

'How touching.'

The voice came from the purple brambles. As Frith and Sebastian moved rapidly away from the broken wall, the branches began to writhe and turn in on themselves, becoming a huge, unsightly knot. And then a dark hole opened in the middle, and Sebastian saw that it was a face: a wild face of sharp thorns and thin, bruise-coloured bark. The spreading branches on the wall behind it were its unruly hair, and when it spoke again he recognised the voice.

'My dear Oster is licking his wounds,' said Y'Gria through bramble lips. 'This happens with the younger ones sometimes. They become confused. They become confused, and they turn against their own families. And Oster wasn't given his songs and stories like the rest of us were, the poor pup.'

'What do you want?' Sebastian was surprised by the heat of sudden anger in his own voice. 'Do you wish us to tear you apart again?' Next to him, Frith stood ready with his staff.

'That? If that is your best, then you are as weak as the mages,' said Y'Gria, although Sebastian thought her tone was too casual. 'It was rude of you to destroy the gardens though, especially after I had shown you such hospitality. No, I only wish to tell you three things. First, that Oster has seen the error of his ways and will not be debasing himself with mortals any more.' Sebastian looked away from the thorny face for a moment. 'Second, that we know of the Citadel, and what your mage friends had planned. Estenn was kind enough to explain it all for me.' The thorns writhed and twisted in on themselves, scoring the thin bark with white lines. 'And third, we will be coming for you. My brothers and my sisters and I will descend on the fetid hole that is Krete, and we will burn you all to embers. Every person, every child and animal, every brick and stone and piece of glass will be ground down to blood and gristle and dust, in vengeance for the insult that is the Citadel. And when that's done, we will come for the rest of your kind.'

'Oh, do give it a rest,' said a familiar voice. Sebastian turned to see Wydrin stalking up to them. She looked as though she'd recently taken a dunk in the sea, but the heat of Relios was rapidly drying her off.

'You! Thief! See how your city burns now?' crowed Y'Gria. 'This will be nothing compared to Krete! The mages there will suffer like no one on Ede.'

'That's where you're wrong,' said Wydrin. 'Because your time is over here. Ede doesn't need your kind any more. I don't think it ever did.' She walked up to the wall and unceremoniously kicked at the bramble face, thumping her big leather boot into the bricks over and over again until the branches broke into pieces and scattered onto the dry red ground. There were a few outraged squawks from Y'Gria, but within seconds her face of branches and thorns was gone, and she had no mouth to speak with. When it was done, Wydrin carefully wiped the bottom of her boots on a clean patch of ground. She turned back to them, looking sharp, amused, and very, very angry.

'You know, I always thought she was supposed to be the nice one. That'll teach me.'

82

Ephemeral awoke to a cloud of pain and misery. Gasping and flailing against it, she turned over, curling up into a ball. There was water soaking into her clothes, and there were small stones poking into her all over, but it was nothing to the silvery web of grief that held her. She made a choked noise, trapped by it. *What is this?*

'Ephemeral?' A cool hand on her arm, a familiar voice. 'By all the spirits, you are alive.'

She opened her eyes. It was daylight again, a weak washed-out sort of light, and Terin stood over her. He had a nasty graze on one side of his face, and his long hair was tangled with leaves and sticks. They were in a sparse-wooded area, the flat ground covered in standing water. 'Where is everyone?'

Terin helped her to her feet. There were a handful of dragon-kin in the clearing with them, huddled together. She reached out to them, but the pain there was still raw. Inky was at the centre of their group, holding them together, and Ephemeral felt a tiny flicker of gratitude at that, before pulling her mind away from them. It was too much.

'You two, are you all right?' Devinia staggered towards them. The woman looked pale, her red hair plastered to her back with black mud. 'Have you seen . . .?'

Her voice trailed off, her attention caught by something Ephemeral couldn't see. Devinia strode past them and knelt by a shape lying in the water. She went very still.

It was Augusta. The old woman had taken a hard blow to the temple, and even the floodwater hadn't been able to wash away all the blood. Her eyelids flickered, and incredibly a ghost of a smile passed over her face.

'Nan? Nan, are you all right?' Devinia sounded very young. Ephemeral swayed on her feet, and she felt Terin's arm loop around her waist.

'Come on,' he said, his voice a quiet breath in her ear. 'Let's give them some time alone.'

They moved a few steps away. Ristanov the Banshee was nearby, half leaning against the trunk of a tree. She no longer looked like anything human, but her eyes were moving wetly in her head, looking around at the saturated ground as if she didn't know where she was. Perhaps she didn't.

'This is wrong,' said Ephemeral quietly. 'I do not like this. I can't . . . There is too much sorrow.' She shivered once, and looked around. There were other dead bodies here, the bodies of the pirates they had killed, but no sign of the great golden figure, or the red one that commanded it.

'Any sorrow is too much,' he said. After a little while, Devinia lowered her head and sat unmoving for a time. Terin left Ephemeral then and went to the red-headed pirate's side, speaking soft words. Together, they moved Augusta's body, finding a raised piece of ground the water hadn't reached. There, Terin spoke more words – Ephemeral couldn't hear them, watching instead the sorrow and the kindness on her husband's face – while Devinia collected rocks to cover up the body. Eventually, Devinia stood alone over Augusta's makeshift cairn, her face set and still, while Terin returned to Ephemeral's side, his head down.

'Augusta Grint was kind to me.' Ephemeral felt like the words floated from her mouth, strange and inadequate. 'She was curious, and she did not think we were monsters. Why would this happen? Why?'

Terin just shook his head. After some small time had passed, Devinia left the cairn and, splashing through the water, went over to the sorry shape that was Ristanov the Banshee. Without saying anything to her, or to either of them, she wrapped both hands around the woman's head and twisted sharply to the left. There was a brittle crack, too loud in the dripping forest, and Ristanov the Banshee, Mayor of Two-Birds, slumped lifelessly to one side. Devinia stood up, wiping her hands on her trousers. Her eyes were dry.

'We carry on to the centre,' she said. 'We go there now.'

83

'You are looking better.'

They had made a small camp away from the abandoned trading post and its collection of brambles, building a fire as the sun turned the west into a confusion of red and orange light. The city appeared to have its own flames under control, and the thick pall of smoke was gradually being blown out to sea. Frith thought it likely that the people of Raistinia would never know how close they had come to being wiped out in one terrible moment. And perhaps that was for the best.

'Do you think so?' Wydrin smirked at him, her green eyes merry, and it was so unlike the Wydrin who had turned away from him on Umbria that he felt his heart soar. 'Because I feel like every inch of the sea lined up to give me a beating.'

'You look more yourself,' he said firmly. 'And the mark on your face has changed.'

The livid red mark on Wydrin's cheek had been replaced with a silver smudge – it looked as though she had been dusted with the powder of some exotic moth's wing. Much of the time it looked to be the colour of steel, but then she would move and it glittered faintly, like starlight on the sea.

'It has?' She reached up to touch it, and looked faintly puzzled. Smiling, he pressed his own fingers lightly to the mark. It felt no different to the rest of her skin.

'It is silver now,' he said. 'What is it?'

She smiled back at him ruefully. 'A warning, or a promise, or just a way of saying I belong to them. Probably all of the above.' When he opened his mouth to ask more questions, she leaned forward and stopped him with a kiss. 'I am sorry about everything that happened before,' she said when she drew away. 'It wasn't me, not really. I mean, what Estenn did to me, it took a small part of me and made it blot everything else out. I was full of fear. Frozen with it.'

'When I thought you had died within Joah's Rivener, I also did things I regret,' said Frith. 'And I didn't have strange god magic addling my head.'

'Yes. Well. I can say now that I'm really glad you weren't stabbed to death by that bitch, because I fucking love you, Lord Aaron Frith.'

There was a polite cough, and Frith looked up to see Sebastian standing over them. He was holding three dead rabbits, and like Wydrin, he looked better than when Frith had seen him last – his face was still lined and his beard and hair were unkempt, but there was a peace in the big knight's eyes that Frith hadn't seen before, and something else, too. An alertness, a hint of steel behind his smile.

'Did you just chase those down?' asked Wydrin. She stood as she spoke and matter-of-factly hugged Sebastian tightly, caring nothing for the dead rabbits. 'That was bloody quick.'

Sebastian shrugged. 'I find I am a decent hunter these days, and I thought we might be in need of dinner. And a bit of space to talk.'

And that was how they passed the next hour. Sebastian spitted the rabbits and cooked all three until they were browned and running with fat. The knight ate one himself, tearing the meat from the bones while it was still so hot it steamed, while Wydrin and Frith shared one between them. The last would go in their pack. Sebastian spoke of his time trapped with Y'Gria, describing the gods and Oster's conflict with them. Frith sensed that there was a part of the story Sebastian wasn't mentioning, but he also knew that he would not hide something important from them. Wydrin related much of their own journey, her face twisting as she spoke of Frith's apparent death on the roofs of Lan-Hellis

512

and then she looked down at the sand as she told them of the last moments of the Red Echo.

'Any other time I could have taken Estenn down, but she'd already poisoned me, back in the artefact room. I was just too stupid to notice.'

'What happened to her?'

Wydrin shrugged. 'No idea. I didn't see her again after I jumped from the tower. We can hope that she was caught in the fires she created, but I doubt it somehow. That one has the luck of the gods on her side. At least what she has left of the Red Echo is useless now.'

'We should be vigilant then,' said Frith. 'She has a particular knack for being where you don't expect her to be.' He remembered the sword piercing his back, cold and hot at the same time. Clearing his throat, he added, 'The Red Echo did a lot of damage, but it didn't wipe out the city as she'd hoped. We have to assume she will want revenge, and that she will want to be a part of what the gods do at Krete.'

'What do you reckon to that, Seb?' Wydrin chewed at a bone, and then pointed at him with it. 'You said the other gods wanted no part of an alliance.'

Sebastian shifted where he sat. 'They are unpredictable.' He paused, then half laughed. 'And that is an understatement. Res'na stands back from it, wanting to avoid the chaos, whereas Res'ni actively courts it. She seemed to think that Y'Gria was afraid of Y'Ruen. But now that the mages have been significantly weakened? With such a devastating blow dealt here, and their leader infected with Res'ni's madness, they are as weak as they have ever been. I wouldn't be surprised if Y'Gria managed to talk them into it, for the sake of finally wiping out the mages. And we know that in our own history they did all finally come to the Citadel together, even if it was in competition with each other. Something about it feels inevitable.'

There were a few moments of silence. The sun had almost set, turning the sky a mottled purple and indigo. The first stars hung over them, and beyond the circle of their small fire Frith could feel the temperature dropping.

'So what is our plan now?' he asked into the silence. He looked at Wydrin, the silver mark on her cheek a bright patch on her pale skin, and then at Sebastian, who was smiling faintly. 'The Black Feather Three ride again?'

Wydrin grinned at them both. 'Of course. It has to be us, doesn't it? Anyone else would fuck it up. Which reminds me,' she came gracefully to her feet and stepped around the fire to where Feveroot was still tightly curled in his fox shape. 'I think we might have a new temporary member. Hey, Feveroot, how are you doing?'

The demon creature stirred, the red mark on his black fur flaring into life. 'I have had better days.'

As if Feveroot were some particularly lazy cat and not a shapeshifting demon, Wydrin leaned down and picked him up, settling him easily in her arms before sitting back down.

'Human. You smell of the sea.'

'I do at that. Now, I thought I might have seen the last of you, demon, but you took the phial and you helped us anyway.'

'I've no doubt we only survived Y'Gria's palace with . . . this creature's help.' Frith looked up at Sebastian. The knight looked unconvinced; of them all, Sebastian had the most reason not to trust a demon.

'You talked to me,' said Feveroot. He sounded uncertain, his long fox's snout pointed towards the ground. 'Before, when I was in the tree, I never needed to talk to anyone. I would listen to the birds and the other small creatures, but listening was enough. Then Joah drew me from the tree and trapped me, and I was a specimen to him. You, though, you asked questions. You listened to my answers.' The small fox shape sat up. 'That seemed . . . it seemed like something that shouldn't go unmarked.'

Wydrin nodded. 'And you are still wounded?'

'I ebb,' said Feveroot, as if this explained everything.

'You need blood, right?' To Frith's surprise, Wydrin reached down for the dagger at her waist.

'Wydrin, what are you doing?' Sebastian's tone was sharp. There was a flash of that steel behind his eyes again.

'What I am doing is helping a friend,' she said firmly. She pressed the edge of her blade to the back of her hand. Frostling was as sharp as ever, and a thick beaded necklace of blood grew on her skin in an instant. She held it out to Feveroot, who hesitated. 'Does it matter if it's freely given?'

'No, it doesn't. And thank you.' The shining black shape of Feveroot grew fluid again and flowed over Wydrin's hand and arm. There was a second where the red patch on the demon's back grew brighter, rivalling the glow of their small fire, and then he drew back. Wydrin flexed her fingers.

'That tickled.'

'And I am replenished. Thank you.'

'Where is the glass phial now?' asked Frith. 'Wydrin gave it back to you?'

'It is still here.' Feveroot's form became liquid once more, parting to reveal the crystal bottle. It was there, and then in moments covered over again. 'I'm not sure it's what you intended, Wydrin of Crosshaven, but I have my freedom now. Joah will not be happy.'

'Oh what a shame,' Wydrin waved an idle hand. 'I can't tell you how much I don't care about Joah's feelings on the matter. So will you come with us, Feveroot? We're still rather stuck for transport.'

'Eventually, I will return to the tree.' The demon paused. 'Or a tree, somewhere. Joah burned my old one. But for now I will travel with you.'

'It will take Y'Gria some time to gather the gods together, and then more to convince them to follow her,' said Sebastian. 'That might give us a head start.'

'That is our plan, then?' asked Frith. 'We are going to Krete?'

'Where better?' Wydrin leaned back from the fire. She was smiling but her eyes were cold. 'We're going back to the Citadel to kill us some gods.'

84

As they approached the eastern gate of Krete, Frith found his stomach churning with a mixture of relief and dismay. The city was still standing, the half-built Citadel still perched at its highest point, and the gates were as busy as ever. Men and women and children came and went with carts and horses and caravans, and the walls barely contained the miasma of smoke and noise that was the aura of a busy city. The gods had not yet attacked and they still had time. Time to do what, though, he wasn't sure.

'So we get in there, go straight to the palace, and warn the mages,' said Wydrin. 'I doubt they'll be glad to see us, but if they've some warning they can put up extra barriers or something.' She shrugged. Feveroot, who, after flying them across Relios in the form of an eagle, was now perched on her shoulder in the shape of a small monkey with red eyes.

'Or it could give them a chance to get people out of the city,' said Sebastian. He narrowed his eyes at the surrounding desert. 'Although where they would go to, I don't know. Perhaps it would be better to be behind the walls at least, than trying to hide behind sand dunes.'

They passed through the busy gate. There were mages stationed there, Frith saw, their long robes marking them out from the other men and women. They were watching the beacons rather than the sky, he noticed.

'If all the gods appeared together at once, they would be

516

overwhelmed,' he said in a low voice. 'For too long they have counted on the reluctance of the gods to work as a single unit.'

No sooner were they through the gate and into the main body of the city than a figure in a hooded robe approached them; it kept its head down and its face in shadow, but the voice was familiar.

'There you are! It is good to see you alive, goodness knows we feared the worst from the reports that have been coming in. This is Sebastian, is it, your friend? Hello! Yes, well, he certainly seems . . . large enough. Will you come with me? Xinian's face will be a picture, she assumed we'd seen the last of you, and certainly that I'd never see you coming back into Krete.'

'Selsye?' Wydrin grinned. 'Is that you?'

The figure dipped her head and briefly pulled the hood back. Selsye winked at them, before letting the fabric fall back into place. 'Come on. Follow me.'

Selsye led them down a side street, and then down several winding alleys. Her caution made Frith uneasy, and he found himself glancing up at the windows for who might be marking their progress, and watching the people they passed closely. Eventually, they came to what looked like an abandoned building – a narrow place built of red brick, squeezed between a tannery and an especially seedy-looking tavern. It was still early, and the tavern windows were dark; it was clearly a place that opened late and stayed open through the early hours. Selsye approached the partially boarded-up door of the red brick building, and up close it was possible to see that the nails had been carefully removed from the planks on one side. She knocked four times, and then they slipped inside, closing the door quietly behind them. Inside was a low-ceilinged dusty room that smelled strongly of damp clothes, with a single oil lamp burning low in the corner. Xinian marched out of the shadows towards them, and for one disorientating moment Frith remembered Joah's bunk room; how she had formed out of the darkness in pieces of grey shadow.

'You made it to Krete!' Immediately she turned to Selsye. 'Were you followed here?'

Even in the poor light Frith saw Selsye frown. 'No, my love, but the news isn't good. Reis has half the mages here looking for us, and the walls are barely manned at all.'

'We have bad news too, I'm afraid,' started Wydrin, but Xinian cut her off with a gesture.

'About Raistinia? We know. Or at least, we guessed. I have been doing my best to monitor the messages coming in from the city.' She took a pained breath. 'At least there are still some people left there to send messages, I suppose. The Red Echo was deployed then, I take it?'

'I am afraid so,' said Sebastian. 'But Wydrin managed to stop it at least partially. A good portion of the city was burned, and I imagine a huge number of people perished.' He paused. 'I am sorry. But it wasn't the complete genocide Estenn intended.'

'And the fanatic herself?'

'We don't know what happened to her, Xinian, but listen,' said Wydrin. 'The gods, they're coming here. Y'Gria promised as much. You have to get the mages ready, or you have to evacuate.'

Xinian snorted. She walked away from them towards a crate, from which she pulled a dark, stoppered bottle. 'That will not be possible. I have no authority here. Why do you imagine I am hiding in this hovel and not in my apartments at the Arkanium?'

'What happened?' asked Frith. 'What happened at Lan-Hellis after we left?'

'When it was realised that Wydrin had escaped, Xinian was inevitably connected to it and declared a heretic,' said Selsye. As she spoke, Xinian produced a number of tin cups and filled them from the bottle. The warm smell of brandy filled the room. 'Reis accused her of, well, a lot of ridiculous things, and the orders are to kill her on sight. I managed to leave Whittenfarne on the pretence of bringing the rest of the artefact collection here to be stored in the Citadel, and we met up in secret. Shortly after I got to Krete, though, Reis disbanded the Citadel project.' Selsye shook her head, brows furrowed. 'Truly, he has lost his wits. It was our best chance of ending this war, and now he has his soldiers taking it to pieces! Xinian and I have been hiding out here, learning what we can. None of it is good.'

'And it's even worse than that,' said Wydrin. 'Y'Gria knows what you were planning with the Citadel, so they all do by now. There's no way they'd fall for that trick. The Citadel is useless.'

They fell silent for a moment. Xinian passed out glasses of brandy, and Frith drank his down gratefully. He had the beginnings of an idea, but the scope of it frightened him. The burning of the alcohol in his stomach was a good distraction.

'Then we are defenceless?' Selsye's voice was very quiet. 'If the gods band together, they can wipe us from the map in moments. And even if they don't, we are doomed to endless war.'

'Do you have any food here?' asked Wydrin.

'Perhaps it's not completely hopeless,' said Frith. They all turned to look at him, and he wondered at the madness he was leading them to now. 'If we cannot bring them to the Citadel, perhaps we can bring the Citadel to them. Where is Joah now?' He swallowed down the surge of bitterness in the back of his throat. 'I will need his assistance.'

There was food, much to Wydrin's relief. From her pack Selsye produced a block of hard cheese, a loaf of black bread, and a greasy roll of ham tied with white string. She passed this to them and left, promising to retrieve Joah; he was there in Krete with them, finding out what he could. Not as well known as Xinian or Selsye, it was easier for him to move without drawing attention. The ham was cut down to the bone by the time Selsye returned with Joah in her wake, and with the food and brandy in her stomach, Wydrin felt better than she had in days. She stood up as they came into the room, taking note of the grave look that passed over Sebastian's face – no doubt he was remembering the thing whose life she had finally ended on the cobbled streets of Skaldshollow. Joah, his young brow unlined, looked very little like that creature.

'I am glad to see you all live,' said Joah in a low voice. 'When we guessed the news from Raistinia, I feared the worst.'

At the sound of his voice, Feveroot uncurled himself from his spot on the floor, red eyes glowing in the poor light.

'And you still have the demon! I have a great deal more I would like to—'

'Feveroot's his own creature now, kid, and you won't be getting him back. Now you need to shut your trap and listen to Lord Frith here, because he has an idea that you might be able to help with, and we don't have much time.'

Joah opened his mouth to argue and Wydrin shifted her posture slightly, one hand resting on her dagger. After a moment the young mage moved to sit on the crates with the others. Frith nodded at her, looking simultaneously amused and slightly pained. He hadn't spoken of his idea while they had been eating; he'd said he needed to think some more.

'I am going to speak now,' he said quietly. 'Some of what I say will sound unlikely. But I ask you to let me tell it all, and to trust that I know what I'm talking about.' He took a slow breath, his narrow face sharp as a dagger in the light from the oil lamp. 'I was once familiar with a device that could tear the Edenier from inside a living being.'

Immediately, Xinian, Selsye and Joah all began to speak at once.

'Enough, mages!' Wydrin gave them all a severe look. 'Do you need to be reminded how little time we have before Y'Gria and associated arseholes turn up to burn your city to the ground?'

Reluctantly, they grew quiet, and Frith continued.

'This device targeted the Edenier inside a person and tore it away from them, storing it in a chamber for later use. Now, if I am not mistaken, the gods are beings largely composed of pure Edenier.' He shifted on the crate, his eyes downcast. Wydrin felt a pang of sympathy – she knew what it had cost him to use the demon-tainted magic. 'I propose that rather than luring them inside the Citadel, where the wards will trap them, we make the entire city of Krete a trap.'

'I have never heard of such magic,' said Joah. Wydrin shot him a look, and he held up a hand. 'Please, wait. It sounds outlandish, yes, but it reverberates with something I have wondered about for some years. The fact that Edenier is a measurable force within us. Something that could, potentially, be extracted. Do you believe you could build such a device here, Lord Frith?'

'With the magical artefacts already stored in the Citadel, yes,' said Frith. 'It would need a combination of Edeian crafting, and Edenier. And . . . some other techniques that are difficult to describe. I will require your assistance, Joah.'

The young mage raised his eyebrows at that. 'What makes you think that I would be able to help?'

Frith looked away for a moment. When he met Joah's eyes again his face was carefully blank. 'I think there's a good chance you will have a natural affinity for this.'

'When you say turn Krete into a giant trap, what do you mean?' asked Sebastian. 'There are a lot of people in this city, Frith.'

'I know. First, we need to reverse the barriers on the walls keeping the gods out.'

'Are you out of your mind?' cried Selsye. Next to her, Xinian's face was grim.

'No. You must listen. We get them all in here, and once they are within the city walls, I will activate the Edenier trap within the Citadel, and as it once tore the Edenier from living beings, it will tear them from the skies. They will be powerless against it. They will be dragged into the chambers designed to hold them, and contained there by Joah's web of spells. It is important that they cannot leave again when they realise what is happening. That is why we must reverse the barriers, to keep them in. Do you see?'

'If you say you can make such a thing, then it is worth taking the chance.' Xinian looked up at them all. 'We cannot go on fighting this war for ever. It will end us all. But if your trap targets Edenier, then will it not drag all the mages into the Citadel as well? Or at least make us powerless? You would end the gods, but you would end us as well.'

Frith sat back. 'Yes, that is a problem.'

'A problem?' cried Selsye. 'It's a bit more than a problem, it's a disaster!'

'But there may be a way around it!' Joah's voice was tight with excitement. 'We can paint a target on their backs. Lord Frith, do you remember what I was working on when we first met at Lan-Hellis?'

Frith frowned. 'A way of applying words directly to skin. You

521

were developing a method of sinking a word directly into the flesh so that mages would not need to rely on silk strips or tattoos.'

'Could we not use that?' asked Joah. 'The right words, something that marks the gods as the true targets of your device. Once marked, your Edenier trap will work only on them, leaving the mages alone.'

Frith sat up. 'Yes. It's possible. With the right words. But we would have to mark the gods directly, which would mean getting close enough to apply your skins.'

'Leave that to me and Feveroot,' said Wydrin. 'I've been up close and personal with a god before. Perhaps not as close and personal as Sebastian, but still.' She grinned at the look Sebastian gave her.

'This is madness,' said Selsye. She took another gulp of brandy. 'But it seems that madness is our only path now. Ye gods.'

'Reversing the barriers on the city walls,' said Frith. 'Can you do it?'

'We will have to avoid being seen,' said Xinian. 'But it is certainly something we can do.'

'Then it is our job to get Frith and Joah inside the Citadel,' said Sebastian. He smiled faintly. 'Just like old times.'

'It won't be easy,' said Selsye. 'The Citadel is riddled with Reis's people now.' She scowled. 'They've taken down the bloody roof.'

'Don't worry,' said Wydrin. She drank down the last of the brandy and grinned around at them all. Despite everything, they had a plan. It was a ridiculous plan and they would likely all be killed, but they weren't going down without a fight. 'If it was easy, it wouldn't be any fun, would it?'

85

It was dusk by the time Xinian and Selsye made their way to the nearest portion of the city wall. To reverse the barriers they would need to visit the ward stations to the north, east, west and south. The Eastern station was the closest. Xinian pulled her hood closer, keeping her eyes down while Selsye watched the mages that passed them.

'Any thoughts on how we're going to do this?' asked Selsye.

'I could go in there and shout at them,' said Xinian. 'Put the fear of the gods into them, make out that Reis has sent new orders.' She paused. 'I'm good at shouting.'

'Xin, we have to at least try to be discreet. If they realise at any point that the barriers have been meddled with, they'll just change them straight back.' They walked hurriedly down narrow streets. To Xinian's eyes everyone looked outrageously unconcerned, as though this were just a normal day, and for a brief moment she felt a searing anger towards them – why should she and her lover be putting themselves at risk? But this was exactly what they were fighting for – the right to live without the threat of the gods hanging over them. 'Perhaps we're thinking about this the wrong way,' said Selsye. 'The barriers are generated from the beacons, right? So we could reverse the magic on the beacons. Or, we could change the walls themselves. Yes, I think that would work.'

'What are you talking about?' The walls loomed in front of them now. Xinian could see the pale blue lights of the beacons, quiet for the moment, and the shadowed shapes of the guards patrolling the top of the wall. The sky beyond them was a brilliant indigo.

'The walls, Xinian. We could craft the walls themselves.' Selsye turned towards her, and she caught a glance of her smile, half hidden by the hood. 'The mage word for "Reverse" should do it. The magic that thrums through the walls and creates the barriers would be reversed. Do you see?'

'Right, fine, if you say so. And how do we do that?'

'Let's go out the gate. I'll burn the word into the wall outside the ward station.'

'There are people on the walls, Selsye. They'll see you.'

'That's where you come in, my love.'

Minutes later, Xinian stood in the deepest shadows at the edge of the gate. There was a small market here, looking to sell food and other wares to travellers arriving at Krete. Such places tended to stay open late, and bright white lamps were being lit over the collection of stalls and crates. Amongst them was a cart piled high with watermelons, and next to it a wooden butt full of drinking water – one of the most popular purchases after a trip across the Creos desert was a skin of water for a parched throat.

She glanced behind her to see the slim form of Selsye moving out into the desert night.

'I am Commander Battleborn,' muttered Xinian. 'I commanded armies, slaughtered demons.' She sighed abruptly, and lifted her hand, turning it towards the water butt. A brief gesture, and the wooden barrel burst open, spraying water everywhere. There was a chorus of cries as those nearby were soaked, and a bellow of outrage from the man selling the water. Another gesture, and the growing pool of water frosted over in seconds, becoming a wide patch of ice.

'I used to have a dignified job.'

Xinian formed another word in her mind, and the cart holding the watermelons tipped violently to one side, spilling its load onto the icy ground. Within seconds the small market was full of skidding, bouncing fruit, being chased by skidding, shouting men and women. Those coming in and out of the gate stopped to watch, and a general murmur of laughter grew in the small space. Xinian stepped partially out of the shadows and looked up towards the wall – the guards were leaning out over the battlement, watching the action avidly. A few minutes later, when the last of the melons were still being chased across the street, Selsye reappeared at the gate, taking Xinian's hand in the dark.

'There are vines growing on the walls out there, so I burned the word underneath them. Fiddly, but less noticeable.' Selsye paused, taking in the scene in front of them. 'A good distraction, my love.' She stood on her toes and stole a quick kiss. 'Only three more to go!'

'Oh, great,' said Xinian.

'I am here to remove some of the magical artefacts. Archmage Reis has requested them.'

They stood on the outer steps of the Citadel, just beyond the black iron gate. As night approached the mages gradually dismantling the stronghold had left, leaving behind a handful of guards. Wydrin had suggested killing those that were left, as she had the first time they had come here, but Joah had stiffened slightly and claimed that as he was, as yet, not implicated in Xinian's treason, he would be able to talk their way in. Sebastian thought it had a reasonable chance of succeeding – there was something inherently trustworthy in the young mage's face – but he stood ready anyway, a borrowed longsword across his back. If they were refused entry, it would be the work of moments to cut them down. He did not relish the thought, but if it was necessary, he would do it. Distantly, he was aware of the bright silvery minds of several small lizards crawling through the newly constructed gardens nearby. He touched their minds lightly, and he felt their curious regard. It was a comfort.

'Why are there so many of you?' asked the guard. 'And why do you come at night? We weren't told about this.' He was peering past Joah with a vaguely perplexed expression. Before they'd left Xinian's hideout, Selsye had bound their arms with the silk strips the mages traditionally wore in an attempt to disguise them, but it had to be said, Wydrin still made the world's least likely mage. Cover her in as much silk as you wanted, the eyes were still drawn to the well-used dagger at her hip, and Sebastian had yet to see a mage wearing so much boiled leather.

'The artefacts have particular properties at night,' said Joah dismissively. 'And there are a lot of them to carry. Will you really keep me waiting out here all night? I have important work to do!'

The guard looked as though he might argue further, but in the end he stood to one side and they passed into the grounds of the Citadel proper. Sebastian shivered despite the warmth of the night. In his memories this place had been a broken, dusty ruin, the statues and carvings worn with the passing of a thousand years, but in this time it was an imposing structure, obviously crafted to reflect the grandeur of the mages. The statues showed mages doing battle with monsters, alongside scenes from mythology that he vaguely recognised. They had intended this to be not only the prison of the gods, but also a monument to their victory. All would look upon the Citadel and see the mastery of the mages wrought in stone. Sebastian smiled bitterly. It had not worked out that way, in the end.

Joah led them in towards a pile of red stone, near black in the growing darkness, and beyond it to a set of steps leading down into a confusion of shadows and rock. The large drum-shaped building that they had once entered, a thousand years in the future, had been partially built and then torn down again, leaving the top level of the Citadel open to the air.

'The men and women taking it apart must question Reis's orders,' said Frith quietly as they headed down the steps. 'They must see that it is madness to disable your only weapon.'

'You underestimate the influence of Reis,' said Joah. He lifted his hand and summoned a small ball of light as they headed down into the dark. The workers had extinguished the lamps as they left – Frith lit them again as they passed. 'He is our greatest mage. There are factions working against him who have been against the Citadel since the start. His sudden change of heart has them confused and on the back foot. At the moment, no one speaks against him because they are not sure what his plan is. Ah, here we are – this is where the artefacts are stored.'

Joah had led them into a low hall filled with crates and boxes and other half-identified shapes in the poor light. Frith looked around.

'And how far is the prison chamber from here?'

'Down several more sets of steps. It sits underneath the rest of the Citadel.'

Frith pulled a hand through his hair. He looked distracted. 'We will gather what is needed from here, and then build the device in the final chamber. You will explain the artefacts to me, and then you will need to start making the skins. Wydrin, Sebastian, now we are in here, you will have to keep everyone else out. Can you do that?'

Sebastian glanced at Wydrin, who shrugged extravagantly.

'I imagine we can keep them off your backs, my lord,' said Sebastian. 'It seems we're back to being your muscle. How long will you need?'

'As long as you can give me,' he said. 'We will be working through the night.'

'All hands on deck,' said Wydrin. She stepped up to Frith and kissed him firmly on the mouth. The young lord pulled her close, almost seeming to gain strength from her. Sebastian had to smile at Joah's startled look. Wydrin let go of Frith with obvious regret, and then punched Sebastian lightly on the arm. 'Come on, Seb, let's go and show off our muscles to any guards that might still be lurking.'

'What do you think?'

Sebastian peered around the column to look at the two guards stationed on the far side of the gardens. They were standing with their heads together, the posture of men who aren't entirely sure what's going on, and looking to hash it out between them. The dark desert night hung above them like a shroud, while the lights of Krete burned all the brighter. He turned back to Wydrin and sighed.

'I think that they are already questioning whether we should be here, and it will be a short while before they send a message to their superiors. You and Frith are hardly inconspicuous. Reis will know whom they describe.'

Wydrin tapped the dagger at her waist. 'So will we be cutting a few throats under the moonlight?'

Sebastian raised an eyebrow at her, and she laughed. 'Yeah, I don't really have the appetite for killing idiots. These are just people caught up in a war between bastards with power. It's funny how when gods are involved, it's the normal people who end up dead, whether that's on a battlefield somewhere, or just minding their own business doing their jobs.' She thought of the heat she'd felt on her face before she'd dropped into the sea at Raistinia; the dust of a thousand dead bodies on the streets of Temerayne. 'And we'll never be free of them either, because the Eye of Euriale apparently keeps vomiting them up. Your friend might not be the only lost god wandering Ede, now that the Spinner is gone.' She glanced up at Sebastian. 'What do you think happened to Oster?'

'He's alive,' said Sebastian softly. His eyes were still on the guards. 'I can feel that. Y'Gria promised him a family and a history, but when he disagreed with her, she locked him away. He feels lost without that connection, without the knowledge the Spinner was supposed to give to him. I think he's probably having to make some difficult decisions at the moment.' Wydrin put her hand on his arm, and he looked down at her, the hint of a smile at the corner of his mouth. 'I've come to realise that I can't be responsible for everyone.'

'You can still be responsible for me, if you like,' she said, squeezing his arm. 'You know, when we've been in the tavern all night and I can't see straight.'

He snorted. 'What are we going to do about these poor souls, then?'

'There are some big rooms back there, with some sturdy doors. I vote that we give them all an early night and stash them away as best we can.' She paused. 'If the gods come before we're ready, inside the Citadel might be the safest place to be.'

Sebastian nodded. 'We'll circuit the grounds while Frith works. If anyone else turns up, they can join their brother guards.'

'Right then.' Not entirely sure why she needed to do it, Wydrin slipped her arm through Sebastian's and gave him a slightly awkward sideways hug. 'I'm glad you're back with us, Seb. Stay safe, brother.'

'Don't I always, little sister?' He kissed the top of her head, and she slipped away into the darkness.

86

Frith paced the room, trying to take in everything at once. He could feel Joah's eyes on him, watching and waiting to hear what to do next. It was strange to be here with a Joah that was so young, so unsure. It was almost possible to feel sorry for him. They had lit all the torches in the room, and warm orange light flickered and danced over a multitude of strange objects.

'You know what all these things are, yes?'

'Yes, of course.' Joah stepped forward. 'I helped Mistress Selsye to catalogue everything we should need.'

'Tell me what these things are.' Frith gestured to a low table scattered with pieces of what looked like twisted metal.

'The remnants of the Armour of Ogren,' said Joah at once. 'Crafted hundreds of years ago and said to be indestructible, it finally failed its wearer during the volcano eruption of—'

'And this?' Frith pointed at a large yellow clay bowl, painted with swirling blue patterns. In the very centre was a red stain.

'The blood chalice of the Zevrast,' said Joah evenly. 'It is said that any potion crafted in the chalice doubles its potency.'

'What of these?' Frith pulled back the blanket covering a crate. Inside it was a bundle of brightly shining knives.

'Morrigan's Regret,' said Joah. 'A cut with one of these blades grants a vision of the future, but the wound never stops bleeding.'

'Yes, that's right,' said Frith faintly. His mind was spinning with knowledge. Everything in this room was familiar, because he had once shared Joah's memories so deeply – and as Joah named them, their purpose and potential came back to him. The version of the Rivener he wished to build grew in his mind by the moment, called into existence as each magical artefact revealed itself. There was Joah's knowledge, yes, but there was also the warring magics inside him – the echo of Edenier, the shadow of the Eye of Euriale. It was similar to how he had felt on the banks of the muddy pond, and his desperation to find Wydrin had guided his hands. There was more than memories at work here – he could see how it would all fit together, and it was dizzying. He took a slow breath and turned back to Joah. The young mage was watching him with wide eyes.

'I know what we need to do. Come, gather up what I tell you to and show me where the prison chamber is. We don't have much time.'

When they had grabbed what they could, Joah led him to a door at the far side of the chamber where a set of stairs curled down into the dark. On his way out of the artefact room, Frith paused, his eyes caught by the imposing form of Tia'mast's skull, or at least the remaining piece of it; a decaying remnant of something that once stood outside time, but no longer. Looking at it as it glowed an eerie green under the torches, Frith felt the germ of an idea blossom at the back of his mind, and then Joah was next to him, half hidden under the pile of boxes in his arms.

'This way, my lord.'

Frith shook his head as if to clear it, and followed Joah down into the depths of the Citadel. A deep chill settled over his flesh, and inevitably he was reminded of his first visit here – the way the corridors and steps had seemed to go on for ever, the strange sense that something was watching them in the dark. And the soreness of his shattered leg, like shards of glass working their way into his flesh. At least, he reflected, he no longer suffered from the effects of Fane's torture. He pushed that thought away, and Joah abruptly stepped to one side and put the boxes he was carrying down on the ground.

'This is the entrance to the prison chamber, Lord Frith. Once the Citadel is complete and the gods are caught, it is my intention that we make the journey down here much more arduous, but for now it is a relatively short walk.'

The young mage produced a ball of pale blue light from the ends of his fingers, and the chamber blossomed into life. Frith's breath caught in his throat.

The chamber was like being inside the belly of some strange creature. It was rounded and carved directly out of the dark red rock native to Creos. There were ridges in the walls, adding to the impression that they were surrounded by the bones of a living thing, and the surface was carved all over with mages' words – thousands upon thousands of them. Here and there were thick leather-bound volumes, no doubt also filled with more mage words, and these were joined together with a thick black iron chain that travelled the circumference of the room. There were tall clay jars too, as big as men, and these caused a shiver of recognition down Frith's spine – he remembered the room where Sebastian had been stabbed by Gallo, and knew that the tops of the jars would be covered with a thick blue wax. The floor of the chamber was rent by a long crack that stretched from one end to the other, about three feet across at its widest point. Joah's light didn't even begin to touch the darkness lurking beneath them.

'So many words . . .' breathed Frith.

'Yes, a great web of spells,' agreed Joah. 'We have been working on it for some years.' He gestured to the walls with their confusion of interlocking mage words. 'In recent years I had a breakthrough in the application of using one word on top of another, and from there it was possible to construct what we needed.' He pointed to the entrance of the chamber. 'In our original plan, the gods would be led down here, where all the artefacts would finally be stored – but once in here the spells act like a sort of funnel. They would push the gods away from the walls and ceiling, and into the prison chamber.' He pointed to the long slash of darkness in the floor. 'Down there is where they would be held for ever. We then planned to build on top of it, floors and floors containing more spells, to keep them there.'

They both stood in silence for a moment. Frith found that part of him wanted to go to the rent in the floor and look down into it. He scowled.

'Then as they will no longer willingly come to this room, it is our job to build a device that will pluck them from the skies over Krete and force them down here. Help me spread out what we have gathered so far, and I will get to work. Do you have what you need to make our targets?'

'I do.' With his hair hanging to either side of his face, Joah's face was hidden in shadow. All at once it was too easy to remember the monster he had become at the end of his life – the strange, stretched shape of his skull, the long fingers of sharpened bone. Frith looked away, busying himself with laying out the artefacts he had chosen. It was already there in his mind, a shape waiting to become real. There were demon sigils on that shape, and he recoiled from the thought of using them again, but there was nothing else for it – the knowledge of the demon Bezcavar was built into the very fabric of the Rivener, and it was impossible to extract it.

'Can I ask you a question?'

Frith looked up to see Joah staring at him.

'If you are quick.'

'You do not seem to like me very much. May I ask why that is?'

Frith turned back to the artefacts. 'I am not the easiest person to get on with. Ask anyone.'

'Yet you seem very friendly with the mercenaries.'

Frith looked up in surprise at the tone in Joah's voice. The young mage had his arms crossed over his chest and suddenly looked very much like a petulant teenager. For a moment Frith wasn't sure he could trust himself not to laugh.

'Wydrin is . . . Wydrin is the woman I love.'

'She is unbound,' said Joah, slightly too quickly. 'There is nothing magical about her at all.'

'You are very wrong there.'

'You have an extraordinary talent, Lord Frith,' continued Joah, almost tripping over his words, 'a type of magic never seen before, and you waste your time with the unbound, on a woman who would likely never bear you mage children. You have a duty to your people, to focus—'

Frith stood, feeling anger crackle through him like electricity. His fists bunched at his sides, he rounded on Joah. 'You dare to speak to me of family? Of duty?' There was no time for this, but there was equally no stepping back from this sudden quickening of rage. 'You know nothing of what I have suffered in the name of such things. And you ask me why I don't seem to like you much?' He laughed suddenly. 'Because you see the unbound as empty, hollow, when in truth any one of them is worth a thousand of you.' He bit off the rest of his words. 'Now, I suggest you get to work, or you *will* see your precious mages destroyed by the gods.'

Joah had taken a step backwards at the force of Frith's anger, and now he nodded once, a blank sort of acceptance on his face. He moved back to the bag of tools and materials he'd brought with him, and Frith turned away, wondering how he had ever, even briefly, felt sorry for the mage.

87

Oster pressed his fingers against the silver cuff in his hand. It had shattered into pieces when he'd broken free from Y'Gria's make-shift prison, but he had kept hold of this piece. It was a reminder of what she had done.

The palace was a wreck now, a sprawling mess of stone and earth across the hard desert dirt, but they lingered there. Y'Gria stalked through her ruined gardens with her green hair a dirty tangle down her back. He was angry with her still, but he also felt a rage coming off her like a fever, and instinctively he stayed out of her way. His human friends had tainted her expected glory at Raistinia, and worse than that, destroyed the place she inhab-ited. Initially, she had brushed it off – she was a god, she could build something new within seconds, it wouldn't even be an effort – but he had seen her running her hands over the broken stones, the uprooted trees looking raw and exposed under the relentless sun. Instead of building a new palace, she had summoned her siblings, and now they were here. Or at least, mostly here.

Res'ni padded across the exposed black dirt, her bare feet like the bellies of fish, while her twin Res'na sat on the rubble that had once been a towering archway. They both watched Y'Gria warily, as if she were a wounded animal that might bite them if they got too close. And, much to Oster's surprise, there was an envoy from Y'Ruen: one of her so-called daughters. She stood aside from the others, scaled arms at her sides, her leathery bat wings folded against her back. There was a sense of great stillness from her, and her yellow eyes were vacant.

'So you are willing to listen to me now, are you?' said Y'Gria. Her mouth was stretched into what Oster supposed some people might generously label a smile. 'You have seen what I wrought upon Raistinia and suddenly you respond to my summons.'

'It's a nice mess you made, I'll give you that,' said Res'ni. She bent and picked up a fistful of dirt, squeezing it between her fingers. 'Although it looks like you made an even bigger mess of your palace.'

Before Y'Gria could respond Res'na spoke smoothly over them both. 'The people of Raistinia are already rebuilding. They move to re-establish their order. I question whether what you have done will make any difference in the long run.'

'Then I question your understanding of humans, brother!' cried Y'Gria. 'Raistinia was where they raised their families, where they spawned their little mage creatures. I halved their population at a stroke, and they will all feel it. Humans greatly prize their spawn, and this will have weakened them. Tell them, Oster.'

Oster stared at her until she looked away.

'Oh pay no attention to him, he's sulking because his human pet abandoned him. Y'Ruen, what say you?'

The dragon's daughter shivered, and then opened her fang-filled mouth. A voice that was not her own issued from her throat – it was fire and ashes and the end of all things.

'*It was a good fire you made, little sister*,' said Y'Ruen. '*Not as fine as my own, of course.*'

Oster found himself staring at the dragon's daughter. He had yet to lay eyes on Y'Ruen, but he could almost feel the shape of her through her voice, a lethal silver shadow.

'Then you will agree? The mages are as weak as they have ever been, and we are at our strongest. If we band together now, with new blood on our side, if we work together as a family, we can finally destroy them. Brothers, sisters, come with me to Krete and let us show them their deaths. They dared to plan to trap us within their city. Do they not deserve to be wiped from the face of Ede for that alone?'

For a few moments there was silence amongst the group. Oster looked down at the silver cuff in his fingers, thinking about Sebastian. He could almost hear his voice, and he could well imagine what he would say.

'If we come together now, we come together as equals,' said Res'ni. 'Mother of the garden and growing things, you are not *our* mother. We stand side by side in this fight, with no leader.'

There was a murmur of what sounded like laughter from the dragon's daughter, but Y'Gria ignored it. 'Of course,' she said, bowing her head. 'I ask only to fight alongside you, sister-wolf.'

'I suppose there is a time for an ending,' said Res'na. He stood up from his perch on the broken archway. 'This could well be it.'

'Then you will all join me?' Y'Gria's golden skin shimmered. Her eyes were bright. 'You will come to Krete?'

'*I will be with you*,' said Y'Ruen, her voice rolling flat against the broken stones. '*I will be with you at the end, little sister.*'

At first it had been easy.

Joah worked on the far side of the cavernous room, imprinting on the diaphanous skins the combination of mage words they had agreed on – the same combination of words would be marbled throughout Frith's version of the Rivener, so that the two would be inextricably linked. The young mage worked quietly and swiftly, all his attention now focussed on the task at hand, and Frith found it easy enough to ignore him while he sketched out his complex designs on the floor of the cavern with a piece of chalk Selsye had provided from one of her many pockets. Eventually, however, he came to a place where he could advance no further – without the Edenier within him, he could not weld the pieces into the shapes he needed, and could not etch upon them the necessary mage words. He briefly considered trying to use Selsye's staff for the task, but although he suspected it wouldn't be impossible, the staff was really a blunt instrument, and this required the most delicate use of the Edenier – layering word upon word, creating a web of spells. The Edeian crafting that came naturally to him now only carried him so far.

Reluctantly, he stood up and crossed to where Joah was crouched.

In the light of their many lamps and torches the young mage was holding up a piece of transparent material so thin that it barely seemed to be there at all. It was pale yellow in colour, and a pair of mage words was inked delicately over the surface, like some sort of elaborate birthmark. Sensing Frith behind him, he turned round.

'What do you think?' He held the skin up higher. 'I think we may be there.'

Frith peered closely at the patterns, and nodded. It was right, he could feel it – the words seemed to sing with potential magic. 'Are you sure they will work on the gods? That they will stay in place?'

Joah shrugged. Consumed by the work, he seemed to have forgotten their earlier differences. Frith suppressed a shiver at the memory of a man whose moods went from amiable to murderous in a second. 'I can't say for sure, obviously,' he said, oblivious to Frith's discomfort. 'Mages don't generally get to test their spells on gods. But the material is made to bond with anything, and I think the gods themselves will be too distracted with trying to destroy this city to notice a tiny mark like this.'

'What's to stop them bonding to someone before we get them where they need to be?'

'Ah, that's the really clever bit.' Joah turned the skin around – on the other side was a very pale shape, a word he almost recognised. 'It says "Y'Gria", in their language,' said Joah, guessing his question. 'I have tailored each skin for them, so they don't end up in the wrong place. It will still be a very delicate process but . . .' He trailed off, and then shrugged. 'You trust the mercenary woman to do this.' It wasn't quite a question.

'I trust her with my life. Then you are nearly finished?'

'Indeed.' He placed the skin back on top of a thin slab of Edeian-enriched rock. 'You need me for something?'

'I do. I have gone as far as I can on my own. I will need you to assist me.'

Frith led him back to his portion of the floor, and falteringly began to explain his elaborate sketches. Joah listened attentively, and gradually his eyes grew bright with excitement. When Frith finished and began to gather together the artefacts they would be bastardising for parts, Joah shook his head wonderingly.

'But this is incredible,' he breathed. He was staring at the plans with a bright hunger that Frith remembered all too well. 'The complexity of it, the ambition. You have no Edenier of your own, and yet you have brought all this together in your mind.' Joah looked up at him, his face filled with frank admiration. 'You must be the greatest crafter of our age. Of any age.'

Frith found himself briefly unable to speak. How much of this was plundered from the memories future Joah had shared with him, and how much was formed of his own instincts and the shimmering half-knowledge of the time magic? The Rivener was not as it had been, that was for certain. Rather than powered by the Heart-Stone it was maintained by a grid of smaller Edeian sources – the gem from an enchanted necklace, the steel of the blades of Morrigan's Regret – and it was infinitely more sophisticated than Joah's original. Instead of simply tearing away the Edenier from victims that passed through its influence, this device would fling out a magical net and pluck from the air those it sought and pull them back into this chamber. He could feel how it would all fit together, web upon web of spells and influences. There was no question that it would work, not really – he could *feel* the rightness of it, and whereas part of him wanted to pretend that it was all Joah, he also knew that wasn't the truth. The device was as much him as the rogue mage. Briefly, he wondered if the time magic was simply allowing him to glimpse the future of the device and from there build it backwards, but the very idea made him dizzy.

'Lord Frith, are you quite well?'

Frith closed his eyes tightly and opened them again. 'Yes. Do you understand everything I've told you?'

'I do. It has its own beautiful logic, like a thing that was just waiting to exist.'

'Good. Then let us get to work.'

Joah gestured, and a piece of broken armour floated gently into the air. It started to turn ruby-red, and twist into a new shape. Frith watched it carefully, already knowing where it would fit within the device. The trap would work; the only question now was whether they could make it in time.

88

The dragon-kin had grown so large that they could no longer travel close to their small group. They thundered through the forest all around them, and Ephemeral would catch glimpses of their leathery hides through the trees, still heading north to the centre of the island. However, when Ephemeral opened her mind fully to them, she felt their curiosity turning outwards now. The memories of their lost siblings travelled with them, but the grief had already lessened, a wound that had scabbed over. Ephemeral reminded herself of the books she had read about wildlife, how an animal that produced so many eggs would expect to lose a certain percentage of them to disease or predators. Perhaps the dragon-kin carried within their blood a certain expectation of grief.

Thinking of such loss, she looked ahead to where Devinia the Red marched through the thick foliage. Since Augusta had died, the woman had barely stopped moving. She ate little and spoke less, just marched with her head held high, as if she dared the island to attack her again. Terin was also quiet, although this was more to do with the increasing temperature. She knew that he suffered again, and that he said nothing about it because there was nothing to be done. For a brief moment, Ephemeral felt a surge of despair such as she'd never known before, and her feet seemed too heavy on the path. Sebastian gone, Augusta Grint dead, Terin dying, and her sisters impossibly far away. She had been so foolish.

What is wrong?

It was Inky, her mind never far from Ephemeral's. She closed her eyes and tried to hold her feelings away from that silvery link.

I am fine. She pushed the idea of exploration towards the dragon-kin, hoping to distract her. *The island is yours now. You can hunt, protect yourselves.*

There was a sense of reluctance from Inky. *The others want to go,* she admitted. *It is time to run alone.*

Then you should go, replied Ephemeral, trying to sound firm. There was a silvery flicker from the other dragon-kin minds, so she opened herself to all of them. *Go, find new hunting grounds. Make your own choices.*

We will protect you, as you protected us. Inky's mind, but she felt it echoed in others.

No. Ephemeral clenched her fists, remembering the terrible noises as the Dawning Man plucked the flying dragon-kin from the air and crushed them, the flat sound of their bodies hitting the wet ground. *Please, no. Not for me. Go, live your own lives. Go!*

She closed her mind to them, and after a few moments, the continual low-level thunder that was the dragon-kin began to grow more distant. A few, she knew, took to the wing and left that way; she felt the wind against her face. Others tramped off into the deeper forest, not looking back. Ephemeral took a shaky breath.

'What happened?' asked Terin. He stood and waited for her to catch up, his blue eyes serious.

'They have – flown the roost? I believe that is the phrase.' Ephemeral forced a smile. 'I have lost enough family.'

Devinia gave no sign that she had noticed the departure of the dragon-kin. They kept walking, mostly in silence, until on the afternoon of the next day, when Terin came to a stop and lifted his head.

'It's close now,' he said. 'Just beyond this treeline.'

Devinia looked up, her eyes bright for the first time in days. 'Let's see what we have, then.'

They stepped blinking into bright sunshine. Beyond the trees was a rising circle of concentric stones, made of a rough greenish rock. They were covered in thick swathes of what looked like a spider's web, and the air was still. Ephemeral felt the flesh on her arms break out in goosebumps. She could feel the power Terin spoke of, like an echo in a room where people had recently been shouting, but there was no sign of anyone.

'This is it,' said Devinia. Her voice cracked a little, and she stumbled as she walked towards the stones. 'The Eye of Euriale. This is where we would have ended up, if –' She shook her head. 'Where are they? Wydrin! There must be something here. A reason for all this. Wydrin!' There was no answer to her calls, and Ephemeral could not feel Sebastian. She swallowed hard against the emptiness in her chest.

The stones were just tall enough to be difficult to climb. Terin, in particular, took frequent breaks as the sun beat down on his uncovered head, until eventually he sat on the edge of one of the stones and waved at her to keep climbing without him.

'I'll get there,' he assured her. 'Just keep an eye on our captain.'

Ephemeral scrambled up after Devinia, who had had a renewed burst of energy. They cut the spider webs away as they moved, chopping methodically and dragging themselves up, from one stone to the next. Eventually they stood looking down into an enormous, shadowed pit. There was a faint green glow from the very bottom, and a distant, whistling sound, like the wind across the desert at night. The sense of echoing power was very strong here, but still not quite present.

'What is this?' Devinia scowled down into the dark. 'What is this supposed to be?'

'It is the heart of the island,' said Ephemeral. She didn't know what else to say.

Devinia looked around, and then back into the hole. 'There should at least be a weapon. There should be power. Something I can use. Not a fucking hole in the ground.'

'There is power here,' said Ephemeral softly. 'But I do not think it is for humans to use.'

Terin appeared at that moment, his face pale from the long

climb. Devinia glared from one to the other. 'After all this, nothing. I should kill you both,' she said, although there was no heat to her words. She went to the outer edge of the stone ring and sat down heavily. 'How can my daughter not be here? How can I have lost so much, for nothing?'

Terin sat down next to her, and to Ephemeral's surprise, briefly touched a hand to Devinia's shoulder. 'What do we do now, Captain?'

They were all silent for some time. In the distance, there was a great thundering crash. The Dawning Man pushing down more trees, still following them, still alive. They had all heard it in the last few days, but no one had spoken of it.

'Let him come,' said Devinia eventually. 'Let the bastard come for me. I will peel that crown from his diseased head, and I'll crush him with his own weapon.' She lifted her head and looked at the other two. 'You should go, now. Find some shade, and try not to die on this stinking island.'

'That's what we *should* do,' agreed Terin.

'What did Augusta say to you, at the end?' asked Ephemeral.

'She told me . . . she told me to put Ristanov out of her misery. That there had been enough pain.'

Ephemeral nodded. She agreed with Augusta. For a few moments the only sounds were the calls of birds and monkeys. Somewhere out there, Inky was taking her first steps in her own life. Her own, independent life.

'If you take the crown, you will be infected too,' said Ephemeral.

'What does it matter now?' said Devinia. 'I'll likely die here anyway, but I'm not going without taking that bastard with me. I have no choice.'

'There is always a choice. I have learned that.' Ephemeral seated herself on the step between Devinia and Terin. It was good to sit down. 'Choices are important. So we will stay with you to the end, blood-of-Wydrin.'

89

Wydrin walked the shadowed streets of Krete, her footfalls silent out of long habit. It was a clear night, the stars overhead dizzyingly clear, but there was a strong desert wind blowing, and it smelt of a change in the weather. A storm, she thought, but then that might just have been her jangling nerves. Augusta had always been best at predicting the weather, much to Devinia's endless annoyance. She smiled at the thought.

She had left the Citadel to fetch them some provisions – it wasn't clear when they would get to eat again, after all – and Joah had distractedly given her directions to a market in the centre of the city that stayed open until the early hours. She was trusting Sebastian to keep the Citadel free of guards or nosy mages, and she realised she had no concerns on that front any more; Sebastian seemed different after his time at Y'Gria's palace. The grim introspection had gone, to be replaced by a steely poise. He seemed comfortable in his own skin again, and for that she was glad. There had been no time to talk to him about it, but she wondered if he had forgiven himself in some part for what had happened with Prince Dallen and the brood sisters. She hoped so. It was about bloody time.

It was late, but the city, like all cities, was not quiet. Men and women still walked the streets, many the worse for drink, and the taverns she passed were lively; chatter and the sour stench of beer poured through the open doors into the night. Even so, there was an unmistakable tension everywhere; the laughter a little too loud, the eyes a little too bright. They would know now what had happened in Raistinia, or at least they would have heard rumours of it, and in their hearts they knew that eventually the fury of the gods would come upon them. For a brief moment, as she paused at the doorway of another tavern, she was filled with the urge to run inside and shout at them all to leave. Get out of the city, get away. Find the furthest corner of the world and hide, and hope the gods won't find you.

Except, of course, that wouldn't be enough. Smiling sourly in the dark she remembered standing and watching the sunset with Sebastian in the Blackwood, telling him that there was nothing they could do – that the dragon wasn't really their problem, anyway. In the end, the reality of that had caught up with her. It had caught up with all of them.

She walked away from the tavern without going inside and followed the streets down and down, until she came to the small market Joah had spoken of. She picked up the scents of fried meat, and quickly purchased several bags of food to take back to the Citadel; chunks of pork on a stick, covered in a sticky glaze that smelt of plums; thick slices of crusty bread fried in butter and dusted with salt; golden pastries filled with a minced mixture of lamb and spices. From another stall she bought a couple of bottles of wine to wash it down and made to go, but her eye fell on a small table to the side of the food stalls. A short woman with black hair and rings clustered on her fingers like virulent barnacles was watching the people passing by with a solemn expression.

Pushing her newly purchased wares into her pack Wydrin approached her, nodding at the items on the table.

'And what are these for, exactly?'

'Charms against the gods, my girl. This one here will hide you from Y'Ruen's baleful gaze – as she passes over, she will not see you,' she indicated a collection of silver rods and coloured beads tied together with a tangle of blue thread. There was a tiny mouse skull hanging from the end. 'And if you have ever felt the evil influence of Res'ni the wolf-sister, then wearing this charm against your bare skin will cleanse you.'

Wydrin snorted with something close to delight. 'Where have you been all my life, woman?'

The charm seller's lips pinched together, sensing mockery. 'I make all of these myself, with my own crafting magic. My customers come back and tell me how these charms have changed their lives.'

'Well, I suppose if it doesn't work, they're too busy being dead to complain.' Seeing the look on the woman's face, Wydrin relented. These people had enough problems without her taking the piss. 'Do they sell well?'

The woman nodded, and some of the energy seemed to go out of her. 'The gods grow angrier by the day. People are frightened, all the time. They are trying to go about their daily lives and pretend that nothing is wrong, but the gods will come for the mages one day, and then we all –' She raised her hands in the air and dropped them. 'I do not come from here. I come from Kurensten, a cold place. The great lakes would freeze in the winter and then when spring came, the ice would get thinner and thinner. Eventually, it would crack and shatter, but until that happened there was a strange noise at night. My mother said it was ghosts, but I knew it was the ice, waiting to break. Krete is like that now. We think we are talking and living our lives, but we are the wailing of ghosts.' She paused and took a breath. 'The charms sell very well, although I don't know if anyone believes in them any more.'

Wydrin nodded slowly. 'They're not gods, not really. They're bullies. Here, I'll take three. The ones for Y'Gria, Y'Ruen and Res'ni. I think that will do us nicely.'

At first the charm maker looked uncertain, as though she thought Wydrin might still be mocking her, but when the coin purse came out she packed up the charms quickly enough, wrapping them in scraps of stiff paper and tying them with ribbon. Wydrin thanked her and turned to go, but the woman caught at her sleeve.

'You must wear them next to your skin, girl, at your throat or at your wrist. That is where they work the best.'

'Sure.'

'Here.' The woman came out from behind the table and gestured

545

for the packages back. 'Which one is for you? I will put it on myself, so I know you have it on correctly.'

Faintly bemused, Wydrin handed her the charm for Res'ni. The woman took it and fastened the leather thong around Wydrin's neck, fussing with the beads and the silver charms until it rested comfortably against her breastbone.

'There,' she said, when finally she was happy with the arrangement. 'That will work well for you, child.'

'Thank you,' said Wydrin, and she was surprised to find that she meant it. There were few things as comforting as being fussed over by a woman old enough to be your grandmother.

'I've seen too many young people die,' said the woman, her voice tight. 'It makes me older than I wish to be. Go on, go. Be blessed, child.'

Wydrin headed away from the market and back towards the Citadel, the charm hanging cold against her throat. She was halfway up the steps that wound around the hill to the Citadel when there was a strange crackle of energy that set her hair on end. For a moment she thought it was simply the storm she had sensed earlier, an errant bolt of lightning perhaps, but then the night lit up with strange green light. She looked up and across the city towards the distant northern gate. The sky above the city wall was filled with boiling cloud, and a twitching mass of squirming tentacles was reaching from the centre. The gods had arrived.

'Fuck me sideways,' she spat, before sprinting up the rest of the steps.

The light from the lamps cast Joah's eyes into deep shadow, making his face gaunt as he bent over his work. His hands were held out in front of him and he was pressing the angular shapes of the demonic pictograms into softened metal with the Edenier. He hadn't spoken for some time now, and Frith did not like the way he stared at the device, his mouth pursed into a thin line of concentration. When the piece was finished, the young mage sat back and without needing to be told to, cooled the hot metal with a thin layer of ice. Still he did not speak. Frith couldn't stand it any longer.

'Well?'

Joah looked up, startled, as though he'd forgotten that Frith was there at all.

'They are extraordinary,' he said earnestly. 'I've never seen anything like them, and yet magic is evident in every line. I can feel it working.' Absently he wiped his fingers on his robe, as though he'd been touching something dirty. 'It is not a pleasant sensation.'

'No,' said Frith. 'It is not.'

'And where did you say you found these runes?'

'I did not say.' Frith shifted where he sat, bringing the finished pieces together and slotting them into place. It was very close to being done now, and he could feel the aura of the thing pressing at his mind. The device looked a little like the Edenier trap had – a serrated ball of black and silver metal, imprinted with the demon's own strange language – but it was larger, and more open. The top peeled back like a flower in bloom, and at its heart were pieces of broken green crystal: not the Heart-Stone, but the pieces of pure Edeian they had been able to salvage from the artefacts in the room above them. Looping around it like a crown was a band of eroded gold, into which Frith had instructed Joah to etch more mage words. This combination of both the mages' and the demon's magic was both beautiful and frightening; it did not repel him in the same way the Edenier trap had, but he felt deeply uneasy, knowing that he had designed it. He stood up, trying to get some blood back into his stiff legs.

'But you must tell me,' Joah ran his hands over the device, his eyes bright. 'This is a whole new branch of magic unrelated to the Edenier, and I must master it.' He glanced up at Frith, and his look was avaricious. 'You are full of mysteries.'

'There is no time, as well you know.' Frith deliberately looked away from him to the last pieces of the trap. 'Quickly, let's get this done.'

'Fine.' Joah picked up one of the artefacts and turned it over in his hands. It was an eroded piece of stone dotted with shards of brittle green crystal. It had obviously been made to resemble something once and had been much larger, but time had reduced it. Joah shook his head. 'There is not enough Edeian here. We need more.'

'That is the last of it,' said Frith. 'Give it to me.'

Joah passed it up to him, and without thinking too closely about it, Frith summoned the time magic. The artefact grew in his hands, becoming a great four-legged animal with a long snout – back in its original form, the statuette had a pair of tusks curving from under its mouth, and they were both formed of the pure Edeian crystal. Frith handed it back. 'Will that do?'

Joah shook his head slightly, in wonder rather than denial, and with a delicate push from the Edenier, broke the crystal free of the stone. He melted more of the silver they had left, and dancing it through the air like a snake, used it to fuse the Edeian shards to the inside of the device. At that moment, there was a clatter of boots on the steps leading from the room, and Wydrin crashed into the chamber with Sebastian at her heels. She was pale, with two points of colour high on her cheeks.

'They're here,' she gasped. 'They're outside the city walls.'

Frith went to them, and took a hold of their arms. 'The device is almost ready, and there are just the targets to place.' He took a breath. It all felt too fast. Wydrin put her hand over his and squeezed it.

'Don't worry, Feveroot and I will get those in place before the gods even know what is happening.' She reached into a pocket and pulled out what appeared to be a pair of charms on lengths of twine. 'Here, you two, humour me and put these on. I'm suddenly feeling very superstitious.'

'What are these?'

'Just extra luck, hopefully.'

He exchanged a look with Sebastian, and then slipped the charm over his head. The big knight did the same.

'I will be up on the roof, watching,' said Sebastian. 'The mages are already attacking and they may delay the gods for a time. Let's hope it's enough.'

Frith nodded. 'When you are ready, Wydrin, signal Sebastian. I will activate the device straight away, and if everything works –' he paused, knowing that she would object to his next words, 'if

548

everything works as it should, the gods will be drawn here immediately.'

'What are you talking about?' Wydrin frowned. 'You need to be out of the chamber before that happens. You understand that, right? There will be four very angry gods sharing this very small space. You do not want to be here.'

'There is no other way. Once the gods are inside the barriers Xinian and Selsye have set, they will know we have something planned. We cannot give them any time to act against it, or they could simply force their way back out again, or focus their efforts on destroying the Citadel.' He paused. 'Besides which, I am the only one that can activate the device. I have to be here.'

'Nonsense,' Wydrin scowled at him. 'If that is the case, then I will come and bloody get you. As soon as the last target is on, Feveroot and I will be here, and you had better be ready to leave.'

There was a rumble and a crash so loud they all felt it through their boots.

'There's no more time,' said Sebastian, his voice low. 'Wydrin, we have to go now.'

Joah appeared at his elbow, carrying a leather pack with a long strap on it. 'Here. The targets are in here. I have labelled each in a language you will understand.' The contempt in his voice was briefly as clear and as cold as ice. Frith saw Wydrin raise an eyebrow at that before dismissing it as unimportant. 'Get in close, put it against their flesh. My magic will do the rest.'

'Got it.' She took the pack from him and slung the strap over her shoulder. 'No time for rousing speeches or last-minute declarations.' She put her arms around Frith and kissed him; he barely had time to respond before she was stepping away again. 'But I will be back for you, princeling. Don't you bloody forget it.'

She and Sebastian headed back up the steps. Frith turned back to the device, trying not to wonder if he'd ever see either of them again.

'Back to work,' he said to Joah. 'We need this done *now*.'

90

They pounded up the steps and out into the night air, Sebastian's heart in his throat. They were met by the creature Wydrin called Feveroot, currently in the form of a small nondescript cat. The red markings on its back throbbed with light as it spoke.

'Krete has its unwanted guests.'

'Yeah,' said Wydrin. 'They're difficult to miss.'

Sebastian stopped next to her and looked out across the city. For the moment, neither of them moved. The sight seemed to freeze his blood in his veins.

Finally, the gods had come to Krete.

It was still dark but the eastern horizon showed a bruising of pink, and in this hot, flat land the morning would soon be upon them. The strange silver light of dawn turned the red-brick buildings of Krete into dusty toys, the gods looming above them like a nightmare. The sirens on the walls were wailing, sending their piercing flashes of blue light up into an uncaring night, and Sebastian realised he could hear the people – he could hear the screaming, the panic as the city awoke. Well he could imagine their horror as they realised that the magical barriers they had relied upon for so long had failed them, and he felt a stab of guilt – they had invited the gods in, and the men and women dying now were their responsibility. Already there were bursts of flame and ice as the mages flew into action, throwing what forces they could against the invading presence. It was difficult to imagine that it had any hope of even holding them off, let alone driving them back.

There was Y'Gria, apparently fully recovered from the loss of her palace. She was a green storm hanging above the city, a confusion of boiling cloud and stretching, reaching tendrils. They slithered down to the buildings below and Sebastian clearly saw them scooping people up from the streets; the roots curling around men and women and lifting them up into the air, before flexing violently, breaking bones and tearing flesh. The bodies were discarded like errant blossoms. Deep in the heart of the roots and the swirling green cloud Sebastian could just about make out Y'Gria's human form, or at least part of it. Her arms were spread wide, and there was an expression of fierce joy on her face.

Y'Gria attacked the west of the city, the beginnings of the dawn light casting her in a growing silver halo, while to the east, Res'na stalked. As literal as a god of order might be expected to be, he was in the form of a giant white wolf, so huge it simply stepped over the walls of Krete, great shaggy head hanging low. His eyes were violet and shone like lamps, and slivers of white light peeled away from his back and his flanks. As Sebastian watched, rooted to the spot, the great wolf bent his head and savaged something on the ground. There had been a volley of fireballs heading from that direction, but abruptly they stopped. Sebastian wondered how many mages had just died in that handful of seconds.

And to the north was what Sebastian took to be Res'ni, god of chaos. It took him a few moments to work out exactly what it was he was seeing. Like Res'na, it was almost wolf-shaped, and black rather than white – a four-legged giant stalking over the walls. But Res'ni was a creature composed of thousands of snapping jaws and hungry mouths. They covered the giant, from its long legs, across its shaggy flanks, and down its narrow back. The wolf-shaped head was barely that; it was a writhing, tortured thing of teeth and tongues and raw, red flesh. Sebastian found he had to look away. It was an insult to reality itself.

'Well,' said Wydrin, 'this plan looks pretty fucking stupid now, doesn't it?'

'I don't see Y'Ruen,' he said, briefly scanning the horizon. There was no sign of the dragon. 'And Oster doesn't appear to be with them. Wydrin, let me come with you. Feveroot can make himself big enough to carry us both. It's got to be better to have as many sword arms up there as possible.'

Wydrin was already shaking her head. 'Don't you see? Our best chance is if Feveroot stays as small as possible. Their weakness is that they are so huge. If they don't notice me, I might actually get out of this alive.' She turned and grinned up at him, and he noted the manic look in her eye. 'Besides which, you need to tell Frith when to activate his trap. Watch for my signal.'

Sebastian felt a wave of despair flow through him. It was unbearable to stand here and watch the massacre. Something inside him, the silvery tide of his dragon blood, was uncurling. 'Wydrin, I have to fight. I have to do something.'

'You may well have to,' she said. 'Remember, watch for my signal, brother.'

She squeezed his arm and then turned to Feveroot. 'Can you make yourself griffin-shaped, my friend?'

Feveroot the cat uncurled itself from the floor and stretched. 'Of course, although surely any bird shape would do?'

'Just for old times' sake.'

There was a swirl of inky darkness and in seconds a black griffin stood before them, its wickedly curved beak slashed with red, its eyes glowing like coals. Wydrin climbed onto its back and seated herself, adjusting the leather pack so that it lay in her lap. When she was settled she reached for Sebastian, and he took her hand.

'The Black Feather Three, remember?' she said. 'Don't let him do anything stupid.'

With that she drew away and hunched over the demon's back before it leapt up into the air, black wings unfurling silently. Sebastian watched her go with one hand curled around the pommel of his sword. Already the day was lighter than it had been.

'I don't know,' he murmured. 'We all seem so intent on doing stupid things, after all.'

Xinian threw herself around the corner of the building, stumbling as a shower of broken brick pattered against her cloak and scratched the back of her head. She glanced back to see the upper level of the building behind her dissolve into a cloud of red powder as the towering white wolf above them nudged it with one enormous paw. Next to her Selsye leaned against the wall, her chest rising and falling rapidly, her eyes wide.

'This is our fault,' she said. 'We let them in.'

'Come on.' Xinian took her hand and half led, half dragged Selsye up the street. They came out into an intersection of several streets. There were a few mages gathered there of many different disciplines, their faces turned up to the suddenly dangerous skies with expressions of horror and panic. Some of them, she noticed approvingly, were readying spells, tying fresh lengths of silk to their arms. Others were simply looking around as if they didn't know where to flee to. Res'na in his great wolf form loomed off to their right, growing ever closer, while it was possible to see the writhing storm that was Y'Gria blotting out half the sky to their left. She turned to Selsye, squeezing her hand.

'Damage control,' she said. 'That's all we can do at this point. Hold them off, keep them busy, and hope the plan works. It's too late to regret our choices now, Selsye.'

Her lover looked uncertain for the barest moment, and then a determined expression settled over her face. She nodded. 'Divide into two factions? One attack, one defence?'

'Yes.' Xinian felt a surge of relief. Without Selsye, this situation would be much too dark to face. 'You take defence, my love.'

They ran into the crowd together, and Xinian started bellowing orders. She saw them all turn to her, eyes sharp with surprise or suspicion, but she saw something else too: relief that someone was taking charge.

'Any military training at all, you're with me. The rest of you to my partner here.' Selsye was already forming her people into lines, taking charge with quiet confidence. 'What are you waiting for? You all knew this day would come. Now let's show them what we can do!'

Faster than she would have hoped, they had two groups of well-ordered mages in rows, their arms bared to show the lines and lines of spell bindings. They all looked frightened, but they also looked ready to fight. There was a thunderous crash, and the square filled with a plume of orange dust as another nearby building was crushed under an errant paw. The twin violet lamps of Res'na's eyes loomed above them, enormous jaws falling open to reveal teeth as tall as the men and women he sought to devour. Xinian was struck by the lack of malice in those eyes – to Res'na they were just a problem to be solved, their destruction the next logical step. It didn't make him any less deadly than the rest of the gods.

There was a shimmer in the air around her mages, and Xinian almost felt rather than saw the tenuous barrier Selsye and her people had erected over them all.

'First three rows, I want repeated walls of flame arching up into this bastard's face. Last three, ice around his legs. We'll see if we can immobilise him. Go!'

She raised her arms and added her own arc of fire to the conflagration. In moments the sky lit up with searing lines of orange flame, and Res'na took a startled step backwards as they hissed against his snout. Clusters of glittering ice sprouted into existence at the tops of the god's legs, slowing him down, and Xinian felt a fierce moment of triumph as the god reared back, shaking his head like a dog with a porcupine quill in its nose. When he came crashing back down one giant paw landed on the roof of the building in front of them.

'Look out!'

The top two floors of the building exploded, sending a shower of brick and splintered wood down on them. There was a shout from Selsye and the barrier over them thrummed with increased energy – the worst of the debris bounced clear, but a few men and women at the edge were caught by smaller pieces of rock. One woman climbed back to her feet, her face covered in a sheet of blood from a scalp wound, but the man next to her stayed sprawled on the cobbles, a shard of wood protruding from his chest. Above them, Res'na shifted in the wreckage, bringing his great head around to focus on them again.

'More fire!' Xinian bellowed, sending a fireball flying up even as she spoke. It hissed against the god's white fur. 'Keep him back and keep him distracted!'

A flurry of fire briefly blotted out her view of the god and she heard Selsye shouting more instructions to her mages. The sky was the luminous deep blue now of early dawn, and Xinian felt a wave of desperation. When would the trap be activated? Would they have to hold off the gods all day? She opened her mouth to issue more commands, when a wave of force crashed into her from her right side. Taken unawares, she dived to the ground, shouting with pain as her elbow struck the cobbles.

'You should be in the dungeon at Lan-Hellis!'

Scarcely able to believe it, she looked up to see Reis marching towards her from one of the side streets. He had around twenty mages at his back, all wearing the colours of his service. Incredibly, he did not look at the gods destroying the city around him, but at her. His eyes were wild with hate.

'Reis?' Xinian climbed warily to her feet.

'I have issued a warrant for your arrest!' He marched up to her and glared around at the other mages in the square. 'This woman is an outlaw! Why do none of you seek to detain her?'

'We have been somewhat busy,' said Xinian faintly. The man looked unwell; his eyes were bloodshot and were bulging out of his head, his robes were dirty, and there was a smudge of grime on his cheek. This was not the man she had known and served for so many years. 'Reis, this is not the time—'

'I will not speak to you, agent of the gods!' With that he threw another wave of pure force at her, but she was faster, erecting her own field of force and throwing it back at him. He fell back, confused that she was even capable of such a thing, and she finally saw how much weaker he had become. Pressing her advantage, she lifted her hand and summoned a localised blizzard, welding his boots to the spot.

'Enough, Reis.' Behind and above them, the fight against Res'na went on. She could hear Selsye shouting orders to both groups now, taking over without question. She felt a surge of love for her, and savoured it. 'There is no time for this.' With Xinian standing over him, the man cowered as though he didn't know where he was. 'I officially relieve you of command.'

He lifted his hands ready to send another barrage of Edenier, his face twisting with hate. Xinian reached down with her hand, grabbed a fistful of his robe and brought her head down sharply to meet his nose. There was a satisfying crunch and Reis sagged in her grip. She dropped him to the cobbles and eyed his men, a smear of his blood across her forehead.

'You lot. Get into formation, if you know what's good for you.'

Soaring high above the city, Wydrin peered over Feveroot's shoulder and felt her stomach turn over. The view was dizzying enough – the demon had taken her up high at her request, so that they might get an overview of the gods' attack – but the scale of the destruction already being visited on Krete turned her blood cold. Y'Gria for her part appeared to be concentrating her efforts on murdering the people fleeing in the streets, her roots surging after the tiny figures like a long dry river rushing to fill its banks, while Res'na and Res'ni were delighting in a wider sense of destruction. Walls and buildings fell, so that Wydrin's view was partially obscured by great clouds of red and grey dust.

'Where first?' Feveroot's voice thrummed through the red slashes on his torso and wings.

Wydrin bit her lip. 'There are so many attractive options, it's hard to say. Here, look.' She pointed down towards Res'na, where half-moons of bright orange flame were exploding into existence in front of his long snout. 'The mages are keeping him nicely distracted for us. Let's approach the bastard from behind, and hopefully he'll never know we were there.'

Feveroot dived and Wydrin clung to his neck with one arm, while her other hand slid inside the leather satchel in her lap. A quick glance and she had her fingers around the target marked with Res'na's name, while Feveroot brought them round in a wide circle, skirting the very edge of the city wall before curving in to approach Res'na's back.

'That's it, that's it,' murmured Wydrin. 'Nice and quiet. Bring me in as low as you can.'

Below them was now a landscape of strange white fur. Up close, it seemed to glow with its own inner light, and it looked oddly glassy, not soft at all. Up ahead, Res'na's huge pointed ears were angled forward, the ruff around his neck standing up on end. The mages were still sending showers of fire up into the god's face, and as they watched he shook his head in irritation.

'Now,' said Wydrin urgently. 'While he's thinking of something else.'

Feveroot in his griffin form dropped like a stone, bringing Res'na's white fur abruptly closer. Sliding the target from the bag Wydrin leaned out and over, holding on to Feveroot with her legs. She stretched and slapped the skin down, her fingers brushing the white surface of the god – it wasn't warm and furry at all, but cold and slick, like crystal – and saw the mages' words on the target glow briefly with yellow light as they sank into the surface. She was still grinning at how easy it had been when Res'na's great head whipped round to snap at them, like a dog stung by a bee.

Wydrin yelped as Feveroot flew up and away, twisting desperately out of the god's reach as jaws as long as her mother's ships crashed shut inches away from them. There was a blast of hot, fetid breath and a glance of eyes like violet moons, and then they were falling away. Luckily at that moment there was a blast of fresh flames from the mages and the god turned back, just as Feveroot swooped down, diving to street level to take them out of view.

'Well, that was easy, wasn't it?' gasped Wydrin, slapping the demon companionably on the flank. She wondered if her stomach would ever come back down from its new location in her throat. 'Who's next?'

91

The device crackled with energy, white and green lights peeling across its surface like beads of condensation on a kettle. Frith felt his hair trying to stand on end.

'It's finished,' breathed Joah.

Frith sat back, watching as the trap he had built for the gods began to fill with its own energy, drawing off the pure Edeian placed inside it and the demon's words etched on its warped surface. There was a great deal of power surging inside the thing, a result of the merging of so many forms of magic. He could feel it pressing against his mind, and like the Edenier trap, it was difficult to look at.

'Yes,' agreed Frith, eventually. He realised he felt relieved. The thing was done, and he would only have to touch it again to turn it on. And once the gods were in here, it would be lost for ever, along with them. He stood up and looked away from it, rubbing his eyes as if he'd been staring into the sun.

'This is extraordinary.' Joah still knelt in front of the device, his hands resting lightly on its surface. 'Do you realise what we have made here? Such a combination of magics has barely even been imagined, let alone created. This will lead to other, extraordinary creations. We have the power now to remove Edenier and store it.' Joah laughed, delighted. 'We will be the greatest mages who ever lived.'

Frith closed his eyes for a moment. He had heard Joah say words like those before.

'No,' he said, and as he said it, a wave of relief crashed over him. He was, in the end, not like Joah. Ambition and the thirst for power did not obliterate everything else in his heart. He was still capable of that choice. 'No, Joah. When I walk away from here, you will not see me again.' He knew that wasn't exactly true, but he dearly wished it was. He wondered if the Joah he would meet in the future would know him, but he thought not. Over a thousand years of death could cloud anyone's mind, and Joah had never been especially clear on his past. 'Everything I know will go with me, and this device,' he gestured at the trap without looking at it, 'will be closed off to you, too. I will not help you.'

Joah stood up slowly. His long brown hair had come loose from its tie during the final stages of building the device, and now it hung around his face in greasy tails. Looking at him, it wasn't difficult to see the mad man he would become.

'You can't mean that,' he said in a low voice, before coming to stand before Frith. 'You have singlehandedly brought magical knowledge forward by years, and you will just take it back again? That cannot be!' In his desperation he took hold of Frith's arm.

'That is exactly what I am going to do.' Frith shook off Joah's hand, and started to walk away. He would go up to see Sebastian now, to watch Wydrin's progress. 'With this contraption, one mage could dominate all others. I must end it here.'

'Then I will force you to give it to me!'

The young mage lifted both his hands, calling into existence two crackling globes of electrical energy. Twisting white worms of light crawled up his arms, casting his face in stark, shifting light. All trace of the meek, polite young man had vanished; there was only hunger in his eyes. And murder.

'You must give it to me! Even if I must – if I must hurt you, I will have it.' Joah advanced on him, his eyes wild. 'You waste your life on these people. What you know, what we could learn together, is worth so much more!'

Frith stared at him. He knew, with a certainty, that Joah was wrong, and a shadow that had haunted his heart since Skaldshollow suddenly lifted. He smiled.

'You will get out now,' he said softly. 'You will leave this place right now, or I will use my own magic on you, and faster than you will be able to counteract. How would you like to turn to dust in seconds, Joah? Nothing would give me greater pleasure, believe me. Know that I give you this choice because I am a better man than you.'

Joah stared at him, his mouth a wet line within his neat beard. For a second it looked as though he would say something more, but then the globes of churning light winked out, and he ran from the chamber. Frith watched him go.

Flying over Res'ni was like descending into a nightmare.

Wydrin bent low over Feveroot, peering down at the monstrosity that was the god, feeling the press of bile against the back of her throat. Res'ni was a seething confusion of gaping mouths, white teeth against wet flesh, snapping and grinning and rending. The wolf shape had its own giant set of jaws, just as Res'na did, but rather than eyes or any other features, there were just endless protruding, snapping mouths. As they watched, the creature surged through the streets of Krete, snapping up any humans foolish enough to get too close, messily devouring them so that the cobbles of the streets were awash with blood.

'Bring us down low,' she murmured into Feveroot's ear. 'And we'll see if there's a bare inch of this thing that doesn't want to eat us.'

Feveroot spread his wings and brought them in low, passing around the back legs of Res'ni and past several tall towers; there were shadows moving there, but they were human, so she dismissed them, focussing instead on Res'ni. Everywhere she looked there were ravenous mouths, and now that they were closer, she could hear the wet, keening noises they made.

'I could shove it down one of their throats, I suppose,' she said. 'But I'm not sure if the spell will work if it gets eaten.'

A shadow from one of the buildings suddenly leapt, and Feveroot rocked to one side as a figure landed on his back. Wydrin spun around, her mouth open to shout a few of her favourite swearwords, when she came face to face with Estenn.

The woman looked close to death. More than three quarters of her face and neck were badly burned, the skin red raw and seeping where it wasn't crisped black, and her eyes were glassy with pain. Her nose was still crusted with black blood from where Wydrin had broken it, and the tattoo of the twin wolves at her throat was now only present on a few tattered rags of skin, like pieces of an old ruined tapestry.

Wydrin brought an elbow round to crash into the woman's face, but Estenn leaned back out of the way and slammed her own fist down into Wydrin's stomach. The blow was too awkward to do any real damage, but it made Wydrin twist to one side and the world spun around her sickeningly.

'Land us!' she gasped to Feveroot. 'Quickly!'

They dropped from the air and crashed into the cobbles. Wydrin rolled clear, one hand checking that the satchel was still around her neck while the other drew Glassheart from its scabbard. Back on her feet and moving, Estenn was already attacking, a small knife flashing silver in the dawn light. Her head was low, the remnants of her black hair hanging in a tangle to either side of her face. Wydrin held her off easily, pushing away her strikes almost lightly.

'Look at what they've done to you,' she said. Above and to their right, the huge form of Res'ni was moving slowly past. Wydrin could hear the desperate screams of her victims.

'They – have given me – glory.'

'Really? Is that what it looks like to you? Because to me it looks like they've chewed you up and spat you out. Did they even come for you after Raistinia? Did they bear your broken body from the burning streets? Or did you do that yourself?'

'I am the Emissary. A servant of the true gods.'

Estenn lunged again, and Wydrin beat her back with a flurry of strikes. The older woman bared her teeth at her like a rabid dog.

'You are a fool,' said Wydrin, and was surprised at the genuine frustration in her own voice. 'Everything you have done, you have done yourself. Surviving Euriale, building up your own community. All right, so it was a community of cannibals and

561

murderers, but it was yours. *You* are the strong one, Estenn. Can you still not see it?'

Estenn screamed wordlessly and charged, getting in under Wydrin's guard so that her short sword was useless. Wydrin punched Estenn hard across the face, breaking open the partially scabbed burns. The woman gave a yelp of pain but did not retreat, instead bringing her knife down in a stabbing motion at Wydrin's throat. It should have been a killing blow, but instead it struck the charm Wydrin had brought from the night market and skidded clear, slicing instead across Wydrin's collarbone – a painful cut, but a shallow one. Wydrin shouted and pushed her back.

'I don't have time for this, Estenn! I will kill you if you make me.'

Estenn came at her again, arms wide. Wydrin brought her blade up and caught the woman in the midriff, sinking the sword home with a grunt. Estenn hissed between bloody teeth, and staggered. One hand went to the blade and the fingers wrapped around it, as if to pull it free again, but there was no strength left in her.

'That's for the Spinner,' said Wydrin, before twisting the blade. Hot blood gushed over her hand and spattered her face. 'And that's for Frith.'

She tore the sword free, grimacing at the hot stench as the woman's stomach was split open. Estenn fell to her knees, the knife dropping from her fingers.

Breathing heavily, Wydrin wiped her bloody blade against her thigh and watched the woman, but she did not look up again. Her tangled hair hid her face.

'What a bloody waste.'

'Her choices were her own, at least.'

Wydrin looked around to see Feveroot, still in his griffin form, watching from the other side of the street. Without another word she went to him and mounted again, before urging him to take flight. She steered him straight at Res'ni now, a strange reckless-ness in her heart, and took them straight under the creature's belly. There were, as she had guessed, fewer mouths there, and she slapped the target home without any difficulty. Unlike her brother, Res'ni's form did not seem as controlled, and therefore

562

not as aware. Wydrin and Feveroot flew out and up into the clear air again without looking back. The sun had risen and the sky was crowded with light and the sound of people dying.

92

Sebastian stared out across Krete, one hand gripping the pommel of his sword so tightly his fingers ached. His eyes followed the tiny shape of Wydrin and Feveroot as they danced across the morning sky, his heart in his mouth – for some time they had vanished from view, and he had gone to the very edge of the Citadel gardens, caught in an agony of uncertainty, but then they had emerged again. Now they were picking their way towards Y'Gria, still trying to keep out of the eye line of the gods, but hampered by the growing light and by the attacks of the mages themselves. As he watched, they dived to one side to avoid a flurry of fireballs meant for the cluster of tentacles that was Y'Gria. Uneasily, he took his eyes from them to survey the damage already done to Krete – large portions of the city were collapsed into rubble, and he dreaded to think of the human cost.

'It's taking too long,' he murmured to himself. It was the hardest thing he had ever done, to stand here and watch while others died. He reminded himself of the plan again, but it did little to lessen the bitter taste in his mouth. 'There will be nothing left to save.'

There was a clatter of boots on stone behind him and he turned to see Joah, running from the Citadel entrance. The young mage didn't look up at him, but kept his head down as he stalked past. A few moments later, Frith appeared at the entrance. Sebastian raised his eyebrows.

'The device is finished,' was all Frith had to say. He came over to stand by Sebastian. 'When Wydrin gives the signal, I will—'

A great shadow fell over them, and Sebastian felt the silver tide of his dragon blood suddenly sing with mingled fury and terror. Y'Ruen passed on overhead, the width of her wings dwarfing all below her, blue scales shining in the early light like sapphires. She did not look down at them, flying out over the city instead, but Sebastian felt the press of her mind briefly against his – it was a wolf passing by a mouse, and he was considered too small a meal to be worth bothering with.

'She comes,' was all he could say. There were a few moments of awful silence, as the city below realised what had finally come for them, and then Y'Ruen opened her terrible jaws and a stream of fire too bright to look at cascaded down into the city, turning all to ruin.

'This won't work,' he said, his voice faint to his own ears. 'She will destroy everything long before Wydrin has a chance to put the final targets in place. Everyone in the city, dead and charred to pieces. It is what she is made to do.'

Fire boiled across the city like an avalanche. The mage attacks increased in power and volume, but they had very little effect on the scaled hide of the dragon.

'I have an idea,' said Frith. Sebastian turned to look at him. The young lord was pale, his white hair stuck to his forehead with sweat, but he looked determined. 'It's a fairly terrible one, I'm afraid.' He met Sebastian's eyes steadily. 'Come with me.'

Frith led Sebastian down into the heart of the Citadel again, hurrying down stairs and corridors until they came to the artefact room. He stopped in front of a plinth where a great shard of green crystal rested.

'Help me carry this outside.'

Sebastian did as he was bid, taking the thicker end of the shard while Frith wrestled with the narrower edge. 'What is this, Frith?'

'It is part of the skull of the ancient dragon-god, Tia'mast. A tiny part, judging by the shape of it.'

They shuffled back towards the exit, moving as quickly as they could. 'And what are you going to do with it, exactly?'

'I'm going to bring the god back.'

Sebastian almost dropped his end. 'Forgive me, I thought for a moment there you said—'

'The gods are natural enemies, yes? That is what Oster told you? They have, in fact, been fighting each other for centuries before they decided to turn their attentions to the mages.'

Sebastian nodded reluctantly. They moved down the corridors, careful not to knock the piece of skull on the walls. 'Yes. They are naturally in competition with each other.'

'What do you suppose will happen if we introduce a new one into their midst, at this very moment?'

Frith looked up and caught Sebastian's eye across the shard. To his surprise, the young lord grinned. 'I think it would be interesting, don't you?'

They carted the skull shard outside into the Citadel gardens. Below them the city was aflame. Sebastian searched the sky and found Wydrin and Feveroot again, still dancing around Y'Gria. The god of growth and life was obviously proving difficult to target, while Y'Ruen was lazily circling the city, pouring fire down onto its streets. There was a flicker of golden light to the east, and Sebastian felt his heart beat heavily in his chest – Oster was there, at the eastern wall. His dragon form was so much smaller than the other gods, but it burned with its own inner light. As he watched, he snapped and harried at the back of Y'Gria's spreading roots, severing them and rending them between his jaws. He had made his choice, after all.

'Frith, are you sure about this? We could be about to make everything a hundred times worse. Assuming we survive, how do we get rid of *this* dragon?'

The young lord was crouching by the skull piece, his hands pressed against its smooth surface. He looked up at Sebastian, his grey eyes serious.

'The time magic would not work against Y'Gria. She stands outside time, ageless somehow, as I'm sure all the gods are, and I could not get a grip on her. But this . . .' He looked down at the skull fragment. 'This is a remnant, a piece of something that has succumbed to the tide of history. The shadow of Tia'mast exists within it still, so I can bring it back. And I'm reasonably certain I can reverse the process too.'

Sebastian shook his head slowly. It was madness, but the sound of the city being destroyed was pressing in all around them.

'Then do it. We have very little time left.'

Frith nodded once. 'Stand back. I've no real idea how big this thing will be.'

Sebastian retreated to the remains of the drum-shaped building that topped the Citadel, and watched as Frith lit up with burning white light like a torch. The piece of green crystal shivered, and then began to grow, bulging and twisting. He had time to recognise the shape of it, the sockets where eyes would rest, the rows and rows of jagged teeth, and then a gigantic shape flowered out from it almost faster than he could follow. He saw a long flexible spine, the delicate filigree of bat-like wings spreading over them, and then the dragon took on its own flesh. Sebastian looked up in helpless wonder; where once there had been the sky, there was an enormous dragon, bigger even than Y'Ruen. The Citadel was dwarfed beneath it, and they stood under its belly. It was the deep green of ancient forests, and its eyes as it turned towards them were the boiling orange of the deepest flame. Its head was fringed with a mane of long twisting horns, and its nostrils flared as it took in their scent. Sebastian was dimly aware that Frith had collapsed onto the stones, the magic having stolen all his strength, but he was unable to tear his eyes from the dragon. It was looking at him. He could feel its mind, questing. The silver tide surged over him, and he fought to assert himself.

Who are you, dragon-kin?

The dragon's voice thundered in his head. There was a wetness at his nose, and he realised he was bleeding, but it seemed distant, unimportant. This dragon's mind was a simple, curious thing – a creature of a darker, more brutal age. Touching its mind, he could almost see what ancient Ede had been; the people were small, insignificant. The world was wild, and full of magic. It had been glorious.

I am your friend, he answered.

The dragon seemed to accept this. *And these others?*

He spoke of the other gods. Sebastian could already feel his mild irritation with them. The dragon's mind was so close to his. He no longer felt overwhelmed. He felt powerful.

They are your enemies, he said firmly. *Would you fight them? With me?*

The dragon, Tia'mast, was confused. He did not know where he was, and these other beings of Edenier were alien to him. Amazingly, he feared to fight them, in case they had tricks he did not know. Sebastian found himself smiling, and he reached out to the dragon.

My friend, do not fear. I will show you. His smile broke into a grin. *I will show you how to kill them. We will hunt together.*

The dragon lowered his great head until it rested on the stones next to Sebastian. The invitation was clear. Sebastian climbed up the twisted horns until he was seated in their midst, just behind the dragon's great, broad head. He felt the dragon's mind cushion him, ready to listen to his commands. The power that coursed beneath him was unbelievable. He opened himself to it.

We will hunt, Tia'mast said, all doubt gone, and he took to the sky.

Wydrin swung Glassheart back and forth, severing roots as they snaked through the air towards them, but as fast as she sliced they came back, sprouting anew from the churning horror that was Y'Gria.

The god of growth and life, the mother of the garden and all newly born creatures, was proving to be very difficult to target. She was a storm of questing roots, surging through the buildings of Krete and clogging the streets, her tentacles throttling and destroying at every turn. Her human form was hidden in the midst of it, but getting close to her was impossible – wave after wave of tentacle held them back. Wydrin didn't think Y'Gria was even aware of their presence.

'We have to get in closer. Time is running out.'

Indeed, the city of Krete was close to ruin, and the mages

themselves appeared to be running out of energy; their attacks were coming slower, and less frequently. Since the arrival of Y'Ruen, much of the city was lost to fire.

'If we can just dart in—'

Without warning, one of the questing tentacles wrapped around Feveroot's neck, squeezing and dragging them towards the ground. The demon squawked and struggled, while Wydrin bent forward and hacked at the feeler with her sword. It was surprisingly tough.

'You'll have to change your shape, push your way out of it.' She felt Feveroot begin to shift under her legs, and then they were thrown clear as a tremendous force crashed into Y'Gria. Spinning away and barely keeping upright, Wydrin glanced over her shoulder to see an enormous green dragon raking its claws across the tentacled mass. She blinked rapidly, thinking that the light must have changed Y'Ruen's colours somehow, but it was no optical illusion – this was a new dragon, bigger than Y'Ruen, and it was the colour of emeralds. She was just taking this in when she spotted Sebastian perched on the creature's head. Her friend had his hands wrapped around the horns sprouting from the dragon's head, and his face was steely in its determination. She could almost *feel* him, imposing his will on the dragon, and then Feveroot was diving away.

'Ye gods and little fishes,' she said faintly. 'Someone has some explaining to do.' She shook her head. 'Quickly now.' They skirted in close, weaving through the fronds of Y'Gria's questing body, now distracted by the attacking dragon, until abruptly they parted to reveal the god herself. She was human at the very centre, although many times the size of a normal human being – her green hair was a wild tangle, and her face was contorted with rage. Her lower half was a cascading confusion of tentacles, and she pushed herself up on these, confronting the dragon. Sliding the target from the satchel, Wydrin leaned out as they flew past and slapped it on the god's shoulder. She saw it glow as the mages' words sank home, but Y'Gria was too occupied by her new attacker, and in moments they were diving away below roof level, keeping out of sight.

'One more to go,' said Wydrin. 'And it's a biggun.'

93

Sebastian's blood soared with the silver tide.

Tia'mast followed his commands eagerly, the two of them working together as one. There was a fierce joy to this: to the hunt, to the destruction of those who would act against them. He took the dragon first to Y'Gria, tearing her roots aside as easily as sweeping his sword through long grass. The rage and the terror on her face was like a balm, and he urged Tia'mast on.

This one seeks to rule us all, he said. *She wishes to impose her wishes on the great god Tia'mast.*

The dragon roared his disapproval and sent a blanket of flame crawling over the rival god. Y'Gria screeched, striking out with her roots, but they all fell away into blackened pieces. There was a flicker of golden lights, and Oster was there, attacking with them – the golden dragon leapt at the heart of the woman and slashed with crystal claws. Sebastian felt Tia'mast's focus sharpen on the newcomer, aggression growing in his heart.

No, there is no danger here. Sebastian opened the link between them a little wider, showing the dragon his regard for Oster, the love he felt for him. For the first time, he acknowledged it himself, and shared that with the dragon, also. *This is a friend. And my bond-mate.*

Tia'mast accepted this easily enough, and Sebastian relaxed. He pulled the great dragon back from Y'Gria, who was now having enough difficulty dealing with Oster, and turned him towards Y'Ruen.

There is someone else you should meet.

Wydrin slapped the final target home, watching with satisfaction as the mage words sank into Y'Ruen's shining blue scales. The beast herself, so mighty and so fearsome, was busy clawing desperately for her life against the enormous bulk of Sebastian's dragon.

They fought now some distance above Krete, roiling and snapping and lunging at each other, like a nest of celestial snakes. It was such an extraordinary sight that Wydrin could feel her mind recoiling from it, refusing to believe the truth of it. She urged Feveroot away, swooping down over the city and coming in fast towards the Citadel. Reaching into her bag, she pulled out the flare Selsye had given her to use as the signal.

'Be ready now, my friend,' she said. 'I will need you to fly as fast as you have ever flown. Can you do that?'

'I preferred being a tree, less rushing about,' said Feveroot. When she kicked at his side, he continued. 'Of course. One last push.'

Holding the flare above her head, she bent low over Feveroot and pulled the fuse. There was a crackle, and they were bathed in a deep red glow.

'I'm coming for you, princeling. Be ready.'

Slowly Frith opened his eyes. He was lying on his back in the half-built Citadel garden, and directly overhead a pair of dragons were locked in violent combat. The wind from their wings battered him, blowing his hair into his eyes. Groaning, he turned over, looking out across the city. His vision was still dark at the edges, and it was difficult to focus, but beyond the fire and the smoke he could see a single point of red light, far across the other side of Krete. The signal. It was time to activate the trap – and not a moment too soon. If Krete had not already fallen, then the end was seconds away.

Summoning the last of his strength, Frith dragged himself to his feet, and then stood for a moment, fighting to stay upright.

His heart thudded sickly in his chest as if every movement was a grievous injury, and his head felt as though he stood on the deck of a ship during the worst of storms. Just the thought of running down to the chamber made his stomach churn, but there was no choice. The final moments had come.

Falling more than walking, Frith forced himself across the gardens to the entrance, and then down the stone steps. His legs felt full of water, and as he descended, his mind presented any number of unhelpful memories – their first journey below the Citadel, the monsters that waited for them there, the agony of the mages' lake. Forcing those thoughts aside he pounded his way down the steps, down into the chamber Selsye and Joah had made to house the gods. There, the device waited for him.

He wondered if Wydrin would get to him in time. If anyone could, it would be her.

Laying his hands on the device, he pushed the last pieces into place, and there was a blinding flash of light. For the briefest second he could see the bones in his own fingers, and then a pulse of tremendous energy passed through him and out, a widening circle of magic. Frith sank to his knees, the last of his strength gone.

'I won't be alone for long, at least,' he whispered to the chamber.

Wydrin and Feveroot tore across Krete, an arrow of black through the smoke and flames.

There was a pressure against her ears and then she felt a rippling shiver move through her. She knew without question that it was Frith's trap, reaching out for the gods she had painted with targets, ready to drag them all to their final resting places. There would be very little time now. Very little time at all.

The Citadel burst into view through the smoke and Feveroot dived towards it, heedless of what would happen if they crashed straight into the stones. Instead, he swept down into the entrance and into the corridors, moving so fast that Wydrin could see nothing but a blur of stone as they swept past. There was a rumble from behind them, and Wydrin felt a cold hand walk down her spine. The gods were coming.

In moments they were in the chamber itself, skidding to a halt and crashing into the far wall. Wydrin stumbled from Feveroot's back to see Frith, lying on his side next to the device. 'Frith!'

At the sound of her voice he stirred, lifting his head with some difficulty. 'My love?'

'Ye gods. Quickly!' She ran to him and dragged him up, pushing him with little care for his dignity onto Feveroot's back. Climbing on behind him, she wrapped her arms around his midriff and held on for dear life.

'If you were holding out on me, Feveroot, now's the time to show off!'

The demon sprang forward, his griffin form dissolving and becoming something else, something more streamlined and more snakelike. Wydrin had a moment to wonder if this was closer to his true form before they were racing up, up to the outside world. They had almost made it when the passageway they fled down was filled with roaring noise and blinding light. There was something else in there with them, something huge. Wydrin screwed her eyes shut against the light, but the voice thundered in her ears. It was Y'Gria.

You cannot do this to us! You will all die!

The god was struggling against the force that dragged her to her confinement, roots filling the narrow passageway as she scrambled for purchase. Wydrin felt several loop around her and Frith, pulling tight and dragging them back with the god. She heard Feveroot cry out in distress as the tentacles wrapped around his slipping, changing form.

'Your time is over!' screamed Wydrin. 'Accept it!'

NEVER!

A thick root slipped around her throat and began to squeeze. Desperately she tried to push her fingers under it, to loosen it somehow, but it was much too strong. They were still moving slowly backwards towards the chamber, inch by inch, despite Y'Gria's desperate crawling. Wydrin tried to take comfort in that – they would go to their deaths, but so would the gods.

'Wydrin, are you with me?' Frith sounded confused.

She let go of the tentacle and wrapped her arms around Frith again, holding him close and pressing her cheek to his neck. 'Always,' she said. 'I'll always be with you, my love.'

Her fingers slipped over something tucked into his shirt, and she realised it was the charm she had bought for him; the one that supposedly protected against Y'Gria. In a small act of defiance, she pulled it free and threw it behind them. The charm maker would be glad, at least, although she was likely dead now too.

The effect was immediate. There was a deafening shriek and the tendrils holding them in place whipped away like they had been scalded. Losing her grip, the god was sucked back down the tunnel away from them, and abruptly they were free.

Feveroot shot forward, and within seconds they were out in the blessed light.

Sebastian saw the last of it from his vantage point on Tia'mast.

One moment he and the dragon were locked in deadly combat with Y'Ruen, claws scrabbling against scales as strong as steel, jaws snapping at flesh, and the next she was gone, torn away from him as Frith's spell dragged her to her prison within the Citadel. For a few dizzying seconds Sebastian felt an enormous void of disappointment in his heart – to have the hunt taken away when he had yet to finish his kill – and then his attention was taken by the other gods being dragged across Krete.

Y'Gria was the first to go, shrinking and becoming lesser, somehow, as the magic took her within its grasp, and then Res'ni and Res'na. They struggled and they bellowed their fury, but the spell was relentless. They churned up the ground as they went, boiling it with the heat of their anger and then they vanished, one by one, into the Citadel. Res'ni was the last to go, her anguished howl echoing across the city, and then she was gone. Sebastian felt Y'Ruen's presence diminish as the spells closed over her, trapping her with her brother and sisters for the next thousand years. A strange silence fell. The Citadel itself shook once, as the beings encased inside it tested their boundaries, and a ring of dust gusted out from around it as though the building itself shifted in its foundations, and then all was still.

The city looked half destroyed, many of the buildings stamped flat or on fire, but Sebastian could already see efforts to control the flames. Some of the mages still lived. Many of the people had survived. He took a slow breath, consciously drawing himself back from the battle rage that had consumed him.

Brother, our enemies have fled. Tia'mast's voice was partly victorious, partly disappointed. Sebastian knew how he felt. Down to the west of the city, the shining shape of Oster was still visible along the wall, and then he vanished. He would be in his human form now, lest he attract the ire of the mages himself. Sebastian felt his chest grow tight; he would have to find Oster. He needed to talk to him. Suddenly, the silver tide seemed unimportant. Absently, he reassured the dragon.

They are gone, yes. We no longer have to fight.

There was silence from the dragon. And then, *There are other magical beings down there. Small creatures. They will be easy prey, but my blood-thirst has been awakened, brother.*

No. Sebastian attempted to reassert control, but now that their mutual enemies were gone, Tia'mast's solitary nature was resurfacing. Unbidden, the dragon began to descend towards the city. *They mean you no harm!*

That is not what I can taste in their magic, said Tia'mast, and Sebastian felt the hunt-hunger come over the dragon once more.

'You know,' said Wydrin. 'We *really* need to stop unleashing dragons.'

They stood together on the Citadel steps, Frith leaning heavily on Wydrin, watching as the giant dragon – the ancient god of an ancient Ede – descended towards Krete, jaws open. Fire was already starting to boil in the back of its throat.

'I can do it,' said Frith. 'I can send him back.'

Wydrin looked at him sceptically. 'You are dead on your feet already for summoning him in the first place.'

'I *can* do it, my love.' He smiled at her. In the morning light her hair was the colour of beaten gold, her eyes like jade. He thought he'd never seen anything more beautiful. 'Sebastian took control of the dragon when I summoned it, I felt him do it, but he has lost that control now. What other choice do we have?'

'Then we'll have to go and fetch Sebastian, I suppose.' She looked down at Feveroot, who was back in his griffin form, panting heavily. 'Up for one more flight, Feveroot?'

The demon turned his head. 'Do I have a choice?'

Wydrin grinned. 'Of course you do, now. That's the point, isn't it?'

They clambered back onto Feveroot's back, the demon making himself slightly larger without needing to be asked, and they were back up in the smoke-smeared sky in seconds. Frith sat ahead of Wydrin, and he squeezed the hand that circled his waist.

'Hold on to me,' he told her. 'I might pass out.' He paused, and then added. 'This really is like old times, isn't it?'

'Too much so,' replied Wydrin. 'We need to get some new times.'

Feveroot took them fast and close, not giving the giant dragon time to notice them, until they were hovering over its head like a fly over a restless sow. Wydrin leaned out and waved.

'Sebastian!'

The knight looked up, and to Frith's relief, reached out for them. Feveroot swept in as close as he could get, and Wydrin hauled the big knight up onto the griffin's back. Below them the dragon's great neck twisted, as though listening to something far away.

'Quickly,' said Sebastian. 'I am doing my best to calm him, but he is confused and fast becoming angry. If you can do something, do it now.'

Feeling Wydrin's arms circle around his waist, Frith held out one hand towards the dragon and summoned the time magic. Faster than ever before, everything around him grew blessedly still – the magic grew stronger every time he used it, even as it burned away his strength – and he reached out for the god, feeling for the relic it had once been. *Your time is over,* he thought, not unkindly, *it was over long ago.* Stronger than anything he'd experienced, he felt the dragon trying to turn within his grip; it wanted to see who or what was commanding him so. Frith pushed with the last of his strength and the dragon's brilliant emerald scales grew dull and dusty, its glaring eyes sinking into its head. The flesh fell away into fibres and dust, and then the brilliant bones of pure Edeian were exposed to the light, until they, too, were washed away by time. At last, there was the final piece, the shard of Tia'mast's skull, and Frith let go, the magic winking out like a candle in a storm. He saw it falling away, tumbling down to smash to pieces on the streets of Krete, and then exhaustion swept in to claim him.

94

The fires were out, but the city still smelled of smoke.

Sebastian stood by the tall window, listening to the sounds of a place putting itself back together again. The mages, he knew, were working in shifts – resting and then building, resting and then healing. The days and nights would be long for them, for some time.

Xinian and Selsye had found them at the Citadel, and immediately Selsye had set to work double checking all the seals and spells, an expression of fierce concentration on her face, while Xinian had sent them back to the palace, telling them to use her apartments as a place to recover and take stock. He guessed from Xinian's wry expression that she would not see her own bed for some hours, particularly now that she appeared to be in charge of everyone. Eventually, he knew, they would put in place all the secrets and the traps that would keep the Citadel sealed off to everyone but the mages – the Culoss, the Mages' Lake – these things would be in their future.

He took a sip from his goblet of wine, and allowed himself to relax. The gods were where they needed to be, and they had lived through the final battle. There was no reason to feel sad.

As if he had summoned him, Sebastian felt a shiver in his dragon blood and turned to the door just before Oster stepped through it. He put the goblet down on a nearby table.

'Oster.' He wasn't sure what else to say. Oster nodded to him, and there were a few moments of awkward silence.

'I saw your friend in the corridor,' said Oster eventually. He had changed into clean clothes, a cream tunic and a red jacket that suited him very well. There was a bruise on his cheek. Sebastian tried to remember if he'd seen him injured so before. 'Wydrin. She embraced me, and then told me that I should "knock off all that god stuff". She said everyone should.'

Sebastian smiled, despite himself. 'Yes, well. She's not exactly a fan of gods these days.'

Oster nodded thoughtfully and came further into the room, walking towards the window where Sebastian was and then stopping, as if thinking better of it. He didn't quite meet Sebastian's eyes as he continued speaking. 'Your other friend, the one with white hair, says he can take us back to . . . where we came from.'

The silver link between them thrummed. Sebastian caught his breath and turned away. How could he feel so close to someone, and yet not have words for what he needed to say? He busied himself with finding another goblet and filling it with wine, although when it came time to offer it to Oster he avoided his eyes. 'Frith is fairly confident.' He cleared his throat. 'The magic he gained travelling through Euriale is the key, apparently. We'll go back to the island, and he will pull us through time.' He shook his head slightly. 'I don't pretend to understand it, but Xinian has already offered us the use of a carapacer to get there. I think she will be relieved when we're gone.'

More silence. Sebastian set his fingers to the lip of the goblet, waiting.

'I have decided not to go back,' said Oster. 'I will stay here, in this time.'

Sebastian turned to him, nearly spilling the wine in his haste. 'What do you mean, not go back?'

'You see, I think your red-headed friend is right. I do not wish to be a god. It seems to me,' he paused, taking a breath, 'it seems to me that the best times I have had have been quiet, human times, with you. When we were together in the gardens, I was happy. At peace. When I was caught in the machinations of my family, I was . . . not happy. That power, and the desperate grasping for it – it twists us all out of shape. And Sebastian, if I return to our Ede, there will be a place waiting for me. Eventually the Eye of Euriale will find some way to regulate itself again – perhaps a new Spinner will be born, to birth new brothers and sisters for me – and I would have to take up the mantle of a god again. I would have no choice. Here,' he gestured out the window. 'Here I can slip away into the crowds, and try being human. No expectations here, no roles. No gap waiting to be filled. I want to be myself.'

Sebastian stood very still. He could feel the surge of the other man's emotions along the link they shared. He wondered if Oster could sense his, too.

'Sebastian,' Oster took a few steps towards him, and then stopped. He looked away, and then back, an expression of mingled anguish and hope on his face. 'I love you. Please, stay with me. Have a life here, with me.'

'Oster, I . . .'

Oster stepped into the circle of his arms and then he kissed him, hesitantly at first, as if unsure of Sebastian's reaction, and then fiercely. Sebastian savoured the taste of him, the rasp of stubble against his cheek, the solid press of his body. The link between them widened and became almost too sweet to bear. For a time they were lost in that silver tide, and Sebastian knew peace for the first time in years.

Wydrin knelt in the red dust of the courtyard, her overly stuffed pack by her side. Feveroot sat before her in the form of a fox, paws folded neatly together. She thought the form suited him.

'Without you, we would all be dead,' she said quietly. 'All of these mages here too. We all owe you an enormous debt, my friend.'

'You gave me my freedom,' replied Feveroot. 'The debt is already paid. Although perhaps I would ask that in future mages could let us be.'

Wydrin frowned slightly. No one had seen Joah since he had fled the Citadel. She suspected he would go to ground for a few years, and that was possibly the worst outcome. There would be no one keeping an eye on him. 'I'm not sure I am able to promise that,' she said, truthfully. 'What will you do now?'

The fox demon tipped his head to one side. 'Find another tree. Far away from people, perhaps. Fare you well, Wydrin of Crosshaven.'

With that, Feveroot's form melted away into black ink, seeping into the cracks of the flagstones and vanishing. Wydrin stood up and brushed herself down. To the far side of the courtyard, Xinian was preparing their carapacer, while Frith loaded bags into the back of it: food, drink, medical supplies. He had slept for an entire day after he had banished the ancient dragon, and he still looked paler than she would have liked, but then, he was tougher than he looked. He always had been.

'Wydrin.'

She turned to see Sebastian walking towards her. He wasn't wearing his sword, which struck her as odd, and he had no bags with him.

'Hey you. We're almost ready to go.' She punched him lightly on the arm. 'Back to Euriale, and then *back* to Euriale, if you see what I mean. And then I am getting the fuck *away* from Euriale, because I have had more than enough of that shit hole.' He was watching her too closely. 'What is it? What's wrong?'

He took a breath, and for a moment he didn't say anything at all. Eventually he took her hand in both of his, and although he smiled his eyes were sad. 'Wydrin, I'm going to stay here. I'm going to stay with Oster.'

'Stay here? What are you talking about? You can't stay here!'

'If Oster goes back, he will have to be a god again. And I love him, Wydrin. I think we could be happy here.'

'But, if you stay here – Wydrin looked away from him, the sun suddenly too bright for her eyes. 'Does he love you?'

'He does.'

She bit her lip. Sebastian's hands around her own were very warm, and the idea of not seeing him again was a sudden physical pain, like a great tearing deep inside. She thought of how he had left the *Poison Chalice*, how he had walked away from them in his misery and his pain, and she forced herself to look up into his eyes. There was peace there now, she could see it. 'I want you to be happy, Sebastian. More than anything, I want that.'

'Wydrin,' his eyes were too bright. He cleared his throat. 'Do you want me to come to Euriale with you? See you off?'

'No, stay here, be happy. Live your life.' Her voice broke a little, and he pulled her close, folding his arms around her and squeezing her like she might fly away. 'I love you, brother.'

'I love you too, Wydrin. My Copper Cat.'

When the carapacer was packed and ready, Frith climbed down and went to Sebastian. Wydrin didn't know exactly how he knew, but he looked at both their faces and his grey eyes grew solemn. He took Sebastian's hand in his, and they exchanged some words she didn't hear, and then they embraced as brothers. When he joined Wydrin back in the carapacer he didn't offer words of comfort but instead pushed her hair back from where it hung in her face and kissed her cheekbone. She didn't trust herself to meet his eyes.

'Are we ready?' called Xinian from the front of the carapacer. Wydrin forced herself to look at Sebastian, standing with his arms crossed over his chest. He smiled at her, and she nodded.

'We're ready, Xinian,' she said, as firmly as she was able, but then when the carapacer wobbled its way uncertainly to hover above the ground, she leaned over the side of it and reached out for him. Sebastian took her hand, and she grinned back.

'I will expect your stories to be good ones, Sir Sebastian Carverson.'

'And I expect you to go on having adventures, Wydrin of Crosshaven.'

The carapacer bumped up into the air then, and his fingers slipped through hers. Xinian took them up into the clear blue sky, and Wydrin's last sight of Sebastian was his face turned up to hers, a man about to go on living his life. She settled back and let Frith put his arm around her. It was going to be a long journey home.

95

'Well, it has certainly been interesting.'

They stood back amongst the greenery in the sweltering heat of Euriale. Xinian had put them down where Frith had directed them, as close to the Eye as he dared to come – he had no wish to attempt to explain any of that to Xinian, particularly as he barely understood it himself. Xinian, clearly keen for them to be gone, had helped them unpack, and was now looking faintly uncomfortable. It reminded him of his father, who had never particularly enjoyed the social functions that came with being a lord, and was never sure how to get people to leave after a banquet. The unexpected memory made him smile.

'It's definitely been that, Xinian.' Wydrin had been quiet during their journey to Euriale, but she was putting a brave face on it now. She would miss Sebastian a great deal. *We both will*, thought Frith. 'Take care of yourself, Xinian the Battleborn. Give Selsye a kiss for me. I hope –' She paused, and her smile faltered, but Frith thought that she recovered well. 'I hope you have long, happy lives together.'

Xinian gave a faintly puzzled smile, and then reached for one of the bags still in the carapacer. 'I thought I would make you a gift of these,' she said, opening the bag. 'Do not tell anyone I gave them to you, though. I wouldn't last long in my new position if people knew I went around gifting magical artefacts to the unbound.'

Wydrin pulled a pair of glittering, delicate gauntlets out of the bag, and her face split into a genuine smile. 'Oh, thank you. I will get some good use out of these, believe me.'

They watched Xinian leave, and then turned and walked into the deepest part of the forest. The concentric stone rings of the Eye loomed through the trees ahead of them. It looked exactly the same as it did in a thousand years' time. *Perhaps there are fixed points in time*, thought Frith. *Or perhaps some places never change.*

'So, how do we do this then?' asked Wydrin. They stopped at the bottom-most circle, looking up. The air was full of green light and the ripe, alien smell of the island. It felt wild and strange.

'It's a reversal of how I've been using the magic so far. Instead of pushing an object through time, I will push us through time. Or I will push everything *but* us through time.' He shook his head. 'It's difficult to describe.'

'I can't say that sounds particularly reassuring, princeling. We do not need to travel through the Eye, then?'

Frith shook his head. 'It is just a landmark. We know this exists in the future. We know the rough shape of it. We won't . . .' He struggled for the right words. 'We won't pop back into existence in the middle of a tree. And we'll know where we are.'

'And maybe my mother will be there, somewhere.' Wydrin sighed. 'We have to try, at least.'

'I can do it,' he said, trying to sound more confident than he felt. He held out his hand, and she took it. 'Hold tight to me, Wydrin, and I'll take us home.'

They stood close together, Wydrin's hands holding Frith's belt, Frith's arms around her waist. He looked into her eyes, reached out with the magic, and *pushed*.

Time sang through them both, surging like a riptide and pulling them on, and on. The history of Ede flowed past them, leaving them gasping in its wake but alive. The magic twinned and flowed and crashed together again, and it was almost possible to see how they all worked together; separate chords in a song, different colours coming together to become light – the secret soul of Ede. Frith reached for it even as he held them together, needing to know, finally, how it all worked . . .

And then mud, the smell of rain, and the sound of Wydrin laughing next to him.

* * *

The Dawning Man stepped out of the trees into the clearing, and Devinia the Red stood to meet him.

'Finally.' She allowed herself a small smile. Here, at last, it would be over. She had lost her ship, she had lost Augusta, and she had lost her daughter. This fight was all that was left to her, and she went to it gladly. Next to her, Ephemeral and Terin stood ready.

'I can summon the cold,' said the Narhl, although he sounded less than certain. They had had a run of hot days, and he was on his last reserves of strength. Devinia met his eyes, and nodded. He had nothing left to give, but he was standing with her anyway. That was what a crew did.

Ephemeral stretched, like a cat getting ready to hunt. 'Do you have any orders, Captain Devinia?'

Kellan was in sight now, an emaciated crimson corpse. He shuffled along beneath the legs of the Dawning Man, and with him were five pirates. Devinia was surprised at that. She had expected the red disease to have killed them all by now.

'Terin, if you can, slow that big golden bastard down. Ephemeral, I expect you to make short work of those walking corpses. Kellan is mine.'

'As you say, Captain.'

Devinia paused. 'Thank you,' she said, suddenly shamed by how her voice cracked. 'Thank you both.'

Ephemeral squeezed her shoulder, and then Kellan opened his mouth to speak. Whatever words he said, Devinia didn't hear them, because she was already running, already leaping down the stone steps with her sword at the ready. Battle-rage settled over her like a red shroud, and the next few moments came to her in vivid flashes.

She saw the Dawning Man looming above her, giant golden fists raised to crush her, and then its shining surface crackled with hoarfrost. It shuddered to a halt, held in place for the moment by thickening ice, while the last of Kellan's desperate pirates came to meet them. She saw Ephemeral, as lithe and as dangerous as a length of severed rigging, dancing her blade to meet the throat of some unfortunate creature crusted in red moss. She saw blood bursting over her own hand as she sank her sword deep into the stomach of someone else, and then she was pushing them to one side. Kellan stood just beyond, just out of reach. If only she could—

There was a thunderous crash, and abruptly she was on her side in the dirt, the breath knocked from her lungs. The Dawning Man had pushed past its icy manacles and had thrown its fists at the ground. Scrambling to her feet, Devinia found herself face to face with a wall of golden crystal, speeding towards her. There was no chance of getting out of its way. She had a moment to think that Augusta would find this amusing – a pirate, killed by gold – when a red-headed blur jumped in front of her, silver fists swinging. There was a deafening crump, and the wall of golden crystal skidded back and away, a serious dent in the middle of it. The scruffy-looking red-head turned to her and grinned.

'All right, Mum?'

Devinia opened her mouth, but no words came out. Lord Frith appeared at her side, his staff held in one hand, but when he raised his arms he burned all over with a bright white light. The Dawning Man shuddered ominously, turning a dark, burnished copper in front of her eyes. The glowing red pattern traced over the golden figure dimmed and sputtered out, and then, unceremoniously, the whole thing fell to pieces, collapsing into a collection of shattered crystals. When it had settled, there was a stunned silence. Devinia could hear the calls of distant startled birds, and the wind picking up. She was vaguely aware that she was swaying on her feet slightly.

'This looks like a bloody mess.' Wydrin lowered her gauntlets. 'So I'm guessing we need to go and—'

Devinia cupped her daughter's face in her hands, and then kissed her on the cheek.

'It's good to see you, Wyd. Now shut up for a moment, please.'

Stepping past Wydrin and her Lord Frith, skirting the pieces of the Dawning Man, she found Kellan, cowering in the dirt. He was holding his claw-like hands over his head.

'But I am the Red King,' he said. 'I am the Red King reborn.'

'You are fuck all, is what you are,' said Devinia, and she thrust her blade into his chest. She waited for his eyes to grow still before she pulled it back out. There was no blood. 'Fuck all.'

96

At the sound of the bell the librarian shelved his stack of papers and hurried along the towering aisles. It was very unusual for someone to visit here at this time of year, let alone at this time of night. It must, he reasoned, be someone very important in need of vital information. In the midst of his alarm he felt a small flicker of irritation. Did no one pay attention to the formal visiting hours these days?

When he reached the front desk he was surprised to find three figures in shadow, conferring amongst each other just as if they weren't wasting his time. The librarian cleared his throat and peered at them pointedly.

'May I *help* you?'

Two of the figures turned towards him, stepping eagerly into the small circle of his lamplight. There was a man with mottled skin – untidy, hardly fit for a library visit, but then he had seen students who gave even less thought to their appearance – and then there was the woman. The woman was a *monster*. She had green skin and eyes like a snake, and when she smiled she revealed pointed fangs. The librarian made a small strangled noise in his throat.

'I do hope you can,' said the green-skinned monster. 'We would like to look at the books. At all the books. We have coin to pay, if you wish.'

'Coin?' squeaked the librarian.

'Lots of it,' said the man. He had a strange accent. 'We have been very busy.'

The librarian took a strangled breath. Once, a student had suggested he keep a weapon behind the desk for occasions when people insisted on speaking too loudly or folding over the pages of a book, and the librarian had laughed politely. What a fool he had been. Still, dignity at all times.

'It is not a question of *coin*.' He summoned his chilliest voice, the one reserved for people who dared to bring food into the library. 'We do not allow your sort in here. This is a civilised place, for civilised people. It is not a place for . . . monsters.'

'Is that right?'

The third figure stepped fully into the light for the first time, and somehow she managed to be more frightening than the other two. She was an older woman, her tan skin riddled with scars, her blue eyes full of barely concealed rage. Was that a bone tied in her hair? She unsheathed a dagger, of all things, and struck the desk, embedding the blade deep within its polished wood.

'Well, I, that is to say—'

'I am Devinia the Red, you snivelling bookworm, and these are my *civilised* friends.' She leaned over the desk towards the librarian, baring her teeth at him in a madwoman's snarl. 'They have a mind to visit some libraries. All of them, in fact. And we're starting with yours, my good man. So go find me some fucking books.'

Wydrin wiped the sweat from her forehead, and took the letter from her pack again. It was already crumpled and stained, and the ink was smudged, but it barely mattered; she knew the thing by heart by now anyway.

'Do you think this is it?' asked Frith. They had spent all day travelling to the very bottom of this valley, the sun beating down on the tops of their heads, and finally they had come to a collection of stones and rocks, the shadows they painted as black as ink on the scrubby ground. If you squinted and tipped your head to one side, it was possible to see how they had once been a building of some sort.

'I bloody well hope so,' she replied, but she knew it was, in her heart. She followed Frith into the ruins, where a rough archway still towered over their heads, offering thick bands of shade. Beyond that there was a wall that still had part of the roof attached – Wydrin supposed that was how the mural hadn't been washed away by a thousand years' worth of weather. Frith poked around the stones, looking for other magical artefacts that might have survived – he had developed a keen interest in such things, just as Wydrin had found a renewed interest in the history of Ede. Wydrin held the letter up to the light. The handwriting was still that of someone who was new to the concept, but it was also the hand of someone who enjoyed the act of writing very much. She smoothed her thumb across the page, smiling.

My dear friend Wydrin Threefellows, the Copper Cat of Crosshaven,

Let me say first of all that your mother sends her regards. She travels with us and seems to enjoy it. I think she enjoys looking out for us. She calls this being 'our muscle'. We have visited many places and I have read many books. Ede is an extraordinary place. I am glad I am getting to see it, and not just destroy parts of it. Thank you.

I believe that we share a particular interest in certain sections of Ede's history. In my readings, I have found some references that I believe you may find edifying. Go to the western region of Relios. There are ruins in the valley of Lankh that I think you should see. Perhaps, when we meet again, you will tell me of them, or we can visit them together.

Yours in sorrow and joy,

Ephemeral

Ephemeral and Terin hadn't been the only ones to visit libraries. With hearts in their throats, Wydrin and Frith had searched through books and scrolls for scraps of information, clues to tell them whether their appearance in the past had changed anything. As far as they could tell, it hadn't; Xinian and Selsye had still died stopping Joah, and he had still succumbed to the wiles of the demon Bezcavar. The time magic itself had faded when they left Euriale; Frith had been disappointed but also, Wydrin thought, slightly relieved.

'We should have done more,' said Wydrin. She turned the letter around in her fingers. 'We should have killed the bastard then, before he did any real harm. Xinian and Selsye could have lived full lives together. It could have – more people would be alive today, if Joah had died before he met the demon.'

Frith looked over to her. It was a conversation they'd had many times since their return. 'We couldn't know what that might do,' he said. 'You know that, Wyd. Joah was responsible for much of the magic that trapped the gods inside the Citadel. If he wasn't there to maintain it, it could have led to the gods escaping. We just don't know.' He sighed and looked down at his boots. 'It would be like taking away the foundation stones of a tower, and hoping that it still stands true.'

Wydrin kicked at the dusty ground. 'Yeah. I know. Every time you say it, I know it's true. Time is a tapestry – remove one thread and it could all unravel. I still wish we had, though.'

Frith was standing before the wall now, and after a moment she joined him there. Carved into the pale yellow stone were the figures of two men standing together, and above them, two dragons, their tails intertwined. All around them, mountains loomed, and a sword lay underneath them all. A broadsword. Wydrin reached out and touched her fingers to the shape of one of the men, feeling the roughness of the stone there and the distance of a thousand years.

'They did great things,' she said with certainty. 'There are stories of them. Ephemeral will find them all, eventually, I've no doubt.' She reached into her pocket and drew out Sebastian's badge of Isu and the small blue-glass globe Crowleo had made him. 'He should have had these with him,' she said. She bent down and placed them at the bottom of the wall. 'But I don't suppose he needs them any more.'

'It feels strange,' said Frith. 'Knowing they are in the past, looking for their future.' He smiled, and took her hand. 'While we are in the future, looking at their past.'

'Perhaps we all live in the past and the future, at the same time,' said Wydrin. It was suddenly hard to see clearly, so she turned her watery smile on him. 'I think we all do that, in a way.'

'As ever, my love, I think you are right.'

They kissed in the ruins, the certainty of each other and the warmth of the sun filling their hearts, and then they turned and set out east, in search of the nearest decent tavern.

Acknowledgements

So I've come to the end of an epic journey I never expected to take. I can't begin to tell you what it's meant to me (I really don't have room for another 200,000 words, after all) so instead I will attempt to thank the people who have taken the journey with me – without them, I would have been Legolas without his lembas bread.

Thank you to John Wordsworth, who started the Copper Cat books on their journey, and big love and gratitude to Claire Baldwin and Emily Griffin – editors who are not only brilliant, but a genuine pleasure to work with, bringing a sharp eye and boundless enthusiasm to everything. The design team at Headline have provided me with some of the best covers I've ever seen, so big thanks to them and Patrick Insole. Thank you also to Caitlin Raynor, on hand to herd me from one thing to another.

I remain forever indebted to my agent, the fantastic Juliet Mushens – not just the best agent in the 'verse, but also one of my very favourite people. For support, cheerleading and the occasional rowdy dinner, thanks must go Team Mushens at large, and particularly to: Den Patrick, who has ushered in another year of Super Relaxed Fantasy Club with me; the tremendous Andrew Reid, who reads the books first and writes pithy comments in the margins; Pete Newman for the cider and all the many emails; and Liz de Jager for being a firecracker and looking after us this last Christmas. Thanks also to Roy Butlin for beta reading duties and the ridiculous amounts of confidence in me, and of course to Adam Christopher, my longest serving writing buddy.

Since this is the final book in the trilogy, I will indulge myself and say a quiet thank you to Sir Terry Pratchett, who brought so much joy to my reading, and consequently, to my writing. We only met once (and you complimented me on my nail varnish) but I will miss you an awful lot.

This particular book is dedicated to my mum, who with infinite patience and only slight exasperation put up with me, the untidiest person in the universe, throughout the years where I was much more interested in books than going outside. Thanks, as ever, to Jenni, who played Zelda through the 90s with me. And as usual the biggest thanks must go to my partner Marty, the brightest part of every day.

Thanks lastly to all the readers who came this far with Wydrin, Frith and Sebastian. I'm sure the Black Feather Three are raising a toast to you all, in some tavern somewhere, sometime. Mine's a mead, if you're buying.

Ye gods and little fishes . . .

Read the full Copper Cat Trilogy

  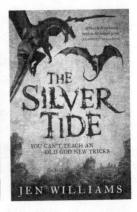

'Gripping, fast-paced adventure' *SciFiNow*

'A force to be reckoned with in the fantasy genre' *Starburst*

'Highly recommended' *Independent*

headline

The Copper Promise

Jen Williams

There are some tall stories about the caverns beneath the Citadel – about magic and mages and monsters and gods.

Wydrin of Crosshaven has heard them all, but she's spent long enough trawling caverns and taverns with her companion Sir Sebastian to learn that there's no money to be made in chasing rumours.

But then a crippled nobleman with a dead man's name offers them a job: exploring the Citadel's darkest depths. It sounds like just another quest with gold and adventure...if they're lucky, they might even have a tale of their own to tell once it's over.

These reckless adventurers will soon learn that sometimes there is truth in rumour. Sometimes a story can save your life.

'A fast-paced and original new voice in heroic fantasy' Adrian Tchaikovsky

978 1 4722 1112 5

headline

The Iron Ghost

Jen Williams

Wydrin of Crosshaven and her companions, Sir Sebastian and Lord Aaron Frith, are experienced in the perils of stirring up the old gods. They are also familiar with defeating them, and are now enjoying being very much in demand for their services.

When a job comes up in the distant city of Skaldshollow, it looks like easy coin – retrieve a stolen item, admire the views, get paid. But in a place haunted by ancient magic, our heroes soon find themselves threatened on all sides. And in the frozen mountains, the stones are walking...

Join the reckless adventurers of THE COPPER PROMISE as they face darker challenges than they could ever have imagined.

'A fresh take on classic tropes... 21st century fantasy at its best' *SFX*

978 1 4722 1114 9

headline

If you loved THE SILVER TIDE,
look out for the first novel in a brand-new trilogy,
coming February 2017.

The Ninth Rain

Jen Williams

The great wall of Ebora is crumbling. Wolves walk streets that
once shone with gold.

Tormalin the Oathless, last son of Ebora, has had enough.
Better to enjoy life's pleasures than to waste away under the
blind gaze of a long-dead god. Talk about a guilt trip. When
the eccentric explorer Lady de Grazon offers him employment,
he foresees an easy life escorting a rich old woman from one
side of Sarn to the other. Even when they are joined by a
fugitive witch with a tendency to set things on fire, the
prospect of facing down monsters and retrieving ancient
artefacts is still preferable to the abomination he left behind.

But not everyone is willing to let the Eboran empire collapse.

The Jure'lia are coming, and the Ninth Rain will fall...

Pre-order online now.

headline